THREE GREAT LORD PETER NOVELS

Dorothy L. Sayers

THREE GREAT LORD PETER NOVELS

STRONG POISON
MURDER MUST ADVERTISE
THE NINE TAILORS

LONDON
VICTOR GOLLANCZ LTD
1978

STRONG POISON First published 1930

MURDER MUST ADVERTISE First published 1933

THE NINE TAILORS First published 1934

ISBN 0 575 02415 1

MADE AND PRINTED IN GREAT BRITAIN BY
THE GARDEN CITY PRESS LIMITED
LETCHWORTH, HERTFORDSHIRE
SG6 1JS

Contents

STRONG POISON

"*Where gat ye your dinner, Lord Rendal, my son?*
Where gat ye your dinner, my handsome young man?"
"*—O I dined with my sweetheart, Mother; make my bed soon,*
For I'm sick to the heart and I fain wad lie down."

"*O that was strong poison, Lord Rendal, my son,*
O that was strong poison, my handsome young man."
"*—O yes, I am poisoned, Mother; make my bed soon,*
For I'm sick to the heart, and I fain wad lie down."

OLD BALLAD

CHAPTER I

THERE WERE CRIMSON roses on the bench; they looked like splashes of blood.

The judge was an old man; so old, he seemed to have outlived time and change and death. His parrot-face and parrot-voice were dry, like his old, heavily-veined hands. His scarlet robe clashed harshly with the crimson of the roses. He had sat for three days in the stuffy court, but he showed no sign of fatigue.

He did not look at the prisoner as he gathered his notes into a neat sheaf and turned to address the jury, but the prisoner looked at him. Her eyes, like dark smudges under the heavy square brows, seemed equally without fear and without hope. They waited.

"Members of the jury——"

The patient old eyes seemed to sum them up and take stock of their united intelligence. Three respectable tradesmen—a tall, argumentative one, a stout, embarrassed one with a drooping moustache, and an unhappy one with a bad cold; a director of a large company, anxious not to waste valuable time; a publican, incongruously cheerful; two youngish men of the artisan class; a nondescript, elderly man, of educated appearance, who might have been anything; an artist with a red beard disguising a weak chin; three women—an elderly spinster, a stout capable woman who kept a sweet-shop, and a harassed wife and mother whose thoughts seemed to be continually straying to her abandoned hearth.

"Members of the jury—you have listened with great patience and attention to the evidence in this very distressing case, and it is now my duty to sum up the facts and arguments which have been put before you by the learned Attorney-General and by the learned counsel for the defence, and to put them in order as clearly as possible, so as to help you in forming your decision.

"But first of all, perhaps I ought to say a few words with regard to that decision itself. You know, I am sure, that it is a great principle of English law that every accused person is held to be innocent unless and until he is proved otherwise. It is not necessary for him, or her, to prove innocence; it is, in the modern slang phrase, 'up to' the Crown to prove guilt, and unless you are quite satisfied that the Crown has done this beyond all reasonable doubt, it is your duty to return a verdict of 'Not guilty'. That does not necessarily mean that the prisoner has established her innocence by proof; it simply means that the Crown has failed to produce in your minds an undoubted conviction of her guilt."

Salcombe Hardy, lifting his drowned-violet eyes for a moment from his reporter's note-book, scribbled two words on a slip of paper and pushed them over to Waffles Newton. "Judge hostile." Waffles nodded. They were old hounds on this blood-trail.

The judge creaked on.

"You may perhaps wish to hear from me exactly what is meant by those words 'reasonable doubt'. They mean, just so much doubt as you might have in everyday life about an ordinary matter of business. This is a case of murder, and it might be natural for you to think that, in such a case, the words mean more than this. But that is not so. They do not mean that you must cast about for fantastical solutions of what seems to you plain and simple. They do not mean those nightmare doubts which sometimes torment us at four o'clock in the morning when we have not slept very well. They only mean that the proof must be such as you would accept about a plain matter of buying and selling, or some such commonplace transaction. You must not strain your belief in favour of the prisoner any more, of course, than you must accept proof of her guilt without the most careful scrutiny.

"Having said just these few words, so that you may not feel too much overwhelmed by the heavy responsibility laid upon you by your duty to the State, I will now begin at the beginning and try to place the story that we have heard, as clearly as possible before you.

"The case for the Crown is that the prisoner, Harriet Vane, murdered Philip Boyes by poisoning him with arsenic. I need not detain you by going through the proofs offered by Sir James Lubbock and the other doctors who have given evidence as to the cause of death. The Crown say he died of arsenical poisoning, and the defence do not dispute it. The evidence is, therefore, that the death was due to arsenic, and you must accept that as a fact. The only question that remains for you is whether, in fact, that arsenic was deliberately administered by the prisoner with intent to murder.

"The deceased, Philip Boyes, was, as you have heard, a writer. He was thirty-six years old, and he had published five novels and a large number of essays and articles. All these literary works were of what is sometimes called an 'advanced' type. They preached doctrines which may seem to some of us immoral or seditious, such as atheism, and anarchy, and what is known as 'free love'. His private life appears to have been conducted, for some time at least, in accordance with these doctrines.

"At any rate, at some time in the year 1927 he became acquainted with Harriet Vane. They met in some of those artistic and literary circles where 'advanced' topics are discussed, and after a time they became very friendly. The prisoner is also a novelist by profession, and it is very important to remember that she is a writer of so-called 'mystery' or 'detective' stories, such as deal with various ingenious methods of committing murder and other crimes.

"You have heard the prisoner in the witness-box, and you have heard the various people who came forward to give evidence as to her character. You have been told that she is a young woman of great ability, brought up on strictly religious principles, who, through no fault of her own, was left, at the age of twenty-three, to make her own way in the world. Since that time—and she is now twenty-nine years old—she has worked industriously to keep herself, and it is very much to her credit that she has, by her own exertions, made herself independent in a legitimate way, owing nothing to anybody and accepting help from no one.

"She has told us herself, with great candour, how she became deeply attached to Philip Boyes, and how, for a considerable time, she held out against his persuasions to live with him in an irregular manner. There was, in fact, no reason at all why he should not have married her honourably; but apparently he represented himself as being conscientiously opposed to any formal marriage. You have the evidence of Sybil Marriott and Eiluned Price that the prisoner was made very unhappy by this attitude which he chose to take up, and you have heard also that he was a very handsome and attractive man, whom any woman might have found it difficult to resist.

"At any rate, in March of 1928, the prisoner, worn out, as she tells us, by his unceasing importunities, gave in, and consented to live on terms of intimacy with him, outside the bonds of marriage.

"Now you may feel, and quite properly, that this was a very wrong thing to do. You may, after making all allowances for this young woman's unprotected position, still feel that she was a person of unstable moral character. You will not be led away by the false glamour which certain writers contrive to throw about 'free love' into thinking that this was anything but an ordinary, vulgar act of misbehaviour. Sir Impey Biggs, very rightly using all his great eloquence on behalf of his client, has painted this action of Harriet Vane's in very rosy colours; he has spoken of unselfish sacrifice and self-immolation, and has reminded you that, in such a situation, the woman always has to pay more heavily than the man. You will not, I am sure, pay too much attention to this. You know quite well the difference between right and wrong in such matters, and you may think that, if Harriet Vane had not become to a certain extent corrupted by the unwholesome influences among which she lived, she would have shown a truer heroism by dismissing Philip Boyes from her society.

"But, on the other hand, you must be careful not to attach the wrong kind of importance to this lapse. It is one thing for a man or woman to live an immoral life, and quite another thing to commit murder. You may perhaps think that one step into the path of wrong-doing makes the next one easier, but you must not give too much weight to that consideration. You are entitled to take it into account, but you must not be too much prejudiced."

The judge paused for a moment, and Freddy Arbuthnot jerked an elbow into the ribs of Lord Peter Wimsey, who appeared to be a prey to gloom.

"I should jolly well hope not. Damn it, if every little game led to murder, they'd be hanging half of us for doin' in the other half."

"And which half would *you* be in?" enquired his lordship, fixing him for a moment with a cold eye and then returning his glance to the dock.

"Victim," said the Hon. Freddy, "victim. Me for the corpse in the library."

"Philip Boyes and the prisoner lived together in this fashion," went on the judge, "for nearly a year. Various friends have testified that they appeared to live on terms of the greatest mutual affection. Miss Price said that, although Harriet Vane obviously felt her unfortunate position very acutely—cutting herself off from her family friends and refusing to thrust herself into company where her social outlawry might cause embarrassment and so on—yet she was extremely loyal to her lover and expressed herself proud and happy to be his companion.

"Nevertheless, in February 1929 there was a quarrel, and the couple separated. It is not denied that the quarrel took place. Mr. and Mrs. Dyer, who occupy the flat immediately above Philip Boyes', say that they heard loud talking in angry voices, the man swearing and the woman crying, and that the next day Harriet Vane packed up all her things and left the house for good. The curious feature in the case, and one which you must consider very carefully, is the reason assigned for the quarrel. As to this, the only evidence we have is the prisoner's own. According to Miss Marriott, with whom Harriet Vane took refuge after the separation, the prisoner steadily refused to give any information on the subject, saying only that she had been painfully deceived by Boyes and never wished to hear his name spoken again.

"Now it might be supposed from this that Boyes had given the prisoner cause for grievance against him, by unfaithfulness, or unkindness, or simply by a continued refusal to regularise the situation in the eyes of the world. But the prisoner absolutely denies this. According to her statement—and on this point her evidence is confirmed by a letter which Philip Boyes wrote to his father—Boyes did at length offer her legal marriage, and this was the cause of the quarrel. You may think this a very remarkable statement to make, but that is the prisoner's evidence on oath.

"It would be natural for you to think that this proposal of marriage takes away any suggestion that the prisoner had a cause of grievance against Boyes. Anyone would say that, under such circumstances, she could have no motive for wishing to murder this young man, but rather the contrary. Still, there is the fact of the quarrel, and the prisoner herself states that this honourable, though belated, proposal was unwelcome to her. She does not say—as she might very reasonably say, and as her counsel has most forcefully and impressively said for her—that this marriage-offer completely does away with any pretext for enmity on her part towards Philip Boyes. Sir Impey Biggs says so, but that is not what the prisoner says. She says—and you must try to put yourselves in her place and understand her point of view if you can—that she was angry with Boyes because, after persuading her against her will to adopt his principles of conduct, he then renounced those principles and so, as she says, 'made a fool of her'.

"Well, that is for you to consider: whether the offer which was in fact made could reasonably be construed into a motive for murder. I must impress upon you that no other motive has been suggested in evidence."

At this point the elderly spinster on the jury was seen to be making a note —a vigorous note, to judge from the action of her pencil on the paper. Lord Peter Wimsey shook his head slowly two or three times and muttered something under his breath.

"After this," said the judge, "nothing particular seems to have happened to these two people for three months or so, except that Harriet Vane left Miss Marriott's house and took a small flat of her own in Doughty Street, while Philip Boyes, on the contrary, finding his solitary life depressing, accepted the invitation of his cousin, Mr. Norman Urquhart, to stay at the latter's house in Woburn Square. Although living in the same quarter of London, Boyes and the accused do not seem to have met very often after the separation. Once or twice there was an accidental encounter at the house of a friend. The dates of these occasions cannot be ascertained with any certainty—they were informal parties—but there is some evidence that there was a meeting towards the end of March, another in the second week in April, and a third some time in May. These times are worth noting, though, as the exact day is left doubtful, you must not attach too much importance to them.

"However, we now come to a date of the very greatest importance. On April 10th, a young woman, who has been identified as Harriet Vane, entered the chemist's shop kept by Mr. Brown in Southampton Row, and purchased two ounces of commercial arsenic, saying that she needed it to destroy rats. She signed the poison-book in the name of Mary Slater, and the handwriting has been identified as that of the prisoner. Moreover, the prisoner herself admits having made this purchase, for certain reasons of her own. For this reason it is comparatively unimportant—but you may think it worth noting—that the housekeeper of the flats where Harriet Vane lives has come here and told you that there are no rats on the premises, and never have been in the whole time of her residence there.

"On May 5th we have another purchase of arsenic. The prisoner, as she herself states, this time procured a tin of arsenical weed-killer, of the same brand that was mentioned in the Kidwelly poisoning case. This time she gave the name of Edith Waters. There is no garden attached to the flats where she lives, nor could there be any conceivable use for weed-killer on the premises.

"On various occasions also, during the period from the middle of March to the beginning of May, the prisoner purchased other poisons, including prussic acid (ostensibly for photographic purposes) and strychnine. There was also an attempt to obtain aconitine, which was not successful. A different shop was approached and a different name given in each case. The arsenic is the only poison which directly concerns this case, but these other purchases are of some importance, as throwing light on the prisoner's activities at this time.

"The prisoner has given an explanation of these purchases which you must consider for what it is worth. She says that she was engaged at that time in writing a novel about poisoning, and that she bought the drugs in order to prove by experiment how easy it was for an ordinary person to get hold of deadly poisons. In proof of this, her publisher, Mr. Trufoot, has produced the manuscript of the book. You have had it in your hands, and you will be given it again, if you like, when I have finished my summing-up, to look at in your own room. Passages were read out to you, showing that the subject of the book was murder by arsenic, and there is a description in it of a young woman going to a chemist's shop and buying a considerable quantity of this deadly substance. And I must mention here what I should have mentioned before, namely, that the arsenic purchased from Mr. Brown was the ordinary commercial arsenic, which is coloured with charcoal or indigo, as the law requires, in order that it may not be mistaken for sugar or any other innocent substance."

Salcombe Hardy groaned: "How long, O Lord, how long shall we have to listen to all this tripe about commercial arsenic? Murderers learn it now at their mother's knee."

"I particularly want you to remember those dates—I will give them to you again—the 10th of April and the 5th of May." (The jury wrote them down. Lord Peter Wimsey murmured: "They all wrote down on their slates, 'She doesn't believe there's an atom of meaning in it'." The Hon. Freddy said "What? what?" and the judge turned over another page of his notes.)

"About this time, Philip Boyes began to suffer from renewed attacks of a gastric trouble to which he had been subject from time to time during his life. You have read the evidence of Dr. Green, who attended him for something of the sort during his University career. That is some time ago; but there is also Dr. Weare, who in 1925 prescribed for a similar attack. Not grave illnesses, but painful and exhausting, with sickness and so on, and aching in the limbs. Plenty of people have such troubles from time to time. Still, there is a coincidence of dates here which may be significant. We get these attacks—noted in Dr. Weare's case-book—one on March 31st, one on April 15th, and one on May 12th. Three sets of coincidences—as you may perhaps think them to be—Harriet Vane and Philip Boyes meet 'towards the end of March', and he has an attack of gastritis on March 31st; on April 10th, Harriet Vane purchases two ounces of arsenic—they meet again 'in the second week in April', and on April 15th he has another attack; on May 5th there is the purchase of weed-killer—'some time in May' there is another meeting, and on May 12th he is taken ill for the third time. You may think that is rather curious, but you must not forget that the Crown have failed to prove any purchase of arsenic before the meeting in March. You must bear that in mind when considering this point.

"After the third attack—the one in May—the doctor advises Boyes to go away for a change, and he selects the north-west corner of Wales. He goes to Harlech, and spends a very pleasant time there and is much better. But he has a friend to accompany him, Mr. Ryland Vaughan, whom you have seen, and this friend says that 'Philip was not happy'. In fact, Mr. Vaughan formed the opinion that he was fretting after Harriet Vane. His bodily health improved, but he grew mentally depressed. And so on June 16th we find him writing a letter to Miss Vane. Now that is an important letter, so I will read it to you once more:

" 'DEAR HARRIET,—Life is an utter mess-up. I can't stick it out here any longer. I've decided to cut adrift and take a trip out West. But before I go, I want to see you once again and find out if it isn't possible to put things straight again. You must do as you like, of course, but I still cannot understand the attitude you take up. If I can't make you see the thing in the right perspective this time I'll chuck it for good. I shall be in town on the 20th. Let me have a line to say when I can come round.

'Yours,

'P.'

"Now that, as you have realised, is a most ambiguous letter. Sir Impey Biggs, with arguments of great weight, has suggested that by the expressions 'cut adrift and take a trip out West', 'I can't stick it out here', and 'chuck it for good', the writer was expressing his intention to make away with himself if he could not effect a reconciliation with the accused. He points out that 'to go west' is a well-known metaphor for dying, and that, of course, may be convincing to you. But Mr. Urquhart, when examined on the subject by the Attorney-General, said that he supposed the letter to refer to a project which he himself had suggested to the deceased, of taking a voyage across the Atlantic to Barbados, by way of change of scene. And the learned Attorney-General makes this other point that when the writer says 'I can't stick it out *here* any longer', he means, here in Britain, or perhaps merely 'here at Harlech', and that if the phrase had reference to suicide it would read simply 'I can't stick it out any longer'.

"No doubt you have formed your own opinion on this point. It is important to note that the deceased asks for an appointment on the 20th. The reply to this letter is before us; it reads:

" 'DEAR PHIL,—You can come round at 9.30 on the 20th if you like, but you certainly will not make me change my mind.'

"And it is signed simply 'H'. A very cold letter, you may think—almost hostile in tone. And yet the appointment is made for 9.30.

"I shall not have to keep your attention very much longer, but I do ask for it at this point, specially—though you have been attending most patiently and industriously all the time—because we now come to the actual day of the death itself."

The old man clasped his hands one over the other upon the sheaf of notes and leaned a little forward. He had it all in his head, though he had known nothing of it until the last three days. He had not reached the time to babble of green fields and childhood ways; he still had firm hold of the present; he held it pinned down flat under his wrinkled fingers with their grey, chalky nails.

"Philip Boyes and Mr. Vaughan came back to town together on the evening of the 19th, and there would seem to be no doubt at all that Boyes was then in the best of health. Boyes spent the night with Mr. Vaughan and they breakfasted together in the usual way upon bacon and eggs, toast, marmalade, and coffee. At 11 o'clock Boyes had a Guinness, observing that, according to the advertisements, it was 'Good for you'. At 1 o'clock he ate a hearty lunch at his club, and in the afternoon he played several sets at tennis with Mr. Vaughan and some other friends. During the game the remark was made by one of the players that Harlech had done Boyes good, and he replied that he was feeling fitter than he had done for many months.

"At half-past seven he went round to have dinner with his cousin, Mr. Norman Urquhart. Nothing at all unusual in his manner or appearance was noticed, either by Mr. Urquhart or by the maid who waited at table. Dinner was served at 8 o'clock exactly, and I think it would be a good thing if you were to write down that time (if you have not already done so) and also the list of things eaten and drunk.

"The two cousins dined alone together, and first, by way of cocktail, each had a glass of sherry. The wine was a fine Oloroso of 1847, and the maid decanted it from a fresh bottle and poured it into the glasses as they sat in the library. Mr. Urquhart retains the dignified old-fashioned custom of having the maid in attendance throughout the meal, so that we have here the advantage of two witnesses during this part of the evening. You saw the maid, Hannah Westlock, in the box, and I think you will say she gave the impression of being a sensible and observant witness.

"Well, there was the sherry. Then came a cup of cold bouillon, served by Hannah Westlock from the tureen on the sideboard. It was very strong, good soup, set to a clear jelly. Both men had some, and, after dinner, the bouillon was finished by the cook and Miss Westlock in the kitchen.

"After the soup came a piece of turbot with sauce. The portions were again carved at the sideboard, the sauce-boat was handed to each in turn, and the dish was then sent out to be finished in the kitchen.

"Then came a *poulet en casserole*—that is, chicken cut up and stewed slowly with vegetables in a fireproof cooking utensil. Both men had some of this, and the maids finished the dish.

"The final course was a sweet omelette, which was made at the table in a chafing-dish by Philip Boyes himself. Both Mr. Urquhart and his cousin were very particular about eating an omelette the moment it came from the pan—and a very good rule it is, and I advise you all to treat omelettes in the same way and never to allow them to stand, or they will get tough. Four eggs were brought to the table in their shells, and Mr. Urquhart broke them one by one into a bowl, adding sugar from a sifter. Then he handed the bowl to Mr. Boyes, saying: 'You're the real dab at omelettes, Philip—I'll leave this to you.' Philip Boyes then beat the eggs and sugar together, cooked the omelette in the chafing-dish, filled it with hot jam, which was brought in by Hannah Westlock, and then himself divided it into two portions, giving one to Mr. Urquhart and taking the remainder himself.

"I have been a little careful to remind you of all these things, to show that we have good proof that every dish served at dinner was partaken of by two people at least, and in most cases by four. The omelette—the only dish which did not go out to the kitchen—was prepared by Philip Boyes himself and shared by his cousin. Neither Mr. Urquhart, Miss Westlock, nor the cook, Mrs. Pettican, felt any ill-effects from this meal.

"I should mention also that there was one article of diet which was partaken of by Philip Boyes alone, and that was a bottle of Burgundy. It was a fine old Corton, and was brought to table in its original bottle. Mr. Urquhart drew the cork and then handed the bottle intact to Philip Boyes, saying that he himself would not take any—he had been advised not to drink at meal-times. Philip Boyes drank two glassfuls and the remainder of the bottle was fortunately preserved. As you have already heard, the wine was later analysed and found to be quite harmless.

"This brings us to 9 o'clock. After dinner, coffee is offered, but Boyes excuses himself on the ground that he does not care for Turkish coffee, and moreover will probably be given coffee by Harriet Vane. At 9.15 Boyes leaves Mr. Urquhart's house in Woburn Square, and is driven in a taxi to the house where Miss Vane has her flat, No. 100 Doughty Street—a distance of about half a mile. We have it from Harriet Vane herself, from Mrs. Bright, a resident in the ground-floor flat, and from Police Constable D. 1234, who was passing along the street at the time, that he was standing on the doorstep, ringing the prisoner's bell, at twenty-five minutes past nine. She was on the look-out for him and let him in immediately.

"Now, as the interview was naturally a private one, we have no account of it to go upon but that of the prisoner. She has told us that as soon as he came in she offered him 'a cup of coffee which was standing ready upon the gas-ring'. Now, when the learned Attorney-General heard the prisoner say that, he immediately asked what the coffee was standing ready in. The prisoner, apparently not quite understanding the purport of the question, replied 'in the fender, to keep hot'. When the question was repeated more clearly, she explained that the coffee was made in a saucepan, and that it was this which was placed upon the gas-ring in the fender. The Attorney-General then drew the prisoner's attention to her previous statement made to the police, in which this expression appeared: 'I had a cup of coffee ready for him on his arrival.' You will see at once the importance of this. If the cups of coffee were prepared and poured out separately before the arrival of the deceased, there was every opportunity to place poison in one of the cups beforehand and offer the prepared cup to Philip Boyes; but if the coffee was poured out from the saucepan in the deceased's presence, the opportunity would be rather less, though of course the thing might easily be done while Boyes' attention was momentarily distracted. The prisoner explained that in her statement she used the phrase 'a cup of coffee' merely as denoting 'a certain quantity of coffee'. You yourselves will be able to judge whether that is a usual and natural form of expression. The deceased is said by her to have taken no milk or sugar in his coffee, and you have the testimony of Mr. Urquhart and Mr. Vaughan that it was his usual habit to drink his after-dinner coffee black and unsweetened.

"According to the prisoner's evidence, the interview was not a satisfactory one. Reproaches were uttered on both sides, and at 10 o'clock or thereabouts the deceased expressed his intention of leaving her. She says that he appeared uneasy, and remarked that he was not feeling well, adding that her behaviour had greatly upset him.

"At ten minutes past ten—and I want you to note these times very carefully—the taxi-driver Burke, who was standing on the rank in Guilford Street, was approached by Philip Boyes and told to take him to Woburn Square. He says that Boyes spoke in a hurried and abrupt tone, like that of a person in distress of mind or body. When the taxi stopped before Mr. Urquhart's house, Boyes did not get out, and Burke opened the door to see what was the matter. He found the deceased huddled in a corner with his hand pressed over his stomach and his face pale and covered with perspiration. He asked him whether he was ill, and the deceased replied: 'Yes, rotten.' Burke helped him out and rang the bell, supporting him with one arm as they stood on the door-step. Hannah Westlock opened the door. Philip Boyes seemed hardly able to walk; his body was bent almost double, and he sank groaning into a hall-chair and asked for brandy. She brought him a stiff brandy-and-soda from the dining-room, and, after drinking this, Boyes recovered sufficiently to take money from his pocket and pay for the taxi.

"As he still seemed very ill, Hannah Westlock summoned Mr. Urquhart from the library. He said to Boyes, 'Hullo, old man—what's the matter with you?' Boyes replied, 'God knows! I feel awful. It can't have been the chicken.' Mr. Urquhart said he hoped not, he hadn't noticed anything wrong with it, and Boyes answered, No, he supposed it was one of his usual attacks, but he'd never felt anything like this before. He was taken upstairs to bed, and Dr. Grainger was summoned by telephone, as being the nearest physician available.

"Before the doctor's arrival, the patient vomited violently, and thereafter continued to vomit persistently. Dr. Grainger diagnosed the trouble as acute gastritis. There was a high temperature and rapid pulse, and the patient's abdomen was acutely painful to pressure, but the doctor found nothing indicative of any trouble in the nature of appendicitis or peritonitis. He therefore went back to his surgery, and made up a soothing medicine to control the vomiting—a mixture of bicarbonate of potash, tincture of oranges, and chloroform—no other drugs.

"Next day the vomiting still persisted, and Dr. Weare was called in to consult with Dr. Grainger, as he was well acquainted with the patient's constitution."

Here the judge paused and glanced at the clock.

"Time is getting on, and as the medical evidence has still to be passed in review, I will adjourn the Court now for lunch."

"He would," said the Hon. Freddy, "just at the beastliest moment when everybody's appetite is thoroughly taken away. Come on, Wimsey, let's go and fold a chop into the system, shall we?—Hullo!"

Wimsey had pushed past without heeding him, and was making his way down into the body of the court, where Sir Impey Biggs stood conferring with his juniors.

"Seems to be in a bit of a stew," said Mr. Arbuthnot, meditatively. "Gone to put an alternative theory of some kind, I expect. Wonder why I came to this bally show. Tedious, don't you know, and the girl's not even pretty. Don't think I'll come back after grub."

He struggled out, and found himself face to face with the Dowager Duchess of Denver.

"Come and have lunch, Duchess," said Freddy, hopefully. He liked the Dowager.

"I'm waiting for Peter, thanks, Freddy. Such an interesting case and interesting people, too, don't you think, though what the jury make of it I don't know, with faces like hams most of them, except the artist, who wouldn't have any features at all if it wasn't for that dreadful tie and his beard, looking like Christ, only not really Christ but one of those Italian ones in a pink frock and blue top thing. Isn't that Peter's Miss Climpson on the jury, how does she get there, I wonder?"

"He's put her into a house somewhere round about, I fancy," said Freddy, "with a typewriting office to look after and live over the shop and run those comic charity stunts of his. Funny old soul, isn't she? Stepped out of a magazine of the 'nineties. But she seems to suit his work all right and all that."

"Yes—such a good thing too, answering all those shady advertisements and then getting the people shown up and so courageous too, some of them the horridest oily people, and murderers I shouldn't wonder with automatic thingummies and life-preservers in every pocket, and very likely a gas-oven full of bones like Landru, so clever, wasn't he? And really *such* women—born murderers as somebody says quite pig-faced but not of course deserving it and possibly the photographs don't do them justice, poor things."

The Duchess was even more rambling than usual, thought Freddy, and as she spoke her eyes wandered to her son with a kind of anxiety unusual in her.

"Top-hole to see old Wimsey back, isn't it?" he said, with simple kindness. "Wonderful how keen he is on this sort of thing, don't you know. Rampages off the minute he gets home like the jolly old war-horse sniffing the T.N.T. Regularly up to the eyes in it."

"Well, it's one of Chief Inspector Parker's cases, and they're such great friends, you know, quite like David and Beersheba—or do I mean Daniel?"

Wimsey joined them at this complicated moment, and tucked his mother's arm affectionately in his own.

"Frightfully sorry to keep you waiting, Mater, but I had to say a word to Biggy. He's having a rotten time, and that old Jeffreys of a judge looks as though he was getting measured for a black cap. I'm going home to burn my books. Dangerous to know too much about poisons, don't you think? Be thou as chaste as ice, as pure as snow, thou shalt not escape the Old Bailey."

"The young woman doesn't seem to have tried that recipe, does she?" remarked Freddy.

"You ought to be on the jury," retorted Wimsey, with unusual acidity, "I bet that's what they're all saying at this moment. I'm convinced that the foreman is a teetotaller—I saw ginger-beer going into the jury-room, and I only hope it explodes and blows his inside through the top of his skull."

"All right, all right," returned Mr. Arbuthnot, soothingly; "what you want is a drink."

CHAPTER II

THE SCRAMBLE FOR places subsided; the jury returned; the prisoner reappeared in the dock suddenly, like a jack-in-the-box; the judge resumed his seat. Some petals had spilt from the red roses. The old voice took up its tale where it had left off.

"Members of the jury—there is no need, I think, for me to recall the course of Philip Boyes' illness in great detail. The nurse was called in on June 21st, and during that day the doctors visited the patient three times. His condition grew steadily worse. There was persistent vomiting and diarrhoea, and he could not keep any food or medicine down at all. On the day after, the 22nd, he was worse still—in great pain, the pulse growing weaker, and the skin about the mouth getting dry and peeling off. The doctors gave him every attention, but could do nothing for him. His father was summoned, and when he arrived he found his son conscious, but unable to lift himself. He was able to speak, however, and in the presence of his father and Nurse Williams he made the remark, 'I'm going out, Dad, and I'm glad to be through with it. Harriet'll be rid of me now—I didn't know she hated me quite so much.' Now that was a very remarkable speech, and we have heard two very different interpretations put upon it. It is for you to say whether, in your opinion, he meant: 'She has succeeded in getting rid of me; I didn't know she hated me enough to poison me,' or whether he meant, 'When I realised she hated me so much, I decided I did not want to live any longer'—or whether, perhaps, he meant neither of these things. When people are very ill, they sometimes get fantastic ideas, and sometimes they wander in their minds; perhaps you may feel that it is not profitable to take too much for granted. Still, those words are part of the evidence, and you are entitled to take them into account.

"During the night he became gradually weaker and lost consciousness, and at 3 o'clock in the morning he died, without ever regaining it. That was on the 23rd of June.

"Now, up to this time, no suspicion of any kind had been aroused. Both Dr. Grainger and Dr. Weare formed the opinion that the cause of death was acute gastritis, and we need not blame them for coming to this conclusion, because it was quite consistent both with the symptoms of the illness and with the past history of the patient. A death-certificate was given in the usual way, and the funeral took place on the 28th.

"Well, then something happened which frequently does happen in cases of this kind, and that is that somebody begins to talk. It was Nurse Williams who talked in this particular case, and while you will probably think that this was a very wrong and very indiscreet thing for a nurse to do, yet, as it turns out, it was a good thing that she did. Of course, she ought to have told Dr. Weare or Dr. Grainger of her suspicions at the time, but she did not do this, and we may at least feel glad to know that, in the doctors' opinions, even if she had done so, and if they had discovered that the illness was caused by arsenic, they would not have been able to do anything more to save the life of this unfortunate man. At any rate, what happened was that Nurse Williams was sent, during the last week of June, to nurse another patient of Dr. Weare's, who happened to belong to the same literary set in Bloomsbury as Philip Boyes and Harriet Vane, and while she was there, she spoke about Philip Boyes, and said that, in her opinion, the illness looked very much like poisoning, and she even mentioned the word arsenic. Well, you know how a thing like that gets about. One person tells another, and it is discussed at tea parties, or what are known, I believe, as cocktail parties, and very soon a story gets spread about, and people mention names and take sides. Miss Marriott and Miss Price were told about it, and it also got to the ears of Mr. Vaughan. Now Mr. Vaughan had been greatly distressed and surprised by Philip Boyes' death, especially as he had been with him in Wales, and knew how much he had improved in health while on his holiday, and he also felt very strongly that Harriet Vane had behaved badly about the love-affair. Mr. Vaughan felt that some action ought to be taken about the matter, and went to Mr. Urquhart and put the story before him. Now Mr. Urquhart is a solicitor, and is therefore inclined to take a cautious view of rumours and suspicions, and he warned Mr. Vaughan that it was not wise to go about making accusations against people, for fear of an action for libel. At the same time, he naturally felt uneasy that such a thing should be said about a relation who had died in his house. He took the course—the very sensible course—of consulting Dr. Weare and suggesting that, if he was quite certain that the illness was due to gastritis and nothing else, he should take steps to rebuke Nurse Williams and put an end to the talk. Dr. Weare was naturally very much surprised and upset to hear what was being said, but, since the suggestion had been made, he could not deny that—taking the symptoms only into account—there was just the bare possibility of something of the sort, because, as you have already heard in the medical evidence, the symptoms of arsenical poisoning and of acute gastritis are really indistinguishable.

"When this was communicated to Mr. Vaughan, he was confirmed in his suspicions, and wrote to the elder Mr. Boyes suggesting an enquiry. Mr. Boyes was naturally very much shocked, and said at once that the matter should be taken up. He had known of the liaison with Harriet Vane, and had noticed that she did not come to enquire after Philip Boyes, nor attend the funeral, and this had struck him as heartless behaviour. In the end, the police were communicated with and an exhumation order obtained.

"You have heard the result of the analysis made by Sir James Lubbock and Mr. Stephen Fordyce. There was a great deal of discussion about methods of analysis and the way that arsenic behaves in the body and so on, but I think we need not trouble too much about those fine details. The chief points in the evidence seemed to me to be these, which you may note down if you care to do so.

"The analysts took certain organs of the body—the stomach, intestines, kidneys, liver and so on—and analysed portions of these and found that they all contained arsenic. They were able to weigh the quantity of arsenic found in these various portions, and they calculated from that the quantity of arsenic present in the whole body. Then they had to allow so much for the amount of arsenic eliminated from the body by the vomiting and diarrhoea and also through the kidneys, because the kidneys play a very large part in the elimination of this particular poison. After making allowance for all these things, they formed the opinion that a large and fatal dose of arsenic—four or five grains, perhaps—had been taken about three days before the death.

"I do not know whether you quite followed all the technical arguments about this. I will try to tell you the chief points as I understood them. The nature of arsenic is to pass through the body very quickly, especially if it is taken with food or immediately following a meal, because the arsenic irritates the lining of the internal organs and speeds up the process of elimination. The action would be quicker if the arsenic were taken in liquid than if it were taken in the form of a powder. Where arsenic was taken with, or immediately on top of, a meal, nearly the whole of it would be evacuated within twenty-four hours after the onset of the illness. So you see that, although the actual quantities found in the body may seem to you and me very small indeed, the mere fact that they were found there at all, after three days of persistent vomiting and diarrhoea and so on, points to a large dose having been taken at some time.

"Now there was a great deal of discussion about the time at which the symptoms first set in. It is suggested by the defence that Philip Boyes may have taken the arsenic himself at some time between leaving Harriet Vane's flat and hailing the taxi in Guilford Street; and they bring forward books which show that in many cases the onset of symptoms takes place in a very short time after the arsenic—a quarter of an hour, I think, was the shortest time mentioned where the arsenic was taken in liquid form. Now the prisoner's statement—and we have no other—is that Philip Boyes left her at 10 o'clock, and at ten minutes past he was in Guilford Street. He was then looking ill. It would not take many minutes to drive to Woburn Square at that hour of night, and by the time he got there, he was already in acute pain and hardly able to stand. Now Guilford Street is a very short way from Doughty Street—perhaps three minutes' walk—and you must ask yourselves, if the prisoner's statement is correct, what he did with those ten minutes. Did he occupy himself in going to some quiet spot and taking a dose of arsenic, which he must in that case have brought with him in anticipation of an unfavourable interview with the prisoner? And I may remind you here that the defence have brought no evidence to show that Philip Boyes ever bought any arsenic, or had access to any arsenic. That is not to say he could not have obtained it—the purchases made by Harriet Vane show that the law about the sale of poisons is not always as effective as one would like it to be—but the fact remains that the defence have not been able to show that the deceased ever had arsenic in his possession. And while we are on this subject, I will mention that, curiously enough, the analysts could find no traces of the charcoal, or indigo, with which commercial arsenic is supposed to be mixed. Whether it was bought by the prisoner or by the deceased himself, you would expect to find traces of the colouring matter. But you may think it likely that all such traces would be removed from the body by the vomiting and purging which took place.

"As regards the suggestion of suicide, you will have to ask yourselves about those ten minutes—whether Boyes was taking a dose of arsenic, or whether, as is also possible, he felt unwell and sat down somewhere to recover himself, or whether, perhaps, he was merely roaming about in the vague way we sometimes do when we are feeling upset and unhappy. Or you may think that the prisoner was mistaken, or not speaking the truth, about the time he left the flat.

"You have also the prisoner's statement that Boyes mentioned, before he left her, that he was feeling unwell. If you think this had anything to do with the arsenic, it of course disposes of the suggestion that he took poison after leaving the flat.

"Then, when one looks into it, one finds that this question about the onset of symptoms is left very vague. Various doctors came here and told you about their own experiences and the cases quoted by medical authorities in books, and you will have noticed that there is no certainty at all about the time when the symptoms may be expected to appear. Sometimes it is a quarter of an hour, sometimes two hours, sometimes as much as five or six, and, I believe, in one case as much as seven hours after taking the poison."

Here the Attorney-General rose respectfully and said: "In that case, me lud, I think I am right in saying that the poison was taken on an empty stomach."

"Thank you, I am much obliged to you for the reminder. That was a case in which the poison was taken on an empty stomach. I only mention these cases to show that we are dealing with a very uncertain phenomenon, and that is why I was particular to remind you of all the occasions on which Philip Boyes took food during the day—the 20th of June—since there is always the possibility that you may have to take them into consideration."

"A beast, but a just beast," murmured Lord Peter Wimsey.

"I have purposely left out of consideration until now another point which arose out of the analysis, and that is the presence of arsenic in the hair. The deceased had curly hair, which he wore rather long; the front portion, when straightened out, measured about six or seven inches in places. Now, in this hair arsenic was found, at the end closest to the head. It did not extend to the tips of the longest hair, but it was found near the roots, and Sir James Lubbock says that the quantity was greater than could be accounted for in any natural way. Occasionally, quite normal people are found to have minute traces of arsenic in the hair and skin and so on, but not to the amount found here. That is Sir James' opinion.

"Now you have been told—and the medical witnesses all agree in this—that if a person takes arsenic, a certain proportion of it will be deposited in the skin, nails, and hair. It will be deposited in the root of the hair, and as the hair grows, the arsenic will be carried along with the growth of the hair, so that you get a rough idea, from seeing the position of the arsenic in the hair, how long the administration of arsenic has been going on. There was a good deal of discussion about this, but I think there was a fairly general agreement that, if you took a dose of arsenic, you might expect to find traces of it in the hair, close to the scalp, after about ten weeks. Hair grows at the rate of about six inches in a year, and the arsenic will grow out with it till it reaches the far end and is cut off. I am sure that the ladies on the jury will understand this very well, because I believe that the same thing occurs in the case of what is termed a 'permanent wave'. The wave is made in a certain portion of the hair, and after a time it grows out, and the hair near the scalp comes up straight and has to be waved again. You can tell by the position of the wave how long ago the waving was done. In the same way, if a finger-nail is bruised, the discoloration will gradually grow up the nail until it reaches the point where you can cut it off with the scissors.

"Now it has been said that the presence of arsenic in and about the roots of Philip Boyes' hair indicates that he must have taken arsenic three months at least before his death. You will consider what importance is to be attached to this in view of the prisoner's purchases of arsenic in April and May, and of the deceased's attacks of sickness in March, April and May. The quarrel with the prisoner took place in February; he was ill in March and died in June. There are five months between the quarrel and the death, and four months between the first illness and the death, and you may think that there is some significance in these dates.

"We now come to the enquiries made by the police. When suspicion was aroused, detectives investigated Harriet Vane's movements and subsequently went to her flat to take a statement from her. When they told her that Boyes was found to have died of arsenic poisoning, she appeared very much surprised, and said, 'Arsenic? What an extraordinary thing!' And then she laughed, and said, 'Why, I am writing a book all about arsenic poisoning.' They asked her about the purchases of arsenic and other poisons which she had made, and she admitted them quite readily and at once gave the same explanation that she gave here in court. They asked what she had done with the poisons, and she replied that she had burnt them because they were dangerous things to have about. The flat was searched, but no poisons of any kind were found, except such things as aspirin and a few ordinary medicines of that kind. She absolutely denied having administered arsenic or any kind of poison to Philip Boyes. She was asked whether the arsenic could possibly have got into the coffee by accident, and replied that was quite impossible, as she had destroyed all the poisons before the end of May."

Here Sir Impey Biggs interposed and begged with submission to suggest that his lordship should remind the jury of the evidence given by Mr. Challoner.

"Certainly, Sir Impey, I am obliged to you. You remember that Mr. Challoner is Harriet Vane's literary agent. He came here to tell us that he had discussed with her as long ago as last December the subject of her forthcoming book, and she then told him that it was to be about poisons, and very probably about arsenic. So you may think it is a point in the prisoner's favour that this intention of studying the purchase and administration of arsenic was already in her mind some time before the quarrel with Philip Boyes took place. She evidently gave considerable thought to the subject, for there were a number of books on her shelves dealing with forensic medicine and toxicology, and also the reports of several famous poison trials, including the Madeleine Smith case, the Seddon case, and the Armstrong case—all of which were cases of arsenical poisoning.

"Well, I think that is the case as it is presented to you. This woman is charged with having murdered her former lover by arsenic. He undoubtedly did take arsenic, and if you are satisfied that she gave it to him, with intent to injure or kill him, and that he died of it, then it is your duty to find her guilty of murder.

"Sir Impey Biggs, in his able and eloquent speech, has put it to you that she had very little motive for such a murder, but I am bound to tell you that murders are very often committed for what seem to be most inadequate motives—if, indeed, any motive can be called adequate for such a crime. Especially where the parties are husband and wife, or have lived together as husband and wife, there are likely to be passionate feelings which may tend to crimes of violence in persons with inadequate moral standards and of unbalanced mind.

"The prisoner had the means—the arsenic—she had the expert knowledge, and she had the opportunity to administer it. The defence say that this is not enough. They say the Crown must go further and prove that the poison could not have been taken in any other way—by accident, or with suicidal intent. That is for you to judge. If you feel that there is any reasonable doubt that the prisoner gave this poison to Philip Boyes deliberately, you must bring her in 'Not guilty' of murder. You are not bound to decide how it was given, if it was not given by her. Consider the circumstances of the case as a whole, and say what conclusion you have come to."

CHAPTER III

"THEY WON'T BE long, I shouldn't think," said Waffles Newton; "it's pretty damned obvious. Look here, old man, I'm going to push my stuff in. Will you let me know what happens?"

"Sure," said Salcombe Hardy, "if you don't mind dropping mine in at our place as you go. You couldn't send me a drink by 'phone, could you? My mouth's like the bottom of a parrot's cage." He looked at his watch. "We shall miss the 6.30 edition, I'm afraid, unless they hurry up. The old man is careful, but he's damned slow."

"They can't in decency not make a pretence of consulting about it," said Newton. "I give them twenty minutes. They'll want a smoke. So do I. I'll be back at ten to, in case."

He wriggled his way out. Cuthbert Logan, who reported for a morning paper, and was a man of more leisure, settled down to write up a word-picture of the trial. He was a phlegmatic and sober person, and could write as comfortably in court as anywhere else. He liked to be on the spot when things happened, and to note down glances, tones of voice, colour effects, and so forth. His copy was always entertaining, and sometimes even distinguished.

Freddy Arbuthnot, who had not, after all, gone home after lunch, thought it was time to do so now. He fidgeted, and Wimsey frowned at him. The Dowager Duchess made her way along the benches and squeezed in next to Lord Peter. Sir Impey Biggs, having watched over his client's interests to the last, disappeared, chatting cheerfully to the Attorney-General, and followed by the smaller legal fry. The dock was deserted. On the bench the red roses stood solitary, their petals dropping.

Chief Inspector Parker, disengaging himself from a group of friends, came slowly up through the crowd and greeted the Dowager. "And what do you think of it, Peter?" he added, turning to Wimsey. "Rather neatly got up, eh?"

"Charles," said Wimsey, "you ought not to be allowed out without me. You've made a mistake, old man."

"Made a mistake?"

"She didn't do it."

"Oh, come!"

"She did not do it. It's very convincing and watertight, but it's all wrong."

"You don't really think that."

"I do."

Parker looked distressed. He had confidence in Wimsey's judgment, and, in spite of his own interior certainty, he felt shaken.

"My dear man, where's the flaw in it?"

"There isn't one. It's damnably knife-proof. There's nothing wrong about it at all, except that the girl's innocent."

"You're turning into a common or garden psychologist," said Parker, with an uneasy laugh, "isn't he, Duchess?"

"I wish I had known that girl," replied the Dowager, in her usual indirect manner, "so interesting and a really remarkable face, though perhaps not strictly good-looking, and all the more interesting for that, because good-looking people are so often cows. I have been reading one of her books, really quite good and so well-written, and I didn't guess the murderer till page 200, rather clever, because I usually do it about page 15. So very curious to write books about crimes and then be accused of a crime one's self, some people might say it was a judgment. I wonder whether, if she didn't do it, she has spotted the murderer herself? I don't suppose detective writers detect much in real life, do they, except Edgar Wallace of course, who always seems to be everywhere and dear Conan Doyle and the black man what was his name and of course the Slater person, such a scandal, though now I come to think of it that was in Scotland where they have such very odd laws about everything particularly getting married. Well I suppose we shall soon know now, not the truth, necessarily, but what the jury have made of it."

"Yes; they are being rather longer than I expected. But, I say, Wimsey, I wish you'd tell me——"

"Too late, too late, you cannot enter now. I have locked my heart in a silver box and pinned it wi' a golden pin. Nobody's opinion matters now, except the jury's. I expect Miss Climpson is telling 'em all about it. When once she starts she doesn't stop for an hour or two."

"Well, they've been half an hour now," said Parker.

"Still waiting?" said Salcombe Hardy, returning to the press-table.

"Yes—so this is what you call twenty minutes! Three-quarters of an hour, I make it."

"They've been out an hour and a half," said a girl to her fiancé, just behind Wimsey. "What can they be discussing?"

"Perhaps they don't think she did it after all."

"What nonsense! Of course she did it. You could see it by her face. Hard, that's what I call it, and she never once cried or anything."

"Oh, I dunno," said the young man.

"You don't mean to say you admired her, Frank?"

"Oh, well, I dunno. But she didn't look to me like a murderess."

"And how do you know what a murderess looks like? Have you ever met one?"

"Well, I've seen them at Madame Tussaud's."

"Oh, waxworks. Everybody looks like a murderer in a waxworks."

"Well, p'raps they do. Have a choc."

"Two hours and a quarter," said Waffles Newton, impatiently. "They must have gone to sleep. Have to be a special edition. What happens if they are all night about it?"

"We sit here all night, that's all."

"Well, it's my turn for a drink. Let me know, will you?"

"Right-ho!"

"I've been talking to one of the ushers," said the Man Who Knows the Ropes, importantly, to a friend. "The judge has just sent round to the jury to ask if he can help them in any way."

"Has he? And what did they say?"

"I don't know."

"They've been out three hours and a half now," whispered the girl behind Wimsey. "I'm getting fearfully hungry."

"Are you, darling? Shall we go?"

"No—I want to hear the verdict. We've waited so long now, we may as well stop on."

"Well, I'll go out and get some sandwiches."

"Oh, that would be nice. But don't be long, because I'm sure I shall get hysterics when I hear the sentence."

"I'll be as quick as ever I can. Be glad you're not the jury—they're not allowed anything at all."

"What, nothing to eat or drink?"

"Not a thing. I don't think they're supposed to have light or fire either."

"Poor things! But it's central-heated, isn't it?"

"It's hot enough here, anyway. I'll be glad of a breath of fresh air."

Five hours.

"There's a terrific crowd in the street," said the Man Who Knows the Ropes, returning from a reconnaissance "Some people started booing the prisoner and a bunch of men attacked them, and one fellow has been carried off in an ambulance."

"Really, how amusing! Look! There's Mr. Urquhart; he's come back. I'm so sorry for him, aren't you? It must be horrid having somebody die in your house."

"He's talking to the Attorney-General. They've all had a proper dinner, of course."

"The Attorney-General isn't as handsome as Sir Impey Biggs. Is it true he keeps canaries?"

"The Attorney-General?"

"No, Sir Impey."

"Yes, quite true. He takes prizes with them."

"What a funny idea!"

"Bear up, Freddy," said Lord Peter Wimsey. "I perceive movements. They are coming, my own, my sweet, were it never so airy a tread."

The Court rose to its feet. The judge took his seat. The prisoner, very white in the electricity, reappeared in the dock. The door leading to the jury-room opened.

"Look at their faces," said the fiancée. "They say if it's going to be 'Guilty' they never look at the prisoner. Oh, Archie, hold my hand!"

The Clerk of Assizes addressed the jury in tones in which formality struggled with reproach.

"Members of the jury, have you all agreed upon your verdict?"

The foreman rose with an injured and irritable countenance.

"I am sorry to say that we find it impossible to come to an agreement."

A prolonged gasp and murmur went round the court. The judge leaned forward, very courteous and not in the least fatigued.

"Do you think that with a little more time you may be able to reach an agreement?"

"I'm afraid not, my lord." The foreman glanced savagely at one corner of the jury-box, where the elderly spinster sat with her head bowed and her hands tightly clasped. "I see no prospect at all of our ever agreeing."

"Can I assist you in any way?"

"No, thank you, my lord. We quite understand the evidence, but we cannot agree about it."

"That is unfortunate. I think perhaps you had better try again, and then, if you are still unable to come to a decision, you must come back and tell me. In the meantime, if my knowledge of the law can be of any assistance to you, it is, of course, quite at your disposal."

The jury stumbled sullenly away. The judge trailed his scarlet robes out at the back of the bench. The murmur of conversation rose and swelled into a loud rumble.

"By Jove," said Freddy Arbuthnot, "I believe it's your Miss Climpson that's holdin' the jolly old show up, Wimsey. Did you see how the foreman glared at her?"

"Good egg," said Wimsey. "Oh, excellent, excellent egg! She has a fearfully tough conscience—she may stick it out yet."

"I believe you've been corrupting the jury, Wimsey. Did you signal to her or something?"

"I didn't," said Wimsey. "Believe me or believe me not, I refrained from so much as a lifted eyebrow."

"And he himself has said it," muttered Freddy, "and it's greatly to his credit. But it's damned hard on people who want their dinners."

Six hours. Six hours and a half.

"At last!"

As the jury filed back for the second time, they showed signs of wear and tear. The harassed woman had been crying and was still choking into her handkerchief. The man with a bad cold looked nearly dead. The artist's hair was rumpled into an untidy bush. The company director and the foreman looked as though they would have liked to strangle somebody, and the elderly spinster had her eyes shut and her lips moving as though she were praying.

"Members of the jury, are you agreed upon your verdict?"

"No; we are quite sure that it is impossible for us ever to agree."

"You are quite sure?" said the judge. "I do not wish to hurry you in any way. I am quite prepared to wait here as long as ever you like."

The snarl of the company director was audible even in the gallery. The foreman controlled himself, and replied in a voice ragged with temper and exhaustion:

"We shall never agree, my lord—not if we was to stay here till Doomsday."

"That is very unfortunate," said the judge, "but in that case, of course, there is nothing for it but to discharge you and order a fresh trial. I feel sure that you have all done your best and that you have brought all the resources of your intelligence and conscience to bear on this matter to which you have listened with so much patient and zealous attention. You are discharged, and you are entitled to be excused from all further jury service for the next twelve years."

Almost before the further formalities were completed, and while the judge's robes still flared in the dark little doorway, Wimsey had scrambled down into the well of the court. He caught the defending counsel by the gown.

"Biggy—well done! You've got another chance. Let me in on this and we'll pull it off."

"You think so, Wimsey? I don't mind confessing that we've done better than I ever expected."

"We'll do better still next time. I say, Biggy, swear me in as a clerk or something. I want to interview her."

"Who, my client?"

"Yes. I've got a hunch about this case. We've got to get her off, and I know it can be done."

"Well, come and see me to-morrow. I must go and speak to her now. I'll be in my chambers at ten. Good-night."

Wimsey darted off and rushed round to the side-door, from which the jury were emerging. Last of them all, her hat askew and her mackintosh dragged awkwardly round her shoulders, came the elderly spinster. Wimsey dashed up to her and seized her hand.

"Miss Climpson!"

"Oh, Lord Peter. Oh, dear! What a dreadful day it has been. Do you know, it was me that caused the trouble, mostly, though two of them most bravely backed me up, and oh, Lord Peter, I hope I haven't done wrong, but I couldn't, no, I *couldn't* in conscience say she had done it when I was sure she hadn't, could I? Oh, dear, oh, dear!"

"You're absolutely right. She didn't do it, and thank God you stood up to them and gave her another chance. I'm going to prove she didn't do it. And I'm going to take you out to dinner, and—I say, Miss Climpson!"

"Yes?"

"I hope you won't mind, because I haven't shaved since this morning, but I'm going to take you round the next quiet corner and kiss you."

CHAPTER IV

THE FOLLOWING DAY was a Sunday, but Sir Impey Biggs cancelled an engagement to play golf (with the less regret as it was pouring cats and dogs), and held an extraordinary council of war.

"Well, now, Wimsey," said the advocate, "what is your idea about this? May I introduce Mr. Crofts, of Crofts & Cooper, solicitors for the defence."

"My idea is that Miss Vane didn't do it," said Wimsey. "I dare say that's an idea which has already occurred to you, but, with the weight of my great mind behind it, no doubt it strikes the imagination more forcibly."

Mr. Crofts, not being quite clear whether this was funny or fatuous, smiled deferentially.

"Quite so," said Sir Impey, "but I should be interested to know how many of the jury saw it in that light."

"Well, I can tell you that, at least, because I know one of them. One woman and half a woman and about three-quarters of a man."

"Meaning precisely?"

"Well, the woman I know stuck out for it that Miss Vane wasn't that sort of person. They bullied her a great deal, of course, because she couldn't lay a finger on any real weakness in the chain of evidence, but she said the prisoner's demeanour was part of the evidence and that she was entitled to take that into consideration. Fortunately, she is a tough, thin, elderly woman with a sound digestion and a militant High-Church conscience of remarkable staying-power, and her wind is excellent. She let 'em all gallop themselves dead, and then said she still didn't believe it and wasn't going to say she did."

"Very useful," said Sir Impey. "A person who can believe all the articles of the Christian faith is not going to boggle over a trifle of adverse evidence. But we can never hope for a whole jury-box full of ecclesiastical die-hards. How about the other woman and the man?"

"Well, the woman was rather unexpected. She was the stout, prosperous party who keeps a sweet-shop. She said she didn't think the case was proved, and that it was perfectly possible that Boyes had taken the stuff himself, or that his cousin had given it to him. She was influenced, rather oddly, by the fact that she had attended one or two arsenic trials, and had not been satisfied by the verdict in some other cases—notably the Seddon trial. She has no opinion of men in general (she has buried her third) and she disbelieves all expert evidence on principle. She said that, personally, she thought Miss Vane might have done it, but she wouldn't really hang a dog on medical evidence. At first she was ready to vote with the majority, but she took a dislike to the foreman, who tried to bear her down by his male authority, and eventually she said she was going to back up my friend Miss Climpson."

Sir Impey laughed.

"Very interesting. I wish we always got this inside information about juries. We sweat like hell to prepare evidence, and then one person makes up her mind on what isn't really evidence at all, and another supports her on the ground that evidence can't be relied on. How about the man?"

"The man was the artist, and the only person who really understood the kind of life these people were leading. He believed your client's version of the quarrel, and said that, if the girl really felt like that about the man, the last thing she would want to do would be to kill him. She'd rather stand back and watch him ache, like the man with the hollow tooth in the comic song. He was also able to believe the whole story about purchasing the poisons, which to the others, of course, seemed extremely feeble. He also said that Boyes, from what he had heard, was a conceited prig, and that anybody who disposed of him was doing a public service. He had had the misfortune to read some of his books, and considered the man an excrescence and a public nuisance. Actually he thought it more than likely that he had committed suicide, and if anybody was prepared to take that point of view he was ready to second it. He also alarmed the jury by saying that he was accustomed to late hours and a stale atmosphere, and had not the slightest objection to sitting up all night. Miss Climpson also said that, in a righteous cause, a little personal discomfort was a trifle, and added that her religion had trained her to fasting. At that point, the third woman had hysterics and another man, who had an important deal to put through next day, lost his temper, so, to prevent bodily violence, the foreman said he thought they had better agree to disagree. So that's how it was."

"Well, they've given us another chance," said Mr. Crofts, "so it's all to the good. It can't come on now till the next sessions, which gives us about a month, and we'll probably get Bancroft next time, who's not such a severe judge as Crossley. The thing is, can we do anything to improve the look of our case?"

"I'm going to have a strenuous go at it," said Wimsey. "There must *be* evidence somewhere, you know. I know you've all worked like beavers, but I'm going to work like a king beaver. And I've got one big advantage over the rest of you."

"More brains?" suggested Sir Impey, grinning.

"No—I should hate to suggest that, Biggy. But I do believe in Miss Vane's innocence."

"Damn it, Wimsey, didn't my eloquent speeches convince you that I was a whole-hearted believer?"

"Of course they did. I nearly shed tears. Here's old Biggy, I said to myself, going to retire from the Bar and cut his throat if this verdict goes against him, because he won't believe in British justice any more. No—it's your triumph at having secured a disagreement that gives you away, old horse. More than you expected. You said so. By the way, if it's not a rude question, who's paying you, Biggy?"

"Cofts & Cooper," said Sir Impey, slyly.

"They're in the thing for their health, I take it?"

"No, Lord Peter. As a matter of fact, the costs in this case are being borne by Miss Vane's publishers and by a—well, a certain newspaper, which is running her new book as a serial. They expect a scoop as the result of all this. But frankly, I don't quite know what they'll say to the expense of a fresh trial. I'm expecting to hear from them this morning."

"The vultures," said Wimsey. "Well, they'd better carry on, but tell 'em I'll see they're guaranteed. Don't bring my name in, though."

"This is very generous——"

"Not at all. I wouldn't lose the fun of all this for the world. Sort of case I fairly wallow in. But in return you must do something for me. I want to see Miss Vane. You must get me passed in as part of your outfit, so that I can hear her version of the story in reasonable privacy. Get me?"

"I expect that can be done," said Sir Impey. "In the meantime you have nothing to suggest?"

"Haven't had time yet. But I'll fish out something, don't you worry. I've already started to undermine the confidence of the police. Chief Inspector Parker has gone home to twine willow-wreaths for his own tombstone."

"You'll be careful," said Sir Impey. "Anything we can discover will come in much more effectively if the prosecution don't know of it beforehand."

"I'll walk as on egg-shells. But if I find the real murderer (if any), you won't object to my having him or her arrested, I take it?"

"No; I won't object to that. The police may. Well, gentlemen, if there's nothing further at the moment, we'd better adjourn the meeting. You'll get Lord Peter the facilities he wants, Mr. Crofts?"

Mr. Crofts exerted himself with energy, and on the following morning Lord Peter presented himself at the gates of Holloway Gaol, with his credentials.

"Oh, yes, my lord. You are to be treated on the same footing as the prisoner's solicitor. Yes, we have had a separate communication from the police, and that will be quite all right, my lord. The warder will take you down, and explain the regulations to you."

Wimsey was conducted through a number of bare corridors to a small room with a glass door. There was a long deal table in it and a couple of repellent chairs, one at either end of the table.

"Here you are, my lord. You sit at one end and the prisoner at the other, and you must be careful not to move from your seats, nor to pass any object over the table. I shall be outside and see you through the glass, my lord, but I shan't be able to overhear nothing. If you will take a seat, they'll bring the prisoner in, my lord."

Wimsey sat down and waited, a prey to curious sensations. Presently there was a noise of footsteps, and the prisoner was brought in, attended by a female wardress. She took the chair opposite to Wimsey, the wardress withdrew, and the door was shut. Wimsey, who had risen, cleared his throat.

"Good morning, Miss Vane," he said, unimpressively.

The prisoner looked at him.

"Please sit down," she said, in the curious, deep voice which had attracted him in court. "You are Lord Peter Wimsey, I believe, and have come from Mr. Crofts."

"Yes," said Wimsey. Her steady gaze was unnerving him. "Yes. I—er—I heard the case and all that, and—er—I thought there might be something I could do, don't you know."

"That was very good of you," said the prisoner.

"Not at all, not at all, dash it! I mean to say, I rather enjoy investigating things, if you know what I mean."

"I know. Being a writer of detective stories, I have naturally studied your career with interest."

She smiled suddenly at him and his heart turned to water.

"Well, that's rather a good thing in a way, because you'll understand that I'm not really such an ass as I'm looking at present."

That made her laugh.

"You're not looking an ass—at least, not more so than any gentleman should under the circumstances. The background doesn't altogether suit your style, but you are a very refreshing sight. And I'm really very grateful to you, though I'm afraid I'm rather a hopeless case."

"Don't say that. It can't be hopeless, unless you actually did it, and I know you didn't."

"Well, I didn't, as a matter of fact. But I feel it's like one book I wrote, in which I invented such a perfectly watertight crime that I couldn't devise any way for my detective to prove it, and had to fall back on the murderer's confession."

"If necessary, we'll do the same. You don't happen to know who the murderer is, I suppose?"

"I don't think there is one. I really believe Philip took the stuff himself. He was rather a defeatist sort of person, you know."

"I suppose he took your separation pretty hard?"

"Well, I daresay it was partly that. But I think it was more that he didn't feel he was sufficiently appreciated. He was apt to think that people were in league to spoil his chances."

"And were they?"

"No, I don't think so. But I do think he offended a great many people. He was rather apt to demand things as a right—and that annoys people, you know."

"Yes, I see. Did he get on all right with his cousin?"

"Oh, yes; though of course he always said it was no more than Mr. Urquhart's duty to look after him. Mr. Urquhart is fairly well off, as he has quite a big professional connection, but Philip really had no claim on him, as it wasn't family money or anything. His idea was that great artists deserved to be boarded and lodged at the expense of the ordinary man."

Wimsey was fairly well acquainted with this variety of the artistic temperament. He was struck, however, by the tone of the reply, which was tinged, he thought, with bitterness and even some contempt. He put his next question with some hesitation.

"Forgive me asking, but—you were very fond of Philip Boyes?"

"I must have been, mustn't I—under the circumstances?"

"Not necessarily," said Wimsey, boldly; "you might have been sorry for him—or bewitched by him—or even badgered to death by him."

"All those things."

Wimsey considered for a moment.

"Were you friends?"

"No." The word broke out with a kind of repressed savagery that startled him. "Philip wasn't the sort of man to make a friend of a woman. He wanted devotion. I gave him that. I did, you know. But I couldn't stand being made a fool of. I couldn't stand being put on probation like an office-boy, to see if I was good enough to be condescended to. I quite thought he was honest when he said he didn't believe in marriage—and then it turned out that it was a test, to see whether my devotion was abject enough. Well, it wasn't. I didn't like having matrimony offered as a bad-conduct prize."

"I don't blame you," said Wimsey.

"Don't you?"

"No. It sounds to me as if the fellow was a prig—not to say a bit of a cad. Like that horrid man who pretended to be a landscape-painter and then embarrassed the unfortunate young woman with the burden of an honour unto which she was not born. I've no doubt he made himself perfectly intolerable about it, with his ancient oaks and family plate, and the curtseying tenantry and all the rest of it."

Harriet Vane laughed once more.

"Yes—it's ridiculous—but humiliating too. Well, there it is. I thought

Philip had made both himself and me ridiculous, and the minute I saw that—well, the whole thing simply shut down—flop!"

She sketched a gesture of finality.

"I quite see that," said Wimsey. "Such a Victorian attitude, too, for a man with advanced ideas. He for God only, she for God in him, and so on. Well, I'm glad you feel like that about it."

"Are you? It's not going to be exactly helpful in the present crisis."

"No; I was looking beyond that. What I mean to say is, when this is over, I want to marry you, if you can put up with me and all that."

Harriet Vane, who had been smiling at him, frowned, and an indefinable expression of distaste came into her eyes.

"Oh, are you another of them? That makes forty-seven."

"Forty-seven what?" asked Wimsey, much taken aback.

"Proposals. They come in by every post. I suppose there are a lot of imbeciles who want to marry anybody who's at all notorious."

"Oh," said Wimsey. "Dear me, that makes it very awkward. As a matter of fact, you know, I don't need any notoriety. I can get into the papers off my own bat. It's no treat to me. Perhaps I'd better not mention it again."

His voice sounded hurt, and the girl eyed him rather remorsefully.

"I'm sorry—but one gets rather a bruised sort of feeling in my position. There have been so many beastlinesses."

"I know," said Lord Peter. "It was stupid of me——"

"No, I think it was stupid of me. But why——?"

"Why? Oh, well—I thought you'd be rather an attractive person to marry. That's all. I mean, I sort of took a fancy to you. I can't tell you why. There's no rule about it, you know."

"I see. Well, it's very nice of you."

"I wish you wouldn't sound as if you thought it was rather funny. I know I've got a silly face, but I can't help that. As a matter of fact, I'd like somebody I could talk sensibly to, who would make life interesting. And I could give you a lot of plots for your books, if that's any inducement."

"But you wouldn't want a wife who wrote books, would you?"

"But I should; it would be great fun. So much more interesting than the ordinary kind that is only keen on clothes and people. Though, of course, clothes and people are all right too, in moderation. I don't mean to say I object to clothes."

"And how about the old oaks and the family plate?"

"Oh, you wouldn't be bothered with them. My brother does all that. I collect first editions and incunabula, which is a little tedious of me, but you wouldn't need to bother with them either unless you liked."

"I don't mean that. What would your family think about it?"

"Oh, my mother's the only one that counts, and she likes you very much from what she's seen of you."

"So you had me inspected?"

"No—dash it all, I seem to be saying all the wrong things to-day. I was absolutely stunned that first day in court, and I rushed off to my mater, who's an absolute dear, and the kind of person who really understands things, and

I said, 'Look here! here's the absolutely one and only woman, and she's being put through a simply ghastly awful business and for God's sake come and hold my hand!' You simply don't know how foul it was."

"That does sound rather rotten. I'm sorry I was brutal. But, by the way, you're bearing in mind, aren't you, that I've had a lover?"

"Oh, yes. So have I, if it comes to that. In fact, several. It's the sort of thing that might happen to anybody. I can produce quite good testimonials. I'm told I make love rather nicely—only I'm at a disadvantage at the moment. One can't be very convincing at the other end of a table with a bloke looking in at the door."

"I will take your word for it. But, 'however entrancing it is to wander unchecked through a garden of bright images, are we not enticing your mind from another subject of almost equal importance?' It seems probable——"

"And if you can quote *Kai Lung*, we should certainly get on together."

"It seems very probable that I shall not survive to make the experiment."

"Don't be so damned discouraging," said Wimsey. "I have already carefully explained to you that this time *I* am investigating this business. Anybody would think you had no confidence in me."

"People have been wrongly condemned before now."

"Exactly; simply because I wasn't there."

"I never thought of that."

"Think of it now. You will find it very beautiful and inspiring. It might even help to distinguish me from the other forty-six, if you should happen to mislay my features or anything. Oh, by the way—I don't positively repel you or anything like that, do I? Because, if I do, I'll take my name off the waiting-list at once."

"No," said Harriet Vane, kindly and a little sadly, "no, you don't repel me."

"I don't remind you of white slugs or make you go goose-flesh all over?"

"Certainly not."

"I'm glad of that. Any minor alterations, like parting the old mane, or growing a toothbrush, or cashiering the eye-glass, you know, I should be happy to undertake, if it suited your ideas."

"Don't," said Miss Vane, "please don't alter yourself in any particular."

"You really mean that?" Wimsey flushed a little. "I hope it doesn't mean that nothing I could do would make me even passable? I'll come in a different set of garments each time, so as to give you a good all-round idea of the subject. Bunter—my man, you know—will see to that. He has excellent taste in ties, and socks, and things like that. Well, I suppose I ought to be going. You—er—you'll think it over, won't you, if you have a minute to spare? There's no hurry. Only don't hesitate to say if you think you couldn't stick it at any price. I'm not trying to blackmail you into matrimony, you know. I mean, I should investigate this for the fun of the thing, whatever happened, don't you see."

"It's very good of you——"

"No, no, not at all. It's my hobby. Not proposing to people, I don't mean, but investigating things. Well, cheer-frightfully-ho and all that. And I'll call again, if I may."

"I will give the footman orders to admit you," said the prisoner, gravely; "you will always find me at home."

Wimsey walked down the dingy street with a feeling of being almost light-headed.

"I do believe I'll pull it off—she's sore, of course—no wonder, after that rotten brute—but she doesn't feel repelled—one couldn't cope with being repulsive—her skin is like honey—she ought to wear deep red—and old garnets—and lots of rings, rather old-fashioned ones—I could take a house, of course—poor kid, I would damn well work to make it up to her—she's got a sense of humour too—brains—one wouldn't be dull—one would wake up, and there'd be a whole day for jolly things to happen in—and then one would come home and go to bed—that would be jolly, too—and while she was writing, I could go out and mess round, so we shouldn't either of us be dull—I wonder if Bunter was right about this suit—it's a little dark, I always think, but the line is good——"

He paused before a shop window to get a surreptitious view of his own reflection. A large coloured window-bill caught his eye:

GREAT SPECIAL OFFER
ONE MONTH ONLY

"Oh, God!" he said, softly, sobered at once. "One month—four weeks—thirty-one days. There isn't much time. And I don't know where to begin."

CHAPTER V

"WELL, NOW," SAID Wimsey, "why do people kill people?"

He was sitting in Miss Katharine Climpson's private office. The establishment was ostensibly a typing bureau, and indeed there were three efficient female typists who did very excellent work for authors and men of science from time to time. Apparently the business was a large and flourishing one, for work frequently had to be refused on the ground that the staff was working at full pressure. But on other floors of the building there were other activities. All the employees were women—mostly elderly, but a few still young and attractive—and if the private register in the steel safe had been consulted, it would have been seen that all these women were of the class unkindly known as "superfluous". There were spinsters with small incomes, or no income at all; widows without family; women deserted by peripatetic husbands and living on a restricted alimony, who, previous to their engagement by Miss Climpson, had had no resources but bridge and boarding-house gossip. There were retired and disappointed schoolteachers; out-of-work actresses; courageous people who had failed with hat-shops and tea-parlours; and even a few Bright Young Things, for whom the cocktail party and the night-club had grown boring. These women seemed to spend most of their time in answering advertisements. Unmarried gentlemen who desired to meet ladies possessed of competences, with a view to matrimony; sprightly sexagenarians, who wanted housekeepers for remote country districts; ingenious gentlemen with financial schemes, on the look-out for capital; literary gentlemen, anxious for female collaborators; plausible gentlemen about to engage talent for productions in the provinces; benevolent gentlemen, who could tell people how to make money in their spare time—gentlemen such as these were very liable to receive applications from members of Miss Climpson's staff. It may have been coincidence that these gentlemen so very often had the misfortune to appear shortly afterwards before the magistrate on charges of fraud, blackmail, or attempted procuration, but it is a fact that Miss Climpson's office boasted a private telephone-line to Scotland Yard, and that few of her ladies were quite so unprotected as they appeared. It is also a fact that the money which paid for the rent and upkeep of the premises might, by zealous enquirers, have been traced to Lord Peter Wimsey's banking account. His lordship was somewhat reticent about this venture of his, but occasionally, when closeted with Chief Inspector Parker or other intimate friends, referred to it as "My Cattery".

Miss Climpson poured out a cup of tea before replying. She wore a quantity of little bangles on her spare, lace-covered wrists, and they clinked aggressively with every movement.

"I really don't know," she said, apparently taking the problem as a psychological one, "it is so *dangerous*, as well as so terribly *wicked*, one wonders that anybody has the *effrontery* to undertake it. And very often they gain so *little* by it."

"That's what I mean," said Wimsey, "what do they set out to gain? Of course, some people seem to do it for the fun of the thing, like that German female, what's her name, who enjoyed seeing people die."

"Such a *strange* taste," said Miss Climpson. "No sugar, I think?—You know, dear Lord Peter, it has been my melancholy duty to attend *many* death-beds, and, though a number of them—such as my dear father's—were *most* Christian and beautiful, I could not call them *fun*. People have very different ideas of fun, of course, and personally I have never greatly cared for George Robey, though Charlie Chaplin always makes me laugh—still, you know, there are *disagreeable details* attending *any* death-bed which one would think could hardly be to anybody's taste, however depraved."

"I quite agree with you," said Wimsey. "But it must be fun, in one sense, to feel that you can control the issues of life and death, don't you know."

"That is an *infringement* upon the prerogative of the Creator," said Miss Climpson.

"But rather jolly to know yourself divine, so to speak. Up above the world so high, like a tea-tray in the sky. I admit the fascination. But for practical purposes that theory is the devil—I beg your pardon, Miss Climpson, respect for sacred personages—I mean, it's unsatisfactory, because it would suit one person just as well as another. If I've got to find a homicidal maniac, I may as well cut my throat at once."

"Don't say *that*," pleaded Miss Climpson, "even in jest. Your work here—so good, so valuable—would be worth living for in spite of the *saddest* personal disappointments. And I have known jokes of that kind turn out very badly, in the most surprising ways. There was a young man we used to know, who was giving to talking in a sadly *random* way—a long time ago, dear Lord Peter, while you were still in the nursery, but young men were wild, even then, whatever they say now about the 'eighties—and he said one day to my poor, dear mother, 'Mrs. Climpson, if I don't make a good bag to-day, I shall shoot myself' (for he was very fond of sport), and he went out with his gun and as he was getting over a stile, he caught the trigger in the hedge and the gun went off and blew his head to pieces. I was quite a girl, and it upset me *dreadfully*, because he was a very handsome young man, with whiskers which we all admired very much, though to-day they would be smiled at, and they were burnt *right off* him with the explosion, and a shocking hole in the side of his head, so they said, for of course I was not allowed to see him."

"Poor chap," said his lordship. "Well, let's dismiss homicidal mania from our minds for the moment. What else do people kill people for?"

"There is—passion," said Miss Climpson, with a slight hesitation at the word, "for I should not like to call it *love*, when it is so unregulated."

"That is the explanation put forward by the prosecution," said Wimsey. "I don't accept it."

"Certainly not. But—it might be possible, might it not, that there was some other unfortunate young woman who was attached to this Mr. Boyes, and felt vindictively towards him?"

"Yes, or a man who was jealous. But the time is the difficulty. You've got to have some plausible pretext for giving a bloke arsenic. You can't just catch him standing on a doorstep, and say, 'Here, have a drink of this', can you?"

"But there were ten minutes unaccounted for," said Miss Climpson, shrewdly. "Might he not have entered some public-house for refreshment, and there met an enemy?"

"By Jove, that's a possibility." Wimsey made a note, and shook his head dubiously. "But it's rather a coincidence. Unless there was a previous appointment to meet there. Still, it's worth looking into. At any rate, it's obvious that Mr. Urquhart's house and Miss Vane's flat were not the only conceivable places where Boyes might have eaten or drunk between 7 and 10.10 that evening. Very well: under the head 'Passion' we find: (1) Miss Vane (ruled out *ex hypothesi*); (2) jealous lover; (3) ditto rival. Place, public-house (query). Now we go on to the next motive, and that's Money. A very good motive for murdering anybody who has any, but a poor one in Boyes' case. Still, let us say, Money. I can think of three sub-headings for that: (1) robbery from the person (very improbable); (2) insurance; (3) inheritance."

"What a clear mind you have," said Miss Climpson.

"When I die you will find 'Efficiency' written on my heart. I don't know what money Boyes had on him, but I shouldn't think it was much. Urquhart and Vaughan might know; still, it's not very important, because arsenic isn't a sensible drug to use on anyone you want to rob. It takes a long time, comparatively, to begin business, and it doesn't make the victim helpless enough. Unless we suppose the taxi-driver drugged and robbed him, there was no one who could possibly profit by such a silly crime."

Miss Climpson agreed, and buttered a second tea-cake.

"Then, insurance. Now we come to the region of the possible. Was Boyes insured? It doesn't seem to have occurred to anybody to find out. Probably he wasn't. Literary blokes have very little forethought, and are careless about trifles like premiums. But one ought to know. Who might have an insurable interest? His father, his cousin (possibly), other relations (if any), his children (if any) and—I suppose—Miss Vane, if he took out the policy while he was living with her. Also anybody who may have lent him money on the strength of such insurance. Plenty of possibilities there. I'm feeling better already, Miss Climpson, fitter and brighter in every way. Either I'm getting a line on the thing, or else it's your tea. That's a good, stout-looking pot. Has it got any more in it?"

"Yes, indeed," said Miss Climpson, eagerly. "My dear father used to say I was a great hand at getting the *utmost* out of a tea-pot. The secret is to *fill* up as you *go* and never empty the pot completely."

"Inheritance," pursued Lord Peter. "Had he anything to leave? Not much, I shouldn't think. I'd better hop round and see his publisher. Or had he lately come into anything? His father or cousin would know. The father is a parson —'slashing trade, that', as the naughty bully says to the new boy in one of Dean Farrar's books. He has a threadbare look. I shouldn't think there was much money in the family. Still, you never know. Somebody might have left Boyes a fortune for his *beaux yeux* or out of admiration for his books. If so, to whom did Boyes leave it? Query: did he make a will? But surely the defence must have thought of these things. I am getting depressed again."

"Have a sandwich," said Miss Climpson.

"Thank you," said Wimsey, "or some hay. There is nothing like it when you are feeling faint, as the White King truly remarked. Well, that more or less disposes of the money motive. There remains Blackmail."

Miss Climpson, whose professional connection with "The Cattery" had taught her something about blackmail, assented with a sigh.

"Who was this fellow Boyes?" enquired Wimsey rhetorically. "I know nothing about him. He may have been a blackguard of the deepest dye. He may have known unmentionable things about all his friends. Why not? Or he may have been writing a book to show somebody up, so that he had to be suppressed at all costs. Dash it all, his cousin's a solicitor. Suppose he has been embezzling trust deeds or something, and Boyes was threatening to split on him? He'd been living in Urquhart's house, and had every opportunity for finding out. Urquhart drops some arsenic into his soup, and—— Ah! there's the snag. He puts arsenic into the soup and eats it himself. That's awkward. I'm afraid Hannah Westlock's evidence rather knocks that on the head. We shall have to fall back on the mysterious stranger in the pub."

He considered a little, and then said:

"And there's suicide, of course, which is what I'm really rather inclined to believe in. Arsenic is tom-fool stuff to commit suicide with, but it has been done. There was the Duc de Praslin, for instance—if his *was* suicide. Only, where's the bottle?"

"The bottle?"

"Well, he must have carried it in something. It might be in a paper, if he took the powdered form, though that would be awkward. Did anybody look for a bottle or paper?"

"Where would they look for it?" asked Miss Climpson.

"That's the rub. If it wasn't on him, it would be anywhere round about Doughty Street, and it's going to be a job looking for a bottle or paper that was chucked away six months ago. I do loathe suicides—they're so difficult to prove. Oh, well, faint heart never won so much as a scrap of paper. Now look here, Miss Climpson. We've got about a month to work this out in. The Michaelmas Term ends on the 21st; this is the 15th. They can't very well bring it up before then, and the Hilary Term starts on January 12th. They'll probably take it early, unless we can show reason for delay. Four weeks to get fresh evidence. Will you reserve the best efforts of yourself and the staff? I don't know yet what I shall want, but I shall probably want something done."

"Of course I will, Lord Peter. You know that it is only *too* great a pleasure to do *anything* for you—even if the whole office were not your own property, which it *is*. Only let me know, at *any* minute of the night or day, and I will do my *very* best to help you."

Wimsey thanked her, made a few enquiries about the work of the bureau, and departed. He hailed a taxi and was immediately driven to Scotland Yard.

Chief Detective-Inspector Parker was, as usual, delighted to see Lord Peter, but there was a worried expression on his plain though pleasant face as he greeted his visitor.

"What is it, Peter? The Vane case again?"

"Yes. You've come a mucker over this, old man, you really have."

"Well, I don't know. It looked pretty straightforward to us."

"Charles, acushla, distrust the straightforward case, the man who looks you straight in the eye, and the tip straight from the horse's mouth. Only the most guileful deceiver can afford to be so aggressively straight. Even the path of the light is curved—or so they tell us. For God's sake, old man, do what you can to put the thing right before next assizes. If you don't, I'll never forgive you. Damn it, you don't *want* to hang the wrong person, do you?—especially a woman and all that."

"Have a fag," said Parker. "You're looking quite wild about the eyes. What have you been doing with yourself? I'm sorry if we've got the wrong pig by the ear, but it's the defence's business to point out where we're wrong, and I can't say they put up a very convincing show."

"No, confound them. Biggy did his best, but that fool and beast Crofts gave him no materials at all. Blast his ugly eyes! I know the brute thinks she did it. I hope he will fry in hell and be served up with cayenne pepper on a red-hot dish!"

"What eloquence!" said Parker, unimpressed. "Anybody would think you'd gone goopy over the girl."

"That's a damned friendly way to talk," said Wimsey, bitterly. "When you went off the deep end about my sister, I may have been unsympathetic—I daresay I was—but I swear I didn't dance on your tenderest feelings and call your manly devotion 'going goopy over a girl'. I don't know where you pick up such expressions, as the clergyman's wife said to the parrot. 'Goopy', indeed! I never heard anything so vulgar."

"Good Lord," exclaimed Parker, "you don't seriously say——"

"Oh, no!" retorted Wimsey, bitterly. "I'm not expected to be serious. A buffoon, that's what I am. I now know exactly what Jack Point feels like. I used to think the *Yeomen* sentimental tosh, but it is all too true. Would you like to see me dance in motley?"

"I'm sorry," said Parker, taking his cue rather from the tone than the words. "If it's like that, I'm damned sorry, old man. But what can I do?"

"Now you're talking. Look here—the most likely thing is that this unsavoury blighter Boyes committed suicide. The unspeakable defence haven't been able to trace any arsenic to his possession—but then they probably couldn't trace a herd of black cattle over a snow-bound field in broad noonday with a microscope. I want your people to take it up."

"Boyes—query arsenic," said Parker, making a note on a pad. "Anything else?"

"Yes. Find out if Boyes visited any pub in the neighbourhood of Doughty Street between, say, 9.50 and 10.10 on the night of June 20th—if he met anybody, and what he took to drink."

"It shall be done. Boyes—query pub." Parker made another note. "Yes?"

"Thirdly, if any bottle or paper that might have contained arsenic was picked up in that district."

"Oh, indeed? And would you like me to trace the 'bus ticket dropped by Mrs. Brown outside Selfridge's in the last Christmas rush? No use making it too easy."

"A bottle is more likely than a paper," went on Wimsey, ignoring him, "because I think the arsenic must have been taken in liquid form to work so quickly."

Parker made no further protest, but noted down "Boyes—Doughty Street—query bottle," and paused expectantly.

"Yes?"

"That's all for the moment. By the way, I should try the garden in Mecklenburgh Square. A thing might lie quite a long time under those bushes."

"Very well. I'll do my best. And if you find out anything which really proves that we've been on the wrong tack, you'll let us know, won't you? We don't want to make large and ignominious public mistakes."

"Well—I've just earnestly promised the defence that I'll do no such thing. But if I spot the criminal, I'll let you arrest him."

"Thanks for small mercies. Well, good luck! Funny for you and me to be on opposite sides, isn't it?"

"Very," said Wimsey. "I'm sorry about it, but it's your own fault."

"You shouldn't have been out of England. By the way——"

"Yes?"

"You realise that probably all our young friend did during those missing ten minutes was to stand about in Theobalds Road or somewhere, looking for a stray taxi?"

"Oh, shut up!" said Wimsey, crossly, and went out.

CHAPTER VI

THE NEXT DAY dawned bright and fair, and Wimsey felt a certain exhilaration as he purred down to Tweedling Parva. "Mrs. Merdle", the car, so called because, like that celebrated lady, she was averse to "row", was sparking merrily on all twelve cylinders, and there was a touch of frost in the air. These things conduce to high spirits.

Wimsey reached his destination about 10 o'clock, and was directed to the vicarage, one of those large, rambling, and unnecessary structures which swallow the incumbent's income during his life and land his survivors with a heavy bill for dilapidations as soon as he is dead.

The Rev. Arthur Boyes was at home, and would be happy to see Lord Peter Wimsey.

The clergyman was a tall, faded man, with lines of worry deeply engraved upon his face, and mild blue eyes a little bewildered by the disappointing difficulty of things in general. His black coat was old, and hung in depressed folds from his stooping, narrow shoulders. He gave Wimsey a thin hand and begged him to be seated.

Lord Peter found it a little difficult to explain his errand. His name evidently aroused no associations in the mind of this gentle and unworldly parson. He decided not to mention his hobby of criminal investigation, but to represent himself, with equal truth, as a friend of the prisoner's. That might be painful, but it would be at least intelligible. Accordingly, he began, with some hesitation:

"I'm fearfully sorry to trouble you, especially as it's all so very distressin' and all that, but it's about the death of your son, and the trial and so on. Please don't think I'm wanting to make an interfering nuisance of myself, but I'm deeply interested—personally interested. You see, I know Miss Vane—I—in fact I like her very much, don't you know, and I can't help thinking there's a mistake somewhere and—and I should like to get it put right if possible."

"Oh—oh, yes!" said Mr. Boyes. He carefully polished a pair of pince-nez and balanced them on his nose, where they sat crookedly. He peered at Wimsey and seemed not to dislike what he saw, for he went on:

"Poor misguided girl! I assure you, I have no vindictive feelings—that is to say, nobody would be more happy than myself to know that she was innocent of this dreadful thing. Indeed, Lord Peter, even if she were guilty, it would give me great pain to see her suffer the penalty. Whatever we do, we cannot bring back the dead to life, and one would infinitely prefer to leave all vengeance in the hand of Him to whom it belongs. Certainly, nothing could be more terrible than to take the life of an innocent person. It would haunt me to the end of my days if I thought there were the least likelihood of it. And I confess that, when I saw Miss Vane in court, I had grievous doubts whether the police had done rightly in accusing her."

"Thank you," said Wimsey, "it is very kind of you to say that. It makes the job much easier. Excuse me, you say 'when you saw her in court'. You hadn't met her previously?"

"No. I knew, of course, that my unhappy son had formed an illicit connection with a young woman, but I could not bring myself to see her—and indeed, I believe that she, with very proper feeling, refused to allow Philip to bring her into contact with any of his relations. Lord Peter, you are a younger man than I am, you belong to my son's generation, and you will perhaps understand that—though he was not bad, not depraved, I will never think that—yet somehow there was not that full confidence between us which there should be between father and son. No doubt I was much to blame. If only his mother had lived——"

"My dear sir," mumbled Wimsey, "I perfectly understand. It often happens. In fact, it's continually happening. The post-war generation and so on. Lots of people go off the rails a bit—no real harm in 'em at all. Just can't see eye to eye with the older people. It generally wears off in time. Nobody really to blame. Wild oats and—er—all that sort of thing."

"I could not approve," said Mr. Boyes, sadly, "of ideas so opposed to religion and morality—perhaps I spoke my mind too openly. If I had sympathised more——"

"It can't be done," said Wimsey. "People have to work it out for themselves. And, when they write books and so on, and get into that set of people, they tend to express themselves rather noisily, if you see what I mean."

"Maybe, maybe. But I reproach myself. Still, this does not help you at all. Forgive me. If there is any mistake, and the jury were evidently not satisfied, we must use all our endeavours to put it right. How can I assist?"

"Well, first of all," said Wimsey, "and I'm afraid this is rather a hateful question, did your son ever say anything, or write anything to you which might lead you to think that he—was tired of his life or anything of that kind? I'm sorry."

"No, no—not at all. I was, of course, asked the same question by the police and by the counsel for the defence. I can truly say that such an idea never occurred to me. There was nothing at all to suggest it."

"Not even when he parted company with Miss Vane?"

"Not even then. In fact, I gathered that he was rather more angry than despondent. I must say that it was a surprise to me to hear that, after all that had passed between them, she was unwilling to marry him. I still fail to comprehend it. Her refusal must have come as a great shock to him. He wrote so cheerfully to me about it beforehand. Perhaps you remember the letter?" He fumbled in an untidy drawer. "I have it here, if you would like to look at it."

"If you would just read the passage, sir," suggested Wimsey.

"Yes, oh, certainly. Let me see. Yes. 'Your morality will be pleased to hear, Dad, that I have determined to regularise the situation, as the good people say.' He had a careless way of speaking and writing sometimes, poor boy, which doesn't do justice to his good heart. Dear me. Yes. 'My young woman is a good little soul, and I have made up my mind to do the thing properly. She really deserves it, and I hope that when everything is made respectable, you will extend your paternal recognition to her. I won't ask you to officiate—as you know, the registrar's office is more in my line, and though she was brought up in the odour of sanctity, like myself, I don't think she will insist on the "Voice that Breathed o'er Eden". I will let you know when it's to be, so that you can come and give us your blessing (*qua* father if not *qua* parson) if you should feel so disposed.' You see, Lord Peter, he quite meant to do the right thing, and I was touched that he should wish for my presence."

"Quite so," said Lord Peter, and thought, "if only that young man were alive, how dearly I should love to kick his bottom for him."

"Well, then there is another letter, saying that the marriage had fallen through. Here it is. 'Dear Dad,—Sorry, but I'm afraid your congratulations must be returned with thanks. The wedding is off, and the bride has run away. There's no need to go into the story. Harriet has succeeded in making a fool of herself and me, so there's no more to be said.' Then later I heard that he had not been feeling well—but all that you know already."

"Did he suggest any reason for these illnesses of his?"

"Oh, no—we took it for granted that it was a recurrence of the old gastric trouble. He was never a very robust lad. He wrote in very hopeful mood from Harlech, saying that he was much better, and mentioning his plan of a voyage to Barbados."

"He did?"

"Yes. I thought it would do him a great deal of good, and take his mind off other things. He spoke of it only as a vague project, not as though anything were settled."

"Did he say anything more about Miss Vane?"

"He never mentioned her name to me again until he lay dying."

"Yes—and what did you think of what he said then?"

"I didn't know what to think. We had no idea of any poisoning then, naturally, and I fancied it must refer to the quarrel between them that had caused the separation."

"I see. Well now, Mr. Boyes. Supposing it was not self-destruction——"

"I really do not think it could have been."

"Now is there anybody else at all who could have an interest in his death?"

"Who could there be?"

"No—no other woman, for instance?"

"I never heard of any. And I think I should have done. He was not secretive about these things, Lord Peter. He was remarkably open and straightforward."

"Yes," commented Wimsey internally, "liked to swagger about it, I suppose. Anything to give pain. Damn the fellow." Aloud he merely said: "There are other possibilities. Did he, for instance, make a will?"

"He did. Not that he had much to leave, poor boy. His books were very cleverly written—he had a fine intellect, Lord Peter—but they did not bring him in any great sums of money. I helped him with a little allowance, and he managed on that and on what he made from his articles in the periodicals."

"He left his copyrights to somebody, though, I take it?"

"Yes. He wished to leave them to me, but I was obliged to tell him that I could not accept the bequest. You see, I did not approve of his opinions, and I should not have thought it right to profit by them. No; he left them to his friend Mr. Vaughan."

"Oh!—may I ask when this will was made?"

"It is dated at the period of his visit to Wales. I believe that before that he had made one leaving everything to Miss Vane."

"Indeed!" said Wimsey. "I suppose she knew about it." His mind reviewed a number of contradictory possibilities, and he added: "But it would not amount to an important sum, in any case?"

"Oh, no. If my son made fifty pounds a year by his books, that was the utmost. Though they tell me," added the old gentleman, with a sad smile, "that after this, his new book will do better."

"Very likely," said Wimsey. "Provided you get into the papers, the delightful reading public don't mind what it's for. Still—— Well, that's that. I gather he would have no private money to leave?"

"Nothing whatever. There has never been any money in our family, Lord Peter, nor yet in my wife's. We're quite the proverbial Church mice." He smiled faintly at this little clerical jest. "Except, I suppose, for Cremorna Garden."

"For—I beg your pardon?"

"My wife's aunt, the notorious Cremorna Garden of the 'sixties."

"Good Lord, yes—the actress?"

"Yes. But she, of course, was never, never mentioned. One did not enquire into the way she got her money. No worse than others, I daresay—but in those days we were very easily shocked. We have seen and heard nothing of her for well over fifty years. I believe she is quite childish now."

"By Jove! I'd no idea she was still alive!"

"Yes, I believe she is, though she must be well over ninety. Certainly Philip never had any money from her."

"Well, that rules money out. Was your son's life insured, by any chance?"

"Not that I ever heard of. We found no policy among his papers, and, so far as I know, nobody has made any claim."

"He left no debts?"

"Only trifling ones—tradesmen's accounts and so on. Perhaps fifty pounds' worth altogether."

"Thank you so much," said Wimsey, rising; "that has cleared the ground a good deal."

"I am afraid it has not got you much farther."

"It tells me where not to look, at any rate," said Wimsey, "and that all saves time, you know. It's frightfully decent of you to be bothered with me."

"Not at all. Ask me anything you want to know. Nobody would be more glad than myself to see that unfortunate young woman cleared."

Wimsey again thanked him and took his leave. He was a mile up the road before a regretful thought overtook him. He turned Mrs. Merdle's bonnet round, skimmed back to the church, stuffed a handful of Treasury notes with some difficulty into the mouth of a box labelled "Church Expenses", and resumed his way back to town.

As he manoeuvred the car through the City, a thought struck him, and, instead of heading for Piccadilly, where he lived, he turned off into a street south of the Strand, in which was situated the establishment of Messrs. Grimsby & Cole, who published the works of Mr. Philip Boyes. After a little delay, he was shown into Mr. Cole's office.

Mr. Cole was a stout and cheerful person, and was much interested to hear that the notorious Lord Peter Wimsey was concerning himself with the affairs of the equally notorious Mr. Boyes. Wimsey represented that, as a collector of first editions, he would be glad to secure copies of all Philip Boyes' works. Mr. Cole regretted extremely that he could not help him, and, under the influence of an expensive cigar, became quite confidential.

"Without wishing to seem callous, my dear Lord Peter," he said, throwing himself back in his chair, and creasing his three chins into six or seven as he did so, "between you and me, Mr. Boyes could not have done better for himself than to go and get murdered like this. Every copy was sold out a week after the result of the exhumation became known, two large editions of his last book were disposed of before the trial came on—at the original price of seven and sixpence, and the libraries clamoured so for the early volumes that we had to reprint the lot. Unfortunately we had not kept the type standing, and the printers had to work night and day, but we did it. We are rushing the three-and-sixpennies through the binders now, and the shilling edition is arranged for. Positively, I don't think you could get a first edition in London for love or money. We have nothing here but our own file copies, but we are putting out a special memorial edition, with portraits, on hand-made paper, limited and numbered, at a guinea. Not the same thing of course, but——"

Wimsey begged to put his name down for a set at a guinea a-piece, adding:

"Sad and all that, don't you know, that the author can't benefit by it, what?"

"Deeply distressing," agreed Mr. Cole, compressing his fat cheeks by two longitudinal folds from the nostril to the mouth. "And sadder still that there can be no more work to come from him. A very talented young man, Lord Peter. We shall always feel a melancholy pride, Mr. Grimsby and myself, in knowing that we recognised his quality, before there was any likelihood of financial remuneration. A *succès d'estime*, that was all, until this very grievous occurrence. But, when the work is good, it is not our habit to boggle about monetary returns."

"Ah, well!" said Wimsey, "it sometimes pays to cast your bread upon the waters. Quite religious, isn't it—you know, the bit about 'plenteously bringing out good works may of thee be plenteously rewarded'. Twenty-fifth after Trinity."

"Quite," said Mr. Cole, with a certain lack of enthusiasm, possibly because he was imperfectly acquainted with the Book of Common Prayer, or possibly because he detected a hint of mockery in the other's tone. "Well, I have very much enjoyed this chat. I am sorry I can do nothing for you about first editions."

Wimsey begged him not to mention it, and with a cordial farewell ran hastily down the stairs.

His next visit was to the office of Mr. Challoner, Harriet Vane's agent. Challoner was an abrupt, dark, militant-looking little man, with untidy hair and thick spectacles.

"Boom?" said he, when Wimsey had introduced himself and mentioned his interest in Miss Vane. "Yes, of course there is a boom. Rather disgusting, really, but one can't help that. We have to do our best for our client, whatever the circumstances. Miss Vane's books have always sold reasonably well—round about the three or four thousand mark in this country—but of course this business has stimulated things enormously. The last book has gone to three new editions, and the new one has sold seven thousand before publication."

"Financially, all to the good, eh?"

"Oh, yes—but frankly I don't know whether these artificial sales do very much good to an author's reputation in the long run. Up like a rocket, down like the stick, you know. When Miss Vane is released——"

"I am glad you say 'when'."

"I am not allowing myself to contemplate any other possibility. But *when* that happens, public interest will be liable to die down very quickly. I am, of course, securing the most advantageous contracts I possibly can at the moment, to cover the next three or four books, but I can only really control the advances. The actual receipts will depend on the sales, and that is where I foresee a slump. I am, however, doing well with serial rights, which are important from the point of view of immediate returns."

"On the whole, as a business man, you are not altogether glad that this has happened?"

"Taking the long view, I am not. Personally, I need not say that I am extremely grieved, and feel quite positive that there is some mistake."

"That's my idea," said Wimsey.

"From what I know of your lordship, I may say that your interest and assistance are the best stroke of luck Miss Vane could have had."

"Oh, thanks—thanks very much. I say—this arsenic book—you couldn't let me have a squint at it, I suppose?"

"Certainly, if it would help you." He touched a bell. "Miss Warburton, bring me a set of galleys of *Death in the Pot*. Trufoot's are pushing publication on as fast as possible. The book was still unfinished when the arrest took place. With rare energy and courage, Miss Vane has put the finishing touches and corrected the proofs herself. Of course, everything had to go through the hands of the prison authorities. However, we were anxious to conceal nothing. She certainly knows all about arsenic, poor girl. These are complete, are they, Miss Warburton? Here you are. Is there anything else?"

"Only one thing. What do you think of Messrs. Grimsby & Cole?"

"I never contemplate them," said Mr. Challoner. "Not thinking of doing anything with them, are you, Lord Peter?"

"Well, I don't know that I am—seriously."

"If you do, read your contract carefully. I won't say bring it to us——"

"If ever I do publish with Grimsby & Cole," said Lord Peter, "I'll promise to do it through you."

CHAPTER VII

LORD PETER WIMSEY almost bounced into Holloway Prison the next morning. Harriet Vane greeted him with a kind of rueful smile.

"So you've reappeared?"

"Good Lord, yes! Surely you expected me to? I fancied I'd left that impression. I say—I've thought of a good plot for a detective story."

"Really?"

"Top-hole. You know, the sort people bring out and say, 'I've often thought of doing it myself, if I could only find time to sit down and write it.' I gather that sitting down is all that is necessary for producing masterpieces. Just a moment, though. I must get through my business first. Let me see——" He made belief to consult a note-book. "Ah, yes. Do you happen to know whether Philip Boyes made a will?"

"I believe he did, when we were living together."

"In whose favour?"

"Oh, in mine. Not that he had much to leave, poor man. It was chiefly that he wanted a literary executor."

"Are you, in point of fact, his executrix now?"

"Good heavens! I never thought of that. I took it for granted he would have altered it when we parted. I think he must have, or I should have heard about it when he died, shouldn't I?"

She looked candidly at him, and Wimsey felt a little uncomfortable.

"You didn't *know* he had altered it, then? Before he died, I mean?"

"I never thought a word more about it, as a matter of fact. If I had thought—of course I should have assumed it. Why?"

"Nothing," said Wimsey. "Only I'm rather glad the will wasn't brought up at the thingummybob."

"Meaning the trial? You needn't be so delicate about mentioning it. You mean, if I had thought I was still his heir, I might have murdered him for his money. But it didn't amount to a hill of beans, you know. I was making four times as much as he was."

"Oh, yes. It was only this silly plot I'd got in my mind. But it *is* rather silly, now I come to think of it."

"Tell me."

"Well, you see——" Wimsey choked a little, and then rattled his idea out with an exaggerated lightness.

"Well—it's about a girl (or a man would do, but we'll call it a girl) who writes novels—crime stories, in fact. And she has a—a friend who also writes. Neither of them best-sellers, you see, but just ordinary novelists."

"Yes? That's a kind of thing that might happen."

"And the friend makes a will, leaving his money—receipts from books and so on—to the girl."

"I see."

"And the girl—who has got rather fed up with him, you know—thinks of a grand scoop that will make both of them best-sellers."

"Oh, yes?"

"Yes. She polishes him off by the same method she has used in her latest crime-thriller."

"A daring stroke," said Miss Vane, with grave approval.

"Yes. And, of course, his books immediately become best-sellers. And she grabs the pool."

"That's really ingenious. An entirely new motive for murder—the thing I've been looking for for years. But—don't you think it would be a little dangerous? She might even be suspected of the murder."

"Then *her* books would become best-sellers, too."

"How true that is! But possibly she wouldn't live to enjoy the profits."

"That, of course," said Wimsey, "is the snag."

"Because, unless she were suspected and arrested and tried, the scoop would only half come off."

"There you are," said Wimsey. "But, as an experienced mystery-monger, couldn't you think of a way round that?"

"I daresay. She might prove an ingenious alibi, for instance. Or, if she were very wicked, manage to push the blame on somebody else. Or lead people to suppose that her friend had made away with himself."

"Too vague," said Wimsey. "How would she do that?"

"I can't say, off-hand. I'll give it careful thought and let you know. Or—here's an idea!"

"Yes?"

"She is a person with a monomania—no, no—not a homicidal one. That's dull, and not really fair to the reader. But there is somebody she wishes to benefit—somebody, say a father, mother, sister, lover, or cause, that badly needs money. She makes a will in his, her, or its favour, and let's herself be hanged for the crime, knowing that the beloved object will then come in for the money. How's that?"

"Great!" cried Wimsey, carried away. "Only—wait a minute. They wouldn't give her the friend's money, would they? You're not allowed to profit by a crime."

"Oh, hang! That's true. It would only be her own money, then. She could make that over by a deed of gift. Yes—look! If she did that immediately after the murder—a deed of gift of everything she possessed—that would include everything she came into under the friend's will. It would then all go direct to the beloved object, and I don't believe the law could stop it!"

She faced him with dancing eyes.

"See here," said Wimsey. "You're not safe. You're too clever by half. But, I say, it's a good plot, isn't it?"

"It's a winner! Shall we write it?"

"By Jove, let's!"

"Only, you know, I'm afraid we shan't get the chance."

"You're not to say that. Of course we're going to write it. Damn it, what am I here for? Even if I could be reconciled to losing you, I couldn't lose the chance of writing my best-seller!"

"But what you've done so far is to provide me with a very convincing motive for murder. I don't know that that's going to help us a great lot."

"What I've done," said Wimsey, "is to prove that that was not the motive, anyway."

"Why?"

"You wouldn't have told me if it had been. You would have gently led me away from the subject. And besides——"

"Well?"

"Well, I've seen Mr. Cole of Grimsby & Cole, and I know who is going to get the major part of Philip Boyes' profits. And I don't somehow fancy that he is the beloved object."

"No?" said Miss Vane, "and why not? Don't you know that I passionately dote on every chin on his face?"

"If it's chins you admire," said Wimsey, "I will try to grow some, though it will be rather hard work. Anyway, keep smiling—it suits you."

"It's all very well, though," he thought to himself, when the gates had closed behind him. "Bright back-chat cheers the patient, but gets us no forrarder. How about this fellow Urquhart? He looked all right in court, but you never can tell. I think I'd better pop round and see him."

He presented himself accordingly in Woburn Square, but was disappointed. Mr. Urquhart had been called away to a sick relative. It was not Hannah Westlock who answered the door, but a stout elderly woman, whom Whimsey supposed to be the cook. He would have liked to question her, but felt that Mr. Urquhart would hardly receive him well if he discovered that his servants had been pumped behind his back. He therefore contented himself with enquiring how long Mr. Urquhart was likely to be away.

"I couldn't rightly say, sir. I understand it depends how the sick lady gets on. If she gets over it, he'll be back at once, for I know he is very busy just now. If she should pass away, he would be engaged some time, with settling up the estate."

"I see," said Wimsey. "It's a bit awkward, because I wanted to speak to him rather urgently. You couldn't give me his address, by any chance?"

"Well, sir, I don't rightly know if Mr. Urquhart would wish it. If it's a matter of business, sir, they could give you information at his office in Bedford Row."

"Thanks very much," said Wimsey, noting down the number. "I'll call there. Possibly they'd be able to do what I want without bothering him."

"Yes, sir. Who should I say called?"

Wimsey handed over his card, writing at the top, "*In re* R. *v.* Vane", and added:

"But there is a chance he may be back quite soon?"

"Oh, yes, sir. Last time he wasn't away more than a couple of days, and a merciful providence I am sure that was, with poor Mr. Boyes dying in that dreadful manner."

"Yes, indeed," said Wimsey, delighted to find the subject introducing itself of its own accord. "That must have been a shocking upset for you all."

"Well, there," said the cook. "I don't hardly like to think of it, even now. A gentleman dying in the house like that, and poisoned too, when one's had the cooking of his dinner—it do seem to bring it home to one, like."

"It wasn't the dinner that was at fault, anyway," said Wimsey, genially.

"Oh, dear, no, sir—we proved that most careful. Not that any accident could happen in my kitchen—I should like to see it! But people do say such things if they get half a chance. Still, there wasn't a thing ate but master and Hannah and I had some of it, and very thankful I was for that, I needn't tell you."

"You must be, I am sure." Wimsey was framing a further enquiry, when the violent ringing of the area bell interrupted them.

"There's that butcher," said the cook. "You'll excuse me, sir. The parlourmaid's in bed with the influenza, and I'm single-handed this morning. I'll tell Mr. Urquhart you called."

She shut the door, and Wimsey departed for Bedford Row, where he was received by an elderly clerk, who made no difficulty about supplying Mr. Urquhart's address.

"Here it is, my lord. Care of Mrs. Wrayburn, Applefold, Windle, Westmorland. But I shouldn't think he would be very long away. In the meantime, could we do anything for you?"

"No, thanks. I rather wanted to see him personally, don't you know. As a matter of fact, it's about that very sad death of his cousin, Mr. Philip Boyes."

"Indeed, my lord? Shocking affair, that. Mr. Urquhart was greatly upset, with it happening in his own house. A very fine young man was Mr. Boyes. He and Mr. Urquhart were great friends, and he took it greatly to heart. Were you present at the trial, my lord?"

"Yes. What did you think of the verdict?"

The clerk pursed up his lips.

"I don't mind saying I was surprised. It seemed to me a very clear case. But juries are very unreliable, especially nowadays, with women on them. We see a good deal of the fair sex in this profession," said the clerk, with a sly smile, "and very few of them are remarkable for possessing the legal mind."

"How true that is," said Wimsey. "If it wasn't for them, though, there'd be much less litigation, so it's all good for business."

"Ha, ha! Very good, my lord. Well, we have to take things as they come, but in my opinion—I'm an old-fashioned man—the ladies were most adorable when they adorned and inspired and did not take an active part in affairs. Here's our young lady clerk—I don't say she wasn't a good worker—but a whim comes over her and away she goes to get married, leaving me in the lurch, just when Mr. Urquhart is away. Now, with a young man, marriage steadies him, and makes him stick closer to his job, but with a young woman, it's the other way about. It's right she should get married, but it's inconvenient, and in a solicitor's office one can't get temporary assistance very well. Some of the work is confidential, of course, and, in any case, an atmosphere of permanence is desirable."

Wimsey sympathised with the head-clerk's grievance, and bade him an affable good-morning. There is a telephone-box in Bedford Row, and he darted into it and immediately rang up Miss Climpson.

"Lord Peter Wimsey speaking—oh, hullo, Miss Climpson! How is everything? All bright and beautiful? Good!—Yes, now listen. There's a vacancy for a confidential female clerk at Mr. Norman Urquhart's, the solicitor's, in Bedford Row. Have you got anybody?—Oh, good!—Yes, send them all along—I particularly want to get someone in there.—Oh, no! no special enquiry—just to pick up any gossip about the Vane business.—Yes, pick out the steadiest-looking, not too much face-powder, and see that their skirts are the regulation four inches below the knee—the head-clerk's in charge, and the last girl left to be married, so he's feeling anti-sex-appeal. Right ho! Get her in and I'll give her her instructions. Bless you, may your shadow never grow bulkier!"

CHAPTER VIII

"BUNTER!"

"My lord?"

Wimsey tapped with his fingers a letter he had just received.

"Do you feel at your brightest and most truly fascinating? Does a livelier iris, winter weather notwithstanding, shine upon the burnished Bunter? Have you got that sort of conquering feeling? The Don Juan touch, so to speak?"

Bunter, balancing the breakfast tray on his fingers, coughed deprecatingly.

"You have a good, upstanding, impressive figure, if I may say so," pursued

Wimsey, "a bold and roving eye when off duty, a ready tongue, Bunter—and, I am persuaded, you have a way with you. What more should any cook or house-parlourmaid want?"

"I am always happy," replied Bunter, "to exert myself to the best of my capacity in your lordship's service."

"I am aware of it," admitted his lordship. "Again and again I say to myself, 'Wimsey, this cannot last. One of these days this worthy man will cast off the yoke of servitude and settle down in a pub or something', but nothing happens. Still, morning by morning, my coffee is brought, my bath is prepared, my razor laid out, my ties and socks sorted, and my bacon and eggs brought to me in a lordly dish. No matter. This time I demand a more perilous devotion —perilous for us both, my Bunter, for if you were to be carried away, a helpless martyr to matrimony, who then would bring my coffee, prepare my bath, lay out my razor, and perform all those other sacrificial rites? And yet——"

"Who is the party, my lord?"

"There are two of them, Bunter, two ladies in a bower, Binnorie, O Binnorie! The parlourmaid you have seen. Her name is Hannah Westlock. A woman in her thirties, I fancy, and not ill-favoured. The other, the cook—I cannot lisp the tender syllables of her name, for I do not know it, but doubtless it is Gertrude, Cecily, Magdalen, Margaret, Rosalys, or some other sweet symphonious sound—a fine woman, Bunter, on the mature side, perhaps, but none the worse for that."

"Certainly not, my lord. If I may say so, the woman of ripe years and queenly figure is frequently more susceptible to delicate attentions than the giddy and thoughtless young beauty."

"True. Let us suppose, Bunter, that you were to be the bearer of a courteous missive to one Mr. Norman Urquhart of Woburn Square. Could you, in the short space of time at your disposal, insinuate yourself, snakelike, as it were, into the bosom of the household?"

"If you desire it, my lord, I will endeavour to insinuate myself to your lordship's satisfaction."

"Noble fellow. In case of an action for breach, or any consequence of that description, the charges will, of course, be borne by the management."

"I am obliged to your lordship. When would your lordship wish me to commence?"

"As soon as I have written a note to Mr. Urquhart. I will ring."

"Very good, my lord."

Wimsey moved over to the writing-desk. After a few moments he looked up, a little peevishly.

"Bunter, I have a sensation of being hovered over. I do not like it. It is unusual and it unnerves me. I implore you not to hover. Is the proposition distasteful, or do you want me to get a new hat? What is troubling your conscience?"

"I beg your lordship's pardon. It had occurred to my mind to ask your lordship, with every respect——"

"Oh, God, Bunter—don't break it gently. I can't bear it. Stab and end the creature—to the heft! What is it?"

"I wish to ask you, my lord, whether your lordship thought of making any changes in your establishment?"

Wimsey laid down his pen and stared at the man.

"Changes, Bunter? When I have just so eloquently expressed to you my undying attachment to the loved routine of coffee, bath, razor, socks, eggs and bacon, and the old, familiar faces? You're not giving me warning, are you?"

"No, indeed, my lord. I should be very sorry to leave your lordship's service. But I had thought it possible that, if your lordship was about to contract new ties——"

"I *knew* it was something in the haberdashery line! By all means, Bunter, if you think it necessary. Had you any particular pattern in mind?"

"Your lordship misunderstands me. I referred to domestic ties, my lord. Sometimes, when a gentleman reorganises his household on a matrimonial basis, the lady may prefer to have a voice in the selection of the gentleman's personal attendant, in which case——"

"Bunter!" said Wimsey, considerably startled, "may I ask where you have contracted these ideas?"

"I ventured to draw an inference, my lord."

"This comes of training people to be detectives. Have I been nourishing a sleuth-hound on my own hearth-stone? May I ask if you have gone so far as to give a name to the lady?"

"Yes, my lord."

There was a pause.

"Well?" said Wimsey, in a rather subdued tone, "what about it, Bunter?"

"A very agreeable lady, if I may say so, my lord."

"It strikes you that way, does it? The circumstances are unusual, of course."

"Yes, my lord. I might perhaps make so bold as to call them romantic."

"You may make so bold as to call them damnable, Bunter."

"Yes, my lord," said Bunter, in a tone of sympathy.

"You won't desert the ship, Bunter?"

"Not on any account, my lord."

"Then don't come frightening me again. My nerves are not what they were. Here is the note. Take it round and do your best."

"Very good, my lord."

"Oh, and Bunter."

"My lord?"

"It seems that I am being obvious. I have no wish to be anything of the kind. If you see me being obvious, will you drop me a hint?"

"Certainly, my lord."

Bunter faded gently out, and Wimsey stepped anxiously to the mirror.

"I can't see anything," he said to himself. "No lily on my cheek with anguish moist and fever-dew. I suppose, though, it's hopeless to try and deceive Bunter. Never mind. Business must come first. I've stopped one, two, three, four earths. What next? How about this fellow Vaughan?"

When Wimsey had any researches to do in Bohemia, it was his custom to enlist the help of Miss Marjorie Phelps. She made figurines in porcelain for a living, and was therefore usually to be found either in her studio or in someone else's studio. A telephone-call at 10 a.m. would probably catch her scrambling eggs over her own gas-stove. It was true that there had been passages, about the time of the Bellona Club affair, between her and Lord Peter which made it a little embarrassing and unkind to bring her in on the subject of Harriet Vane, but, with so little time in which to pick and choose his tools, Wimsey was past worrying about gentlemanly scruples. He put the call through and was relieved to hear an answering "Hullo!"

"Hullo, Marjorie! This is Peter Wimsey. How goes it?"

"Oh, fine, thanks. Glad to hear your melodious voice again. What can I do for the Lord High Investigator?"

"Do you know one Vaughan, who is mixed up in the Philip Boyes murder mystery?"

"Oh, Peter! Are you on to that? How gorgeous! Which side are you taking?"

"For the defence."

"Hurray!"

"Why this pomp of jubilee?"

"Well, it's much more exciting and difficult, isn't it?"

"I'm afraid it is. Do you know Miss Vane, by the way?"

"Yes and no. I've seen her with the Boyes-Vaughan crowd."

"Like her?"

"So-so."

"Like him? Boyes, I mean?"

"Never stirred a heart-beat."

"I said, did you like him?"

"One didn't. One either fell for him or not. He wasn't the merry bright-eyed pal of the period, you know."

"Oh! What's Vaughan?"

"Hanger-on."

"Oh?"

"House-dog. Nothing must interfere with the expansion of my friend the genius. That sort."

"Oh!"

"Don't keep saying 'Oh!' Do you want to meet the man Vaughan?"

"If it's not too much trouble."

"Well, turn up to-night with a taxi and we'll go the rounds. We're certain to drop across him somewhere. Also the rival gang, if you want them—Harriet Vane's supporters."

"Those girls who gave evidence?"

"Yes. You'll like Eiluned Price, I think. She scorns everything in trousers, but she's a good friend at a pinch."

"I'll come, Marjorie. Will you dine with me?"

"Peter, I'd adore to, but I don't think I will. I've got an awful lot to do."

"Right-ho! I'll roll round about nine, then."

Accordingly, at 9 o'clock, Wimsey found himself in a taxi with Marjorie Phelps, headed for a round of the studios.

"I've been doing some intensive telephoning," said Marjorie, "and I think we shall find him at the Kropotkys'. They are pro-Boyes, Bolshevik, and musical, and their drinks are bad, but their Russian tea is safe. Does the taxi wait?"

"Yes; it sounds as if we might want to beat a retreat."

"Well, it's nice to be rich. It's down the court here on the right, over the Petrovitchs' stable. Better let me grope first."

They stumbled up a narrow and encumbered stair, at the top of which a fine confused noise of a piano, strings, and the clashing of kitchen utensils announced that some sort of entertainment was in progress.

Marjorie hammered loudly on a door, and, without waiting for an answer, flung it open. Wimsey, entering on her heels, was struck in the face, as by an open hand, by a thick muffling wave of heat, sound, smoke, and the smell of frying.

It was a very small room, dimly lit by a single electric bulb, smothered in a lantern of painted glass, and it was packed to suffocation with people, whose silk legs, bare arms, and pallid faces loomed at him like glow-worms out of the obscurity. Coiling wreaths of tobacco-smoke swam slowly to and fro in the midst. In one corner an anthracite stove, glowing red and mephitical, vied with a roaring gas-oven in another corner to raise the atmosphere to roasting-pitch. On the stove stood a vast and steaming kettle; on a side-table stood a vast and steaming samovar; over the gas, a dim figure stood turning sausages in a pan with a fork, while an assistant attended to something in the oven, which Wimsey, whose nose was selective, identified among the other fragment elements in this compound atmosphere, and identified, rightly, as kippers. At the piano, which stood just inside the door, a young man with bushy red hair was playing something of a Czechoslovakian flavour, to a violin obligato by an extremely loose-jointed person of indeterminate sex in a Fair Isle jumper. Nobody looked round at their entrance. Marjorie picked her way over the scattered limbs on the floor and, selecting a lean young woman in red, bawled into her ear. The young woman nodded and beckoned to Wimsey. He negotiated a passage, and was introduced to the lean woman by the simple formula: "Here's Peter—this is Nina Kropotky."

"So pleased," shouted Madame Kropotky through the clamour. "Sit by me. Vanya will get you something to drink. It is beautiful, yes? That is Stanislas—such a genius—his new work on the Piccadilly Tube station—great, *n'est-ce pas*? Five days he was continually travelling upon the escalator to absorb the tone-values."

"Colossal!" yelled Wimsey.

"So—you think? Ah! you can appreciate! You understand it is really for the big orchestra. On the piano it is nothing. It needs the brass, the effects, the tympani—b'rrrrrrr!—So! But one seizes the form, the outline. Ah! it finishes! Superb! magnificent!"

The enormous clatter ceased. The pianist mopped his face and glared haggardly round. The violinist put down its instrument and stood up, revealing itself, by its legs, to be female. The room exploded into conversation. Madame Kropotky leapt over her seated guests and embraced the perspiring Stanislas on both cheeks. The frying-pan was lifted from the stove in a fusillade of spitting fat, a shriek went up for "Vanya" and presently a cadaverous face was pushed down to Wimsey's, and a deep guttural voice barked at him: "What will you drink?" while simultaneously a plate of kippers came hovering perilously over his shoulder.

"Thanks," said Wimsey, "I have just dined—just *dined*," he roared despairingly, "full up, *complet*!"

Marjorie came to the rescue with a shriller voice and more determined refusal.

"Take those dreadful things away, Vanya. They make me sick. Give us some tea, tea, tea!"

"Tea!" echoed the cadaverous man, "they want tea! What do you think of Stanislas' tone-poem? Strong, modern, eh? The soul of rebellion in the crowd—the clash, the revolt at the heart of the machinery. It gives the bourgeois something to think of, oh, yes!"

"Bah!" said a voice in Wimsey's ear, as the cadaverous man turned away, "it is nothing. Bourgeois music. Programme music. Pretty!—You should hear Vrilovitch's 'Ecstasy on the letter Z'. That is pure vibration with no antiquated pattern in it. Stanislas—he thinks much of himself, but it is old as the hills—you can sense the resolution at the back of all his discords. Mere harmony in camouflage. Nothing in it. But he takes them all in because he has red hair and reveals his bony structure."

The speaker certainly did not err along these lines, for he was as bald and round as a billiard-ball. Wimsey replied soothingly:

"Well, what can you do with the wretched and antiquated instruments of our orchestra? A diatonic scale, bah! Thirteen miserable, bourgeois semi-tones, pooh! To express the infinite complexity of modern emotion, you need a scale of thirty-two notes to the octave."

"But why cling to the octave?" said the fat man. "Till you can cast away the octave and its sentimental associations, you walk in fetters of convention."

"That's the spirit!" said Wimsey. "I would dispense with all definite notes. After all, the cat does not need them for his midnight melodies, powerful and expressive as they are. The love-hunger of the stallion takes no account of octave or interval in giving forth the cry of passion. It is only man, trammelled by a stultifying convention—oh, hullo, Marjorie, sorry—what is it?"

"Come and talk to Ryland Vaughan," said Marjorie. "I have told him you are a tremendous admirer of Philip Boyes' books. Have you read them?"

"Some of them. But I think I'm getting light-headed."

"You'll feel worse in an hour or so. So you'd better come now." She steered him to a remote spot near the gas-oven, where an extremely elongated man was sitting curled up on a floor cushion, eating caviare out of a jar with a pickle-fork. He greeted Wimsey with a sort of lugubrious enthusiasm.

"Hell of a place," he said, "hell of a business altogether. This stove's too hot. Have a drink. What the devil else can one do? I come here because Philip used to come here. Habit, you know. I hate it, but there's nowhere else to go."

"You knew him very well, of course," said Wimsey, seating himself in a waste-paper basket, and wishing he was wearing a bathing-suit.

"I was his only real friend," said Ryland Vaughan, mournfully. "All the rest only cared to pick his brains. Apes! parrots! all the bloody lot of them."

"I've read his books and thought them very fine," said Wimsey, with some sincerity. "But he seemed to me an unhappy soul."

"Nobody understood him," said Vaughan. "They called him difficult—who wouldn't be difficult with so much to fight against? They sucked the blood out of him, and his damned thieves of publishers took every blasted coin they could lay their hands on. And then that bitch of a woman poisoned him. My god, what a life!"

"Yes, but what made her do it—if she did do it?"

"Oh, she did it all right. Sheer, beastly spite and jealousy, that's all there was to it. Just because she couldn't write anything but tripe herself. Harriet Vane's got the bug all these damned women have got—fancy they can do things. They hate a man and they hate his work. You'd think it would have been enough for her to help and look after a genius like Phil, wouldn't you? Why, damn it, he used to ask her advice about his work—her advice! Good Lord!"

"Did he take it?"

"Take it? She wouldn't give it. Told him she never gave opinions on other authors' work. *Other* authors! The impudence of it! Of course she was out of things among us all, but why couldn't she realise the difference between her mind and his? Of course it was hopeless from the start for Philip to get entangled with that kind of woman. Genius must be served, not argued with. I warned him at the time, but he was infatuated. And then, to want to marry her——!"

"Why did he?" asked Wimsey.

"Remains of parsonical upbringing, I suppose. It was really pitiful. Besides, I think that fellow Urquhart did a lot of mischief. Sleek family lawyer—d'you know him?"

"No."

"He got hold of him—put up to it by the family, I imagine. I saw the influence creeping over Phil long before the real trouble began. Perhaps it's a good thing he's dead. It would have been ghastly to watch him turn conventional and settle down."

"When did this cousin start getting hold of him, then?"

"Oh—about two years ago—a little more, perhaps. Asked him to dinner and that sort of thing. The minute I saw him I knew he was out to ruin Philip, body and soul. What he wanted—what Phil wanted, I mean—was freedom and room to turn about in, but what with the woman and the cousin and the father in the background—oh, well! It's no use crying about it now. His work is left, and that's the best part of him. He's left me that to look after, at least. Harriet Vane didn't get her finger in that pie, after all."

"I'm sure it's absolutely safe in your hands," said Wimsey.

"But when one thinks what there might have been," said Vaughan, turning his bloodshot eyes miserably on Lord Peter, "it's enough to make one cut one's throat, isn't it?"

Wimsey expressed agreement.

"By the way," he said, "you were with him all that last day, till he went to his cousin's. You don't think he had anything on him in the way of poison or anything? I don't want to seem unkind—but he was unhappy—it would be rotten to think that he——"

"No," said Vaughan, "no. That I'll swear he never did. He would have told me—he trusted me in those last days. I shared all his thoughts. He was miserably hurt by that damned woman, but he wouldn't have gone without telling me or saying good-bye. And besides—he wouldn't have chosen that way. Why should he? I could have given him——"

He checked himself, and glanced at Wimsey, but, seeing nothing in his face beyond sympathetic attention, went on:

"I remember talking to him about drugs. Hyoscine—veronal—all that sort of thing. He said, 'If ever I want to go out, Ryland, you'll show me the way.' And I would have—if he'd really wanted it. But arsenic! Philip, who loved beauty so much—do you think he would have chosen arsenic? the suburban poisoner's outfit? That's absolutely impossible."

"It's not an agreeable sort of thing to take, certainly," said Wimsey.

"Look here," said Vaughan, hoarsely and impressively—he had been putting a constant succession of brandies on top of the caviare, and was beginning to lose his reserve—"look here! See this!" He pulled a small bottle from his breast pocket. "That's waiting till I've finished editing Phil's books. It's a comfort to have it there to look at, you know. Peaceful. Go out through the ivory gate—that's classical—they brought me up on the classics. These people would laugh at a fellow, but you needn't tell them I said it—funny, the way it sticks—'*tendebantque manus ripæ ulterioris amore, ulterioris amore*'—what's that bit about the souls thronging thick as leaves in Vallombrosa—no, that's Milton—*amorioris ultore—ultoriore*—damn it—poor Phil!"

Here Mr. Vaughan burst into tears and patted the little bottle.

Wimsey, whose head and ears were thumping as though he were sitting in an engine-room, got up softly and withdrew. Somebody had begun a Hungarian song, and the stove was white-hot. He made signals of distress to Marjorie, who was sitting in a corner with a group of men. One of them appeared to be reading his own poems with his mouth nearly in her ear, and another was sketching something on the back of an envelope, to the accompaniment of yelps of merriment from the rest. The noise they made disconcerted the singer, who stopped in the middle of a bar, and cried angrily:

"Ach! this noise! these interruptions! they are intolerable! I lose myself! Stop! I begin all over again, from the beginning."

Marjorie sprang up, apologising.

"I'm a brute—I'm not keeping your menagerie in order, Nina. We're being perfect nuisances. Forgive me, Marya, I'm in a bad temper. I'd better pick up Peter and toddle away. Come and sing to me another day, darling, when I'm feeling better and there is more room for my feelings to expand. Good-night, Nina—we've enjoyed it frightfully—and Boris, that poem's the best thing you've done, only I couldn't hear it properly. Peter, tell them what a rotten mood I'm in to-night and take me home."

"That's right," said Wimsey, "nervy, you know—bad effect on the manners and so on."

"Manners," said a bearded gentleman suddenly and loudly, "are for the bourgeois."

"Quite right," said Wimsey. "Beastly bad form, and gives you repressions in the what-not. Come on, Marjorie, or we shall all be getting polite."

"I begin again," said the singer, "from the beginning."

"Whew!" said Wimsey, on the staircase.

"Yes, I know. I think I'm a perfect martyr to put up with it. Anyway, you've seen Vaughan. Nice dopey specimen, isn't he?"

"Yes, but I don't think he murdered Philip Boyes, do you? I had to see him to make sure. Where do we go next?"

"We'll try Joey Trimbles'. That's the stronghold of the opposition show."

Joey Trimbles occupied a studio over a mews. Here there was the same crowd, the same smoke, more kippers, still more drinks, and still more heat and conversation. In addition there was a blaze of electric light, a gramophone, five dogs, and a strong smell of oil-paints. Sylvia Marriott was expected. Wimsey found himself involved in a discussion of free love, D. H. Lawrence, the prurience of prudery, and the immoral significance of long skirts. In time, however, he was rescued by the arrival of a masculine-looking middle-aged woman with a sinister smile and a pack of cards, who proceeded to tell everybody's fortune. The company gathered around her, and at the same time a girl came in and announced that Sylvia had sprained her ankle and couldn't come. Everybody said warmly, "Oh, how sickening, poor dear!" and forgot the subject immediately.

"We'll scoot off," said Marjorie. "Never mind about saying good-bye. Nobody marks you. It's good luck about Sylvia, because she'll be at home and can't escape us. I sometimes wish they'd all sprain their ankles. And yet, you know, nearly all those people are doing very good work. Even the Kropotky crowd. I used to enjoy this kind of thing myself once."

"We're getting old, you and I," said Wimsey. "Sorry, that's rude. But do you know, I'm getting on for forty, Marjorie."

"You wear well. But you are looking a bit fagged to-night, Peter dear. What's the matter?"

"Nothing at all but middle-age."

"You'll be settling down if you're not careful."

"Oh, I've been settled for years."

"With Bunter and the books. I envy you sometimes, Peter."

Wimsey said nothing. Marjorie looked at him almost in alarm, and tucked her arm in his.

"Peter—do please be happy. I mean, you've always been the comfortable sort of person that nothing could touch. Don't alter, will you?"

That was the second time Wimsey had been asked not to alter himself; the first time, the request had exalted him; this time, it terrified him. As the taxi lurched along the rainy Embankment, he felt for the first time the dull and angry helplessness which is the first warning stroke of the triumph of mutability. Like the poisoned Athulf in the *Fool's Tragedy*, he could have cried, "Oh, I am changing, changing, fearfully changing." Whether his present enterprise failed or succeeded, things would never be the same again. It was not that his heart would be broken by a disastrous love—he had outlived the luxurious agonies of youthful blood, and in this very freedom from illusion he recognised the loss of something. From now on, every hour of light-heartedness would be, not a prerogative, but an achievement—one more axe or case-bottle or fowling-piece, rescued, Crusoe-fashion, from a sinking ship.

For the first time, too, he doubted his own power to carry through what he had undertaken. His personal feelings had been involved before this in his investigations, but they had never before clouded his mind. He was fumbling —grasping uncertainly here and there at fugitive and mocking possibilities. He asked questions at random, doubtful of his object, and the shortness of the time, which would once have stimulated, now frightened and confused him.

"I'm sorry, Marjorie," he said, rousing himself, "I'm afraid I'm being damned dull. Oxygen-starvation, probably. D'you mind if we have the window down a bit? That's better. Give me good food and a little air to breathe and I will caper, goat-like, to a dishonourable old age. People will point me out, as I creep, bald and yellow and supported by discreet corsetry, into the night-clubs of my great-grandchildren, and they'll say, 'Look, darling! that's the wicked Lord Peter, celebrated for never having spoken a reasonable word for the last ninety-six years. He was the only aristocrat who escaped the guillotine in the revolution of 1960. We keep him as a pet for the children.' And I shall wag my head and display my up-to-date dentures and say, 'Ah, ha! They don't have the fun we used to have in my young days, the poor, well-regulated creatures!' "

"There won't be any night-clubs then for you to creep into, if they're as disciplined as all that."

"Oh, yes—nature will have her revenge. They will slink away from the Government Communal Games to play solitaire in catacombs over a bowl of unsterilised skim-milk. Is this the place?"

"Yes; I hope there's someone to let us in at the bottom, if Sylvia's bust her leg. Yes—I hear footsteps. Oh, it's you, Eiluned; how's Sylvia?"

"Pretty all right, only swelled up—the ankle, that is. Coming up?"

"Is she visible?"

"Yes, perfectly respectable."

"Good, because I'm bringing Lord Peter Wimsey up, too."

"Oh," said the girl. "How do you do? You detect things, don't you? Have you come for the body or anything?"

"Lord Peter's looking into Harriet Vane's business for her."

"Is he? That's good. Glad somebody's doing something about it." She was a short, stout girl with a pugnacious nose and a twinkle. "What do you say it was? I say he did it himself. He was the self-pitying sort, you know. Hullo, Syl—here's Marjorie, with a bloke who's going to get Harriet out of jug."

"Produce him instantly!" was the reply from within. The door opened upon a small bed-sitting-room, furnished with the severest simplicity, and inhabited by a pale, spectacled young woman in a Morris chair, her bandaged foot stretched out upon a packing-case.

"I can't get up, because, as Jenny Wren said, my back's bad and my legs queer. Who's the champion, Marjorie?"

Wimsey was introduced, and Eiluned Price immediately enquired, rather truculently:

"Can he drink coffee, Marjorie? Or does he require masculine refreshment?"

"He's perfectly godly, righteous, and sober, and drinks anything but cocoa and fizzy lemonade."

"Oh! I only asked because some of your male belongings need stimulating, and we haven't got the wherewithal, and the pub's just closing."

She stumped over to a cupboard, and Sylvia said:

"Don't mind Eiluned; she likes to treat 'em rough. Tell me, Lord Peter, have you found any clues or anything?"

"I don't know," said Wimsey. "I've put a few ferrets down a few holes. I hope something may come up the other end."

"Have you seen the cousin yet—the Urquhart creature?"

"Got an appointment with him for to-morrow. Why?"

"Sylvia's theory is that he did it," said Eiluned.

"That's interesting. Why?"

"Female intuition," said Eiluned, bluntly. "She doesn't like the way he does his hair."

"I only said he was too sleek to be true," protested Sylvia. "And who else could it have been? I'm sure it wasn't Ryland Vaughan; he's an obnoxious ass, but he is genuinely heart-broken about it all."

Eiluned sniffed scornfully, and departed to fill a kettle at a tap on the landing.

"And, whatever Eiluned thinks, I can't believe Phil Boyes did it himself."

"Why not?" asked Wimsey.

"He talked such a lot," said Sylvia. "And he really had too high an opinion of himself. I don't think he would have wilfully deprived the world of the privilege of reading his books."

"He would," said Eiluned. "He'd do it out of spite, to make the grown-ups sorry. No, thanks"—as Wimsey advanced to carry the kettle—"I'm quite capable of carrying six pints of water."

"Crushed again!" said Wimsey.

"Eiluned disapproves of conventional courtesies between the sexes," said Marjorie.

"Very well," replied Wimsey, amiably. "I will adopt an attitude of passive decoration. Have you any idea, Miss Marriott, why this over-sleek solicitor should wish to make away with his cousin?"

"Not the faintest. I merely proceed on the old Sherlock Holmes basis that when you have eliminated the impossible, then whatever remains, however improbable, must be true."

"Dupin said that before Sherlock. I grant the conclusion, but in this case I question the premises. No sugar, thank you."

"I thought all men liked to make their coffee into syrup."

"Yes, but then I am very unusual. Haven't you noticed it?"

"I haven't had much time to observe you, but I'll count the coffee as a point in your favour."

"Thanks frightfully. I say—can you people tell me just what was Miss Vane's reaction to the murder?"

"Well——" Sylvia considered a moment. "When he died—she was upset, of course——"

"She was startled," said Miss Price, "but it's my opinion she was thankful to be rid of him. And no wonder. Selfish beast! He'd made use of her and nagged her to death for a year and insulted her at the end. And he was one of your greedy sort that wouldn't let go. She *was* glad, Sylvia—what's the good of denying it?"

"Yes, perhaps. It was a relief to know he was finished with. But she didn't know then that he'd been murdered."

"No. The murder spoilt it a bit—if it was a murder, which I don't believe. Philip Boyes was always determined to be a victim, and it was very irritating of him to succeed in the end. I believe that's what he did it for."

"People do do that kind of thing," said Wimsey, thoughtfully. "But it's difficult to prove. I mean, a jury is much more inclined to believe in some tangible sort of reason, like money. But I can't find any money in this case."

Eiluned laughed.

"No, there never was much money, except what Harriet made. The ridiculous public didn't appreciate Phil Boyes. He couldn't forgive her that, you know."

"Didn't it come in useful?"

"Of course, but he resented it all the same. She ought to have been ministering to his work, not making money for them both with her own independent trash. But that's men all over."

"You haven't much opinion of us, what?"

"I've known too many borrowers," said Eiluned Price, "and too many that wanted their hands held. All the same, the women are just as bad, or they wouldn't put up with it. Thank heaven, I've never borrowed and never lent—except to women, and they pay back."

"People who work hard usually do pay back, I fancy," said Wimsey, "—except geniuses."

"Women geniuses don't get coddled," said Miss Price, grimly, "so they learn not to expect it."

"We're getting rather off the subject, aren't we?" said Marjorie.

"No," replied Wimsey, "I'm getting a certain amount of light on the central figures in the problem—what journalists like to call the protagonists." His mouth gave a wry little twist. "One gets a lot of illumination in that fierce light that beats upon a scaffold."

"Don't say that," pleaded Sylvia.

A telephone rang somewhere outside, and Eiluned Price went out to answer it.

"Eiluned's anti-man," said Sylvia, "but she's a very reliable person."

Wimsey nodded.

"But she's wrong about Phil—she couldn't stick him, naturally, and she's apt to think——"

"It's for you, Lord Peter," said Eiluned, returning. "Fly at once—all is known. You're wanted by Scotland Yard."

Wimsey hastened out.

"That you, Peter? I've been scouring London for you. We've found the pub."

"Never!"

"Fact. And we're on the track of a packet of white powder."

"Good God!"

"Can you run down first thing to-morrow? We may have it for you."

"I will skip like a ram and hop like a high hill. We'll beat you yet, Mr. Bleeding Chief Inspector Parker."

"I hope you will," said Parker, amiably, and rang off.

Wimsey pranced back into the room.

"Miss Price's price has gone to odds on," he announced. "It's suicide, fifty to one and no takers. I am going to grin like a dog and run about the city."

"I'm sorry I can't join you," said Sylvia Marriott, "but I'm glad if I'm wrong."

"I'm glad I'm right," said Eiluned Price, stolidly.

"And you are right and I am right and everything is quite all right," said Wimsey.

Marjorie Phelps looked at him and said nothing. She suddenly felt as though something inside her had been put through a wringer.

CHAPTER IX

BY WHAT INGRATIATING means Mr. Bunter had contrived to turn the delivery of a note into the acceptance of an invitation to tea was best known to himself. At half-past four on the day which ended so cheerfully for Lord Peter, he was seated in the kitchen of Mr. Urquhart's house, toasting crumpets. He had been trained to a great pitch of dexterity in the preparation of crumpets, and if he was somewhat lavish in the matter of butter, that hurt nobody except Mr. Urquhart. It was natural that the conversation should turn to the subject of murder. Nothing goes so well with a hot fire and buttered crumpets as a wet day without and a good dose of comfortable horrors within. The heavier the lashing of the rain and the ghastlier the details, the better the flavour seems to be. On the present occasion, all the ingredients of an enjoyable party were present in full force.

" 'Orrible white, he looked, when he came in," said Mrs. Pettican the cook. "I see him when they sent for me to bring up the 'ot bottles. Three of them, they 'ad, one to his feet and one to his back and the big rubber one to 'is stummick. White and shiverin', he was, and that dreadful sick, you never would believe. And he groaned pitiful."

"Green, he looked to me, Cook," said Hannah Westlock, "or you might perhaps call it a greenish-yellow. I thought it was jaundice a-coming on—more like them attacks he had in the spring."

"He was a bad colour then," agreed Mrs. Pettican, "but nothink like to what he was that last time. And the pains and cramps in his legs was agonising. That struck Nurse Williams very forcible—a nice young woman she was, and not stuck-up like some as I could name. 'Mrs. Pettican', she said to me, which I call it better manners than callin' you Cook as they mostly do, as though they paid your wages for the right of callin' you out of your name—'Mrs. Pettican,' said she, 'never did I see anything to equal them cramps except in one other case that was the dead spit of this one,' she said, 'and you mark my words, Mrs. Pettican, them cramps ain't there for nothin'.' Ah! little did I understand her meanin' at the time."

"That's a regular feature of these arsenical cases, or so his lordship tells me," replied Bunter. "A very distressing symptom. Had he ever had anything of the sort before?"

"Not what you could call cramps," said Hannah, "though I remember when he was ill in the spring he complained of getting the fidgets in the hands and feet. Something like pins-and-needles, by what I understood him to say. It was a worrit to him, because he was finishing one of his articles in a hurry, and what with that and his eyes being so bad, the writing was a trial to him, poor thing."

"From what the gentleman for the prosecution said, talking it out with Sir James Lubbock," said Mr. Bunter, "I gathered that those pins-and-needles, and bad eyes and so on, were a sign he'd been given arsenic regularly, if I may so phrase it."

"A dreadful wicked woman she must 'a been," said Mrs. Pettican, "—'ev another crumpet, do, Mr. Bunter—a-torturin' of the poor soul that long-winded way. Bashin' on the 'ed or the 'asty use of a carvin' knife when roused I can understand, but the 'orrors of slow poisonin' is the work of a fiend in 'uman form, in my opinion."

"Fiend is the only word, Mrs. Pettican," agreed the visitor.

"And the wickedness of it," said Hannah, "quite apart from the causing of a painful death to a fellow-being. Why, it's only the mercy of Providence we weren't all brought under suspicion."

"Yes, indeed," said Mrs. Pettican. "Why, when master told us about them diggin' poor Mr. Boyes up and findin' him full of that there nasty arsenic, it give me sech a turn, I felt as if the room was a-goin' round like the gallopin' 'orses at the roundabouts. 'Oh, sir!' I ses, 'what, in our 'ouse!' That's what I ses, and he ses, 'Mrs. Pettican,' he ses, 'I sincerely hope not.' "

Mrs. Pettican, having imparted this Macbeth-like flavour to the story, was pleased with it, and added:

"Yes, that's what I said to 'im. 'In our 'ouse,' I said, and I'm sure I never slep' a wink for three nights afterwards, what with the police and the fright and one thing and another."

"But of course you had no difficulty in proving that it hadn't happened in this house?" suggested Bunter. "Miss Westlock gave her evidence so beautifully at the trial, I'm sure she made it clear as clear could be to judge and jury. The judge congratulated you, Miss Westlock, and I'm sure he didn't say nearly enough—so plainly and well as you spoke up before the whole Court."

"Well, I never was one to be shy," confessed Hannah, "and then, what with going through it all so careful with the master and then with the police, I knew what the questions would be and was prepared, as you might say."

"I wonder you could speak so exactly to every little detail, all that time ago," said Bunter, with admiration.

"Well, you see, Mr. Bunter, the very morning after Mr. Boyes was took ill, master comes down to us and he says, sitting in that chair ever so friendly, just as you might be yourself, 'I'm afraid Mr. Boyes is very ill,' he says. 'He thinks he must have ate something as disagreed with him,' he says, 'and perhaps as it might be the chicken. So I want you and Cook,' he says, 'to run through with me everything we had for dinner last night to see if we can think what it could have been.' 'Well, sir,' I said, 'I don't see that Mr. Boyes could have ate anything unwholesome here, for Cook and me had just the same, put aside yourself, sir, and it was all as sweet and good as it could be,' I said."

"And I said the same," said the Cook. "Sech a plain, simple dinner as it was, too—no oysters nor mussels nor anythink of that sort, as it's well known shell-fish is poison to some people's stummicks, but a good stren'thenin' drop o' soup, and a bit of nice fish, and a casseroled chicken with turnips and carrots done in the gravy, and a omelette, wot could be lighter and better? Not but there's people as can't relish eggs in any form, my own mother was just the same, give her so much as a cake what had bin made with a egg in it and she'd be that sick and come out all over spots like nettle-rash, you'd be surprised. But Mr. Boyes was a great gentleman for eggs, and omelettes was his particular favourite."

"Yes, he made the omelette himself that very night, didn't he?"

"He did," said Hannah, "and well I remember it, for Mr. Urquhart asked particular after the eggs, was they new-laid, and I reminded him they was some he had brought in himself that afternoon from that shop on the corner of Lamb's Conduit Street where they always have them fresh from the farm, and I reminded him that one of them was a little cracked and he'd said, 'We'll use that in the omelette to-night, Hannah,' and I brought out a clean bowl from the kitchen and put them straight in—the cracked one and three more besides, and never touched them again till I brought them to table. 'And what's more, sir,' I said, 'there's the other eight still here out of the dozen, and you can see for yourself they're as good and fresh as they can be.' Didn't I, Cook?"

"Yes, Hannah. And as for the chicken, that was a little beauty. It was that young and tender, I says to Hannah at the time as it seemed a shame to casserole it, for it would 'ave roasted beautiful. But Mr. Urquhart is very partial to a casseroled chicken; he says as there's more flavour to 'em that way, and I dunno but what he's right."

"If done with a good beef stock," pronounced Mr. Bunter, judicially, "the vegetables well packed in layers, on a foundation of bacon, not too fat, and the whole well seasoned with salt, pepper, and paprika, there are few dishes to beat a casseroled chicken. For my own part, I would recommend a *soupçon* of garlic, but I am aware that such is not agreeable to all tastes."

"I can't a-bear the smell or sight of the stuff," said Mrs. Pettican, frankly, "but as for the rest, I'm with you, always allowing that the giblets is added to the stock, and I would personally favour mushrooms when in season, but not them tinned or bottled sorts as looks pretty but has no more taste to 'em than boot-buttons if so much. But the secret is in the cooking, as you know well, Mr. Bunter, the lid being kep' well sealed down to 'old the flavour and the cookin' bein' slow to make the juices perambulate through *and* through each other as you might say. I'm not denyin' as sech is very 'ighly enjoyable, and so Hannah and me found it, though fond of a good roast fowl also, when well-basted with a good rich stuffing to rejuice the dryness. But as to roasting it, Mr. Urquhart wouldn't hear of it, and bein' as it's him that pays the bills, he has the right to give his orders."

"Well," said Bunter, "it's certain if there had been anything unwholesome about the casserole, you and Miss Westlock could scarcely have escaped it."

"No, indeed," said Hannah, "for I won't conceal that, being blessed with hearty appetites, we finished it every bit, except a little piece I gave to the cat. Mr. Urquhart asked to see the remains of it next day, and seemed quite put out to find it was all gone and the dish washed up—as though any washing-up was ever left overnight in *this* kitchen."

"I couldn't a-bear myself if I had to begin the day with dirty dishes," said Mrs. Pettican. "There was a drop of the soup left—not much, jest a wee drain, and Mr. Urquhart took that up to show to the doctor, and he tasted it and said it was very good, so Nurse Williams told us, though she didn't have none of it herself."

"And as for the Burgundy," said Hannah Westlock, "which was the only thing Mr. Boyes had to himself, like, Mr. Urquhart told me to cork it up tight and keep it. And just as well we did, because, of course, the police asked to see it when the time came."

"It was very far-seeing of Mr. Urquhart to take such precautions," said Bunter, "when there wasn't any thought at the time but that the poor man died naturally."

"That's what Nurse Williams said," replied Hannah, "but we put it down to him being a solicitor and knowing what ought to be done in a case of sudden death. Very particular he was, too—got me to put a bit of sticking-plaster over the mouth of the bottle and write my initials on it, so that it shouldn't be opened accidental. Nurse Williams always said he expected an inquest, but Dr. Weare being there to speak to Mr. Boyes having had these kind of bilious attacks all his life, of course there was no question raised about giving the certificate."

"Of course not," said Bunter, "but it's very fortunate, as it turns out, that

Mr. Urquhart should have understood his duty so well. Many's the case his lordship has seen in which an innocent man has been brought near to the gallows for lack of a simple little precaution like that."

"And when I think how near Mr. Urquhart was to being away from 'ome at the time," said Mrs. Pettican, "the thought fair gives me palpitations. Called away, he was, to that tiresome old woman what's always a-dying and never dies. Why, he's there now—Mrs. Wrayburn, up in Windle. Rich as Sneezes, she is, by all accounts, and no good to nobody, for she's gone quite childish, so they say. A wicked old woman she was, too, in 'er day, and 'er other relations wouldn't 'ave nothink to do with 'er, only Mr. Urquhart, and I don't suppose 'e wouldn't, neither, only 'e's her solicitor and it's his duty so to do."

"Duty does not always lie in pleasant places," commented Mr. Bunter, "as you and I well know, Mrs. Pettican."

"Them that are rich," said Hannah Westlock, "find no difficulty about getting their duties performed for them. Which I will make bold to say, Mrs. Wrayburn would not have done if she had been poor, great-aunt or no great-aunt, knowing Mr. Urquhart."

"Ah!" said Bunter.

"I pass no comments," said Miss Westlock, "but you and me, Mr. Bunter, know how the world goes."

"I suppose Mr. Urquhart stands to gain something when the old woman does peg out," suggested Bunter.

"That's as may be; he's not a talker," said Hannah, "but it stands to reason he wouldn't be always giving up his time and tearing off to Westmorland for nothing. Though I wouldn't care myself to put my hand to money that's wickedly come by. It would not bring a blessing with it, Mr. Bunter."

"It's easy talking, my girl, when you ain't likely to be put in the way of temptation," said Mrs. Pettican. "There's many great families in the kingdom what never would 'a bin 'eard of if somebody 'adn't bin a little easier in their ways than what we've bin brought up to. There's skelintons in a many cupboards if the truth was known."

"Ah!" said Bunter, "I believe you. I've seen diamond necklaces and fur coats that should have been labelled 'Wages of Sin' if deeds done in the dark were to be proclaimed upon the house-tops, Mrs. Pettican. And there are families that hold their heads high that wouldn't ever have existed but for some king or other taking his amusements on the wrong side of the blanket, as the old saying goes."

"They say as some that was high up wasn't too high to take notice of old Mrs. Wrayburn in her young days," said Hannah, darkly. "Queen Victoria wouldn't never allow her to act before the Royal Family—she knew too much about her goings-on."

"An actress, was she?"

"And a very beautiful one, they say, though I can't rightly recollect what her stage name was," mused Mrs. Pettican. "It was a queer one, I know——'Yde Park, or somethink of that. This Wrayburn as she married, 'e was nobody—jest to kiver up the scandal, that's what she married 'im for. Two children she 'ad—but 'ose I would not take it upon me to say—and they both died in the cholera, which no doubt it was a judgment."

"That's not what Mr. Boyes called it," said Hannah, with a self-righteous sniff. "The Devil took care of his own, that was his way of putting it."

"Ah! he talked careless," said Mrs. Pettican, "and no wonder, seeing the folks he lived with. But he'd a sobered down in time if he'd bin spared. A very pleasant way 'e 'ad with 'im when 'e liked. Come in here, he would, and chat upon one thing and another, very amusing-like."

"You're too soft with the gentlemen, Mrs. Pettican," said Hannah. "Anyone as has taking ways and poor health is ewe-lambs to you."

"So Mr. Boyes knew all about Mrs. Wrayburn?"

"Oh, yes—it was all in the family, you see, and no doubt Mr. Urquhart would 'a told him more than he'd say to us. Which train did Mr. Urquhart say he was a-comin' by, Hannah?"

"He said dinner for half-past seven. That'll be the six-thirty, I should think."

Mrs. Pettican glanced at the clock and Bunter, taking this as a hint, rose and made his farewells.

"And I 'opes as you'll come again, Mr. Bunter," said the Cook, graciously. "The master makes no objections to respectable gentlemen visitors at tea-time. Wednesday is my 'arf-day."

"Mine is Friday," added Hannah, "and every other Sunday. If you should be Evangelical, Mr. Bunter, the Rev. Crawford in Judd Street is a beautiful preacher. But maybe you'll be going out of town for Christmas."

Mr. Bunter replied that that season would undoubtedly be spent at Duke's Denver, and departed in a shining halo of vicarious splendour.

CHAPTER X

"HERE YOU ARE, Peter," said Chief Inspector Parker, "and here is the lady you are anxious to meet. Mrs. Bulfinch, allow me to introduce Lord Peter Wimsey."

"Pleased, I am sure," said Mrs. Bulfinch. She giggled, and dabbed her large, blonde face with powder.

"Mrs. Bulfinch, before her union with Mr. Bulfinch, was the life and soul of the saloon bar at the Nine Rings in Gray's Inn Road," said Mr. Parker, "and well known to all for her charm and wit."

"Go on," said Mrs. Bulfinch, "you're a one, aren't you? Don't you pay no attention to him, your lordship. You know what these police fellows are."

"Sad dogs," said Wimsey, shaking his head. "But I don't need his testimonials; I can trust my own eyes and ears, Mrs. Bulfinch, and I can only say that, if I had had the happiness to make your acquaintance before it was too late, it would have been my lifetime's ambition to wipe Mr. Bulfinch's eye."

"You're every bit as bad as he is," said Mrs. Bulfinch, highly gratified, "and what Bulfinch would say to you I *don't* know. Quite upset, he was, when the officer came round to ask me to pop along to the Yard. 'I don't like it, Gracie,' he says, 'we've always bin respectable in this house and no trouble with disorderlies nor drinks after hours, and once you get among them fellows you don't know the things you may be asked.' 'Don't be so soft,' I tells him; 'the boys all know me and they haven't got nothing against me, and if it's just to tell them about the gentleman that left the packet behind him at the Rings, I haven't no objection to tell them, having nothing to reproach myself with. What'd they think,' I said, 'if I refused to go? Ten to one they'd think there was something funny about it.' 'Well,' he says, 'I'm coming with you.' 'Oh, are you?' I says, 'and how about the new barman you was going to engage this morning? For,' I said, 'serve in the jug and bottle I will not, never having been accustomed to it, so you can do as you like.' So I came away and left him to it. Mind you, I like him for it. I ain't saying nothing against Bulfinch, but, police or no police, I reckon I know how to take care of myself."

"Quite so," said Parker, patiently. "Mr. Bulfinch need feel no alarm. All we want you to do is to tell us, to the best of your recollection, about that young man you spoke of and help us to find the white paper packet. You may be able to save an innocent person from being convicted, and I am sure your husband could not object to that."

"Poor thing!" said Mrs. Bulfinch, "I'm sure when I read the account of the trial I said to Bulfinch——"

"Just a moment. If you wouldn't mind beginning at the beginning, Mrs. Bulfinch, Lord Peter would understand better what you have to tell us."

"Why, of course. Well, my lord, before I was married I was barmaid at the Nine Rings, as the Chief Inspector says. Miss Montague I was then—it's a better name than Bulfinch, and I was almost sorry to say goodbye to it, but there! a girl has to make a lot of sacrifices when she marries and one more or less is nothing to signify. I never worked there but in the saloon bar, for I wouldn't undertake the four-ale business, it not being a refined neighbourhood, though there's a lot of very nice legal gentlemen drops in of an evening on the saloon side. Well, as I was saying, I was working there up to my marriage, which was last August Bank Holiday, and I remember one evening a gentleman coming in——"

"Could you remember the date, do you think?"

"Not within a day or so I couldn't, for I wouldn't wish to swear to a fib, but it wasn't far off the longest day, for I remember making that same remark to the gentleman for something to say, you know."

"That's near enough," said Parker. "Round about June 20th, or 21st, or something like that?"

"That's right, as near as I can speak to it. And as to the time of night, that I *can* tell you—knowing how keen you 'tecs always are on the hands of the clock." Mrs. Bulfinch giggled again and looked archly round for applause.

"There was a gentleman sitting there—I didn't know him, he was a stranger to the district—and he asked what was our closing time and I told him 11 o'clock, and he said, 'Thank God! I thought I was going to be turned out at 10.30,' and I looked at the clock and said, 'Oh, you're all right, anyway, sir; we always keep that clock a quarter of an hour fast.' The clock said twenty past, so I know it must have been five past ten really. So we got talking a bit about these prohibitionists and the way they had been trying it on again to get our licensing-hour altered to half-past ten, only we had a good friend on the Bench in Mr. Judkins, and while we were discussing it, I remember so well, the door was pushed open hurried-like and a young gentleman comes in, almost falls in, I might say, and he calls, 'Give me a double brandy, quick.' Well, I didn't like to serve him at once, he looked so white and queer, I thought he'd had one or two over the eight already, and the boss was most particular about that sort of thing. Still, he spoke all right—quite clear and not repeating himself nor nothing, and his eyes, though they did look a bit funny, weren't fixed-like, if you understand me. We get to size folks up pretty well in our business, you know. He sort of held on to the bar, all scrunched up together and bent double, and he says, 'Make it a stiff one, there's a good girl. I'm feeling awful bad.' The gentleman I'd been talking to, he says to him, 'Hold up,' he says, 'what's the matter?' and the gentleman says, 'I'm going to be ill.' And he puts his hands across his waistcoat like so!"

Mrs. Bulfinch clasped her waist and rolled her big blue eyes dramatically.

"Well, then I see he wasn't drunk, so I mixed him a double Martell with just a splash of soda and he gulps it down, and says 'That's better'. And the other gentleman puts his arm round him and helps him to a seat. There was a good many other people in the bar, but they didn't notice much, being full of the racing news. Presently the gentleman asks me for a glass of water, and I fetched it to him, and he says: 'Sorry if I frightened you, but I've just had a bad shock, and it must have gone to my inside. I'm subject to gastric trouble,' he says, 'and any worry or shock always affects my stomach. However,' he says, 'perhaps this will stop it.' And he takes out a white paper packet with some powder in it, and drops it into the glass of water and stirs it up with a fountain-pen and drinks it off."

"Did it fizz or anything?" asked Wimsey.

"No; it was just a plain powder, and it took a bit of a time to mix. He drank it off and said, 'That settles it', or 'That'll settle it', or something of that sort. And then he says, 'Thanks very much. I'm better now and I'd better get home in case it takes me again.' And he raised his hat—he was quite the gentleman—and off he goes."

"How much powder do you think he put in?"

"Oh, a good dollop. He didn't measure it or anything, just shot it in out of the packet. Near a dessertspoonful it might have been."

"And what happened to the packet?" prompted Parker.

"Ah, there you are." Mrs. Bulfinch took a glance at Wimsey's face and seemed pleased with the effect she was producing.

"We'd just got the last customer out—about five past eleven, that would be—and George was locking the door, when I see something white on the seat. Somebody's handkerchief I thought it was, but when I picked it up, I see it was the paper packet. So I said to George, 'Hullo! the gentleman's left his medicine behind him', and he said, 'What is it?' and I looked, but the label had been torn off. It was just one of them chemist's packets, you know, with the ends turned up and a label stuck across, but there wasn't a bit of the label left."

"You couldn't even see whether it had been printed in black or in red?"

"Well, now." Mrs. Bulfinch considered. "Well, no, I couldn't say that. Now you mention it, I do seem to recollect that there was something red about the packet, somewhere, but I can't clearly call it to mind. I wouldn't swear. I know there wasn't any name or printing of any kind, because I looked to see what it was."

"You didn't try tasting it, I suppose?"

"Not me. It might have been poison or something. I tell you, he was a funny-looking customer." (Parker and Wimsey exchanged glances.)

"Was that what you thought at the time?" enquired Wimsey, "or did it only occur to you later on—after you'd read about the case, you know?"

"I thought it at the time, of course," retorted Mrs. Bulfinch, snappishly. "Aren't I telling you that's why I didn't taste it? I said so to George at the time, what's more. Besides, if it wasn't poison, it might be 'snow' or something. 'Best not touch it,' that's what I said to George, and he said: 'Chuck it in the fire.' But I wouldn't have that. The gentleman might have come back for it. So I stuck it up on the shelf behind the bar, where they keep the spirits, and never thought of it again from that day to yesterday, when your policeman came round about it."

"It's been looked for there," said Parker, "but they can't seem to find it anywhere."

"Well, I don't know about that. I put it there and I left the Rings in August, so what's gone with it I can't say. Daresay they threw it away when they were cleaning. Wait a bit, though—I'm wrong when I say I never thought about it again. I did just wonder about it when I read the report of the trial in the *News of the World*, and I said to George, 'I wouldn't be surprised if that was the gentleman who came into the Rings one night and seemed so poorly—just fancy!' I said—just like that. And George said, 'Now don't you get fancies, Gracie my girl; you don't want to get mixed up in a police case.' George has always held his head high, you see."

"It's a pity you didn't come forward with this story," said Parker, severely.

"Well, how was I to know it was important? The taxi-driver had seen him a few minutes afterwards and he was ill then, so the powder couldn't have had anything to do with it, if it was him, which I couldn't swear to. And anyhow, I didn't see about it till the trial was all over and finished with."

"There will be a new trial, though," said Parker, "and you may have to give evidence at that."

"You know where to find me," said Mrs. Bulfinch, with spirit. "I shan't run away."

"We're very much obliged to you for coming now," added Wimsey, pleasantly.

"Don't mention it," said the lady. "Is that all you want, Mr. Chief Inspector?"

"That's all at present. If we find the packet, we may ask you to identify it. And, by the way, it's advisable not to discuss these matters with your friends, Mrs. Bulfinch. Sometimes ladies get talking, and one thing leads to another, and in the end they remember incidents that never took place at all. You understand."

"I never was one for talking," said Mrs. Bulfinch, offended. "And it's my opinion, when it comes to putting two and two together to make five of 'em, the ladies aren't in it with the gentlemen."

"I may pass this on to the solicitors for the defence, I suppose?" said Wimsey, when the witness had departed.

"Of course," said Parker, "that's why I asked you to come and hear it—for what it's worth. Meanwhile, we shall of course have a good hunt for the packet."

"Yes," said Wimsey, thoughtfully, "yes—you will have to do that—naturally."

Mr. Crofts did not look best pleased when this story was handed on to him.

"I warned you, Lord Peter," he said, "what might come of showing our hand to the police. Now they've got hold of this incident, they will have every opportunity to turn it to their own advantage. Why didn't you leave it to us to make the investigation?"

"Damn it," said Wimsey, angrily, "it was left to you for about three months and you did absolutely damn all. The police dug it up in three days. Time's important in this case, you know."

"Very likely, but don't you see that the police won't rest now till they've found this precious packet."

"Well?"

"Well, and suppose it isn't arsenic at all? If you'd left it in our hands, we could have sprung the thing on them at the last moment, when it was too late to make enquiries, and then we should have knocked the bottom out of the prosecution. Give the jury Mrs. Bulfinch's story as it stands and they'd have to admit there was some evidence that the deceased poisoned himself. But now, of course, the police will find or fake something and show that the powder was perfectly harmless."

"And supposing they find it and it *is* arsenic?"

"In *that* case, of course," said Mr. Crofts, "we shall get an acquittal. But do you believe in that possibility, my lord?"

"It's perfectly evident that *you* don't," said Wimsey, hotly. "In fact, you think your client's guilty. Well, I don't."

Mr. Crofts shrugged his shoulders.

"In our client's interests," he said, "we are bound to look at the unfavourable side of all evidence, so as to anticipate the points that are likely to be made by the prosecution. I repeat, my lord, that you have acted indiscreetly."

"Look here," said Wimsey, "I'm not out for a verdict of 'Not proven'. As far as Miss Vane's honour and happiness are concerned, she might as well be found guilty as acquitted on a mere element of doubt. I want to see her absolutely cleared and the blame fixed in the right quarter. I don't want any shadow of doubt about it."

"Highly desirable, my lord," agreed the solicitor, "but you will allow me to remind you that it is not merely a question of honour or happiness, but of saving Miss Vane's neck from the gallows."

"And I say," said Wimsey, "that it would be better for her to be hanged outright than to live and have everybody think her a murderess who got off by a fluke."

"Indeed?" said Mr. Crofts. "I fear that this is not an attitude that the defence can very well adopt. May I ask if it is adopted by Miss Vane herself?"

"I shouldn't be surprised if it was," said Wimsey. "But she's innocent, and I'll make you damn well believe it before I've done."

"Excellent, excellent," said Mr. Crofts, suavely; "nobody will be more delighted than myself. But I repeat that, in my humble opinion, your lordship will be wiser not to betray too many confidences to Chief Inspector Parker."

Wimsey was still simmering inwardly from this encounter when he entered Mr. Urquhart's office in Bedford Row. The head clerk remembered him and greeted him with the deference due to an exalted and expected visitor. He begged his lordship to take a seat for a moment, and vanished into an inner office.

A woman typist, with a strong, ugly, rather masculine face, looked up from her machine as the door closed, and nodded abruptly to Lord Peter. Wimsey recognised her as one of the "The Cattery", and put a commendatory mental note against Miss Climpson's name for quick and efficient organisation. No words passed, however, and in a few moments the head clerk returned and begged Lord Peter to step inside.

Norman Urquhart rose from his desk and held out a friendly hand of greeting. Wimsey had seen him at the trial, and noted his neat dress, thick, smooth, dark hair, and general appearance of brisk and business-like respectability. Seeing him now more closely, he noticed that he was rather older than he had appeared at a distance. He put him down as being somewhere about the middle forties. His skin was pale and curiously clear, except for a number of little freckles, like sun-spots, rather unexpected at that time of the year, and in a man whose appearance conveyed no other suggestion of an outdoor life. The eyes, dark and shrewd, looked a little tired, and were bistred about the orbits, as though anxiety were not unknown to them.

The solicitor welcomed his guest in a high, pleasant voice and asked what he could do for him.

Wimsey explained that he was interested in the Vane poisoning trial, and that he had the authority of Messrs. Crofts & Cooper to come and bother Mr. Urquhart with questions, adding, as usual, that he was afraid he was being a nuisance.

"Not at all, Lord Peter, not at all. I'm only too delighted to help you in any way, though really I'm afraid you have heard all I know. Naturally, I was very much taken aback by the result of the autopsy, and rather relieved,

I must admit, to find that no suspicion was likely to be thrown on me, under the rather peculiar circumstances."

"Frightfully tryin' for you," agreed Wimsey. "But you seem to have taken the most admirable precautions at the time."

"Well, you know, I suppose we lawyers get into a habit of taking precautions. Not that I had any idea of poison at the time—or, needless to say, I should have insisted on an enquiry then and there. What was in my mind was more in the nature of some kind of food-poisoning; not botulism—the symptoms were all wrong for that—but some contamination from cooking utensils or from some bacillus in the food itself. I am glad it turned out not to be that, though the reality was infinitely worse in one way. I suppose, really, in all cases of sudden and unaccountable illness, an analysis of the secretions ought to be made as a routine part of the business, but Dr. Weare appeared perfectly satisfied, and I trusted entirely to his judgment."

"Obviously," said Wimsey. "One doesn't naturally jump to the idea that people are bein' murdered—though I daresay it happens more often than one is apt to suppose."

"It probably does, and if I'd ever had the handling of a criminal case, the suspicion might have occurred to me, but my work is almost entirely conveyancing and that sort of business—and probate and divorce and so on."

"Talkin' of probate," said Wimsey, carelessly, "had Mr. Boyes any sort of financial expectations?"

"None at all that I know of. His father is by no means well off—the usual country parson with a small stipend and a huge vicarage and tumbledown church. In fact, the whole family belongs to the unfortunate professional middle-class—overtaxed and with very little financial stamina. I shouldn't think there were more than a few hundred pounds to come to Philip Boyes, even if he had outlived the lot of them."

"I had an idea there was a rich aunt somewhere."

"Oh, no—unless you're thinking of old Cremorna Garden. She's a great-aunt, on the mother's side. But she hasn't had anything to do with them for very many years."

At this moment Lord Peter had one of those bursts of illumination which come suddenly when two unrelated facts make contact in the mind. In the excitement of hearing Parker's news about the white paper packet, he had paid insufficient attention to Bunter's account of the tea-party with Hannah Westlock and Mrs. Pettican, but now he remembered something about an actress "with a name like 'Yde Park, or something of that". The readjustment made itself so smoothly and mechanically in his mind that his next question followed almost without a pause.

"Isn't that Mrs. Wrayburn of Windle in Westmorland?"

"Yes," said Mr. Urquhart. "I've just been up to see her, as a matter of fact. Of course, yes, you wrote to me there. She's been quite childish, poor old lady, for the last five years or so. A wretched life—dragging on like that, a misery to herself and everybody else. It always seems to me a cruel thing that one may not put these poor old people out of the way, as one would a favourite animal—but the law will not let us be so merciful."

"Yes, we'd be hauled over the coals by the N.S.P.C.A. if we let a cat linger on in misery," said Wimsey. "Silly, isn't it? But it's all of a piece with the people who write to the papers about keepin' dogs in draughty kennels and don't give a hoot—or a penny—to stop landlords allowin' a family of thirteen to sleep in an undrained cellar with no glass in the windows and no windows to put it in. It really makes me quite cross, sometimes, though I'm a peaceful sort of idiot as a rule. Poor old Cremorna Garden—she must be gettin' on now, though. Surely she can't last much longer."

"As a matter of fact, we all thought she'd gone the other day. Her heart is giving out—she's over ninety, poor soul, and she gets these attacks from time to time. But there's amazing vitality in some of these ancient ladies."

"I suppose you're about her only living relation now."

"I suppose I am, except for an uncle of mine in Australia." Mr. Urquhart accepted the fact of the relationship without enquiring how Wimsey came to know about it. "Not that my being there can do her any good. But I'm her man of business, too, so it's just as well I should be on the spot when anything happens."

"Oh, quite, quite. And, being her man of business, of course you know how she has left her money."

"Well, yes, of course. Though I don't quite see, if you'll forgive me saying so, what that has to do with the present problem."

"Why, don't you see," said Wimsey, "it just occurred to me that Philip Boyes might have got himself into some kind of financial mess-up—it happens to the best of men—and have, well, taken the short way out of it. But, if he had any expectations from Mrs. Wrayburn, and the old girl—I mean, the poor old lady—was so near shuffling off this mortal thingummy, why then, don't you know, he would have waited, or raised the wind on the strength of a post-obit or something or the other. You get my meaning, what?"

"Oh, I see—you are trying to make out a case for suicide. Well, I agree with you that it's the most hopeful defence for Miss Vane's friends to put up, and as far as that goes I can support you. Inasmuch, that is, as Mrs. Wrayburn did not leave Philip anything. Nor, so far as I know, had he the smallest reason to suppose she would do so."

"You're positive of that?"

"Quite. As a matter of fact"—Mr. Urquhart hesitated—"well, I may as well tell you that he asked me about it one day, and I was obliged to tell him that he hadn't the least chance of getting anything from her."

"Oh—he did actually ask?"

"Well, yes, he did."

"That's rather a point, isn't it? How long ago would that be?"

"Oh—about eighteen months ago, I fancy. I couldn't be sure."

"And as Mrs. Wrayburn is now childish, I suppose he couldn't entertain any hope that she would ever alter the will?"

"Not the slightest."

"No, I see. Well, I think we might make something of that. Great disappointment, of course—one would make out that he had counted a good deal upon it. Is it much, by the way?"

"Pretty fair—about seventy or eighty thousand."

"Very sickening, to think of all that good stuff going west and not getting a look-in one's self. By the way, how about you? Don't you get anything? I beg your pardon, fearfully inquisitive and all that, but I mean to say, considering you've been looking after her for years and are her only available relation, so to speak, it would be a trifle thick, what?"

The solicitor frowned, and Wimsey apologised.

"I know, I know—I've been fearfully impudent. It's a failing of mine. And, anyhow, it'll all be in the papers when the old lady does pop off, so I don't know why I should be so anxious to pump you. Wash it out—I'm sorry."

"There's no real reason why you shouldn't know," said Mr. Urquhart, slowly, "though one's professional instinct is to avoid disclosing one's clients' affairs. As a matter of fact, I am the legatee myself."

"Oh?" said Wimsey, in a disappointed voice. "But in that case—that rather weakens the story, doesn't it? I mean to say, your cousin might very well have felt, in that case, that he could look to you for—that is—of course I don't know what your ideas might have been——"

Mr. Urquhart shook his head.

"I see what you are driving at, and it is a very natural thought. But actually, such a disposal of the money would have been directly contrary to the expressed wish of the testatrix. Even if I could legally have made it over, I should have been morally bound not to do so, and I had to make that clear to Philip. I might, of course, have assisted him with casual gifts of money from time to time, but, to tell the truth, I should hardly have cared to do so. In my opinion, the only hope of salvation for Philip would have been to make his way by his own work. He was a little inclined—though I don't like speaking ill of the dead—to—to rely too much on other people."

"Ah, quite. No doubt that was Mrs. Wrayburn's idea also?"

"Not exactly. No. It went rather deeper than that. She considered that she had been badly treated by her family. In short—well, as we have gone so far, I don't mind giving you her *ipsissima verba*."

He rang a bell on his desk.

"I haven't got the will itself here, but I have the draft. Oh, Miss Murchison, would you kindly bring me in the deed-box labelled 'Wrayburn'? Mr. Pond will show it to you. It isn't heavy."

The lady from "The Cattery" departed silently in quest of the box.

"This is all rather irregular, Lord Peter," went on Mr. Urquhart, "but there are times when too much discretion is as bad as too little, and I should like you to see exactly why I was forced to take up this rather uncompromising attitude towards my cousin. Ah, thank you, Miss Murchison."

He opened the deed-box with a key attached to the bunch which he took from his trousers pocket, and turned over a quantity of papers. Wimsey watched him with the expression of a rather foolish terrier who expects a tit-bit.

"Dear, dear," ejaculated the solicitor, "it doesn't seem to be—oh! of course, how forgetful of me. I'm so sorry; it's in my safe at home. I got it out for reference last June, when the previous alarm occurred about Mrs. Wrayburn's illness, and in the confusion which followed on my cousin's death I quite forgot to bring it back. However, the gist of it was——"

"Never mind," said Wimsey, "there's no hurry. If I called at your house to-morrow, perhaps I could see it then."

"By all means, if you think it important. I do apologise for my carelessness. In the meantime, is there anything else I can tell you about the matter?"

Wimsey asked a few questions, covering the ground already traversed by Bunter in his investigations, and took his departure. Miss Murchison was again at work in the outer office. She did not look up as he passed.

"Curious," mused Wimsey, as he pattered along Bedford Row, "everybody is so remarkably helpful about this case. They cheerfully answer questions which one has no right to ask and burst into explanations in the most unnecessary manner. None of them seems to have anything to conceal. It's quite astonishing. Perhaps the fellow really did commit suicide. I hope he did. I wish I could question *him*. I'd put him through it, blast him. I've got about fifteen different analyses of his character already—all different.... It's very ungentlemanly to commit suicide without leaving a note to say you've done it—gets people into trouble. When I blow my brains out——"

He stopped.

"I hope I shan't want to," he said. "I hope I shan't need to want to. Mother wouldn't like it, and it's messy. But I'm beginning to dislike this job of getting people hanged. It's damnable for their friends.... I won't think about hanging. It's unnerving."

CHAPTER XI

WIMSEY PRESENTED HIMSELF at Mr. Urquhart's house at 9 o'clock the next morning, and found that gentleman at breakfast.

"I thought I might catch you before you went down to the office," said his lordship, apologetically. "Thanks awfully, I've had my morning nosebag. No, really, thanks—I never drink before eleven. Bad for the inside."

"Well, I've found the draft for you," said Mr. Urquhart pleasantly. "You can cast your eye over it while I drink my coffee, if you'll excuse my going on. It exposes the family skeleton a little, but it's all ancient history now."

He fetched a sheet of typescript from a side-table and handed it to Wimsey, who noticed, mechanically, that it had been typed on a Woodstock machine, with a chipped lower-case p, and an A slightly out of alignment.

"I'd better make quite clear the family connection of the Boyeses and the Urquharts," he went on, returning to the breakfast-table, "so that you will understand the will. The common ancestor is old John Hubbard, a highly respectable banker at the beginning of the last century. He lived in Nottingham, and the bank, as usual in those days, was a private, family concern. He had three daughters, Jane, Mary, and Rosanna. He educated them well, and they ought to have been heiresses in a mild way, but the old boy made the usual mistakes, speculated unwisely, allowed his clients too much rope—the old story. The bank broke, and the daughters were left penniless. The eldest, Jane, married a man called Henry Brown. He was a schoolmaster, and very poor and quite repellently moral. They had one daughter, Julia, who eventually married a curate, the Rev. Arthur Boyes, and was the mother of Philip Boyes. The second daughter, Mary, did rather better financially, though socially she married beneath her. She accepted the hand of one Josiah Urquhart, who was engaged in the lace-trade. This was a blow to the old people, but Josiah came originally of a fairly decent family, and was a most worthy person, so they made the best of it. Mary had a son, Charles Urquhart, who contrived to break away from the degrading associations of trade. He entered a solicitor's office, did well, and finally became a partner in the firm. He was my father, and I am his successor in the legal business.

"The third daughter, Rosanna, was made of different stuff. She was very beautiful, a remarkably fine singer, a graceful dancer, and altogether a particularly attractive and spoilt young person. To the horror of her parents, she ran away and went on the stage. They erased her name from the family Bible. She determined to justify their worst suspicions. She became the spoilt darling of fashionable London. Under her stage name of Cremorna Garden, she went from one disreputable triumph to another. And, mind you, she had brains—nothing of the Nell Gwynne business about her. She was the take-it-and-keep-it sort. She took everything—money, jewels, *appartements meublés*, horses, carriages, all the rest of it, and turned it into good consolidated funds. She was never prodigal of anything except her person, which she considered to be a sufficient return for all favours, and I daresay it was. I never saw her till she was an old woman, but, before she had the stroke which destroyed her brain and body, she still kept the remains of remarkable beauty. She was a shrewd old woman in her way, and grasping. She had those tight little hands, plump and narrow, that give nothing away—except for cash down. You know the sort.

"Well, the long and the short of it was that the eldest sister, Jane—the one who married the schoolmaster—would have nothing to do with the family black sheep. She and her husband wrapped themselves up in their virtue and shuddered when they saw the disgraceful name of Cremorna Garden billed outside the Olympic or the Adelphi. They returned her letters unopened and forbade her the house, and the climax was reached when Henry Brown tried to have her turned out of the church on the occasion of his wife's funeral.

"My grandparents were less strait-laced. They didn't call on her and didn't invite her, but they occasionally took a box for her performances and they sent her a card for their son's wedding, and were polite in a distant kind of way. In consequence, she kept up a civil acquaintance with my father, and eventually put her business into his hands. He took the view that property was property, however acquired, and said that if a lawyer refused to handle dirty money he would have to show half his clients the door.

"The old lady never forgot or forgave anything. The very mention of the Brown-Boyes connection made her foam at the mouth. Hence, when she came to make her will, she put in that paragraph you have before you now. I pointed out to her that Philip Boyes had had nothing to do with the persecution, as, indeed, neither had Arthur Boyes, but the old sore rankled still, and she wouldn't hear a word in his favour. So I drew up the will as she wanted it; if I hadn't, somebody else would have done so, you know."

Wimsey nodded, and gave his attention to the will, which was dated eight years previously. It appointed Norman Urquhart as sole executor, and, after a few legacies to servants and to theatrical charities, it ran as follows:

> "All the rest of my property whatsoever and wheresoever situated I give to my great-nephew Norman Urquhart of Bedford Row Solicitor for his lifetime and at his death to be equally divided among his legitimate issue but if the said Norman Urquhart should decease without legitimate issue the said property to pass to [here followed the names of the charities previously specified]. And I make this disposition of my property in token of gratitude for the consideration shown to me by my said great-nephew Norman Urquhart and his father the late Charles Urquhart throughout their lives and to ensure that no part of my property shall come into the hands of my great-nephew Philip Boyes or his descendants. And to this end and to mark my sense of the inhuman treatment meted out to me by the family of the said Philip Boyes I enjoin upon the said Norman Urquhart as my dying wish that he neither give lend nor convey to the said Philip Boyes any part of the income derived from the said property enjoyed by him the said Norman Urquhart during his lifetime nor employ the same to assist the said Philip Boyes in any manner whatsoever."

"H'm!" said Wimsey, "that's pretty clear, and pretty vindictive."

"Yes, it is—but what are you to do with old ladies who won't listen to reason? She looked pretty sharply to see I had got the wording fierce enough before she would put her name to it."

"It must have depressed Philip Boyes all right," said Wimsey. "Thank you—I'm glad I've seen that; it makes the suicide theory a good deal more probable."

In theory it might do so, but the theory did not square as well as Wimsey could have wished with what he had heard about the character of Philip Boyes. Personally, he was inclined to put more faith in the idea that the final interview with Harriet had been the deciding factor in the suicide. But this, too, was not quite satisfactory. He could not believe that Philip had felt that particular kind of affection for Harriet Vane. Perhaps, though, it was merely that he did not want to think well of the man. His emotions were, he feared, clouding his judgment a little.

He went back home and read the proofs of Harriet's novel. Undoubtedly she could write well, but undoubtedly she knew only too much about the administration of arsenic. Moreover, the book was about two artists who lived in Bloomsbury and led an ideal existence, full of love and laughter and poverty, till somebody unkindly poisoned the young man and left the young woman inconsolable and passionately resolved to avenge him. Wimsey ground his teeth and went down to Holloway Gaol, where he very nearly made a jealous exhibition of himself. Fortunately, his sense of humour came to the rescue when he had cross-examined his client to the verge of exhaustion and tears.

"I'm sorry," he said; "the fact is, I'm most damnably jealous of this fellow Boyes. I oughtn't to be, but I am."

"That's just it," said Harriet, "and you always would be."

"And if I was, I shouldn't be fit to live with. Is that it?"

"You would be very unhappy. Quite apart from all the other drawbacks."

"But, look here," said Wimsey, "if you married me I shouldn't be jealous, because then I should know that you really liked me and all that."

"You think you wouldn't be. But you would."

"Should I? Oh, surely not. Why should I? It's just the same as if I married a widow. Are all second husbands jealous?"

"I don't know. But it's not quite the same. You'd never really trust me, and we should be wretched."

"But, damn it all," said Wimsey, "if you would once say you cared a bit about me it would be all right. I should believe that. It's because you won't say it that I imagine all sorts of things."

"You would go on imagining things in spite of yourself. You couldn't give me a square deal. No man ever does."

"Never?"

"Well, hardly ever."

"That would be rotten," said Wimsey, seriously. "Of course, if I turned out to be that sort of idiot, things would be pretty hopeless. I know what you mean. I knew a bloke once who got that jealous bug. If his wife wasn't always hanging round his neck, he said it showed he meant nothing to her, and if she did express her affection he called her a hypocrite. It got quite impossible, and she ran away with somebody she didn't care twopence for, and he went about saying that he had been right about her all along. But everybody else said it was his own silly fault. It's all very complicated. The advantage seems to be with the person who gets jealous first. Perhaps you could manage to be jealous of me. I wish you would, because it would prove that you took a bit of interest in me. Shall I give you some details of my hideous past?"

"Please don't."

"Why not?"

"I don't want to know about all the other people."

"Don't you, by Jove? I think that's rather hopeful. I mean, if you just felt like a mother to me, you would be anxious to be helpful and understanding. I loathe being helped and understood. And, after all, there was nothing in any of them—except Barbara, of course."

"Who was Barbara?" asked Harriet, quickly.

"Oh, a girl. I owe her quite a lot, really," replied Wimsey, musingly. "When she married the other fellow, I took up sleuthing as a cure for wounded feelings, and it's really been great fun, take it all in all. Dear me, yes—I was very much bowled over that time. I even took a special course in logic for her sake."

"Good gracious!"

"For the pleasure of repeating 'Barbara celarent darii ferio baralipton'. There was a kind of mysterious romantic lilt about the thing which was somehow expressive of passion. Many a moonlight night have I murmured it to the nightingales which haunt the gardens of St. John's—though, of course, I was a Balliol man myself, but the buildings are adjacent."

"If anybody ever marries you, it will be for the pleasure of hearing you talk piffle," said Harriet, severely.

"A humiliating reason, but better than no reason at all."

"I used to piffle rather well myself," said Harriet, with tears in her eyes, "but it's got knocked out of me. You know—I was really meant to be a cheerful person—all this gloom and suspicion isn't the real me. But I've lost my nerve, somehow."

"No wonder, poor kid. But you'll get over it. Just keep on smiling, and leave it to Uncle Peter."

When Wimsey got home, he found a note awaiting him.

"DEAR LORD PETER,—As you saw, I got the job. Miss Climpson sent six of us, all with different stories and testimonials, of course, and Mr. Pond (the head clerk) engaged me, subject to Mr. Urquhart's approval.

"I've only been here a couple of days, so there isn't very much I can tell you about my employer, personally, except that he has a sweet tooth and keeps secret stores of chocolate cream and Turkish delight in his desk, which he surreptitiously munches while he is dictating. He seems pleasant enough.

"But there's just one thing. I fancy it would be interesting to investigate his financial activities. I've done a good bit one way and another with stockbroking, you know, and yesterday in his absence I took a call for him which I wasn't meant to hear. It wouldn't have told the ordinary person anything, but it did me, because I knew something about the man at the other end. Find out if Mr. U. had been doing anything with the Megatherium Trust before their big crash.

"Further reports when anything turns up.

"Yours sincerely,
"JOAN MURCHISON."

"Megatherium Trust?" said Wimsey. "That's a nice thing for a respectable solicitor to get mixed up with. I'll ask Freddy Arbuthnot. He's an ass about everything except stocks and shares, but he does understand them for some ungodly reason."

He read the letter again, mechanically noting that it was typed on a Woodstock machine, with a chipped lower-case p, and a capital A that was out of alignment.

Suddenly he woke up and read it a third time, noticing, by no means mechanically, the chipped p and the irregular capital A.

Then he sat down, wrote a line on a sheet of paper, folded it, addressed it to Miss Murchison, and sent Bunter out to post it.

For the first time, in this annoying case, he felt the vague stirring of the waters as a living idea emerged slowly and darkly from the inmost deeps of his mind.

CHAPTER XII

WIMSEY WAS ACCUSTOMED to say, when he was an old man and more talkative even than usual, that the recollection of that Christmas at Duke's Denver had haunted him in nightmares, every night regularly, for the following twenty years. But it is possible that he remembered it with advantages. There is no doubt that it tried his temper severely. It began inauspiciously at the tea-table, when Mrs. "Freak" Dimsworthy fluted out in her high, overriding voice: "And is it true, Lord Peter, dear, that you are defending that frightful poisoning woman?" The question acted like the drawing of a champagne cork. The whole party's bottled-up curiosity about the Vane case creamed over in one windy gust of stinging froth.

"I've no doubt she did it, and I don't blame her," said Captain Tommy Bates; "perfectly foul blighter. Has his photograph on the dust-cover of his books, you know—that's the sort of squit he was. Wonderful, the rotters these highbrow females will fall for. The whole lot of 'em ought to be poisoned like rats. Look at the harm they do to the country."

"But he was a very fine writer," protested Mrs. Featherstone, a lady in her thirties, whose violently compressed figure suggested that she was engaged in a perpetual struggle to compute her weight in terms of the first syllables of her name rather than the last. "His books are positively Gallic in their audacity and restraint. Audacity is not rare—but that perfect concision of style is a gift which——"

"Oh, if you like dirt," interrupted the Captain, rather rudely.

"I wouldn't call it that," said Mrs. Featherstone. "He is frank, of course, and that is what people in this country will not forgive. It is part of our national hypocrisy. But the beauty of the writing puts it all on a higher plane."

"Well, I wouldn't have the muck in the house," said the Captain, firmly. "I caught Hilda with it, and I said, 'Now you send that book straight back to the library.' I don't often interfere, but one must draw the line somewhere."

"How did you know what it was like?" asked Wimsey, innocently.

"Why, James Douglas' article in the *Express* was good enough for me," said Captain Bates. "The paragraphs he quoted were filthy—positively filthy."

"Well, it's a good thing we've all read them," said Wimsey. "Forewarned is forearmed."

"We owe a great debt of gratitude to the Press," said the Dowager Duchess; "so kind of them to pick out all the plums for us and save us the trouble of reading the books, don't you think, and such a joy for the poor dear people who can't afford seven and sixpence, or even a library subscription, I suppose, though I'm sure that works out cheaply enough if one is a quick reader. Not that the cheap ones will take those books for I asked my maid, such a superior girl and so keen on improving her mind, which is more than I can say for most of my friends, but no doubt it is all due to free education for the people and I suspect her in my heart of voting Labour though I never ask because I don't think it's fair, and besides, if I did, I couldn't very well take any notice of it, could I?"

"Still, I don't suppose the young woman murdered him on that account," said her daughter-in-law. "From all accounts she was just as bad as he was."

"Oh, come," said Wimsey, "you can't think that, Helen. Damn it, she writes detective stories, and in detective stories virtue is always triumphant. They're the purest literature we have."

"The Devil is always ready to quote Scripture when it pays him to do so," said the younger Duchess, "and they say the wretched woman's sales are going up by leaps and bounds."

"It's my belief," said Mr. Harringay, "that the whole thing is a publicity stunt gone wrong." He was a large, jovial man, extremely rich and connected with the City. "You never know what these advertising fellows are up to."

"Well, it looks like a case of hanging the goose that lays the golden eggs this time," said Captain Bates, with a loud laugh. "Unless Wimsey means to pull off one of his conjuring tricks."

"I hope he does," said Miss Titterton. "I adore detective stories. I'd commute the sentence to penal servitude on condition that she turned out a new story every six months. It would be much more useful than picking oakum or sewing mail-bags for the post-office to mislay."

"Aren't you being a bit previous?" suggested Wimsey, mildly. "She's not convicted yet."

"But she will be next time. You can't fight facts, Peter."

"Of course not," said Captain Bates. "The police know what they're about. They don't put people into the dock if there isn't something pretty shady about 'em."

Now this was a fearful brick, for it was not so many years since the Duke of Denver had himself stood his trial on a mistaken charge of murder. There was a ghastly silence, broken by the Duchess, who said icily: "Really, Captain Bates!"

"What? Eh? Oh, of course, I mean to say, I know mistakes do happen sometimes, but that's a very different thing. I mean to say, this woman, with no morals at all, that is, I mean——"

"Have a drink, Tommy," said Lord Peter, kindly; "you aren't quite up to your usual standard of tact to-day."

"No, but do tell us, Lord Peter," cried Mrs. Dimsworthy, "what the creature is *like*. Have you talked to her? I thought she had rather a nice voice, though she's as plain as a pancake."

"Nice voice, Freakie? Oh, no," said Mrs. Featherstone. "I should have called it rather sinister. It absolutely thrilled me. I got shudders all the way down my spine. A genuine *frisson*. And I think she would be quite attractive, with those queer, smudgy eyes, if she were properly dressed. A sort of *femme fatale,* you know. Does she try to hypnotise you, Peter?"

"I saw in the papers," said Miss Titterton, "that she had had hundreds of offers of marriage."

"Out of one noose into the other," said Harringay, with his noisy laugh.

"I don't think I should care to marry a murderess," said Miss Titterton, "especially one that's been trained on detective stories. One would be always wondering whether there was anything funny about the taste of the coffee."

"Oh, these people are all mad," said Mrs. Dimsworthy. "They have a morbid longing for notoriety. It's like the lunatics who make spurious confessions and give themselves up for crimes they haven't committed."

"A murderess might make quite a good wife," said Harringay. "There was Madeleine Smith, you know—she used arsenic too, by the way—she married somebody and lived happily to a respectable old age."

"But did her husband live to a respectable old age?" demanded Miss Titterton. "That's more to the point, isn't it?"

"Once a poisoner, always a poisoner, *I* believe," said Mrs. Featherstone. "It's a passion that grows upon you—like drink or drugs."

"It's the intoxicating sensation of power," said Mrs. Dimsworthy. "But Lord Peter, *do* tell us——"

"Peter!" said his mother, "I do wish you'd go and see what's happened to Gerald. Tell him his tea is getting cold. I think he's in the stables talking to Freddy about thrush or cracked heels or something, so tiresome the way horses are always getting something the matter with them. You haven't trained Gerald properly, Helen, he used to be quite punctual as a boy. Peter was always the tiresome one, but he's becoming almost human in his old age. It's that wonderful man of his who keeps him in order, really a remarkable character and so intelligent, quite one of the old sort, you know, a perfect autocrat, and such manners too. He would be worth thousands to an American millionaire, most impressive, I wonder Peter isn't afraid he'll give warning one of these days, but I really believe he is positively attached to him, Bunter attached to Peter, I mean, though the other way on would be true too, I'm sure Peter pays more attention to his opinion than he does to mine."

Wimsey had escaped, and was by now on his way to the stables. He met Gerald, Duke of Denver, returning, with Freddy Arbuthnot in tow. The former received the Dowager's message with a grin.

"Got to turn up, I suppose," he said. "I wish nobody had ever invented tea. Ruins your nerves and spoils your appetite for dinner."

"Beastly sloppy stuff," agreed the Hon. Freddy. "I say, Peter, I've been wanting to get hold of you."

"Same here," said Wimsey, promptly. "I'm feelin' rather exhausted with conversation. Let's wander through the billiard-room and build our constitutions up before we face the barrage."

"To-day's great thought," said Freddy, enthusiastically. He pattered happily after Wimsey into the billiard-room, and flung himself down in a large chair. "Great bore, Christmas, isn't it? All the people one hates most gathered together in the name of goodwill and all that."

"Bring a couple of whiskies," said Wimsey to the footman. "And, James, if anybody asks for Mr. Arbuthnot or me, you rather think we have gone out. Well, Freddy, here's luck! Has anything transpired, as the journalists say?"

"I've been sleuthing like stink on the tracks of your man," said Mr. Arbuthnot. "Really, don't you know, I shall soon be qualified to set up in your line of business. Our financial column, edited by Uncle Buthie—that sort of thing. Friend Urquhart has been very careful though. Bound to be—respectable family lawyer and all that. But I saw a man yesterday who knows a fellow who had it from a chappie that said Urquhart had been dipping himself a bit recklessly off the deep end."

"Are you sure, Freddy?"

"Well, not to say sure. But this man, you see, owes me one, so to speak, for having warned him off the Megatherium before the band began to play, and he thinks, if he can get hold of the chappie that knows—not the fellow that told him, you understand, but the other one—that he might be able to get something out of him, don't you see, especially if I was able to put this other chappie in the way of something or the other, what?"

"And no doubt you have secrets to sell."

"Oh, well, I daresay I could make it worth this other chappie's while, because I've got an idea, through this other fellow that my bloke knows, that the chappie is rather up against it, as you might say, through being caught short on some Airways stock, and if I was to put him in touch with Goldberg, don't you see, it might get him out of a hole and so on, he's a cousin of old Levy's, who was murdered, you know, and all these Jews stick together like leeches, and, as a matter of fact, I think it's very fine of them."

"But what has old Levy got to do with it?" asked Wimsey, his mind running over the incidents in that half-forgotten murder-episode.

"Well, as a matter of fact," said the Hon. Freddy, a little nervously, "I've—er—done the trick as you might say. Rachel Levy is—er—in fact—going to become Mrs. Freddy and all that sort of thing."

"The devil she is," said Wimsey, ringing the bell. "Tremendous congratters and all that. It's been a long time working up, hasn't it?"

"Why, yes," said Freddy. "Yes, it has. You see, the trouble was that I was a Christian—at least, I was christened and all that, though I pointed out I wasn't at all a good one, except, of course, that one keeps up the family pew and turns out on Christmas Day and so on. Only it seems they didn't mind that so much as my bein' a Gentile. Well that, of course, is past prayin' for. And then there was the difficulty about the kids—if any. But I explained that I didn't mind what they counted them as—and I don't, you know, because, as I was saying, it would be all to the little beggars' advantage to be in with the Levy and Goldberg crowd, especially if the boys were to turn out anything in the financial way. And then I rather got round Lady Levy by sayin' I had served nearly seven years for Rachel—that was rather smart, don't you think?"

"Two more whiskies, James," said Lord Peter. "It was brilliant, Freddy. How did you come to think of it?"

"In church," said Freddy, "at Diana Rigby's wedding. The bride was fifty minutes late and I had to do something, and somebody had left a Bible in the pew. I saw that—I say, old Laban was a bit of a tough, wasn't he?—and I said to myself, 'I'll work that off next time I call,' and so I did, and the old lady was uncommonly touched by it."

"And the long and the short of it is, you're fixed up," said Wimsey. "Well, cheerio, here's to it. Am I best man, Freddy, or do you bring it off at the Synagogue?"

"Well, yes—it is to be at the Synagogue—I had to agree to that," said Freddy, "but I believe some sort of bridegroom's friend comes into it. You'll stand by me, old bean, won't you? You keep your hat on, don't forget."

"I'll bear it in mind," said Wimsey, "and Bunter will explain the procedure to me. He's bound to know. He knows everything. But look here, Freddy, you won't forget about this little enquiry, will you?"

"I won't, old chap—upon my word I won't. I'll let you know the very second I hear anything. But I really think you may count on there being something in it."

Wimsey found some consolation in this. At any rate, he so far pulled himself together as to be the life and soul of the rather restrained revels at Duke's Denver. The Duchess Helen, indeed, observed rather acidly to the Duke that Peter was surely getting too old to play the buffoon, and that it would be better if he took things seriously and settled down.

"Oh, I dunno," said the Duke, "Peter's a weird fish—you never know what he's thinkin' about. He pulled me out of the soup once and I'm not going to interfere with him. You leave him alone, Helen."

Lady Mary Wimsey, who had arrived late on Christmas Eve, took another view of the matter. She marched into her younger brother's bedroom at 2 o'clock on the morning of Boxing Day. There had been dinner and dancing and charades of the most exhausting kind. Wimsey was sitting thoughtfully over the fire in his dressing-gown.

"I say, old Peter," said Lady Mary, "you're being a bit fevered, aren't you? Anything up?"

"Too much plum-pudding," said Wimsey, "and too much county. I'm a martyr, that's what I am—burning in brandy to make a family holiday."

"Yes, it's ghastly, isn't it? But how's life? I haven't seen you for an age. You've been away such a long time."

"Yes—and you seem very much taken up with this house-decorating job you're running."

"One must do something. I get rather sick of being aimless, you know."

"Yes. I say, Mary, do you ever see anything of old Parker these days?"

Lady Mary stared into the fire.

"I've had dinner with him once or twice, when I was in town."

"Have you? He's a very decent sort. Reliable, homespun—that sort of thing. Not amusing, exactly."

"A little solid."

"As you say—a little solid." Wimsey lit a cigarette. "I should hate anything upsettin' to happen to Parker. He'd take it hard. I mean to say, it wouldn't be fair to muck about with his feelin's and so on."

Mary laughed.

"Worried, Peter?"

"N-no. But I'd rather like him to have fair play."

"Well, Peter—I can't very well say yes or no till he asks me, can I?"

"Can't you?"

"Well, not to him. It would upset his ideas of decorum, don't you think?"

"I suppose it would. But it would probably upset them just as much if he did ask you. He would feel that the mere idea of hearing a butler announce 'Chief Detective-Inspector and Lady Mary Parker' would have something shocking about it."

"It's stalemate, then, isn't it?"

"You could stop dining with him."

"I could do that, of course."

"And the mere fact that you don't—I see. Would it be any good if I demanded to know his intentions in the true Victorian manner?"

"Why this sudden thirst for getting your family off your hands, old man? Peter—nobody's being horrible to you, are they?"

"No, no. I'm just feeling rather like a benevolent uncle, that's all. Old age creeping on. That passion for being useful which attacks the best of us when we're getting past our prime."

"Like me with the house-decorating. I designed these pyjamas, by the way. Don't you think they're rather entertaining? But I expect Chief Inspector Parker prefers the old-fashioned nightgown, like Dr. Spooner or whoever it was."

"That would be a wrench," said Wimsey.

"Never mind. I'll be brave and devoted. Here and now I cast off my pyjamas for ever!"

"No, no," said Wimsey, "not here and now. Respect a brother's feelings. Very well. I am to tell my friend Charles Parker that if he will abandon his natural modesty and propose, you will abandon your pyjamas and say yes."

"It will be a great shock for Helen, Peter."

"Blast Helen. I daresay it won't be the worst shock she'll get."

"Peter, you're plotting something devilish. All right. If you want me to administer the first shock and let her down by degrees—I'll do it."

"Right-ho!" said Wimsey, casually.

Lady Mary twisted one arm about his neck and bestowed on him one of her rare sisterly caresses.

"You're a decent old idiot," she said, "and you look played-out. Go to bed."

"Go to blazes," said Lord Peter, amiably.

CHAPTER XIII

MISS MURCHISON FELT a touch of excitement in her well-regulated heart as she rang the bell of Lord Peter's flat. It was not caused by the consideration of his title or his wealth or his bachelorhood, for Miss Murchison had been a business woman all her life, and was accustomed to visiting bachelors of all descriptions without giving a second thought to the matter. But his note had been rather exciting.

Miss Murchison was thirty-eight, and plain. She had worked in the same financier's office for twelve years. They had been good years on the whole, and it was not until the last two that she had even begun to realise that the brilliant financier who juggled with so many spectacular undertakings was juggling for his life under circumstances of increasing difficulty. As the pace grew faster, he added egg after egg to those which were already spinning in the air. There is a limit to the number of eggs which can be spun by human hands. One day an egg slipped and smashed—then another—then a whole omelette of eggs. The juggler fled from the stage and escaped abroad, his chief assistant blew out his brains, the audience booed, the curtain came down, and Miss Murchison, at thirty-seven, was out of a job.

She had put an advertisement in the papers and had answered many others. Most people appeared to want their secretaries young and cheap. It was discouraging.

Then her own advertisement had brought an answer from a Miss Climpson, who kept a typing bureau.

It was not what she wanted, but she went. And she found that it was not quite a typing bureau after all, but something more interesting.

Lord Peter Wimsey, mysteriously at the back of it all, had been abroad when Miss Murchison entered "The Cattery", and she had never seen him till a few weeks ago. This would be the first time she had actually spoken to him. An odd-looking person, she thought, but people said he had brains. Anyhow——

The door was opened by Bunter, who seemed to expect her and showed her at once into a sitting-room lined with bookshelves. There were some fine prints on the walls, an Aubusson carpet, a grand piano, a vast Chesterfield, and a number of deep and cosy chairs, upholstered in brown leather. The curtains were drawn, a wood-fire blazed on the hearth, and before it stood a table, with a silver tea-service whose lovely lines were delightful to the eye.

As she entered, her employer uncoiled himself from the depths of an arm-chair, put down a black-letter folio which he had been studying, and greeted her in the cool, husky and rather languid tones which she had already heard in Mr. Urquhart's office.

"Frightfully good of you to come round, Miss Murchison. Beastly day, isn't it? I'm sure you want your tea. Can you eat crumpets? Or would you prefer something more up-to-date?"

"Thanks," said Miss Murchison, as Bunter hovered obsequiously at her elbow, "I like crumpets very much."

"Oh, good! Well, Bunter, we'll struggle with the tea-pot ourselves. Give Miss Murchison another cushion and then you can toddle off. Back at work, I suppose? How's our Mr. Urquhart?"

"He's all right." Miss Murchison had never been a chatty girl. "There's one thing I wanted to tell you——"

"Plenty of time," said Wimsey. "Don't spoil your tea." He waited on her with a kind of anxious courtesy which pleased her. She expressed admiration of the big bronze chrysanthemums heaped here and there about the room.

"Oh! I'm glad you like them. My friends say they give a feminine touch to the place, but Bunter sees to it, as a matter of fact. They make a splash of colour and all that, don't you think?"

"The books look masculine enough."

"Oh, yes—they're my hobby, you know. Books—and crime, of course. But crime's not very decorative, is it? I don't care about collecting hangmen's ropes and murderers' overcoats. What are you to do with 'em? Is the tea all right? I ought to have asked you to pour out, but it always seems to me rather unfair to invite a person and then make her do all the work. What do you do when you're not working, by the way? Do you keep a secret passion for anything?"

"I go to concerts," said Miss Murchison. "And when there isn't a concert I put something on the gramophone."

"Musician?"

"No—never could afford to learn properly. I ought to have been, I daresay. But there was more money in being a secretary."

"I suppose so."

"Unless one is absolutely first-class, and I should never have been that. And third-class musicians are a nuisance."

"They have a rotten time, too," said Wimsey. "I hate to see them in cinemas, poor beasts, playing the most ghastly tripe, sandwiched in with snacks of Mendelssohn and torn-off gobbets of the 'Unfinished'. Have a sandwich. Do you like Bach? Or only the moderns?"

He wriggled on to the piano stool.

"I'll leave it to you," said Miss Murchison, rather surprised.

"I feel rather like the Italian Concerto this evening. It's better on the harpsichord, but I haven't got one here. I find Bach good for the brain. Steadying influence and all that."

He played the Concerto through, and then, after a few seconds' pause, went on to one of the "Forty-eight". He played well, and gave a curious impression of controlled power, which, in a man so slight and so fantastical in manner, was unexpected and even a little disquieting. When he had finished, he said, still sitting at the piano:

"Did you make the inquiry about the typewriter?"

"Yes; it was bought new three years ago."

"Good. I gather, by the way, that you are probably right about Urquhart's connection with the Megatherium Trust. That was a very helpful observation of yours. Consider yourself highly commended."

"Thank you."

"Anything fresh?"

"No—except that the evening after you called at Mr. Urquhart's office, he stayed on a long time after we had gone, typing something."

Wimsey sketched an arpeggio with his right hand and demanded:

"How do you know how long he stayed and what he was doing if you had all gone?"

"You said you wanted to know of anything, however small, that was in the least unusual. I thought it might be unusual for him to stay on by himself, so I walked up and down Princeton Street and round Red Lion Square till half-past seven. Then I saw him put the light out and go home. Next morning I noticed that some papers I had left just inside my typewriter cover had been disturbed. So I concluded that he had been typing."

"Perhaps the charwoman disturbed them?"

"Not she. She never disturbs the dust, let alone the cover."

Wimsey nodded.

"You have the makings of a first-class sleuth, Miss Murchison. Very well. In that case, our little job will have to be undertaken. Now, look here—you quite understand that I'm going to ask you to do something illegal?"

"Yes, I understand."

"And you don't mind?"

"No. I imagine that if I'm taken up you will pay any necessary costs."

"Certainly."

"And if I go to prison?"

"I don't think it will come to that. There's a slight risk, I admit—that is, if I'm wrong about what I think is happening—that you might be brought up for attempted theft or for being in possession of safe-breaking tools, but that is the most that could happen."

"Oh, well, it's all in the game, I suppose."

"You mean that?"

"Yes."

"Splendid. Well—you know that deed-box you brought in to Mr. Urquhart's room the day I was there?"

"Yes, the one marked Wrayburn."

"Where is it kept? In the outer office, where you could get hold of it?"

"Oh, yes—on a shelf with a lot of others."

"Good. Would it be possible for you to get left alone in the office any day for, say, half an hour?"

"Well—at lunch-time I'm supposed to go out at half-past twelve and come back at half-past one. Mr. Pond goes out then, but Mr. Urquhart sometimes comes back. I couldn't be certain that he wouldn't pop out on me. And it would look funny if I wanted to stay on after four-thirty, I expect. Unless I pretend I had made a mistake and wanted to stay and put it right. I could do that. I might come extra early in the morning when the charwoman is there—or would it matter her seeing me?"

"It wouldn't matter very much," said Wimsey, thoughtfully. "She'd probably think you had legitimate business with the box. I'll leave it to you to choose the time."

"But what am I to do? Steal the box?"

"Not quite. Do you know how to pick a lock?"

"Not in the least, I'm afraid."

"I often wonder what we go to school for," said Wimsey. "We never seem to learn anything really useful. I can pick quite a pretty lock myself, but, as we haven't much time and as you'll need some rather intensive training, I think I'd better take you to an expert. Should you mind putting your coat on and coming round with me to see a friend?"

"Not at all. I should be delighted."

"He lives in the Whitechapel Road, but he's a very pleasant fellow, if you can overlook his religious opinions. Personally, I find them rather refreshing. Bunter! Get us a taxi, will you?"

On the way to the East End, Wimsey insisted upon talking music—rather to Miss Murchison's disquietude; she began to think there was something a little sinister in this pointed refusal to discuss the object of their journey.

"By the way," she ventured, interrupting something Wimsey was saying about fugal form, "this person we are going to see—has he a name?"

"Now you mention it, I believe he has, but he's never called by it. It's Rumm."

"Not very, perhaps, if he—er—gives lessons in lock-picking."

"I mean, his name's Rumm."

"Oh; what is it then?"

"Dash it! I mean, Rumm is his name."

"Oh! I beg your pardon."

"But he doesn't care to use it, now that he is a total abstainer."

"Then what does one call him?"

"*I* call him Bill," said Wimsey, as the taxi drew up at the entrance to a narrow court, "but when he was at the head of his profession they called him 'Blindfold Bill'. He was a very great man in his time."

Paying off the taxi-man (who had obviously taken them for welfare workers till he saw the size of his tip, and now did not know what to make of them), Wimsey steered his companion down the dirty alley-way. At the far end was a small house, from whose lighted windows poured forth the loud strains of a chorus of voices, supported by a harmonium and other instruments.

"Oh, dear!" said Wimsey, "we've struck a meeting. It can't be helped. Here goes."

Pausing until the strains of "Glory, glory, glory" had been succeeded by a sound as of fervent prayer, he hammered lustily at the door. Presently a small girl put her head out and, seeing Lord Peter, uttered a shrill cry of delight.

"Hullo, Esmeralda Hyacinth!" said Wimsey. "Is Dad in?"

"Yes, sir, please, they'll be so pleased, will you step in and oh, please?"

"Well?"

"Please, sir, will you sing 'Nazareth'?"

"No, I will not sing 'Nazareth' on any account, Esmeralda; I'm surprised at you."

"Daddy says 'Nazareth' isn't worldly, and you do sing it so beautifully," said Esmeralda, her mouth drooping.

Wimsey hid his face in his hands.

"This comes of having done a foolish thing once," he said. "One never lives it down. I won't promise, Esmeralda, but we'll see. But I want to talk business with Dad when the meeting's over."

The child nodded; at the same moment, the praying voice within the room ceased, amid ejaculations of "Alleluia!" and Esmeralda, profiting by this momentary pause, pushed open the door and said loudly:

"Here's Mr. Peter and a lady."

The room was small, very hot, and very full of people. In one corner was the harmonium, with the musicians grouped about it. In the middle, standing by a round table covered with a red cloth, was a stout, square man, with a face like a bulldog. He had a book in his hand, and appeared to be about to announce a hymn, but, seeing Wimsey and Miss Murchison, he came forward, stretching out a large and hearty hand.

"Welcome one and welcome all!" he said. "Brethren, 'ere is a dear brother and sister in the Lord as is come out of the 'aunts of the rich and the riotous living of the West End to join with us in singing the Songs of Zion. Let us sing and give praise. Alleluia! We know that many shall come from the East *and* from the West and sit down at the Lord's feast, while many that thinks theirselves chosen shall be cast into outer darkness. Therefore let us not say, because this man wears a shiny eye-glass, that he is not a chosen vessel, or, because this woman wears a di'mond necklace and rides in 'er Rolls-Royce, she will not therefore wear a white robe and a gold crown in the New Jerusalem, nor because these people travels in the Blue Train to the Rivereera, therefore they shall not be seen a-castin' down their golden crowns by the River of the Water of Life. We 'ears that there talk sometimes in 'Yde Park o' Sundays, but it's bad and foolish and leads to strife and envyings and not to charity. All we like sheep 'ave gone astray and well I may say so, 'avin' been a black and wicked sinner myself till this 'ere gentleman for such 'e truly is laid 'is 'and upon me as I was a-bustin' of 'is safe and was the instrument under God of turnin' me from the broad way that leadeth to destruction. Oh, brethren, what a 'appy day that was for me, alleluia! What a shower of blessings come to me by the grace of the Lord! Let us unite now in thanksgiving for 'Eaven's mercies in Number One 'Undred and Two. (Esmeralda, give our dear friends a 'ymn-book.)"

"I'm sorry," said Wimsey to Miss Murchison. "Can you bear it? I fancy this is the final outbreak."

The harmonium, harp, sackbut, psaltery, dulcimer, and all kinds of music burst out with a blare which nearly burst the ear-drum, the assembly lifted its combined voices, and Miss Murchison, to her amazement, found herself joining—at first self-consciously and then with a fine fervour—in that stirring chant—

"Sweeping through the gates,
Sweeping through the gates of the New Jerusalem,
Washed in the Blood of the Lamb."

Wimsey, who appeared to find it all very good fun, carolled away happily, without the slightest embarrassment; whether because he was accustomed to the exercise, or merely because he was one of those imperturbably self-satisfied people who cannot conceive of themselves as being out of place in any surroundings, Miss Murchison was unable to determine.

To her relief, the religious exercise came to an end with the hymn, and the company took their leave, with many hand-shakings all round. The musicians emptied the condensed moisture from their wind-instruments politely into the fireplace and the lady who played the harmonium drew the cover over the keys and came forward to welcome the guests. She was introduced simply as Bella, and Miss Murchison concluded, rightly, that she was the wife of Mr. Bill Rumm and the mother of Esmeralda.

"Well, now," said Bill, "it's dry work preachin' and singin'—you'll take a cup of tea or coffee, now, won't you?"

Wimsey explained that they had just had tea, but begged that the family might proceed with their own meal.

"It ain't 'ardly supper-time yet," said Mrs. Rumm. "P'raps if you was to do your business with the lady and gentleman, Bill, they might feel inclined to take a bite with us later. It's trotters," she added, hopefully.

"It's very kind of you," said Miss Murchison, hesitatingly.

"Trotters want a lot of beating," said Wimsey, "and since our business will take a little time we'll accept with pleasure—if you're sure we're not putting you out."

"Not at all," said Mrs. Rumm, heartily. "Eight beautiful trotters they is, and with a bit of cheese they'll go round easy. Come along, 'Meraldy—your Dad's got business."

"Mr. Peter's going to sing," said the child, fixing reproachful eyes on Wimsey.

"Now don't you worrit his lordship," rebuked Mrs. Rumm. "I declare I'm ashamed of you."

"I'll sing after supper, Esmeralda," said Wimsey. "Hop along now like a good girl or I'll make faces at you. Bill, I've brought you a new pupil."

"Always 'appy to serve you, sir, knowing as it's the Lord's work. Glory be."

"Thank you," said Wimsey, modestly. "It's a simple matter, Bill, but as the young lady is inexperienced with locks and so on, I've brought her along to be coached. You see, Miss Murchison, before Bill here saw the light——"

"Praise God!" put in Bill.

"He was the most accomplished burglar and safe-breaker in the three kingdoms. He doesn't mind my telling you this, because he's taken his medicine and finished with it all and is now a very honest and excellent locksmith of the ordinary kind."

"Thanks be to Him that giveth the victory!"

"But from time to time, when I need a little help in a righteous cause, Bill gives me the benefit of his great experience."

"And oh! what 'appiness it is, miss, to turn them talents w'ich I so wickedly abused to the service of the Lord. His 'oly Name be blessed that bringeth good out of evil."

"That's right," said Wimsey, with a nod. "Now, Bill, I've got my eye on a solicitor's deed-box, which may or may not contain something which will help me to get an innocent person out of trouble. This young lady can get access to the box, Bill, if you can show her the way inside it."

"If?" grunted Bill, with sovereign contempt. "'Course I can! Deed-box, that's nuffin'. That ain't no field for a man's skill. Robbin' the kid's money-box, that's what it is with they trumpery little locks. There ain't a deed-box in this 'ere city wot I couldn't open blindfold in boxing-gloves with a stick of boiled macaroni."

"I know, Bill; but it isn't you that's got to do it. Can you teach the lady how to work it?"

"Sure I can. What kinder lock is it, lidy?"

"I don't know," said Miss Murchison. "An ordinary lock, I think. I mean, it has the usual sort of key—not a Bramah, or anything of that kind. Mr.—that is the solicitor has one set of keys and Mr. Pond has another—just plain keys with barrels and wards."

"Ho!" said Bill, "then 'arf an hour will teach you all you want, miss." He went to a cupboard and brought out half a dozen lock-plates and a bunch of curious thin wire hooks, strung on a ring like keys.

"Are those pick-locks?" asked Miss Murchison, curiously.

"That's what they are, miss. Ingines of Satan!" He shook his head as he lovingly fingered the bright steel. "Many's the time sech keys as these 'ave let pore sinners in by the back gate into 'ell."

"This time," said Wimsey, "they'll let a poor innocent out of prison into the sunshine—if any, in this beastly climate."

"Praise Him for His manifold mercies! Well, miss, the fust thing is to understand the construction of a lock. Now jest you look 'ere."

He picked up one of the locks and showed how, by holding up the spring, the catch could be thrust back.

"There ain't no need of all them fancy wards, you see, miss. The barrel and the spring—that's all there is to it. Jest you try."

Miss Murchison accordingly tried, and forced several locks with an ease that astonished her.

"Well now, miss, the difficulty is, you see, that when the lock's in place, you can't use your eyes. But you 'as your 'earin' and you 'as the feelin' in your fingers, giv' you by Providence (praise His Name!) for that purpose. Now what you 'as to do, miss, is to shet your eyes and see with your fingers, like, w'en you've got your spring 'ooked back sufficient ter let the catch go past."

"I'm afraid I'm very clumsy," said Miss Murchison, at the fifth or sixth attempt.

"Now don't you fret, miss. Jest take it easy and you'll find the right way of it come to you all of a sudden, like. Jest feel when it seems to go sweet and use your 'ands independent. Would you like to 'ave a little go at a combination while you're 'ere, sir? I've got a beauty 'ere. Giv' to me it was by Sam, you know 'oo I mean. Many's the time I've tried to show 'im the error of 'is ways. 'No, Bill,' 'e ses, 'I ain't got no use for religion,' 'e ses, pore lost sheep, 'but I ain't got no quarrel with you, Bill,' ses 'e, 'and I'd like for ter give you this 'ere little sooverneer.' "

"Bill, Bill," said Wimsey, shaking a reproachful finger, "I'm afraid this wasn't honestly come by."

"Well, sir, if I knowed the owner I'd 'and it over to 'im with the greatest of pleasure. It's quite good, you see. Sam put the soup in at the 'inges and it blowed the 'ole front clean off, lock and all. It's small, but it's a real beauty —new pattern to me, that is. But I mastered it," said Bill, with unregenerate pride, "in an hour or two."

"It'd have to be a good bit of work to beat you, Bill"; Wimsey set the lock up before him, and began to manipulate the knob, his fingers moving with micrometer delicacy and his ear bent to catch the fall of the tumblers.

"Lord!" said Bill—this time with no religious intention—"wot a cracksman you'd a-made, if you'd a-given your mind to it—which the Lord in His mercy forbid you should!"

"Too much work in that life for me, Bill," said Wimsey. "Dash it! I lost it that time."

He turned the knob back and started over again.

By the time the trotters arrived, Miss Murchison had acquired considerable facility with the more usual types of lock and a greatly enhanced respect for burglary as a profession.

"And don't you let yourself be 'urried, miss," was Bill's final injunction, "else you'll leave scratches on the lock and do yourself no credit. Lovely bit of work, that, ain't it, Lord Peter, sir?"

"Beyond me, I'm afraid," said Wimsey, with a laugh.

"Practice," said Bill, "that's all it is. If you'd a-started early enough you'd a-been a beautiful workman." He sighed. "There ain't many of 'em nowadays —glory be!—that can do a real artistic job. It fair goes to my 'eart to see a elegant bit o' stuff like that blowed all to bits with gelignite. Wot's gelignite? Any fool can 'andle it as doesn't mind makin' a blinkin' great row. Brutal, I calls it."

"Now, don't you get 'ankerin' back after them things, Bill," said Mrs. Rumm, reprovingly. "Come along, do, now and eat yer supper. Ef anybody's goin' ter do sech a wicked thing as breakin' safes, wot do it matter whether it's done artistic or inartistic?"

"Ain't that jest like a woman?—beggin' yer pardon, miss."

"Well, you know it's true," said Mrs. Rumm.

"I know those trotters look very artistic," said Wimsey, "and that's quite enough for me."

The trotters having been eaten, and "Nazareth" duly sung, to the great admiration of the Rumm family, the evening closed pleasantly with the performance of a hymn, and Miss Murchison found herself walking up the Whitechapel Road, with a bunch of pick-locks in her pocket and some surprising items of knowledge in her mind.

"You make some very amusing acquaintances, Lord Peter."

"Yes—rather a jape, isn't it? But Blindfold Bill is one of the best. I found him on my premises one night and struck up a sort of an alliance with him. Took lessons from him and all that. He was a bit shy at first, but he got converted by another friend of mine—it's a long story—and the long and short of it was, he got hold of this locksmith business, and is doing very well at it. Do you feel quite competent about locks now?"

"I think so. What am I to look for when I get the box open?"

"Well," said Wimsey, "the point is this. Mr. Urquhart showed me what purported to be the draft of a will made five years ago by Mrs. Wrayburn. I've written down the gist of it on a bit of paper for you. Here it is. Now the snag about it is that that draft was typed on a machine which, as you tell me, was bought new from the makers only three years ago."

"Do you mean that's what he was typing that evening he stayed late at the office?"

"It looks like it. Now, why? If he had the original draft, why not show me that? Actually, there was no need for him to show it to me at all, unless it was to mislead me about something. Then, though he said he had the thing at home, and must have known he had it there, he pretended to search for it in Mrs. Wrayburn's box. Again, why? To make me think that it was already in existence when I called. The conclusion I drew is that, if there is a will, it's not along the lines of the one he showed me."

"It looks rather like that, certainly."

"What I want you to look for is the real will—either the original or the copy ought to be there. Don't take it away, but try to memorise the chief points in it, especially the names of the chief legatee or legatees and of the residuary legatee. Remember that the residuary legatee gets everything which isn't specifically left to somebody else, or anything which falls in by a legatee's dying before the testatrix. I specially want to know whether anything was left to Philip Boyes or if any mention of the Boyes family is made in the will. Failing a will, there might be some other interesting document, such as a secret trust, instructing the executor to dispose of the money in some special way. In short, I want particulars of any document which may seem to be of interest. Don't waste too much time making notes. Carry the provisions in your head if you can and note them down privately when you get away from the office. And be sure you don't leave those skeleton keys about for people to find."

Miss Murchison promised to observe these instructions, and, a taxi coming up at that moment, Wimsey put her into it and sped her to her destination.

CHAPTER XIV

MR. NORMAN URQUHART glanced at the clock, which stood at 4.15, and called through the open door:

"Are those affidavits nearly ready, Miss Murchison?"

"I am just on the last page, Mr. Urquhart."

"Bring them in as soon as you've finished. They ought to go round to Hansons' to-night."

"Yes, Mr. Urquhart."

Miss Murchison galloped noisily over the keys, slamming the shift-lever over with unnecessary violence, and causing Mr. Pond once more to regret the intrusion of female clerks. She completed her page, ornamented the foot of it with a rattling row of fancy lines and dots, threw over the release, span the roller, twitching the foolscap sheets from under it in vicious haste, flung the carbons into the basket, shuffled the copies into order, slapped them vigorously on all four edges to bring them into symmetry, and bounced with them into the inner office.

"I haven't had time to read them through," she announced.

"Very well," said Mr. Urquhart.

Miss Murchison retired, shutting the door after her. She gathered her belongings together, took out a hand-mirror and unashamedly powdered her rather large nose, stuffed a handful of odds-and-ends into a bulging handbag, pushed some papers under her typewriter cover ready for the next day, jerked her hat from the peg and crammed it on her head, tucking wisps of hair underneath it with vigorous and impatient fingers.

Mr. Urquhart's bell rang—twice.

"Oh, bother!" said Miss Murchison, with heightened colour.

She snatched the hat off again, and answered the summons.

"Miss Murchison," said Mr. Urquhart, with an expression of considerable annoyance, "do you know that you have left out a whole paragraph on the first page of this?"

Miss Murchison flushed still more deeply.

"Oh, have I? I'm very sorry."

Mr. Urquhart held up a document resembling in bulk that famous one of which it was said that there was not truth enough in the world to fill so long an affidavit.

"It is very annoying," he said. "It is the longest and most important of the three, and is urgently required first thing to-morrow morning."

"I can't think how I could have made such a silly mistake," muttered Miss Murchison. "I will stay on this evening and re-type it."

"I'm afraid you will have to. It is unfortunate, as I shall not be able to look it through myself, but there is nothing else to be done. Please check it carefully this time, and see that Hansons' have it before 10 o'clock to-morrow."

"Yes, Mr. Urquhart. I will be extremely careful. I am very sorry indeed. I will make sure that it is quite correct and take it round myself."

"Very well, that will do," said Mr. Urquhart. "Don't let it happen again."

Miss Murchison picked up the papers and came out, looking flustered. She dragged the cover off the typewriter with much sound and fury, jerked out the desk-drawers till they slammed against the drawer-stops, shook the top sheet, carbons, and flimsies together as a terrier shakes a rat, and attacked the machine tempestuously.

Mr. Pond, who had just locked his desk, and was winding a silk scarf about his throat, looked at her in mild astonishment.

"Have you some more typing to do to-night, Miss Murchison?"

"Got to do the whole bally thing again," said Miss Murchison. "Left out a paragraph on page one—it would be page one, of course—and he wants the tripe round at Hansons' by 10 o'clock."

Mr. Pond groaned slightly and shook his head.

"Those machines make you careless," he reproved her. "In the old days, clerks thought twice about making foolish mistakes, when it meant copying the whole document out again by hand."

"Glad I didn't live then," said Miss Murchison, shortly, "one might as well have been a galley-slave."

"And we didn't knock off at half-past four, either," said Mr. Pond. "We *worked* in those days."

"You may have worked longer," said Miss Murchison, "but you didn't get through as much in the time."

"We worked accurately and neatly," said Mr. Pond, with emphasis, as Miss Murchison irritably disentangled two keys which had jammed together under her hasty touch.

Mr. Urquhart's door opened, and the retort on the typist's lips was silenced. He said good-night and went out. Mr. Pond followed him.

"I suppose you will have finished before the cleaner goes, Miss Murchison," he said. "If not, please remember to extinguish the light and to hand the key to Mrs. Hodges in the basement."

"Yes, Mr. Pond. Good-night."

"Good-night."

His steps pattered through the entrance, sounded again loudly as he passed the window, and died away in the direction of Brownlow Street. Miss Murchison continued typing till she calculated that he was safely on the tube at Chancery Lane. Then she rose, with a quick glance round her, and approached a high tier of shelves, stacked with black deed-boxes, each of which bore the name of a client in bold white letters.

WRAYBURN was there, all right, but had mysteriously shifted its place. This in itself was unaccountable. She clearly remembered having replaced it, just before Christmas, on top of the pile MORTIMER—SCROGGINS—LORD COOTE—DOLBY BROS. and WINGFIELD; and here it was, on the day after Boxing Day, at the bottom of a pile, heaped over and kept down by BODGERS—SIR J. PENKRIDGE—FLATSBY & COATEN—TRUBODY LTD. and UNIVERSAL BONE

TRUST. Somebody had been spring-cleaning, apparently, over the holidays, and Miss Murchison thought it improbable that it was Mrs. Hodges.

It was tiresome, because all the shelves were full, and it would be necessary to lift down all the boxes and stand them somewhere before she could get out WRAYBURN. And Mrs. Hodges would be in soon, and though Mrs. Hodges didn't really matter, it might look odd. . . .

Miss Murchison pulled the chair from her desk (for the shelf was rather high) and, standing on it, lifted down UNIVERSAL BONE TRUST. It was heavyish, and the chair (which was of the revolving kind, and not the modern type with one spindly leg and a stiffly sprung back, which butts you in the lower spine and keeps you up to your job) wobbled unsteadily, as she carefully lowered the box and balanced it on the narrow top of the cupboard. She reached up again and took down TRUBODY LTD., and placed it on BONE TRUST. She reached up for the third time and seized FLATSBY & COATEN. As she stooped with it a step sounded in the doorway and an astonished voice said behind her:

"Are you looking for something, Miss Murchison?"

Miss Murchison started so violently that the treacherous chair swung through a quarter-turn, nearly shooting her into Mr. Pond's arms. She came down awkwardly, still clasping the black deed-box.

"How you startled me, Mr. Pond! I thought you had gone."

"So I had," said Mr. Pond, "but when I got to the Underground I found I had left a little parcel behind me. So tiresome—I had to come back for it. Have you seen it anywhere? A little round jar, done up in brown paper."

Miss Murchison set FLATSBY & COATEN on the seat of the chair and gazed about her.

"It doesn't seem to be in my desk," said Mr. Pond. "Dear, dear, I shall be so late. And I can't go without it, because it's wanted for dinner—in fact, it's a little jar of caviare. We have guests to-night. Now, where can I have put it?"

"Perhaps you put it down when you washed your hands," suggested Miss Murchison, helpfully.

"Well, now, perhaps I did." Mr. Pond fussed out and she heard the door of the little lavabo in the passage open with a loud creak. It suddenly occurred to her that she had left her handbag open on her desk. Suppose the skeleton keys were visible. She darted towards the bag, just as Mr. Pond returned in triumph.

"Much obliged to you for your suggestion, Miss Murchison. It was there all the time. Mrs. Pond would have been so much upset. Well, good-night again." He turned towards the door. "Oh, by the way, were you looking for something?"

"I was looking for a mouse," replied Miss Murchison with a nervous giggle. "I was just sitting working when I saw it run along the top of the cupboard and—er—up the wall behind those boxes."

"Dirty little beasts," said Mr. Pond. "The place is overrun with them. I have often said we ought to have a cat here. No hope of catching it now, though. You're not afraid of mice apparently?"

"No," said Miss Murchison, holding her eyes, by a strenuous physical effort, on Mr. Pond's face. If the skeleton keys were—as it seemed to her they must be—indecently exposing their spidery anatomy on her desk it would be madness to look in that direction. "No. In your days I suppose all women were afraid of mice."

"Yes, they were," admitted Mr. Pond, "but then, of course, their garments were longer."

"Rotten for them," said Miss Murchison.

"They were very graceful in appearance," said Mr. Pond. "Allow me to assist you in replacing those boxes."

"You will miss your train," said Miss Murchison.

"I have missed it already," replied Mr. Pond, glancing at his watch. "I shall have to take the 5.30." He politely picked up FLATSBY & COATEN and climbed perilously with it in his hands to the unsteady seat of the rotatory chair.

"It's extremely kind of you," said Miss Murchison, watching him as he restored it to its place.

"Not at all. If you would kindly hand me up the others——"

Miss Murchison handed him TRUBODY LTD. and UNIVERSAL BONE TRUST.

"There!" said Mr. Pond, completing the pile and dusting his hands. "Now let us hope the mouse has gone for good. I will speak to Mrs. Hodges about procuring a suitable kitten."

"That would be a very good idea," said Miss Murchison. "Good-night, Mr. Pond."

"Good-night, Miss Murchison."

His footsteps pattered down the passage, sounded again more loudly beneath the window, and for the second time died away in the direction of Brownlow Street.

"Whew!" said Miss Murchison. She darted to her desk. Her fears had deceived her. The bag was shut and the keys invisible.

She pulled her chair back to its place and sat down, as a clash of brooms and pails outside announced the arrival of Mrs. Hodges.

"Ho!" said Mrs. Hodges, arrested on the threshold at sight of the lady clerk industriously typing away, "beg your pardon, miss, but I didn't know as how anybody was here."

"Sorry, Mrs. Hodges. I've got a little bit of work to finish. But you carry on. Don't mind me."

"Thet's all right, miss," said Mrs. Hodges. "I can do Mr. Partridge's office fust."

"Well, if it's all the same to you," said Miss Murchison. "I've just got to type a few pages and—er—make a précis—notes, you know—of some documents for Mr. Urquhart."

Mrs. Hodges nodded and vanished again. Presently a loud bumping noise overhead proclaimed her presence in Mr. Partridge's office.

Miss Murchison waited no longer. She dragged her chair to the shelves again, took down swiftly, one after the other, BONE TRUST, TRUBODY LTD., FLATSBY & COATEN, SIR J. PENKRIDGE, and BODGERS. Her heart beat heavily as at last she seized WRAYBURN and carried it across to her desk.

She opened her bag and shook out its contents. The bunch of pick-locks clattered upon the desk, mixed up with a handkerchief, a powder compact, and a pocket-comb. The thin and shining steel barrels seemed to burn her fingers.

As she picked the bunch over, looking for the most suitable implement, there came a loud rap at the window.

She wheeled round, terrified. There was nothing there. Thrusting the pick-locks into the pocket of her sports-coat, she tiptoed across and looked out. In the lamplight she observed three small boys engaged in climbing the iron railings which guard the sacred areas of Bedford Row. The foremost child saw her and gesticulated, pointing downwards. Miss Murchison waved her hand and cried "Be off with you!"

The child shouted something unintelligible and pointed again. Putting two and two together, Miss Murchison deduced from the rap at the window, the gesture, and the cry, that a valuable ball had fallen into the area. She shook her head with severity and returned to her task.

But the incident had reminded her that the window had no blinds and that, under the glare of the electric light, her movements were as visible to anybody in the street as though she stood on a lighted stage. There was no reason to suppose that Mr. Urquhart or Mr. Pond was about, but her uneasy conscience vexed her. Moreover, if a policeman should pass by, would he not be able to recognise pick-locks a hundred yards away? She peered out again. Was it her agitated fancy, or was that a sturdy form in dark blue emerging from Hand Court?

Miss Murchison fled in alarm and, snatching up the deed-box, carried it bodily into Mr. Urquhart's private office.

Here, at least, she could not be overlooked. If anybody came in—even Mrs. Hodges—her presence might cause surprise, but she would hear them coming and be warned in advance.

Her hands were cold and shaking, and she was not in the best condition to profit by Blindfold Bill's instructions. She drew a few deep breaths. She had been told not to hurry herself. Very well, then, she would not.

She chose a key with care and slipped it into the lock. For years, as it seemed to her, she scratched about aimlessly, till at length she felt the spring press against the hooked end. Pushing and lifting steadily with one hand, she introduced her second key. She felt the lever move—in another moment there was a sharp click and the lock was open.

There were not a great many papers in the box. The first document was a long list of securities, endorsed "Securities deposited with Lloyd's Bank". Then came the copies of some title-deeds, of which the originals were similarly deposited. Then came a folder filled with correspondence. Some of this consisted of letters from Mrs. Wrayburn herself, the latest letter being dated five years previously. In addition there were letters from tenants, bankers, and stockbrokers, with copies of the replies written from the office and signed by Norman Urquhart.

Miss Murchison hastened impatiently through all this. There was no sign of a will or copy of a will—not even of the dubious draft that the solicitor had shown to Wimsey. Two papers only now remained at the bottom of the box.

Miss Murchison picked up the first. It was a Power of Attorney, dated January 1925, giving Norman Urquhart full powers to act for Mrs. Wrayburn. The second was thicker and tied neatly with red tape. Miss Murchison slipped this off and unfolded the document.

It was a Deed of Trust, making over the whole of Mrs. Wrayburn's property to Norman Urquhart, in trust for herself, and providing that he should pay into her current account, from the estate, a certain fixed annual sum for personal expenses. The deed was dated July 1920, and attached to it was a letter, which Miss Murchison hastily read through:

"Applefold,
"Windle.
"May 15th, 1920.

"MY DEAR NORMAN,—Thank you very much, my dear boy, for your birthday letter and the pretty scarf. It is good of you to remember your old aunt so faithfully.

"It has occurred to me that, now that I am over eighty years old, it is time that I put my business into your hands entirely. You and your father have managed very well for me all these years, and you have, of course, always very properly consulted me before taking any steps with regard to investments. But I am getting such a *very old woman now* that I am quite out of touch with the modern world, and I cannot pretend that my opinions are of any real value. I am a *tired* old woman, too, and though you always explain everything *most clearly*, I find the *writing of letters* a *gêne* and a burden to me at my advanced age.

"So I have determined to put my property in Trust with you for my lifetime, so that you may have full power to handle everything according to your own discretion, without having to consult me every time. And also, though I am strong and healthy yet, I am glad to say, and have my wits quite about me, still, that happy state of things might alter at any time. I might become paralysed or feeble in my head, or want to make some foolish use of my money, as silly old women have done before now.

"So will you draw up a deed of this kind and bring it to me and I will sign it. And at the same time I will give you instructions about my will.

"Thanking you again for your good wishes,

"Your affec. Great-Aunt,
"ROSANNA WRAYBURN."

"Hurray!" said Miss Murchison. "There *was* a will, then! And this trust—that's probably important, too."

She read the letter again, skimmed through the clauses of the trust, taking particular notice that Norman Urquhart was named as sole trustee, and finally made a mental note of some of the larger and more important items in the list of securities. Then she replaced the documents in their original order, relocked the box—which yielded to treatment like an angel—carried it out, replaced it, piled the other boxes above it, and was back at her machine, just as Mrs. Hodges re-entered the office.

"Just finished, Mrs. Hodges," she called out cheerfully.

"I wondered ef yer would be," said Mrs. Hodges, "I didn't hear the typewriter a-going."

"I was making notes by hand," said Miss Murchison. She crumpled together the spoiled front page of the affidavit and threw it into the waste-paper basket together with the re-type which she had begun. From her desk-drawer she produced a correctly typed first page, provided beforehand for the purpose, added it to the bundle of script, put the top copy and the required sets of flimsies into an envelope, sealed it, addressed it to Messrs. Hanson & Hanson, put on her hat and coat, and went out, bidding a pleasant farewell to Mrs. Hodges at the door.

A short walk brought her to Messrs Hansons' office, where she delivered the affidavit through the letter-box. Then, with a brisk step and humming to herself, she made for the 'bus-stop at the junction of Theobald's Road and Gray's Inn Road.

"I think I deserve a little supper in Soho," said Miss Murchison.

She was humming again as she walked from Cambridge Circus into Frith Street. "What *is* this beastly tune?" she asked herself abruptly. A little consideration reminded her that it was "Sweeping through the gates, Sweeping through the gates . . ."

"Bless me!" said Miss Murchison. "Going dotty, that's what I am."

CHAPTER XV

LORD PETER CONGRATULATED Miss Murchison and gave her a rather special lunch at Rules, where there is a particularly fine old cognac for those that appreciate such things. Indeed, Miss Murchison was a little late in returning to Mr. Urquhart's office, and in her haste omitted to hand back the skeleton keys. But when the wine is good and the company agreeable one cannot always think of everything.

Wimsey himself, by a great act of self-control, had returned to his own flat to think, instead of bolting away to Holloway Gaol. Although it was a work of charity and necessity to keep up the spirits of the prisoner (it was in this way that he excused his almost daily visits), he could not disguise from himself that it would be even more useful and charitable to get her innocence proved. So far, he had not made much real progress.

The suicide theory had been looking very hopeful when Norman Urquhart had produced the draft of the will; but his belief in that draft had now been thoroughly undermined. There was still a faint hope of retrieving the packet of white powder from the Nine Rings, but as the days passed remorselessly on, that hope diminished almost to vanishing-point. It irked him to be taking no action in the matter—he wanted to rush to the Gray's Inn Road, to cross-question, bully, bribe, ransack every person and place in and about the Rings, but he knew that the police could do this better than he could.

Why had Norman Urquhart tried to mislead him about the will? He could so easily have refused all information. There must be some mystery about it. But if Urquhart were not, in fact, the legatee, he was playing rather a dangerous game. If the old lady died, and the will was proved, the facts would probably be published—and she might die any day.

How easy it would be, he thought, regretfully, to hasten Mrs. Wrayburn's death a trifle. She was ninety-three and very frail. An overdose of something—a shake—a slight shock, even—— It did not do to think after that fashion. He wondered idly who lived with the old woman and looked after her. . . .

It was the 30th of December, and he still had no plan. The stately volumes on his shelves, rank after rank of saint, historian, poet, philosopher, mocked his impotence. All that wisdom and all that beauty, and they could not show him how to save the woman he imperiously wanted from a sordid death by hanging. And he had thought himself rather clever at that kind of thing. The enormous and complicated imbecility of things was all round him like a trap. He ground his teeth and raged helplessly, striding about the suave, wealthy, futile room. The great Venetian mirror over the fireplace showed him his own head and shoulders. He saw a fair, foolish face, with straw-coloured hair sleeked back; a monocle clinging incongruously under a ludicrously-twitching brow; a chin shaved to perfection, hairless, epicene; a rather high collar, faultlessly starched, a tie elegantly knotted and matching in colour the handkerchief which peeped coyly from the breast-pocket of an expensive Savile-Row-tailored suit. He snatched up a heavy bronze from the mantelpiece—a beautiful thing; even as he snatched it, his fingers caressed the patina—and the impulse seized him to smash the mirror and smash the face—to break out into great animal howls and gestures.

Silly! One could not do that. The inherited inhibitions of twenty civilised centuries tied one hand and foot in bonds of ridicule. What if he did smash the mirror? Nothing would happen. Bunter would come in, unmoved and unsurprised, would sweep up the débris in a dust-pan, would prescribe a hot bath and massage. And next day a new mirror would be ordered, because people would come in and ask questions, and civilly regret the accidental damage to the old one. And Harriet Vane would still be hanged, just the same.

Wimscy pulled himself together, called for his hat and coat, and went away in a taxi to call on Miss Climpson.

"I have a job," he said to her, more abruptly than was his wont, "which I should like you to undertake yourself. I can't trust anybody else."

"How *kind* of you to put it like that," said Miss Climpson.

"The trouble is, I can't in the least tell you how to set about it. It all depends on what you find when you get there. I want you to go to Windle in Westmorland and get hold of an imbecile and paralysed old lady called Mrs. Wrayburn, who lives at a house called Applefold. I don't know who looks after her, or how you are to get into the house. But you've got to do it, and you've got to find out where her will is kept, and, if possible, see it."

"Dear me!" said Miss Climpson.

"And what's worse," said Wimsey, "you've only got about a week to do it in."

"That's a very short time," said Miss Climpson.

"You see," said Wimsey, "unless we can give some very good reason for delay, they're bound to take the Vane case almost first thing next sessions. If I could persuade the lawyers for the defence that there is the least chance of securing fresh evidence, they could apply for a postponement. But at present I have nothing that could be called evidence—only the vaguest possible hunch."

"I see," said Miss Climpson. "Well, none of us can do more than our best, and it is very necessary to have faith. That moves mountains, we are told."

"Then for Heaven's sake lay in a good stock of it," said Wimsey, gloomily, "because, as far as I can see, this job is like shifting the Himalayas and the Alps, with a spot of frosty Caucasus and a touch of the Rockies thrown in."

"You may count on me to do my poor best," replied Miss Climpson, "and I will ask the dear vicar to say a Mass of special intention for one engaged in a difficult undertaking. When would you like me to start?"

"At once," said Wimsey. "I think you had better go just as your ordinary self, and put up at the local hotel—no—a boarding-house; there will be more opportunities for gossip. I don't know much about Windle, except that there is a boot-factory there and rather a good view, but it's not a large place, and I should think everybody would know about Mrs. Wrayburn. She is very rich, and was notorious in her time. The person you'll have to cotton on to is the female—there must be one of some sort—who nurses and waits on Mrs. Wrayburn and is, generally speaking, about her path and about her bed and all that. When you find out her special weakness, drive a wedge into it like one o'clock. Oh! by the way—it's quite possible the will isn't there at all, but in the hands of a solicitor-fellow called Norman Urquhart who hangs out in Bedford Row. If so, all you can do is to get the pump to work and find out anything—anything at all—to his disadvantage. He's Mrs. Wrayburn's great-nephew, and he goes to see her sometimes."

Miss Climpson made a note of these instructions.

"And now I'll tootle off and leave you to it," said Wimsey. "Draw on the firm for any money you want. And if you need any special outfit, send me a wire."

On leaving Miss Climpson, Lord Peter Wimsey again found himself a prey to *Weltschmerz* and self-pity. But it now took the form of a gentle, pervading melancholy. Convinced of his own futility, he determined to do what little good lay in his power before retiring to a monastery or to the frozen wastes of the Antarctic. He taxi'd purposefully round to Scotland Yard, and asked for Chief Inspector Parker.

Parker was in his office, reading a report which had just come in. He greeted Wimsey with an expression which seemed more embarrassed than delighted.

"Have you come about that packet of powder?"

"Not this time," said Wimsey. "I don't suppose you'll ever hear anything more of that. No. It's—rather a more—er—delicate matter. It's about my sister."

Parker started and pushed the report to one side.

"About Lady Mary?"

"Er—yes. I understand she's been going about with you—er—dining—and all that sort of thing, what?"

"Lady Mary has honoured me—on one or two occasions—with her company," said Parker. "I did not think—I did not know—that is, I understood——"

"Ah! but *did* you understand, that's the point?" said Wimsey, solemnly. "You see, Mary's a very nice-minded sort of girl, though I say it, and——"

"I assure you," said Parker, "that there is no need to tell me that. Do you suppose that I should misinterpret her kindness? It is the custom nowadays for women of the highest character to dine unchaperoned with their friends, and Lady Mary has——"

"I'm not suggesting a chaperon," said Wimsey. "Mary wouldn't stick it for one thing, and I think it's all bosh, anyhow. Still, bein' her brother, and all that—it's Gerald's job really, of course, but Mary and he don't altogether hit it off, you know, and she wouldn't be likely to burble any secrets into his ear, especially as it would all be handed on to Helen—what was I going to say? Oh, yes—as Mary's brother, you know, I suppose it's my so to speak duty to push round and drop the helpful word here and there."

Parker jabbed the blotting-paper thoughtfully.

"Don't do that," said Wimsey, "it's bad for your pen. Take a pencil."

"I suppose," said Parker, "I ought not to have presumed——"

"What did you presume, old thing?" said Wimsey, his head cocked, sparrow-fashion.

"Nothing to which anybody could object," said Parker, hotly. "What are you thinking of, Wimsey? I quite see that it is unsuitable, from your point of view, that Lady Mary Wimsey should dine in public restaurants with a policeman, but if you imagine I have ever said a word to her that could not be said with the greatest propriety——"

"—in the presence of her mother, you wrong the purest and sweetest woman that ever lived, and insult your friend," interrupted Peter, snatching the words from his mouth and rattling them to a glib conclusion. "What a perfect Victorian you are, Charles. I should like to keep you in a glass case. Of course you haven't said a word. What I want to know is, why?"

Parker stared at him.

"For the last five years or so," said Wimsey, "you have been looking like a demented sheep at my sister, and starting like a rabbit whenever her name is mentioned. What do you mean by it? It is not ornamental. It is not exhilarating. You unnerve the poor girl. You give me a poor idea of your guts, if you will pardon the expression. A man doesn't like to see a man go all wobbly about his sister—at least, not with such a prolonged wobble. It's unsightly. It's irritating. Why not slap the manly thorax and say, 'Peter, my dear old mangel-wurzel, I have decided to dig myself into the old family trench and be a brother to you'? What's stopping you? Is it Gerald? He's an ass, I know, but he's not a bad old stick, really. Is it Helen? She's a bit of a wart, but you needn't see much of her. Is it me? Because, if so, I'm thinking of becoming a hermit—there was a Peter the Hermit, wasn't there?—so I shouldn't be in your way. Cough up the difficulty, old thing, and we will have it removed in a plain van. Now, then!"

"Do you—are you asking me——?"

"I'm asking you your intentions, damn it!" said Wimsey, "and if that's not Victorian enough, I don't know what is. I quite understand your having given Mary time to recover from that unfortunate affair with Cathcart and the Goyles fellow, but dash it all, my dear man, one can overdo the delicacy business. You can't expect a girl to stand on and off for ever, can you? Are you waiting for leap-year, or what?"

"Look here, Peter, don't be a damned fool. How can I ask your sister to marry me?"

"*How* you do it is your affair. You might say: 'What about a spot of matrimony, old dear?' That's up-to-date, and plain and unmistakable. Or you could go down on one knee and say, 'Will you honour me with your hand and heart?' which is pretty and old-fashioned and has the merit of originality in these times. Or you could write, or wire, or telephone. But I leave that to your own individual fancy."

"You're not serious."

"Oh, God! Shall I ever live down this disastrous reputation for tomfoolery? You're making Mary damned unhappy, Charles, and I wish you'd marry her and have done with it."

"Making her unhappy?" said Parker, almost in a shout. "Me—her—unhappy?"

Wimsey tapped his forehead significantly.

"Wood—solid wood! But the last blow seems to have penetrated. Yes, you—her—unhappy—do you get it now?"

"Peter—if I really thought that——"

"Now don't go off the deep end," said Wimsey; "it's wasted on me. Keep it for Mary. I've done my brotherly duty and there's an end of it. Calm yourself. Return to your reports——"

"Oh, Lord, yes," said Parker. "Before we go any farther, I've got a report for you."

"You have? Why didn't you say so at first?"

"You wouldn't let me."

"Well, what is it?"

"We've found the packet."

"What?"

"We've found the packet."

"Actually found it?"

"Yes. One of the barmen——"

"Never mind the barmen. You're sure it's the right packet?"

"Oh, yes; we've identified it."

"Get on. Have you analysed it?"

"Yes, we've analysed it."

"Well, what is it?"

Parker looked at him with the eyes of one who breaks bad news, and said, reluctantly:

"Bicarbonate of soda."

CHAPTER XVI

MR. CROFTS, EXCUSABLY enough, said, "I told you so"; Sir Impey Biggs observed curtly, "Very unfortunate."

To chronicle Lord Peter Wimsey's daily life during the ensuing week would be neither kind nor edifying. An enforced inactivity will produce irritable symptoms in the best of men. Nor did the imbecile happiness of Chief Inspector Parker and Lady Mary Wimsey tend to soothe him, accompanied as it was by tedious demonstrations of affection for himself. Like the man in Max Beerbohm's story, Wimsey "hated to be touching". He was only moderately cheered by hearing from the industrious Freddy Arbuthnot that Mr. Norman Urquhart was found to be more or less deeply involved in the disasters of the Megatherium Trust.

Miss Kitty Climpson, on the other hand, was living in what she herself liked to call a "whirl of activity". A letter, written the second day after her arrival in Windle, furnishes us with a wealth of particulars.

"Hillside View,
"Windle,
"Westmorland.
"Jan. 1st, 1930.

"MY DEAR LORD PETER,—I feel sure you will be anxious to hear, at the *earliest possible* moment, *how* things are *going*, and though I have only been here *one* day, I really think I have *not* done so *badly*, all things considered!

"My train got in quite late on Monday night, after a *most dreary* journey, with a *lugubrious* wait at *Preston*, though thanks to your kindness in insisting that I should travel *First-class*, I was not really at all tired! Nobody can realise what a *great* difference these extra comforts make, especially when one is *getting on* in years, and after the *uncomfortable* travelling which I had to endure in my days of poverty, I feel that I am living in almost *sinful* luxury! The carriage was *well* heated—indeed, *too much* so and I should have liked the window down, but that there was a *very fat* business man, *muffled* up to the eyes in *coats* and *woolly waistcoats* who *strongly* objected to fresh air! Men are such HOT-HOUSE PLANTS nowadays, are they not, quite unlike my dear father, who would never permit a *fire* in the house *before* November the 1st, or *after* March 31st, even though the thermometer was at *freezing-point*!

"I had *no* difficulty in getting a comfortable room at the Station Hotel, *late* as it was. In the old days, an *unmarried* woman arriving *alone* at *midnight* with a *suitcase* would hardly have been considered *respectable*—what a wonderful difference one finds to-day! I am *grateful* to have lived to see such changes, because whatever old-fashioned people may say about the greater *decorum* and *modesty* of women in Queen Victoria's time, those who can remember the old conditions know how *difficult* and *humiliating* they were!

"Yesterday morning, of course, my *first* object was to find a *suitable boarding-house,* in accordance with your instructions, and I was *fortunate* enough to hit upon this house at the *second* attempt. It is very well run and *refined*, and there were three *elderly ladies* who are *permanent* boarders here, and are *well up* in all the GOSSIP of the town, so that nothing could be more *advantageous* for our purpose!!

"As soon as I had engaged my room, I went out for a little *voyage of discovery*. I found a very helpful *policeman* in the High Street, and asked him where to find Mrs. Wrayburn's house. He knew it quite well, and told me to take the *omnibus* and it would be a penny ride to the Fisherman's Arms and then about 5 minutes' walk. So I followed his directions, and the 'bus took me right out into the country to a *cross-roads* with the Fisherman's Arms at the corner. The conductor was most polite and helpful and showed me the way, so I had *no difficulty* in finding the house.

"It is a *beautiful old place,* standing in its own grounds—quite a *big* house, built in the *eighteenth century,* with an *Italian* porch and a lovely green lawn with a cedar-tree and formal flower-beds, and in summer must be really a *garden of Eden.* I looked at it from the road for a little time—I did not think this would be at all *peculiar* behaviour, if anybody saw me, because *anybody* might be interested in such a fine old place. Most of the *blinds* were down, as though the greater part of the house were *uninhabited*, and I could not see any *gardener* or anybody about—I suppose there is not very much to be done in the garden this time of the year. One of the *chimneys* was smoking, however, so there were *some* signs of life about the place.

"I took a little *walk* down the road and then turned back and passed the house again, and this time I saw a servant just passing round the corner of the house, but of course she was *too far off* for me to speak to. So I took the omnibus back again and had lunch at Hillside View, so as to make acquaintance with my fellow-boarders.

"Naturally I did not want to seem *too eager* all at once, so I said nothing about Mrs. Wrayburn's house *at first,* but just talked generally about Windle. I had some difficulty in parrying the *questions* of the good ladies, who *wondered* very much *why* a stranger had come to Windle at this time of the year, but without telling many actual *untruths* I think I left them with the *impression* that I had come into a little fortune (!) and was visiting the Lake District to find a suitable spot in which to settle next *summer*! I talked about *sketching*—as girls we were *all* brought up to dabble a little in water-colours, so that I was able to display quite sufficient *technical knowledge* to satisfy them!

"That gave me quite a *good* opportunity to ask about the *house*!! Such a *beautiful* old place, I said, and did anybody live there? (Of *course* I did not blurt this out *all at once*—I waited till they had told me of the many *quaint spots* in the district that would interest an artist!) Mrs. Pegler, a very *stout*, PUSSY old lady with a LONG TONGUE (!) was able to tell me *all* about it. My dear Lord Peter, what I do *not* know now about the *abandoned wickedness* of Mrs. Wrayburn's early life is really NOT WORTH KNOWING!! But what was *more to the point* is that she told me the *name* of Mrs. Wrayburn's *nurse-companion*. She is a MISS BOOTH, a retired nurse, about *sixty* years old, and she lives *all alone* in the house with Mrs. Wrayburn, except for the *servants*, and a *housekeeper*. When I heard that Mrs. Wrayburn was so *old*, and *paralysed* and *frail*, I said was it not very *dangerous* that Miss Booth should be the only attendant, but Mrs. Pegler said the housekeeper was a *most trustworthy* woman who had been with Mrs. Wrayburn for many years, and was *quite* capable of looking after her any time when Miss Booth was out. So it appears that Miss Booth does go out sometimes! Nobody in this house seems to *know* her *personally*, but they say she is often to be seen in the town in *nurse's uniform*. I managed to extract quite a good description of her, so if I should happen to meet her, I daresay I shall be *smart* enough to *recognise* her!

"That is really *all* I have been able to discover in *one* day. I hope you will not be *too* disappointed, but I was obliged to listen to a terrible amount of *local history* of one kind and another, and of course I could not FORCE the conversation round to Mrs. Wrayburn in any suspicious way.

"I will let you know as *soon* as I get the *least bit* more information.

"Most sincerely yours,

"KATHARINE ALEXANDRA CLIMPSON."

Miss Climpson finished her letter in the privacy of her bedroom, and secured it carefully in her capacious handbag before going downstairs. A long experience of boarding-house life warned her that to display openly an envelope addressed even to a minor member of the nobility would be to court a quite unnecessary curiosity. True, it would establish her status, but at that moment Miss Climpson hardly wished to move in the limelight. She crept quietly out at the hall-door, and turned her steps towards the centre of the town.

On the previous day, she had marked down one principal tea-shop, two rising and competitive tea-shops, one slightly *passé* and declining tea-shop, a Lyons, and four obscure and, on the whole, negligible tea-shops which combined the service of refreshments with a trade in sweets. It was now half-past ten. In the next hour and a half she could, with a little exertion, pass in review all that part of the Windle population which indulged in morning coffee.

She posted her letter and then debated with herself where to begin. On the whole, she inclined to leave the Lyons for another day. It was an ordinary plain Lyons, without orchestra or soda-fountain. She thought that its clientèle would be chiefly housewives and clerks. Of the other four, the most likely was, perhaps, the Central. It was fairly large, well-lighted and cheerful, and strains of music issued from its doors. Nurses usually like the large, well-lighted, and melodious. But the Central had one drawback. Anyone coming from the direction of Mrs. Wrayburn's house would have to pass all the others to get to it. This fact unfitted it for an observation-post. From this point of view, the advantage lay with Ye Cosye Corner, which commanded the 'bus-stop. Accordingly, Miss Climpson decided to start her campaign from that spot. She selected a table in the window, ordered a cup of coffee and a plate of digestive biscuits, and entered upon her vigil.

After half an hour, during which no woman in nurse's costume had been sighted, she ordered another cup of coffee and some pastries. A number of people—mostly women—dropped in, but none of them could by any possibility be identified with Miss Booth. At half-past eleven, Miss Climpson felt that to stay any longer would be conspicuous and might annoy the management. She paid her bill and departed.

The Central had rather more people in it than Ye Cosye Corner, and was in some ways an improvement, having comfortable wicker chairs instead of fumed oak settles, and brisk waitresses instead of languid semi-gentlewomen in art-linen. Miss Climpson ordered another cup of coffee and a roll and butter. There was no window-table vacant, but she found one close to the orchestra from which she could survey the whole room. A fluttering dark-blue veil at the door made her heart beat, but it proved to belong to a lusty young person with two youngsters and a perambulator, and hope withdrew once more. By twelve o'clock, Miss Climpson decided that she had drawn blank at the Central.

Her last visit was to the Oriental—an establishment singularly ill-adapted for espionage. It consisted of three very small rooms of irregular shape, dimly lit by forty-watt bulbs in Japanese shades, and further shrouded by bead curtains and draperies. Miss Climpson, in her inquisitive way, wandered into all its nooks and corners, disturbing several courting couples, before returning to a table near the door and sitting down to consume her fourth cup of coffee. Half-past twelve came, but no Miss Booth. "She can't come now," thought Miss Climpson; "she will have to get back and give her patient lunch."

She returned to Hillside View with but little appetite for the joint of roast mutton.

At half-past three she sallied out again, to indulge in an orgy of teas. This time she included the Lyons and the fourth tea-shop, beginning at the far end of the town and working her way back to the 'bus-stop. It was while she was struggling with her fifth meal, in the window of Ye Cosye Corner, that a hurrying figure on the pavement caught her eye. The winter evening had closed in, and the street lights were not very brilliant, but she distinctly saw a stoutish, middle-aged nurse in a black veil and grey cloak pass along on the nearer pavement. By craning her neck, she could see her make a brisk spurt, scramble on the 'bus at the corner, and disappear in the direction of the Fisherman's Arms.

"How vexatious!" said Miss Climpson, as the vehicle disappeared. "I must have just missed her somewhere. Or perhaps she was having tea in a private house. Well, I'm afraid this is a blank day. And I do feel so *full* of tea!"

It was fortunate that Miss Climpson had been blest by Heaven with a sound digestion, for the next morning saw a repetition of the performance. It was possible, of course, that Miss Booth only went out two or three times a week, or that she only went out in the afternoon, but Miss Climpson was taking no chances. She had at least achieved the certainty that the 'bus-stop was the place to watch. This time she took up her post at Ye Cosye Corner at 11 o'clock and waited till twelve. Nothing happened and she went home.

In the afternoon she was there again at three. By this time the waitress had got to know her, and betrayed a certain amused and tolerant interest in her comings and goings. Miss Climpson explained that she liked so much to watch the people pass, and spoke a few words in praise of the café and its service. She admired a quaint old inn on the opposite side of the street, and said she thought of making a sketch of it.

"Oh, yes," said the girl, "there's a many artists comes here for that."

This gave Miss Climpson a bright idea, and the next morning she brought a pencil and sketch-book with her.

By the extraordinary perversity of things in general, she had no sooner ordered her coffee, opened the sketch-book, and started to outline the gables of the inn, than a 'bus drew up, and out of it stepped the stout nurse in the black and grey uniform. She did not enter Ye Cosye Corner, but marched on at a brisk pace down the opposite side of the street, her veil flapping like a flag.

Miss Climpson uttered a sharp exclamation of annoyance, which drew the waitress's attention.

"How provoking!" said Miss Climpson. "I have left my rubber behind. I must just run out and buy one."

She dropped the sketch-book on the table and made for the door.

"I'll cover your coffee up for you, miss," said the girl, helpfully. "Mr. Bulteel's, down near the Bear, is the best stationer's."

"Thank you, thank you," said Miss Climpson, and darted out.

The black veil was still flapping in the distance. Miss Climpson pursued breathlessly, keeping to the near side of the road. The veil dived into a chemist's shop. Miss Climpson crossed the road a little behind it and stared into a window full of baby-linen. The veil came out, fluttered undecidedly on the pavement, turned, passed Miss Climpson, and went into a boot-shop.

"If it's shoe-laces, it'll be quick," thought Miss Climpson, "but if it's trying-on it may be all morning." She walked slowly past the door. By good luck a customer was just coming out, and, peering past him, Miss Climpson just caught a glimpse of the black veil vanishing into the back premises. She pushed the door boldly open. There was a counter for sundries in the front of the shop, and the doorway through which the nurse had vanished was labelled "Ladies' Department".

While buying a pair of brown silk laces, Miss Climpson debated with herself. Should she follow and seize this opportunity? Trying on shoes is usually a lengthy business. The subject is marooned for long periods in a chair, while the assistant climbs ladders and collects piles of cardboard boxes. It is also comparatively easy to enter into conversation with a person who is trying on shoes. But there is a snag in it. To give colour to your presence in the fitting department, you must yourself try on shoes. What happens? The assistant first disables you by snatching off your right-hand shoe, and then disappears. And supposing, meanwhile, your quarry completes her purchase and walks out? Are you to follow, hopping madly on one foot? Are you to arouse suspicion by hurriedly replacing your own footgear and rushing out with laces flying and an unconvincing murmur about a forgotten engagement? Still worse, suppose you are in an amphibious condition, wearing one shoe of your own and one of the establishment's? What impression will you make by suddenly bolting with goods to which you are not entitled? Will not the pursuer very quickly become the pursued?

Having weighed this problem in her mind, Miss Climpson paid for her shoe-laces and retired. She had already bilked a tea-shop, and one misdemeanour in a morning was about as much as she could hope to get away with.

The male detective, particularly when dressed as a workman, an errand-boy, or a telegraph-messenger, is favourably placed for "shadowing". He can loaf without attracting attention. The female detective must not loaf. On the other hand, she can stare into shop-windows for ever. Miss Climpson selected a hat-shop. She examined all the hats in both windows attentively, coming back to gaze in a purposeful manner at an extremely elegant model with an eye-veil and a pair of excrescences like rabbits'-ears. Just at the moment when any observer might have thought that she had at last made up her mind to go in and ask the price, the nurse came out of the boot-shop. Miss Climpson shook her head regretfully at the rabbits'-ears, darted back to the other window, looked, hovered, hesitated—and tore herself away.

The nurse was now about thirty yards ahead, moving well, with the air of a horse that sights his stable. She crossed the street again, looked into a window piled with coloured wools, thought better of it, passed on, and turned in at the door of the Oriental Café.

Miss Climpson was in the position of one who, after prolonged pursuit, has clapped a tumbler over a moth. For the moment the creature is safe and the pursuer takes breath. The problem now is to extract the moth without damage.

It is easy, of course, to follow a person into a café and sit down at her table, if there is room there. But she may not welcome you. She may feel it perverse in you to thrust yourself upon her when other tables are standing empty. It is better to offer some excuse, such as restoring a dropped handkerchief or drawing attention to an open handbag. If the person will not provide you with an excuse, the next best thing is to manufacture one.

The stationer's shop was only a few doors off. Miss Climpson went in and purchased an indiarubber, three picture post-cards, a BB pencil, and a calendar, and waited while they were made up into a parcel. Then she slowly made her way across the street and turned into the Oriental.

In the first room she found two women and a small boy occupying one recess, an aged gentleman drinking milk in another, and a couple of girls consuming coffee and cakes in a third.

"Excuse me," said Miss Climpson to the two women, "but does this parcel belong to you? I picked it up just outside the door."

The elder woman, who had evidently been shopping, hastily passed in review a quantity of miscellaneous packages, pinching each one by way of refreshing her memory as to the contents.

"I don't think it's mine, but really I can't say for certain. Let me see. That's eggs and that's bacon and—what's this, Gertie? Is that the mouse-trap? No, wait a minute, that's cough-mixture, that is—and that's Aunt Edith's cork soles, and that's Nugget—no, bloater paste, this here's the Nugget—why, bless my soul, I believe I *have* been and gone and dropped the mouse-trap—but that don't look like it to me."

"No, Mother," said the younger woman, "don't you remember, they were sending round the mouse-trap with the bath."

"Of course, so they were. Well, that accounts for that. The mouse-trap and the two frying-pans, they was all to go with the bath, and that's all except the soap, which you've got, Gertie. No, thank you very much, all the same, but it isn't ours; somebody else must have dropped it."

The old gentleman repudiated it firmly but politely, and the two girls merely giggled at it. Miss Climpson passed on. Two young women with their attendant young men duly thanked her in the second room, but said the parcel was not theirs.

Miss Climpson passed on into the third room. In one corner was a rather talkative party of people with an Airedale, and at the back, in the most obscure and retired of all the Oriental nooks and corners, sat the nurse, reading a book.

The talkative party had nothing to say to the parcel, and Miss Climpson, with her heart beating fast, bore down upon the nurse.

"Excuse me," she said, smiling graciously, "but I think this little parcel must be yours. I picked it up just in the doorway and I've asked all the other people in the café."

The nurse looked up. She was a grey-haired, elderly woman, with those curious large blue eyes which disconcert the beholder by their intense gaze, and are usually an index of some emotional instability. She smiled at Miss Climpson and said pleasantly:

"No, no, it isn't mine. So kind of you. But I have all my parcels here."

She vaguely indicated the cushioned seat which ran round three sides of the alcove, and Miss Climpson, accepting the gesture as an invitation, promptly sat down.

"How very odd," said Miss Climpson. "I made sure someone must have dropped it coming in here. I wonder what I had better do with it." She pinched it gently. "I shouldn't think it was valuable, but one never knows. I suppose I ought to take it to the police-station."

"You could hand it to the cashier," suggested the nurse, "in case the owner came back here to claim it."

"Well now, so I could," cried Miss Climpson. "How clever of you to think of it. Of course, yes, that would be the best way. You must think me very foolish, but the idea never occurred to me. I'm not a very practical person, I'm afraid, but I do so admire the people who are. I should never do to take up *your* profession, should I? Any little emergency leaves me *quite* bewildered."

The nurse smiled again.

"It's largely a question of training," she said. "And of *self*-training, too, of course. All these little weaknesses can be cured by placing the mind under a Higher Control—don't you believe that?"

Her eyes rested hypnotically upon Miss Climpson's.

"I suppose that is true."

"It is such a mistake," pursued the nurse, closing her book and laying it down on the table, "to imagine that anything in the mental sphere is large or small. Our least thoughts and actions are equally directed by the higher centres of spiritual power, if we can bring ourselves to believe it."

A waitress arrived to take Miss Climpson's order.

"Oh, dear! I seem to have intruded myself upon your table . . ."

"Oh, don't get up," said the nurse.

"Are you sure? Really? Because I don't want to interrupt you——"

"Not at all. I live a very solitary life, and I am always glad to find a friend to talk to."

"How nice of you. I'll have scones and butter, please, and a pot of tea. This is such a nice little café, don't you think?—so quiet and peaceful. If only those people wouldn't make such a noise with that dog of theirs. I don't like those great, big animals, and I think they're quite dangerous, don't you?"

The reply was lost on Miss Climpson, for she had suddenly seen the title of the book on the table, and the Devil, or a Ministering Angel (she was not quite sure which), was, so to speak, handing her a full-blown temptation on a silver salver. The book was published by the Spiritualist Press and was called *Can the Dead Speak?*

In a single moment of illumination, Miss Climpson saw her plan complete and perfect in every detail. It involved a course of deception from which her conscience shrank appalled, but it was certain. She wrestled with the demon. Even in a righteous cause, could anything so wicked be justified?

She breathed what she thought was a prayer for guidance, but the only answer was a small whisper in her ear, "Oh, jolly good work, Miss Climpson!" and the voice was the voice of Peter Wimsey.

"Pardon me," said Miss Climpson, "but I see you are a student of spiritualism. How interesting that is!"

If there was one subject in the world about which Miss Climpson might claim to know something, it was spiritualism. It is a flower which flourishes bravely in a boarding-house atmosphere. Time and again, Miss Climpson had listened while the apparatus of planes and controls, correspondences and veridical communications, astral bodies, auras, and ectoplastic materialisations was displayed before her protesting intelligence. That to the Church it was a forbidden subject she knew well enough, but she had been paid companion to so many old ladies and had been forced so many times to bow down in the House of Rimmon.

And then there had been the quaint little man from the Psychical Research Society. He had stayed a fortnight in the same private hotel with her at Bournemouth. He was skilled in the investigation of haunted houses and the detection of poltergeists. He had rather liked Miss Climpson, and she had passed several interesting evenings hearing about the tricks of mediums. Under his guidance she had learnt to turn tables and produce explosive cracking noises; she knew how to examine a pair of sealed slates for the marks of the wedges which let the chalk go in on a long black wire to write spirit-messages. She had seen the ingenious rubber gloves which leave the impression of spirit hands in a bucket of paraffin-wax, and which, when deflated, can be drawn delicately from the hardened wax through a hole narrower than a child's wrist. She even knew theoretically, though she had never tried it, how to hold her hands to be tied behind her back so as to force that first deceptive knot which makes all subsequent knots useless, and how to flit about the room banging tambourines in the twilight in spite of having been tied up in a black cabinet with both fists filled with flour. Miss Climpson had wondered greatly at the folly and wickedness of mankind.

The nurse went on talking, and Miss Climpson answered mechanically.

"She's only a beginner," said Miss Climpson to herself. "She's reading a text-book. . . . And she is quite uncritical. . . . Surely she knows that that woman was exposed long ago. . . . People like her shouldn't be allowed out alone—they're living incitements to fraud. . . . I don't know this Mrs. Craig she is talking about, but I should say she was as twisty as a corkscrew. . . . I must avoid Mrs. Craig; she probably knows too much. . . . If the poor deluded creature will swallow that, she'll swallow anything."

"It does seem *most* wonderful, doesn't it?" said Miss Climpson, aloud. "But isn't it a wee bit *dangerous*? I've been told I'm sensitive myself, but I have never dared to *try*. Is it *wise* to open one's mind to these supernatural influences?"

"It's not dangerous if you know the right way," said the nurse. "One must learn to build up a shell of pure thoughts about the soul, so that no evil influences can enter it. I have had the most marvellous talks with the dear ones who have passed over . . ."

Miss Climpson refilled the tea-pot and sent the waitress for a plate of sugary cakes.

". . . unfortunately I am not mediumistic myself—not yet, that is. I can't get anything when I'm alone. Mrs. Craig says that it will come by practice and concentration. Last night I was trying with the ouija board, but it would only write spirals."

"Your conscious mind is too active, I expect," said Miss Climpson.

"Yes, I daresay that is it. Mrs. Craig says that I am wonderfully sympathetic. We get the most wonderful results when we sit together. Unfortunately she is abroad just now."

Miss Climpson's heart gave a great leap, so that she nearly spilled her tea.

"You yourself are a medium, then?" went on the nurse.

"I have been told so," said Miss Climpson, guardedly.

"I wonder," said the nurse, "whether if we sat together——"

She looked hungrily at Miss Climpson.

"I don't really like——"

"Oh, do! You are such a sympathetic person. I'm sure we should get good results. And the spirits are so pathetically anxious to communicate. Of course, I wouldn't like to try unless I was sure of the person. There are so many fraudulent mediums about"—("So you do know that much!" thought Miss Climpson)—"but with somebody like yourself one is absolutely safe. You would find it make such a difference in your life. I used to be so unhappy over all the pain and misery in the world—we see so much of it, you know—till I realised the certainty of survival and how all our trials are merely sent to fit us for life on a higher plane."

"Well," said Miss Climpson, slowly, "I'm willing just to try. But I can't say I really *believe* in it, you know."

"You would—you would."

"Of course, I've seen one or two strange things happen—things that couldn't be tricks, because I knew the people—and which I couldn't explain——"

"Come up and see me this evening, now do!" said the nurse, persuasively. "We'll just have one quiet sitting and then we shall see whether you really are a medium. I've no doubt you are."

"Very well," said Miss Climpson. "What is your name, by the way?"

"Caroline Booth—Miss Caroline Booth. I'm nurse to an old, paralysed lady in the big house along the Kendal Road."

"Thank goodness for that, anyway," thought Miss Climpson. Aloud she said:

"And my name is Climpson; I think I've got a card somewhere. No—I've left it behind. But I'm staying at Hillside View. How do I get to you?"

Miss Booth mentioned the address and the time of the 'bus, and added an invitation to supper, which was accepted. Miss Climpson went home and wrote a hurried note:

"MY DEAR LORD PETER,—I am sure you have been *wondering* what has *happened* to me. But *at last* I have NEWS! I have STORMED THE CITADEL!!! I am going to the house TO-NIGHT and you may expect GREAT THINGS!!!

"In *haste*,

"Yours very sincerely,

"KATHARINE A. CLIMPSON."

Miss Climpson went out into the town again after lunch. First, being an honest woman, she retrieved her sketch-book from Ye Cosye Corner and paid her bill, explaining that she had run across a friend that morning and been detained. She then visited a number of shops. Eventually she selected a small metal soap-box which suited her requirements. Its sides were slightly convex, and, when closed and pinched slightly, it sprang back with a hearty cracking noise. This, with a little contrivance and some powerful sticking-plaster, she fixed to a strong elastic garter. When clasped about Miss Climpson's bony knee and squeezed sharply against the other knee, the box emitted a series of cracks so satisfying as to convince the most sceptical. Miss Climpson, seated before the looking-glass, indulged in an hour's practice before tea, till the crack could be produced with the minimum of physical jerk.

Another purchase was a length of stiff black-bound wire, such as is used for making hat-brims. Used double, neatly bent to a double angle and strapped to the wrist, this contrivance was sufficient to rock a light table. The weight of a heavy table would be too much for it, she feared, but she had had no time to order blacksmith's work. She could try, anyway. She hunted out a black velvet rest-gown with long, wide sleeves, and satisfied herself that the wires could be sufficiently hidden.

At six o'clock, she put on this garment, fastened the soap-box to her leg—turning the box outward, lest untimely cracks should startle her fellow-travellers, muffled herself in a heavy rain-cloak of Inverness cut, took hat and umbrella, and started on her way to steal Mrs. Wrayburn's will.

CHAPTER XVII

SUPPER WAS OVER. It had been served in a beautiful old panelled room with an Adam ceiling and fireplace, and the food had been good. Miss Climpson felt braced and ready.

"We'll sit in my own room, shall we?" said Miss Booth. "It's the only really comfortable place. Most of this house is shut up, of course. If you'll excuse me, dear, I will just run up and give Mrs. Wrayburn her supper and make her comfortable, poor thing, and then we can begin. I shan't be more than half an hour or so."

"She's quite helpless, I suppose?"

"Yes, quite."

"Can she speak?"

"Not to say speak. She mumbles sometimes, but one can't make anything of it. It's sad, isn't it, and her so rich. It will be a happy day for her when she passes over."

"Poor soul!" said Miss Climpson.

Her hostess led her into a small, gaily-furnished sitting-room and left her there among the cretonne covers and the ornaments. Miss Climpson ran her eyes rapidly over the books, which were mostly novels, with the exception of some standard works on spiritualism, and then turned her attention to the mantelpiece. It was crowded with photographs, as the mantelpieces of nurses usually are. Conspicuous among hospital groups and portraits inscribed "From your grateful patient" was a cabinet photograph of a gentleman in the dress and moustache of the 'nineties, standing beside a bicycle, apparently upon a stone balcony in mid-air, with a distant view over a rocky gorge. The frame was silver, heavy, and ornate.

"Too young for a father," said Miss Climpson, as she turned it over and pushed back the catch of the frame; "either sweetheart or favourite brother. H'm! 'My dearest Lucy, from her ever-loving Harry'. Not a brother, I fancy. Photographer's address, Coventry. Cycle trade, possibly. Now what happened to Harry? Not matrimony, obviously. Death, or infidelity. First-class frame and central position; bunch of hot-house narcissi in a vase—I think Harry has passed over. What next? Family group? Yes. Names conveniently beneath. Dearest Lucy in a fringe, Papa and Mamma, Tom and Gertrude. Tom and Gertrude are older, but they may be still alive. Papa is a parson. Largish house—country rectory, perhaps. Photographer's address, Maidstone. Wait a minute. Here's Papa in another group, with a dozen small boys. Schoolmaster, or takes private pupils. Two boys have straw hats with zig-zag ribbons—school, probably, then. What's that silver cup? Thos. Booth and three other names—Pembroke College Fours, 1883. Not an expensive college. Wonder whether Papa objected to Harry on account of the cycle-manufacturing connection? That book over there looks like a school prize. It is. Maidstone Ladies' College—for distinction in English Literature. Just so. Is she coming back?—No, false alarm. Young man in khaki, 'Your loving nephew, G. Booth'—ah! Tom's son, I take it. Did he survive, I wonder? Yes—she is coming, this time."

When the door opened, Miss Climpson was sitting by the fire, deeply engaged in *Raymond*.

"So sorry to keep you waiting," said Miss Booth, "but the poor old dear is rather restless this evening. She'll do now for a couple of hours, but I shall have to go up again later. Shall we begin at once? I'm *so* eager to try."

Miss Climpson readily agreed.

"We usually use this table," said Miss Booth, bringing forward a small, round table of bamboo, with a shelf between its legs. Miss Climpson thought she had never seen a piece of furniture more excellently adapted for the faking of phenomena, and heartily approved of Mrs. Craig's choice.

"Do we sit in the light?" she enquired.

"Not in full light," said Miss Booth. "Mrs. Craig explained to me that the blue rays of daylight or electricity are too hard for the spirits. They shatter the vibrations, you see. So we usually put out the light and sit in the firelight, which is quite bright enough for taking notes. Will you write down, or shall I?"

"Oh, I think you had better do it as you're more accustomed to it," said Miss Climpson.

"Very well." Miss Booth fetched a pencil and a pad of paper and switched off the light.

"Now we just sit down and place our thumbs and finger-tips lightly on the table, near the edge. It's better to make a circle, of course, but one can't do that with two people. And just at first, I think it's better not to talk—till a *rapport* is established, you know. Which side will you sit?"

"Oh, this will do for me," said Miss Climpson.

"You don't mind the fire on your back?"

Miss Climpson most certainly did not.

"Well, that's a good arrangement, because it helps to screen the rays from the table."

"That's what I thought," said Miss Climpson, truthfully.

They placed thumbs and finger-tips on the table and waited.

Ten minutes passed.

"Did you feel any movement?" whispered Miss Booth.

"No."

"It sometimes takes a little time."

Silence.

"Ah! I thought I felt something then."

"I've got a feeling like pins and needles in my fingers."

"So have I. We shall get something soon."

A pause.

"Would you like to rest a little?"

"My wrists ache rather."

"They do till you get used to it. It's the power coming through them."

Miss Climpson lifted her fingers and rubbed each wrist gently. The thin black hooks came quietly down to the edge of her black velvet sleeve.

"I feel sure there is power all about us. I can feel a cold thrill on my spine."

"Let's go on," said Miss Climpson. "I'm quite rested now."

Silence.

"I feel," whispered Miss Climpson, "as though something was gripping the back of my neck."

"Don't move."

"And my arms have gone dead from the elbow."

"Hush! so have mine."

Miss Climpson might have added that she had a pain in her deltoids, if she had known the name for them. This is not an uncommon result of sitting with the thumbs and fingers on a table without support for the wrist.

"I'm tingling from head to foot," said Miss Booth.

At this moment the table gave a violent lurch. Miss Climpson had over-estimated the force necessary to move bamboo furniture.

"Ah!"

After a slight pause for recuperation, the table began to move again, but more gently, till it was rocking with a regular see-saw motion. Miss Climpson found that by gently elevating one rather large foot, she could take practically all the weight off her wrist-hooks. This was fortunate, as she was doubtful whether their constitution would stand the strain.

"Shall we speak to it?" asked Miss Climpson.

"Wait a moment," said Miss Booth. "It wants to go sideways."

Miss Climpson was surprised by this statement, which seemed to argue a high degree of imagination, but she obligingly imparted a slight gyratory movement to the table.

"Shall we stand up?" suggested Miss Booth.

This was disconcerting, for it is not easy to work a vibrating table while stooping and standing on one leg. Miss Climpson decided to fall into a trance. She dropped her head on her chest and uttered a slight moan. At the same time she pulled back her hands, releasing the hooks, and the table continued to revolve jerkily, spinning beneath their fingers.

A coal fell from the fire with a crash, sending up a bright jet of flame. Miss Climpson started, and the table ceased spinning and came down with a little thud.

"Oh, dear!" exclaimed Miss Booth. "The light has dispersed the vibrations. Are you all right, dear?"

"Yes, yes," said Miss Climpson, vaguely. "Did anything happen?"

"The power was tremendous," said Miss Booth. "I've never felt it so strong."

"I think I must have fallen asleep," said Miss Climpson.

"You were entranced," said Miss Booth. "The control was taking possession. Are you very tired, or can you go on?"

"I feel quite all right," said Miss Climpson, "only a little drowsy."

"You're a wonderfully strong medium," said Miss Booth.

Miss Climpson, surreptitiously flexing her ankle, was inclined to agree.

"We'll put a screen before the fire this time," said Miss Booth. "That's better. Now!"

The hands were replaced on the table, which began to rock again almost immediately.

"We won't lose any more time," said Miss Booth. She cleared her throat slightly, and addressed the table.

"Is there a spirit here?"

Crack!

The table ceased moving.

"Will you give me one knock for 'Yes' and two for 'No'?"

Crack!

The advantage of this method of interrogation is that it obliges the enquirer to put leading questions.

"Are you the spirit of one who has passed over?"

"Yes."

"Are you Fedora?"

"No."

"Are you one of the spirits who have visited me before?"

"No."

"Are you friendly to us?"

"Yes."

"Are you pleased to see us?"

"Yes. Yes. Yes."

"Are you happy?"

"Yes."

"Are you here to ask anything for yourself?"

"No."

"Are you anxious to help us personally?"

"No."

"Are you speaking on behalf of another spirit?"

"Yes."

"Does he want to speak to my friend?"

"No."

"To me, then?"

"Yes. Yes. Yes. Yes." (The table rocked violently.)

"Is it the spirit of a woman?"

"No."

"A man?"

"Yes."

A little gasp.

"Is it the spirit I have been trying to communicate with?"

"Yes."

A pause and a tilting of the table.

"Will you speak to us by means of the alphabet? One knock for A, two for B, and so on?"

("Belated caution," thought Miss Climpson.)

Crack!

"What is your name?"

Eight taps, and a long indrawn breath.

One tap——

"H-A——"

A long succession of taps.

"Was that an R? You go too fast."

Crack!

"H-A-R—is that right?"

"Yes."

"Is it Harry?"

"Yes, yes, yes."

"Oh, Harry! At last! How are you? Are you happy?"

"Yes—no—lonely."

"It wasn't my fault, Harry."

"Yes. Weak."

"Ah, but I had my duty to think of. Remember who came between us."

"Yes. F-A-T-H-E-"

"No, no, Harry! It was mo——"

"—A-D!" concluded the table, triumphantly.

"How can you speak so unkindly?"

"Love comes first."

"I know that now. But I was only a girl. Won't you forgive me now?"

"All forgiven. Mother forgiven too."

"I'm so glad. What do you do where you are, Harry?"

"Wait. Help. Atone."

"Have you any special message for me?"

"Go to Coventry!" (Here the table became agitated.)

This message seemed to overwhelm the seeker.

"Oh, it really is you, Harry! You haven't forgotten the dear old joke. Tell me——"

The table showed great signs of excitement at this point and poured out a volley of unintelligible letters.

"What do you want?"

"G-G-G——"

"It must be somebody else interrupting," said Miss Booth. "Who is that, please?"

"G-E-O-R-G-E" (very rapidly).

"George! I don't know any George, except Tom's boy. Has anything happened to him, I wonder."

"Ha! ha! ha! not George Booth, George Washington."

"George Washington?"

"Ha! ha!" (The table became convulsively agitated, so much so that the medium seemed hardly able to hold it. Miss Booth, who had been noting down the conversation, now put her hands back on the table, which stopped capering and began to rock.)

"Who is here now?"

"Pongo."

"Who is Pongo?"

"Your control."

"Who was that talking just now?"

"Bad spirit. Gone now."

"Is Harry still there?"

"Gone."

"Does anybody else want to speak?"

"Helen."

"Helen who?"

"Don't you remember? Maidstone."

"Maidstone? Oh, do you mean Ellen Pate?"

"Yes, Pate."

"Fancy that! Good-evening, Ellen. How nice to hear from you."

"Remember row."

"Do you mean the big row in the dormitory?"

"Kate bad girl."

"No, I don't remember Kate, except Kate Hurley. You don't mean her, do you?"

"Naughty Kate. Lights out."

"Oh, I *know* what she's trying to say. The cakes after lights were out."

"That's right."

"You still spell badly, Ellen."

"Miss—Miss——"

"Mississippi? Haven't you learnt it yet?"

"Funny."

"Are there many of our class where you are?"

"Alice and Mabel. Send love."

"How sweet of them. Give them my love too."

"Yes. All love. Flowers. Sunshine."

"What do you——"

"P," said the table, impatiently.

"Is that Pongo again?"

"Yes. Tired."

"Do you want us to stop?"

"Yes. Another time."

"Very well, good-night."

"Good-night."

The medium leaned back in her chair with an air of exhaustion which was perfectly justified. It is very tiring to rap out letters of the alphabet, and she was afraid the soap-box was slipping.

Miss Booth turned on the light.

"That was wonderful!" said Miss Booth.

"Did you get the answers you wanted?"

"Yes, indeed. Didn't you hear them?"

"I didn't follow it all," said Miss Climpson.

"It is a little difficult, counting, till you're used to it. You must be dreadfully tired. We'll stop now and make some tea. Next time perhaps we could use the ouija. It doesn't take nearly so long to get the answers with that."

Miss Climpson considered this. Certainly it would be less wearisome, but she was not sure of being able to manipulate it.

Miss Booth put the kettle on the fire and glanced at the clock.

"Dear me! it's nearly eleven. How the time has flown! I must run up and see to my old dear. Would you like to read through the questions and answers? I don't suppose I shall be many minutes."

Satisfactory so far, thought Miss Climpson. Confidence was well established. In a few days' time, she would be able to work her plan. But she had nearly tripped up over George. And it was stupid to have said "Helen". Nellie would have done for either—there was a Nellie in every school forty-five years ago. But, after all, it didn't much matter what you said—the other person was sure to help you out of it. How desperately her legs and arms were aching. Wearily she wondered if she had missed the last 'bus.

"I'm afraid you have," said Miss Booth, when the question was put to her on her return. "But we'll ring up a taxi. At my expense, of course, dear. I insist, as you were so good in coming all this way, entirely to please me. Don't you think the communications are too marvellous? Harry would never come before—poor Harry! I'm afraid I was very unkind to him. He married, but you see he has never forgotten me. He lived at Coventry, and we used to have a joke about it—that's what he meant by saying that. I wonder which Alice and Mabel that was. There was an Alice Gibbons and an Alice Roach—both such nice girls; I think Mabel must be Mabel Herridge. She married and went out to India years and years ago. I can't remember her married name, and I've never heard from her since, but she must have passed to the other side. Pongo is a new control. We must ask him who he is. Mrs. Craig's control is Fedora—she was a slave-girl at the Court of Poppæa."

"Really!" said Miss Climpson.

"She told us her story one night. So romantic. She was thrown to the lions because she was a Christian and refused to have anything to do with Nero."

"How very interesting."

"Yes, isn't it? But she doesn't speak very good English, and it's sometimes rather hard to understand her. And she sometimes lets the tiresome ones in. Pongo was very quick at getting rid of George Washington. You will come again, won't you? To-morrow night?"

"Certainly, if you like."

"Yes, please do. And next time you must ask for a message for yourself."

"I will indeed," said Miss Climpson. "It has all been *such* a revelation—quite *wonderful*. I never *dreamed* that I had such a gift."

And that was true, also.

CHAPTER XVIII

IT WAS, OF course, useless for Miss Climpson to try to conceal from the boarding-house ladies where she had been and what she had been doing. Her return at midnight in a taxi had already aroused the liveliest curiosity, and she told the truth to avoid being accused of worse dissipations.

"My dear Miss Climpson," said Mrs. Pegler, "you will not, I trust, think me interfering, but I must caution you against having anything to do with Mrs. Craig or her friends. I have no doubt Miss Booth is an excellent woman, but I do not like the company she keeps. Nor do I approve of spiritualism. It is a prying into matters which we are not intended to know about, and may lead to very undesirable results. If you were a married woman, I could explain myself more clearly, but you may take it from me that these indulgences may have serious effects upon the character in more ways than one."

"Oh, Mrs. Pegler," said Miss Etheredge, "I don't think you should say that. One of the most beautiful characters I know—a woman whom it is a privilege to call one's friend—is a spiritualist, and she is a real saint in her life and influence."

"Very likely, Miss Etheredge," replied Mrs. Pegler, drawing her stout figure to its most impressive uprightness, "but that is not the point. I do not say that a spiritualist may not live a good life, but I *do* say that the majority of them are most unsatisfactory people, and far from truthful."

"I have happened to meet with a number of so-called mediums in the course of my life," agreed Miss Tweall, acidly, "and all of them, without *any* exception, were people I would not have trusted any further than I could see them—if as far."

"That is very true of a great many of them," said Miss Climpson, "and

I am sure *nobody* could have better opportunities of judging than *myself*. But I think and hope that some of them are at least *sincere* if *mistaken* in their claims. What do *you* think, Mrs. Liffey?" she added, turning to the proprietress of the establishment.

"We-ll," said Mrs. Liffey—obliged, in her official capacity, to agree as far as possible with all parties—"I must say, from what I have read, and that is not a great deal, for I have little time for reading—still, I think there is a certain amount of evidence to show that, in certain cases and under strictly safeguarded conditions, there is possibly some foundation of truth beneath the spiritualists' claims. Not that I should care to have anything to do with it personally; as Mrs. Pegler says, I do not as a rule care very much for the sort of people who go in for it, though doubtless there are many exceptions. I think perhaps that the subject should be left to properly qualified investigators."

"There I agree with you," said Mrs. Pegler. "No words can express the disgust I feel at the intrusion of women like this Mrs. Craig into realms that should be sacred to us all. Imagine, Miss Climpson, that that woman—whom I do not know and have no intention of knowing—actually had the impertinence once to write to me and say that she had received a message at one of her *séances*, as she calls them, purporting to come from my dear husband. I cannot tell you what I felt. To have the General's name actually brought up, in public, in connection with such wicked nonsense! And of course it was the purest invention, for the General was the *last* man to have anything to do with goings-on. 'Pernicious poppycock' he used to call it in his bluff military way. And when it came to telling me, his widow, that he had come to Mrs. Craig's house and played the accordion and asked for special prayers to deliver him from a place of punishment, I could only look on it as a calculated insult. The General was a regular church-goer and entirely opposed to prayers for the dead or anything popish; and as to being in any undesirable place, he was the best of men, even if he was a little abrupt at times. As for accordions, I hope, wherever he is, he has something better to do with his time."

"A most shameful business," said Miss Tweall.

"Who is this Mrs. Craig?" asked Miss Climpson.

"Nobody knows," said Mrs. Pegler, ominously.

"She is said to be a doctor's widow," said Mrs. Liffey.

"It's my opinion," said Miss Tweall, "that she is no better than she should be."

"A woman of her age," said Mrs. Pegler, "with henna'd hair and earrings a foot long——"

"And going about in those extraordinary clothes," said Miss Tweall.

"And having such very odd people to stay with her," said Mrs. Pegler. "You remember that black man, Mrs. Liffey, who wore a green turban and used to say his prayers in the front garden, till the police interfered."

"What I should like to know," said Miss Tweall, "is where she gets her money from."

"If you ask me, my dear, the woman's on the make. Heaven knows what she persuades people to do in these spiritualistic meetings."

"But what brought her to Windle?" asked Miss Climpson. "I should have thought London, or some big town, would have been a better place for her if she is the kind of person you describe."

"I shouldn't be surprised if she was in hiding," said Miss Tweall, darkly. "There is such a thing as making a place too hot to hold you."

"Without altogether subscribing to your wholesale condemnation," said Miss Climpson, "I must agree that psychical research can be *very dangerous indeed* in the *wrong hands*, and, from what Miss Booth tells me, I do doubt very *much* whether Mrs. Craig is a suitable guide for the inexperienced. Indeed, I quite felt it my *duty* to put Miss Booth on her guard, and that is what I am endeavouring to do. But, as you know, one has to do that kind of thing *very* tactfully—otherwise one may merely, so to speak, put the person's back up. The first step is to gain her *confidence*, and then, little by little, one may be able to induce a more wholesome frame of mind."

"That's *so* true," said Miss Etheredge, eagerly, her pale blue eyes lighting with something that was almost animation. "I very nearly fell under the influence of a dreadful, fraudulent person myself, till my dear friend showed me a better way."

"Maybe," said Mrs. Pegler, "but in my opinion the whole thing is best left alone."

Undeterred by this excellent advice, Miss Climpson kept her appointment. After a spirited exhibition of table-rocking, Pongo consented to communicate by means of the ouija board, though at first he was rather awkward with it. He attributed this, however, to the fact that he had never learned to write while on earth. Asked who he was, he explained that he was an Italian acrobat of the Renaissance period, and that his full name was Pongocelli. He had lived a sadly irregular life, but had redeemed himself by heroically refusing to abandon a sick child during the time of the Great Plague in Florence. He had caught the plague and died of it, and was now working out the period of probation for his sins by serving as guide and interpreter to other spirits. It was a touching story, and Miss Climpson was rather proud of it.

George Washington was rather intrusive, and the *séance* also suffered from a number of mysterious interruptions from what Pongo described as a "jealous influence". Nevertheless, "Harry" reappeared and delivered some consolatory messages, and there were further communications from Mabel Herridge, who gave a vivid description of her life in India. On the whole, and taking the difficulties into account, a successful evening.

On Sunday there was no *séance*, owing to the revolt of the medium's conscience. Miss Climpson felt that she could not, really could not bring herself to do it. She went to church instead, and listened to the Christian message with a distracted mind.

On Monday, however, the two enquirers again took their seats about the bamboo table, and the following is the report of the *séance*, as noted down by Miss Booth:

7.30 p.m.

On this occasion proceedings were begun at once with the ouija board; after a few minutes, a loud succession of raps announced the presence of a control.

Question: Good-evening. Who is that?

Answer: Pongo here. Good-evening! Heaven bless you.

Q. We are very glad to have you with us, Pongo.

A. Good—very good. Here we are again!

Q. Is that you, Harry?

A. Yes, only to give my love. Such a crowd.

Q. The more the better. We are glad to meet all our friends. What can we do for you?

A. Attend. Obey the spirits.

Q. We will do all we can, if you will tell us what to do.

A. Boil your heads!

Q. Go away, George, we don't want you.

A. Get off the line, silly.

Q. Pongo, can't you send him away?

(Here the pencil drew the sketch of an ugly face.)

Q. Is that your portrait?

A. That's me. G. W. Ha, ha!

(The pencil zigzagged violently and drove the board right over the edge of the table. When it was replaced it started to write in the hand we associate with Pongo.)

A. I have sent him away. Very noisy to-night. F. jealous and sends him to disturb us. Never mind. Pongo more powerful.

Q. Who do you say is jealous?

A. Never mind. Bad person. *Maladetta.*

Q. Is Harry still there?

A. No. Other business. There is a spirit here who wishes your help.

Q. Who is it?

A. Very hard. Wait.

(The pencil made a series of wide loops.)

Q. What letter is that?

A. Silly! don't be impatient. There is difficulty. I will try again.

(The pencil scribbled for a few minutes and then wrote a large C.)

Q. We have got the letter C. Is that right?

A. C.-C.-C——

Q. We have got C.

A. C-R-E——

(Here there was another violent interruption.)

A. (in Pongo's writing): She is trying, but there is much opposition. Think helpful thoughts.

Q. Would you like us to sing a hymn?

A. (Pongo again, very angry): Stupid! Be quiet! (Here the writing changed again.) M-O——

Q. Is that part of the same word?

A. R-N-A.

Q. Do you mean Cremorna?

A. (in the new writing): Cremorna, Cremorna. Through! Glad, glad, glad!

At this point, Miss Booth turned to Miss Climpson and said in a puzzled voice:

"This is very strange. Cremorna was Mrs. Wrayburn's stage name. I do hope—surely she can't have passed away suddenly. She was perfectly comfortable when I left her. Had I better go and see?"

"Perhaps it's another Cremorna?" suggested Miss Climpson.

"But it's such an unusual name."

"Why not ask who it is?"

Q. Cremorna—what is your second name?

A. (the pencil writing very fast): Rosegarden—easier now.

Q. I don't understand you.

A. Rose—Rose—Rose—silly!

Q. Oh! (my dear, she's mixing up the two names.) Do you mean Cremorna Garden?

A. Yes.

Q. Rosanna Wrayburn?

A. Yes.

Q. Have you passed over?

A. Not yet. In exile.

Q. Are you still in the body?

A. Neither in the body nor out of the body. Waiting. (*Pongo interposing*) When what you call the mind is departed, the spirit waits in exile for the Great Change. Why can't you understand? Make haste. Great difficulties.

Q. We are so sorry. Are you in trouble about something?

A Great trouble.

Q. I hope it isn't anything in Dr. Brown's treatment, or mine——

A. (*Pongo*) Do not be so foolish. (*Cremorna*) My will.

Q. Do you want to alter your will?

A. No.

Miss Climpson. That is fortunate, because I don't think it would be legal. What do you want us to do about it, dear Mrs. Wrayburn?

A. Send it to Norman?

Q. To Mr. Norman Urquhart?

A. Yes. He knows.

Q. He knows what is to be done with it?

A. He wants it.

Q. Very well. Can you tell us where to find it?

A. I have forgotten. Search.

Q. Is it in the house?

A. I tell you I have forgotten. Deep waters. No safety. Failing, failing . . . (Here the writing became very faint and irregular.)

Q. Try to remember.

A. In the B—B—B—(a confusion and the pencil staggering wildly) No good. (Suddenly, in a different hand and very vigorously) Get off the line, get off the line, get off the line.

Q. Who is that?

A. (*Pongo*) She has gone. The bad influence back. Ha, ha! Get off! Finished now. (The pencil ran right out of the medium's control, and, on being replaced on the table, refused to answer any further questions.)

"How dreadfully vexatious!" exclaimed Miss Booth.

"I suppose you have no idea where the will is?"

"Not the least. 'In the B——' she said. Now, what could that be?"

"In the Bank, perhaps," suggested Miss Climpson.

"It might be. If so, of course, Mr. Urquhart would be the only person who could get it out."

"Then why hasn't he? She said he wanted it."

"Of course. Then it must be somewhere in the house. What could B stand for?"

"Box, Bag, Bureau——?"

"Bed? It might be almost anything."

"What a pity she couldn't finish the message. Shall we try again! Or shall we look in all the likely places?"

"Let's look first, and then, if we can't find it, we can try again."

"That's a good idea. There are some keys in one of the bureau drawers that belong to her boxes and things."

"Why not try them?" said Miss Climpson, boldly.

"We will. You'll come and help, won't you?"

"If you think it advisable. I'm a stranger, you know."

"The message came to you as much as to me. I'd rather you came with me. You might be able to suggest places."

Miss Climpson made no further ado, and then went upstairs. It was a queer business—practically robbing a helpless woman in the interests of someone she had never seen. Queer. But the motive must be a good one, if it was Lord Peter's.

At the top of the beautiful staircase with its ample curve was a long, wide corridor, the walls hung thickly from floor to ceiling with portraits, sketches, framed autograph letters, programmes, and all the reminiscent bric-a-brac of the green-room.

"All her life is here and in these two rooms," said the nurse. "If this collection was to be sold, it would fetch a lot of money. I suppose it will be, some day."

"Whom does the money go to, do you know?"

"Well, I've always thought it would be to Mr. Norman Urquhart—he's a relation of hers; about the only one, I believe. But I've never been told anything about it."

She pushed open a tall door, graceful with curved panels and classical architrave, and turned on the light.

It was a stately great room, with three tall windows and a ceiling gracefully moulded with garlands of flowers and flambeaux. The purity of its lines was, however, defaced and insulted by a hideous rose-trellised wallpaper, and heavy plush curtains of a hot crimson with thick gold fringes and ropes, like the drop-curtain of a Victorian play-house. Every foot of space was crammed thick with furniture—buhl cabinets incongruously jostling mahogany chiffoniers; whatnot tables strewn with ornaments cuddling the bases of heavy German marbles and bronzes; lacquer screens, Sheraton bureaux, Chinese vases, alabaster lamps, chairs, ottomans of every shape, colour, and period, clustered thick as plants wrestling for existence in a tropical jungle. It was the room of a woman without taste or moderation, who refused nothing and surrendered nothing, to whom the fact of possession had become the one steadfast reality in a world of loss and change.

"It may be in here or in the bedroom," said Miss Booth. "I'll get her keys."

She opened a door on the right. Miss Climpson, endlessly inquisitive, tiptoed in after her.

The bedroom was even more of a nightmare than the sitting-room. A small electric reading-lamp burned dimly by the bed, huge and gilded, with hangings of rose brocade cascading in long folds from a tester supported by fat golden cupids. Outside the narrow circle of light loomed monstrous wardrobes, more cabinets, tall chests of drawers. The dressing-table, frilled and flounced, held a wide, threefold mirror, and a monstrous cheval-glass in the centre of the room darkly reflected the towering and shadowy outlines of the furniture.

Miss Booth opened the middle door of the largest wardrobe. It swung back with a creak, letting out a great gush of frangipani. Nothing, evidently, had been altered in this room since silence and paralysis had struck the owner down.

Miss Climpson stepped softly up to the bed. Instinct made her move cautiously as a cat, though it was evident that nothing would ever startle or surprise its occupant.

An old, old face, so tiny in the vast expanse of sheet and pillow that it might have been a doll, stared up at her with unblinking, unseeing eyes. It was covered with fine surface-wrinkles, like a hand sodden with soapy water, but all the great lines carved by experience had been smoothed out with the relaxing of the helpless muscles. It was both puffed and crumpled. It reminded Miss Climpson of a child's pink balloon, from which nearly all the air has leaked away. The escaping breath puffed through the lax lips in little blowing, snorting sounds and added to the resemblance. From under the frilled night-cap straggled a few lank wisps of whitened hair.

"Funny, isn't it," said Miss Booth, "to think that with her lying like that, her spirit can communicate with us."

Miss Climpson was overcome by a sense of sacrilege. It was only by a great effort that she prevented herself from confessing the truth. She had pulled the garter with the soap-box above her knee for safety, and the elastic was cutting painfully into the muscles of her leg—a kind of reminder of her iniquities.

But Miss Booth had already turned away, and was pulling open the drawers of one of the bureaux.

Two hours passed, and they were still searching. The letter B opened up a particularly wide field of search. Miss Climpson had chosen it on that account, and her foresight was rewarded. By a little ingenuity, that useful letter could be twisted to fit practically any hiding-place in the house. The things that were neither bureaux, beds, bags, boxes, baskets, nor bibelot-tables could usually be described as big, black, brown, or buhl, or, at a pinch, as being bedroom or boudoir furniture, and since every shelf, drawer, and pigeon-hole in every object was crammed full of newspaper-cuttings, letters, and assorted souvenirs, the searchers soon found their heads, legs, and backs aching with effort.

"I'd no idea," said Miss Booth, "that there could be so many possible places."

Miss Climpson, sitting on the floor, with her back hair uncoiling itself and her decent black petticoats rucked up nearly to the soap-box, agreed wearily.

"It's dreadfully exhausting isn't it?" said Miss Booth. "Wouldn't you like to stop? I can go on searching to-morrow by myself. It's a shame to tire you out in this way."

Miss Climpson turned this over in her mind. If the will were found in her absence and sent to Norman Urquhart, would Miss Murchison be able to get hold of it before it was again hidden away or destroyed? She wondered.

Hidden away, not destroyed. The mere fact that the will had been sent to him by Miss Booth would prevent the solicitor from making away with it, for there would be a witness to its existence. But he might successfully conceal it for a considerable time—and time was of the essence of the adventure.

"Oh, I'm not a scrap tired," she said brightly, sitting up on her heels and restoring her coiffure to something more like its usual neatness. She had a black note-book in her hand, taken from a drawer in one of the Japanese cabinets, and was turning its pages mechanically. A line of figures caught her eye: 12, 18, 4, 0, 9, 3, 15, and she wondered vaguely what they referred to.

"We've looked through everything here," said Miss Booth. "I don't believe we've missed anything—unless, of course, there is a secret drawer somewhere."

"Could it be in a book, do you think?"

"A book! Why, of course it might. How silly of us not to think of that! In detective stories, wills are always hidden in books."

"More often than in real life," thought Miss Climpson, but she got up and dusted herself and said cheerfully:

"So they are. Are there many books in the house?"

"Thousands," said Miss Booth. "Downstairs in the library."

"I shouldn't have expected Mrs. Wrayburn to be a great reader, somehow."

"Oh, I don't think she was. The books were bought with the house, so Mr. Urquhart told me. They're nearly all old ones, you know—big things bound in leather. Dreadfully dull. I've never found a thing to read there. But they're just the sort of books to hide wills in."

They emerged into the corridor.

"By the way," said Miss Climpson, "won't the servants think it funny of us to be wandering about the place so late?"

"They all sleep in the other wing. Besides, they know that I sometimes have visitors. Mrs. Craig has often been here as late as this when we have had interesting sittings. There's a spare bedroom where I can put people up when I want to."

Miss Climpson made no more objections, and they went downstairs and along the hall into the library. It was big, and books filled the walls and bays in serried ranks—a heart-breaking sight.

"Of course," said Miss Booth, "if the communication hadn't insisted on something beginning with B——"

"Well?"

"Well—I should have expected any papers to be in the safe down here."

Miss Climpson groaned in spirit. The obvious place, naturally! If only her misplaced ingenuity—well! one must make the best of it.

"Why not look?" she suggested. "The letter B may have been referring to something quite different. Or it may have been an interruption from George Washington. It would be quite like him to use words beginning with a B, don't you think?"

"But if it was in the safe, Mr. Urquhart would know about it."

Miss Climpson began to feel that she had let her invention play about too freely.

"It wouldn't do any harm to make sure," she suggested.

"But I don't know the combination," said Miss Booth. "Mr. Urquhart does, of course. We could write and ask him."

An inspiration came to Miss Climpson.

"I believe I know it," she exclaimed. "There was a row of seven figures in that black note-book I was looking at just now, and it passed through my mind that they must be a memorandum of something."

"Black Book!" cried Miss Booth. "Why, there you are! How could we have been so silly! Of course Mrs. Wrayburn was trying to tell us where to find the combination!"

Miss Climpson again blessed the all-round utility of the letter B.

"I'll run up and fetch it," she cried.

When she came down again, Miss Booth was standing before a section of the bookshelves, which had swung out from the wall, disclosing the green door of a built-in safe. With trembling hands, Miss Climpson touched the milled knob and turned it.

The first attempt was unsuccessful, owing to the fact that the note did not make it clear which way the knob should be turned first, but at the second attempt the pointer swung over on the seventh figure with a satisfying click.

Miss Booth seized the handle, and the heavy door moved and stood open. A bundle of papers lay inside. On the top, staring them in the face, was a long, sealed envelope. Miss Climpson pounced upon it.

"Will of Rosanna Wrayburn
June 5th 1920."

"Well, isn't that marvellous?" cried Miss Booth.

On the whole, Miss Climpson agreed with her.

CHAPTER XIX

MISS CLIMPSON STAYED the night in the spare bedroom.

"The best thing," she said, "will be for you to write a little letter to Mr. Urquhart, explaining about the *séance,* and saying that you thought it best and safest to send the will on to him."

"He will be very much surprised," said Miss Booth. "I wonder what he will say. Lawyers don't believe in spirit communications as a rule. And he'll think it rather funny that we should have managed to open the safe."

"Well, but the spirit led us directly to the combination, didn't it? He could hardly expect you to ignore a message like that, could he? The proof of your good faith is that you are sending the will straight to him. And it would be as well, don't you think, if you asked him to come up and check the other contents of the safe and have the combination altered?"

"Wouldn't it be better if I kept the will and asked him to come for it?"

"But perhaps he requires it urgently."

"Then why hasn't he been to fetch it?"

Miss Climpson noted with some irritation that, where spiritualistic messages were not concerned, Miss Booth showed signs of developing an independent judgment.

"Perhaps he doesn't know yet that he wants it. Perhaps the spirits foresaw an urgent need that will only arise to-morrow."

"Oh, yes, that's quite likely. If only people would avail themselves more fully of the marvellous guidance given to them, so much might be foreseen and provided for! Well, I think you are right. We will find a big envelope to fit it, and I will write a letter and we will send it by the first post to-morrow."

"It had better be registered," said Miss Climpson. "If you will entrust it to me, I will take it down to the post-office first thing."

"Will you? That will be a great relief to my mind. Well now, I'm sure you're as tired as I am, so I'll put on a kettle for the hot-water bottles and we'll turn in. Will you make yourself comfy in my sitting-room? I've only got to put the sheets on your bed. What? No, indeed, I can do it in a moment; *please* don't bother. I'm so used to making beds."

"Then I'll see to the kettles," said Miss Climpson. "I simply *must* make myself useful."

"Very well. It won't take long. The water is quite hot in the kitchen boiler."

Left alone in the kitchen, with a kettle bumping and singing on its way to boiling-point, Miss Climpson wasted no time. She tiptoed quickly out again and stood with ear cocked at the foot of the stairs, listening to the nurse's footsteps as they pattered into the distance. Then she slipped into the little sitting-room, took up the will in its sealed envelope, and a long thin paper-knife which she had already marked down as a useful weapon, and hastened back to the kitchen.

It is astonishing how long a kettle which seems to be on the verge of boiling will take before the looked-for jet of steady steam emerges from its spout. Delusive little puffs and deceptive pauses in the song tantalise the watcher interminably. It seemed to Miss Climpson that there would have been time to make twenty beds before the kettle boiled that evening. But even a watched pot cannot absorb heat for ever. After what appeared to be an hour, but was actually about seven minutes, Miss Climpson, guilty and furtive, was holding the flap of the envelope before the scalding steam.

"I mustn't hurry," said Miss Climpson, "oh, blessed saints, I mustn't hurry, or I shall tear it."

She slipped the paper-knife under the flap; it lifted; it opened cleanly, just as Miss Booth's step resounded in the passage.

Miss Climpson adroitly dropped the paper-knife behind the stove and thrust the envelope, with the flap doubled back to prevent it from re-sticking itself, behind a dish-cover on the wall.

"The water's ready!" she cried blithely. "Where are the bottles?"

It is a tribute to her nerve that she filled them with a steady hand. Miss Booth thanked her, and departed upstairs, a bottle in each hand.

Miss Climpson pulled the will from its hiding-place, drew it from its envelope, and glanced swiftly through it.

It was not a long document, and, in spite of the legal phraseology, its purport was easily gathered. Within three minutes she had replaced it, moistened the gum and stuck the flap down again. She put it in her petticoat-pocket—for her garments were of a useful and old-fashioned kind—and went to hunt in the pantry. When Miss Booth returned, she was making tea peacefully.

"I thought it would refresh us after our labours," she remarked.

"A very good idea," said Miss Booth; "in fact, I was just going to suggest it."

Miss Climpson carried the tea-pot to the sitting-room, leaving Miss Booth to follow with the cups, milk, and sugar on a tray. With the tea-pot on the hob and the will once more lying innocently on the table, she smiled and breathed deeply. Her mission was accomplished.

Letter from Miss Climpson to
Lord Peter Wimsey

"*Tuesday, Jan. 7th 1930.*

"MY DEAR LORD PETER,—As my *telegram* this morning will have informed you, I have SUCCEEDED!! Though what excuse I can find in my *conscience* for the *methods* I have used, I *don't* KNOW! but I believe the Church takes into account the necessity of *deception* in certain *professions*, such as that of a *police-detective* or a SPY in time of WARFARE, and I *trust* that my *subterfuges* may be allowed to come under that *category*. However, you will not want to hear about my *religious scruples*! So I will hasten to let you know *what* I have DISCOVERED!!

"In my last letter I explained the *plan* I had in mind, so you will know what to do about the *Will itself*, which was duly *despatched* by *Registered*

Post this morning under cover to *Mr. Norman Urquhart.* How surprised he will be to get it!!! Miss Booth wrote an excellent *covering letter*, which I *saw* before it went, which explains the circumstances and *mentions* NO NAMES!! I have wired to Miss Murchison to *expect* the package, and I hope that when it comes she will contrive to be *present* at the opening, so as to constitute *yet another* WITNESS to its existence. In any case, I should not think he would *venture* to *tamper* with it. Perhaps Miss Murchison may be able to INVESTIGATE it in detail, which I had not *time* to do (it was all *most* adventurous! and I am looking forward to *telling* you ALL ABOUT IT when I come back), but in case she is *not* able to do so, I will give you the *rough outline.*

"The property consists of *real estate* (the house and grounds) and a *personalty* (am I not *good* at legal terms??) which I am not able to calculate *exactly*. But the gist of it is this:

"The *real estate* is left to *Philip Boyes*, absolutely.

"*Fifty thousand pounds* is left to *Philip Boyes* also, in *cash.*

"The remainder (is not this called the residue?) is left to NORMAN URQUHART, who is appointed sole executor.

"There are a few *small legacies* to Stage Charities, of which I did not manage to memorise any *particulars.*

"There is a special paragraph, explaining that the greater part of the property is left to *Philip Boyes* in token that the testatrix FORGIVES the ill-treatment meted out to her by *his family*, for which he was *not responsible.*

"The date of the Will is June 5th 1920, and the *witnesses* are *Eva Gubbins*, housekeeper, and *John Briggs*, gardener.

"I hope, dear Lord Peter, that this information will be enough for your purpose. I had hoped that even *after* Miss Booth had enclosed the Will in a *covering envelope* I might be able to take it out and *peruse it at leisure,* but unfortunately she *sealed* it for greater security with Mrs. Wrayburn's *private seal*, which I had not sufficient *dexterity* to *remove and replace,* though I understand it is possible to *do so* with a *hot knife.*

"You will *understand* that I cannot leave Windle *just yet*—it would look so odd to do so immediately after this occurrence. Besides, I am hoping, in a further series of 'sittings', to *warn* Miss Booth against Mrs. Craig and her 'control' Fedora, as I am *quite sure* that this person is *quite* as great a *charlatan* as I AM!!!—and without my *altruistic* motives!! So you will not be surprised if I am away from Town for, say, *another week*! I am a little worried about the *extra expense* of this, but if you do not think it *justified* for the sake of safety, *let me know*—and I will alter my arrangements accordingly.

"Wishing you *all success*, dear Lord Peter,

"Most sincerely yours,

"KATHARINE A. CLIMPSON.

"P.S.—I managed to do the 'job' *very nearly* within the stipulated week, you see. I am *so sorry* it was not *quite* finished yesterday, but I was so *terrified* of *spoiling* the WHOLE THING by *rushing it*!!"

"Bunter," said Lord Peter, looking up from this letter, "I *knew* there was something fishy about that will."

"Yes, my lord."

"There is something about wills which brings out the worst side of human nature. People who under ordinary circumstances are perfectly upright and amiable, go as curly as corkscrews and foam at the mouth whenever they hear the words 'I devise and bequeath'. That reminds me, a spot of champagne in a silver tankard is no bad thing to celebrate on. Get up a bottle of the Pommery and tell Chief Inspector Parker I should be glad of a word with him. And bring me those notes of Mr. Arbuthnot's. And oh, Bunter!"

"My lord?"

"Get Mr. Crofts on the phone and give him my compliments, and say I have found the criminal and the motive and hope presently to produce proof of the way the crime was done, if he will see that the case is put off for a week or so."

"Very good, my lord."

"All the same, Bunter, I really don't know how it *was* done."

"That will undoubtedly suggest itself before long, my lord."

"Oh, yes," said Wimsey, airily. "Of course. Of course. I'm not worrying about a trifle like that."

CHAPTER XX

"T'CH! T'CH!" SAID Mr. Pond, clicking his tongue against his denture.

Miss Murchison looked up from her typewriter.

"Is anything the matter, Mr. Pond?"

"No, nothing," said the head clerk, testily. "A foolish letter from a foolish member of your sex, Miss Murchison."

"That's nothing new."

Mr. Pond frowned, conceiving the tone of his subordinate's voice to be impertinent. He picked up the letter and its enclosure and took them into the inner office.

Miss Murchison nipped swiftly across to his desk and glanced at the registered envelope which lay upon it, open. The post-mark was "Windle".

"That's luck," said Miss Murchison, to herself. "Mr. Pond is a better witness than I should be. I'm glad he opened it."

She regained her place. In a few minutes Mr. Pond emerged, smiling slightly.

Five minutes later, Miss Murchison, who had been frowning over her shorthand note-book, rose up and came over to him.

"Can you read shorthand, Mr. Pond."

"No," said the head clerk. "In my day it was not considered necessary."

"I can't make out this outline," said Miss Murchison. "It looks like 'give consent to', but it may be only 'give consideration to'—there's a difference, isn't there?"

"There certainly is," said Mr. Pond, drily.

"P'raps I'd better not risk it," said Miss Murchison. "It's got to go off this morning. I'd better ask him."

Mr. Pond snorted—not for the first time—over the carelessness of the female typist.

Miss Murchison walked briskly across the room and opened the inner door without knocking—an informality which left Mr. Pond groaning again.

Mr. Urquhart was standing up with his back to the door, doing something or other at the mantelpiece. He turned round sharply, with an exclamation of annoyance.

"I have told you before, Miss Murchison, that I like you to knock before entering."

"I am very sorry; I forgot."

"Don't let it happen again. What is it?"

He did not return to his desk, but stood leaning against the mantelshelf. His sleek head, outlined against the drab-painted panelling, was a little thrown back, as though—Miss Murchison thought—he were protecting or defying somebody.

"I could not quite make out my shorthand note of your letter to Tewke & Peabody," said Miss Murchison, "and I thought it better to come and ask you."

"I wish," said Mr. Urquhart, fixing a stern eye upon her, "that you would take your notes clearly at the time. If I am going too fast for you, you should tell me so. It would save trouble in the end—wouldn't it?"

Miss Murchison was reminded of a little set of rules which Lord Peter Wimsey—half in jest and half in earnest—had once prepared for the guidance of "The Cattery". Of Rule Seven in particular, which ran: "Always distrust the man who looks you straight in the eyes. He wants to prevent you from seeing something. Look for it."

She shifted her eyes under her employer's gaze.

"I'm very sorry, Mr. Urquhart. I won't let it occur again," she muttered. There was a curious dark line at the edge of the panelling just behind the solicitor's head, as though the panel did not quite fit its frame. She had never noticed it before.

"Well, now, what is the trouble?"

Miss Murchison asked her question, got her answer, and retired. As she went, she cast a glance over the desk. The will was not there.

She went back and finished her letters. When she took them in to be signed, she seized the opportunity to look at the panelling again. There was no dark line to be seen.

Miss Murchison left the office promptly at half-past four. She had a feeling that it would be unwise to linger about the premises. She walked briskly away through Hand Court, turned to the right along Holborn, dived to the right again through Featherstone Buildings, made a detour through Red Lion Street, and debouched into Red Lion Square. Within five minutes she was at her old walk round the square, and up Princeton Street. Presently, from a safe distance, she saw Mr. Pond come out, thin, stiff, and stooping, and walk down Bedford Row towards Chancery Lane Station. Before very long, Mr. Urquhart followed. He stood a moment on the threshold, glancing to left and right, then came straight across the street towards her. For a moment she thought he had seen her, and she dived hurriedly behind a van that was standing at the kerb. Under its shelter, she withdrew to the corner of the street, where there is a butcher's shop, and scanned a windowful of New Zealand lamb and chilled beef. Mr. Urquhart came nearer. His steps grew louder—then paused. Miss Murchison glued her eyes on a round of meat marked 4½ lb., 3*s.* 4*d.* A voice said. "Good-evening, Miss Murchison. Choosing your supper-chop?"

"Oh! good-evening, Mr. Urquhart. Yes—I was just wishing that Providence had seen fit to provide more joints suitable for single people."

"Yes—one gets tired of beef and mutton."

"And pork is apt to be indigestible."

"Just so. Well, you should cease to be single, Miss Murchison."

Miss Murchison giggled.

"But this is so sudden, Mr. Urquhart."

Mr. Urquhart flushed under his curious freckled skin.

"Good-night," he said abruptly, and with extreme coldness.

Miss Murchison laughed to herself as he strode off.

"Thought that would settle him. It's a great mistake to be familiar with your subordinates. They take advantage of you."

She watched him out of sight on the far side of the square, then returned along Princeton Street, crossed Bedford Row, and re-entered the office building. The charwoman was just coming downstairs.

"Well, Mrs. Hodges, it's me again! Do you mind letting me in? I've lost a pattern of silk. I think I must have left it in my desk, or dropped it on the floor. Have you come across it?"

"No, miss, I ain't done your office yet."

"Then I'll have a hunt round for it. I want to get up to Bourne's before half-past six. It's such a nuisance."

"Yes, miss, and such a crowd always with the 'buses and things. Here you are, miss."

She opened the door, and Miss Murchison darted in.

"Shall I 'elp you to look for it, miss?"

"No, thank you, Mrs. Hodges, please don't bother. I don't expect it's far off."

Mrs. Hodges took up a pail and went to fill it at a tap in the back yard. As soon as her heavy steps had ascended again to the first floor, Miss Murchison made for the inner office.

"I must and will see what's behind that panelling."

The houses in Bedford Row are Hogarthian in type, tall, symmetrical, with the glamour of better days upon them. The panels in Mr. Urquhart's room, though defaced by many coats of paint, were handsomely designed, and over the mantelpiece ran a festoon of flowers and fruit, rather florid for the period, with a ribbon and basket in the centre. If the panel was controlled by a concealed spring, the boss that moved it was probably to be found among this decorative work. Pulling a chair to the fireplace, Miss Murchison ran her fingers quickly over the festoon, pushing and pressing with both hands, while keeping her ear cocked for intruders.

This kind of investigation is easy for experts, but Miss Murchison's knowledge of secret hiding-places was only culled from sensational literature; she could not find the trick of the thing. After nearly a quarter of an hour, she began to despair.

Thump—thump—thump—Mrs. Hodges was coming downstairs.

Miss Murchison sprang away from the panelling so hastily that the chair slipped, and she had to thrust hard at the wall to save herself. She jumped down, restored the chair to its place, glanced up—and saw the panel standing wide open.

At first she thought it was a miracle, but soon realised that in slipping she had thrust sideways at the frame of the panel. A small square of woodwork had slipped away sideways, and exposed an inner panel with a keyhole in the middle.

She heard Mrs. Hodges in the outer room, but she was too excited to bother about what Mrs. Hodges might be thinking. She pushed a heavy chair across the door, so that nobody could enter without noise and difficulty. In a moment Blindfold Bill's keys were in her hand—how fortunate that she had not returned them! How fortunate, too, that Mr. Urquhart had relied on the secrecy of the panel, and had not thought it worth while to fit his cache with a patent lock!

A few moments' quick work with the keys, and the lock turned. She pulled the little door open.

Inside was a bundle of papers. Miss Murchison ran them over—at first quickly—then again, with a puzzled face. Receipts for securities—share certificates—Megatherium Trust—surely the names of those investments were familiar—where had she . . .?

Suddenly Miss Murchison sat down, feeling quite faint, the bundle of papers in her hand.

She realised now what had happened to Mrs. Wrayburn's money, which Norman Urquhart had been handling under that confiding Deed of Trust, and why the matter of the will was so important. Her head whirled. She picked up a sheet of paper from the desk and began jotting down in hurried shorthand the particulars of the various transactions of which these documents were the evidence.

Somebody bumped at the door.

"Are you in here, miss?"

"Just a moment, Mrs. Hodges. I think I must have dropped it on the floor in here."

She gave the big chair a sharp push, effectually closing the door.

She must hurry. Anyway, she had got down enough to convince Lord Peter that Mr. Urquhart's affairs needed looking into. She put the papers back into the cupboard, in the exact place from which she had taken them. The will was there, too, she noticed, laid on one side by itself. She peered in. There was something else, tucked away at the back. She thrust her hand in and pulled the mysterious object out. It was a white paper packet, labelled with the name of a foreign chemist. The end had been opened and tucked in again. She pulled the paper apart, and saw that the packet contained about two ounces of a fine white powder.

Next to hidden treasure and mysterious documents, nothing is more full of sensational suggestion than a packet of anonymous white powder. Miss Murchison caught up another sheet of clean paper, tipped a thimbleful of the powder into it, replaced it at the back of the cupboard, and re-locked the door with the skeleton key. With trembling fingers she pushed the panel back into place, taking care to shut it completely, so as to show no betraying dark line.

She rolled the chair away from the door and cried out gaily:

"I've got it, Mrs. Hodges!"

"There, now!" said Mrs. Hodges, appearing in the doorway.

"Just fancy!" said Miss Murchison. "I was looking through my patterns when Mr. Urquhart rang, and this one must have stuck to my frock and dropped on the floor in here."

She held up a small piece of silk triumphantly. She had torn it from the lining of her bag in the course of the afternoon—a proof, if any were needed, of her devotion to her work, for the bag was a good one.

"Dearie me," said Mrs. Hodges. "What a good thing you found it, wasn't it, miss?"

"I nearly didn't," said Miss Murchison; "it was right in this dark corner. Well, I must fly to get there before the shop shuts. Good-night, Mrs. Hodges."

But long before the accommodating Messrs. Bourne & Hollingsworth had closed their doors, Miss Murchison was ringing the second floor bell at 110*a* Piccadilly.

She found a council in progress. There was the Hon. Freddy Arbuthnot, looking amiable; Chief Inspector Parker, looking worried; Lord Peter, looking somnolent; and Bunter, who, having introduced her, retired to a position on the fringe of the assembly and hovered there looking correct.

"Have you brought us news, Miss Murchison? If so, you have come at the exact right moment to find the eagles gathered together. Mr. Arbuthnot, Chief Inspector Parker, Miss Murchison. Now let's all sit down and be happy together. Have you had tea? or will you absorb a spot of something?"

Miss Murchison declined refreshment.

"H'm!" said Wimsey. "The patient refuses food. Her eyes glitter wildly. The expression is anxious. The lips are parted. The fingers fumble with the clasp of the bag. The symptoms point to an acute attack of communicativeness. Tell us the worst, Miss Murchison."

Miss Murchison needed no urging. She told her adventures, and had the pleasure of holding her audience enthralled from the first word to the last.

When she finally produced the screw of paper containing the white powder, the sentiments of the company expressed themselves in a round of applause, in which Bunter joined discreetly.

"Are you convinced, Charles?" asked Wimsey.

"I admit that I am heavily shaken," said Parker. "Of course, the powder must be analysed——"

"It shall, embodied caution," said Wimsey. "Bunter, make ready the rack and thumbscrew. Bunter has been taking lessons in Marsh's test, and performs it to admiration. You know all about it too, Charles, don't you?"

"Enough for a rough test."

"Carry on then, my children. In the meanwhile, let us sum up our findings."

Bunter went out and Parker, who had been making entries in a note-book, cleared his throat.

"Well," he said, "the matter stands, I take it, like this. You say that Miss Vane is innocent, and you undertake to prove this by bringing a convincing accusation against Norman Urquhart. So far, your evidence against him is almost entirely concerned with motive, bolstered up by proofs of intent to mislead enquiry. You say that your investigations have brought the case against Urquhart to a point at which the police can, and ought to, take it up, and I am inclined to agree with you. I warn you, however, that you still have to establish evidence as to means and opportunity."

"I know that. Tell us a new one."

"All right, as long as you know it. Very well. Now Philip Boyes and Norman Urquhart are the only surviving relations of Mrs. Wrayburn, or Cremorna Garden, who is rich, and has money to leave. A number of years ago, Mrs. Wrayburn put all her affairs into the hands of Urquhart's father, the only member of the family with whom she remained on friendly terms. On his father's death, Norman Urquhart took over those affairs himself, and in 1920, Mrs. Wrayburn executed a Deed of Trust, giving him sole authority to handle her property. She also made a will, dividing her property unequally between her two great-nephews. Philip Boyes got all the real estate and £50,000, while Norman Urquhart took whatever was left and was also sole executor. Norman Urquhart, when questioned about this will, deliberately told you an untruth, saying that the bulk of the money was left to him, and even went so far as to produce a document purporting to be a draft of such a will. The pretended date of this draft is subsequent to that of the will discovered by Miss Climpson, but there is no doubt that the draft itself was drawn out by Urquhart, certainly within the last three years and probably within the last few days. Moreover, the fact that the actual will, though lying in a place accessible to Urquhart, was not destroyed by him, suggests that it was not, in fact, superseded by any subsequent testamentary disposition. By the way, Wimsey, why didn't he simply take the will and destroy it? As the sole surviving heir, he would then inherit without dispute."

"Perhaps it didn't occur to him. Or there might even be other relatives surviving. How about that uncle in Australia?"

"True. At any rate, he didn't destroy it. In 1925. Mrs. Wrayburn became completely paralysed and imbecile, so that there was no possibility of her ever enquiring into the disposition of her estate or making another will.

"About this time, as we know from Mr. Arbuthnot, Urquhart took the dangerous step of plunging into speculation. He made mistakes, lost money, plunged more deeply to recover himself, and was involved to a large extent in the great crash of Megatherium Trust, Ltd. He certainly lost far more than he could possibly afford, and we now find, from Miss Murchison's discoveries—of which I must say that I should hate to have to take official notice—that he had been consistently abusing his position as trustee and employing Mrs. Wrayburn's money for his private speculations. He deposited her holdings as security for large loans, and embarked the money thus raised in the Megatherium and other wild-cat schemes.

"As long as Mrs. Wrayburn lived, he was fairly safe, for he only had to pay to her the sums necessary to keep up her house and establishment. In fact, all the household bills and so on were settled by him as her man of affairs under Power of Attorney, all salaries were paid by him, and, so long as he did this, it was nobody's business to ask what he had done with the capital. But as soon as Mrs. Wrayburn died, he would have to account to the other heir, Philip Boyes, for the capital which he had misappropriated.

"Now in 1929, just about the time that Philip Boyes quarrelled with Miss Vane, Mrs. Wrayburn had a serious attack of illness and very nearly died. The danger passed, but might recur at any moment. Almost immediately afterwards we find him becoming friendly with Philip Boyes and inviting him to stay at his house. While living with Urquhart, Boyes has three attacks of illness, attributed by his doctor to gastritis, but equally consistent with arsenical poisoning. In June 1929, Philip Boyes goes away to Wales and his health improves.

"While Philip Boyes is absent, Mrs. Wrayburn has another alarming attack, and Urquhart hastens up to Windle, possibly with the idea of destroying the will in case the worst happens. It does not happen, and he comes back to London, just in time to receive Boyes on his return from Wales. That night, Boyes is taken ill with symptoms similar to those of the previous spring, but much more violent. After three days he dies.

"Urquhart is now perfectly safe. As residuary legatee, he will receive, at Mrs. Wrayburn's death, all the money bequeathed to Philip Boyes. That is, he will not get it, because he has already taken it and lost it, but he will no longer be called upon to produce it and his fraudulent dealings will not be exposed.

"So far, the evidence as to motive is extremely cogent, and far more convincing than the evidence against Miss Vane.

"But here is your snag, Wimsey. When and how was the poison administered? We know that Miss Vane possessed arsenic and that she could easily have given it to him without witnesses. But Urquhart's only opportunity was at the dinner he shared with Boyes, and if anything in this case is certain, it is that the poison was not administered at that dinner. Everything which Boyes ate or drank was equally eaten and drunk by Urquhart and/or the servants, with the single exception of the Burgundy, which was preserved and analysed and found to be harmless."

"I know," said Wimsey, "but that is what is so suspicious. Did you ever hear of a meal hedged round with such precautions? It's not natural, Charles. There's the sherry, poured out by the maid from the original bottle; the soup, fish and casseroled chicken—so impossible to poison in one portion without poisoning the whole—the omelette, so ostentatiously prepared at table by the hands of the victim—the wine, sealed up and marked—the remnants consumed in the kitchen—you would think the man had gone out of his way to construct a suspicion-proof meal. The wine is the final touch which makes the thing incredible. Do you tell me that at that earliest moment when everybody supposes the illness to be a natural one, and when the affectionate cousin ought to be overwhelmed with anxiety for the sick man, it is natural or believable that an innocent person's mind should fly to accusations of poisoning? If he was innocent himself, then he suspected something. If he did suspect, why didn't he tell the doctor and have the patient's secretions and so on analysed? Why should he ever have thought of protecting himself against accusation when no accusation had been made, unless he knew that an accusation would be well-founded? And then there's the business about the nurse."

"Exactly. The nurse did have her suspicions."

"If he knew about them, he ought to have taken steps to refute them in the proper way. But I don't think he did know about them. I was referring to what you told us to-day. The police have got in touch with the nurse again, Miss Williams, and she tells them that Norman Urquhart took special pains never to be left alone with the patient, and never to give him any food or medicine, even when she herself was present. Doesn't that argue a bad conscience?"

"You won't find any lawyer or jury to believe it, Peter."

"Yes, but look here, doesn't it strike you as funny? Listen to this, Miss Murchison. One day the nurse was doing something or the other in the room, and she had got the medicine there on the mantelpiece. Something was said about it, and Boyes remarked, 'Oh, don't bother, Nurse. Norman can give me my dope.' Does Norman say, 'Right-ho, old man!' as you or I would? No! He says: 'No, I'll leave it to Nurse—I might make a mess of it.' Pretty feeble, what?"

"Lots of people are nervous about looking after invalids," said Miss Murchison.

"Yes, but most people can pour stuff out of a bottle into a glass. Boyes wasn't *in extremis*—he was speaking quite rationally and all that. I say the man was deliberately protecting himself."

"Possibly," said Parker, "but after all, old man, when *did* he administer the poison?"

"Probably not at the dinner at all," said Miss Murchison. "As you say, the precautions seem rather obvious. They may have been intended to make people concentrate on the dinner and forget other possibilities. Did he have a whisky when he arrived or before he went out or anything?"

"Alas, he did not. Bunter has been cultivating Hannah Westlock almost to breach of promise point, and she says that she opened the door to Boyes on his arrival, that he went straight upstairs to his room, that Urquhart was out at the time and only came in a quarter of an hour before dinner-time, and that the two met for the first time over the famous glass of sherry in the library. The folding-doors between the library and dining-room were open and Hannah was buzzing round the whole time laying the table, and she is sure that Boyes had the sherry and nothing but the sherry."

"Not so much as a digestive tablet?"

"Nothing."

"How about after dinner?"

"When they had finished the omelette, Urquhart said something about coffee. Boyes looked at his watch and said, 'No time, old chap; I've got to be getting along to Doughty Street.' Urquhart said he would ring up a taxi, and went out to do so. Boyes folded up his napkin, got up, and went into the hall. Hannah followed and helped him on with his coat. The taxi arrived. Boyes got in, and off he went without seeing Urquhart again."

"It seems to me," said Miss Murchison, "that Hannah is an exceedingly important witness for Mr. Urquhart's defence. You don't think—I hardly like to suggest it—but you don't think that Bunter is allowing his feelings to overcome his judgment?"

"He says," replied Lord Peter, "that he believes Hannah to be a sincerely religious woman. He has sat beside her in chapel and shared her hymn-book."

"But that may be the merest hypocrisy," said Miss Murchison, rather warmly, for she was militantly rationalist. "I don't trust these unctuous people."

"I didn't offer that as a proof of Hannah's virtue," said Wimsey, "but of Bunter's unsusceptibility."

"But he looks like a deacon himself."

"You've never seen Bunter off duty," said Lord Peter, darkly. "I have, and I can assure you that a hymn-book would be about as softening to his heart as neat whisky to an Anglo-Indian liver. No; if Bunter says Hannah is honest, then she *is* honest."

"Then that definitely cuts out the drinks and the dinner," said Miss Murchison, unconvinced, but willing to be open-minded. "How about the water-bottle in the bedroom?"

"The devil!" cried Wimsey. "That's one up to you, Miss Murchison. We didn't think of that. The water-bottle—yes—a perfectly fruity idea. You recollect, Charles, that in the Bravo case it was suggested that a disgruntled servant had put tartar emetic in the water-bottle. Oh, Bunter—here you are! Next time you hold Hannah's hand, will you ask her whether Mr. Boyes drank any water from his bedroom water-bottle before dinner?"

"Pardon me, my lord, the possibility had already presented itself to my mind."

"It had?"

"Yes, my lord."

"Do you never overlook anything, Bunter?"

"I endeavour to give satisfaction, my lord."

"Well, then, don't talk like Jeeves. It irritates me. What about the water-bottle?"

"I was about to observe, my lord, when this lady arrived, that I had elicited a somewhat peculiar circumstance relating to the water-bottle."

"Now we're getting somewhere," said Parker, flattening out a new page of his note-book.

"I would not go so far as to say that, sir. Hannah informed me that she showed Mr. Boyes into his bedroom on his arrival and withdrew, as it was her place to do. She had scarcely reached the head of the staircase when Mr. Boyes put his head out of the door and recalled her. He then asked her to fill his water-bottle. She was considerably astonished at this request, since she had a perfect recollection of having previously filled it when she put the room in order."

"Could he have emptied it himself?" asked Parker, eagerly.

"Not into his interior, sir—there had not been time. Nor had the drinking-glass been utilised. Moreover, the bottle was not merely empty, but dry inside. Hannah apologised for the neglect, and immediately rinsed out the bottle and filled it from the tap."

"Curious," said Parker. "But it's quite likely she never filled it at all."

"Pardon me, sir. Hannah was so much surprised by the episode that she mentioned it to Mrs. Pettican, the cook, who said that she distinctly recollected seeing her fill the bottle that morning."

"Well, then," said Parker, "Urquhart or somebody must have emptied it and dried it out. Now, why? What would one naturally do if one found one's water-bottle empty?"

"Ring the bell," said Wimsey, promptly.

"Or shout for help," added Parker.

"Or," said Miss Murchison, "if one wasn't accustomed to be waited on, one might use the water from the bedroom jug."

"Ah! . . . of course, Boyes was used to a more or less Bohemian life."

"But surely," said Wimsey, "that's idiotically roundabout. It would be much simpler just to poison the water in the bottle. Why direct attention to the thing by making it more difficult? Besides, you couldn't count on the victim's using the jug-water—and, as a matter of fact, he didn't."

"And he *was* poisoned," said Miss Murchison, "so the poison wasn't either in the jug or the bottle."

"No—I'm afraid there's nothing to be got out of the jug and bottle department. Hollow, hollow, hollow all delight, Tennyson."

"All the same," said Parker, "that incident convinces me. It's too complete, somehow. Wimsey's right; it's not natural for a defence to be so perfect."

"My God," said Wimsey, "we have convinced Charles Parker. Nothing more is needed. He is more adamantine than any jury."

"Yes," said Parker, modestly, "but I'm more logical, I think. And I'm not being flustered by the Attorney-General. I should feel happier with a little evidence of a more objective kind."

"You would. You want some real arsenic. Well, Bunter, what about it?"

"The apparatus is quite ready, my lord."

"Very good. Let us go and see if we can give Mr. Parker what he wants. Lead and we follow."

In a small apartment usually devoted to Bunter's photographic work, and furnished with a sink, a bench, and a bunsen burner, stood the apparatus necessary for making a Marsh's test of arsenic. The distilled water was already bubbling gently in the flask, and Bunter lifted the little glass tube which lay across the flame of the burner.

"You will perceive, my lord," he observed, "that the apparatus is free from contamination."

"I see nothing at all," said Freddy.

"That, as Sherlock Holmes would say, is what you may expect to see when there is nothing there," said Wimsey, kindly. "Charles, you will pass the water and the flask and the tube, old Uncle Tom Cobley and all, as being arsenic-free."

"I will."

"Wilt thou love, cherish, and keep her, in sickness or in health—sorry! turned over two pages at once. Where's that powder? Miss Murchison, you identify this sealed envelope as being the one you brought from the office, complete with mysterious white powder from Mr. Urquhart's secret hoard?"

"I do."

"Kiss the Book. Thank you. Now then——"

"Wait a sec," said Parker, "you haven't tested the envelope separately."

"That's true. There's always a snag somewhere. I suppose, Miss Murchison, you haven't such a thing as another office envelope about you?"

Miss Murchison blushed, and fumbled in her handbag.

"Well—there's a little note I scribbled this afternoon to a friend——"

"*In* your employer's time, *on* your employer's paper," said Wimsey. "Oh, how right Diogenes was when he took his lantern to look for an honest typist! Never mind. Let's have it. Who wills the end, wills the means."

Miss Murchison extracted the envelope and freed it from the enclosure. Bunter, receiving it respectfully on a developing dish, cut it into small pieces, which he dropped into the flask. The water bubbled brightly, but the little tube still remained stainless from end to end.

"Does something begin to happen soon?" enquired Mr. Arbuthnot. "Because I feel this show's a bit lackin' in pep, what?"

"If you don't sit still I shall take you out," retorted Wimsey. "Carry on, Bunter. We'll pass the envelope."

Bunter accordingly opened the second envelope, and delicately dropped the white powder into the wide mouth of the flask. All five heads bent eagerly over the apparatus. And instantly, definitely, magically, a thin silver stain began to form in the tube where the flame impinged upon it. Second by second it spread and darkened to a deep brownish-black ring with a shining metallic centre.

"Oh, lovely, lovely," said Parker, with professional delight.

"Your lamp's smoking or something," said Freddy.

"Is that arsenic?" breathed Miss Murchison, gently.

"I hope so," said Wimsey, gently detaching the tube and holding it up to the light. "It's either arsenic or antimony."

"Allow me, my lord. The addition of a small quantity of solute chlorinated lime should decide the question beyond reach of cavil."

He performed this further test amid an anxious silence. The stain dissolved and vanished under the bleaching solution.

"Then it is arsenic," said Parker.

"Oh, yes," said Wimsey, nonchalantly, "of course it is arsenic. Didn't I tell you?" His voice wavered a little with suppressed triumph.

"Is that all?" enquired Freddy, disappointed.

"Isn't it enough?" said Miss Murchison.

"Not quite," said Parker, "but it's a long way towards it. It proves that Urquhart has arsenic in his possession, and by making an official enquiry in France, we can probably find out whether this packet was already in his possession last June. I notice, by the way, that it is ordinary white arsenious acid, without any mixture of charcoal or indigo, which agrees with what was found at the post-mortem. That's satisfactory, but it would be even more satisfactory if we could provide an opportunity for Urquhart to have administered it. So far, all we have done is to demonstrate clearly that he couldn't have given it to Boyes either before, during, or after dinner, during the period required for the symptoms to develop. I agree that an impossibility so bolstered up by testimony is suspicious in itself, but, to convince a jury, I should prefer something better than a *credo quia impossibilè*."

"Riddle-me-right, and riddle-me-ree," said Wimsey, imperturbably. "We've overlooked something, that's all. Probably something quite obvious. Give me the statutory dressing-gown and ounce of shag, and I will undertake to dispose of this little difficulty for you in a brace of shakes. In the meantime, you will no doubt take steps to secure, in an official and laborious manner, the evidence which our kind friends here have already so ably gathered in by unconventional methods, and will stand by to arrest the right man when the time comes?"

"I will," said Parker, "gladly. Apart from all personal considerations, I'd far rather see that oily-haired fellow in the dock than any woman, and if the Force has made a mistake, the sooner it's put right the better for all concerned."

Wimsey sat late that night in the black-and-primrose library, with the tall folios looking down at him. They represented the world's accumulated hoard of mellow wisdom and poetical beauty, to say nothing of thousands of pounds in cash. But all these counsellors sat mute upon their shelves. Strewn on tables and chairs lay the bright scarlet volumes of the *Notable British Trials*—Palmer, Pritchard, Maybrick, Seddon, Armstrong, Madeleine Smith—the great practitioners in arsenic—huddled together with the chief authorities on forensic medicine and toxicology.

The theatre-going crowds surged home in saloon and taxi, the lights shone over the empty width of Piccadilly, the heavy night-lorries rumbled slow and seldom over the black tarmac, the long night waned and the reluctant winter dawn struggled wanly over the piled roofs of London. Bunter, silent and anxious, sat in his kitchen, brewing coffee on the stove and reading the same page of the *British Journal of Photography* over and over again.

At half-past eight the library bell rang.

"My lord?"

"My bath, Bunter."

"Very good, my lord."

"And some coffee."

"Immediately, my lord."

"And put back all the books except these."

"Yes, my lord."

"I know now how it was done."

"Indeed, my lord? Permit me to offer my respectful congratulations."

"I've still got to prove it."

"A secondary consideration, my lord."

Wimsey yawned. When Bunter returned a minute or two later with the coffee, he was asleep.

Bunter put the books quietly away, and looked with some curiosity at the chosen few left open on the table. They were: *The Trial of Florence Maybrick*; Dixon Mann's *Forensic Medicine and Toxicology*; a book with a German title which Bunter could not read; and A. E. Housman's *A Shropshire Lad.*

Bunter studied these for a few moments, and then slapped his thigh softly.

"Why, of course!" he said under his breath. "Why, what a mutton-headed set of chumps we've all been!" He touched his master lightly on the shoulder.

"Your coffee, my lord."

CHAPTER XXI

"THEN YOU WON'T marry me?" said Lord Peter.

The prisoner shook her head.

"No. It wouldn't be fair to you. And besides——"

"Well?"

"I'm frightened of it. One couldn't get away. I'll live with you, if you like, but I won't marry you."

Her tone was so unutterably dreary that Wimsey could feel no enthusiasm for this handsome offer.

"But that sort of thing doesn't always work," he expostulated. "Dash it all, you ought to know—forgive my alluding to it and all that—but it's frightfully inconvenient, and one has just as many rows as if one was married."

"I know that. But you could cut loose any time you wanted to."

"But I shouldn't want to."

"Oh, yes, you would. You've got a family and traditions, you know. Cæsar's wife and that sort of thing."

"Blast Cæsar's wife! And as for the family traditions—they're on my side, for what they're worth. Anything a Wimsey does is right and Heaven help the person who gets in the way. We've even got a damned old family motto about it—'I hold by my Whimsy'—quite right too. I can't say that when I look in the glass I exactly suggest to myself the original Gerald de Wimsey, who bucked about on a cart-horse at the Siege of Acre, but I do jolly well intend to do what I like about marrying. Who's to stop me? They can't eat me. They can't even cut me, if it comes to that. Joke, unintentional, officers, for the use of."

Harriet laughed.

"No, I suppose they can't cut you. You wouldn't have to slink abroad with your impossible wife and live at obscure Continental watering-places like people in Victorian novels."

"Certainly not."

"People would forget I'd had a lover?"

"My dear child, they're forgetting that kind of thing every day. They're experts at it."

"And was supposed to have murdered him?"

"And were triumphantly acquitted of having murdered him, however greatly provoked."

"Well, I won't marry you. If people can forget all that, they can forget we're not married."

"Oh, yes, *they* could. I couldn't, that's all. We don't seem to be progressing very fast with this conversation. I take it the general idea of living with me does not hopelessly repel you?"

"But this is all so preposterous," protested the girl. "How can I say what I should or shouldn't do if I were free and certain of—surviving?"

"Why not? I can imagine what I should do even in the most unlikely circumstances, whereas this really is a dead cert, straight from the stables."

"I can't," said Harriet, beginning to wilt. "Do please stop asking me. I don't know. I can't think. I can't see beyond the—beyond the—beyond the next few weeks. I only want to get out of this and be left alone."

"All right," said Wimsey, "I won't worry you. Not fair. Abusing my privilege and so on. You can't say 'Pig' and sweep out, under the circs., so I won't offend again. As a matter of fact, I'll sweep out myself, having an appointment—with a manicurist. Nice little girl, but a trifle refained in her vowels. Cheerio!"

The manicurist, who had been discovered by the help of Chief Inspector Parker and his sleuths, was a kitten-faced child with an inviting manner and a shrewd eye. She made no bones about accepting her client's invitation to dine, and showed no surprise when he confidentially murmured that he had a little proposition to put before her. She put her plump elbows on the table, cocked her head at a coy angle, and prepared to sell her honour dear.

As the proposition unfolded itself, her manner underwent an alteration that was almost comical. Her eyes lost their rounded innocence, her very hair seemed to grow less fluffy, and her eyebrows puckered in genuine astonishment.

"Why, of course I could," she said finally, "but whatever do you want them for? Seems funny to me."

"Call it just a joke," said Wimsey.

"No." Her mouth hardened. "I wouldn't like it. It doesn't make sense, if you see what I mean. What I mean, it sounds a queer sort of joke and that kind of thing might get a girl into trouble. I say, it's not one of those, what do they call 'em?—there was a bit about it in Madame Crystal's column last week in *Susie's Snippets*—spells, you know, witchcraft—the occult, that sort of thing? I wouldn't like it if it was to do any harm to anybody."

"I'm not going to make a waxen image, if that's what you mean. Look here, are you the sort of girl who can keep a secret?"

"Oh, I don't talk. I never was one to let my tongue wag around. I'm not like ordinary girls."

"No, I thought you weren't. That's why I asked you to come out with me. Well, listen, and I'll tell you."

He leaned forward and talked. The little painted face upturned to his grew so absorbed and so excited that a bosom friend, dining at a table some way off, grew quite peevish with envy, making sure that darling Mabel was being offered a flat in Paris, a Daimler car, and a thousand-pound necklace, and quarrelled fatally with her own escort in consequence.

"So you see," said Wimsey, "it means a lot to me."

Darling Mabel gave an ecstatic sigh.

"Is that all true? You're not making it up? It's better than any of the talkies."

"Yes, but you mustn't say one word. You're the only person I've told. You won't give me away to him?"

"Him? He's a stingy pig. Catch me giving him anything. I'm on. I'll do it for you. It'll be a bit difficult, 'cause I'll have to use the scissors, which we don't do as a rule. But I'll manage. You trust me. They won't be big ones, you know. He comes in pretty often, but I'll give you all I get. And I'll fix Fred. He always has Fred. Fred'll do it if I ask him. What'll I do with them when I get them?"

Wimsey drew an envelope from his pocket.

"Sealed up inside this," he said, impressively, "there are two little pill-boxes. You mustn't take them out till you get the specimens, because they've been carefully prepared so as to be absolutely chemically clean, if you see what I mean. When you're ready, open the envelope, take out the pill-boxes, put the parings into one and the hair into the other, shut them up at once, put them into a clean envelope, and post them to this address. Get that?"

"Yes." She stretched out an eager hand.

"Good girl. And not a word."

"Not—one—word!" She made a gesture of exaggerated caution.

"When's your birthday?"

"Oh, I don't have one. I never grow up."

"Right; then I can send you an unbirthday present any day in the year. You'd look nice in mink, I think."

"Mink, I think," she mocked him. "Quite a poet, aren't you?"

"You inspire me," said Wimsey, politely.

CHAPTER XXII

"I HAVE COME round," said Mr. Urquhart, "in answer to your letter. I am greatly interested to hear that you have some fresh information about my unfortunate cousin's death. Of course, I shall be delighted to give you any assistance I can."

"Thank you," said Wimsey. "Do sit down. You have dined, of course? But you will have a cup of coffee. You prefer the Turkish variety, I fancy. My man brews it rather well."

Mr. Urquhart accepted the offer, and complimented Bunter on having achieved the right method of concocting that curiously syrupy brew, so offensive to the average Occidental.

Bunter thanked him gravely for his good opinion, and proffered a box of that equally nauseating mess called Turkish delight which not only gluts the palate and glues the teeth, but also smothers the consumer in a floury cloud of white sugar. Mr. Urquhart immediately plugged his mouth with a large lump of it, murmuring indistinctly that it was the genuine Eastern variety. Wimsey, with an austere smile, took a few sips of strong black coffee without sugar or milk, and poured himself out a glass of old brandy. Bunter retired, and Lord Peter, laying a note-book open upon his knee, glanced at the clock and began his narrative.

He recapitulated the circumstances of Philip Boyes' life and death at some length. Mr. Urquhart, yawning surreptitiously, ate, drank, and listened.

Wimsey, still with his eye on the clock, then embarked upon the story of Mrs. Wrayburn's will.

Mr. Urquhart, considerably astonished, set his coffee-cup aside, wiped his sticky fingers upon his handkerchief, and stared.

Presently he said:

"May I ask how you have obtained this very remarkable information?"

Wimsey waved his hand.

"The police," he said; "wonderful thing, police organisation. Surprisin' what they find out when they put their minds to it. You're not denying any of it, I presume?"

"I am listening," said Mr. Urquhart, grimly. "When you have finished this extraordinary statement, I may perhaps discover exactly what it is I have to deny."

"Oh, yes," said Wimsey. "I'll try to make that clear. I'm not a lawyer, of course, but I'm tryin' to be as lucid as I can."

He droned remorselessly on, and the hands of the clock went round.

"So far as I make it out," he said, when he had reviewed the whole question of motive, "it was very much to your interest to get rid of Mr. Philip Boyes. And indeed the fellow was, in my opinion, a pimple and a wart, and in your place I should have felt much the same about him."

"And is this the whole of your fantastic accusation?" enquired the solicitor.

"By no means. I am now coming to the point. 'Slow but sure' is the motto of yours faithfully. I notice that I have taken up seventy minutes of your valuable time, but, believe me, the hour has not been unprofitably spent."

"Allowing that all this preposterous story were true, which I most emphatically deny," observed Mr. Urquhart, "I should be greatly interested to know how you imagine that I administered the arsenic. Have you worked out something ingenious for that? Or am I supposed to have suborned my cook and parlourmaid to be my accomplices? A little rash of me, don't you think, and affording remarkable opportunities for blackmail?"

"So rash," said Wimsey, "that it is quite out of the question for a man so full of forethought as yourself. The sealing-up of that bottle of Burgundy, for example, argues a mind alive to possibilities—unusually so. In fact, the episode attracted my attention from the start."

"Indeed?"

"You ask me how and when you administered the poison. It was not before dinner, I think. The thoughtfulness shown in emptying the bedroom water-bottle—oh, no! that point was not missed—the care displayed in meeting your cousin before a witness and never being left alone with him—I think that rules out the period before dinner."

"I should think it might."

"The sherry," perused Wimsey, thoughtfully. "It was a new bottle, freshly decanted. The disappearance of the remains might be commented on. I fancy we can absolve the sherry."

Mr. Urquhart bowed ironically.

"The soup—it was shared by the cook and parlourmaid and they survived. I am inclined to pass the soup, and the same thing applies to the fish. It would be easy to poison a portion of fish, but it would involve the co-operation of Hannah Westlock, and that conflicts with my theory. A theory is a sacred thing to me, Mr. Urquhart—almost a what d'you call it—a dogma."

"An unsafe attitude of mind," remarked the lawyer, "but in the circumstances I will not quarrel with it."

"Besides," said Wimsey, "if the poison had been given in the soup or the fish, it might have started to work before Philip—I may call him so, I hope? —had left the house. We come to the casserole. Mrs. Pettican and Hannah Westlock can give the casserole a clean bill of health, I fancy. And, by the way, from the description it must have been most delicious. I speak as a man with some considerable experience in gastronomic matters, Mr. Urquhart."

"I am well aware of it," said Mr. Urquhart, politely.

"And now there remains only the omelette. A most admirable thing when well made and eaten—that is so important—eaten immediately. A charming idea to have the eggs and sugar brought to the table and prepared and cooked on the spot. By the way, I take it there was no omelette left over for the kitchen? No, no! One does not let a good thing like that go out half-eaten. Much better that the good cook should make a fine, fresh omelette for herself and her colleague. Nobody but yourself and Philip partook of the omelette, I am sure."

"Quite so," said Mr. Urquhart. "I need not trouble to deny it. But you will bear in mind that I did partake of it, without ill-effects. And, moreover, that my cousin made it himself."

"So he did. Four eggs, if I remember rightly, with sugar and jam from what I may call the common stock. No—there would be nothing wrong with the sugar or the jam. Er—I believe I am right in saying that one of the eggs was cracked when it came to table?"

"Possibly. I do not really remember."

"No? Well, you are not on oath. But Hannah Westlock remembers that when you brought the eggs in—you purchased them yourself, you know, Mr. Urquhart—you mentioned that one was cracked and particularly desired that it should be used for the omelette. In fact, you yourself laid it in the bowl for that purpose."

"What about it?" asked Mr. Urquhart, perhaps a trifle less easily than before.

"It is not very difficult to introduce powdered arsenic into a cracked egg," said Wimsey. "I have made the experiment myself with a small glass tube. Perhaps a small funnel would be even easier. Arsenic is a fairly heavy substance—seven or eight grains will go into a teaspoon. It collects at one end of the egg, and any traces on the exterior of the shell can be readily wiped off. Liquid arsenic could be poured in still more easily, of course, but for a particular reason I made my experiment with the ordinary white powder. It is fairly soluble."

Mr. Urquhart had taken a cigar from his case, and was making rather a business of lighting it.

"Do you suggest," he enquired, "that in the whisking together of four eggs, one particular poisoned egg was somehow kept miraculously separated from the rest and deposited with its load of arsenic at one end of the omelette only? Or that my cousin deliberately helped himself to the poisoned end and left the rest to me?"

"Not at all, not at all," said Wimsey. "I suggest merely that the arsenic was in the omelette and came there by way of the egg."

Mr. Urquhart threw his match into the fireplace.

"There seem to be some flaws in your theory, as well as in the egg."

"I haven't finished the theory yet. My next bit of it is built up from very trifling indications. Let me enumerate them. Your disinclination to drink at dinner, your complexion, a few nail-parings, a snipping or so from your very well-kept hair—I put these together, add a packet of white arsenic from the secret cupboard in your office, rub the hands a little—so—and produce—hemp, Mr. Urquhart, hemp."

He sketched the shape of a noose lightly in the air.

"I don't understand you," said the solicitor, hoarsely.

"Oh, *you* know," said Wimsey. "Hemp—what they make ropes of. Great stuff, hemp. Yes, well, about this arsenic. As you know, it's not good for people in a general way, but there are some people—those tiresome peasants in Styria one hears so much about—who are supposed to eat it for fun. It improves their wind, so they say, and clears their complexions, and makes their hair sleek, and they give it to their horses for the same reasons; bar the complexion, that is, because a horse hasn't much complexion, but you know what I mean. Then there was that horrid man Maybrick—he used to take it, or so they say. Anyhow, it's well known that some people do take it and manage to put away large dollops after a bit of practice—enough to kill any ordinary person. But you know all this."

"This is the first time I've heard of such a thing."

"Where *do* you expect to go to? Never mind. We'll pretend this is all new to you. Well, some fellow—I've forgotten his name,* but it's all in Dixon Mann—wondered how the dodge was worked, and he got going on some dogs and things and he dosed 'em and killed a lot of 'em I daresay, and in the end he found that whereas liquid arsenic was dealt with by the kidneys and was uncommonly bad for the system, solid arsenic could be given day by day, a little bigger dose each time, so that in time the doings—what an old lady I knew in Norfolk called 'the tubes'—got used to it and could push it along without taking any notice of it, so to speak. I read a book somewhere which said it was all done by leucocytes—those jolly little white corpuscles, don't you know—which sort of got round the stuff and bustled it along so that it couldn't do any harm. At all events, the point is that if you go on taking solid arsenic for a good long time—say a year or so—you establish a what-not, an immunity, and can take six or seven grains at a time without so much as a touch of indijaggers."

"Very interesting," said Mr. Urquhart.

"Apparently these beastly Styrian peasants do it that way, and they're very careful not to drink for two hours or thereabouts after taking it, for fear it should all get washed into the kidneys and turn poisonous on 'em. I'm not bein' very technical, I'm afraid, but that's the gist of it. Well, it occurred to me, don't you see, old horse, that if you'd had the bright idea to immunise yourself first, you could easily have shared a jolly old arsenical omelette with a friend. It would kill him and it wouldn't hurt you."

"I see."

The solicitor licked his lips.

"Well, as I say, you have a nice clear complexion—except that I notice the arsenic has pigmented the skin here and there (it does sometimes), and you've got the sleek hair and so on, and I noticed you were careful not to drink at dinner, and I said to myself, 'Peter, my bright lad, what about it?' And when

*Valetta

they found a packet of white arsenic in your cupboard—never mind how for the moment!—I said, "Hullo, hullo, how long has this been going on?' Your handy foreign chemist has told the police two years—is that right? About the time of the Megatherium crash that would be, wouldn't it? All right, don't tell me if you don't want to. Then we got hold of some bits of your hair and nails, and lo and behold! they were bung-full of arsenic. And we said, 'What-ho!' So that's why I asked you to come along and have a chat with me. I thought you might like to offer some sort of suggestion, don't you know."

"I can only suggest," said Urquhart, with a ghastly face but a strictly professional manner, "that you should be careful before you communicate this ludicrous theory to anybody. What you and the police—whom, frankly, I believe to be capable of anything—have been planting on my premises I do not know, but to give out that I am addicted to drug-taking habits is slander and criminal. It is quite true that I have for some time been taking a medicine which contains slight traces of arsenic—Dr. Grainger can furnish the prescription—and that may very likely have left a deposit in my skin and hair, but, further than that, there is no foundation for this monstrous accusation."

"None?"

"None."

"Then how is it," asked Wimsey, coolly, but with something menacing in his rigidly controlled voice, "how is it that you have this evening consumed, without apparent effect, a dose of arsenic sufficient to kill two or three ordinary people? That disgusting sweetmeat on which you have been gorging yourself in, I may say, a manner wholly unsuited to your age and position, is smothered in white arsenic. You ate it, God forgive you, an hour and a half ago. If arsenic can harm you, you should have been rolling about in agonies for the last hour."

"You devil!"

"Couldn't you try to get up a few symptoms?" said Wimsey, sarcastically. "Shall I bring you a basin? Or fetch the doctor? Does your throat burn? Is your inside convulsed with agony? It is rather late in the day, but with a little goodwill you could surely produce *some* display of feeling, even now."

"You are lying. You wouldn't dare to do such a thing! It would be murder."

"Not in this case, I fancy. But I am willing to wait and see."

Urquhart stared at him. Wimsey got out of his chair in a single swift movement and stood over him.

"I wouldn't use violence if I were you. Let the poisoner stick to his bottle. Besides, I am armed. Pardon the melodrama. Are you going to be sick or not?"

"You're mad."

"Don't say that. Come, man—pull yourself together. Have a shot at it. Shall I show you the bathroom?"

"I'm ill."

"Of course; but your tone is not convincing. Through the door, along the passage, and third on the left."

The lawyer stumbled out. Wimsey returned to the library and rang the bell.

"I think, Bunter, Mr. Parker may require some assistance in the bathroom."

"Very good, my lord."

Bunter, departed, and Wimsey waited. Presently there were sounds of a scuffle in the distance. A group appeared at the door—Urquhart, very white, his hair and clothes disordered, flanked by Parker and Bunter, who held him firmly by the arms.

"Was he sick?" asked Wimsey, with interest.

"No, he wasn't," said Parker, grimly, snapping the handcuffs on his prey. "He cursed you fluently for five minutes, then tried to get out of the window, saw it was a three-storey drop, charged in through the dressing-room door, and ran straight into me. Now don't struggle, my lad; you'll only hurt yourself."

"And he still doesn't know whether he's poisoned or not?"

"He doesn't seem to think he is. At any rate, he made no effort about it. His one idea was to hop it."

"That's feeble," said Wimsey; "if I wanted people to think I'd been poisoned I'd put up a better show than that."

"Stop talking, for God's sake," said the prisoner. "You've got me by a vile, damnable trick. Isn't that enough? You can shut up about it."

"Oh," said Parker, "we've got you, have we? Well, I warned you not to talk, and if you *will* do it, it's not my fault. By the way, Peter, I don't suppose you did actually poison him, did you? It doesn't seem to have hurt him, but it'll affect the doctor's report."

"No, I didn't, as a matter of fact," said Wimsey. "I only wanted to see how he'd react to the suggestion. Well, cheerio! I can leave it to you now."

"We'll look after him," said Parker. "But you might let Bunter ring up a taxi."

When the prisoner and his escort had departed, Wimsey turned thoughtfully to Bunter, glass in hand.

"*Mithridates he died old*, says the poet. But I doubt it, Bunter. In this case I very much doubt it."

CHAPTER XXIII

THERE WERE GOLDEN chrysanthemums on the judge's bench; they looked like burning banners.

The prisoner, too, had a look in her eyes that was a challenge to the crowded court, as the clerk read the indictment. The judge, a plump, elderly man with an eighteenth-century face, looked expectantly at the Attorney-General.

"My lord, I am instructed that the Crown offers no evidence against this prisoner."

The gasp that went round the room sounded like the rustle of trees in a rising wind.

"Do I understand that the charge against the prisoner is withdrawn?"

"Those are my instructions, my lord."

"In that case," said the judge, impassively, turning to the jury, "there is nothing left for you but to return a verdict of 'Not Guilty'. Usher, keep those people quiet in the gallery."

"One moment, my lord." Sir Impey Biggs rose up, large and majestic.

"On my client's behalf—on Miss Vane's behalf, my lord, I beg your lordship's indulgence for a few words. A charge has been brought against her, my lord, the very awful charge of murder, and I should like it to be made clear, my lord, that my client leaves this court without a stain upon her character. As I am informed, my lord, this is not a case of the charge being withdrawn in default of evidence. I understand, my lord, that further information has came to the police which definitely proves the entire innocence of my client. I also understand, my lord, that a further arrest has been made and that an enquiry will follow, my lord, in due course. My lord, this lady must go forth into the world acquitted, not only at this bar, but at the bar of public opinion. Any ambiguity would be intolerable, and I am sure, my lord, that I have the support of the learned Attorney-General for what I say."

"By all means," said the Attorney. "I am instructed to say, my lord, that in withdrawing the charge against the prisoner, the Crown proceeds from complete conviction of her absolute innocence."

"I am very glad to hear it," said the judge. "Prisoner at the bar, the Crown, by unreservedly withdrawing this dreadful charge against you, has demonstrated your innocence in the clearest possible way. After this, nobody will be able to suppose that the slightest imputation rests upon you, and I most heartily congratulate you on this very satisfactory ending to your long ordeal. Now, please—I sympathise very much with the people who are cheering, but this is not a theatre or a football match, and if they are not quiet, they will have to be put out. Members of the jury, do you find the prisoner 'Guilty' or 'Not Guilty'?"

"Not guilty, my lord."

"Very good. The prisoner is discharged without a stain upon her character. Next case."

So ended, sensational to the last, one of the most sensational murder trials of the century.

Harriet Vane, a free woman, found Eiluned Price and Sylvia Marriott waiting for her as she descended the stairs.

"Darling!" said Sylvia.

"Three loud cheers!" said Eiluned.

Harriet greeted them a little vaguely.

"Where is Lord Peter Wimsey?" she enquired. "I must thank him."

"You won't," said Eiluned, bluntly. "I saw him drive off the moment the verdict was given."

"Oh!" said Miss Vane.

"He'll come and see you," said Sylvia.

"No, he won't," said Eiluned.

"Why not?" said Sylvia.

"Too decent," said Eiluned.

"I'm afraid you're right," said Harriet.

"I like that young man," said Eiluned. "You needn't grin. I do like him. He's not going to do the King Cophetua stunt, and I take off my hat to him. If you want him, you'll have to send for him."

"I won't do that," said Harriet.

"Oh, yes, you will," said Sylvia. "I was right about who did the murder, and I'm going to be right about this."

Lord Peter Wimsey went down to Duke's Denver that same evening. He found the family in a state of perturbation, all except the Dowager, who sat placidly making a rug in the midst of the uproar.

"Look here, Peter," said the Duke, "you're the only person with any influence over Mary. You've got to do something. She wants to marry your policeman friend."

"I know," said Wimsey. "Why shouldn't she?"

"It's ridiculous," said the Duke.

"Not at all," said Lord Peter. "Charles is one of the best."

"Very likely," said the Duke, "but Mary can't marry a policeman."

"Now, look here," said Wimsey, tucking his sister's arm in his, "you leave Polly alone. Charles made a bit of a mistake at the beginning of this murder case, but he doesn't make many, and one of these days he'll be a big man, with a title, I shouldn't wonder, and everything handsome about him. If you want to have a row with somebody, have it with me."

"My God!" said the Duke, "you're not going to marry a policewoman?"

"Not quite," said Wimsey. "I intend to marry the prisoner."

"What?" said the Duke. "Good Lord, what, what?"

"If she'll have me," said Lord Peter Wimsey.

MURDER MUST ADVERTISE

AUTHOR'S NOTE

I do not suppose that there is a more harmless and law-abiding set of people in the world than the Advertising Experts of Great Britain. The idea that any crime could possibly be perpetrated on Advertising premises is one that could only occur to the ill-regulated fancy of a detective novelist, trained to fasten the guilt upon the Most Unlikely Person. If, in the course of this fantasy, I have unintentionally used a name or slogan suggestive of any existing person, firm or commodity, it is by sheer accident, and is not intended to cast the slightest reflection upon any actual commodity, firm or person.

CONTENTS

CHAPTER I

Death Comes to Pym's Publicity

"AND BY THE way," said Mr. Hankin, arresting Miss Rossiter as she rose to go, "there is a new copy-writer coming in to-day."

"Oh, yes, Mr. Hankin?"

"His name is Bredon. I can't tell you much about him; Mr. Pym engaged him himself; but you will see that he is looked after."

"Yes, Mr. Hankin."

"He will have Mr. Dean's room."

"Yes, Mr. Hankin."

"I should think Mr. Ingleby could take him in hand and show him what to do. You might send Mr. Ingleby along if he can spare me a moment."

"Yes, Mr. Hankin."

"That's all. And, oh, yes! Ask Mr. Smayle to let me have the Dairyfields guard-book."

"Yes, Mr. Hankin."

Miss Rossiter tucked her note-book under her arm, closed the glass-panelled door noiselessly after her and tripped smartly down the corridor. Peeping through another glass-panelled door, she observed Mr. Ingleby seated on a revolving chair with his feet on the cold radiator, and talking with great animation to a young woman in green, perched on the corner of the writing-table.

"Excuse me," said Miss Rossiter, with perfunctory civility, "but Mr. Hankin says can you spare him a moment, Mr. Ingleby?"

"If it's Tom-Boy Toffee," replied Mr. Ingleby defensively, "it's being typed. Here! you'd better take these two bits along and make it so. That will lend an air of verisimilitude to an otherwise——"

"It isn't Tom-Boy. It's a new copy-writer."

"What, already?" exclaimed the young woman. "Before those shoes were old! Why, they only buried little Dean on Friday."

"Part of the modern system of push and go," said Mr. Ingleby. "All very distressing in an old-fashioned, gentlemanly firm. Suppose I've got to put this blighter through his paces. Why am I always left with the baby?"

"Oh, rot!" said the young woman, "you've only got to warn him not to use the directors' lav., and not to tumble down the iron staircase."

"You are the most callous woman, Miss Meteyard. Well, as long as they don't put the fellow in with me——"

"It's all right, Mr. Ingleby. He's having Mr. Dean's room."

"Oh! What's he like?"

"Mr. Hankin said he didn't know, Mr. Pym took him on."

"Oh, gosh! friend of the management," Mr. Ingleby groaned.

"Then I think I've seen him," said Miss Meteyard. "Tow-coloured, supercilious-looking blighter. I ran into him coming out of Pymmie's room yesterday. Horn-rims. Cross between Ralph Lynn and Bertie Wooster."

"Death, where is thy sting? Well, I suppose I'd better push off and see about it."

Mr. Ingleby lowered his feet from the radiator, prised up his slow length from the revolving chair, and prowled unhappily away.

"Oh, well, it makes a little excitement," said Miss Meteyard.

"Oh, don't you think we've had rather too much of that lately? By the way, could I have your subscription for the wreath? You told me to remind you."

"Yes, rather. What is it? A bob? Here's half-a-crown, and you'd better take the sweep-money out of it as well."

"Thanks awfully, Miss Meteyard. I do hope you get a horse this time."

"High time I did. I've been five years in this beastly office and never even been placed. I believe you wangle the draw."

"Indeed we don't, Miss Meteyard, or we shouldn't let all the horses go to those people in the Printing. Wouldn't you like to come and draw for us this time? Miss Parton's just typing out the names."

"All right." Miss Meteyard scrambled down leggily and followed Miss Rossiter to the typist's room.

This was a small, inconvenient cubicle, crowded at the moment to bursting point. A plump girl in glasses, with head tilted back and brows twisted to keep the smoke of a cigarette out of her eyes, was rattling off the names of Derby runners on her typewriter, assisted by a bosom friend who dictated the list from the columns of the *Morning Star*. A languid youth in shirt-sleeves was cutting the names of sweep subscribers from a typed sheet, and twisting the papers into secretive little screws. A thin, eager young man, squatting on an upturned waste-paper basket, was turning over the flimsies in Miss Rossiter's tray and making sarcastic comments upon the copy to a bulky, dark youth in spectacles, immersed in a novel by P. G. Wodehouse and filching biscuits from a large tin. Draped against the door-posts and blocking the entrance to all comers, a girl and another young man, who seemed to be visitors from another department, were smoking gaspers and discussing lawn-tennis.

"Hullo, angels" said Miss Rossiter, brightly. "Miss Meteyard's going to draw for us. And there's a new copy-writer coming."

The bulky young man glanced up to say "Poor devil!" and retreated again into his book.

"Bob for the wreath and sixpence for the sweep," went on Miss Rossiter, scrabbling in a tin cash-box. "Has anybody got two shillings for a florin? Where's your list, Parton? Scratch Miss Meteyard off, will you? Have I had your money, Mr. Garrett?"

"No money till Saturday," said the Wodehouse-reader.

"Hark at him!" cried Miss Parton, indignantly. "You'd think we were millionaires, the way we have to finance this department."

"Pick me a winner," replied Mr. Garrett, "and you can knock it off the prize-money. Hasn't that coffee come yet?"

"Have a look, Mr. Jones," suggested Miss Parton, addressing the gentleman on the door-post, "and see if you can see the boy. Just check these runners over with me, duckie. Meteor Bright, Tooralooral, Pheidippides II, Roundabout——"

"Roundabout's scratched," said Mr. Jones. "Here's the boy just coming."

"Scratched? No, when? What a shame! I put him down in the *Morning Star* competition. Who says so?"

"*Evening Banner* lunch special. Slip in the stable."

"Damn!" said Miss Rossiter, briefly. "There goes my thousand quid! Oh, well, that's life. Thank you, sonnie. Put it on the table. Did you remember the cucumber? Good boy. How much? One-and-five? Lend me a penny, Parton. There you are. Mind out a minute, Mr. Willis, do you mind? I want a pencil and rubber for the new bloke."

"What's his name?"

"Bredon."

"Where's he come from?"

"Hankie doesn't know. But Miss Meteyard's seen him. She says he's like Bertie Wooster in horn-rims."

"Older though," said Miss Meteyard. "A well-preserved forty."

"Oh, gosh! When's he coming?"

"'Smorning. If I'd been him I'd have put it off till tomorrow and gone to the Derby. Oh, here's Mr. Ingleby. He'll know. Coffee, Mr. Ingleby? Have you heard anything?"

"Star of Asia, Twinkletoes, Sainte-Nitouche, Duke Humphrey . . ."

"Forty-two," said Mr. Ingleby. "No sugar, thanks. Never been in advertising before. *Balliol*."

"Golly!" said Miss Meteyard.

"As you say. If there is one thing more repulsive than another it is Balliolity," agreed Mr. Ingleby, who was a Trinity man.

> "*Bredon went to Balliol*
> *And sat at the feet of Gamaliel*"

chanted Mr. Garrett, closing his book.

> "*And just as he ought*
> *He cared for nought,*"

added Miss Meteyard. "I defy you to find another rhyme for Balliol."

"Flittermouse, Tom Pinch, Fly-by-Night . . ."

> "*And his language was sesquipedalial.*"

"It isn't sesquipedalial, it's sesquipedalian."

"Bother!"

"Twist those papers up tight, duckie. Put them in the lid of the biscuit-tin. Damn! that's Mr. Armstrong's buzzer. Stick a saucer over my coffee. Where's my note-book?"

". . . two double-faults running, so I said . . ."

". . . I can't find the carbon of that Magnolia whole-treble . . ."

". . . started at fifty to one . . ."

"Who's bagged my scissors?"

"Excuse me, Mr. Armstrong wants his Nutrax carbons . . ."

". . . and shake 'em up well . . ."

". . . hail you all, impale you all, jail you all . . ."

"Mr. Ingleby, can you spare me a moment?"

At Mr. Hankin's mildly sarcastic accents, the scene dislimned as by magic. The door-post drapers and Miss Parton's bosom friend melted out into the passage, Mr. Willis, rising hurriedly with the tray of carbons in his hand, picked a paper out at random and frowned furiously at it, Miss Parton's cigarette dropped unostentatiously to the floor, Mr. Garrett, unable to get rid of his coffee-cup, smiled vaguely and tried to look as though he had picked it up by accident and didn't know it was there, Miss Meteyard, with great presence of mind, put the sweep counterfoils on a chair and sat on them, Miss Rossiter, clutching Mr. Armstrong's carbons in her hand, was able to look businesslike, and did so. Mr. Ingleby alone, disdaining pretence, set down his cup with a slightly impudent smile and advanced to obey his chief's command.

"This," said Mr. Hankin, tactfully blind to all evidences of disturbance, "is Mr. Bredon. You will—er—show him what he has to do. I have had the Dairyfields guard-books sent along to his room. You might start him on margarine. Er—I don't think Mr. Ingleby was up in your time, Mr. Bredon—he was at Trinity. Your Trinity, I mean, not ours." (Mr. Hankin was a Cambridge man.)

Mr. Bredon extended a well-kept hand.

"How do you do?"

"How do you do?" echoed Mr. Ingleby. They gazed at one another with the faint resentment of two cats at their first meeting. Mr. Hankin smiled kindly at them both.

"And when you've produced some ideas on margarine, Mr. Bredon, bring them along to my room and we'll go over them."

"Right-ho!" said Mr. Bredon, simply.

Mr. Hankin smiled again and padded gently away.

"Well, you'd better know everybody," said Mr. Ingleby, rapidly. "Miss Rossiter and Miss Parton are our guardian angels—type our copy, correct our grammar, provide us with pencils and paper and feed us on coffee and cake. Miss Parton is the blonde and Miss Rossiter the brunette. Gentlemen prefer blondes but personally I find them both equally seraphic."

Mr. Bredon bowed.

"Miss Meteyard—of Somerville. One of the brighter ornaments of our department. She makes the vulgarest limericks ever recited within these chaste walls."

"Then we shall be friends," said Mr. Bredon cordially.

"Mr. Willis on your right, Mr. Garrett on your left—both comrades in affliction. That is the whole department, except Mr. Hankin and Mr. Armstrong who are directors, and Mr. Copley, who is a man of weight and experience and does not come and frivol in the typists' room. He goes out for his elevenses, and assumes seniority though he hath it not."

Mr. Bredon grasped the hands extended to him and murmured politely.

"Would you like to be in on the Derby sweep?" inquired Miss Rossiter, with an eye to the cash-box. "You're just in time for the draw."

"Oh, rather," said Mr. Bredon. "How much?"

"Sixpence."

"Oh, yes, rather. I mean, it's jolly good of you. Of course, absolutely—must be in on the jolly old sweep, what?"

"That brings the first prize up to a pound precisely," said Miss Rossiter, with a grateful sigh. "I was afraid I should have to take two tickets myself. Type Mr. Bredon's for him, Parton. B,R,E,D,O,N—like summer-time on Bredon?"

"That's right."

Miss Parton obligingly typed the name and added another blank ticket to the collection in the biscuit-box.

"Well, I suppose I'd better take you along to your dog-kennel," said Mr. Ingleby, with gloom.

"Right-ho!" said Mr. Bredon. "Oh, rather. Yes."

"We're all along this corridor," added Mr. Ingleby, leading the way. "You'll find your way about in time. That's Garrett's room and that's Willis's, and this is yours, between Miss Meteyard and me. That iron staircase opposite me goes down to the floor below; mostly group managers and conference rooms. Don't fall down it, by the way. The man whose room you've got tumbled down it last week and killed himself."

"No, did he?" said Mr. Bredon, startled.

"Bust his neck and cracked his skull," said Mr. Ingleby. "On one of those knobs."

"Why do they put knobs on staircases?" expostulated Mr. Bredon. "Cracking fellows' skulls for them? It's not right."

"No, it isn't," said Miss Rossiter, arriving with her hands full of scribbling-blocks and blotting-paper. "They're supposed to prevent the boys from sliding down the handrail, but it's the stairs themselves that are so—oh, I say, push on. There's Mr. Armstrong coming up. They don't like too much being said about the iron staircase."

"Well, here you are," said Mr. Ingleby, adopting this advice. "Much the same as the rest, except that the radiator doesn't work very well. Still, that won't worry you just at present. This was Dean's room."

"Chap who fell downstairs?"

"Yes."

Mr. Bredon gazed round the small apartment, which contained a table, two chairs, a rickety desk and a bookshelf, and said:

"Oh!"

"It *was* awful," said Miss Rossiter.

"It must have been," agreed Mr. Bredon, fervently.

"Mr. Armstrong was just giving me dictation when we heard the most *frightful* crash. He said, 'Good God, what's that?' I thought it must be one of the boys, because one of them fell down last year carrying an Elliot-Fisher typewriter and it sounded exactly like it, only worse. And I said, 'I think one of the boys must have fallen downstairs, Mr. Armstrong,' and he said, 'Careless little devil,' and went on dictating and my hand was so shaky I could hardly make my outlines and then Mr. Ingleby ran past and Mr. Daniels' door opened and then we heard the most terrific shriek, and Mr. Armstrong said, 'Better go and see what's happened,' so I went out and looked down and I couldn't see anything because there was such a bunch of people standing round and then Mr. Ingleby came tearing up, with *such* a look on his face—you were as white as a sheet, Mr. Ingleby, you really were."

"Possibly," said Mr. Ingleby, a little put out. "Three years in this soul-searing profession have not yet robbed me of all human feeling. But that will come in time."

"Mr. Ingleby said, 'He's killed himself!' And I said, 'Who?' and he said 'Mr. Dean,' and I said, 'You don't mean that,' and he said, 'I'm afraid so,' and I went back to Mr. Armstrong and said, 'Mr. Dean's killed himself,' and he said, 'What do you mean, killed himself?' and then Mr. Ingleby came in and Mr. Armstrong gave one look at him and went out and I went down by the other staircase and saw them carrying Mr. Dean along to the board-room and his head was all hanging sideways."

"Does this kind of thing happen often?" inquired Mr. Bredon.

"Not with such catastrophic results," replied Mr. Ingleby, "but that staircase is definitely a death-trap."

"I fell down it myself one day," said Miss Rossiter, "and tore the heels off both my shoes. It was awfully awkward, because I hadn't another pair in the place and——"

"I've drawn a horse, darlings!" announced Miss Meteyard, arriving without ceremony. "No luck for you, Mr. Bredon, I'm afraid."

"I always was unlucky."

"You'll feel unluckier still after a day with Dairyfields Margarine," said Mr. Ingleby, gloomily. "Nothing for me, I suppose?"

"Nothing, I'm afraid. Of course Miss Rawlings has drawn the favourite—she always does."

"I hope it breaks its beastly leg," said Mr. Ingleby. "Come in, Tallboy, come in. Do you want me? Don't mind butting in on Mr. Bredon. He will soon become used to the idea that his room is a public place within the meaning of the act. This is Mr. Tallboy, group-manager for Nutrax and a few other wearisome commodities. Mr. Bredon, our new copy-writer."

"How do you do?" said Mr. Tallboy, briefly. "Look here, about this Nutrax 11-inch double. Can you possibly cut out about thirty words?"

"No, I can't," said Mr. Ingleby. "I've cut it to the bone already."

"Well, I'm afraid you'll have to. There isn't room for all this guff with a two-line sub-head."

"There's plenty of room for it."

"No, there isn't. We've got to get in the panel about the Fifty-six Free Chiming Clocks."

"Damn the clocks and the panel! How do they expect to display all that in a half-double?"

"Dunno, but they do. Look here, can't we take out this bit about 'When your nerves begin to play tricks on you,' and start off with 'Nerves need Nutrax'?"

"Armstrong liked that bit about playing tricks. Human appeal and all that. No, take out that rot about the patent spring-cap bottle."

"They won't stand for dropping that," said Miss Meteyard. "That's their pet invention."

"Do they think people buy nerve-food for the sake of the bottle? Oh, well! I can't do it straight away. Hand it over."

"The printer wants it by two o'clock," said Mr. Tallboy, dubiously.

Mr. Ingleby damned the printer, seized the proof and began cutting the copy, uttering offensive ejaculations between his teeth.

"Of all the beastly days of the week," he observed, "Tuesday is the foulest. There's no peace till we get this damned 11-inch double of our chests. There! I've cut out twenty-two words, and you'll have to make it do. You can take that 'with' up into the line above and save a whole line, and that gives you the other eight words."

"All right, I'll try," agreed Mr. Tallboy. "Anything for a quiet life. It'll look a bit tight, though."

"Wish *I* was tight," said Mr. Ingleby. "Take it away, for God's sake, before I murder anybody."

"I'm going, I'm going," said Mr. Tallboy, and vanished hastily. Miss Rossiter had departed during the controversy, and Miss Meteyard now took herself out of the way, remarking, "If Pheidippides wins, you shall have a cake for tea."

"Now we'd better start *you* off," observed Mr. Ingleby. "Here's the guard-book. You'd better have a look through it to see the kind of thing, and then think up some headlines. Your story is, of course, that Dairyfields' 'Green Pastures' Margarine is everything that the best butter ought to be and only costs ninepence a pound. And they like a cow in the picture."

"Why? Is it made of cow-fat?"

"Well, I daresay it is, but you mustn't say so. People wouldn't like the idea. The picture of the cow suggests the taste of butter, that's all. And the name—Green Pastures—suggests cows, you see."

"It suggests niggers to me," said Mr. Bredon. "The play, you know."

"You mustn't put niggers in the copy," retorted Mr. Ingleby. "Nor, of course, religion. Keep Psalm 23 out of it. Blasphemous."

"I see. Just something about 'Better than Butter and half the price.' Simple appeal to the pocket."

"Yes, but you mustn't knock butter. They sell butter as well."

"Oh!"

"You can say it's as good as butter."

"But in that case," objected Mr. Bredon, "what does one find to say in favour of butter? I mean, if the other stuff's as good and doesn't cost so much, what's the argument for buying butter?"

"You don't need an argument for buying butter. It's a natural, human instinct."

"Oh, I see."

"Anyway, don't bother about butter. Just concentrate on Green Pastures Margarine. When you've got a bit done, you take it along and get it typed, and then you buzz off to Mr. Hankin with the result. See? Are you all right now?"

"Yes, thanks," said Mr. Bredon, looking thoroughly bewildered.

"And I'll push along about 1 o'clock and show you the decentest place for lunch."

"Thanks frightfully."

"Well, cheerio!" Mr. Ingleby returned to his own room.

"*He* won't stay the course," he said to himself. "Goes to a damned good tailor, though. I wonder——"

He shrugged his shoulders and sat down to concoct a small, high-class folder about Slider's Steel Office Tables.

Mr. Bredon, left alone, did not immediately attack the subject of margarine. Like a cat, which, in his soft-footed inquisitiveness, he rather resembled, he proceeded to make himself acquainted with his new home. There was not very much to see in it. He opened the drawer in his writing-table and found a notched and inky ruler, some bitten-looking pieces of india-rubber, a number of bright thoughts on tea and margarine scribbled on scraps of paper, and a broken fountain-pen. The book-case contained a dictionary, a repellent volume entitled *Directory of Directors*, a novel by Edgar Wallace, a pleasingly got-up booklet called *All about Cocoa, Alice in Wonderland*, Bartlett's *Familiar Quotations*, the *Globe* edition of the *Works of Wm. Shakespeare*, and five odd numbers of the *Children's Encylopaedia.* The interior of the sloping desk offered more scope for inquiry; it was filled with ancient and dusty papers, including a Government Report on the Preservatives in Food (Restrictions) Act of 1926, a quantity of rather (in every sense) rude sketches by an amateur hand, a bundle of pulls of advertisements for Dairyfields commodities, some private correspondence and some old bills. Mr. Bredon, dusting fastidious fingers, turned from this receptacle, inventoried a hook and a coat-hanger on the wall and a battered paper-file in a corner, and sat down in the revolving-chair before the table. Here, after a brief glance at a pastepot, a pair of scissors, a new pencil and a blotting-pad, two scribbling-blocks and a grubby cardboard box-lid full of oddments, he propped up the Dairyfields guard-book before him, and fell to studying his predecessor's masterpieces on the subject of Green Pastures Margarine.

An hour later, Mr. Hankin pushed open the door and looked in upon him. "How are you getting on?" he inquired kindly.

Mr. Bredon sprang to his feet.

"Not frightfully well, I'm afraid. I don't seem to get the atmosphere altogether, if you follow me."

"It will come," said Mr. Hankin. He was a helpfully-minded man, who believed that new copy-writers throve on encouragement. "Let me see what you are doing. You are starting with the headlines? Quite right. The headline is more than half the battle. IF YOU WERE A COW—no, no, I'm afraid we mustn't call the customer a cow. Besides, we had practically the same headline in—let me see—about 1923, I think. Mr. Wardle put it up, you'll find it in the last guard-book but three. It went 'IF YOU KEPT A COW IN THE KITCHEN you could get no better bread-spread than G.P. Margarine'—and so on. That was a good one. Caught the eye, made a good picture, and told the whole story in a sentence."

Mr. Bredon bowed his head, as one who hears the Law and the Prophets. The copy-chief ran a thoughtful pencil over the scribbled list of headlines, and ticked one of them.

"I like that.

BIGGER AND BUTTER
VALUE FOR MONEY

That has the right feel about it. You might write copy for that, and perhaps for this one,

YOU'D BE READY TO BET
IT WAS BUTTER—

though I'm not quite sure about it. These Dairyfields people are rather strait-laced about betting."

"Oh, are they? What a pity! I'd done several about that. 'HAVE A BIT ON—' Don't you like that one?"

Mr. Hankin shook his head regretfully.

"I'm afraid that's too direct. Encouraging the working classes to waste their money."

"But they all do it—why, all these women like a little flutter."

"I know, I know. But I'm sure the client wouldn't stand for it. You'll soon find the biggest obstacle to good advertising is the client. They all have their fads. That headline would do for Darling's, but it won't do for Dairyfields. We did very well with a sporting headline in '26—'PUT YOUR SHIRT ON Darling's Non-collapsible Towel-Horse'—sold 80,000 in Ascot week. Though that was partly accident, because we mentioned a real horse in the copy and it came in at 50 to 1, and all the women who'd won money on it rushed out and bought Non-collapsible Towel-Horses out of sheer gratitude. The public's very odd."

"Yes," said Mr. Bredon. "They must be. There seems to be more in advertising than, so to speak, meets the eye."

"There is," said Mr. Hankin, a little grimly. "Well, get some copy written and bring it along to me. You know where to find my room?"

"Oh, yes—at the end of the corridor, near the iron staircase."

"No, no, that's Mr. Armstrong. At the other end of the corridor, near the other staircase—not the iron staircase. By the way——"

"Yes?"

"Oh, nothing," said Mr. Hankin, vaguely. "That is to say—no, nothing."

Mr. Bredon gazed after his retreating figure, and shook his fair head in a meditative manner. Then, applying himself to his task, he wrote out, rather quickly, a couple of paragraphs in praise of margarine and wandered out with them. Turning to the right, he paused opposite the door of Ingleby's room and stared irresolutely at the iron staircase. As he stood there, the glass door of a room on the opposite side of the corridor opened and a middle-aged man shot out. Seeing Bredon, he paused in his rush for the stair-head and inquired:

"Do you want to know how to get anywhere or anything?"

"Oh! thanks awfully. No—I mean, yes. I'm the new copy-writer. I'm looking for the typists' room."

"Other end of the passage."

"Oh, I see, thanks frightfully. This place is rather confusing. Where does this staircase go to?"

"Down to a whole lot of departments—mostly group-managers' rooms and board-rooms and Mr. Pym's room and several of the Directors' rooms and the Printing."

"Oh, I see. Thanks ever so. Where does one wash?"

"That's downstairs too. I'll show you if you like."

"Oh, thanks—thanks most awfully."

The other man plunged down the steep and rattling spiral as though released by a spring. Bredon followed more gingerly.

"A bit precipitous, isn't it?"

"Yes, it is. You'd better be careful. One fellow out of your department smashed himself up here the other day."

"No, really?"

"Broke his neck. Dead when we picked him up."

"No, did he? was he? How on earth did he come to do that? Couldn't he see where he was going?"

"Slipped, I expect. Must have been going too fast. There's nothing really wrong with the staircase. I've never had an accident. It's very well-lit."

"Well-lit?" Mr. Bredon gaped vaguely at the skylight and up and down the passage, surrounded, like the one on the floor above, with glass partitions. "Oh, yes, to be sure. It's very well-lit. Of course he must have slipped. Dashed easy thing to slip on a staircase. Did he have nails in his shoes?"

"I don't know. I wasn't noticing his shoes. I was thinking about picking up the pieces."

"Did you pick him up?"

"Well, I heard the racket when he went down, and rushed out and got there one of the first. My name's Daniels, by the way."

"Oh, is it? Daniels, oh, yes. But didn't it come out at the inquest about his shoes?"

"I don't remember anything about it."

"Oh! then I suppose he didn't have nails. I mean, if he had, somebody would have mentioned it. I mean, it would be a sort of excuse, wouldn't it?"

"Excuse for whom?" demanded Daniels.

"For the firm; I mean, when people put up staircases and other people come tumbling down them, the insurance people generally want to know why. At least, I'm told so. I've never fallen down any staircases myself—touch wood."

"You'd better not try," retorted Daniels, evading the question of insurance. "You'll find the wash-place through that door and down the passage on the left."

"Oh, thanks frightfully."

"Not at all."

Mr. Daniels darted away into a room full of desks, leaving Mr. Bredon to entangle himself in a heavy swing door.

In the lavatory, Bredon encountered Ingleby.

"Oh!" said the latter. "You've found your way. I was told off to show you, but I forgot."

"Mr. Daniels showed me. Who's he?"

"Daniels? He's a group-manager. Looks after a bunch of clients—Sliders and Harrogate Bros. and a few more. Sees to the lay-outs and sends the stereos down to the papers and all that. Not a bad chap."

"He seems a bit touchy about the iron staircase. I mean, he was quite matey till I suggested that the insurance people would want to look into that fellow's accident—and then he kind of froze on me."

"He's been a long time in the firm and doesn't like any nasturtiums cast at it. Certainly not by a new bloke. As a matter of fact, it's better not to throw one's weight about here till one's been ten years or so in the place. It's not encouraged."

"Oh? Oh, thanks awfully for telling me."

"This place is run like a Government office," went on Ingleby. "Hustle's not wanted and initiative and curiosity are politely shown the door."

"That's right," put in a pugnacious-looking red-headed man, who was scrubbing his fingers with pumice-stone as though he meant to take the skin off. "I asked them for £50 for a new lens—and what was the answer? Economy, please, in all departments—the Whitehall touch, eh?—and yet they pay you fellows to write more-you-spend-more-you-save copy! However, I shan't be here long, that's one comfort."

"This is Mr. Prout, our photographer," said Ingleby. "He has been on the point of leaving us for the last five years, but when it comes to the point he realises that we couldn't do without him and yields to our tears and entreaties."

"Tcha!" said Mr. Prout.

"The management think Mr. Prout so precious," went on Ingleby, "that they have set his feet in a large room——"

"That you couldn't swing a kitten in," said Mr. Prout, "and no ventilation. Murder, that's what they do here. Black holes of Calcutta and staircases that break people's heads open. What we want in this country is a Mussolini to organise trade conditions. But what's the good of talking? All the same, one of these days, you'll see."

"Mr. Prout is our tame firebrand," observed Ingleby, indulgently. "You coming up, Bredon?"

"Yes. I've got to take this stuff to be typed."

"Right-ho! Here you are. Round this way and up this staircase by the lift, through the Dispatching and here you are—right opposite the home of British Beauty. Children, here's Mr. Bredon with a nice bit of copy for you."

"Hand it here," said Miss Rossiter, "and oh! Mr. Bredon, do you mind putting down your full name and address on this card—they want it downstairs for the file."

Bredon took the card obediently.

"Block letters please," added Miss Rossiter, glancing with some dismay at the sheets of copy she had just received.

"Oh, do you think my handwriting's awful? I always think it's rather neat, myself. Neat, but not gaudy. However, if you say——"

"Block letters," repeated Miss Rossiter, firmly. "Hullo! here's Mr. Tallboy. I expect he wants you, Mr. Ingleby."

"What, again?"

"Nutrax have cancelled that half-double," announced Mr. Tallboy with gloomy triumph. "They've just sent up from the conference to say that they want something special to put up against the new Slumbermalt campaign, and Mr. Hankin says will you get something out and let him have it in half an hour."

Ingleby uttered a loud yell, and Bredon, laying down the index-card, gazed at him open-mouthed.

"Damn and blast Nutrax," said Ingleby. "May all its directors get elephantiasis, locomotor ataxy and ingrowing toe-nails."

"Oh, quite," said Tallboy. "You'll let us have something, won't you? If I can get it passed before 3 o'clock the printer—— Hullo!"

Mr. Tallboy's eye, roving negligently round, had fallen on Bredon's index-card. Miss Rossiter's glance followed his. Neatly printed on the card stood the one word

DEATH

"Look at that!" said Miss Rossiter.

"Oh!" said Ingleby, looking over his shoulder. "That's who you are, is it, Bredon? Well, all I can say is, your stuff ought to come home to everybody. Universal appeal, and so forth."

Mr. Bredon smiled apologetically.

"You startled me so," he said. "Popping off that howl in my ear." He took up the card and finished his inscription:

DEATH BREDON,
12A, Great Ormond Street,
W.C.1.

CHAPTER II

Embarrassing Indiscretion of Two Typists

FOR THE TWENTIETH time, Mr. Death Bredon was studying the report of the coroner's inquest on Victor Dean.

There was the evidence of Mr. Prout, the photographer:

"It would be about tea-time. Tea is served at 3.30, more or less. I was coming out of my room on the top floor, carrying my camera and tripod. Mr. Dean passed me. He was coming quickly along the passage in the direction of the iron staircase. He was not running—he was walking at a good pace. He was carrying a large, heavy book under one arm. I know now that it was *The Times Atlas.* I turned to walk in the same direction that he was going. I saw him start down the iron staircase; it is rather a steep spiral. He had taken about half a dozen steps when he seemed to crumple together and disappear. There was a tremendous crash. You might call it a clatter—a prolonged crashing noise. I started to run, when Mr. Daniels' door opened and he came out and collided with the legs of my tripod. While we were mixed up together, Mr. Ingleby ran past us down the corridor. I heard a shrill scream from below. I put the camera down and Mr. Daniels and I went to the head of the staircase together. Some other people joined us—Miss Rossiter, I think, and some of the copy-writers and clerks. We could see Mr. Dean lying huddled together at the foot of the staircase. I could not say whether he had fallen down the stairs or through the banisters. He was lying all in a heap. The staircase is a right-handed spiral, and makes one complete turn. The treads are composed of pierced ironwork. The hand-rail has a number of iron knobs on it, about the size of small walnuts. The stairs are apt to be slippery. The stair is well lit. There is a skylight above, and it receives light through the glass panels of Mr. Daniels' room and also from the glass-panelled corridor on the floor below. I have here a photograph taken by myself at 3.30 p.m. yesterday—that is the day after the accident. It shows the head of the spiral staircase. It was taken by ordinary day-light. I used an Actinax Special Rapid plate with the H & D number 450. The exposure was 1/5 second with the lens stopped down to *f*.16. The light was then similar to what it was at the time of Mr. Dean's death. The sun was shining on both occasions. The corridor runs, roughly, north and south. As deceased went down the staircase, the light would be coming from above and behind him; it is not possible that he could have the sun in his eyes."

Then came Mr. Daniels' account:

"I was standing at my desk consulting with Mr. Freeman about an advertising lay-out. I heard the crash. I thought one of the boys must have fallen down again. A boy did fall down that staircase on a previous occasion. I do not consider it a dangerous structure. I consider that the boy was going too fast. I do not recollect hearing Mr. Dean go along the passage. I did not see him. My back was to the door. People pass along that passage continuously; I should not be paying attention. I went quickly out when I heard the noise of the fall. I encountered Mr. Prout and tripped over his tripod. I did not exactly fall down, but I stumbled and had to catch hold of him to steady myself. There was nobody in the corridor when I came out except Mr. Prout. I will swear to that. Mr. Ingleby came past us while we were recovering from the collision. He did not come from his own room, but from the south end of the passage. He went down the iron staircase and Mr. Prout and I followed as quickly as we could. I heard somebody shriek downstairs. I think it was just before, or just after I ran into Mr. Prout. I was rather confused at the time and cannot say for certain. We saw Mr. Dean lying at the bottom of the staircase. There were a number of people standing round. Then Mr. Ingleby came up the stairs very hastily and called out: 'He's dead!' or 'He's killed himself'. I cannot speak to the exact words. I did not believe him at first; I thought he was exaggerating. I went on down the staircase. Mr. Dean was lying bundled together, head downwards. His legs were partly up the staircase. I think somebody had already tried to lift him before I got there. I have had some experience of death and accidents. I was a stretcher-bearer in the War. I examined him and give it as my opinion that he was dead. I believe Mr. Atkins had already expressed a similar opinion. I helped to lift the body and carry it into the board-room. We laid him on the table and endeavoured to administer first-aid, but I never had any doubt that he was dead. It did not occur to us to leave him where he was till the police were summoned, because, of course, he might not have been dead, and we could not leave him head downwards on the staircase."

Then came Mr. Atkins, who explained that he was a group-secretary, working in one of the downstairs rooms.

"I was just coming out of my room, the door of which commands a view of the iron staircase. It is not directly opposite the foot of the staircase, but it commands a view of the lower half of the staircase. Anyone coming down the staircase would have his back turned to me as he stepped off. I heard a loud crash, and saw the deceased falling all of a heap down the stairs. He did not appear to make any attempt to save himself. He was clutching a large book in his arms. He did not loose his grip of the book as he fell. He seemed to cannon from one side of the staircase to the other and fall like a sack of potatoes, so to speak. He pitched on his head at the bottom. I was carrying a large tray full of glass jars. I set this down and ran towards him. I endeavoured to lift him up, but the moment I touched him I felt sure that he was dead. I formed the opinion that he had broken his neck. Mrs. Crump was in the passage at the time. Mrs. Crump is the head charwoman. I said to her: 'Good God! he's broken his neck,' and she screamed loudly. A number of other people arrived almost immediately upon the scene. Somebody said, 'Perhaps it's only dislocated.' Mr. Daniels said to me: 'We can't leave him here.' I think it was Mr. Armstrong who suggested that he should be taken into the board-room. I assisted to carry him there. The book was held by the deceased in such a tight grip that we had difficulty in getting it away from him. He made no movement of any kind after he fell, and no attempt at speech. I never had the least doubt that he was dead from the moment that he fell."

Mrs. Crump confirmed this account to the best of her ability. She said:

"I am head charwoman to the firm of Pym's Publicity, Ltd. It is my duty to take the tea-wagon round the office building at about 3.30 each afternoon. That is, I start my round at about 3.15 and finish at about 3.45. I had nearly finished doing the first floor, and was returning on my way to the lift to take tea up to the top floor. That would make the time about 3.30. I was coming along the corridor and was facing the foot of the iron staircase. I saw Mr. Dean fall. He fell all in a bunch-like. It was dreadful. He did not shout out or make any exclamation in falling. He fell like a dead thing. My heart seemed to stop. I was struck so I couldn't move for a minute or two. Then Mr. Atkins came running along to pick him up. He said: 'He's broke his neck,' and I let out a scream. I couldn't help myself, I was that upset. I think that staircase is a wicked dangerous place. I am always warning the other women against it. If you was to slip you couldn't hardly save yourself, not if you was carrying anything. People run up and downstairs on it all day, and the edges of the steps gets that polished you wouldn't believe, and some of them is wore down at the edges."

The medical evidence was given by Dr. Emerson. "I reside in Queen's Square, Bloomsbury. It is about five minutes from my house to the offices of Pym's Publicity in Southampton Row. I received a telephone message at 3.40 p.m. and went round immediately. Deceased was dead when I arrived. I concluded that he had then been dead about 15 minutes. His neck was broken at the fourth cervical vertebra. He also had a contused wound on the right temple which had cracked the skull. Either of these injuries was sufficient to cause death. I should say he had died instantly upon falling. He had also the tibia of the left leg broken, probably through catching in the banister of the staircase. There were also, of course, a quantity of minor scratches and contusions. The wound on the head is such as might be caused through pitching upon one of the knobs on the handrail in falling. I could not say whether this or the broken vertebra was the actual cause of death, but in either case, death would be instantaneous. I agree that it is not a matter of great importance. I found no trace of any heart disease or any other disease which might suggest that deceased was subject to vertigo or fainting-fits. I observed no traces of alcoholic tendency or of addiction to drugs. I have seen the staircase, and consider that it would be very easy to slip upon it. So far as I can tell, deceased's eyesight would appear to have been normal."

Miss Pamela Dean, sister of deceased, gave evidence that her brother had been in good health at the time of the accident, and that he had never been subject to fits or fainting. He was not short-sighted. He occasionally suffered from liverish attacks. He was a good dancer and usually very neat and nimble on his feet. He had once sprained his ankle as a boy, but so far as she knew, no permanent weakness of the joint had resulted.

Evidence was also called which showed that accidents had occurred on several previous occasions to persons descending the staircase; other witnesses expressed the opinion that the staircase was not dangerous to anybody exercising reasonable care. The jury returned a verdict of accidental death, with a rider to the effect that they thought the iron spiral should be replaced by a more solid structure.

Mr. Bredon shook his head. Then he drew a sheet of paper from the rack before him and wrote down:

1. He seemed to crumple together.
2. He did not make any attempt to save himself.
3. He did not loose his grip of the book.
4. He pitched on his head at the bottom.
5. Neck broken, skull cracked; either injury fatal.
6. Good health; good sight; good dancer.

He filled himself a pipe and sat for some time staring at this list. Then he searched in a drawer and produced a piece of notepaper, which seemed to be an unfinished letter, or the abandoned draft of one.

"DEAR MR. PYM—I think it only right that you should know that there is something going on in the office which is very undesirable, and might lead to serious——"

After a little more thought, he laid this document aside and began to scribble on another sheet, erasing and rewriting busily. Presently a slow smile twitched his lips.

"I'll swear there's something in it," he muttered, "something pretty big. But the job is, to handle it. One's got to go for the money—but where's it coming from? Not from Pym, I fancy. It doesn't seem to be his personal show, and you can't blackmail a whole office. I wonder, though. After all, he'd probably pay a good bit to prevent——"

He relapsed into silence and meditation.

"And what," demanded Miss Parton, spearing another chocolate éclair, "do you think of our Mr. Bredon?"

"The Pimlico Pet?" said Miss Rossiter. "You'll put on pounds and pounds if you eat all that sweet stuff, duckie. Well, I think he's rather a lamb, and his shirts are simply too marvellous. He won't be able to keep that up on Pym's salary, bonus or no bonus. Or the silk socks either."

"He's been brought up silk-lined all right," agreed Miss Parton. "One of the new poor, I expect. Lost all his money in the slump or something."

"Either that, or his family have got tired of supporting him and pushed him out to scratch for himself," suggested Miss Rossiter. She slimmed more strenuously than her colleague, and was less inclined to sentiment. "I sort of asked him the other day what he did before he came here, and he said, all sorts of things, and mentioned that he'd had a good bit to do with motors. I expect he's been one of these gilded johnnies who used to sell cars on commission, and the bottom's dropped out of that and he's got to do a job of work—if you call copy-writing work."

"I think he's very clever," said Miss Parton. "Did you see that idiotic headline he put up for Margarine yesterday: 'IT'S A FAR, FAR BUTTER THING'? Hankie nearly sniggered himself sick. I think the Pet was pulling his leg. But what I mean is, he wouldn't think of a silly thing like that if he hadn't got brains."

"He'll make a copy-writer," declared Miss Rossiter, firmly. She had seen so many new copy-writers come and pass like ships in the night, that she was as well able to size them up as the copy-chiefs themselves. "He's got the flair if you know what I mean. He'll stay all right."

"I hope he does," said Miss Parton. "He's got beautiful manners. Doesn't chuck the stuff at you as if you were dirt like young Willis. And he pays his tea-bill like a little gentleman."

"Early days," said Miss Rossiter. "He's paid *one* tea-bill. Gives me the pip, the way some of them make a fuss about it. There's Garrett. He was quite rude when I went to him on Saturday. Hinted that I made money out of the teas. I suppose he thinks it's funny. I don't."

"He means it for a joke."

"No, he doesn't. Not altogether. And he's always grumbling. Whether it's Chelsea buns or jam roll, there's always something wrong with it. I said to him, 'Mr. Garrett,' I said, 'if *you* like to give up *your* lunch-time every day to trying to find something that *everybody* will enjoy, you're welcome to do it.' 'Oh, no,' he said, 'I'm not the office-boy.' 'And who do you think I am,' I said, 'the errand-girl?' So he told me not to lose my temper. It's all very well, but you get very tired of it, especially this hot weather, fagging round."

Miss Parton nodded. The teas were a perennial grievance.

"Anyhow," she said, "friend Bredon is no trouble. A plain biscuit and a cup of tea every day. That's his order. And he said he was quite ready to pay the same subscription as everybody else, though really he ought to be let off with sixpence. I do like a man to be generous and speak to you nicely."

"Oh, the Pet's tongue runs on ball-bearings," said Miss Rossiter. "And talk of being a nosey-parker!"

"They all are," replied Miss Parton. "But I say, do you know what I did yesterday? It was dreadful. Bredon came in and asked for Mr. Hankin's carbons. I was in an awful rush with some of old Copley's muck—he always wants everything done in five minutes—and I said, 'Help yourself.' Well, what do you think? Ten minutes afterwards I went to look for something on the shelf and I found he'd gone off with Mr. Hankin's private letter-file. He must have been blind, because it's marked PRIVATE in red letters an inch high. Of course Hankie'd be in an awful bait if he knew. So I hared off to Bredon and there he was, calmly reading Hankie's private letters, if you please! 'You've got the wrong file, Mr. Bredon,' I said. And he wasn't a bit ashamed. He just handed it back with a grin and said, 'I was beginning to think I might have. It's very interesting to see what salary everybody gets.' And, my dear, he was reading Hankie's departmental list. And I said, 'Oh, Mr. Bredon, you *oughtn't* to be reading that. It's frightfully confidential.' And he said, 'Is it?' He seemed quite surprised."

"Silly ass!" said Miss Rossiter. "I hope you told him to keep it to himself. They *are* all so sensitive about their salaries. I'm sure I don't know why. But they're all dying to find out what the others get and terrified to death anybody should find out what they get themselves. If Bredon goes round shooting his mouth off, he'll stir up some awful trouble."

"I warned him," said Miss Parton, "and he seemed to think it was awfully funny and asked how long it would take him to reach Dean's salary."

"Let's see, how much was Dean getting?"

"Six," replied Miss Parton, "and not worth much more in my opinion. The department will be better-tempered without him, I must say. He did rile 'em sometimes."

"If you ask me," said Miss Rossiter, "I don't think this business of mixing the University people with the other sort works very well. With the Oxford and Cambridge lot it's all give-and-take and bad language, but the others don't seem to fit in with it. They always think they're being sneered at."

"It's Ingleby upsets them. He never takes anything seriously."

"None of them do," said Miss Rossiter, putting an unerring experienced finger on the point of friction. "It's all a game to them, and with Copley and Willis it's all deadly serious. When Willis starts on metaphysics, Ingleby recites limericks. Personally, I'm broadminded. I rather like it. And I will say the 'varsity crowd don't quarrel like the rest of them. If Dean hadn't fallen downstairs, there'd have been a good old bust-up between him and Willis."

"I never could understand what that was all about," observed Miss Parton, thoughtfully stirring her coffee.

"*I* believe there was a girl in it," said Miss Rossiter. "Willis used to go about with Dean quite a lot at the weekend, and then it all stopped suddenly. They had an awful row one day last March. Miss Meteyard heard them going at it hammer and tongs in Dean's room."

"Did she hear what the fuss was?"

"No. Being Miss Meteyard, she first pounded on the partition and then went in and told them to shut up. She's no use for people's private feelings. Funny woman. Well, I suppose we'd better push off home, or we shan't be fit for anything in the morning. It was quite a good show, wasn't it? Where's the check? You had two cakes more than me. Yours is one-and-a-penny and mine's ninepence. If I give you a bob and you give me twopence and the waitress twopence and settle up at the desk, we shall be all square."

The two girls left the Corner House by the Coventry Street entrance, and turned to the right and crossed the Piccadilly merry-go-round to the Tube entrance. As they regained the pavement, Miss Rossiter clutched Miss Parton by the arm:

"Look! the Pet! got up regardless!"

"Go on!" retorted Miss Parton. "It isn't the Pet. Yes it is! Look at the evening cloak and the gardenia, *and*, my dear, the monocle!"

Unaware of this commentary, the gentleman in question was strolling negligently towards them, smoking a cigarette. As he came abreast of them, Miss Rossiter broke into a cheerful grin and said "Hullo!"

The man raised his hat mechanically and shook his head. His face was a well-bred blank. Miss Rossiter's cheeks became flooded with a fiery crimson.

"It isn't him. How *awful*!"

"He took you for a tart," said Miss Parton, with some confusion and perhaps a little satisfaction.

"It's an extraordinary thing," muttered Miss Rossiter, vexed. "I could have sworn——"

"He's not a bit like him, really, when you see him close to," said Miss Parton, wise after the event. "I told you it wasn't him."

"You said it was him." Miss Rossiter glanced back over her shoulder, and was in time to see a curious little incident.

A limousine car came rolling gently along from the direction of Leicester Square and drew up close to the kerb, opposite the entrance to the Criterion Bar. The man in dress-clothes stepped up to it and addressed a few words to the occupant, flinging his cigarette away as he did so, and laying one hand on the handle of the door, as though about to enter the car. Before he could do so, two men emerged suddenly and silently from a shop-entrance. One of them spoke to the chauffeur; the other put his hand on the gentleman's elegant arm. A brief sentence or two were exchanged; then the one man got up beside the chauffeur while the second man opened the door of the car. The man in dress-clothes got in, the other man followed, and the whole party drove off. The whole thing was so quickly done that almost before Miss Parton could turn round in answer to Miss Rossiter's exclamation, it was all over.

"An arrest!" breathed Miss Rossiter, her eyes shining. "Those two were detectives. I wonder what our friend in the monocle's been doing."

Miss Parton was thrilled.

"And we actually spoke to him and thought it was Bredon."

"*I* spoke to him," corrected Miss Rossiter. It was all very well for Miss Parton to claim the credit, but only a few minutes back she had rather pointedly dissociated herself from the indiscretion and she could not be allowed to have it both ways.

"You did, then," agreed Miss Parton. "I'm surprised at you, Rossie, trying to get off with a smart crook. Anyhow, if Bredon doesn't turn up to-morrow, we'll know it was him after all."

But it could hardly have been Mr. Bredon, for he was in his place the next morning just as usual. Miss Rossiter asked him if he had a double.

"Not that I know of," said Mr. Bredon. "One of my cousins is a bit like me."

Miss Rossiter related the incident, with slight modifications. On consideration, she thought it better not to mention that she had been mistaken for a lady of easy virtue.

"Oh, I don't think that would be my cousin," replied Mr. Bredon. "He's a frightfully proper person. Well known at Buckingham Palace, and all that."

"Go on," said Miss Rossiter.

"I'm the black sheep of the family," said Mr. Bredon. "He never even sees me in the street. It must have been someone quite different."

"Is your cousin called Bredon, too?"

"Oh, yes," said Mr. Bredon.

CHAPTER III

Inquisitive Interviews of a New Copy-Writer

MR. BREDON HAD been a week with Pym's Publicity, and had learnt a number of things. He learned the average number of words that can be crammed into four inches of copy; that Mr. Armstrong's fancy could be caught by an elaborately-drawn lay-out, whereas Mr. Hankin looked on art-work as waste of a copy-writer's time; that the word "pure" was dangerous, because, if lightly used, it laid the client open to prosecution by the Government inspectors, whereas the words "highest quality", "finest ingredients", "packed under the best conditions" had no legal meaning, and were therefore safe; that the expression "giving work to umpteen thousand British employees in our model works at so-and-so" was not by any means the same thing as "British made throughout"; that the north of England liked its butter and margarine salted, whereas the south preferred it fresh; that the *Morning Star* would not accept any advertisements containing the word "cure", though there was no objection to such expressions as "relieve" or "ameliorate", and that, further, any commodity that professed to "cure" anything might find itself compelled to register as a patent medicine and use an expensive stamp; that the most convincing copy was always written with the tongue in the cheek, a genuine conviction of the commodity's worth producing—for some reason—poverty and flatness of style; that if, by the most far-fetched stretch of ingenuity, an indecent meaning could be read into a headline, that was the meaning that the great British Public would infallibly read into it; that the great aim and object of the studio artist was to crowd the copy out of the advertisement and that, conversely, the copy-writer was a designing villain whose ambition was to cram the space with verbiage and leave no room for the sketch; that the lay-out man, a meek ass between two burdens, spent a miserable life trying to reconcile these opposing parties; and further, that all departments alike united in hatred of the client, who persisted in spoiling good lay-outs by cluttering them up with coupons, free-gift offers, lists of local agents and realistic portraits of hideous and uninteresting cartons, to the detriment of his own interests and the annoyance of everybody concerned.

He also learned to find his way without assistance over the two floors occupied by the agency, and even up on to the roof, where the messenger boys did their daily physical jerks under the eye of the Sergeant, and whence a fine view of London might be obtained on a clear day. He became acquainted with a number of the group-managers, and was sometimes even able to remember off-hand which clients' accounts were in the control of which manager, while with most of the members of his own department he found himself established on a footing of friendly intimacy. There were the two copy-chiefs, Mr. Armstrong and Mr. Hankin, each brilliant in his own way and each with his own personal fads. Mr. Hankin, for example, would never accept a headline containing the word "magnificent"; Mr. Armstrong disliked any lay-out which involved the picture of a judge or a Jew, and was rendered so acutely wretched when the proprietors of "Whifflets" put out a new brand of smoke called "Good Judge" Mixture that he was obliged to hand the whole account over, lock, stock and barrel to Mr. Hankin. Mr. Copley, an elderly, serious-minded man, who had entered the advertising profession before the modern craze set in for public-school-and-University-trained copy-writers, was remarkable for a tendency to dyspepsia and a perfectly miraculous knack of writing appetising copy for tinned and packeted foodstuffs. Anything that came out of a tin or a packet was poison to him, and his diet consisted of under-cooked beef-steak, fruit and whole-meal bread. The only copy he really enjoyed writing was that for Bunbury's Whole-Meal Flour, and he was perennially depressed when his careful eulogiums, packed with useful medical detail, were scrapped in favour of some light-headed foolishness of Ingleby's, on the story that Bunbury's Whole-Meal Flour took the Ache out of Baking. But on Sardines and Tinned Salmon he was unapproachable.

Ingleby specialised in snobbish copy about Twentyman's Teas ("preferred by Fashion's Favourites"), Whifflets ("in the Royal Enclosure at Ascot, in the Royal Yacht Club at Cowes, you find the discriminating men who smoke Whifflets") and Farley's Footwear ("whether it's a big shoot or a Hunt Ball, Farley puts you on a sound footing"). He lived in Bloomsbury, was communistic in a literary way, and dressed almost exclusively in pull-overs and grey flannels. He was completely and precociously disillusioned and one of the most promising copy-writers Pym's had ever fathered. When released from Whifflets and fashionable footwear, he could be amusing on almost any subject, and had a turn for "clever" copy, wherever cleverness was not out of place.

Miss Meteyard, with a somewhat similar mental makeup, could write about practically anything except women's goods, which were more competently dealt with by Mr. Willis or Mr. Garrett, the former of whom, in particular, could handle corsets and face-cream with a peculiar plaintive charm which made him more than worth his salary. The copy department on the whole worked happily together, writing each other's headlines in a helpful spirit and invading each other's rooms at all hours of the day. The only two men with whom Bredon was unable to establish genial relations were Mr. Copley, who held aloof from everybody, and Mr. Willis, who treated him with a reserve for which he was unable to account. Otherwise he found the department a curiously friendly place.

And it talked. Bredon had never in his life encountered a set of people with such active tongues and so much apparent leisure for gossip. It was a miracle that any work ever got done, though somehow it did. He was reminded of his Oxford days, when essays mysteriously wrote themselves in the intervals of club-meetings and outdoor sports, and when most of the people who took firsts boasted of never having worked more than three hours of any day. The atmosphere suited him well enough. He was a bonhomous soul, with the insatiable curiosity of a baby elephant, and nothing pleased him better than to be interrupted in his encomiums of Sopo ("makes Monday, Fun-day") or the Whoosh Vacuum-cleaner ("one Whoosh and it's clean") by a fellow-member of the department, fed-up with advertising and spoiling for a chat.

"Hullo!" said Miss Meteyard one morning. She had dropped in to consult

Bredon about googlies—the proprietors of Tomboy Toffee having embarked upon a series of cricket advertisements which, starting respectively from "Lumme, what a Lob!" or "Yah! that's a Yorker!" led up by devious routes to the merits of Toffee—and had now reached the point when "Gosh! it's a Googly" had to be tackled. Bredon had demonstrated googlies with pencil and paper, and also in the corridor with a small round tin of Good Judge tobacco (whereby he had nearly caught Mr. Armstrong on the side of the head), and had further discussed the relative merits of "Gosh" and "Golly" in the headline; but Miss Meteyard showed no symptoms of departing. She had sat down at Bredon's table and was drawing caricatures, in which she displayed some skill, and was rummaging in the pencil-tray for an india-rubber when she remarked, as above mentioned, "Hullo!"

"What?"

"That's little Dean's scarab. It ought to have been sent back to his sister."

"Oh, that! Yes, I knew that was there, but I didn't know who it belonged to. It's not a bad thing. It's real onyx, though of course it's not Egyptian and it's not even very old."

"Probably not, but Dean adored it. He thought it was a sure-fire mascot. He always had it in his waistcoat pocket or sitting in front of him while he worked. If he'd had it on him that day, he wouldn't have tumbled downstairs—at least, that's what he'd have said himself."

Bredon poised the beetle on the palm of his hand. It was as big as a man's thumb-nail, heavy and shallowly carved, smooth except for a slight chip at one side.

"What sort of chap was Dean?"

"Well. *De mortuis*, and all that, but I wasn't exactly keen on him. I thought he was rather an unwholesome little beast."

"What way?"

"For one thing, I didn't like the people he went about with."

Bredon twitched an interrogative eyebrow.

"No," said Miss Meteyard, "I don't mean what you mean. At least, I mean, I can't tell you about that. But he used to tag round with that de Momerie crowd. Thought it was smart, I suppose. Luckily, he missed the famous night when that Punter-Smith girl did away with herself. Pym's would never have held its head up again if one of its staff had been involved in a notorious case. Pym's is particular."

"How old did you say this blighter was?"

"Oh, twenty-six or seven, I should think."

"How did he come to be here?"

"Usual thing. Needed cash, I suppose. Had to have some sort of job. You can't lead a gay life on nothing, and he wasn't anybody, you know. His father was a bank-manager, or something, deceased, so I suppose young Victor had to push out and earn his keep. He knew how to look after himself all right."

"Then how did he get in with that lot?"

Miss Meteyard grinned at him.

"Somebody picked him up, I should think. He had a certain kind of good looks. There is a *nostalgie de la banlieue* as well as *de la boue*. And you're pulling my leg, Mr. Death Bredon, because you know that as well as I do."

"Is that a compliment to my sagacity or a reflection on my virtue?"

"How *you* came here is a good deal more interesting than how Victor Dean came here. They start new copy-writers without experience at four quid a week—about enough to pay for a pair of your shoes."

"Ah!" said Bredon, "how deceptive appearances can be! But it is evident, dear lady, that you do not do your shopping in the true West End. You belong to the section of society that pays for what it buys. I revere, but do not imitate you. Unhappily, there are certain commodities which cannot be obtained without cash. Railway fares, for example, or petrol. But I am glad you approve of my shoes. They are supplied by Rudge in the Arcade and, unlike Farley's Fashion Footwear, are actually of the kind that is to be seen in the Royal Enclosure at Ascot and wherever discriminating men congregate. They have a ladies' department, and if you will mention my name——"

"I begin to see why you chose advertising as a source of supply." The look of doubt left Miss Meteyard's angular face, and was replaced by a faintly derisive expression. "Well, I suppose I'd better get back to Tomboy Toffee. Thanks for your dope about googlies."

Bredon shook his head mournfully as the door closed after her. "Careless," he muttered. "Nearly gave the game away. Oh, well, I suppose I'd better do some work and look as genuine as possible."

He pulled towards him a guard-book pasted up with pulls of Nutrax advertising and studied its pages thoughtfully. He was not left long in peace, however, for after a couple of minutes Ingleby slouched in, a foul pipe at full blast and his hands thrust deep into his trousers-pockets.

"I say, is Brewer here?"

"Don't know him. But," added Bredon, waving his hand negligently, "you have my permission to search. The priest's hole and the concealed staircase are at your service."

Ingleby rooted in the bookcase in vain.

"Somebody's bagged him. Anyway, how do you spell Chrononhotonthologos?"

"Oh! I can do that. And Aldiborontophoscophornio, too. Crossword? Torquemada?"

"No, headline for Good Judges. Isn't it hot? And now I suppose we're going to have a week's dust and hammering."

"Why?"

"The fiat has gone forth. The iron staircase is condemned."

"Who by?"

"The Board."

"Oh, rot! they mustn't do that."

"What d'you mean?"

"Admission of liability, isn't it?"

"Time, too."

"Well, I suppose it is."

"You looked quite startled. I was beginning to think you had some sort of personal feeling in the matter."

"Good Lord, no, why should I? Just a matter of principle. Except that the staircase does seem to have had its uses in eliminating the unfit. I gather that the late Victor Dean was not universally beloved."

"Oh, I don't know. I never saw much harm in him, except that he wasn't exactly pukka and hadn't quite imbibed the Pym spirit, as you may say. Of course the Meteyard woman loathed him."

"Why?"

"Oh! she's a decent sort of female, but makes no allowances. My motto is, live and let live, but protect your own interests. How are you getting on with Nutrax?"

"Haven't touched it yet. I've been trying to get out a name for Twentyman's shilling tea. As far as I can make Hankin out, it has no qualities except cheapness to recommend it, and is chiefly made of odds and ends of other teas. The name must suggest solid worth and respectability."

"Why not call it 'Domestic Blend'? Nothing could sound more reliable and obviously nothing could suggest so much dreary economy."

"Good idea. I'll put it up to him." Bredon yawned. "I've had too much lunch. I don't think anybody ought to have to work at half-past two in the afternoon. It's unnatural."

"Everything's unnatural in this job. Oh, my God! Here's somebody with something on a tray! Go away! go a-*way*!"

"I'm sorry," said Miss Parton, brightly, entering with six saucers filled with a grey and steaming mess. "But Mr. Hankin says, will you please taste these samples of porridge and report upon them?"

"My dear girl, look at the time!"

"Yes, I know, it's awful, isn't it? They're numbered A, B and C, and here's the questionnaire paper, and if you'll let me have the spoons back I'll get them washed for Mr. Copley."

"I shall be sick," moaned Ingleby. "Who's this? Peabody's?"

"Yes—they're putting out a tinned porridge, 'Piper Parritch'. No boiling, no stirring—only heat the tin. Look for the Piper on the label."

"Look here," said Ingleby, "run away and try it on Mr. McAllister."

"I did, but his report isn't printable. There's sugar and salt and a jug of milk."

"What we suffer in the service of the public!" Ingleby attacked the mess with a disgusted sniff and a languid spoon. Bredon solemnly rolled the portions upon his tongue, and detained Miss Parton.

"Here, take this down while it's fresh in my mind. Vintage A: Fine, full-bodied, sweet nutty flavour, fully matured; a grand masculine porridge. Vintage B: extra-sec, refined, delicate character, requiring only——"

Miss Parton emitted a delighted giggle, and Ingleby, who hated gigglers, fled.

"Tell me, timeless houri," demanded Mr. Bredon, "what was wrong with my lamented predecessor? Why did Miss Meteyard hate him and why does Ingleby praise him with faint damns?"

This was no problem to Miss Parton.

"Why, because he didn't play fair. He was always snooping round other people's rooms, picking up their ideas and showing them up as his own. And if anybody gave him a headline and Mr. Armstrong or Mr. Hankin liked it, he never said whose it was."

This explanation seemed to interest Bredon. He trotted down the passage and thrust his head round Garrett's door. Garrett was stolidly making out his porridge report, and looked up with a grunt.

"I hope I'm not interrupting you at one of those moments of ecstasy," bleated Bredon, "but I just wanted to ask you something. I mean to say, it's just a question of etiquette, don't you know, and what's done, so to speak. I mean, look here! You see, Hankie-pankie told me to get out a list of names for a shilling tea and I got out some awful rotten ones, and then Ingleby came in and I said, 'What would you call this tea?' just like that, and he said, 'Call it Domestic Blend,' and I said 'What-ho! that absolutely whangs the nail over the crumpet.' Because it struck me, really, as being the caterpillar's boots."

"Well, what about it?"

"Well, just now I was chatting to Miss Parton about that fellow Dean, the one who fell downstairs you know, and why one or two people here didn't seem to be fearfully keen on him, and she said, it was because he got ideas out of other people and showed them up as his own stuff. And what I wanted to know was, isn't it done to ask people? Ingleby didn't say anything, but of course, if I've made a floater——"

"Well, it's like this," said Garrett. "There's a sort of unwritten law—at our end of the corridor, anyway. You take any help you can get and show it up with your initials on it, but if Armstrong or whoever it is simply goes all out on it and starts throwing bouquets about, you're rather expected to murmur that it was the other bird's suggestion really, and you thought rather well of it yourself."

"Oh, I see. Oh, thanks frightfully. And if, on the other hand, he goes right up in the air and says it's the damn-silliest thing he's seen since 1919, you stand the racket, I suppose."

"Naturally. If it's as silly as that you ought to have known better than to put it up to him anyway."

"Oh, yes."

"The trouble with Dean was that he first of all snitched people's ideas without telling them, and then didn't give them the credit for it with Hankin. But, I say, I wouldn't go asking Copley or Willis for too much assistance if I were you. They weren't brought up to the idea of lending round their lecture notes. They've a sort of board-school idea that everybody ought to paddle his own canoe."

Bredon thanked Garrett again.

"And if I were you," continued Garrett, "I wouldn't mention Dean to Willis at all. There's some kind of feeling—I don't know quite what. Anyway, I just thought I'd warn you."

Bredon thanked him with almost passionate gratitude.

"It's so easy to put your foot in it in a new place, isn't it? I'm really most frightfully obliged to you."

Clearly Mr. Bredon was a man of no sensibility, for half an hour later he was in Willis's room, and had introduced the subject of the late Victor Dean. The result was an unequivocal request that Mr. Bredon would mind his own business. Mr. Willis did not wish to discuss Mr. Dean at all. In addition to this, Bredon became aware that Willis was suffering from an acute and painful embarrassment, almost as though the conversation had taken some indecent turn. He was puzzled, but persisted. Willis, after sitting for some moments in gloomy silence, fidgeting with a pencil, at last looked up.

"If you're on Dean's game," he said, "you'd better clear out. I'm not interested."

He might not be, but Bredon was. His long nose twitched with curiosity.

"What game? I didn't know Dean. Never heard of him till I came here. What's the row?"

"If you didn't know Dean, why bring him up? He went about with a gang of people I didn't care about, that's all, and from the look of you, I should have said you belonged to the same bright crowd."

"The de Momerie crowd?"

"It's not much use your pretending you don't know all about it, is it?" said Willis, with a sneer.

"Ingleby told me Dean was a hanger-on of that particular bunch of Bright Young People," replied Bredon, mildly. "But I've never met any of them. They'd think me terribly ancient. They would, really. Besides, I don't think they're nice to know. Some of them are really naughty. Did Mr. Pym know that Dean was a Bright Young Thing?"

"I shouldn't think so, or he'd have buzzed him out double quick. What business is Dean of yours, anyway?"

"Absolutely none. I just wondered about him, that's all. He seems to have been a sort of misfit here. Not quite imbued with the Pym spirit, if you see what I mean."

"No, he wasn't. And if you take my advice, you'll leave Dean and his precious friends alone, or you won't make yourself too popular. The best thing Dean ever did in his life was to fall down that staircase."

"Nothing in life became him like the leaving it? But it seems a bit harsh, all the same. Somebody must have loved him. 'For he must be somebody's son,' as the dear old song says. Hadn't he any family? There is a sister, at least, isn't there?"

"Why the devil do you want to know about his sister?"

"I don't. I just asked, that's all. Well, I'd better tootle off, I suppose. I've enjoyed this little talk."

Willis scowled at his retreating form, and Mr. Bredon went away to get his information elsewhere. As usual, the typists' room was well informed.

"Only the sister," said Miss Parton. "She's something to do with Silkanette Hosiery. She and Victor ran a little flat together. Smart as paint, but rather silly, I thought, the only time I saw her. I've an idea our Mr. Willis was a bit smitten in that direction at one time, but it didn't seem to come to anything."

"Oh, I see," said Mr. Bredon, much enlightened.

He went back to his own room and the guard-books. But his attention wandered. He paced about, sat down, got up, stared out of the window, came back to the desk. Then, from a drawer, he pulled out a sheet of paper. It bore a list of dates in the previous year, and to each date was appended a letter of the alphabet, thus:

Jan.	7	G
„	14	O?
„	21	A
„	28	P
Feb.	5	G

There were other papers in the desk in the same handwriting—presumably Victor Dean's—but this list seemed to interest Mr. Bredon unaccountably. He examined it with an attention that one would have thought it scarcely deserved, and finally folded it carefully away in his pocket-book.

"Who dragged whom, how many times, at the wheels of what, round the walls of where?" demanded Mr. Bredon of the world at large. Then he laughed. "Probably some sublime scheme for selling Sopo to sapheads," he remarked, and this time set himself soberly to work upon his guard-books.

Mr. Pym, the presiding genius of Pym's Publicity, Ltd., usually allowed a week or so to elapse before interviewing new members of his staff. His theory was that it was useless to lecture people about their work till they had acquired some idea of what the work actually was. He was a conscientious man, and was particularly careful to keep before his mind the necessity for establishing a friendly personal relation with every man, woman and child in his employment, from the heads of departments down to the messenger-boys and, not being gifted with any spontaneous ease and charm of social intercourse, had worked out a rigid formula for dealing with this necessity. At the end of a week or so, he sent for any newly-joined recruits, interrogated them about their work and interests, and delivered his famous sermon on Service in Advertising. If they survived this frightful ordeal, under which nervous young typists had been known to collapse and give notice, they were put on the list for the monthly tea-party. This took place in the Little Conference Room. Twenty persons, selected from all ranks and departments, congregated under Mr. Pym's official eye to consume the usual office tea, supplemented by ham sandwiches from the canteen, and cake supplied at cost by Dairyfields, Ltd., and entertained one another for an exact hour. This function was supposed to promote inter-departmental cordiality, and by its means the entire staff, including the Outside Publicity, passed under scrutiny once in every six months. In addition to these delights there were, for department and group managers, informal dinners at Mr. Pym's private residence, where six victims were turned off at a time, the proceedings being hilariously concluded by the formation of two bridge-tables, presided over by Mr. and Mrs. Pym respectively. For the group-secretaries, junior copy-writers and junior artists, invitations were issued to an At Home twice a year, with a band and dancing till 10 o'clock; the seniors were expected to attend these and exercise the functions of stewards. For the clerks and typists, there was the Typists' Garden-Party, with tennis and badminton; and for the office-boys, there was the Office-Boys' Christmas Treat. In May of every year there was the Grand Annual Dinner and Dance for the whole staff, at which the amount of the staff bonus was announced for the year, and the health of Mr. Pym was drunk amid expressions of enthusiastic loyalty.

In accordance with the first item on this onerous programme, Mr. Bredon was summoned to the Presence within ten days of his first appearance at Pym's.

"Well, Mr. Bredon," said Mr. Pym, switching on an automatic smile and switching it off again with nervous abruptness, "and how are you getting on?"

"Oh, pretty well, thank you, sir."

"Find the work hard?"

"It is a little difficult," admitted Bredon, "till you get the hang of it, so to speak. A bit bewildering, if you know what I mean."

"Quite so, quite so," said Mr. Pym. "Do you get on all right with Mr. Armstrong and Mr. Hankin?"

Mr. Bredon said he found them very kind and helpful.

"They give me very good accounts of you," said Mr. Pym. "They seem to think you will make a good copy-writer." He smiled again and Bredon grinned back impudently.

"That's just as well, under the circumstances, isn't it?"

Mr. Pym rose suddenly to his feet and threw open the door which separated his room from his secretary's cubicle.

"Miss Hartley, do you mind going along to Mr. Vickers and asking him to look up the detailed appropriation for Darling's and let me have it? You might wait and bring it back with you."

Miss Hartley, realising that she was to be deprived of hearing Mr. Pym's discourse on Service in Advertising, which—owing to the thinness of the wooden partition and the resonant quality of Mr. Pym's voice—was exceedingly familiar to her, rose and departed obediently. This meant that she would be able to have a nice chat with Miss Rossiter and Miss Parton while Mr. Vickers was getting his papers together. And she would not hurry herself, either. Miss Rossiter had hinted that Mr. Willis had hinted all kinds of frightful possibilities about Mr. Bredon, and she wanted to know what was up.

"Now," said Mr. Pym, passing his tongue rapidly across his lips and seeming to pull himself together to face a disagreeable interview. "What have you got to tell me?"

Mr. Bredon, very much at his ease, leaned across with his elbows on the Managing Director's desk, and spoke for some considerable time in a low tone, while Mr. Pym's cheek grew paler and paler.

CHAPTER IV

Remarkable Acrobatics of a Harlequin

IT HAS ALREADY been hinted that Tuesday was a day of general mortification in Pym's copy-department. The trouble was caused by Messrs. Toule & Jollop, proprietors of Nutrax, Maltogene, and Jollop's Concentrated Lacto-beef Tablets for Travellers. Unlike the majority of clients who, though all tiresome in their degree, exercised their tiresomeness by post from a reasonable distance and at reasonable intervals, Messrs. Toule & Jollop descended upon Pym's every Tuesday for a weekly conference. While there, they reviewed the advertising for the coming week, rescinding the decisions taken at the previous week's conference, springing new schemes unexpectedly upon Mr. Pym and Mr. Armstrong, keeping those two important men shut up in the Conference Room for hours on end, to the interruption of office-business, and generally making nuisances of themselves. One of the items discussed at this weekly séance was the Nutrax 11-inch double for Friday's *Morning Star*, which occupied an important position in that leading news-organ on the top right-hand corner of the Home page, next to the special Friday feature. It subsequently occupied other positions in other journals, of course, but Friday's *Morning Star* was the real matter of importance.

The usual procedure in respect of this exasperating advertisement was as follows. Every three months or so, Mr. Hankin sent out an S.O.S. to the copy-department to the effect that more Nutrax copy was urgently required. By the united ingenuity of the department, about twenty pieces of copy were forthwith produced and submitted to Mr. Hankin. Under his severely critical blue pencil, these were reduced to twelve or so, which went to the Studio to be laid out and furnished with illustrative sketches. They were then sent or handed to Messrs. Toule & Jollop, who fretfully rejected all but half a dozen, and weakened and ruined the remainder by foolish alterations and additions. The copy-department was then scourged into producing another twenty efforts, of which, after a similar process of elimination and amendment, a further half-dozen contrived to survive criticism, thus furnishing the necessary twelve half-doubles for the ensuing three months. The department breathed again, momentarily, and the dozen lay-outs were stamped in purple ink "Passed by Client", and a note was made of the proposed order of their appearance.

On Monday of each week, Mr. Tallboy, group-manager for Nutrax, squared his shoulders and settled down to the task of getting Friday's half-double safely into the *Morning Star*. He looked out the copy for the week and sent round to collect the finished sketch from the Studio. If the finished sketch was really finished (which seldom happened), he sent it down to the block-makers, together with the copy and a carefully drawn lay-out. The block-makers, grumbling that they never were allowed proper time for the job, made a line-block of the sketch. The thing then passed to the printers, who set up the headlines and copy in type, added a name-block of the wrong size, locked the result up in a forme, pulled a proof and returned the result to Mr. Tallboy, pointing out in a querulous note that it came out half an inch too long. Mr. Tallboy corrected the misprints, damned their eyes for using the wrong name-block, made it clear to them that they had set the headlines in the wrong fount, cut the proof to pieces, pasted it up again into the correct size and returned it. By this time it was usually 11 o'clock on Tuesday morning, and Mr. Toule or Mr. Jollop, or both of them, were closeted in the Conference Room with Mr. Pym and Mr. Armstrong, calling loudly and repeatedly for their 11-inch double. As soon as the new proof arrived from the printers, Mr. Tallboy sent it down to the Conference Room by a boy, and escaped, if he could, for his elevenses. Mr. Toule or Mr. Jollop then pointed out to Mr. Pym and Mr. Armstrong a great number of weaknesses in both sketch and copy. Mr. Pym and Mr. Armstrong, sycophantically concurring in everything the client said, confessed themselves at a loss and invited suggestions from Mr. Toule (or Mr. Jollop). The latter, being, as most clients are, better at destructive than constructive criticism, cudgelled his brains into stupor, and thus reduced himself to a condition of utter blankness, upon which the persuasiveness of Mr. Pym and Mr. Armstrong could work with hypnotic effect. After half an hour of skilled treatment, Mr. Jollop (or Mr. Toule) found himself returning with a sense of relief and refreshment to the rejected lay-out. He then discovered that it was really almost exactly what he required. It only needed the alteration of a sentence and the introduction of a panel about gift-coupons. Mr. Armstrong then sent the lay-out up again to Mr. Tallboy, with a request that he would effect these necessary alterations. Mr. Tallboy, realising with delight that these involved nothing more drastic than the making of a new lay-out and the complete re-writing of the copy, sought out the copy-writer whose initials appeared on the original type-script, instructing him to cut out three lines and incorporate the client's improvements, while he himself laid the advertisement out afresh.

When all this had been done, the copy was returned to the printer to be re-set, the forme was sent to the block-makers, a complete block was made of the whole advertisement, and a fresh proof was returned. If, by any lucky chance, there turned out to be no defects in the block, the stereotypers got to work and made a sufficient number of stereos to be sent out to the other papers carrying the Nutrax advertising, with a proof to accompany each. On Thursday afternoon, the stereos were distributed by the despatching department to the London papers by hand, and to the provincial papers by post and train, and if nothing went wrong with these arrangements, the advertisement duly appeared in Friday's *Morning Star* and in other papers on the dates provided for. So long and arduous a history it is, that lies behind those exhortations to "Nourish your Nerves with Nutrax", which smite the reader in the eye as he opens his *Morning Star* in the train between Gidea Park and Liverpool Street.

On this particular Tuesday, exasperation was intensified. To begin with, the weather was exceptionally close, with a thunderstorm impending, and the top floor of Pym's Publicity was like a slow oven beneath the broad lead roof and the great glass skylights. Secondly, a visit was expected from two directors of Brotherhoods, Ltd., that extremely old-fashioned and religiously-minded firm who manufacture boiled sweets and non-alcoholic liquors. A warning had been sent round that all female members of the staff must refrain from smoking, and that any proofs of beer or whisky advertising must be carefully concealed from sight. The former restriction bore hardly upon Miss Meteyard and the copy-department typists, whose cigarettes were, if not encouraged, at least winked at in the ordinary way by the management. Miss Parton had been further upset by a mild suggestion from Mr. Hankin that she was showing rather more arm and neck than the directors of Brotherhoods, Ltd., would think seemly; out of sheer perversity, she had covered the offending flesh with a heavy sweater, and was ostentatiously stewing and grumbling and snapping the head off everyone who approached her. Mr. Jollop, who was, if anything, slightly more captious than Mr. Toule, had arrived particularly early for the weekly Nutrax conference, and had distinguished himself by firmly killing no less than three advertisements which Mr. Toule had previously passed. This meant that Mr. Hankin had been obliged to send out his S.O.S. nearly a month earlier than usual. Mr. Armstrong had toothache, and had been exceptionally short with Miss Rossiter, and something had gone wrong with Miss Rossiter's typewriter, so that its spacing was completely unreliable.

To Mr. Ingleby, perspiring over his guard-books, entered the detested form of Mr. Tallboy, a sheet of paper in his hand.

"Is this your copy?"

Mr. Ingleby stretched out a languid hand, took the paper, glanced at it and returned it.

"How often have I got to tell you blasted incompetents," he demanded amiably, "that those initials are on the copy for the purpose of identifying the writer? If you think my initials are DB you're either blind or potty."

"Who is DB anyway?"

"New fellow, Bredon."

"Where is he?"

Mr. Ingleby jerked his thumb in the direction of the next room.

"Empty," announced Mr. Tallboy, after a brief excursion.

"Well, have a look for him," suggested Ingleby.

"Yes, but look here," said Mr. Tallboy, persuasively, "I only want a suggestion. What the devil are the Studio to do with this? Do you mean to say Hankin passed that headline?"

"Presumably," said Ingleby.

"Well, how does he or Bredon or anybody suppose we're going to get it illustrated? Has the client seen it? They'll never stand for it. What's the point in laying it out? I can't think how Hankin came to pass it."

Ingleby stretched his hand out again.

"Brief, bright and brotherly," he observed. "What's the matter with it?"

The headline was:

——!

IF LIFE'S A BLANK

TAKE NUTRAX

"And in any case," grumbled Tallboy, "the *Morning Star* won't take it. They won't put in anything that looks like bad language."

"Your look-out," said Ingleby. "Why not ask 'em?"

Tallboy muttered something impolite.

"Anyway, if Hankin's passed it, it'll have to be laid out, I suppose," said Ingleby. "Surely the Studio—oh! hullo! here's your man. You'd better worry him. Bredon!"

"That's me!" said Mr. Bredon. "All present and correct!"

"Where've you been hiding from Tallboy? You knew he was on your tail."

"I've been on the roof," admitted Bredon, apologetically. "Cooler and all that. What's the matter. What have I done?"

"Well, this headline of yours, Mr. Bredon. How do you expect them to illustrate it?"

"I don't know. I left it to their ingenuity. I always believe in leaving scope to other people's imagination."

"How on earth are they to draw a blank?"

"Let 'em take a ticket in the Irish Sweep. That'll larn 'em," said Ingleby.

"I should think it would be rather like a muchness," suggested Bredon. "Lewis Carroll, you know. Did you ever see a drawing of a muchness?"

"Oh, don't fool," growled Tallboy. "We've got to do something with it. Do you really think it's a good headline, Mr. Bredon?"

"It's the best I've written yet," said Bredon enthusiastically, "except that beauty Hankie wouldn't pass. Can't they draw a man looking blank? Or just a man with a blank face, like those 'Are these missing features yours?' advertisements?"

"Oh, I suppose they *could*," admitted Tallboy, discontentedly. "I'll put it up to them anyhow. Thanks," he added, belatedly, and bounced out.

"Cross, isn't he?" said Ingleby. "It's this frightful heat. Whatever made you go up on the roof? It must be like a gridiron."

"So it is, but I thought I'd just try it. As a matter of fact, I was chucking pennies over the parapet to that brass band. I got the bombardon twice. The penny goes down with a tremendous whack, you know, and they look up all over the place to see where it comes from and you dodge down behind the parapet. It's a tremendous high parapet, isn't it? I suppose they wanted to make the building look even higher than it is. It's the highest in the street in any case. You do get a good view from up there. 'Earth hath not anything to show more fair.' It's going to rain like billy-ho in about two ticks. See how black it's come over."

"You seem to have come over pretty black, if it comes to that," remarked Ingleby. "Look at the seat of your trousers."

"You do want a lot," complained Bredon, twisting his spine alarmingly. "It is a bit sooty up there. I was sitting on the skylight."

"You look as if you'd been shinning up a pipe."

"Well, I did shin down a pipe. Only one pipe—rather a nice pipe. It took my fancy."

"You're loopy," said Ingleby, "doing acrobatics on dirty pipes in this heat. Whatever made you?"

"I dropped something," said Mr. Bredon, plaintively. "It went down on to the glass roof of the wash-place. I nearly put my foot through. Wouldn't old Smayle have been surprised if I'd tumbled into the wash-basin on top of him? And then I found I needn't have gone down the pipe after all; I came back by the staircase—the roof-door was open on both floors."

"They generally keep them open in hot weather," said Ingleby.

"I wish I'd known. I say, I could do with a drink."

"All right, have a glass of Sparkling Pompayne."

"What's that?"

"One of Brotherhood's non-alcoholic refreshers," grinned Ingleby. "Made from finest Devon apples, with the crisp, cool sparkle of champagne. Definitely anti-rheumatic and non-intoxicant. Doctors recommend it."

Bredon shuddered.

"I think this is an awfully immoral job of ours. I do, really. Think how we spoil the digestions of the public."

"Ah, yes—but think how earnestly we strive to put them right again. We undermine 'em with one hand and build 'em up with the other. The vitamins we destroy in the canning, we restore in Revito, the roughage we remove from Peabody's Piper Parritch we make up into a package and market as Bunbury's Breakfast Bran; the stomachs we ruin with Pompayne, we re-line with Peplets to aid digestion. And by forcing the damn-fool public to pay twice over—once to have its food emasculated and once to have the vitality put back again—we keep the wheels of commerce turning and give employment to thousands—including you and me."

"This wonderful world!" Bredon sighed ecstatically. "How many pores should you say there were in the human skin, Ingleby?"

"Damned if I know. Why?"

"Headline for Sanfect. Could I say, at a guess, ninety million? It sounds a good round number. 'Ninety Million Open Doors by which Germs can Enter—Lock Those Doors with Sanfect.' Sounds convincing, don't you think? Here's another: 'Would you Leave your Child in a Den of Lions?' That ought to get the mothers."

"It'd make a good sketch—— Hullo! here comes the storm and no mistake."

A flash of lightning and a tremendous crack of thunder broke without warning directly over their heads.

"I expected it," said Bredon. "That's why I did my roof-walk."

"How do you mean, that's why?"

"I was on the look-out for it," explained Bredon. "Well, it's here. Phew! that was a good one. I do adore thunder-storms. By the way, what has Willis got up against me?"

Ingleby frowned and hesitated.

"He seems to think I'm not nice to know," explained Bredon.

"Well—I warned you not to talk to him about Victor Dean. He seems to have got it into his head you were a friend of his, or something."

"But what *was* wrong with Victor Dean?"

"He kept bad company. Why are you so keen to know about Dean, anyway?"

"Well, I suppose I'm naturally inquisitive. I always like to know about people. About the office-boys, for instance. They do physical jerks on the roof, don't they? Is that the only time they're allowed on the roof?"

"They'd better not let the Sergeant catch 'em up there in office-hours. Why?"

"I just wondered. They're a mischievous lot, I expect; boys always are. I like 'em. What's the name of the red-headed one? He looks a snappy lad."

"That's Joe—they call him Ginger, of course. What's he been doing?"

"Oh, nothing. I suppose you get a lot of cats prowling about this place."

"Cats? I've never seen any cats. Except that I believe there's a cat that lives in the canteen, but she doesn't seem to come up here. What do you want a cat for?"

"I don't—anyway, there must be dozens of sparrows, mustn't there?"

Ingleby began to think that the heat had affected Bredon's brain. His reply was drowned in a tremendous crash of thunder. A silence followed, in which the street noises came thinly up from without; then heavy drops began to spit upon the panes. Ingleby got up and shut the window.

The rain came down like rods and roared upon the roof. In the lead gutters it danced and romped, rushing in small swift rivers into the hoppers. Mr. Prout, emerging from his room in a hurry, received a deluge of water down his neck from the roof and yelled for a boy to run along and shut the sky-lights. The oppression of heat and misery lifted from the office like a cast-off eiderdown. Standing ot the window of his own room, Bredon watched the hurrying foot-passengers, six storeys below, open their umbrellas to the deluge, or, caught defenceless, scurry into shop doorways. Down below, in the Conference Room, Mr. Jollop suddenly smiled and passed six lay-outs and a three-colour folder, and consented to the omission of the Fifty-six Free Chiming Clocks from the current week's half-double. Harry, the lift-man, ushering a dripping young woman into the shelter of the cage, expressed sympathy with her plight, and offered her a wipe-down with a duster. The young woman smiled at him, assured him that she was quite all right and asked if she could see Mr. Bredon. Harry handed her on to Tompkin, the reception clerk, who said he would send up, and what was her name, please?

"Miss Dean—Miss Pamela Dean—on private business."

The clerk became full of sympathetic interest.

"Our Mr. Dean's sister, miss?"

"Yes."

"Oh, yes, miss. A dreadful sad thing about Mr. Dean, miss. We were all very sorry to lose him like that. If you'll just take a seat, miss, I'll tell Mr. Bredon you're here."

Pamela Dean sat down and looked about her. The reception-hall was on the lower floor of the agency and contained nothing but the clerk's semicircular desk, two hard chairs, a hard settle and a clock. It occupied the space which, on the upper floor, was taken up by the Dispatching, and just outside the door was the lift and the main staircase, which wound round the lift-shaft and went the whole way to the roof, though the lift itself went no further than the top floor. The clock pointed to 12.45, and already a stream of employees was passing through the hall, or clattering down from the floor above for a wash and brush-up before going out to lunch. A message from Mr. Bredon arrived to say that he would be down in a moment, and Pamela Dean entertained herself by watching the various members of the staff as they passed. A brisk, neat young man, with an immaculate head of wavy brown hair, a minute dark moustache and very white teeth (Mr. Smayle, had she known it, group-manager for Dairyfields, Ltd.); a large, bald man with a reddish, clean-shaven face and a masonic emblem (Mr. Harris of the Outdoor Publicity); a man of thirty-five, with rather sulky good looks and restless light eyes (Mr. Tallboy, brooding on the iniquities of Messrs. Toule & Jollop); a thin, prim, elderly man (Mr. Daniels); a plump little man with a good-natured grin and fair hair, chatting to a square-jawed, snub-nosed red-head (Mr. Cole, group-manager for Harrogate Bros. of soap fame, and Mr. Prout, the photographer); a handsome, worried, grey-haired man in the forties, accompanying a prosperous baldpate in an overcoat (Mr. Armstrong escorting Mr. Jollop away to a mollifying and expensive lunch); an untidy, saturnine person with both hands in his trousers-pockets (Mr. Ingleby); a thin, predatory man with a stoop and jaundiced eyeballs (Mr. Copley, wondering whether his lunch was going to agree with him); then a lean, fair-haired, anxious-looking youth, who, at sight of her, stopped dead in his tracks, flushed, and then passed on. This was Mr. Willis; Miss Dean gave him a glance and a cool nod, which was as coolly returned. Tompkin, the reecption clerk, who missed nothing, saw the start, the flush, the glance and the nods and mentally added another item to his fund of useful knowledge. Then came a slim man of forty or so, with a long nose and straw-coloured hair, wearing horn-rimmed glasses and a pair of well-cut grey trousers which seemed to have received recent ill-treatment; he came up to Pamela and said, more as a statement than as a question:

"Miss Dean."

"Mr. Bredon?"

"Yes."

"You ought not to have come here," said Mr. Bredon, shaking his head reproachfully, "it's a little indiscreet, you know. However—hullo, Willis, want me?"

It was evidently not Mr. Willis' lucky day. He had conquered his nervous agitation and turned back with the obvious intention of addressing Pamela, just in time to find Bredon in possession. He replied, "Oh, no, not at all"—with such patent sincerity that Tompkin made another ecstatic mental note, and was, indeed, forced to dive hurriedly behind his counter to conceal his radiant face. Bredon grinned amiably and Willis, after a moment's hesitation, fled through the doorway.

"I'm sorry," said Miss Dean. "I didn't know——"

"Never mind," said Bredon, and then, in a louder tone: "You've come for those things of your brother's, haven't you? I've got them here; I'm working in his room, don't you know. I say, er, how about, er, coming out and honouring me by taking in a spot of lunch with me, what?"

Miss Dean agreed; Bredon fetched his hat and they passed out.

"Ho!" said Tompkin in confidence to himself. "Ho! what's the game, I wonder? She's a smart jane all right, all right. Given the youngster a chuck and now she's out after the new bloke, I shouldn't be surprised. *And* I don't know as I blame her."

Mr. Bredon and Miss Dean went sedately down together in silence, affording no pasture for the intelligent ears of Harry the liftman, but as they emerged into Southampton Row, the girl turned to her companion:

"I was rather surprised when I got your letter . . ."

Mr. Willis, lurking in the doorway of a neighbouring tobacconist's shop, heard the words and scowled. Then, pulling his hat over his eyebrows and buttoning his mackintosh closely about him, he set out in pursuit. They walked through the lessening rain to the nearest cab-rank and engaged a taxi. Mr. Willis, cunningly waiting till they were well started, engaged the next.

"Follow that taxi," he said, exactly like somebody out of a book. And the driver, nonchalant as though he had stepped from the pages of Edgar Wallace, replied, "Right you are, sir," and slipped in his clutch.

The chase offered no excitement, ending up in the tamest possible manner at Simpson's in the Strand. Mr. Willis paid off his taxi, and climbed, in the wake of the couple, to that upper room where ladies are graciously permitted to be entertained. The quarry found a table near the window; Mr. Willis, ignoring the efforts of a waiter to pilot him to a quiet corner, squeezed in at the table next to them, where a man and woman, who obviously wanted to lunch alone, made way for him indignantly. Even so, he was not very well placed, for, though he could see Bredon and the girl, they had their backs to him, and their conversation was perfectly inaudible.

"Plenty of room at the next table, six," suggested the waiter.

"I'm all right here," replied Willis, irritably. His neighbour glared, and the waiter, with a glance as much as to say, 'Loopy—but what can a man do?' presented the bill of fare. Willis vaguely ordered saddle of mutton and red currant jelly with potatoes and gazed at Bredon's slim back.

". . . very nice to-day, sir."

"What?"

"The cauliflower, sir—very nice to-day."

"Anything you like."

The little black hat and the sleek yellow poll seemed very close together. Bredon had taken some small object out of his pocket and was showing it to the girl. A ring? Willis strained his eyes——

"What will you drink, sir?"

"Lager," said Willis, at random.

"Pilsener, sir, or Barclay's London Lager?"

"Oh, Pilsener."

"Light or dark, sir?"

"Light—dark—no, I mean light."

"Large light Pilsener, sir?"

"Yes, yes."

"Tankard, sir?"

"Yes, no—damn it! Bring it in anything that's got a hole in the top." There seemed no end to the questions that could be asked about beer. The girl had taken the object and was doing something with it. What? For heaven's sake, what?

"Roast or new potatoes, sir?"

"New." The man had gone, thank goodness. Bredon was holding Pamela Dean's hand—no, he was turning over the object that lay on her palm. The woman opposite Willis was stretching across for the sugar-basin—her head obstructed his view—deliberately, as it seemed to him. She moved back. Bredon was still examining the object——

A large dinner-wagon, laden with steaming joints under great silver covers, was beside him. A lid was lifted—the odour of roast mutton smote him in the face.

"A little more fat, sir? You like it underdone?"

Great God! What monster helpings they gave one at this place! What sickening stuff mutton was! How vile were these round yellow balls of potato that the man kept heaping on his plate! What disgusting stuff cauliflower could be—a curdle of cabbage! Willis, picking with nauseated reluctance at the finest roast saddle in London, felt his stomach cold and heavy, his feet a-twitch.

The hateful meal dragged on. The indignant couple finished their gooseberry pie and went their affronted way without waiting for coffee. Now Willis could see better. The other two were laughing now and talking eagerly. In a sudden lull a few words of Pamela's floated clearly back to him: "It's to be fancy dress, so you'll slip in all right." Then she dropped her voice again.

"Will you take any more mutton, sir?"

Try as he would, Willis could catch nothing more. He sat on in Simpson's until Bredon, glancing at his watch, appeared to remind himself and his companion that advertising copy-writers must work sometimes. Willis was ready for them. His bill was paid. He had only to shelter behind the newspaper he had brought in with him until they had passed him and then—what? Follow them out? Pursue them again in a taxi, wondering all the time how closely they were clasped together, what they were saying to one another, what appointments they were making, what new devilment there was still in store for Pamela, now that Victor Dean was out of the way, and what he would or could do next to make the world safe for her to live in?

He was spared the decision. As the two came abreast of him, Bredon, suddenly popping his head over the Lunch Edition of the *Evening Banner*, observed cheerfully:

"Hullo, Willis! enjoyed your lunch? Excellent saddle, what? But you should have tried the peas. Can I give you a lift back to the tread-mill?"

"No, thanks," growled Willis; and then realised that if he had said "Yes, please," he would at least have made an ardent tête-à-tête in the taxi impossible. But ride in the same taxi with Pamela Dean and Bredon he could not.

"Miss Dean, unhappily, has to leave us," went on Bredon. "You might come and console me by holding my hand."

Pamela was already half-way out of the room. Willis could not decide whether she knew to whom her escort was speaking and had studied to avoid him, or whether she supposed him to be some friend of Bredon's unknown to her. Quite suddenly he made up his mind.

"Well," he said, "it is getting a bit late. If you're having a taxi, I'll share it with you."

"That's the stuff," said Bredon. Willis rose and joined him and they moved on to where Pamela was waiting.

"I think you know our Mr. Willis?"

"Oh, yes," Pamela smiled a small, frozen smile. "Victor and he were great friends at one time."

The door. The stairs. The entrance. They were outside at last.

"I must be getting along now. Thank you so much for my lunch, Mr. Bredon. And you won't forget?"

"I certainly will not. 'Tisn't likely, is it?"

"Good afternoon, Mr. Willis."

"Good afternoon."

She was gone, walking briskly in her little, high-heeled shoes. The roaring Strand engulfed her. A taxi purred up to them.

Bredon gave the address and waved Willis in before him.

"Pretty kid, young Dean's sister," he remarked, cheerfully.

"See here, Bredon; I don't know quite what your game is, but you'd better be careful. I told Dean and I tell you—if you get Miss Dean mixed up with that dirty business of yours——"

"What dirty business?"

"You know well enough what I mean."

"Perhaps I do. And what then? Do I get my neck broken, like Victor Dean?"

Bredon slewed round as he spoke and looked Willis hard in the eye.

"You'll get——" Willis checked himself. "Never mind," he said, darkly, "you'll get what's coming to you. I'll see to that."

"I've no doubt you'll do it very competently, what?" replied Bredon. "But do you mind telling me exactly where you come into it? From what I can see, Miss Dean does not seem to welcome your championship with any great enthusiasm."

Willis flushed a dusky red.

"It's no business of mine, of course," went on Bredon, airily, while their taxi chugged impatiently in a hold-up at Holborn Tube Station, "but then, on the other hand, it doesn't really seem to be any business of yours, does it?"

"It is my business," retorted Willis. "It's every decent man's business. I heard Miss Dean making an appointment with you," he went on, angrily.

"What a detective you would make," said Bredon, admiringly. "But you really ought to take care, when you are shadowing anybody, that they are not sitting opposite a mirror, or anything that will serve as a mirror. There is a picture in front of the table where we were sitting, that reflects half the room. Elementary, my dear Watson. No doubt you will do better with practice. However, there is no secret about the appointment. We are going to a fancy dress affair on Friday. I am meeting Miss Dean for dinner at Boulestin's at 8 o'clock and we are going on from there. Perhaps you would care to accompany us?"

The policeman dropped his arm, and the taxi lurched forward into Southampton Row.

"You'd better be careful," growled Willis, "I might take you at your word."

"I should be charmed, personally," replied Bredon. "You will decide for yourself whether Miss Dean would or would not be put in an embarrassing position if you joined the party. Well, well, here we are at our little home from home. We must put aside this light badinage and devote ourselves to Sopo and Pompayne and Peabody's Piper Parritch. A delightful occupation, though somewhat lacking in incident. But let us not complain. We can't expect battle, murder and sudden death more than once a week or so. By the way, where were you when Victor Dean fell downstairs?"

"In the lavatory," said Willis, shortly.

"Were you, indeed?" Bredon looked at him once more attentively. "In the lavatory? You interest me strangely."

The atmosphere of the copy-department was much less strained by tea-time. Messrs. Brotherhood had been and gone, having seen nothing to shock their sense of propriety; Mr. Jollop, mellowed by his lunch, had passed three large poster designs with almost reckless readiness and was now with Mr. Pym, being almost persuaded to increase his appropriation for the autumn campaign. The suffering Mr. Armstrong, released from attendance on Mr. Jollop, had taken himself away to visit his dentist. Mr. Tallboy, coming in to purchase a stamp from Miss Rossiter for his private correspondence, announced with delight that the Nutrax half-double had gone to the printers.

"Is that 'KITTLE CATTLE'?" asked Ingleby. "You surprise me. I thought we should have trouble with it."

"I believe we did," said Tallboy. "Was it Scotch, and would people know what it meant? Would it suggest that we were calling women cows? And wasn't the sketch a little modernistic? But Armstrong got it shoved through somehow. May I drop this in your 'Out' basket, Miss Rossiter?"

"Serpently," replied the lady, with gracious humour, presenting the basket to receive the letter. "All billy-doos receive our prompt attention and are immediately forwarded to their destination by the quickest and surest route."

"Let's see," said Garrett. "I bet it's to a lady, and him a married man, too! No, you don't, Tallboy, you old devil—stand still, will you? Tell us who it is, Miss Rossiter."

"K. Smith, Esq.," said Miss Rossiter. "You lose your bet."

"What a swizz! But I expect it's all camouflage. I suspect Tallboy of keeping a harem somewhere. You can't trust these handsome blue-eyed men."

"Shut up, Garrett. I never," said Mr. Tallboy, extricating himself from

Garrett's grasp and giving him a playful punch in the wind, "in my life, met with such a bunch of buttinskis as you are in this department. Nothing is sacred to you, not even a man's business correspondence."

"How should anything be sacred to an advertiser?" demanded Ingleby, helping himself to four lumps of sugar. "We spend our whole time asking intimate questions of perfect strangers and it naturally blunts our finer feelings. 'Mother! has your Child Learnt Regular Habits?' 'Are you Troubled with Fullness after Eating?' 'Are you satisfied about your Drains?' 'Are you *Sure* that your Toilet-Paper is Germ-free?' 'Your most Intimate Friends dare not Ask you this Question'. 'Do you Suffer from Superfluous Hair?' 'Do you Like them to Look at your Hands?' 'Do you ever ask yourself about Body-Odour?' 'If anything Happened to You, would your Loved Ones be Safe?' 'Why Spend so much Time in the Kitchen?' 'You think that Carpet is Clean—but is it?' 'Are you a Martyr to Dandruff?' Upon my soul, I sometimes wonder why the long-suffering public doesn't rise up and slay us."

"They don't know of our existence," said Garrett. "They all think advertisements write themselves. When I tell people I'm in advertising, they always ask whether I design posters—they never think about the copy."

"They think the manufacturer does it himself," said Ingleby.

"They ought to see some of the suggestions the manufacturer does put up when he tries his hand at it."

"I wish they could." Ingleby grinned. "That reminds me. You know that idiotic thing Darling's put out the other day—the air-cushion for travellers with a doll that fits into the middle and sits up holding an 'ENGAGED' label?"

"What for?" asked Bredon.

"Well, the idea is, that you plank the cushion down in the railway carriage and the doll proclaims that the place is taken."

"But the cushion would do that without the doll."

"Of course it would, but you know how silly people are. They like superfluities. Well, anyway, they—Darling's, I mean—got out an ad. for the rubbish all by their little selves, and were fearfully pleased with it. Wanted us to put it through for them, till Armstrong burst into one of his juicy laughs and made them blush."

"What was it?"

"Picture of a nice girl bending down to put the cushion in the corner of a carriage. And the headline? 'DON'T LET THEM PINCH YOUR SEAT'."

"Attaboy!" said Mr. Bredon.

The new copy-writer was surprisingly industrious that day. He was still in his room, toiling over Sanfect ("Wherever there's Dirt there's Danger!" "The Skeleton in the Water-closet", "Assassins Lurk in your Scullery!" "Deadlier than Shell-Fire—GERMS!!") when Mrs. Crump led in her female army to attack the day's accumulated dirt—armed, one regrets to say, not with Sanfect, but with plain yellow soap and water.

"Come in, come in!" cried Mr. Bredon, genially, as the good lady paused reverently at his door. "Come and sweep me and my works away with the rest of the rubbish."

"Well, I'm sure, sir," said Mrs. Crump, "I've no need to be disturbing you."

"I've finished, really," said Bredon. "I suppose there's an awful lot of stuff to clear out here every day."

"That there is, sir—you'd hardly believe. Paper—well, I'm sure paper must be cheap, the amount they waste. Sackfuls and sackfuls every evening goes out. Of course, it's disposed of to the mills, but all the same it must be a dreadful expense. And there's boxes and boards and odds and ends—you'd be surprised, the things we picks up. I sometimes think the ladies and gentlemen brings up all their cast-offs on purpose to throw 'em away here."

"I shouldn't wonder."

"And mostly chucked on the floor," resumed Mrs. Crump, warming to her theme, "hardly ever in the paper-baskets, though goodness knows they makes 'em big enough."

"It must give you a lot of trouble."

"Lor, sir, we don't think nothing of it. We just sweeps the lot up and sends the sacks down by the lift. Though sometimes we has a good laugh over the queer things we finds. I usually just give the stuff a look through to make sure there's nothing valuable got dropped by mistake. Once I found two pound-notes on Mr. Ingleby's floor. He's a careless one and no mistake. And not so long ago—the very day poor Mr. Dean had his sad accident—I found a kind of carved stone lying round in the passage—looked as though it might be a charm or a trinket or something of that. But I think it must have tumbled out of the poor gentleman's pocket as he fell, because Mrs. Doolittle said she'd seen it in his room, so I brought it in here, sir, and put it in that there little box."

"Is this it?" Bredon fished in his waistcoat pocket and produced the onyx scarab, which he had unaccountably neglected to return to Pamela Dean.

"That's it, sir. A comical-looking thing, ain't it? Like it might be a beedle or such. It was lying in a dark corner under the iron staircase and at first I thought it was just a pebble like the other one."

"What other one?"

"Well, sir, I found a little round pebble in the very same place only a few days before. I said at the time, 'Well,' I said, 'that's a funny thing to find there.' But I reckon that one must have come from Mr. Atkins's room, him having take his seaside holiday early this year on account of having been ill, and you know how people do fill up their pockets with sea-shells and pebbles and such."

Bredon hunted in his pocket again.

"Something like that, was it?" He held out a smooth, water-rounded pebble, about the size of his thumbnail.

"Very like it, sir. Did that come out of the passage, sir, might I ask?"

"No—I found that up on the roof."

"Ah!" said Mrs. Crump. "It'll be them boys up to their games. When the Sergeant's eye is off them you never know what they're after."

"They do their drill up there, don't they? Great stuff. Hardens the muscles and develops the figure. When do they perform? In the lunch-hour?"

"Oh, no, sir. Mr. Pym won't have them running about after their dinners.

He says it spoils their digestions and gives them the colic. Very particular, is Mr. Pym. Half-past eight regular they has to be on duty, sir, in their pants and singlets. Twenty minutes they has of it and then changed and ready for their dooties. After dinner they sets a bit in the boys' room and has a read or plays somethink quiet, as it might be, shove ha'penny or tiddley-winks or such. But in their room they must stay, sir; Mr. Pym won't have nobody about the office in the dinner-hour, sir, not without, of course, it's the boy that goes round with the disinfectant, sir."

"Ah, of course! Spray with Sanfect and you're safe."

"That's right, sir, except that they uses Jeyes' Fluid."

"Oh, indeed," said Mr. Bredon, struck afresh by the curious reluctance of advertising firms to use the commodities they extol for a living. "Well, we're very well looked after here, Mrs. Crump, what?"

"Oh, yes, sir. Mr. Pym pays great attention to 'ealth. A very kind gentleman, is Mr. Pym. Next week, sir, we has the Charwomen's Tea, down in the canteen, with an egg-and-spoon race and a bran-tub, and bring the kiddies. My daughter's little girls always look forward to the tea, sir."

"I'm sure they must," said Mr. Bredon, "and I expect they'd like some new hair-ribbons or something of that sort——"

"It's very kind of you, sir," said Mrs. Crump, much gratified.

"Not at all." A couple of coins clinked. "Well, I'll push off now and leave you to it."

A very nice gentleman, in Mrs. Crump's opinion, and not at all proud.

It turned out precisely as Mr. Willis had expected. He had tracked his prey from Boulestin's, and this time he felt quite certain he had not been spotted. His costume—that of a member of the Vehmgericht, with its black cassock and black, eyeletted hood covering the whole head and shoulders—was easily slipped on over his every-day suit. Muffled in an old burberry, he had kept watch behind a convenient van in Covent Garden until Bredon and Pamela Dean came out; his taxi had been in waiting just round the corner. His task was made the easier by the fact that the others were driving, not in a taxi, but in an enormous limousine, and that Bredon had taken the wheel himself. The theatre rush was well over before the chase started, so that there was no need to keep suspiciously close to the saloon. The trail had led westward through Richmond and still west, until it had ended at a large house, standing in its own grounds on the bank of the river. Towards the end of the journey they were joined by other cars and taxis making in the same direction; and on arrival they found the drive a parking-place for innumerable vehicles. Bredon and Miss Dean had gone straight in, without a glance behind them.

Willis, who had put on his costume in the taxi, anticipated some difficulty about getting in, but there was none. A servant had met him at the door and asked if he was a member. Willis had replied boldly that he was and given the name of William Brown, which seemed to him an ingenious and plausible invention. Apparently the club was full of William Browns, for the servant raised no difficulty, and he was ushered straight in to a handsomely furnished hall. Immediately in front of him, on the skirts of a crowd of people drinking cocktails, was Bredon, in the harlequin black and white which had been conspicuous as he stepped into his car after dinner. Pamela Dean, in an exiguous swan's-down costume representing a powder-puff, stood beside him. From a room beyond resounded the strains of a saxophone.

"The place," said Mr. Willis to himself, "is a den of iniquity." And for once, Mr. Willis was not far wrong.

He was amazed by the slackness of the organisation. Without question or hesitation, every door was opened to him. There was gambling. There was drink in oceans. There was dancing. There were what Mr. Willis had heard described as orgies. And at the back of it all, he sensed something else, something that he did not quite understand; something that he was not precisely kept out of, but to which he simply had not the key.

He was, of course, partnerless, but he soon found himself absorbed into a party of exceedingly bright young people, and watching the evolutions of a *danseuse* whose essential nakedness was enhanced and emphasised by the wearing of a top hat, a monocle and a pair of patent-leather boots. He was supplied with drinks—some of which he paid for, but the majority of which were thrust upon him, and he suddenly became aware that he would have made a better detective had he been more hardened to mixed liquors. His head began to throb, and he had lost sight of Bredon and Pamela. He became obsessed with the idea that they had departed into one of the sinister little cubicles he had seen—each heavily curtained and furnished with a couch and a mirror. He broke away from the group surrounding him and began a hurried search through the house. His costume was hot and heavy, and the sweat poured down his face beneath the stifling black folds of his hood. He found a conservatory full of amorous drunken couples, but the pair he was looking for was not among them. He pushed open a door and found himself in the garden. Cries and splashes attracted him. He plunged down a rose-scented alley beneath a pergola and came out upon an open space with a round fountain-pool in the centre.

A man with a girl in his arms came reeling past him, flushed and hiccuping with laughter, his leopard-skin tunic half torn from his shoulders and the vine-leaves scattering from his hair as he ran. The girl was shrieking like a steam-engine. He was a broad-shouldered man, and the muscles of his back gleamed in the moonlight as he swung his protesting burden from him and tossed her, costume and all, into the pool. Yells of laughter greeted this performance, renewed as the girl, draggled and dripping, crawled back over the edge of the basin and burst into a stream of abuse. Then Willis saw the black-and-white harlequin.

He was climbing the statue-group in the centre of the pool—an elaborate affair of twined mermaids and dolphins, supporting a basin in which crouched an amorino, blowing from a conch-shell a high spout of dancing water. Up and up went the slim chequered figure, dripping and glittering like a fantastic water-creature. He caught the edge of the upper basin with his hands, swung for a moment and lifted. Even in that moment, Willis felt a pang of reluctant admiration. It was the easy, unfretted motion of the athlete, a display of muscular strength without jerk or effort. Then his knee was on the basin. He was up and climbing upon the bronze cupid. Yet another moment and he was kneeling upon the figure's stooped shoulders—standing upright upon them, the spray of the fountain blowing about him.

"Good God!" thought Willis, "the fellow's a tight-rope walker—or he's too drunk to fall." There were yells of applause, and a girl began to shriek hysterically. Then a very tall woman, in a moonlight frock of oyster satin, who had made herself the centre of the most boisterous of all the parties, pushed past Willis and stood out on the edge of the basin, her fair hair standing out like a pale aureole round her vivid face.

"Dive!" she called out, "dive in! I dare you to! Dive in!"

"Shut up, Dian!" One of the soberer of the men caught her round the shoulders and put his hand over her mouth. "It's too shallow—he'll break his neck."

She pushed him away.

"You be quiet. He shall dive. I want him to. Go to hell, Dickie. You wouldn't dare do it, but he will."

"I certainly wouldn't. Stow it."

"Come on, Harlequin, dive!"

The black and white figure raised its arms above its fantastic head and stood poised.

"Don't be a fool, man," bawled Dickie.

But the other women were fired with the idea and their screams drowned his voice.

"Dive, Harlequin, dive."

The slim body shot down through the spray, struck the surface with scarcely a splash and slid through the water like a fish. Willis caught his breath. It was perfectly done. It was magnificent. He forgot his furious hatred of the man and applauded with the rest. The girl Dian ran forward and caught hold of the swimmer as he emerged.

"Oh, you're marvellous, you're marvellous!" She clung to him, the water soaking into her draggled satin.

"Take me home, Harlequin—I adore you!"

The Harlequin bent his masked face and kissed her. The man called Dickie tried to pull him away, but was neatly tripped and fell with a jerk into the pool, amid a roar of laughter. The Harlequin tossed the tall girl across his shoulder.

"A prize!" he shouted. "A prize!"

Then he swung her lightly to her feet and took her hand. "Run," he called, "run! Let's run away, and let them catch us if they can."

There was a sudden stampede. Willis saw the angry face of Dickie as he lurched past him and heard his swearing. Somebody caught his hand. He ran up the rose-alley, panting. Something caught his foot, and he tripped and fell. His companion abandoned him, and ran on, hooting. He sat up, found his head enveloped in his hood and struggled to release himself.

A hand touched his shoulder.

"Come on, Mr. Willis," said a mocking voice in his ear, "Mr. Bredon says I am to escort you home."

He succeeded in dragging the black cloth from his head and scrambled to his feet.

Beside him stood Pamela Dean. She had taken off her mask, and her eyes were alight with mischief.

CHAPTER V

Surprising Metamorphosis of Mr. Bredon

LORD PETER WIMSEY had paid a call upon Chief Inspector Parker of Scotland Yard, who was his brother-in-law.

He occupied a large and comfortable arm-chair in the Chief Inspector's Bloomsbury flat. Opposite him, curled upon the chesterfield, was his sister, Lady Mary Parker, industriously knitting an infant's vest. On the window-seat, hugging his knees and smoking a pipe, was Mr. Parker himself. On a convenient table stood a couple of decanters and a soda siphon. On the hearth-rug was a large tabby cat. The scene was almost ostentatiously peaceful and domestic.

"So you have become one of the world's workers, Peter," said Lady Mary.

"Yes; I'm pulling down four solid quid a week. Amazin' sensation. First time I've ever earned a cent. Every week when I get my pay-envelope, I glow with honest pride."

Lady Mary smiled, and glanced at her husband, who grinned cheerfully back. The difficulties which are apt to arise when a poor man marries a rich wife had, in their case, been amicably settled by an ingenious arrangement, under which all Lady Mary's money had been handed over to her brothers in trust for little Parkers to come, the trustee having the further duty of doling out each quarter to the wife a sum precisely equal to the earnings of the husband during that period. Thus a seemly balance was maintained between the two principals; and the trifling anomaly that Chief Inspector Parker was actually a mere pauper in comparison with small Charles Peter and still smaller Mary Lucasta, now peacefully asleep in their cots on the floor above, disturbed nobody one whit. It pleased Mary to have the management of their moderate combined income, and incidentally did her a great deal of good. She now patronised her wealthy brother with all the superiority which the worker feels over the man who merely possesses money.

"But what *is* the case all about, exactly?" demanded Parker.

"Blest if I know," admitted Wimsey, frankly. "I got hauled into it through Freddy Arbuthnot's wife—Rachel Levy that was, you know. She knows old Pym, and he met her at dinner somewhere and told her about this letter that was worrying him, and she said, Why not get somebody in to investigate it, and he said, who? So she said she knew somebody—not mentioning my name, you see—and he said would she ask me to buzz along, so I buzzed and there I am."

"Your narrative style," said Parker, "though racy, is a little elliptical. Could you not begin at the beginning and go on until you come to the end, and then, if you are able to, stop?"

"I'll try," said his lordship, "but I always find the stopping part of the business so difficult. Well, look! On a Monday afternoon—the 25th of May, to be particular—a young man, Victor Dean by name, employed as a copy-writer in the firm of Pym's Publicity, Ltd., Advertising Agents, fell down an iron spiral staircase on their premises, situate in the upper part of Southampton Row, and died immediately of injuries received, to wit: one broken neck, one cracked skull, one broken leg and minor cuts and contusions, various. The time of this disaster was, as nearly as can be ascertained, 3.30 in the afternoon."

"Hum!" said Parker. "Pretty extensive injuries for a fall of that kind."

"So I thought, before I saw the staircase. To proceed. On the day after this occurrence, the sister of deceased sends to Mr. Pym a fragment of a half-finished letter which she has found on her brother's desk. It warns him that there is something of a fishy nature going on in the office. The letter is dated about ten days previous to the death, and appears to have been laid aside as though the writer wanted to think over the wording a bit more carefully. Very good. Now, Mr. Pym is a man of rigid morality—except, of course, as regards his profession, whose essence is to tell plausible lies for money——"

"How about truth in advertising?"

"Of course, there is *some* truth in advertising. There's yeast in bread, but you can't make bread with yeast alone. Truth in advertising," announced Lord Peter sententiously, "is like leaven, which a woman hid in three measures of meal. It provides a suitable quantity of gas, with which to blow out a mass of crude misrepresentation into a form that the public can swallow. Which incidentally brings me to the delicate and important distinction between the words 'with' and 'from'. Suppose you are advertising lemonade, or, not to be invidious, we will say perry. If you say 'Our perry is made from fresh-plucked pears only,' then it's got to be made from pears only, or the statement is actionable; if you just say it is made 'from pears', without the 'only', the betting is that it is probably made chiefly of pears; but if you say, 'made *with* pears', you generally mean that you use a peck of pears to a ton of turnips, and the law cannot touch you—such are the niceties of our English tongue."

"Make a note, Mary, next time you go shopping, and buy nothing that is not 'from, only'. Proceed, Peter—and let us have a little less of your English tongue."

"Yes. Well, here is a young man who starts to write a warning letter. Before he can complete it, he falls downstairs and is killed. Is that, or is it not, a darned suspicious circumstance?"

"So suspicious that it is probably the purest coincidence. But since you have a fancy for melodrama, we will allow it to be suspicious. Who saw him die?"

"I, said the fly. Meaning one Mr. Atkins and one Mrs. Crump, who saw the fall from below, and one Mr. Prout who saw it from above. All their evidence is interesting. Mr. Prout says that the staircase was well-lit, and that deceased was not going extra fast, while the others say that he fell all of a heap, forwards, clutching *The Times Atlas* in so fierce a grip that it could afterwards hardly be prised from his fingers. What does that suggest to you?"

"Only that the death was instantaneous, which it would be if one broke one's neck."

"I know. But look here! You are going downstairs and your foot slips. What happens? Do you crumple forwards and dive down head first? Or do you sit down suddenly on your tail and do the rest of the journey that way?"

"It depends. If it was actually a slip, I should probably come down on my tail. But if I tripped, I should very likely dive forwards. You can't tell, without knowing just how it happened."

"All right. You always have an answer. Well now—do you clutch what you're carrying with a deathly grip—or do you chuck it, and try to save yourself by grabbing hold of the banisters?"

Mr. Parker paused. "I should probably grab," he said, slowly, "unless I was carrying a tray full of crockery, or anything. And even then . . . I don't know. Perhaps it's an instinct to hold on to what one's got. But equally it's an instinct to try and save one's self. I don't know. All this arguing about what you and I would do and what the reasonable man would do is very unsatisfactory."

Wimsey groaned. "Put it this way, doubting Thomas. If the death-grip was due to instantaneous rigor, he must have been dead so quickly that he couldn't think of saving himself. Now, there are two possible causes of death—the broken neck, which he must have got when he pitched on his head at the bottom, and the crack on the temple, which is attributed to his hitting his skull on one of the knobs on the banisters. Now, falling down a staircase isn't like falling off a roof—you do it in instalments, and have time to think about it. If he killed himself by hitting the banisters, he must have fallen first and hit himself afterwards. The same thing applies, with still more force, to his breaking his neck. Why, when he felt himself going, didn't he drop everything and break his fall?"

"I know what you want me to say," said Parker. "That he was sandbagged first and dead before he fell. But I don't see it. I say he would have caught his toe in something and tripped forwards and struck his head straight away and died of that. There's nothing impossible about it."

"Then I'll try again. How's this? That same evening, Mrs. Crump, the head charwoman, picked up this onyx scarab in the passage, just beneath the iron staircase. It is, as you see, rounded and smooth and heavy for its size, which is much about that of the iron knobs on the staircase. It has, as you also see, a slight chip on one side. It belonged to the dead man, who was accustomed to carry it in his waistcoat pocket or keep it sitting on the desk beside him while he worked. What about it?"

"I should say it fell from his pocket when he fell."

"And the chip?"

"If it wasn't there before——"

"It wasn't, his sister says she's sure it wasn't."

"Then it got chipped in falling."

"You think that?"

"I do."

"I think you were meant to think that. To continue: some few days earlier, Mrs. Crump found a smooth pebble of much the same size as the scarab lying in the same passage at the foot of the same iron staircase."

"Did she?" said Parker. He uncurled himself from the window-seat and made for the decanters. "What does she say about it?"

"Says that you'd scarcely believe the queer odds and ends she finds when she's cleaning out the office. Attributes the stone to Mr. Atkins, he having taken his seaside holiday early on account of ill-health."

"Well," said Parker, releasing the lever of the soda-siphon, "and why not?"

"Why not, indeed? This other pebble, which I here produce, was found by me on the roof of the lavatory. I had to shin down a pipe to get it, and ruined a pair of flannel bags."

"Oh, yeah?"

"Okay, captain. That's where I found it. I also found a place where the paint had been chipped off the skylight."

"What skylight?"

"The skylight that is directly over the iron staircase. It's one of those pointed things, like a young greenhouse, and it has windows that open all round—you know the kind I mean—which are kept open in hot weather. It was hot weather when young Dean departed this life."

"The idea being that somebody heaved a stone at him through the skylight?"

"You said it, chief. Or, to be exact, not *a* stone, but *the* stone. Meaning the scarab."

"And how about the other stones?"

"Practice shots. I've ascertained that the office is always practically empty during the lunch-hour. Nobody much ever goes on the roof, except the office-boys for their P.J.'s at 8.30 ack emma."

"People who live in glass skylights shouldn't throw stones. Do you mean to suggest that by chucking a small stone like this at a fellow, you're going to crack his skull open and break his neck for him?"

"Not if you just throw it, of course. But how about a sling or a catapult?"

"Oh, in that case, you've only got to ask the people in the neighbouring offices if they've seen anybody enjoying a spot of David and Goliath exercise on Pym's roof, and you've got him."

"It's not as simple as that. The roof's quite a good bit higher than the roofs of the surrounding buildings, and it has a solid stone parapet all round about three feet high—to give an air of still greater magnificence, I suppose. To sling a stone through on to the iron staircase you'd have to kneel down in a special position between that skylight and the next, and you can't be seen from anywhere—unless somebody happened to be *on* the staircase looking up—which nobody obviously was, except Victor Dean, poor lad. It's safe as houses."

"Very well, then. Find out if any member of the staff has frequently stayed in at lunch-time."

Wimsey shook his head.

"No bon. The staff clock in every morning, but there are no special tabs kept on them at 1 o'clock. The reception clerk goes out to his lunch, and one of the elder boys takes his place at the desk, just in case any message or parcel comes in, but he's not there necessarily every moment of the time. Then there's the lad who hops round with Jeyes' Fluid in a squirt, but he doesn't go on to the roof. There's nothing to prevent anybody from going up, say at half-past twelve, and staying there till he's done his bit of work and then simply walking out down the staircase. The liftman, or his locum tenens, would be on duty, but you've only to keep on the blind side of the lift as you pass and he couldn't possibly see you. Besides, the lift might quite well have gone down to the basement. All the bloke would have to do would just be to bide his time and walk out. There's nothing in it. Similarly, on the day of the death. He goes through towards the lavatory, which is reached from the stairs. When the coast is clear, he ascends to the roof. He lurks there, till he sees his victim start down the iron staircase, which everybody does, fifty times a day. He whangs off his bolt and departs. Everybody is picking up the body and exclaiming over it, when in walks our friend, innocently, from the lav. It's as simple as pie."

"Wouldn't it be noticed, if he was out of his own room all that time?"

"My dear old man, if you knew Pym's! Everybody is always out of his room. If he isn't chatting with the copy-department, or fooling round the typists, he's in the studio, clamouring for a lay-out, or in the printing, complaining about a folder, or in the press-department, inquiring about an appropriation, or in the vouchers, demanding back numbers of something, or if he isn't in any of those places, he's somewhere else—slipping out for surreptitious coffee or hair-cuts. The word alibi has no meaning in a place like Pym's."

"You're going to have a lovely time with it all, I can see that," said Parker. "But what sort of irregularity could possibly be going on in a place like that, which would lead to murder?"

"Now we're coming to it. Young Dean used to tag round with the de Momerie crowd——"

Parker whistled.

"Sinning above his station in life?"

"Very much so. But you know Dian de Momerie. She gets more kick out of corrupting the bourgeois—she enjoys the wrestle with their little consciences. She's a bad lot, that girl. I took her home last night, so I ought to know."

"Peter!" said Lady Mary. "Quite apart from your morals, which alarm me, how did you get into that gang? I should have thought they'd as soon have taken up with Charles, here, or the Chief Commissioner."

"Oh, I went incog. A comedy of masks. And you needn't worry about my morals. The young woman became incapably drunk on the way home, so I pushed her inside her dinky little maisonette in Garlic Mews and tucked her up on a divan in the sitting-room to astonish her maid in the morning. Though she's probably past being astonished. But the point is that I found out a good bit about Victor Dean."

"Just a moment," interrupted Parker, "did he dope?"

"Apparently not, though I'll swear it wasn't Dian's fault if he didn't. According to his sister, he was too strong-minded. Possibly he tried it once and felt so rotten that he didn't try it again. . . . Yes—I know what you're thinking. If he was dopey, he might have fallen downstairs on his own account. But I don't think that'll work. These things have a way of coming out at post-mortems. The question was raised . . . no; it wasn't that."

"Did Dian have any opinion on the subject?"

"She said he wasn't a sport. All the same, she seems to have kept him in tow from about the end of November to the end of April—nearly six months, and that's a long time for Dian. I wonder what the attraction was. I suppose the whelp must have had something engaging about him."

"Is that the sister's story?"

"Yes; but she says that Victor 'had great ambitions'. I don't quite know what she thinks he meant by that."

"I suppose she realised that Dian was his mistress. Or wasn't she?"

"Must have been. But I rather gather his sister thought he was contemplating matrimony."

Parker laughed.

"After all," said Lady Mary, "he probably didn't tell his sister everything."

"Damned little, I should imagine. She was quite honestly upset by last night's show. Apparently the party Dean took her to wasn't quite so hot. Why did he take her? That's another problem. He said he wanted her to meet Dian, and no doubt the kid imagined she was being introduced to a future in-law. But Dean—you'd think he'd want to keep his sister out of it. He couldn't, surely, really have wanted to corrupt her, as Willis said."

"Who is Willis?"

"Willis is a young man who foams at the mouth if you mention Victor Dean, who was once Victor Dean's dearest friend, who is in love with Victor Dean's sister, is furiously jealous of me, thinks I'm tarred with the same brush as Victor Dean, and dogs my footsteps with the incompetent zeal of fifty Watsons. He writes copy about face-cream and corsets, is the son of a provincial draper, was educated at a grammar school and wears, I deeply regret to say, a double-breasted waistcoat. That is the most sinister thing about him—except that he admits to having been in the lavatory when Victor Dean fell downstairs, and the lavatory, as I said before, is the next step to the roof."

"Who else was in the lavatory?"

"I haven't asked him yet. How can I? It's horribly hampering to one's detective work when one isn't supposed to be detecting, because one daren't ask any questions, much. But if whoever it was knew I was detecting, then whatsoever questions I asked, I shouldn't get any answers. It wouldn't matter if only I had the foggiest notion whom or what I was detecting, but looking among about a hundred people for the perpetrator of an unidentified crime is rather difficult."

"I thought you were looking for a murderer."

"So I am—but I don't think I shall ever get the murderer till I know why the murder was done. Besides, what Pym engaged me to do was to look for the irregularity in the office. Of course, murder is an irregularity, but it's not the one I'm commissioned to hunt for. And the only person I can fix a motive for the murder on to is Willis—and it's not the sort of motive I'm looking for."

"What was Willis's row with Dean?"

"Damn silliest thing in the world. Willis used to go home with Dean at week-ends. Dean lived in a flat with his sister, by the way—no parents or anything. Willis fell in love with sister. Sister wasn't sure about him. Dean took sister to one of Dian's hot parties. Willis found out. Willis, being a boob, talked to sister like a Dutch uncle. Sister called Willis a disgusting, stuck-up idiotic, officious prig. Willis rebuked Dean. Dean told Willis to go to hell. Loud row. Sister joined in. Dean family united in telling Willis to go and bury himself. Willis told Dean that if he (Dean) persisted in corrupting his (Dean's) sister he (Willis) would shoot him like a dog. His very words, or so I am told."

"Willis," said Mary, "appears to think in clichés."

"Of course he does—that's why he writes such good corset-copy. Anyhow, there it was. Dean and Willis at daggers drawn for three months. Then Dean fell downstairs. Now Willis has started on me. I told off Pamela Dean to take him home last night, but I don't know what came of it. I've explained to her that those hot-stuff parties are genuinely dangerous, and that Willis has some method in his madness, though a prize juggins as regards tact and knowledge of the sex. It was frightfully comic to see old Willis sneaking in after us in a sort of Ku Klux Klan outfit—incredibly stealthy, and wearing the same shoes he wears in the office and a seal-ring on his little finger that one could identify from here to the Monument."

"Poor lad! I suppose it wasn't Willis who tipped friend Dean down the staircase?"

"I don't think so, Polly—but you never know. He's such a melodramatic ass. He might consider it a splendid sin. But I don't think he'd have had the brains to work out the details. And if he had done it, I fancy he'd have gone straight round to the police-station, smitten the double-breasted waistcoat a resounding blow and proclaimed 'I did it, in the cause of purity'. But against that, there's the undoubted fact that Dean's connection with Dian and Co. definitely came to an end in April—so why should he wait till the end of May to strike the blow? The row with Dean took place in March."

"Possibly, Peter, the sister has been leading you up the garden. The connection may not have stopped when she said it did. She may have kept it up on her own. She may even be a drug-taker or something herself. You never know."

"No; but generally one can make a shrewd guess. No; I don't think there's anything like that wrong with Pamela Dean. I'll swear her disgust last night was genuine. It was pretty foul, I must say. By the way, Charles, where the devil do these people get their stuff from? There was enough dope floating about that house to poison a city."

"If I knew that," said Mr. Parker, sourly, "I should be on velvet. All I can tell you is, that it's coming in by the boat-load from somewhere or other, and is being distributed broadcast from somewhere or other. The question is, where? Of course, we could lay hands to-morrow on half a hundred of the small distributors, but where would be the good of that? They don't know themselves where it comes from, or who handles it. They all tell the same tale. It's handed to them in the street by men they've never seen before and couldn't identify again. Or it's put in their pockets in omnibuses. It isn't always that they won't tell they honestly don't know. And if you did catch the man immediately above them in the scale, he would know nothing either. It's heart-breaking. Somebody must be making millions out of it."

"Yes. Well, to go back to Victor Dean. Here's another problem. He was pulling down six pounds a week at Pym's. How does one manage to run with the de Momerie crowd on £300 a year? Even if he wasn't much of a sport, it couldn't possibly be done for nothing."

"Probably he lived on Dian."

"Possibly he did, the little tick. On the other hand, I've got an idea. Suppose he really did think he had a chance of marrying into the aristocracy—or what he imagines to be the aristocracy. After all, Dian is a de Momerie, though her people have shown her the door, and you can't blame them. Put it that he was spending far more than he could afford in trying to keep up the running. Put it that it took longer than he thought and that he had got heavily dipped. And then see what that half-finished letter to Pym looks like in the light of that theory."

"Well," began Parker.

"Oh, do step on the gas!" broke in Mary. "How you two darlings do love going round and round a subject, don't you? Blackmail, of course. It's perfectly obvious. I've seen it coming for the last hour. This Dean creature is looking round for a spot of extra income and he discovers somebody at Pym's doing something he shouldn't—the head-cashier cooking the accounts, or the office-boy pilfering from the petty cash, or something. So he says, 'if you don't square me, I'll tell Pym', and starts to write a letter. Probably, you know, he never meant that letter to get to Mr. Pym, at all; it was just a threat. The other man stops him for the moment by paying up something on account. Then he thinks: 'This is hopeless, I'd better slug the little beast.' So he slugs him. And there you are."

"Just as simple as that," said Wimsey.

"Of course it's simple, only men love to make mysteries."

"And women love to jump to conclusions."

"Never mind the generalisations," said Parker, "they always lead to bad reasoning. Where do I come into all this?"

"You give me your advice, and stand by ready to rally round with your myrmidons in case there's any rough-housing. By the way, I can give you the address of that house we went to last night. Dope and gambling to be had for the asking, to say nothing of nameless orgies."

He mentioned the address and the Chief Inspector made a note of it. "Though we can't do much," he admitted. "It's a private house, belonging to a Major Milligan. We've had our eye on it for some time. And even if we could get in on it, it probably wouldn't help us to what we want. I don't suppose there's a soul in that gang who knows where the dope comes from. Still, it's something to have definite evidence that that's where it goes. By the way, we got the goods on that couple you helped us to arrest the other night. They'll probably get seven years."

"Good. I was pretty nearly had that time, though. Two of Pym's typists were fooling round and recognised me. I gave them a fishy stare and explained next morning that I had a cousin who closely resembled me. That notorious fellow Wimsey, of course. It's a mistake to be too well known."

"If the de Momerie crowd get wise to you, you'll find yourself in Queer Street," said Parker. "How did you get so pally with Dian?"

"Dived off a fountain into a fish-pond. It pays to advertise. She thinks I'm the world's eighth wonder. Absolutely the lobster's dress-shirt."

"Well, don't kill yourself," said Mary, gently. "We rather like you, and small Peter couldn't spare his best uncle."

"It will do you no end of good," remarked his brother-in-law, callously, "to have a really difficult case for once. When you've struggled for a bit with a death that might have been caused by anybody for any imaginable motive, you may be less sniffy and superior about the stray murders all over the country that the police so notoriously fail to avenge. I hope it will be a lesson to you. Have another spot?"

"Thanks; I'll try to profit by it. In the meantime, I'll go on gulling the public and being Mr. Bredon, to be heard of at your address. And let me know of any developments with the Momerie-Milligan lot."

"I will. Should you care to make one in our next dope-raid?"

"Sure thing. When do you expect it?"

"We've had information about cocaine-smuggling on the Essex coast. Worst thing the Government ever did was to abolish the coast-guard service. It doubles our trouble, especially with all these privately-owned motor-boats about. If you're out for an evening's fun any time, you could come along—and you might bring that car of yours. It's faster than anything we've got."

"I see. Two for yourselves and one for me. Right you are. I'm on. Send me a line any time. I cease work at 5.30."

In the meantime, three hearts were being wrung on Mr. Death Bredon's account.

Miss Pamela Dean was washing a pair of silk stockings in her solitary flat.

"Last night was rather marvellous. . . . I suppose I oughtn't to have enjoyed it, with poor old Victor only just buried, the darling . . . but, of course, I really went for Victor's sake . . . I wonder if that detective man will find out anything about it . . . he didn't say much, but I believe he thinks there was something funny about Victor being killed like that . . . anyhow, Victor suspected there was something wrong, and he'd *want* me to do everything I could to ferret it out. . . . I didn't know private detectives were like that. . . . I thought they were nasty, furtive little men . . . vulgar . . . I like his voice . . . and his hands . . . oh, dear! there's a hole . . . I'll have to catch it together before it runs up the instep . . . and beautiful manners, only I'm afraid he was cross with me for coming to Pym's . . . he must be fearfully athletic to climb up that fountain . . . he swims like a fish . . . my new bathing-dress . . . sun-bathing . . . thank goodness I've got decent legs . . . I'll really have to get some more stockings, these won't go on much longer . . . I wish I didn't look so washed-out in black. . . . Poor Victor! . . . I wonder what I can possibly do with Alec Willis

... if only he wasn't such a prig.... I don't mind Mr. Bredon ... he's quite right about that crowd being no good, but then he really knows what he's talking about, and it isn't just prejudice.... Why will Alec be so jealous and tiresome? ... And looking so silly in that black thing ... following people about.... Incompetent—I do like people to be competent.... Mr. Bredon looks terribly competent ... no, he doesn't exactly look it, but he is ... he looks as though he never did anything but go to dinner-parties.... I suppose high-class detectives have to look like that.... Alec would make a rotten detective.... I don't like ill-tempered men ... I wonder what happened when Mr. Bredon went off with Dian de Momerie ... she is beautiful ... damn her, she's lovely ... she does drink an awful lot ... they say it makes you look old before your time ... you get coarse ... my complexion's all right, but I'm not the fashionable type ... Dian de Momerie is perfectly crazy about people who do mad things ... I don't like aluminium blondes ... I wonder if I could get an aluminium bleach...."

Alec Willis, hammering a rather hard pillow into a more comfortable shape in his boarding-house bedroom, sought slumber in vain:

"Gosh! what a head I had this morning ... that damned, sleek brute! ... there's something up between Pamela and him ... helping her with some business of Victor's my foot! ... He's out to make trouble ... and going off with that white-headed bitch ... it's a damned insult ... of course Pamela would lick his boots ... women ... put up with anything ... wish I hadn't had all those drinks ... damn this bed! damn this foul place ... I'll have to chuck Pym's ... it isn't safe.... Murder? ... anybody interfering with Pamela ... Pamela.... She wouldn't let me kiss her ... that swine Bredon ... down the iron staircase ... get my hands on his throat.... What a hope! damned posturing acrobat ... Pamela ... I'd like to show her ... money, money, money ... if I wasn't so damned hard up ... Dean was a little squirt anyway ... I only told her the truth ... blast all women! ... They like rotters ... I haven't paid for that last suit ... oh, hell! I wish I hadn't had those drinks ... I forgot to get any bicarbonate ... I haven't paid for those boots ... all those naked women in the swimming-pool ... black and silver ... he spotted me, damn his eyes! ... "Hullo, Willis!" this morning, as cool as a fish ... dives like a fish ... fish don't dive ... fish don't sleep ... or do they? ... I can't sleep ... 'Macbeth hath murdered sleep'... Murder ... down the iron staircase ... get my hands on his throat ... oh, damn! damn! damn! ..."

Dian de Momerie was dancing:

"My God! I'm bored.... Get off my feet, you clumsy cow.... Money, tons of money ... but I'm bored.... Can't we do something else? ... I'm sick of that tune ... I'm sick of everything ... he's working up to get all mushy ... suppose I'd better go through with it ... I was sozzled last night ... wonder where the Harlequin man went to ... wonder who he was ... that little idiot Pamela Dean ... these women ... I'll have to make up to her, I suppose, if I'm ever to get his address ... I got him away from her, any old how ... wish I hadn't been so squiffy ... I can't remember ... climbing up the fountain ... black and silver ... he's got a lovely body ... I think he could give me a thrill . . . my God! how bored I am . . . he's exciting . . . rather mysterious . . . I'll have to write to Pamela Dean . . . silly little fool . . . expect she hates me . . . rather a pity I chucked little Victor . . . fell downstairs and broke his silly neck . . . damn good riddance . . . ring her up . . . she's not on the 'phone . . . so suburban not to be on the 'phone . . . if this tune goes on, I shall scream . . . Milligan's drinks are rotten . . . why does one go there? . . . Must do something . . . Harlequin . . . don't even know his name. . . . Weedon . . . Leader . . . something or other . . . oh, hell! perhaps Milligan knows . . . I can't stand this any longer . . . black and silver . . . thank God! that's over!"

All over London the lights flickered in and out, calling on the public to save its body and purse: SOPO SAVES SCRUBBING—NUTRAX FOR NERVES—CRUNCHLETS ARE CRISPER—EAT PIPER PARRITCH—DRINK POMPAYNE—ONE WHOOSH AND IT'S CLEAN—OH, BOY! IT'S TOMBOY TOFFEE—NOURISH NERVES WITH NUTRAX—FARLEY'S FOOTWEAR TAKES YOU FURTHER—IT ISN'T DEAR, IT'S DARLING—DARLING'S FOR HOUSEHOLD APPLIANCES—MAKE ALL SAFE WITH SANFECT—WHIFFLETS FASCINATE. The presses, thundering and growling, ground out the same appeals by the million: ASK YOUR GROCER—ASK YOUR DOCTOR—ASK THE MAN WHO'S TRIED IT—MOTHERS! GIVE IT TO YOUR CHILDREN—HOUSEWIVES! SAVE MONEY—HUSBANDS! INSURE YOUR LIVES—WOMEN! DO YOU REALISE?—DON'T SAY SOAP, SAY SOPO! Whatever you're doing, stop it and do something else! Whatever you're buying, pause and buy something different! Be hectored into health and prosperity! Never let up! Never go to sleep! Never be satisfied. If once you are satisfied, all our wheels will run down. Keep going—and if you can't, Try Nutrax for Nerves!

Lord Peter Wimsey went home and slept.

CHAPTER VI

Singlar Spotlessness of a Lethal Weapon

"YOU KNOW," SAID Miss Rossiter to Mr. Smayle, "our newest copy-writer is perfectly potty."

"Potty?" Mr. Smayle, showing all his teeth in an engaging smile, "you don't say so, Miss Rossiter? How, potty?"

"Well, loopy," explained Miss Rossiter. "Goofy, Blah. He's always up on the roof, playing with a catapult. I don't know *what* Mr. Hankin would say if he knew."

"With a catapult?" Mr. Smayle looked pained. "That doesn't seem quite the thing. But we in other spheres, Miss Rossiter, always envy, if I may say so, the happy youthful spirit of the copy-department. Due, no doubt," added

Mr. Smayle, "to the charming influence of the ladies. Allow me to get you another cup of tea."

"Thanks awfully, I wish you would." The monthly tea was in full swing, and the Little Conference Room was exceedingly crowded and stuffy. Mr. Smayle edged away gallantly in pursuit of tea, and against the long table, presided over by Mrs. Johnson (the indefatigable lady who ruled the Dispatching, the office-boys and the first-aid cupboard) found himself jostled by Mr. Harris of the Outdoor Publicity.

"Pardon, old fellow," said Mr. Smayle.

"Granted," said Mr. Harris, "fascinating young fellows like you are privileged to carry all before them. Ha, ha, *ha!* I saw you doing the polite to Miss Rossiter—getting on like a house a fire, eh?"

Mr. Smayle smirked deprecatingly.

"Wouldn't you like three guesses at our conversation?" he suggested. "One milk and no sugar and one milk and sugar, Mrs. J., please."

"Three's two too many," replied Mr. Harris. "I can tell you. You were talking about Miss Rossiter and Mr. Smayle, hey? Finest subjects of conversation in the world—to Mr. Smayle and Miss Rossiter, hey?"

"Well, you're wrong," said Mr. Smayle, triumphantly. "We were discussing another member of this community. The new copy-writer, in fact. Miss Rossiter was saying he was potty."

"They're all potty in that department, if you ask me," said Mr. Harris, waggling his chins. "Children. Arrested development."

"It looks like it," agreed Mr. Smayle. "Cross-words I am not surprised at, for everybody does them, nor drawing nursery pictures, but playing with catapults on the roof is reely childish. Though what with Miss Meteyard bringing her Yo-Yo to the office with her——"

"I'll tell you what it is, Smayle," pronounced Mr. Harris, taking his colleague by the lapel and prodding him with his forefinger, "it's all this University education. What does it do? It takes a boy, or a young woman for that matter, and keeps him in leading-strings in the playground when he ought to be ploughing his own furrow in the face of reality—Hullo, Mr. Bredon! Was that your toe? Beg pardon, I'm sure. This room's too small for these social gatherings. I hear you are accustomed to seek the wide, open spaces on the roof."

"Oh, yes. Fresh air and all that, you know. Exercise. Do you know, I've been taking pot-shots at the sparrows with a catapult. Frightfully good training for the eye and that sort of thing. Come up one day and we'll have a competition."

"Not for me, thanks," replied Mr. Harris. "Getting too old for that kind of thing. Though when I was a boy I remember putting a pebble through my old aunt's cucumber-frame. Lord! how she did scold, to be sure!"

Mr. Harris suddenly looked rather wistful.

"I haven't had a catapult in my hand for thirty years, I don't suppose," he added.

"Then it's time you took it up again." Mr. Bredon half pulled a tangle of stick and rubber from his side-pocket and pushed it back again, with a wink and a grimace at the back of Mr. Pym, who now came into view, talking condescendingly to a lately-joined junior. "Between you and me, Harris, don't you find this place a bit wearisome at times?"

"Wearisome?" put in Mr. Tallboy, extricating himself from the crowd at the table, and nearly upsetting Mr. Smayle's two cups of tea, now at length achieved, "wearisome? You people don't know the meaning of the word. Nobody but a lay-out man knows what a lay-out man's feelings is."

"You should frivol with us," said Mr. Bredon. "If the lay-out lays you out, rejuvenate your soul in Roof Revels with Copy-writers. I bagged a starling this morning."

"What do you mean, bagged a starling?"

"Father, I cannot tell a lie. I did it with my little catapult. But if it's found," added Mr. Bredon earnestly, "I expect they will lay the blame on the canteen cat."

"—apult," said Mr. Harris. He looked at Mr. Tallboy to see if this play upon words had been appreciated, and seeing that that gentleman looked more than ordinarily blank and unreceptive, he proceeded to rub it in.

"Like the old joke, eh? 'O take a pill! O take a pill! O take a pilgrim home!' "

"What do you say?" asked Mr. Tallboy, frowning in the effort to concentrate.

"O blame the cat, don't you see," persisted Mr. Harris, "Oh blame the cat! O blame the catapult! Got me?"

"Ha, ha! very good!" said Mr. Tallboy.

"There was another," Mr. Harris went on, "O for a man! O for a——"

"Are you a good hand with a catapult, Tallboy?" inquired Mr. Bredon, rather hastily, as though he feared something might explode unless he caused a diversion.

"I haven't the eye for it." Mr. Tallboy shook his head, regretfully.

"Eye for what?" demanded Miss Rossiter.

"For a catapult."

"Oh, go on, Mr. Tallboy! And you such a tennis champion!"

"It's not quite the same thing," explained Mr. Tallboy.

"A games' eye is a games' eye, surely!"

"An eye's an eye for a' that," said Mr. Harris, rather vaguely. "Ever done anything at darts, Mr. Bredon?"

"I won the pewter pot three years running at the Cow and Pump," replied that gentleman, proudly. "With right of free warren—I mean free beer every Friday night for a twelvemonth. It came rather expensive, though, because every time I had my free pot of beer I had to stand about fifteen to the pals who came to see me drink it. So I withdrew myself from the competition and confined myself to giving exhibition displays."

"What's that about darts?"

Mr. Daniels had roamed into view. "Have you ever seen young Binns throw darts? Really quite remarkable."

"I haven't yet the pleasure of Mr. Binns' acquaintance," acknowledged Mr. Bredon. "I am ashamed to say that there are still members of this great staff unknown to me except by sight. Which, of all the merry faces I see flitting about the passages, is the youthful Mr. Binns?"

"You wouldn't have seen him, I don't expect," said Miss Rossiter. "He helps Mr. Spender in the Vouchers. Go along there one day and ask for a back number of some obscure periodical, and Mr. Binns will be sent to fetch it. He's a terrific dab at any sort of game."

"Except bridge," said Mr. Daniels, with a groan. "I drew him one night at a tournament—you remember, Miss Rossiter, the last Christmas party but two, and he went three no trumps on the ace of spades singleton, five hearts to the king, queen and——"

"What a memory you have, Mr. Daniels! You'll never forget or forgive those three no trumps. Poor Mr. Binns! He must miss Mr. Dean—they often lunched together."

Mr. Bredon seemed to pay more attention to this remark than it deserved, for he looked at Miss Rossiter as though he were about to ask her a question, but the conclave was broken up by the arrival of Mrs. Johnson, who, having served out the tea and handed the teapot over to the canteen cook, felt that the time had come for her to join in the social side of the event. She was a large, personable widow, with a surprising quantity of auburn hair and a high complexion, and being built on those majestic lines was, inevitably and unrelentingly, arch.

"Well, well," she said, brightly. "And how is Mr. Daniels to-day?"

Mr. Daniels, having suffered this method of address for nearly twelve years, bore up tolerably well under it, and merely replied that he was quite well.

"This is the first time you have been at one of our monthly gatherings, Mr. Bredon," pursued the widow. "You're *supposed* to make the acquaintance of the rest of the staff, you know, but I see you haven't strayed far from your own department. Ah, well, when we're fat and forty"—here Mrs. Johnson giggled—"we can't expect the same attention from the gentlemen that these young things get."

"I assure you," said Mr. Bredon, "that nothing but an extreme awe of your authority has hitherto prevented me from forcing my impertinent attentions upon you. To tell you the truth, I've been misbehaving myself, and I expect you would give me a rap over the knuckles if you knew what I'd been doing."

"Not unless you've been upsetting my boys," returned Mrs. Johnson, "the young scamps! Take your eye off them a minute and they're up to their games. Would you believe it, that little wretch they call Ginger brought a Yo-Yo to the office with him and broke the window in the boys' room practising 'Round the World' in his lunch-hour. That'll come out of young Ginger's wages."

"I'll pay up when I break a window," promised Mr. Bredon, handsomely. "I shall say: I did it with my little catapult——"

"Catapult!" cried Mrs. Johnson, "I've had quite enough of catapults. There was that Ginger, not a month ago—— Let me catch you at it once again, I said."

Mr. Bredon, with raised and twisted eyebrows, exhibited his toy.

"You've been at my desk, Mr. Bredon!"

"Indeed I have not; I shouldn't dare," protested the accused. "I'm far too pure-minded to burgle a lady's desk."

"I should hope so," said Mr. Daniels. "Mrs. Johnson keeps all her letters from her admirers in that desk."

"That's quite enough of that, Mr. Daniels. But I really did think for a moment that was Ginger's catapult, but I see now it's a bit different."

"Have you still got that poor child's catapult? You are a hard-hearted woman."

"I have to be."

"That's bad luck on all of us," said Mr. Bredon. "Look here, let the kid have it back. I like the boy. He says 'Morning, sir' in a tone that fills me with a pleasant conceit of myself. And I like red hair. To oblige *me*, Mrs. Johnson, let the child have his lethal weapon."

"Well," said Mrs. Johnson, yielding, "I'll hand it over to *you*, Mr. Bredon, and if any more windows are broken it's you will be responsible. Come along to me when the tea-party's over. Now I must go and talk to that other new member."

She bustled away, no doubt to tell Mr. Newbolt, Mr. Hamperley, Mr. Sidebotham, Miss Griggs and Mr. Woodhurst about the childish proclivities of copy-writers. The tea-party dwindled to its hour's end, when Mr. Pym, glancing at the Greenwich-controlled electric clock-face on the wall, bustled to the door, casting vague smiles at all and sundry as he went. The chosen twenty, released from durance, surged after him into the corridor. Mrs. Johnson found Mr. Bredon's slim form drooping deprecatingly beside her.

"Shall I come for the catapult before we both forget about it?"

"Certainly, if you like; you *are* in a hurry," said Mrs. Johnson.

"It promises me a few more minutes in your company," said Mr. Bredon.

"You *are* a flatterer," said Mrs. Johnson, not altogether ill-pleased. After all, she was not very much older than Mr. Bredon, and a plump widowhood has its appeal. She led the way upstairs to the Dispatching department, took a bunch of keys from her handbag and opened a drawer.

"You're careful with your keys, I see. Secrets in the drawer and all that, I suppose?"

"Stamp-money, that's all," said Mrs. Johnson, "and any odds and ends I have to confiscate. Not but what anybody *might* get at my keys if they wanted to, because I often leave my bag on the desk for a few moments. But we've got a very honest set of boys here."

She lifted out a sheet of blotting-paper and a cash-box, and began to rummage at the back of the drawer. Mr. Bredon detained her by laying his left hand on hers.

"What a pretty ring you're wearing."

"Do you like it? It belonged to my mother. Garnets, you know. Old-fashioned, but quaint, don't you think?"

"A pretty ring, and it suits the hand," said Mr. Bredon, gallantly. He held the hand pensively in his. "Allow me." He slipped his right hand into the drawer and brought out the catapult. "This appears to be the engine of destruction—a good, strong one, from the look of it."

"Have you cut your finger, Mr. Bredon?"

"It's nothing; my penknife slipped and it's opened up again. But I think it has stopped bleeding."

Mr. Bredon unwound his handkerchief from his right hand, wrapped it carelessly round the catapult, and dropped both together into his pocket. Mrs. Johnson inspected the finger he held out to her.

"You'd better have a bit of sticking-plaster for that," she pronounced. "Wait a moment, and I'll get you some from the first-aid cupboard." She took up her keys and departed. Mr. Bredon, whistling thoughtfully to himself, looked round. On a bench at the end of the room sat four messenger-boys, waiting to be sent upon any errand that might present itself. Conspicuous among them was Ginger Joe, his red head bent over the pages of the latest *Sexton Blake*.

"Ginger!"

"Yessir."

The boy ran up and stood expectantly by the desk.

"When do you get off duty to-night?"

"'Bout a quarter to six, sir, when I've taken the letters down and cleared up here."

"Come along then and find me in my room. I've got a small job for you. You need not say anything about it. Just a private matter."

"Yessir." Ginger grinned confidentially. A message to a young lady, his experience told him. Mr. Bredon waved him back to his bench as Mrs. Johnson's footsteps approached.

The sticking-plaster was fixed in its place.

"And now," said Mrs. Johnson, playfully, "you must run away, Mr. Bredon. I see Mr. Tallboy's got a little spot of trouble for me, and I've got fifty stereos to pack and dispatch."

"I want this got down to the printer urgently," said Mr. Tallboy, approaching with a large envelope.

"Cedric!" cried Mrs. Johnson.

A boy ran up. Another lad, arriving from the staircase, dumped a large tray full of stereo-blocks on the desk. The interlude was over. Mrs. Johnson addressed herself briskly to the important task of seeing that the right block went to the right newspaper, and that all were safely packed in corrugated cardboard and correctly stamped.

Punctually at a quarter to six, Ginger Joe presented himself at Mr. Bredon's door. The office was almost empty; the cleaners had begun their rounds, and the chink of pails, the slosh of soap and water and the whirr of the vacuum-cleaner resounded through the deserted corridors.

"Come in, Ginger; is this your catapult?"

"Yessir."

"It's a good one. Made it yourself?"

"Yessir."

"Good shot with it?"

"Pretty fair, sir."

"Like to have it back?"

"Yes, please, sir."

"Well, don't touch it for the moment. I want to see whether you're the sort of fellow to be trusted with a catapult."

Ginger grinned a little sheepishly.

"Why did Mrs. Johnson take it away from you?"

"We ain't supposed to carry them sort of things in our uniform pockets, sir. Mrs. Johnson caught me a-showin' it to the other fellows, sir, and con-stickated it."

"Confiscated."

"Confiscated it, sir."

"I see. Had you been shooting with it in the office, Ginger?"

"No, sir."

"H'm. You're the bright lad who's broken a window, aren't you?"

"Yessir. But that wasn't with a catapult. It was a Yo-Yo, sir."

"Quite so. You're sure you've never used a catapult in the office?"

"Oh, no, sir, never, sir."

"What made you bring this thing to the office at all?"

"Well, sir——" Ginger stood on one leg. "I'd been telling the other chaps about me shooting me Aunt Emily's tom-cat, sir, and they wanted to see it, sir."

"You're a dangerous man, Ginger. Nothing is safe from you. Tom-cats and windows and maiden aunts—they're all your victims, aren't they?"

"Yessir." Understanding this to be in the nature of a jest, Joe sniggered happily.

"How long ago did this bereavement take place, Ginger?"

"Bereavement, sir? Did you mean Auntie's cat?"

"No, I meant, how long ago was your catapult confiscated?"

"Bit over a month ago, it would be, sir."

"About the middle of May?"

"That's right, sir."

"And you've never laid hands on it since?"

"No, sir."

"Have you any other catapult?"

"No, sir."

"Has any of the other boys got a catapult?"

"No, sir."

"Or a sling, or any other infernal machine for projecting stones?"

"No, sir; leastways, not here, sir. Tom Faggott has a pea-shooter at home, sir."

"I said stones, not peas. Did you ever shoot with this, or any other catapult, on the roof?"

"On the roof of the office, sir?"

"Yes."

"No, sir."

"Or anybody else that you know of?"

"No, sir."

"Are you absolutely sure?"

"Nobody that I know of, sir."

"Now, look here, son; I've got an idea that you're a straight sort of fellow, that mightn't like to split on a pal. You're quite sure there isn't anything at all about this catapult that you know and don't like to tell me? Because, if there is, I shall quite understand, and I'll explain to you exactly why it would be better that you should tell me."

Ginger's eyes opened very wide in bewilderment.

"Honest injun, sir," he said, with earnest sincerity, "I don't know nothing at all about no catapult, bar Mrs. Johnson taking that one and putting it away in her desk. Cross my heart and wish I may die, sir."

"All right. What was that book I saw you reading just now?"

Ginger, accustomed to the curious habit grown-up people have of interrogating their youngers and betters on any unrelated subjects that happen to strike a roving fancy, replied without hesitation or surprise:

"*The Clue of the Crimson Star*, sir. About Sexton Blake; he's a detective, you know, sir. It's a top-hole yarn."

"Like detective-stories, Ginger?"

"Oh, yes, sir. I reads a lot of them. I'm going to be a detective one day, sir. My eldest brother's in the police, sir."

"Is he? Splendid fellow. Well, the first thing a detective has to learn to do is to keep his mouth shut. You know that?"

"Yessir."

"If I show you something now, can you keep quiet about it?"

"Yessir."

"Very well. Here's a ten-bob note. Hop out to the nearest chemist and get me some grey powder and an insufflator."

"What sort of powder, sir?"

"Grey powder—mercury powder—the man will know. And an insufflator; it's a little rubber bulb with a nozzle to it."

"Yessir."

Ginger Joe hopped with speed.

"An ally," said Mr. Bredon to himself, "an ally—indispensable, I fear, and I fancy I've picked the right one."

Ginger came panting back in record time. He scented adventure. Mr. Bredon, in the meantime, had attached a discreet curtain of brown paper to the glass panel of his door. Mrs. Crump was not surprised. That proceeding was familiar to her. It usually meant that a gentleman was going out, and wished to change his trousers in a decent privacy.

"Now," said Mr. Bredon, shutting the door, "we will see whether your catapult can tell us anything about its adventures since it left your hands." He filled the insufflator with the grey powder and directed an experimental puff upon the edge of the desk. On blowing away the surplus powder, he thus disclosed a surprising collection of greasy finger-prints. Ginger was enthralled.

"Coo!" he said, reverently. "Are you going to test the catapult for prints, sir?"

"I am. It will be interesting if we find any, and still more interesting if we find none."

Ginger, goggle-eyed, watched the proceedings. The catapult appeared to have been well polished by use and presented an admirable surface for finger-prints, had there been any, but though they covered every half-inch of the thick Y-fork with powder, the result was a blank. Ginger looked disappointed.

"Ah!" said Bredon. "Now is it that it will not, or that it cannot speak? We will make that point clear. Catch hold of the thing, Ginger, as though you were whanging a shot off."

Ginger obeyed, clutching grimly with his greasy little paw.

"That ought to give 'em," said his new friend, "the whole of the palms of the fingers round the handle and the ball of the thumb in the fork. Now we'll try again."

The insufflator came once more into play, and this time a noble set of markings sprang into view.

"Ginger," said Mr. Bredon, "what do you, as a detective, deduce from this?"

"Mrs. Johnson must a-wiped it, sir."

"Do you think that's very likely, Ginger?"

"No, sir."

"Then go on deducing."

"Somebody else must a-wiped it, sir."

"And why should somebody else do that?"

Ginger knew where he was now.

"So that the police couldn't fix nothing on him, sir."

"The police, eh?"

"Well, sir, the police—or a detective—or somebody like as it might be yourself, sir."

"I can find no fault with that deduction, Ginger. Can you go further and say why this unknown catapult artist should have gone to all that trouble?"

"No, sir."

"Come, come."

"Well, sir, it ain't as though he stole it—and besides, it ain't worth nothing."

"No; but it looks as though somebody had borrowed it, if he didn't steal it. Who could do that?"

"I dunno, sir. Mrs. Johnson keeps that drawer locked."

"So she does. Do you think Mrs. Johnson has been having a little catapult practice on her own?"

"Oh, no, sir. Women ain't no good with catapults."

"How right you are. Well, now, suppose somebody had sneaked Mrs. Johnson's keys and taken the catapult and broken a window or something with it, and was afraid of being found out?"

"There ain't been nothing broke in this office, not between Mrs. Johnson pinching my catapult and me breaking the window with the Yo-Yo. And if one of the boys has took the catapult, I don't think they'd think about finger-prints, sir."

"You never know. He might have been playing burglars or something and just wiped his finger-prints away out of dramatic instinct, if you know what that is."

"Yessir," agreed Ginger, in a dissatisfied tone.

"Particularly if he'd done some really bad damage with it. Or of course, it might be more than dramatic instinct. Do you realise, Ginger, that a thing like this might easily kill anybody, if it happened to catch him in just the right spot?"

"Kill anybody? Would it, sir?"

"I wouldn't like to try the experiment. Was your aunt's tom-cat killed?"

"Yessir."

"That's nine lives at a blow, Ginger, and a man has only one. You're quite sure, sonny, that nobody you know of was larking about with this catapult the day Mr. Dean fell downstairs?"

Ginger flushed and turned pale; but apparently only with excitement. His small voice was hoarse as he answered:

"No, sir. Wish I may die, sir, I never see nothing of that. You don't think somebody catapulted Mr. Dean, sir?"

"Detectives never 'think' anything," replied Mr. Bredon, reprovingly. "They collect facts and make deductions—God forgive me!" The last three words were a whispered lip-service to truth. "Can you remember who might have happened to be standing round or passing by when Mrs. Johnson took that catapult from you and put it in her desk?"

Ginger considered.

"I couldn't say right off, sir. I was just coming upstairs to the Dispatching when she spotted it. She was behind me, you see, sir, and it made me pocket stick out, like. A-jawing me, she was, all up the stairs, and took it off me at the top and sent me down again with the basket to Mr. 'Ornby. I never see her put it away. But some of the other boys may have. 'Course, I knowed it was there, because all the things as is confisticated——"

"Confiscated."

"Yessir—confiscated, gets put in there. But I'll ask round, sir."

"Don't let them know why you're asking."

"No, sir. Would it do if I said I believed somebody had been borrowing of it and spiled the elastic for me?"

"That would do all right, provided——"

"Yessir. Provided I recollecks to spile the elastic."

Mr. Bredon, who had already jabbed a penknife into his own finger that afternoon in the sacred cause of verisimilitude, smiled lovingly upon Ginger Joe.

"You are the kind of man I am proud to do business with," he said. "Here's another thing. You remember when Mr. Dean was killed. Where were you at the time?"

"Sittin' on the bench in the Dispatching, sir. I got an alibi." He grinned.

"Find out for me, if you can, how many other people had alibis."

"Yessir."

"It's rather a job, I'm afraid."

"I'll do me best, sir. I'll make up somefin', don't you worry. It's easier for me to do it than it is for you, I see that, sir. I say, sir!"

"Yes?"

"Are you a Scotland Yard 'tec?"

"No, I'm not from Scotland Yard."

"Oh! Begging your pardon for asking, sir. But I thought, if you was, you might be able, excuse me, sir, to put in a word for my brother."

"I might be able to do that, all the same, Ginger."

"Thank you, sir."

"Thank *you*," replied Mr. Bredon, with the courtesy which always distinguished him. "And mum's the word, remember."

"Wild 'orses," declared Ginger, finally and completely losing his grasp of the aitches with which a careful nation had endowed him at the expense of the tax-payer, "wild 'orses wouldn't get a word out o' me when I've give me word to 'old me tongue."

He ran off. Mrs. Crump, coming along the passage with a broom, was surprised to find him still hanging about the place. She challenged him, received an impudent answer, and went her way, shaking her head. A quarter of an hour later, Mr. Bredon emerged from his seclusion. As she had expected, he was in evening dress and looking, she thought, very much the gentleman. She obliged by working the lift for him. Mr. Bredon, the ever-polite, expanded and assumed his gibus during the descent, apparently for the express purpose of taking it off to her when he emerged.

In a taxi rolling south-west, Mr. Bredon removed his spectacles, combed out his side-parting, stuck a monocle in his eye, and by the time he reached Piccadilly Circus was again Lord Peter Wimsey. With a vacant wonder he gazed upon the twinkling sky-signs, as though, ignorant astronomer, he knew nothing of the creative hands that had set these lesser lights to rule the night.

CHAPTER VII

Alarming Experience of a Chief Inspector

ON THAT SAME night, or rather in the early hours of the following morning, a very disagreeable adventure befell Chief Inspector Parker. He was the more annoyed by it, in that he had done absolutely nothing to deserve it.

He had had a long day at the Yard—no thrills, no interesting disclosures, no exciting visitors, not so much as a dis-diamonded rajah or a sinister Chinaman—only the reading and summarising of twenty-one reports of interviews with police narks, five hundred and thirteen letters from the public in response to a broadcast S.O.S. about a wanted man, and a score or so of anonymous letters, all probably written by lunatics. In addition, he had had to wait for a telephone call from an inspector who had gone down to Essex to investigate some curious movements of motor-boats in and about the estuary of the Blackwater. The message, if favourable, might call for immediate action, on which account Mr. Parker thought it better to wait for it in his office than go home to bed, with the prospect of being howked out again at 1 o'clock in the morning. There, then, he sat, as good as gold, collating information and drawing up a schedule of procedure for the following day's activities, when the telephone duly rang. He glanced at the clock, and saw that it pointed to 1.10. The message was brief and unsatisfactory. There was nothing to report; the suspected boat had not arrived with that tide; no action was therefore called for; Chief Inspector Parker could go home and get what sleep he could out of the small hours.

Mr. Parker accepted disappointment as philosophically as the gentleman in Browning's poem, who went to the trouble and expense of taking music lessons just in case his lady-love might demand a song with lute *obbligato*. Waste of time, as it turned out, but—supppose it hadn't been. It was all in the day's work. Putting his papers tidily away and locking his desk, the Chief Inspector left the building, walked down to the Embankment, took a belated tram through the subway to Theobald's Road and thence walked soberly to Great Ormond Street.

He opened the front door with his latch-key and stepped inside. It was the same house in which he had long occupied a modest bachelor flat, but on his marriage he had taken, in addition, the flat above his own, and thus possessed what was, in effect, a seven-roomed maisonette, although, on account of a fiddling L.C.C. regulation about access to the roof for the first-floor tenants in case of fire, he was not permitted to shut his two floors completely off by means of a door across the staircase.

The front hall, common to all the tenants, was in darkness when he got in. He switched on the light and hunted in the little glass-fronted box labelled "Flat 3—Parker" for letters. He found a bill and a circular and deduced, quite correctly, that his wife had been at home all evening and too tired or too slack to go down to fetch the 9.30 post. He was turning to go upstairs, when he remembered that there might be a letter for Wimsey, under the name of Bredon, in the box belonging to Flat 4. As a rule, of course, this box was not used, but when Wimsey had begun his impersonation at Pym's, his brother-in-law had provided him with a key to fit it and had embellished the box itself with a written label "Bredon", for the better information of the postman.

There was one letter in the "Bredon" box—the kind that novelists used to call a "dainty missive"; that is to say, the envelope was tinted mauve, had a gilt deckle-edge and was addressed in a flourishing feminine handwriting. Parker took it out, intending to enclose it with a note which he was sending to Wimsey in the morning, pushed it into his pocket and went on up to the first floor. Here he switched out the hall-light which, like the staircase lights, was fitted with two-way wiring, and proceeded to the second floor, containing Flat 3, which comprised his living-room, dining-room and kitchen. Here he hesitated, but, rather unfortunately for himself, decided that he did not really want soup or sandwiches. He switched off the lower light behind him and pressed down the switch that should have supplied light to the top flight. Nothing happened. Parker growled but was not surprised. The staircase lights were the affair of the landlord, who had a penurious habit of putting in cheap bulbs and leaving them there till the filament broke. By this means he alienated his tenants' affections, besides wasting more in electricity than he saved in bulbs, but then he was that kind of man. Parker knew the stairs as well as he knew the landlord's habits; he went on up in the dark, not troubling to light a match.

Whether the little incident had, however, put his professional subconsciousness on the alert, or whether some faint stir of breath or movement gave him last-minute warning, he never afterwards knew. He had his key in his hand, and was about to insert it in the lock when he dodged suddenly and instinctively to the right, and in that very instant the blow fell, with murderous violence, on his left shoulder. He heard his collar-bone crack as he flung himself round to grapple with the villainous darkness, and even as he did so he found himself thinking: "If I hadn't dodged, my bowler would have broken the blow and saved my collar-bone." His right hand found a throat, but it was protected by a thick muffler and a turned-up collar. He struggled to get his fingers inside this obstacle, at the same time that, with his semi-disabled left arm, he warded off the second blow which he felt was about to descend upon him. He heard the other man panting and cursing. Then the resistance suddenly gave way, and before he could loose his grip he was lurching forward, while a jerked knee smote him with brutal violence in the stomach, knocking the wind out of him. He staggered, and his opponent's fist crashed upon his jaw. In his last seconds of consciousness before his head struck the ground, he thought of the weapon in the other's hand and gave up hope.

Probably his being knocked out saved his life. The crash of his fall woke Lady Mary. For a stunned moment she lay, wondering. Then her mind rushed to the children, asleep in the next room. She turned on the light, calling out as she did so to ask whether they were all right. Receiving no answer, she sprang up, threw on a dressing-gown and ran into the nursery. All was peace. She stood puzzled, and asking herself whether she had dreamed the crash. Then she heard feet running down the staircase at headlong speed. She ran back into the bedroom, pulled out the revolver which always lay loaded in the dressing-table drawer and flung open the door which gave upon the landing. The light streaming from behind her showed her the crumpled body of her husband, and as she stared aghast at this unnerving sight, she heard the street-door slam heavily.

"What you ought to have done," said Mr. Parker, acidly, "was not to have bothered about me, but dashed to the window and tried to get a squint at the bloke as he went down the street."

Lady Mary smiled indulgently at this absurd remark, and turned to her brother.

"So that's all I can tell you about it, and he's uncommonly lucky to be alive, and ought to be jolly well thankful instead of grumbling."

"You'd grumble all right," said Parker, "with a bust collar-bone and a headache like nothing on earth and a feeling as though bulls of Bashan had been trampling on your tummy."

"It beats me," said Wimsey, "the way these policemen give way over a trifling accident. In the Sexton Blake book that my friend Ginger Joe has just lent me, the great detective, after being stunned with a piece of lead-piping and trussed up for six hours in ropes which cut his flesh nearly to the bone, is taken by boat on a stormy night to a remote house on the coast and flung down a flight of stone steps into a stone cellar. Here he contrives to release himself from his bonds after three hours' work on the edge of a broken wine-bottle, when the villain gets wise to his activities and floods the cellar with gas. He is most fortunately rescued at the fifty-ninth minute of the eleventh hour and, pausing only to swallow a few ham sandwiches and a cup of strong coffee, instantly joins in a prolonged pursuit of the murderers by aeroplane, during which he has to walk out along the wing and grapple with a fellow who has just landed on it from a rope and is proposing to chuck a hand-grenade into the cockpit. And here is my own brother-in-law—a man I have known for nearly twenty years—giving way to bad temper and bandages because some three-by-four crook has slugged him one on his own comfortable staircase."

Parker grinned ruefully.

"I'm trying to think who it could have been," he said. "It wasn't a burglar or anybody like that—it was a deliberate attempt at murder. The light-bulb had been put out of action beforehand and he had been hiding for hours behind the coal-bunker. You can see the marks of his feet. Now, who in the name of goodness have I got it in for to that extent? It can't be Gentleman Jim or Dogsbody Dan, because that's not their line of country at all. If it had happened last week, it might well have been Knock-out Wally—he uses a cosh—but we jailed him good and hard for that business down in Limehouse on Saturday night. There are one or two bright lads who have it in for me one way or another, but I can't exactly fit it on to any of them. All I know is, that whoever it was, he must have got in here before 11 p.m., when the house-keeper shuts the street door and puts out the hall light. Unless, of course, he had a latch-key, but that's not so likely. He wasn't obliging enough to leave anything behind to identify him, except a Woolworth pencil."

"Oh, he left a pencil, did he?"

"Yes—one of those pocket propelling things—not a wooden one—you needn't hope for a handy mould of his front teeth on it, or anything like that."

"Show, show!" pleaded Wimsey.

"All right; you can see it if you like. I've tried it for finger-prints, but I can't get much—only vague smudges, very much superimposed. I've had our finger-print wallah round to look at 'em, but he doesn't seem to have made anything of 'em. See if you can find the pencil, Mary dear, for your little brother. Oh, and by the way, Peter, there's a letter for you. I've only just remembered. In my left coat-pocket, Mary. I'd just taken it out of the Flat 4 box when all this happened."

Mary sped away, and returned in a few minutes with the pencil and the coat.

"I can't find any letter."

Parker took the coat and, with his available hand, searched all the pockets carefully.

"That's funny," he said. "I know it was there. One of those fancy long-shaped mauve envelopes with gilt edges, and a lady's fist, rather sprawly."

"Oh!" said Wimsey, "the letter's gone, has it?" His eyes glinted with excitement. "That's very remarkable. And what's more, Charles, this isn't a Woolworth pencil—it's one of Darling's."

"I meant Darling's—same thing. Anybody might carry one of them."

"Ah!" said Wimsey, "but this is where my expert knowledge comes in. Darling's don't sell these pencils—they give them away. Anybody buying more than a pound's worth of goods gets a pencil as a good-conduct prize. You observe that it carries an advertising slogan: IT ISN'T DEAR, IT'S DARLING. (One of Pym's best efforts, by the way.) The idea is that, every time you make a note on your shopping list, you are reminded of the superior economy of purchasing your household goods from Darling's. And a very remarkable firm it is, too," added his lordship, warming to the subject. "They've carried the unit system to the pitch of a fine art. You can sit on a Darling chair, built up in shilling and sixpenny sections and pegged with patent pegs at sixpence a hundred. If Uncle George breaks the leg, you buy a new leg and peg it in. If you buy more clothes than will go into your Darling chest of drawers, you unpeg the top, purchase a new drawer for half a crown, peg it on and replace the top. Everything done by numbers, and kindness. And, as I say, if you buy enough, they give you a pencil. If you mount up to five pounds' worth, they give you a fountain pen."

"That's very helpful," said Parker, sarcastically. "It ought to be easy to identify a criminal who has bought a pound's worth of goods at Darling's within the last six months or so."

"Wait a bit; I said I had expert knowledge. This pencil—a natty scarlet, as you observe, with gold lettering—didn't come from any of Darling's branches. It's not on the market yet. There are only three places it could have come from: one, from the pencil manufacturer's; two, from Darling's head office; three, from our place."

"Do you mean Pym's?"

"I do. This is the new pencil design, with an improved propelling mechanism. The old ones only propelled; this repels also, with a handy twist of the what-d'ye-call. Darling's obligingly presented us with a half a gross of them to try out."

Mr. Parker sat up so suddenly that he jarred his shoulder and his head, and groaned dismally.

"I think it highly improbable," went on Lord Peter, lusciously, "that you have a deadly enemy at the pencil manufacturer's or at Darling's head office. It seems to me much more likely that the gentleman with the cosh, or knuckle-duster, or sand-bag, or lead-piping, in short, the blunt instrument, came from Pym's, guided by the address which, with your usual amiability, you kindly allowed me to give as mine. Observing my name neatly inscribed on the letter-box of Flat 4, he mounted confidently, armed with his cosh, knuckle——"

"Well, I'm dashed!" exclaimed Lady Mary, "do you mean to say that it's really you, you devil, who ought to be lying there mangled and bruised in the place of my afflicted husband?"

"I think so," said Wimsey, with satisfaction, "I certainly do think so.

Particularly as the assailant seems to have walked off with my private correspondence. I know who—or to be grammatical, whom—that letter was from, by the way."

"Who?" demanding Parker, disregarding the grammatical nicety.

"Why, from Pamela Dean, to be sure. I recognise your description of the envelope."

"Pamela Dean? The victim's sister?"

"As you say."

"Willis's young woman?"

"Precisely."

"But how should he know about the letter?"

"I don't suppose he did. I rather fancy this is the result of a little bit of self-advertisement I put in yesterday afternoon at the office tea-party. I made it clear to all and sundry that I had been experimenting on the roof with a catapult."

"Did you? Who, exactly, were the all and sundry?"

"The twenty people taking tea and all the other people they mentioned it to."

"Rather a wide limit."

"M'm, yes. I thought I might get some reaction. What a pity it reacted on you and not on me."

"A very great pity," agreed Mr. Parker, with feeling.

"Still, it might have been worse. We've got three lines to go upon. The people who heard about the catapult. The people who knew, or inquired for, my address. And, of course, the bloke who's lost his pencil. But, I say——" Wimsey broke off with a shout of laughter, "what a shock it must have been for whoever it was when I turned up this morning without so much as a black eye! Why in the name of creation didn't you let me have all the details first thing this morning, so that I could have kept a look-out?"

"We were otherwise employed," said Lady Mary.

"Besides, we didn't think it had anything to do with you."

"You should have guessed. Wherever trouble turns up, there am I at the bottom of it. But I'll overlook it this time. You have been sufficiently punished, and no one shall say that a Wimsey could not be magnanimous. But this blighter—you didn't manage to mark him, Charles, did you?"

"Afraid not. I got a clutch on his beastly throat, but he was all muffled up."

"You did that badly, Charles. You should have socked him one. But, as I said before, I forgive you. I wonder if our friend will have another shot at me."

"Not at this address, I hope," said Mary.

"*I* hope not. I'd like to have him under my own eye next time. He must have been pretty smart to get that letter. Why in the world—ah! now I understand."

"What?"

"Why nobody fainted at the sight of me this morning. He must have had a torch with him. He knocks you down and turns on the torch to see if you're properly dead. The first thing he spots is the letter. He grabs that—why? Because—we'll come back to that. He grabs it and then looks at your classic features. He realises that he's slugged the wrong man, and at that very moment he hears Mary making a hullabaloo. So he clears. That's perfectly plain now. But the letter? Would he have taken any letter that happened to be there, or did he know the writing? When was that letter delivered? Yes, of course, the 9.30 post. Suppose, when he came in to look for my flat, he saw the letter in the box and recognised whom it was from. That opens up a wide field of speculation, and possibly even offers us another motive."

"Peter," said Lady Mary, "I don't think you ought to sit here exciting Charles with all this speculation. It'll send his temperature up."

"So it will, by Jove! Well, look here, old boy, I'm really fearfully sorry you copped that packet that was meant for me. It's perfectly damnable luck and I'm dashed thankful it was no worse. I'll buzz off now. I've got to, anyhow. I've got a date. So-long."

Wimsey's first action after leaving the flat was to ring up Pamela Dean, whom he fortunately found at home. He explained that her letter had been lost in transmission, and asked what was in it.

"Only a note from Dian de Momerie. She wants to know who you are. You seem to have made a remarkable hit."

"We aim to please," said Peter. "What have you done about it?"

"Nothing. I didn't know what you would like me to do."

"You didn't give her my address?"

"No. That was what she was asking for. I didn't want to make another mistake, so I passed it all on to you."

"Quite right."

"Well?"

"Tell her—does she know that I'm at Pym's?"

"No, I was very careful to say absolutely nothing about you. Except your name. I did tell her that, but she seems to have forgotten it."

"Good. Listen, now. Tell bright Dian that I'm a most mysterious person. You never know where to find me yourself. Hint that I'm probably miles away—in Paris or Vienna, or anything that sounds fruity. You can convey the right impression, I know. Phillips Oppenheim, with a touch of Ethel M. Dell and Elinor Glyn."

"Oh, yes, I can do that."

"And you might say that she will probably see me some time when she least expects it. Suggest, if you don't mind being so vulgar, that I am a sort of yellow-dog dingo, very truly run after and hard to catch. Be stimulating. Be intriguing."

"I will. Am I at all jealous, by the way?"

"Yes, if you like. Give the impression that you're sort of putting her off. It's a hard chase and you're not keen on competitors."

"All right. That won't be difficult."

"What did you say?"

"Nothing. I said I could manage that all right."

"I know you'll do it beautifully. I rely on you very much."

"Thank you. How is the enquiry getting on?"

"So-so."

"Tell me all about it some time, won't you?"

"Rather! As soon as there's anything to report."

"Will you come to tea one Saturday or Sunday?"

"I should love to."

"I'll keep you to that."

"Oh, yes, rather! Well, good-night."

"Good-night—Yellow-Dog Dingo."

"Bung-ho!"

Wimsey put down the receiver. "I hope," he thought, "she isn't going to make an awkwardness. You cannot trust these young women. No fixity of purpose. Except, of course, when you particularly want them to be yielding."

He grinned with a wry mouth, and went out to keep his date with the one young woman who showed no signs of yielding to him, and what he said or did on that occasion is in no way related to this story.

Ginger Joe hoisted himself cautiously up in bed and looked round the room.

His elder brother—not the policeman, but sixteen-year-old Bert, the nosey one—was reassuringly asleep, curled up dog-fashion, and dreaming, no doubt, of motor-cycles. The faint light from the street lamp outlined the passive hump he made in the bedclothes, and threw a wan gleam across Ginger's narrow bedstead.

From beneath his pillow, Ginger drew out a penny exercise book and a stubby pencil. There was very little privacy in Ginger's life, and opportunities had to be seized when they occurred. He licked the pencil, opened the book, and headed a page in a large, round hand: "Report".

There he paused. It was desirable to do this thing really creditably, and the exercises in English composition they had given him at school did not seem to help. "My Favourite Book", "What I Should Like to Do when I Grow Up", "What I Saw at the Zoo"—very good subjects but not of great assistance to a rising young detective. He had once been privileged to take a glimpse at Wally's note-book (Wally being the policeman), and remembered that the items had all begun somewhat in this fashion: "At 8.30 p.m., as I was proceeding along Wellington Street"—a good opening, but not applicable to the present case. The style of *Sexton Blake*, also, though vigorous, was more suited for the narration of stirring adventures than for the compilation of a catalogue of names and facts. And on the top of all this, there was the awkward question of spelling—always a stumbling-block. Ginger felt vaguely that an ill-spelt report would have an untrustworthy appearance.

In this emergency, he consulted his native commonsense, and found it a good guide.

"I better just begin at the beginning," he said to himself, and, pressing heavily upon the paper and frowning desperately, began to write.

"REPORT
by Joseph L. Potts
(aged 14½)"

On consideration, he thought this needed a little more corroborative detail, and added his address and the date. Then the report proceeded:

"I had a talk with the boys about the *catter* (erased) cattapult. Bill Jones says he reckollects of me standing in the Dispatch and Mrs. Johnson collering of the cattapult. Sam Tabbit and George Pyke was there too. What I says to them was as Mr. Bredon give me back the cattapult and it have the bit of leather tore and I wants to know who done it. They all says they never been to Mrs. Johnson's draw and I think they was tellin the truth sir because Bill and Sam is good sorts and you can always tell if George is fibbing because of the way he looks and he was looking alright. So then I says could it have been any of the others and they says they have not seen none of them with cattapults so I makes out to be very angry and says it's a pitty a boy can't have his cattapult *confist* confiskcated without somebody goes and tears of it. And then Clarence Metcalfe comes along which he is head boy sir and asks what's up so I tells him and he says if anybody's been at Mrs. Johnsons draw its very serious. So he gets arsking them all and they all says no but Jack Bolter remembers of Mrs. Johnson leaving her bag on the desk one day and Miss Parton picking it up and taking of it down to the canteen. I says when? And he says it was about two days after my cattapult was *confik* took away, and the time just after lunch sir. So you see sir it would have been laying there an hour sir when nobody was about.

"Now sir about who else was there and might have seen it took. Now I comes to think I remember Mr. Prout was there at the head of the stairs because he passed a remark to Mrs. Johnson and pulled my ear and there was one of the young ladies I think it was Miss Hartley waiting to get a messenger. And after I gone down to Mr. Hornby Sam says as Mr. Wedderburn came along and him and Mrs. Johnson had a bit of a joke about it. But sir I expecks lots of people knew about it because Mrs. Johnson would tell them in the canteen. She is always telling tales on we boys sir I suppose she thinks its funny.

"This is all I has to report about the cattapult sir. I has not yet made any inquiry about the other matter thinking one was enough at a time or they might think I was askin a lot of questions but I have thought of a plan for that.

"Yours respeckfully
J. POTTS."

"What the devil are you doing there, Joe?"

Ginger, too absorbed in his report to have kept a proper look-out upon Bert, started violently, and thrust the exercise book under his pillow.

"Never you mind," he said, nervously. "It's private."

"Oh, is it?"

Bert flung the bedclothes aside and advanced, a threatening figure.

"Writing poitry?" he demanded, with contempt.

"It's nothing to do with you," retorted Ginger. "You leave me be."

" 'And that there book over," said Bert.

"No, I won't."

"You won't, won't you?"

"No, I won't. Get out!"

Ginger clasped the document with agitated hands.

"I'm going to 'ave a look—leggo!"

Ginger was a wiry child for his years and spirited, but his hands were hampered by the book, and the advantages of height, weight and position were with Bert. The struggle was noisy.

"Let me go, you beastly great bully."

"I'll teach you to call names! Cheeky little beast."

"Ow!" wailed Ginger. "I won't, I won't, I tell you! it's private!"

Whack! wallop!

"Nah then!" said a stately voice, "wot's all this?"

"Wally, tell Bert to leave me be."

"He didn't oughter cheek me. I only wanted ter know wot he was doin', sittin' up writin' poitry w'en he oughter a-bin asleep."

"It's private," persisted Ginger. "Really and truly, it's frightfully private."

"Can't yer leave the kid alone?" said P.C. Potts, magisterially, "makin' all this noise. You'll wake Dad and then you'll both get a 'iding. Now both of you 'op back to bed or I'll 'ave ter take you up for disturbing the peace. And you did oughter be asleep, Joe, and not writing poitry."

"It ain't poitry, It's something I was doing for a gentleman at the office and he said I wasn't to tell nobody."

"Well, see here," said Wally Potts, extending a vast official fist. "You 'and over that there book to me, see? I'll put it away in my drawer and you can 'ave it again in the morning. And now go to sleep for goodness sake, both on yer."

"You won't read it, will yer, Wally?"

"All right, I won't read it if you're so bloomin' perticler."

Ginger, reluctant but confident of Wally's honour, reluctantly released the exercise book.

"That's right," said Wally, "and if I 'ear any more larkin' about you're for it, both of yer. See wot I mean?"

He stalked away, gigantic in his striped pyjamas.

Ginger Joe, rubbing the portions of himself which had suffered in the assault, rolled the bedclothes about him and took comfort in telling himself a fresh instalment of that nightly narrative of which he was both author and hero.

"Bruised and battered, but unshaken in his courage, the famous detective sank back on his straw pallet in the rat-ridden dungeon. In spite of the pain of his wounds, he was happy, knowing that the precious documents were safe. He laughed to think of the baffled Crime King, gnashing his teeth in his gilded oriental saloon. 'Foiled yet again, Hawk-eye!' growled the villainous doctor, 'but it will be my turn next!' Meanwhile . . ."

The life of a detective is a hard one.

CHAPTER VIII

Convulsive Agitation of an Advertising Agency

IT WAS ON the Friday of the week in which all these stirring incidents occurred that Pym's Publicity Ltd. became convulsed by the Great Nutrax Row, which shook the whole office from the highest to the lowest, turned the peaceful premises into an armed camp and very nearly ruined the Staff Cricket Match against Brotherhood's, Ltd.

The hardworking and dyspeptic Mr. Copley was the prime mover of all the trouble. Like most fomenters of schism, he acted throughout with the best intentions—and indeed, when one looks back upon the disturbance in the serene perspective of distance and impartiality, it is difficult to see what he could have done, other than what he did. But as Mr. Ingleby observed at the time, "It isn't what Copley *does*, it's the way he does it"; and in the heat and fury of the battle, when the passions of strong men are aroused, judgment easily becomes warped.

The thing started in this way:

At a quarter past six on the Thursday evening, the office was deserted, except for the cleaners and Mr. Copley, who, by an altogether exceptional accident, was left working overtime upon a rush series of cut-price advertisements for Jamboree Jellies. He was getting along nicely, and hoped to be through by half-past six and home in good time for 7.30 supper, when the telephone in the Dispatching rang violently and insistently.

"Dash it!" said Mr. Copley, annoyed by the din, "they ought to know the office is closed. You'd think they expected us to work all night."

He went on working, trusting that the nuisance would cease of itself. Presently it did cease, and he heard the shrill voice of Mrs. Crump informing the caller that there was nobody in the office. He took a soda-mint tablet. His sentence was shaping itself beautifully. "The authentic flavour of the fresh home-grown orchard fruit—of apricots ripening in the sunny warmth of an old, walled garden . . ."

"Excuse me, sir."

Mrs. Crump, shuffling apologetically in her carpet slippers, poked a nervous head round the door.

"What is it now?" said Mr. Copley.

"Oh, if you please, sir, it's the *Morning Star* on the telephone very urgent, asking for Mr. Tallboy. I told them they was all gone 'ome, but they says it's very important, sir, so I thought I'd better ask you."

"What's it all about?"

"Somethink about the advertisement for to-morrow morning, sir—somethink's gone wrong and they say, did it ought to be left out altogether or can we send them somethink else, sir?"

"Oh, well!" said Mr. Copley, resigned, "I suppose I'd better come and speak to them."

"I dunno whether I done right, sir," continued Mrs. Crump, anxiously pattering after him, "but I thought, sir, if there *is* a gentleman in the office I ought to tell him about it, because I didn't know but what it mightn't be important——"

"Quite right, Mrs. Crump, quite right," said Mr. Copley. "I daresay I can settle it."

He strode competently to the telephone and grasped the receiver.

"Hullo!" he said petulantly, "Pym's here. What's the matter?"

"Oh!" said a voice. "Is that Mr. Tallboy?"

"No. Mr. Tallboy's gone home. Everybody's gone home. You ought to know that by this time. What is it?"

"Well," said the voice, "it's about that Nutrax half-double for to-morrow's feature page."

"What about it? Haven't you had it?"

(Just like Tallboy, thought Mr. Copley. No organisation. You never could trust these younger men.)

"Yes, we've got it," said the voice, doubtfully, "but Mr. Weekes says we can't put it in. You see——"

"Can't put it in?"

"No. You see, Mr.——"

"I'm Mr. Copley. It's not in my department. I really know nothing about it. What's the matter with it?"

"Well, if you had it there before you, you'd see what I mean. You know the headline——"

"No, I don't," snapped Mr. Copley, exasperated. "I tell you it's not my business and I've never seen the thing."

"Oh!" said the voice, with irritating cheerfulness. "Well, the headline is: ARE YOU TAKING TOO MUCH OUT OF YOURSELF? And, taken in conjunction with the sketch, Mr. Weekes thinks it might lay itself open to an unfortunate interpretation. If you had it there before you, I think you'd see what he means."

"I see," said Mr. Copley, thoughtfully. Fifteen years' experience told him that this was disaster. There was no arguing with it. If the *Morning Star* got it into their heads that an advertisement contained some lurking indelicacy, that advertisement would not be printed, though the skies fell. Indeed, it was better that it should not. Errors of this kind lowered the prestige of the product and of the agency responsible. Mr. Copley had no fancy for seeing copies of *Morning Star* sold at half-a-crown a time in the Stock Exchange to provide a pornographer's holiday.

In the midst of his annoyance, he felt the inward exultation of the Jeremiah whose prophecies have come true. He had always said that the younger generation of advertising writers were No Good. Too much of the new-fangled University element. Feather-headedness. No solid business sense. No thought. But he was well-trained. He carried the war instantly into the enemy's camp.

"You ought to let us know earlier," he said, severely. "It's ridiculous to ring up at a quarter past six, when the office is closed. What do you expect us to do about it?"

"Not our fault," said the voice, brightly. "It only came in ten minutes ago. We're always asking Mr. Tallboy to let us have the blocks in better time, just to prevent this kind of situation."

More and more confirmation of Mr. Copley's prophecies. General slackness—that was what it was. Mr. Tallboy had left promptly at 5.30. Mr. Copley had seen him go. Clock-watchers, the whole lot of them. Tallboy had no business to leave before he had got an assurance from the paper that the block was received and that all was in order. Moreover, if the messenger had not delivered the parcel to the *Morning Star* till 6.5, he had either started too late, or had dawdled on the way. More bad management. That Johnson woman—no control, no discipline. Before the War there would have been no women in advertising offices, and none of these silly mistakes.

Still, something must be done.

"Very unfortunate," said Mr. Copley. "Well, I'll see if I can get hold of somebody. What's your last moment for making an alteration?"

"Must have it down here by 7 o'clock," said the voice, ineluctably. "As a mater of fact, the foundry is waiting for that sheet now. We only want your block to lock the forme. But I've spoken to Wilkes, and he says he can give you till seven."

"I'll ring you," said Mr. Copley, and rang off.

Rapidly his mind raced over the list of people who were fitted to cope with the situation. Mr. Tallboy, the group-manager; Mr. Wedderburn, his group-secretary; Mr. Armstrong, the copy-chief responsible; the writer of the copy, whoever he was; in the last resort, Mr. Pym. It was a most unfortunate moment. Mr. Tallboy lived at Croydon, and was probably still swaying and sweltering in the train; Mr. Wedderburn—he really had no idea where he lived, except that it was probably in some still more remote suburb. Mr. Armstrong lived in Hampstead; he was not in the telephone-book, but his private number would doubtless be on the telephone-clerk's desk; there was some hope of catching him. Mr. Copley hurried downstairs, found the list and the number and rang up. After two wrong numbers, he got the house. Mr. Armstrong's housekeeper replied. Mr. Armstrong was out. She could not say where he had gone or when he would return. Could she take a message? Mr. Copley replied that it didn't matter and rang off again. Half-past six.

He consulted the telephonist's list again. Mr. Wedderburn did not appear upon it and presumably was not on the 'phone. Mr. Tallboy's name was there. Without much hope, Mr. Copley got on to the Croydon number, only to hear, as he expected, that Mr. Tallboy had not yet returned. His heart sinking, Mr. Copley rang up Mr. Pym's house. Mr. Pym had just that minute left. Where for? It was urgent. Mr. and Mrs. Pym were dining at Frascati's with Mr. Armstrong. This sounded a little more hopeful. Mr. Copley rang up Frascati's. Oh, yes. Mr. Pym had engaged a table for 7.30. He had not yet arrived. Could they give a message when he did arrive? Mr. Copley left a message to ask Mr. Pym or Mr. Armstrong to ring him up at the office before 7 o'clock if possible, but he felt convinced that nothing could possibly come of it. No doubt these gadding directors had gone to a cocktail party somewhere. He looked at the clock. It was 6.45. As he looked, the telephone rang again.

It was, as he had expected, the *Morning Star,* impatient for instructions.

"I can't get hold of anybody," explained Mr. Copley.

"What are we to do? Leave it out altogether?"

Now, when you see in a newspaper a blank white space, bearing the legend "THIS SPACE RESERVED FOR SO-AND-SO LTD.", it may mean nothing very much to you, but to those who know anything of the working of advertising agencies, those words carry the ultimate, ignominious brand of incompetency and failure. So-and-so's agents have fallen down on their job; nothing can be alleged in mitigation. It is the Thing That Must Not Happen.

Mr. Copley, therefore, while savagely reflecting that it would serve the whole bunch of slackers and half-wits right if the space *was* left blank, ejaculated hastily: "No, no! on no account. Hold the line one moment. I'll see what I can do." In so doing he acted very properly, for it is the first and almost the only rule of business morality that the Firm must come first.

Dashing hastily along the passage, he entered Mr. Tallboy's room, which was on the same floor as the Dispatching and Copy departments, on the far side of the iron staircase. One minute brought him there; another minute, spent rummaging in Mr. Tallboy's drawers, gave him what he wanted—an advance proof of the wretched Nutrax half-double. A glance showed him that Mr. Weeke's doubts were perfectly justified. Each harmless enough in itself, sketch and headline together were deadly. Without waiting to wonder how so obvious a gaffe had escaped the eagle eyes of the department chiefs, Mr. Copley sat down and pulled out his pocket pencil. Nothing now could be done about the sketch; it must stand; his job was to find a new headline which would suit the sketch and the opening line of the copy, and contain approximately the same number of letters as the original.

Hurriedly he jotted down ideas and crossed them out. "WORK AND WORRY SAP NERVE-STRENGTH"—that was on the right lines, but was a few letters short. It was rather flat, too; and besides, it wasn't quite true. Not work—over-work was what the copy was talking about. "WORRY AND OVERWORK"—no good, it lacked rhythm. "OVERWORK AND OVER-WORRY"—far better, but too long. As it stood, the headline filled three lines (too much, thought Mr. Copley, for a half-double), being spaced thus:

Are you Taking
TOO MUCH OUT
OF YOURSELF?

He scribbled desperately, trying to save a letter here and there. "NERVOUS FORCE"? "NERVE-FORCE"? "NERVE-POWER"? The minutes were flying. Ah? how about this?

OVER-WORK &
OVER-WORRY—
waste Nerve-Power!

Not brilliant, but dead on the right note, unexceptionable and offering no difficulties about spacing. On the point of rushing back to the 'phone it occurred to him that the instrument on Mr. Tallboy's desk might have been left connected to the switchboard. He removed the receiver; a reassuring buzz assured him that it was so. He spoke urgently:

"Are you there?"

"Yes."

"Look here. Can you cut away the headline and re-set in Goudy Bold?"

"Ye-es—yes, we can just do that if we get it at once."

"I'll dictate it."

"Right-ho! Fire away."

"Start exactly where you start now with 'ARE YOU TAKING'. First line in caps, same size as the caps you've got there for 'TOO MUCH OUT'. Right. This is the line: 'OVER-WORK &'—with hyphen in Over-work and an ampersand. Got that?"

"Yes."

"Next line. Same size. Start two ems further in, 'OVER-WORRY'. Hyphen. Dash. Got that?"

"Yes."

"Now, the third line, Goudy 24-point upper and lower. Start under the W, 'waste Nerve-Power!' Capital N, capital P, and screamer. Got that?"

"Yes; I'll repeat. First line Goudy caps., starting level with cap A of present headline. O,V,E,R, hyphen, W,O,R,K, ampersand; second line, same fount, 2 ems to the right, O,V,E,R, hyphen, W,O,R,R,Y, dash. Third line. Start under W, Goudy 24 point upper and lower: lower-case w,a,s,t,e, capital N,e,r,v,e, hyphen, capital P,o,w,e,r, screamer. That O.K.?"

"That's right. Much obliged."

"Not at all. Much obliged to you. Sorry to bother you. Good-bye."

"Good-bye."

Mr. Copley sank back, mopping his brow. It was done. The firm was saved. Men had been decorated for less. When it came to an emergency, when all the jumped-up jacks-in-office had deserted their posts, it was on him, Mr. Copley, the old-fashioned man of experience, that Pym's Publicity had to depend. A man who could grapple with a situation. A man not afraid of responsibility. A man whose heart and soul were wrapped up in his job. Suppose he had rushed off home on the stroke of half-past five, like Tallboy, caring nothing whether his work was done or not—what would have happened? Pym's would have been in the cart. He would have something to say about it in the morning. He hoped it would be a jolly good lesson to them.

He pulled the roll-top of Mr. Tallboy's desk down again over the disgracefully untidy set of pigeon-holes and the cluttered mass of paper that it nightly concealed, and as he did so, received fresh proof of the disorderliness of Mr. Tallboy's habits. From some mysterious nook where it had become caught up, a registered envelope dislodged itself, and fell with a plump little flop to the floor.

Mr. Copley stooped at once and picked it up. It was addressed in block letters to J. Tallboy, Esq., at the Croydon address, and had already been opened. Peeping in at the slit end, Mr. Copley observed what could be nothing but a thickish wad of green currency notes. Yielding to a not unnatural impulse, Mr. Copley pulled them out, and counted, to his astonishment and indignation, no less than fifty of them.

If there was one action more than another which Mr. Copley condemned as Thoughtless and Unfair (long advertising practice had given him a trick of thinking in capital letters), it was Putting Temptation in People's Way. Here was the colossal sum of Fifty Pounds, so carelessly secured that the mere opening of the desk sent it skittering to the floor, for Mrs. Crump and her corps of charladies to find. No doubt they were all very honest women, but in these Hard Times, a working woman could hardly be blamed if she succumbed. Worse still, suppose the precious envelope had got swept up and destroyed. Suppose it had fallen into the wastepaper basket and thence made its way to the sack and the paper-makers, or, still worse, to the furnace. Some innocent person might have been Falsely Accused, and laboured for the rest of her life under a Stigma. It was intolerable of Mr. Tallboy. It was Really Wicked.

Of course, Mr. Copley realised exactly what had happened. Mr. Tallboy had received this Large Sum (from whom? there was no covering letter; but that was hardly Mr. Copley's business. Possibly these were winnings on dog-races, or something equally undesirable) and had brought it to the office, intending to bank it at the Metropolitan & Counties Bank at the corner of Southampton Row, where the majority of the staff kept their accounts. By some accident, he had been prevented from doing this before the Bank closed. Instead of bestowing the envelope safely in his pocket, he had thrust it into his desk, and at 5.30 had rushed off home in his usual helter-skelter way, and forgotten all about it. And if he had since given another thought to it, reflected Mr. Copley indignantly, it was probably only to assume that it would be "perfectly all right". The man really ought to be given a lesson.

Very well, he *should* be given a lesson. The notes should be placed in safe custody and he, Mr. Copley, would give Mr. Tallboy a good talking-to in the morning. He hesitated for a moment as to the best plan. If he took the notes away with him, there was the possibility that he might have his pocket picked on the way home, which would be very unfortunate and expensive. It would be better to take them to his own room and lock them securely in the bottom drawer of his own desk. Mr. Copley congratulated himself upon the conscientious foresight that had prompted him to ask for a drawer with a proper lock.

He accordingly carried the packet to his room, put it safely away underneath a quantity of confidential papers dealing with future campaigns for tinned food and jellies, tidied up his own desk and locked it, pocketed the keys, brushed his hat and coat and took his virtuous departure, not forgetting to replace the telephone receiver upon its hook as he passed through the Dispatching.

He emerged from the doorway into the street, and crossed the road before turning south to the Theobalds Road tram-terminus. On gaining the opposite pavement, he happened to glance back, and saw the figure of Mr. Tallboy coming up on the other side from the direction of Kingsway. Mr. Copley stood still and watched him. Mr. Tallboy turned into Pym's entrance and disappeared.

"Aha!" said Mr. Copley to himself, "he's remembered about the money after all."

It is at this point that Mr. Copley's conduct is perhaps open to censure. A charitable fellow-feeling would, one imagines, have prompted him to dodge back through the traffic, to return to Pym's, to take the lift to the top floor, to seek out the anxious Mr. Tallboy and to say to him: "Look here, old man, I found a registered packet of yours sculling about and put it away in safety and, by the bye, about that half-double for Nutrax——" But he did not.

Let us remember, in mitigation, that it was now half-past seven, that there was no chance of his getting back to his evening meal much before half-past eight, that he was of dyspeptic habit and dependent upon regular hours, and that he had had a long day, concluding with an entirely unnecessary piece of worry and hustle occasioned by Mr. Tallboy's tiresomeness.

"Let him suffer for it," said Mr. Copley, grimly. "It serves him right."

He caught his tram and departed on his tedious way to a remote northern suburb. As he jolted and ground along, he planned to himself how, next day, he would score over Mr. Tallboy and earn commendations from the powers that were.

There was one factor with which Mr. Copley, in his anticipatory triumph, had failed to reckon; namely, that to obtain the full effect and splendour of his *coup de théâtre* it was necessary for him to get to the office before Mr. Tallboy. In his day-dream, he had taken this for granted—naturally so, since he was a punctual man at all times, and Mr. Tallboy was apt to be more punctual in departing than in arriving. Mr. Copley's idea was that, after making a stately report to Mr. Armstrong at 9 o'clock, in the course of which Mr. Tallboy would be called in and admonished, he should then take the repentant group-manager privately to one side, read him a little lecture on orderliness and thought for others, and hand him over his fifty pounds with a paternal caution. Meanwhile, Mr. Armstrong would mention the Nutrax incident to the other directors, who would congratulate themselves on having so reliable, experienced, and devoted a servant. The words sang themselves into a little slogan in Mr. Copley's head: "You can Count on Copley in a Crisis."

But things did not turn out that way. To begin with, Mr. Copley's late arrival on the Thursday night plunged him into a domestic storm which lasted into the night and still muttered with thunderous reverberations on the following morning.

"I suppose," said Mrs. Copley, acidly, "that while you were telephoning to all these people, it was too much trouble to think of your *wife*. I don't count at all, naturally. It's nothing to *you* that I should be left imagining all kinds of things. Well, don't blame *me* if the chicken is roasted to a chip and the potatoes are sodden, and you get indigestion."

The chicken *was* roasted to a chip; the potatoes *were* sodden; and, in consequence, Mr. Copley did get a violent indigestion, to which his wife was obliged to minister with soda-mint and bismuth and hot-water bottles, voicing her opinion of him at every application. Not until six o'clock in the morning did he fall into a heavy and unrefreshing slumber, from which he was aroused at a quarter to eight by hearing Mrs. Copley say:

"If you are going to the office to-day, Frederick, you had better get up. If you are *not* going, you may as well say so, and I will send a message. I have called you three times, and your breakfast is getting cold."

Mr. Copley, with a bilious headache over his right eye and a nasty taste in his mouth, would gladly have authorised her to send the message—gladly have turned over upon his pillow and buried his woes in sleep, but the recollection of the Nutrax half-double and the fifty pounds rushed over him in a flood and swept him groaning from between the sheets. Seen in the morning light, to the accompaniment of black spots dancing before his eyes, the prospect of his triumph had lost much of its glamour. Still, he could not let it go with a mere explanation by telephone. He must be on the spot. He shaved hastily, with a shaking hand, and cut himself. The flow of blood would not be staunched. It invaded his shirt. He snatched the garment off, and called to his wife for a clean one. Mrs. Copley supplied it—not without reprimand. It seemed that the putting on of a clean shirt on a Friday morning upset the entire economy of the household. At ten minutes past eight, he came down to a breakfast he could not eat, his cheek ludicrously embellished with a tuft of cotton-wool and his ears ringing with migraine and conjugal rebuke.

It was impossible, now, to catch the 8.15. Sourly, he caught the 8.25.

At a quarter to nine, the 8.25 was hung up for twenty minutes outside King's Cross on account of an accident to a goods train.

At 9.30, Mr. Copley crawled drearily into Pym's, wishing he had never been born.

As he entered the office from the lift, the reception-clerk greeted him with a message that Mr. Armstrong would like to see him at once. Mr. Copley, savagely signing his name far away below the red line which divided the punctual from the dilatory, nodded, and then wished he had not, as a pang of agony shot through his aching head. He mounted the stair and encountered Miss Parton, who said brightly:

"Oh, *here* you are, Mr. Copley! We thought you were lost. Mr. Armstrong would like to see you."

"I'm just going," said Mr. Copley, savagely. He went to his room and took off his coat, wondering whether a phenacetin would cure his headache or merely make him sick. Ginger Joe knocked at the door.

"If you please, sir, Mr. Armstrong says, could you spare him a moment."

"All right, all right," said Mr. Copley. He tottered out into the passage, and nearly fell into the arms of Mr. Ingleby.

"Hullo!" said the latter, "you're wanted, Copley! We were just sending out the town-crier. You'd better nip along to Armstrong pronto. Tallboy's out for your blood."

"Ar'rh!" said Mr. Copley.

He shouldered Mr. Ingleby aside and went on his way, only to encounter Mr. Bredon, lurking at the door of his own room, armed with an imbecile grin and a jew's harp.

"See the conquering hero comes," cried Mr. Bredon, following up this remark with a blast upon his instrument.

"Jackanapes!" said Mr. Copley. Whereupon, to his horror, Mr. Bredon executed three handsome cart-wheels before him down the passage, finishing up accurately before Mr. Armstrong's door, and just out of Mr. Armstrong's line of sight.

Mr. Copley knocked upon the glass panel, through which he could see Mr. Armstrong, seated at his desk, Mr. Tallboy, upright and indignant, and Mr. Hankin standing, with his usual air of mild hesitation, on the far side of the room. Mr. Armstrong looked up and beckoned Mr. Copley in.

"Ah!" said Mr. Armstrong, "here's the man we want. Rather late this morning, aren't you, Mr. Copley?"

Mr. Copley explained that there had been an accident on the line.

"Something must be done about these accidents on the line," said Mr. Armstrong. "Whenever Pym's staff travels, the trains break down. I shall have to write to the Superintendent of the line. Ha, ha!"

Mr. Copley realised that Mr. Armstrong was in one of his frivolous and tiresome moods. He said nothing.

"Now, Mr. Copley," said Mr. Armstrong, "what's all this about the Nutrax half-double? We've just had an agitated telegram from Mr. Jollop. I can't get hold of the *Morning Star* man—what's his name?"

"Weekes," said Mr. Tallboy.

"Weekes—golly, what a name! But I understand—or Mr. Tallboy understands—from somebody or other, that you altered the Nutrax headline last night. I've no doubt you've got an excellent explanation, but I should like to know just what we've got to say to Mr. Jollop."

Mr. Copley pulled himself together and embarked on an account of the previous night's crisis. He felt that he was not doing himself justice. Out of the tail of his eye, he could see the dab of cotton-wool on his cheek waggling absurdly as he spoke. He pointed out with emphasis and acerbity the extremely unfortunate suggestion conveyed by the sketch and the original headline.

Mr. Armstrong burst into a hoot of laughter.

"My God!" he shouted. "They've got us there, Tallboy! Ho, ho, ho! Who wrote the headline? I must tell Mr. Pym about this. Why the devil didn't you catch it, Tallboy?"

"It never occurred to me," said Mr. Tallboy, unaccountably crimson in the face. Mr. Armstrong hooted again.

"I think Ingleby wrote it," added Mr. Tallboy.

"Ingleby, of all people!" Mr. Armstrong's mirth was not to be restrained. He pushed the buzzer on his desk. "Miss Parton, ask Mr. Ingleby to step in here."

Mr. Ingleby arrived, cool and insolent as ever. Mr. Armstrong, half speechless with joy, thrust the original pull of the advertisement at him, with a comment so barbarically outspoken that Mr. Copley blushed.

Mr. Ingleby, unabashed, capped the comment with a remark still more immodest, and Miss Parton, lingering, notebook in hand, gave a refined snigger.

"Well, sir," said Ingleby, "it's not my fault. My original rough was illustrated with a very handsome sketch of a gentleman overwhelmed with business cares. If the innocents in the Studio choose to turn down my refined suggestion in favour of a (male epithet) and a (female epithet) who look as though they'd been making a night of it, I refuse to be responsible."

"Ha, ha!" said Mr. Armstrong. "That's Barrow all over. I don't suppose Barrow——"

The end of the sentence was more complimentary to the Studio-chief's virtue than to his virility. Mr. Hankin suddenly exploded into a loud snicker of laughter.

"Mr. Barrow is rather fond of cashiering any suggestion put forward by the Copy Department," said Mr. Copley. "I hardly like to suggest that there is any inter-departmental jealousy behind it, but the fact remains——"

But Mr. Armstrong was feeling hilarious, and paid no attention. He recited a limerick, amid applause.

"Well, it's all right, Mr. Copley," he said, when he had partially recovered himself. "You did quite right. I'll send an explanation to Mr. Jollop. He'll have a fit."

"He'll be surprised that *you* passed it," said Mr. Hankin.

"Well he may be," agreed Mr. Armstrong, pleasantly. "It isn't often I overlook anything indecent. I must have been off-colour that day. So must you, Tallboy. Oh, dear! Mr. Pym will have something to say about it. I shall enjoy seeing his face. I only wish it had gone through. He'd have sacked the whole department."

"It would have been very serious," said Mr. Copley.

"Of course it would. I'm very glad the *Morning Star* spotted it. All right. Now that's settled. Mr. Hankin, about that whole page for Sopo——"

"I hope," said Mr. Copley, "you are satisfied with what I did. There wasn't much time——"

"Quite all right, quite all right," said Mr. Armstrong. "Very much obliged to you. But, by the way, you might have let somebody know. I was left rather up in the air this morning."

Mr. Copley explained that he had endeavoured to get into touch with Mr. Pym, Mr. Armstrong, Mr. Tallboy and Mr. Wedderburn, but without success.

"Yes, yes, I see," said Mr. Armstrong. "But why didn't you ring up Mr. Hankin?"

"I am always at home by six," added Mr. Hankin, "and it is very seldom that I go out. When I do, I always leave directions where I am to be found." (This was a dig at Mr. Armstrong.)

Dismay seized upon Mr. Copley. He had clean forgotten Mr. Hankin, and he knew well enough that Mr. Hankin, mild as were his manners, was quick to resent anything in the nature of a slight.

"Of course," he stammered. "Of course, yes, I might have done that. But Nutrax being your client, Mr. Armstrong—I thought—it never occurred to me that Mr. Hankin——"

This was a bad tactical error. It was, to begin with, contrary to the great Pym Principle that any member of the Copy Department was supposed to be ready to carry on with any part of the work at any time, if called upon.

And it also suggested that Mr. Hankin was, in that respect, less versatile than Mr. Copley himself.

"Nutrax," said Mr. Hankin, in a thin manner, "is certainly not a favourite account of mine. But I have coped with it in my time." (This was another side-blow at Mr. Armstrong, who had temperamental periods when he was apt to hand all his clients over to Mr. Hankin, pleading nervous exhaustion.) "It is really no further outside my scope than that of the junior copy-writers."

"Well, well," said Mr. Armstrong, perceiving that Mr. Hankin was on the point of doing the undesirable thing, and ticking off a member of the department before a member of another department, "it's not of any great consequence, and you did your best in an awkward crisis. Nobody can think of everything. Now, Mr. Hankin"—he dismissed the small fry with a nod—"let's get this Sopo question settled once and for all. Don't go, Miss Parton, I want you to take a note. I'll see to Nutrax, Mr. Tallboy. Don't worry."

The door closed behind Mr. Copley, Mr. Ingleby and Mr. Tallboy.

"My God!" said Ingleby, "what a howl! Went with a bang from start to finish. It only wanted Barrow to make it complete. That reminds me, I'll have to go and pull his leg. This'll teach him to turn down my intelligent suggestions. Hullo! there's the Meteyard. I must tell her what Armstrong said about old Barrow."

He dived into Miss Meteyard's room, from which unladylike shouts of mirth were soon heard to proceed. Mr. Copley, feeling as though his head were filled with hard knobs of spinning granite that crashed with sickening thuds against his brain-pan, walked stiffly away to his own quarters. As he passed the Dispatching, he had a vision of Mrs. Crump, in tears, standing before Mrs. Johnson's desk, but he paid no attention. His one agonised yearning was to shake off Mr. Tallboy, who padded grimly at his heels.

"Oh, Mr. Tallboy!"

Mrs. Johnson's rather shrill voice came to Mr. Copley like an order of release. He shot home like a bolting rabbit. He must try phenacetin and chance the consequences. Hastily he swallowed three tablets without even troubling to fetch a glass of water, sat down in his revolving chair and closed his eyes.

Crash, crash, crash, went the lumps of granite in his brain. If only he could remain where he was, quite quietly, for half an hour——

The door was flung violently open.

"Look here, Copley," said Mr. Tallboy, in a voice like a pneumatic drill, "when you were hugger-muggering round with my desk last night did you have the unprintable bloody impertinence to interfere with my private belongings?"

"For heaven's sake," moaned Mr. Copley, "don't make such a row. I've got a splitting headache."

"I don't care a highly-coloured damn if you've got a headache or not," retorted Mr. Tallboy, flinging the door to behind him with a slam like the report of an 11-inch gun. "There was an envelope in my desk last night with fifty pounds in it, and it's gone, and that old (epithet) Mrs. Crump says she saw you (vulgar word)-ing about among my papers."

"I have your fifty pounds here," replied Mr. Copley, with as much dignity as he could muster. "I put it away safely for you, and I must say, Tallboy, that I consider it extremely thoughtless of you to leave your property about for the charwomen to find. It's not fair. You should have more consideration. And I did not rummage about in your desk as you suggest. I merely looked for the pull of the Nutrax half-double, and when I was closing the desk, this envelope fell out upon the floor."

He stooped to unlock the drawer, experiencing a ghastly qualm as he did so.

"You mean to tell me," said Mr. Tallboy, "that you had the all-fired cheek to take my money away to your own damned room——"

"In your own interests," said Mr. Copley.

"Interests be damned! Why the devil couldn't you leave it in a pigeon-hole and not be so blasted interfering?"

"You do not realise——"

"I realise this," said Mr. Tallboy, "that you're an expurgated superannuated interfering idiot. What you wanted to come poking your blasted nose in for——"

"Really, Mr. Tallboy——"

"What business was it of yours, anyway?"

"It was anybody's business," said Mr. Copley—so angry that he almost forgot his headache—"who had the welfare of the firm at heart. I am considerably older than you, Tallboy, and in my day, a group-manager would have been ashamed to leave the building before ascertaining that all was well with his advertisement for the next day's paper. How you came to let such an advertisement pass in the first place is beyond my understanding. You were then late with the block. Perhaps you do not know it was not received by the *Morning Star* till five minutes past six—*five minutes past six*. And instead of being at your post to consider any necessary corrections——"

"I don't want you to teach me my job," said Mr. Tallboy.

"Pardon me, I think you do."

"Anyhow, what's that got to do with it? The point is, you stick your nose into my private affairs——"

"I did not. The envelope fell out——"

"That's a bloody lie."

"Pardon me, it is the truth."

"Don't keep saying 'pardon me' like a bloody kitchen-maid."

"Leave my room!" shrieked Mr. Copley.

"I'm not going to leave your damned room till I get an apology."

"I think I ought to receive the apology."

"*You?*" Mr. Tallboy became almost inarticulate. "You——! Why the hell couldn't you have had the decency to ring me up and tell me, anyway?"

"You weren't at home."

"How do you know? Did you try?"

"No. I knew you were out, because I saw you in Southampton Row."

"You saw me in Southampton Row, and you hadn't the ordinary common decency to get hold of me and tell me what you'd been after? Upon my word, Copley, I believe you jolly well *meant* to get me into a row. And collar the cash for yourself, too, I shouldn't wonder."

"How dare you suggest any such thing?"

"And all your rot about consideration for the charwomen! It's sheer damned hypocrisy. Of course I thought one of them had had it. I told Mrs. Crump——"

"You accused Mrs. Crump?"

"I didn't accuse her. I told her I had missed fifty pounds."

"That just shows you," began Mr. Copley.

"And fortunately she'd seen you at my desk. Otherwise, I suppose I should never have heard anything more about my money."

"You've no right to say that."

"I've a damn sight more right to say it than you had to steal the money."

"Are you calling me a thief?"

"Yes, I am."

"And I call you a scoundrel," gasped Mr. Copley, beside himself, "an insolent scoundrel. And I say that if you came by the money honestly, which I doubt, sir, which I very much doubt——"

Mr. Bredon poked his long nose round the door.

"I say," he bleated anxiously, "sorry to butt in, and all that, but Hankie's compliments and he says, would you mind talking a little more quietly? He's got Mr. Simon Brotherhood next door."

A pause followed, in which both parties realised the thinness of the beaver-board partition between Mr. Hankin's room and Mr. Copley's. Then Mr. Tallboy thrust the recovered envelope into his pocket.

"All right, Copley," he said. "I shan't forget your kind interference." He bounced out.

"Oh, dear, oh, dear," moaned Mr. Copley, clasping his head in his hands.

"Is anything up?" queried Mr. Bredon.

"Please go away," pleaded Mr. Copley, "I'm feeling horribly ill."

Mr. Bredon withdrew on catlike feet. His inquisitive face beamed with mischief. He pursued Mr. Tallboy into the Dispatching, and found him earnestly talking to Mrs. Johnson.

"I say, Tallboy," said Mr. Bredon, "what's wrong with Copley? He looks jolly fed-up. Have you been twisting his tail?"

"It's no affair of yours, anyway," retorted Mr. Tallboy, sullenly. "All right, Mrs. J., I'll see Mrs. Crump and put it right with her."

"I hope you will, Mr. Tallboy. And another time, if you have any valuables, I should be obliged if you would bring them to me and let me put them in the safe downstairs. These upsets are not pleasant, and Mr. Pym would be greatly annoyed if he knew about it."

Mr. Tallboy fled for the lift without vouchsafing any reply.

"Atmosphere seems a bit hectic this morning, Mrs. Johnson," observed Mr. Bredon, seating himself on the edge of the good lady's desk. "Even the presiding genius of the Dispatching looks a trifle ruffled. But a righteous indignation becomes you. Gives sparkle to the eyes and a clear rosiness to the complexion."

"Now that'll do, Mr. Bredon. What will my boys think if they hear you making fun of me? Really, though, some of these people are *too* trying. But

I must stand up for my women, Mr. Bredon, and for my boys. There isn't one of them that I wouldn't trust, and it isn't right to bring accusations with nothing to support them."

"It's simply foul," agreed Mr. Bredon. "Who's been bringing accusations?"

"Well, I don't know if I ought to tell tales out of school," said Mrs. Johnson, "but it's really only justice to poor Mrs. Crump to say——"

Naturally, in five minutes time, the insinuating Mr. Bredon was in possession of the whole story.

"But you needn't go and spread it all round the office," said Mrs. Johnson.

"Of course I needn't," said Mr. Bredon. "Hullo! is that the lad with our coffee?"

He sprang alertly from his perch and hastened into the typists' room, where Miss Parton was detailing to a prick-eared audience the more juicy details of the morning's scene with Mr. Armstrong.

"That's nothing," announced Mr. Bredon. "You haven't heard the latest development."

"Oh, *what* is it?" cried Miss Rossiter.

"I've promised not to tell," said Mr. Bredon.

"Shame, shame!"

"At least, I didn't exactly promise. I was asked not to."

"Is it about Mr. Tallboy's money?"

"You do know, then? What a disappointment!"

"I know that poor little Mrs. Crump was crying this morning because Mr. Tallboy had accused her of taking some money out of his desk."

"Well, if you know that," said Mr. Bredon artlessly, "in justice to Mrs. Crump——"

His tongue wagged busily.

"Well, I think it's too bad of Mr. Tallboy," said Miss Rossiter. "He's always being rude to poor old Copley. It's a shame. And it's rotten to accuse the charwomen."

"Yes, it is," agreed Miss Parton, "but I've no patience with that Copley creature. He's a tiresome old sneak. He went and told Hankie once that he'd seen me at the dog-races with a gentleman friend. As if it was any business of his what a girl does out of business hours. He's too nosey by half. Just because anybody's a mere typist it doesn't mean one's a heathen slave. Oh! here's Mr. Ingleby. Coffee, Mr. Ingleby? I say, *have* you heard about old Copley pinching Mr. Tallboy's fifty quid?"

"You don't say so," exclaimed Mr. Ingleby, shooting a miscellaneous collection of oddments out of the waste-paper basket as a preliminary to upturning it and sitting upon it. "Tell me quickly. Golly! what a day we're having!"

"Well," said Miss Rossiter, lusciously taking up the tale, "somebody sent Mr. Tallboy fifty pounds in a registered envelope——"

"What's all this?" interrupted Miss Meteyard, arriving with some sheets of copy in one hand and a bag of bulls' eyes in the other. "Here are some lollipops for my little ones. Now let's hear it all from the beginning. I only wish people would send *me* fifty poundses in registered envelopes. Who was the benefactor?"

"I don't know. Do you know, Mr. Bredon?"

"Haven't the foggiest. But it was all in currency notes, which is suspicious, for a start."

"And he brought them to the office, meaning to take them to the bank."

"But he was busy," chimed in Miss Parton, "and forgot all about them."

"Catch me forgetting about fifty pounds," said Miss Parton's bosom-friend from the Printing.

"Oh, we're only poor hardworking typists. Fifty pounds or so is nothing to Mr. Tallboy, obviously. He put them in his desk—"

"Why not in his pocket?"

"Because he was working in his shirt-sleeves, and didn't like to leave all that wealth hanging on a coat-peg——"

"Nasty suspicious nature the man's got——"

"Yes; well, he forgot them at the lunch-hour. And in the afternoon, he found that the blockmaker had done something silly with the Nutrax block——"

"Was that what delayed it?" inquired Mr. Bredon.

"Yes, that was it. And, I say, I've found out something else. Mr. Drew——"

"Who's Mr. Drew?"

"That stout man from the Cormorant Press. He said to Mr. Tallboy he thought the headline was a bit hot. And Mr. Tallboy said he had a nasty mind and anyhow, everybody had passed it and it was too late to alter it then——"

"Jiminy!" said Mr. Garrett, suddenly bursting into speech, "it's a good thing Copley didn't get hold of that. He'd have rubbed it in, all right. I must say, I think Tallboy ought to have done something about it."

"Who told you that?"

"Mr. Wedderburn. Drew asked him about it this morning. Said he noticed they'd thought better of it after all."

"Well, get on with the story."

"By the time Mr. Tallboy had had the block put right, the bank was shut. So he forgot about it again, and went off, leaving the fifty quid in his desk."

"Does he often do that sort of thing?"

"Goodness knows. And old Copley was working late on his jellies——"

Clack, clack, clack. The story lost nothing in the telling.

"—poor old Mrs. Crump was weeping like a sponge——"

"—Mrs. Johnson was in *such* a bait——"

"—making a most *awful* row. Mr. Bredon heard them. What did he call him, Mr. Bredon?"

"—accused him of stealing the money——"

"—thief and scoundrel——"

"—what Mr. Brotherhood must have thought——"

"—give them the sack, I shouldn't wonder——"

"—my dear, the *thrills* we get in this place!"

"And, by the way," observed Mr. Ingleby, maliciously, "I pulled Barrow's leg all right about that sketch."

"You *didn't* tell him what Mr. Armstrong said?"

"No. At least, I didn't tell him Mr. Armstrong said it. But I gave him a hint to that effect off my own bat."

"You are awful!"

"He's out for the blood of this department—especially Copley's."

"Because Copley went to Hankie last week about a Jamboree display and complained that Barrow didn't follow his directions, and so now he thinks this business is a plot of Copley's to——"

"Shut up!"

Miss Rossiter leapt at her typewriter and began to pound the keys deafeningly.

Amid a pointed silence of tongues, Mr. Copley made his entrance.

"Is that Jelly copy of mine ready, Miss Rossiter? There doesn't seem to be much work being done here this morning."

"You've got to take your turn, Mr. Copley. I have a report of Mr. Armstrong's to finish."

"I shall speak to Mr. Armstrong about the way the work is done," said Mr. Copley. "This room is a bear-garden. It's disgraceful."

"Why not give Mr. Hankin a turn?" snapped Miss Parton, unpleasantly.

"No, but really, Copley, old sport," pleaded Mr. Bredon, earnestly. "You mustn't let these little things get your goat. It's not done, old thing. Positively not done. You watch me squeeze copy out of Miss Parton. She eats out of my hand. A little kindness and putting her hair in papers will work wonders with her. Ask her nicely and she'll do anything for you."

"A man of your age, Bredon, should know better," said Mr. Copley, "than to hang round here all day. Am I the only person in this office with work to do?"

"If you only knew it," replied Mr. Bredon, "I'm working away like anything. Look here," he added, as the unhappy Mr. Copley withdrew, "do the poor old blighter's muck for him. It's a damned shame to tease him. He's looking horribly green about the gills."

"Right-ho!" said Miss Parton, amiably, "I don't mind if I do. May as well get it over."

The typewriters clacked again.

CHAPTER IX

Unsentimental Masquerade of a Harlequin

DIAN DE MOMERIE was holding her own. True, the big Chrysler and the Bentley ahead of her had more horsepower, but young Spenlow was too drunk to last out, and Harry Thorne was a notoriously rotten driver. She had only to tail them at a safe distance till they came to grief. She only wished

"Spot" Lancaster would leave her alone. His clumsy grabs at her waist and shoulders interfered with her handling of the car. She eased the pressure of her slim sandal on the accelerator, and jabbed an angry elbow into his hot face.

"Shut up, you fool! you'll have us into the ditch, and then they'd beat us."

"I say!" protested Spot, "don't do that. It hurts."

She ignored him, keeping her eye on the road. Everything was perfect to-night. There had been a most stimulating and amusing row at Tod Milligan's, and Tod had been very definitely told where he got off. All the better. She was getting tired of Tod's hectoring. She was keyed up just enough and not too much. The hedges flashed and roared past them; the road, lit by the raking headlights, showed like a war-worn surface of holes and hillocks, which miraculously smoothed themselves out beneath the spinning wheels. The car rode the earth-waves like a ship. She wished it were an open car and not this vulgar, stuffy saloon of Spot's.

The Chrysler ahead was lurching perilously, thrashing her great tail like a fighting salmon. Harry Thorne had no business with a car like that; he couldn't hold it on the road. And there was a sharp S-bend coming. Dian knew that. Her senses seemed unnaturally sharpened—she could see the road unrolled before her like a map. Thorne was taking the first bend—far too wide—and young Spenlow was cutting in on the left. The race was hers now—nothing could prevent it. Spot was drinking again from a pocket-flask. Let him. It left her free. The Chrysler, wrenched brutally across the road, caught the Bentley on the inner edge of the bend, smashing it against the bank and slewing it round till it stood across the road. Was there room to pass? She pulled out, her off wheels bumping over the grass verge. The Chrysler staggered on, swaying from the impact—it charged the bank and broke through the hedge. She heard Thorne yell—saw the big car leap miraculously to earth without overturning, and gave an answering cry of triumph. And then the road was suddenly lit up as though by a searchlight, whose powerful beam swallowed her own headlights like a candle in sunlight.

She leant over to Spot.

"Who's that behind us?"

"Dunno," grunted Spot, twisting ineffectually to stare through the small pane at the rear of the car. "Some blighter or other."

Dian set her teeth. Who the hell, who the *hell* had a car like that? The driving mirror showed only the glare of the enormous twin lights. She drove the accelerator down to its limit, and the car leaped forward. But the pursuer followed easily. She swung out on the crown of the road. Let him crash if he wanted to. He held on remorselessly. A narrow, hump-backed bridge sprang out of the darkness. She topped it and seemed to leap the edge of the world. A village, with a wide open square. This would be the man's chance. He took it. A great dark shape loomed up beside her, long, low and open. Out of the tail of her eye she sought the driver. For five seconds he held beside her, neck and neck, and she saw the black mask and skull-cap and the flash of black and silver. Then, in the narrowing of the street, he swept ahead. She remembered what Pamela Dean had told her:

"You will see him when you least expect him."

Whatever happened, she must hold on to him. He was running ahead now, lightly as a panther, his red tail-lamp tantalisingly only a few yards away. She could have cried with exasperation. He was playing with her.

"Is this all your beastly Dutch-oven will do?"

Spot had fallen asleep. His head rolled against her arm and she shook it off violently. Two miles, and the road plunged beneath over-arching trees, with a stretch of woodland on either side. The leading car turned suddenly down a side-road and thence through an open gate beneath the trees; it wound its way into the heart of the wood, and then abruptly stopped; all its lights were shut off.

She jammed on her brakes and was out upon the grass. Overhead the tree-tops swung together in the wind. She ran to the other car; it was empty.

She stared round. Except for the shaft of light thrown by her own head-lamps, the darkness was Stygian. She stumbled over her long skirts among briars and tufts of bracken. She called:

"Where are you? Where are you hiding? Don't be so *silly*!"

There was no answer. But presently, far off and mockingly, there came the sound of a very high, thin fluting. No jazz tune, but one which she remembered from nursery days:

Tom, Tom the piper's son
Learned to play when he was young,
And the only tune that he could play
Was: "*Over the hills and far away——*"

"It's too *stupid*," said Dian.

Over the hills and a great way off
The wind is blowing my top-knot off.

The sound was so bodiless that it seemed to have no abiding-place. She ran forward, and it grew fainter; a thick bramble caught her, tearing her ankles and her sheer silk stockings. She wrenched herself pettishly away and started off in a new direction. The piping ceased. She suddenly became afraid of the trees and the darkness. The good, comforting drinks were taking back the support they gave and offering her instead a horrible apprehensiveness. She remembered Spot's pocket-flask and began scrambling back towards the car. Then the beaconing lights went out, leaving her alone with the trees and the wind.

The high spirits induced by gin and cheerful company do not easily survive siege by darkness and solitude. She was running now, desperately, and screaming as she ran. A root, like a hand about her ankles, tripped her, and she dropped, cowering.

The thin tune began again.

Tom, Tom the piper's son—

She sat up.

"The terror induced by forests and darkness," said a mocking voice from somewhere over her head, "was called by the Ancients, Panic fear, or the fear of the great god Pan. It is interesting to observe that modern progress has not altogether succeeded in banishing it from ill-disciplined minds."

Dian gazed upwards. Her eyes were growing accustomed to the night, and in the branches of the tree above her she caught the pale gleam of silver.

"What do you want to behave like an idiot for?"

"Advertisement, chiefly. One must be different. I am always different. That is why, my dear young lady, I am the pursued and not the pursuer. You may say it is a cheap way of producing an effect, and so it is; but it is good enough for gin-soaked minds. On such as you, if you will pardon my saying so, subtlety would be wasted."

"I wish you would come down."

"Possibly. But I prefer to be looked up to."

"You can't stay there all night. Think how silly you would look in the morning."

"Ah! but by comparison with yourself I shall retain an almost bandbox perfection of appearance. My costume is better suited than yours to acrobatic exercise in a wood at midnight."

"Well, what are you doing it for, anyway?"

"To please myself—which is the only reason you would admit for doing anything."

"Then you can sit up there and do it all alone. I'm going home."

"Your shoes aren't very suitable for a long walk—but if it amuses you, go home by all means."

"Why should I have to walk?"

"Because I have the ignition keys of both cars in my pocket. A simple precaution, my dear Watson. Nor do I think it will be very much good to try to send a message by your companion. He is plunged in the arms of Morpheus—an ancient and powerful god, though not so ancient as Pan."

"I hate you," said Dian.

"Then you are on the high road to loving me—which is only natural. We needs must love the highest when we see it. Can you see me?"

"Not very well. I could see you better if you came down."

"And love me better, perhaps?"

"Perhaps."

"Then I am safer where I am. Your lovers have a knack of coming to bad ends. There was young Carmichael——"

"I couldn't help that. He drank too much. He was an idiot."

"And Arthur Barrington——"

"I told him it wasn't any good."

"Not a bit of good. But he tried, all the same, and blew his brains out. Not that they were very good brains, but they were all the brains he had. And Victor Dean——"

"The little rotter! That wasn't anything to do with me."

"Wasn't it?"

"Why, he fell down a staircase, didn't he?"

"So he did. But why?"

"I haven't the faintest idea."

"Haven't you? I thought you might have. Why did you send Victor Dean about his business?"

"Because he was a silly little bore and just like all the rest."

"You like them to be different?"

"I like everything to be different."

"And when you find them different, you try to make them all alike. Do you know anybody who is different?"

"Yes; you're different."

"Only so long as I stay on my branch, Circe. If I come down to your level, I should be just like all the rest."

"Come down and try."

"I know when I am well off. You had better come up to me."

"You know I can't."

"Of course you can't. You can only go down and down."

"Are you trying to insult me?"

"Yes, but it's very difficult."

"Come down, Harlequin—I want you here."

"That's a new experience for you, isn't it? To want what you can't get. You ought to be grateful to me."

"I always want what I can't get."

"What do you want?"

"Life—thrills——"

"Well, you're getting them now. Tell me all about Victor Dean."

"Why do you want to know about him?"

"That's a secret."

"If I tell you, will you come down?"

"Perhaps."

"What a funny thing to want to know about."

"I'm famous for being funny. How did you pick him up?"

"We all went out one night to some frightful sort of suburban dancing place. We thought it would be such a scream."

"And was it?"

"No, it was rather dull really. But he was there, and he fell for me and I thought he was rather a pet. That's all."

"A simple story in words of one syllable. How long was he your pet?"

"Oh, about six months. But he was terribly, terribly boring. And such a prig. Imagine it, Harlequin darling. He got all cross and wanted bread and cheese and kisses. Are you laughing?"

"Hilariously."

"He wasn't any fun. He was all wet."

"My child, you are telling this story very badly. You made him drink and it upset his little tummy. You made him play high, and he said he couldn't afford it. And you tried to make him take drugs and he didn't like it. Anything else?"

"He was a little beast, Harlequin, really he was. He was out for what he could get."

"Aren't you?"

"Me?" Dian was really surprised. "I'm terribly generous. I gave him everything he wanted. I'm like that when I'm fond of anybody."

"He took what he could get but didn't spend it like a gentleman?"

"That's it. Do you know, he actually called himself a gentleman. Wouldn't that make you laugh? Like the middle ages, isn't it? Ladies and Gentlemen. He said we needn't think he wasn't a gentleman because he worked in an office. Too mirth-making, Harlequin, darling, wasn't it?"

She rocked herself backwards and forwards in amusement.

"Harlequin! Listen! I'll tell you something funny. One night Tod Milligan came in and I told him: 'This is Victor Dean, and he's a gentleman, and he works for Pym's Publicity.' Tod said: 'Oh, you're the chap, are you?' and looked too utterly murderous. And afterwards he asked me, just like you, how I got hold of Victor. That's queer. Did Tod send you out here to ask me?"

"No. No one ever sends me. I go where I like."

"Well, then, why do you all want to know about Victor Dean?"

"Too mystery-making, isn't it? What did Milligan say to Dean?"

"Nothing much, but he told me to string him along. And afterwards, quite suddenly, he told me to give him the push."

"And you did as you were told, like a good girl?"

"I was fed up with Victor, anyhow. And it doesn't do to get wrong with Tod."

"No—he might cut off supplies, mightn't he? Where does he get it from?"

"Coke, do you mean? I don't know."

"No, I suppose you don't. And you can't get him to tell you, either. Not with all your charms, Circe."

"Oh, Tod! he doesn't give anything away. He's a dirty swine. I loathe him. I'd do anything to get away from Tod. But he knows too much. And besides, he's got the stuff. Lots of people have tried to chuck Tod, but they always go back again—on Fridays and Saturdays."

"That's when he hands it out, is it?"

"Mostly. But——" she began to laugh again—"you weren't there to-night, were you? It was too amusing. He'd run short, or something. There was a hellish row. And that septic woman Babs Woodley was screaming all over the place. She scratched him. I do hope he gets blood-poisoning. He promised it would be there to-morrow, but he looked the most perfect idiot, with blood running down his chin. She said she'd shoot him. It was too marvellous."

"Rabelaisian, no doubt."

"Fortunately I'd got enough, so I gave her enough to keep her quiet, and then we thought we'd have a race. I won—at least, I should have, if it hadn't been for you. How did you happen along?"

"Oh, I just happened along. I always happen."

"You don't. You only seem to happen occasionally. You aren't one of Tod's regular lot, are you?"

"Not at present."

"Do you want to be? Because, don't. I'll get the stuff for you if you want it. But Tod's a beast. You'd better keep clear of him."

"Are you warning me for my good?"

"Yes, I am."

"What devotion!"

"No, I mean it. Life's hell, anyway, but it's worse if you get mixed up with Tod."

"Then why don't you cut loose from Tod?"

"I can't."

"Afraid of him?"

"Not so much of him. It's the people behind him. Tod's afraid too. He'd never let me go. He'd kill me first."

"How fascinating! I think I must know Tod better."

"You'd end by being afraid, too."

"Should I? Well, there's a kick in being afraid."

"Come down here, Harlequin, and I'll show you how to get a kick out of life."

"Could you?"

"Try and see."

There was a rustle among the leaves, and he slid down to stand beside her.

"Well?"

"Lift me up. I'm all cramped."

He lifted her, and she felt his hands hard as iron under her breast. She was tall, and as she turned to look at him she could see the glint of his eyeballs, level with her own.

"Well, will I do?"

"For what?"

"For you?"

"For me? What are you good for, to me?"

"I'm beautiful."

"Not so beautiful as you were. In five years time you will be ugly."

"Five years? I wouldn't want you for five years."

"I wouldn't want you for five minutes."

The cold daybreak was beginning to filter through the leaves; it showed her only a long, implacable chin and the thin curl of a smiling mouth. She made a snatch at his mask, but he was too quick for her. Very deliberately he turned her towards him, putting both her arms behind her back and holding them there.

"What next?" she demanded, mockingly.

"Nothing. I shall take you home."

"You will? Ah, you will, then?"

"Yes, as I did once before."

"Exactly as you did before?"

"Not exactly, because you were drunk then. You are sober now. With that trifling difference, the programme will be carried out according to precedent."

"You might kiss me, Harlequin."

"Do you deserve kissing? Once, for your information. Twice, for your disinterested effort to save me from the egregious Mr. Milligan. And the third time, because the fancy takes me that way."

He bestowed the kisses like deliberate insults. Then he picked her up bodily, still holding her arms imprisoned, and dumped her into the back of the open car.

"Here's a rug for you. You'll need it."

She said nothing. He started up the engine, turned the car and drove it slowly along the path. As they came abreast of the saloon, he leaned out and tossed the ignition key on to the knees of Spot Lancaster, happily snoring in his seat. In a few minutes, they had turned out from the wood into the main road. The sky was faintly streaked with the ghostly glimmer of the false dawn.

Dian de Momerie slid from under the rug and leaned forward. He was driving easily, slumped down in his seat, his black poll leaning carelessly back, his hand slack on the wheel. With a twist, she could send him and herself into the ditch, and he would deserve it.

"Don't do it," he said, without turning his head.

"You devil!"

He stopped the car.

"If you don't behave, I shall leave you by the roadside, sitting on a milestone, like the bailiff's daughter of Islington. Or, if you prefer it, I can tie you up. Which is it to be?"

"Be kind to me."

"I am being kind. I have preserved you from boredom for two solid hours. I beg you not to plunge us both into the horrors of an anti-climax. What are you crying for?"

"I'm tired—and you won't love me."

"My poor child, pull yourself together. Who would believe that Dian de Momerie could fall for a fancy-dress and a penny whistle?"

"It isn't that. It's you. There's something queer about you. I'm afraid of you. You aren't thinking about me at all. You're thinking of something horrible. What is it? What is it? Wait!"

She put out a cold hand and clutched his arm.

"I'm seeing something that I can't make out. I've got it now. Straps. They are strapping his elbows and dropping a white bag over his head. The hanged man. There's a hanged man in your thoughts. Why are you thinking of hanging?"

She shrank away from him and huddled into the farthest corner of the car. Wimsey re-started the engine and let in the clutch.

"Upon my word," he thought, "that's the oddest after-effect of drink and drugs I've met yet. Very interesting. But not very safe. Quite a providential interposition in one way. We may get home without breaking our necks. I didn't know I carried such a graveyard aura about with me."

Dian was fast asleep when he lifted her out of the car. She half woke, and slipped her arms round his neck.

"Darling, it's been lovely." Then she came to with a little start. "Where have we got to? What's happened?"

"We're home. Where's your latch-key?"

"Here. Kiss me. Take that mask off."

"Run along in. There's a policeman thinking we look rather disreputable." He opened the door.

"Aren't you coming in?"

She seemed to have forgotten all about the hanged man.

He shook his head.

"Well, good-bye, then."

"Good-bye."

He kissed her gently this time and pushed her into the house. The policeman, stumping inquisitively nearer, revealed a face that Wimsey knew. He smiled to himself as the official gaze swept over him.

"Good morning, officer."

"Morning, sir," said the policeman, stolidly.

"Moffatt, Moffatt," said his lordship, reprovingly, "you will never get promotion. If you don't know me, you should know the car."

"Good lord, your lordship, I beg your pardon. Didn't somehow expect to see you here."

"Not so much of the lordship. Somebody might be listening. You on your beat?"

"Just going home, my—sir."

"Jump in and I'll drive you there. Ever see a fellow called Milligan round this way?"

"Major Tod Milligan? Yes, now and then. He's a bad hat, he is, if ever there was one. Runs that place down by the river. Mixed up with that big drug-gang as Mr. Parker's after. We could pull him in any day, but he's not the real big noise."

"Isn't he, Moffatt?"

"No, my lord. This car's a treat, ain't she? Shouldn't think there's much catches *you* on the road. No. What Mr. Parker wants is to get him to lead us to the top man of all, but there don't seem to be much chance of it. They're as cunning as weasels, they are. Don't suppose he knows himself who the other fellow is."

"How's it worked, Moffatt?"

"Well, my lord, as far as we've been told, the stuff is brought in from the coast once or twice a week and run up to London. We've had a try at catching it on the way more than once, that is to say, Mr. Parker's special squad have, but they've always given us the slip. Then it'll be taken somewhere, but where we don't know, and distributed out again to the big distributors. From them it goes to all kinds of places. We could lay hands on it there—but lord! what's the use? It'd only be in another place next week."

"And whereabouts does Milligan come into it?"

"We think he's one of the high-up distributors, my lord. He hands it out at that house of his, and in other places."

"In the place where you found me, for instance?"

"That's one of them."

"But the point is, where does Milligan get his supplies?"

"That's it, my lord."

"Can't you follow him and find out?"

"Ah! but he don't fetch it for himself, my lord. There's others does that. And you see, if we was to open his parcels and search his tradesmen and so on, they'd just strike him off their list, and we'd be back where we was before."

"So you would. How often does he give parties in that house of his?"

"Most evenings, my lord. Seems to keep open house, like."

"Well, keep an eye open on Friday and Saturday nights, Moffatt."

"Fridays and Saturdays, my lord?"

"Those are the nights when things happen."

"Is that so, my lord? I'm much obliged to you. We didn't know that. That's a good tip, that is. If you'll drop me at the next corner, my lord, that'll do me champion. I'm afraid I've took your lordship out of your way."

"Not a bit, Moffatt, not a bit. Very glad to have seen you. And, by the way, you have not seen me. Not a question of my morals, you understand, but I've a fancy that Major Milligan might not approve of my visiting that particular house."

"That's all right, my lord. Not being on duty at the time, I ain't bound to put in a report. Good morning, my lord, and thank you."

CHAPTER X

Distressing Developments of an Office Row

"ALL VERY WELL for you to talk, Bill Jones," said Ginger Joe, "but bet you sixpence if you was called as a witness in a case, you'd get into a 'owling mess. Why, they might ask you what you was doin' a month ago and what'd you know about that?"

"Bet you I'd know all right."

"Bet you you wouldn't."

"All right, bet you anything I would."

"Bet you if I was a 'tec——"

"Cor lumme, you'd be a good 'tec, you would."

"Bet you I would, anyhow."

"'Oo ever 'eard of a carrotty-'eaded 'tec?"

This objection appeared to Ginger to be irrelevant. He replied, however, automatically:

"Bet you I'd be a better 'tec 'or you."

"Bet you you wouldn't."

"Bet you if I was a 'tec and arst you w'ere you was when Mr. Dean fell downstairs, you wouldn't 'ave no alleybi."

"That's silly, that is," said Bill Jones. "I wouldn't want no alleybi for Mr. Dean falling downstairs, 'cause it was accidental death."

"All right, Suet-face. I was only sayin', supposin' I *was* 'tec an' I was investigatin' Mr. Dean fallin' downstairs, and I arst you wot you was a-doin' of, you wouldn't be able to tell me."

"Bet you I would, then. I was on the lift, that's where I was, and 'Arry could prove it. So just you stick that in your silly face and shut up."

"Oh, you was on the lift was you? 'Ow d'you know that was when it was?"

"When wot was?"

"When Mr. Dean fell downstairs?"

" 'Cos the first thing I 'ears when I comes off the lift is Mr. Tompkin a-telling Sam there all about it. Didn't I, Sam?"

Sam Tabbitt glanced up from a copy of *Radio for Amateurs* and nodded briefly.

"That don't prove nothing," persisted Ginger. "Not without you know 'ow long it took Mr. Tompkin to shoot 'is mouth off."

"Not long it didn't," said Sam. "I'd just come out of the Big Conference room—takin' tea to Mr. Pym and two clients, I was—Muggleton's, if you want ter know—and I hears an awful screeching and I says to Mr. Tompkin, 'Coo, lumme!' I says, 'wot's up?' An' he says as Mr. Dean's fallen down and broke 'is neck an' they've jest rung up for a doctor."

"That's right," added Cyril, who was the boy in attendance on the Executive and the Switchboard. "Mr. Stanley comes running along full pelt into our place and says, 'Oh, Miss Fearney, Mr. Dean's fell downstairs and we're afraid he's killed himself and you're to telephone for a doctor.' So Miss Fearney tells Miss Beit to put the call through and I hops out quick through the other door so as Miss Fearney can't see me—that's the door behind Mr. Tompkin's desk—and I says, 'Mr. Dean's tumbled down and killed hisself,' and he says, 'run and see what's happened, Cyril.' So I runs and I see Sam jest a-comin' out from the Big Conference room. Didn't I, Sam?"

Sam agreed.

"And that's when I heard the screeching," he added.

"Who was a-screeching?"

"Mrs. Crump was a-screeching in the Executive. Said she'd just seen Mr. Dean fall down and kill hisself and they was a-bringin' 'im along. So I looked into the passage and there they was, a-carryin' of him. He did look awful."

"And that was when I come up," said Bill, sticking to the point at issue. "I hears Mr. Tompkin telling Sam about it, and I runs after Sam and I calls to Mr. Tompkin as they're a-bringing him through, and he comes and looks on too. So they takes him into the boardroom, and Miss Fearney says, 'What about telling Mr. Pym?" and Mr. Tompkin says 'He's still in the conference,' and she says, 'I know he is. We don't want the clients to hear about it.' So Mr. Tomkin says, 'Better telephone through to him.' So she does and then she gets hold of me and says, 'Bill, get a sheet of brown paper and run along to the boardroom and tell them to put it over the glass door,' and just as I was a-going, Mr. Atkins comes along and says, 'Is there any dust-sheets?' he says. 'He's gone,' he says, 'and we got to have somethink to put over him.' And Miss Fearney says, sharp-like, 'Dust-sheets is nothing to do with this department,' she says, 'what are you thinking about? Go up and ask Mrs. Johnson.' Coo! that was a set-out, that was." Bill grinned, as one who looks back to a grand gala-day, a brilliant green oasis in a desert of drudgery. Then he remembered once more what the dispute had been about.

"So where's your blinkin' alleybi?" he demanded, sternly. "Where's yours, Ginger, if it comes to that?"

By such methods, serpentine but effective, Ginger Joe pursued his inquiries. The eyes of the office-boy are everywhere, and his memory is retentive. Five days of inquiry brought the whole inside staff of Pym's under review—all that was necessary, since the day of Dean's death had not been the day that brought the Outside Publicity men into the office.

Out of the ninety-odd inside members of the staff, only ten remained unaccounted or partially unaccounted for. These were: in the Copy Department:

Mr. Willis. He had arrived from the outside staircase about five minutes after the accident, had gone straight through the hall, up the stair to the Dispatching and so into his own room, speaking to nobody. About a quarter of an hour later, he had gone to Mr. Dean's room and, not finding him, had gone back to the typists' room. Here, on asking for Mr. Dean, he had been greeted with the news, which appeared to startle and horrify him. (Witness: the boy George Pyke, who had heard Miss Rossiter telling Mrs. Johnson all about it.)

Mr Hankin. He had been absent from the office since half-past two, on private business, and did not return till half-past four. Harry had informed him of the catastrophe as soon as he came in, and, as soon as he stepped out of the lift, Mr. Tompkin had requested him to go and see Mr. Pym. (Witnesses: Harry and Cyril.)

Mr. Copley. Presumably in his room all the time, but this could not be substantiated, since he never took tea and was accustomed to work at his "slope", which was set against the inner wall and not visible to anyone casually passing his door. He was an assiduous worker, and was not likely to emerge from his room, however much noise or running about there might be in the passages. At a quarter to five he had walked in the most ordinary way into the typists' room to ask why his copy had not been typed. Miss Parton had told him, rather tartly, that she didn't see how he could expect anything to be ready under the circumstances. He had then asked what circumstances and, on being told about Mr. Dean's fatal accident, had expressed astonishment and regret, but added that he could see no reason why the work of the department should not be carried on. (Witnesses: four boys who, on separate occasions, had heard this shocking exhibition of callousness discussed with and by Mrs. Johnson.)

In the Vouchers:

Mr. Binns. An elegant youth who had gone out at 3 o'clock to inquire for last September's number of the *Connoisseur* for Mr. Armstrong, and had unaccountably taken an hour and a half over the transaction. (Witness: Sam, whose elder sister was a typist in the Vouchers, and had given it as her opinion that young Binns had had a date for tea with his best girl.) (Note: Mr. Binns was already known to Mr. Bredon as the darts expert who had often lunched with Victor Dean.)

In the various Group-managers' offices:

Mr. Haagedorn (Sopo and allied products). Leave of absence all day to attend aunt's funeral. But said to have been seen during the afternoon attending a matinée at the Adelphi. (Witnesses: Jack Dennis, the boy who thought he had seen him, and Mr. Tompkin's attendance-register consulted by Cyril.)

Mr. Tallboy. Exact location at the moment of the action not quite certain. At. 3.30 or thereabouts, Mr. Wedderburn had come down to the Vouchers to ask for certain back numbers of the *Fishmonger's Gazette*, saying that Mr. Tallboy wanted them in a hurry. On returning ten minutes later, after having the required numbers sorted out for him, Mr. Wedderburn had run into all the excitement about Mr. Dean and had forgotten the *Fishmonger's Gazette.* He had, in fact, been talking to Miss Fearney in the Executive, when Mr. Tallboy had come in and rather abruptly asked whether he was expected to wait all night for them. Mr. Wedderburn had explained that the alarm about Mr. Dean had put the matter out of his head, and Mr. Tallboy had replied that the work had got to be done, notwithstanding. (Witnesses: Horace, the messenger-boy in the Vouchers, and Cyril.)

Mr. McAllister. Group-secretary to Dairyfields, Ltd., under Mr. Smayle. Absent all afternoon on visit to dentist. (Witness: Mr. Tompkin's register.)

In the studio:

Mr. Barrow. At British Museum, studying Greek vases with view to advertising display for Klassika Corsets. (Witness: Mr. Barrow's time-sheet.)

Mr. Vibart. Supposed to be at Westminster, making a sketch of the Terrace of the House of Commons for Farley's Footwear. ("The feet that tread this historic pavement are more often than not, clad in Farley Fashion Footwear.") Absent 2.30—4.30 (Witnesses: Mr. Vibart's time-sheet and the sketch itself.)

Wilfred Cotterill. At 3 o'clock complained of nose-bleeding and sent to lie down by himself in the Boys' Room, the other boys being told to leave him alone. Completely forgotten by everybody till 5 o'clock, when he was discovered, asleep, by the boys going in to change their tunics. Alleged that he had slept through the whole of the excitement. (Witnesses: All the other boys.) Wilfred Cotterill was a small, pale, excitable child of fourteen, but looking much younger. When told what he had missed he merely remarked "Oo-er!"

A very creditable piece of work on Ginger Joe's part, thought Mr. Bredon, if we may continue so to call him during office-hours, but leaving much room for further inquiry. His own investigations were not going too well. In his search for Darling Special Pencils he had been brought face to face with the practical communism of office life. The Copy Department preferred 5B or even 6B drawing-pencils for writing its roughs, and was not much interested in Darling's product, except, of course, Mr. Garrett, who had been drawing up a little panel for display in Darling's advertisements, calling attention to the generous offer of the pencil. He had two specimens, and four, in various stages of decay, were found in the typists' room. There was one on Mr. Armstrong's desk. Mr. Hankin had none. Mr. Ingleby admitted to having thrown his out of the window in a fit of temper, and Miss Meteyard said she thought she had one somewhere if Mr. Bredon really wanted it, but he had better ask Miss Parton. The other departments were even worse. The pencils had been taken home, lost, or thrown away. Mr. McAllister, mysteriously but characteristically, said he had no less than six. Mr. Wedderburn had lost his, but produced one which he had bagged from Mr. Tallboy. Mr. Prout said he couldn't be bothered; the pencil was a silly, gimcrack thing anyway; if Bredon really wanted a propelling pencil he ought to get an Eversharp. He (Mr. Prout) had never seen the thing since he'd had it to photograph; he added that for a first-class photographer to spend his life photographing tin pencils and jelly cartons was enough to drive any sensitive person to suicide. It was heart-breaking work.

In the matter of his own address, Bredon did get one piece of information. Mr. Willis had asked for it one day. Discreet questioning fixed the date to within a day or so, one way or another, of Chief Inspector Parker's unfortunate encounter on the stairs. Nearer than this, Miss Beit (the telephonist, who also presided over the office address-book) could not go. It was all rather unnerving as well as exasperating. Mr. Bredon hoped that the assailant would have been sufficiently alarmed by the failure of his first attempt to forswear blunt instruments and violence for the future; nevertheless, he developed a habit of keeping a careful look-out for following footsteps whenever he left the office. He went home by circuitous routes, and when engaged on his daily duties, found himself avoiding the iron staircase.

Meanwhile, the great Nutrax row raged on with undiminished vigour, developing as it went an extraordinary number of offshoots and ramifications, of which the most important and alarming was a violent breach between Mr. Smayle and Mr. Tallboy.

It began, rather absurdly, at the bottom of the lift, where Mr. Tallboy and Miss Meteyard were standing, waiting for Harry to return and waft them to their sphere of toil above. To them, enter Mr. Smayle, fresh and smiling, his teeth gleaming as though cleaned with Toothshine, a pink rose-bud in his buttonhole, his umbrella neatly rolled.

"Morning, Miss Meteyard, morning, morning," said Mr. Smayle, raising his bowler, and replacing it at a jaunty angle. "Fine day again."

Miss Meteyard agreed that it was a fine day. "If only," she added, "they wouldn't spoil it with income-tax demands."

"Don't talk about income-tax," replied Mr. Smayle with a smile and a shudder. "I said to the wife this morning, 'My dear, we shall have to take our holiday in the back garden, I can see.' And I'm sure it's a fact. Where the money for our usual little trip to Eastbourne is to come from, I don't know."

"The whole thing's iniquitous," said Mr. Tallboy. "As for this last budget——"

"Ah! *you* must be paying super-tax, old man," said Mr. Smayle, giving Mr. Tallboy a prod in the ribs with his umbrella.

"Don't do that," said Mr. Tallboy.

"Tallboy needn't worry," said Mr. Smayle, with a rallying air. "He's got more money than he knows what to do with. We all know that, don't we, Miss Meteyard?"

"He's luckier than most, then," said Miss Meteyard.

"He can afford to chuck his quids over the office, fifty at a time," pursued Mr. Smayle. "Wish I knew where he gets it from. Daresay the income-tax authorities would like to know too. I'll tell you what, Miss Meteyard, this man's a dark horse. I believe he runs a dope-den or a bucket-shop on the sly, eh? You're a one, you are," said Mr. Smayle, extending a roguish forefinger and jabbing it into Mr. Tallboy's second waistcoat button. At this moment the lift descended and Miss Meteyard stepped into it. Mr. Tallboy, rudely thrusting Mr. Smayle aside, stepped in after her.

"Here!" said Mr. Smayle, "manners, manners! The trouble with you, old man," he went on, "is that you can't take a joke. No offence meant, I'm sure—and none taken, I hope."

He clapped Mr. Tallboy on the shoulder.

"Do you mind keeping your hands off me, Smayle," said Mr. Tallboy.

"Oh, all right, all right, your Highness. Got out of bed the wrong side, hasn't he?" He appealed to Miss Meteyard, being troubled by an obscure feeling that men should not quarrel before ladies, and that it was somehow up to him to preserve the decencies by turning the whole thing into a joke.

"Money's a sore point with us all, I'm afraid, Mr. Smayle," replied Miss Meteyard. "Let's talk about something jollier. That's a nice rose you've got there."

"Out of my own garden," replied Mr. Smayle, with pride. "Mrs. Smayle's a wonder with roses. I leave it all to her, bar the digging and mulching, of course." They emerged from the lift and signed their names at the desk. Miss Meteyard and Mr. Smayle passed on through the ante-room and turned by common consent to the left up the stair by the Dispatching. Mr. Tallboy shouldered past them and took a lone and frosty course down the main corridor to ascend by the iron staircase.

"I'm reelly very sorry," said Mr. Smayle, "that Tallboy and I should have indulged in anything approaching to words in your presence, Miss Meteyard."

"Oh, that's nothing. He seems a little irritable. I don't think he likes that little upset of his with Mr. Copley to be talked about."

"No, but reelly," said Mr. Smayle, lingering at the door of Miss Meteyard's room "if a man can't take a harmless joke, it's a great pity, isn't it?"

"It is," said Miss Meteyard. "Hullo! What are all you people doing here?"

Mr. Ingleby and Mr. Bredon, seated on Miss Meteyard's radiator with a volume of the *New Century Dictionary* between them, looked up unabashed.

"We're finishing a Torquemada crossword," said Ingleby, "and naturally the volume we wanted was in your room. Everything always is."

"I forgive you," said Miss Meteyard."

"But I do wish you wouldn't bring Smayle in here with you," said Mr. Bredon. "The mere sight of him makes me think of Green Pastures Margarine. You haven't come to dun me for that copy, have you? Because don't, there's a good fellow. I haven't done it and I can't do it. My brain has dried up. How you can live all day with Margarine and always look so fresh and cheerful passes my understanding."

"I assure you it's an effort," said Mr. Smayle, displaying his teeth. "But it reelly is a great refreshment to see you copy-writers all so cheerful and pleasant together. Not like some people I could name."

"Mr. Tallboy has been unkind to Mr. Smayle," said Miss Meteyard.

"I like to be agreeable with everybody," said Mr. Smayle, "but reelly, when it comes to shoving your way past a person into the lift as if one wasn't there and then telling you to keep your hands off as if a person was dirt, a man may be excused for taking offence. I suppose Tallboy thinks I'm not worth speaking to, just because he's been to a public school and I haven't."

"Public school," said Mr. Bredon, "first I've heard of it. What public school?"

"He was at Dumbleton," said Mr. Smayle, "but what I say is, I went to a Council School and I'm not ashamed of it."

"Where's Dumbleton?" demanded Ingleby. "I shouldn't worry, Smayle. Dumbleton isn't a public school, within the meaning of the act."

"Isn't it?" said Mr. Smayle, hopefully. "Well, you and Mr. Bredon have had college educations, so you know all about it. What schools do *you* call public schools?"

"Eton," said Mr. Bredon, promptly, "—and Harrow," he added, magnanimously, for he was an Eton man.

"Rugby," suggested Mr. Ingleby.

"No, no," protested Bredon, "that's a railway junction."

Ingleby delivered a brisk left-hander to Bredon's jaw, which the latter parried neatly.

"And I've heard," Bredon went on, "that there's a decentish sort of place at Winchester, if you're not too particular."

"I once met a man who'd been to Marlborough," suggested Ingleby.

"I'm sorry to hear that," said Bredon. "They get a terrible set of hearty roughs down there. You can't be too careful of your associates, Ingleby."

"Well," said Mr. Smayle, "Tallboy always says that Dumbleton is a public school."

"I daresay it is—in the sense that it has a Board of Governors," said Ingleby, "but it's nothing to be snobbish about."

"What is, if you come to that?" said Bredon. "Look here, Smayle, if only you people could get it out of your heads that these things matter a damn, you'd be a darn sight happier. You probably got a fifty times better education than I ever did."

Mr. Smayle shook his head. "Oh, no," he said, "I'm not deceiving myself about that, and I'd give anything to have had the same opportunities as you. There's a difference, and I know there's a difference, and I don't mind admitting it. But what I mean is, some people make you feel it and others don't. I don't feel it when I'm talking to either of you, or to Mr. Armstrong or Mr. Hankin, though you've been to Oxford and Cambridge and all that. Perhaps it's just because you've been to Oxford and Cambridge."

He struggled with the problem, embarrassing the other two men by his wistful eyes.

"Look here," said Miss Meteyard, "I know what you mean. But it's just that these two here never think twice about it. They don't have to. And you don't have to, either. But the minute anybody begins to worry about whether he's as good as the next man, then he starts a sort of uneasy snobbish feeling and makes himself offensive."

"I see," said Mr. Smayle. "Well, of course, Mr. Hankin doesn't have to try and prove that he's better than me, because he is and we both know it."

"Better isn't the right word, Smayle."

"Well, better educated. You know what I mean."

"Don't worry about it," said Ingleby. "If I were half as good at my job as you are at yours, I should feel superior to everybody in this tom-fool office."

Mr. Smayle shook his head, but appeared comforted.

"I do wish they wouldn't start that kind of thing," said Ingleby when he had gone, "I don't know what to say to them."

"I thought you were a Socialist, Ingleby," said Bredon, "it oughtn't to embarrass you."

"So I am a Socialist," said Ingleby, "but I can't stand this stuff about Old Dumbletonians. If everybody had the same State education, these things wouldn't happen."

"If everybody had the same face," said Bredon, "there'd be no pretty women."

Miss Meteyard made a grimace.

"If you go on like that, I shall be getting an inferiority complex too."

Bredon looked at her gravely.

"I don't think you'd care to be called pretty," he said, "but if I were a painter I should like to make a portrait of you. You have very interesting bones."

"Good God!" said Miss Meteyard. "I'm going. Let me know when you've finished with my room."

There was a mirror in the typists' room, and in this Miss Meteyard curiously studied her face.

"What's the matter, Miss Meteyard?" asked Miss Rossiter. "Got a spot coming?"

"Something of the sort," said Miss Meteyard, absently. "Interesting bones indeed!"

"Pardon?" said Miss Rossiter.

"Smayle is getting unbearable," grumbled Mr. Tallboy to Mr. Wedderburn. "Vulgar little tick. I hate a fellow who digs you in the ribs."

"He means no harm," rejoined Mr. Wedderburn. "He's quite a decent sort, really."

"Can't stand those teeth," grumbled Mr. Tallboy. "And why must he put that stinking stuff on his hair?"

"Oh, well," said Mr. Wedderburn.

"I'm not going to have him playing in the cricket match, anyhow," pursued Mr. Tallboy, viciously. "Last year he wore white suède shoes with crocodile vamps, and an incredible blazer with Old Borstalian colours."

Mr. Wedderburn looked up, rather startled.

"Oh, but you're not going to leave him out? He's quite a good bat and very nippy on the ball in the field."

"We can do without him," said Mr. Tallboy, firmly. Mr. Wedderburn said no more. There was no regular cricket eleven at Pym's, but every summer a scratch team was got together to play a couple of matches, the selection being entrusted to Mr. Tallboy, who was energetic and had once carried his bat out for 52 against Sopo. He was supposed to submit a list of cricketers for Mr. Hankin's final decision, but Mr. Hankin seldom questioned his selection, for the sufficient reason that there were seldom more than eleven candidates available to choose from. The important point was that Mr. Hankin should bat third, and field at mid-on. If these points were taken note of, he raised no further objections.

Mr. Tallboy pulled out a list.

"Ingleby," he said, "and Garrett. Barrow. Adcock. Pinchley. Hankin. Myself. Gregory can't play; he's going away for the week-end, so we'd better have McAllister. And we can't very well leave out Miller. I wish we could, but he's a Director. Yourself."

"Leave me out," said Mr. Wedderburn. "I haven't touched a bat since last year and I didn't put up much of a show then."

"We've nobody else who can bowl slow spinners," said Mr. Tallboy. "I'll put you down No. 11."

"All right," said Mr. Wedderburn, gratified by the recognition accorded to his bowling, but irrationally provoked by being put down No. 11. He had expected his companion to say, "Oh, but that was a fluke," and send him in higher up the list. "How about a wicket-keeper? Grayson says he won't do it again, not after getting his front tooth knocked out last year. He seems to have got the wind up properly."

"We'll make Haagedorn do it. He's got hands like a pair of hams. Who else? Oh, that chap in the printing—Beesely—he's not much good with a bat, but we can rely on him for a few straight balls."

"What about that new fellow in the Copy Department? Bredon? He's a public school man. Is he any good?"

"Might be. He's a bit ancient, though. We've got two aged stiffs already in Hankin and Miller."

"Aged stiff be blowed. That chap can move, I've seen him do it. I wouldn't be surprised if he could show us a bit of style."

"Well, I'll find out. If he's any good, we'll stick him in instead of Pinchley."

"Pinchley can swipe 'em up," said Mr. Wedderburn.

"He never does anything but swipe. He's jam for the fielders. He gave them about ten chances last year and was caught both innings."

Mr. Wedderburn agreed that this was so.

"But he'll be awfully hurt if he's left out," he said.

"I'll ask about Bredon," said Mr. Tallboy.

He sought out that gentleman, who was, for once, in his own room, singing soup-slogans to himself.

A meal begun with Blagg's Tomato
Softens every husband's heart-oh!

Hubbies hold those wives most dear
Who offer them Blagg's Turtle Clear.

Fit for an Alderman—serve it up quick—
Rum-ti-ty, tum-ti-ty, Blagg's Turtle Thick.

"Rum-ti-ty, tum-ti-ty," said Mr. Bredon. "Hullo, Tallboy, what's the matter? Don't say Nutrax has developed any more innuendos."

"Do you play cricket?"

"Well, I used to play for——" Mr. Bredon coughed; he had been about to say, "for Oxford", but remembered in time that these statements could be checked. "I've played a good deal of country-house cricket in the old days. But I'm rapidly qualifying to be called a Veteran. Why?"

"I've got to scrape up an eleven for a match against Brotherhood's. We play one every year. They always beat us, of course, because they have their own playing-fields and play together regularly, but Pym likes it to be done. He thinks it fosters fellow-feeling between client and agent and all that sort of thing."

"Oh! when does it come off?"

"Saturday fortnight."

"I daresay I might keep my end up for a bit, if you can't get anybody better."

"You anything of a bowler?"

"Nothing."

"Better with the willow than the leather, eh?"

Mr. Bredon, wincing a little at this picturesqueness, admitted that, if he was anything, he was a batsman.

"Right. You wouldn't care to open the ball with Ingleby, I suppose?"

"I'd rather not. Put me down somewhere near the tail."

Tallboy nodded.

"Just as you like."

"Who captains this Eleven?"

"Well, I do, as a rule. At least, we always ask Hankin or Miller, just out of compliment, but they generally decline with thanks. Well, righty-ho! I'll just buzz round and see that the others are O.K."

The selected team went up on the office notice-board at lunch-time. At ten minutes past two, the trouble began with Mr. McAllister.

"I observe," said he, making a dour appearance in Mr. Tallboy's room, "that ye're no askin' Smayle to play for ye, and I'm thinkin' it'll be a wee bit awkward for me if I play and he does not. Workin' in his room all day and under his orders, it will make my poseetion not just so very comfortable."

"Position in the office has nothing to do with playing cricket," said Mr. Tallboy.

"Ay, imph'm, that's so. But I just do not care for it. So ye'll oblige me by leavin' my name oot."

"Just as you like," said Tallboy, annoyed. He struck Mr. McAllister's name off the list, and substituted that of Mr. Pinchley. The next defection was that of Mr. Adcock, a stolid youth from the Voucher Department. He inconsiderately fell off a step-ladder in his own home, while assisting his mother to hang a picture, and broke the small bone of his leg.

In this extremity, Mr. Tallboy found himself compelled to go and eat humble pie to Mr. Smayle, and request him to play after all. But Mr. Smayle had been hurt in his feelings by being omitted from the first list, and showed no eagerness to oblige.

Mr. Tallboy, who was, indeed, a little ashamed of himself, endeavoured to gloss the matter over, by making it appear that his real object in leaving out Mr. Smayle had been to make room for Mr. Bredon, who had been to Oxford and was sure to play well. But Mr. Smayle was not deceived by this specious reasoning.

"If you had come to me in the first instance," he complained, "and put the matter to me in a friendly way, I should say nothing about it. I like Mr. Bredon, and I appreciate that he has had advantages that I haven't had. He's a very gentlemanly fellow, and I should be happy to make way for him. But I do not care for having things done behind my back in a hole-and-corner fashion."

If Mr. Tallboy had said at this point, "Look here, Smayle, I'm sorry; I was rather out of temper at the time over that little dust-up we had, and I apologise"—then Mr. Smayle, who was really an amiable creature enough, would have given way and done anything that was required of him. But Mr. Tallboy chose to take a lofty tone. He said:

"Come, come, Smayle. You're not Jack Hobbs, you know."

Even this might have passed over with Mr. Smayle's ready admission that he was not England's premier batsman, had not Mr. Tallboy been unhappily inspired to say:

"Of course, I don't know about you, but *I* have always been accustomed to have these things settled by whoever was appointed to select the team, and to play or not, according as I was put down."

"Oh, yes," retorted Mr. Smayle, caught on his sensitive point, "you would say that. I am quite aware, Tallboy, that I never was at a public school, but that is no reason why I shouldn't be treated with ordinary, common courtesy. And from those who have been to real public schools, I get it, what's more. You may think a lot of Dumbleton, but it isn't what *I* call a public school."

"And what do *you* call a public school?" inquired Mr. Tallboy.

"Eton," retorted Mr. Smayle, repeating his lesson with fatal facility, "and Harrow, and—er—Rugby, and Winchester and places like those. Places where they send gentlemen's sons to."

"Oh, do they?" said Mr. Tallboy. "I suppose you are sending *your* family to Eton, then."

At this, Mr. Smayle's narrow face became as white as a sheet of paper. "You cad!" he said, choking. "You unspeakable swine. Get out of here or I'll kill you."

"What the devil's the matter with you, Smayle?" cried Mr. Tallboy, in considerable surprise.

"Get out!" said Mr. Smayle.

"Now, I'd just like a word wi' ye, Tallboy," interposed Mr. McAllister. He laid a large, hairy hand on Mr. Tallboy's arm and propelled him gently from the room.

"What on airth possessed ye to say such a thing to him?" he asked, when they were safely in the passage. "Did ye not know that Smayle has but the one boy and him feeble-minded, the poor child?"

Mr. Tallboy was really aghast. He was stricken with shame, and, like many shame-stricken people, took refuge in an outburst of rage against the nearest person handy.

"No, I didn't know. How should I be expected to know anything about Smayle's family? Good God! I'm damned sorry and all that, but why must the fellow be such an ass? He's got a mania about public schools. Eton, indeed! I don't wonder the boy's feeble-minded if he takes after his father."

Mr. McAllister was deeply shocked. His Scottish sense of decency was outraged.

"Ye ought to be damn well ashamed o' yersel'," he said, severely, and releasing Tallboy's arm, stepped back into the room he shared with Mr. Smayle and slammed the door.

Now, it is not very clear at the first glance what this disagreement between Mr. Tallboy and Mr. Smayle about a cricket match had to do with the original disagreement between the former and Mr. Copley. True, one may trace a remote connection at the beginnings of things, since the Tallboy-Smayle row may be said to have started with Mr. Smayle's indiscreet jest about Mr. Tallboy's fifty pounds. But this fact has no very great importance. What is really important is that as soon as Mr. McAllister made known all the circumstances of the Tallboy-Smayle affair (which he did as soon as he could find a listener), public opinion, which in the Tallboy-Copley dispute had been largely on Mr. Tallboy's side, veered round. It was felt that since Mr. Tallboy could behave with so much unkindness to Mr. Smayle, he was probably not guiltless towards Mr. Copley. The office staff was divided like the Red Sea and rose up in walls on either hand. Only Mr. Armstrong, Mr. Ingleby, and Mr. Bredon, sardonic Gallios, held themselves apart, caring little, but fomenting the trouble for their own amusement. Even Miss Meteyard, who abominated Mr. Copley, experienced an unwonted uprush of feminine pity for him, and pronounced Mr. Tallboy's behaviour intolerable. Old Copley, she said, might be an interfering old nuisance, but he wasn't a cad. Mr. Ingleby said he really didn't think Tallboy could have meant what he said to Smayle. Miss Meteyard said: "Tell that to the marines," and, having said so, noted that the phrase would make a good headline for something-or-other. But Mr. Ingleby said, "No, that had been done."

Miss Parton, of course, was an anti-Copleyite whom nothing could move, and therefore smiled on Mr. Tallboy when he happened into the typists' room to borrow a stamp. But Miss Rossiter, though superficially more peppery, prided herself on possessing a well-balanced mind. After all, she insisted, Mr. Copley had probably meant well over the matter of the fifty pounds and, when you came to think of it, he had got Tallboy and all the rest of the Nutrax contingent out of a very tiresome sort of mess. She thought that Mr. Tallboy thought rather a lot of himself, and he had certainly had no business to speak as he had done to poor Mr. Smayle.

"And," said Miss Rossiter, "I don't like his lady friends."

"Lady friends?" said Miss Parton.

"Well, I'm not one to talk, as you know," replied Miss Rossiter, "but when you see a married man coming out of a restaurant at past midnight with somebody who is obviously not his wife——"

"No!" exclaimed Miss Parton.

"My dear! and got up regardless . . . one of those little hats with an eye-veil . . . three-inch diamanté heels . . . such bad taste with a semi-toilette . . . fish-net stockings and all. . . ."

"Perhaps it was his sister."

"My *dear*! . . . And his wife's having a baby, too. . . . He didn't see me. . . . Of course, I wouldn't say a word, but I do think . . ."

Thus the typewriters clacked.

Mr. Hankin, though officially impartial, was a Tallboyite. Himself a precise and efficient man, he was nevertheless perennially irritated by the precision and efficiency of Mr. Copley. He suspected, what was quite true, that Mr. Copley criticised the conduct of the department and would have liked to be given a measure of authority. Mr. Copley had a way of coming to him with suggestions: "Would it not be better, Mr. Hankin, if . . ." "If you will excuse my making a suggestion, Mr. Hankin, could not a stricter control be kept . . .?" "Of course, I know I am in an entirely subordinate position here, Mr. Hankin, but I have had over thirty years' experience of advertising, and in my humble opinion . . ."—excellent suggestions, always, and having only the one drawback that they threatened either to annoy Mr. Armstrong, or to involve a quantity of tedious and time-wasting supervision, or to embroil the whole temperamental Copy Department and put it off its stroke. Mr. Hankin grew weary of saying: "Quite so, Mr. Copley, but Mr. Armstrong and I find it works better, on the whole, to have as few restrictions as possible." Mr. Copley had a way of saying that he quite understood, which always left Mr. Hankin with the impression that Mr. Copley thought him weak and ineffectual, and this impression had been confirmed by the Nutrax incident. When a point had arisen about which Mr. Hankin might, and ought to, have been consulted, Mr. Copley had passed him over—conclusive proof to Mr. Hankin that all Mr. Copley's valuable suggestions about departmental management were so much window-dressing, put forward to show how brilliant Mr. Copley was, and not in the least with the desire of aiding Mr. Hankin or the department. In this, Mr. Hankin's shrewdness saw much more clearly into Mr. Copley's motives than did Mr. Copley himself. He was quite right. Consequently, he was not inclined to bother himself about Mr. Copley, and was determined to give any necessary support to Mr. Tallboy. The Smayle incident was, naturally, not reported to him; he therefore made no comment upon the Cricket Eleven except to ask, mildly, why Mr. Smayle and Mr. McAllister were excluded. Mr. Tallboy replied briefly that they were unable to play, and that was the end of the matter.

Mr. Tallboy had a further ally in Mr. Barrow, who disliked the whole Copy Department on principle, because, as he complained, they were a conceited lot who were always trying to interfere with his artists and dictate to him about his displays. He admitted that, as a general proposition, the sketch was supposed to illustrate the copy, but he maintained (and with truth) that the displays suggested by the copy-writers were often quite impracticable and that the copy-writers took unnecessary offence over the very necessary modifications which he had to make in their "roughs". Further, he had been deeply insulted by Mr. Armstrong's remarks about himself, too faithfully reported by Mr. Ingleby, whom he detested. In fact, he was within an ace of refusing altogether to play in the same match as Mr. Ingleby.

"Oh, but, look here!" protested Mr. Tallboy, "you simply can't let me down like that! You're the best bat we've got."

"Can't you leave Ingleby out?"

This was more than awkward, for in fact Mr. Barrow, though a good and reliable bat, was by no means so good a bat as Mr. Ingleby. Mr. Tallboy hesitated:

"I don't quite see how I can do that. He made 63 last year. But I'll tell you what. I'll put him in fourth and leave you to open with somebody else —say Pinchley. Will you start with Pinchley?"

"You can't put Pinchley in first. He's nothing but a slogger."

"Who else is there?"

Mr. Barrow scanned the list mournfully.

"It's a weak bunch, Tallboy. Is that really the best you can do?"

"Afraid so."

"Pity you've managed to get across Smayle and McAllister."

"Yes—but that can't be helped now. You'll *have* to play, Mr. Barrow, or we'll have to scratch—one or the other."

"I know what you'd better do. Put yourself in first with me."

"They won't like that. They'll think it's swank."

"Then put Garrett in."

"Very well. You'll play, then?"

"I suppose I must."

"That's very sporting of you, Mr. Barrow."

Mr. Talboy ran down, sighing, to pin the revised list on the board:

MATCH AGAINST BROTHERHOOD'S

1. Mr. Barrow
2. Mr. Garrett
3. Mr. Hankin
4. Mr. Ingleby
5. Mr. Tallboy (Captain)
6. Mr. Pinchley
7. Mr. Miller
8. Mr. Beeseley
9 Mr. Bredon
10. Mr. Haagedorn
11. Mr. Wedderburn

He stood for a moment looking at it rather hopelessly. Then he went back to his room and took up a large sheet of foolscap, with the intention of marking off the figures for a client's appropriation over the next three months. But his mind was not on the figures. Presently he pushed the sheet aside, and sat staring blankly out of the window across the grey London roofs.

"What's up, Tallboy?" inquired Mr. Wedderburn.

"Life's the devil," said Mr. Tallboy. Then, in a sudden outburst:

"My God! how I hate this blasted place. It gets on my nerves."

"Time you had your holiday," said Mr. Wedderburn, placidly. "How's the wife?"

"All right," rejoined Mr. Tallboy, "but we shan't be able to get away till September."

"That's the worst of being a family man," replied Mr. Wedderburn. "And that reminds me. Have you done anything about that series for *The Nursing Times* about 'Nutrax for Nursing Mothers'?"

Mr. Tallboy thoughtlessly cursed the nursing mothers, dialled Mr. Hankin's room on the inter-office 'phone and in a mournful tone put in a requisition for six 4-inch doubles on that inspiring subject.

CHAPTER XI

Inexcusable Invasion of a Ducal Entertainment

TO LORD PETER WIMSEY, the few weeks of his life spent in unravelling the Problem of the Iron Staircase possessed an odd dreamlike quality, noticeable at the time and still more insistent in retrospect. The very work that engaged him—or rather, the shadowy simulacrum of himself that signed itself on every morning in the name of Death Bredon—wafted him into a sphere of dim platonic archetypes, bearing a scarcely recognisable relationship to anything in the living world. Here those strange entities, the Thrifty Housewife, the Man of Discrimination, the Keen Buyer and the Good Judge, for ever young, for ever handsome, for ever virtuous, economical and inquisitive, moved to and fro upon their complicated orbits, comparing prices and values, making tests of purity, asking indiscreet questions about each other's ailments, household expenses, bed-springs, shaving cream, diet, laundry work and boots, perpetually spending to save and saving to spend, cutting out coupons and collecting cartons, surprising husbands with margarine and wives with patent washers and vacuum cleaners, occupied from morning to night in washing, cooking, dusting, filing, saving their children from germs, their complexions from wind and weather, their teeth from decay and their stomachs from indigestion, and yet adding so many hours to the day by labour-saving appliances that they had always leisure for visiting the talkies, sprawling on the beach to picnic upon Potted Meats and Tinned Fruit, and (when adorned by So-and-so's Silks, Blank's Gloves, Dash's Footwear, Whatnot's Weatherproof Complexion

Cream and Thingummy's Beautifying Shampoos) even attending Ranelagh, Cowes, the Grand Stand at Ascot, Monte Carlo and the Queen's Drawing-Rooms. Where, Bredon asked himself, did the money come from that was to be spent so variously and so lavishly? If this hell's-dance of spending and saving were to stop for a moment, what would happen? If all the advertising in the world were to shut down to-morrow, would people still go on buying more soap, eating more apples, giving their children more vitamins, roughage, milk, olive oil, scooters and laxatives, learning more languages by gramophone, hearing more virtuosos by radio, re-decorating their houses, refreshing themselves with more non-alcoholic thirst-quenchers, cooking more new, appetising dishes, affording themselves that little extra touch which means so much? Or would the whole desperate whirligig slow down, and the exhausted public relapse upon plain grub and elbow-grease? He did not know. Like all rich men, he had never before paid any attention to advertisements. He had never realised the enormous commercial importance of the comparatively poor. Not on the wealthy, who buy only what they want when they want it, was the vast superstructure of industry founded and built up, but on those who, aching for a luxury beyond their reach and for a leisure for ever denied them, could be bullied or wheedled into spending their few hardly won shillings on whatever might give them, if only for a moment, a leisured and luxurious illusion. Phantasmagoria—a city of dreadful day, of crude shapes and colours piled Babel-like in a heaven of harsh cobalt and rocking over a void of bankruptcy—a Cloud Cuckooland, peopled by pitiful ghosts, from the Thrifty Housewife providing a Grand Family Meal for Fourpence with the aid of Dairyfields Butter Beans in Margarine, to the Typist capturing the affections of Prince Charming by a liberal use of Muggins's Magnolia Face Cream.

Among these phantasms, Death Bredon, driving his pen across reams of office foolscap, was a phantasm too, emerging from this nightmare toil to a still more fantastical existence amid people whose aspirations, rivalries and modes of thought were alien, and earnest beyond anything in his waking experience. Nor, when the Greenwich-driven clocks had jerked on to half-past-five, had he any world of reality to which to return; for then the illusionary Mr. Bredon dislimned and became the still more illusionary Harlequin of a dope-addict's dream; an advertising figure more crude and fanciful than any that postured in the columns of the *Morning Star*; a thing bodiless and absurd, a mouthpiece of stale clichés shouting in dull ears without a brain. From this abominable impersonation he could not now free himself, since at the sound of his name or the sight of his unmasked face, all the doors in that other dream-city—the city of dreadful night—would be closed to him.

From one haunting disquietude, Dian de Momerie's moment of inexplicable insight had freed him. She no longer desired him. He thought she rather dreaded him; yet, at the note of the penny whistle she would come out and drive with him, hour after hour, in the great black Daimler, till night turned to daybreak. He sometimes wondered whether she believed in his existence at all; she treated him as though he were some hateful but fascinating figure in a hashish-vision. His fear now was that her unbalanced fancy might topple her over the edge of suicide. She asked him once what he was and what he wanted, and he told her stark truth, so far as it went.

"I am here because Victor Dean died. When the world knows how he died, I shall go back to the place from which I came."

"To the place from which you came. I've heard that said before, but I can't remember where."

"If you ever heard a man condemned to death, then you heard it said then."

"My God, yes! That was it. I went to a murder trial once. There was a horrible old man, the Judge—I forget his name. He was like a wicked old scarlet parrot, and he said it as though he liked it. 'And may the Lord have mercy upon your soul.' Do we have souls, Harlequin, or is that all nonsense? It is nonsense, isn't it?"

"So far as you are concerned, it probably is."

"But what have I got to do with Victor's death?"

"Nothing, I hope. But you ought to know."

"Of course I had nothing to do with it."

And indeed, she might not have. This was the most phantasmal part of the illusion—the border where day-dream and night-dream marched together in an eternal twilight. The man had been murdered—of that he was now certain; but what hand had struck the blow and why was still beyond all guessing. Bredon's instinct told him to hold fast to Dian de Momerie. She was the guardian of the shadow-frontier; through her, Victor Dean, surely the most prosaic denizen of the garish city of daylight, had stepped into the place of bright flares and black abysses, whose ministers are drink and drugs and its monarch death. But question her as he might, he could get no help from her. She had told him one thing only, and over and over again he pondered it, wondering how it fitted into the plot. Milligan, the sinister Milligan, knew something about Pym's, or somebody who worked at Pym's. He had known of this before he met Dean, for he had said on meeting him: "So you're the chap, are you?" What connection was there? What had Dean, at Pym's, had to do with Milligan, before Milligan knew him? Was it merely that Dian had boasted, laughing, of having a lover from that respectable agency? Had Victor Dean died merely because of Dian's fancy for him?

Wimsey could not believe it; the fancy had died first, and the death of Dean was, after that, surely superfluous. Besides, when they of the city of night slay for passion's sake, they lay no elaborate schemes, wipe off no finger-prints and hold no discreet tongues before or after. Brawls and revolver-shots, with loud sobs and maudlin remorse, are the signs and tokens of fatal passion among leaders of the bright life.

One other piece of information Dian had indeed given him, but at that moment he could not interpret it, and was not even aware that he held it. He could only wait, like a cat at a mouse-hole, till something popped out that he could run after. And so he passed his nights very wearily, driving the car and playing upon a penny whistle, and snatching his sleep in the small hours, before taking up the daily grind at Pym's.

Wimsey was quite right about Dian de Momerie's feeling for him. He excited her and frightened her, and, on the whole, she got a sensation of rather titillating horror at the sound of the penny whistle. But the real reason of her anxiety to propitiate him was founded on a coincidence that he could not have known and that she did not tell him.

On the day after their first encounter, Dian had backed an outsider called Acrobat, and it had come in at 50 to 1. Three days after the adventure in the woods, she had backed another outsider called Harlequin, each way, and it had come in second at 100 to 1. Thereafter, she had entertained no doubt whatever that he was a powerful and heaven-sent mascot. The day after a meeting with him was her lucky day, and it was a fact that on those days she usually succeeded in winning money in one way or another. Horses, after those first two brilliant coups, had been rather disappointing, but her fortune with cards had been good. How much of this good fortune had been due to sheer self-confidence and the will to win, only a psychologist could say; the winnings were there, and she had no doubt at all about the reason for them. She did not tell him that he was a mascot, from a superstitious feeling that to do so would be to break the luck, but she had been to a crystal-gazer, who, reading her mind like a book, had encouraged her in the belief that a mysterious stranger would bring her good fortune.

Major Milligan, sprawling upon the couch in Dian's flat with a whisky-and-soda, turned on her a pair of rather bilious eyes. He was a large, saturnine man, blank as to morals but comparatively sober in his habits, as people must be who make money out of other people's vices.

"Ever see anything of that Dean girl nowadays, Dian?"

"No, darling," said Dian, absently. She was getting rather tired of Milligan, and would have liked to break with him, if only he had not been so useful, and if she had not known too much to make a break-away healthy.

"Well, I wish you would."

"Oh, why? She's one of Nature's worst bores, darling."

"I want to know if she knows anything about that place where Dean used to work."

"The advertising place? But, Tod, how too yawn-making. Why do you want to know about advertising?"

"Oh, never mind why. I was on to something rather useful there, that's all."

"Oh!" Dian considered. This, she thought, was interesting. Something to be made out of this perhaps. "I'll give her a ring if you like. But she's about as wet as a drowned eel. *What* do you want to know?"

"That's my business."

"Tod, I've often wanted to ask you. Why did you say I'd got to chuck Victor? Not that I cared about him, the poor fish, but I just wondered, especially after you'd told me to string him along."

"Because," replied Major Milligan, "the young what-not was trying to double-cross me."

"Good heavens, Tod—you ought to go on the talkies as Dog-faced Dick the Dope-King of the Underworld. Talk sense, darling."

"That's all very well, my girl, but your little Victor was getting to be a nuisance. Somebody had been talking to him—probably you."

"Me? that's good! There wasn't anything I could tell him. You never tell me anything, Tod."

"No—I've got some sense left."

"How rude you are, darling. Well, you see, I couldn't have split to Victor. Did you bump Victor off, Tod?"

"Who says he was bumped off?"

"A little bird told me."

"Is that your friend in the black and white checks?"

Dian hesitated. In an expansive and not very sober moment, she had told Tod about her adventure in the woods, and now rather wished she had not. Milligan took her silence for consent and went on:

"Who is that fellow, Dian?"

"Haven't the foggiest."

"What's he want?"

"He doesn't want me, at any rate," said Dian. "Isn't that humiliating, Tod?"

"It must be." Milligan grinned. "But what's the big idea?"

"I think he's on Victor's lay, whatever that was. He said he wouldn't be here if Victor hadn't popped off. Too thrilling, don't you think?"

"Um," said Milligan. "I think I'd like to meet this friend of yours. When's he likely to turn up?"

"Damned if I know. He just arrives. I don't think I'd have anything to do with him, Tod, if I were you. He's dangerous—queer, somehow. I've got a hunch about him."

"Your brain's going to mush, sweetest," said Milligan, "and he's trading on it, that's all."

"Oh, well," said Dian, "he amuses me, and you don't any more. You're getting to be a bit feeding, Tod." She yawned and trailed over to the looking-glass, where she inspected her face narrowly. "I think I'll give up dope, Tod. I'm getting puffy under the eyes. Do you think it would be amusing to go all good?"

"About as amusing as a Quaker meeting. Has your friend been trying to reform you? That's damn good."

"Reform me, nothing. But I'm looking horribly hag-like to-night. Oh, hell! what's the odds, anyway? Let's do something."

"All right. Come on round to Slinker's. He's throwing a party."

"I'm sick of Slinker's parties. I say, Tod, let's go and gate-crash something really virtuous. Who's the stickiest old cat in London that's got anything on?"

"Dunno."

"Tell you what. We'll scoop up Slinker's party and go round and look for striped awnings, and crash the first thing we see."

"Right-ho! I'm on."

Half an hour later, a noisy gang, squashed into five cars and a taxi, were whooping through the quieter squares of the West End. Even to-day, a few strongholds of the grimly aristocratic are left in Mayfair, and Dian, leaning from the open window of the leading car, presently gave tongue before a tall, old-fashioned house, whose entrance was adorned with a striped awning, a crimson carpet and an array of hothouse plants in tubs upon the steps.

"Whoopee! Hit it up, boys! Here's something! Whose is it?"

"My God!" said Slinger Braithwaite. "We've hit the bull, all right. It's Denver's place."

"You won't get in there," said Milligan. "The Duchess of Denver is heaven's prize frozen-face. Look at the chucker-out in the doorway. Better try something easier."

"Easier be damned. We said the first we came to, and this is the first. No ratting, darlings."

"Well, look here," said Milligan, "we'd better try the back entrance. There's a gate into the garden round the other side, opening on the car-park. We've more chance there."

From the other side, the assault turned out to be easy enough. The cars were parked in a back street, and on approaching the garden gate, they found it wide open, displaying a marquee, in which supper was being held. A bunch of guests came out just as they arrived, while, almost on their heels, two large cars drove up and disgorged a large party of people.

"Blow being announced," said an immaculate person, "we'll just barge right in and dodge the Ambassadors."

"Freddy, you can't."

"Can't I? You watch me." Freddy tucked his partner's arm firmly under his own and marched with determination up to the gate. "We're certain to barge into old Peter or somebody in the garden."

Dian nipped Milligan's arm, and the pair of them fell in behind the new arrivals. The gate was passed—but a footman just inside presented an unexpected obstacle.

"Mr. and Mrs. Frederick Arbuthnot," said the immaculate gentleman. "And party," he added, waving a vague hand behind him.

"Well, *we're* in, anyhow," exulted Dian.

Helen, Duchess of Denver, looked round with satisfaction upon her party. It was all going very nicely indeed. The Ambassador and his wife had expressed delight at the quality of the wine. The band was good, the refreshments more than adequate. A tone of mellow decorum pervaded the atmosphere. Her own dress, she thought, became her, although her mother-in-law, the Dowager Duchess, had said something rather acid about her spine. But then, the Dowager was always a little tiresome and incalculable. One must be fashionable, though one would not, of course, be vulgarly immodest. Helen considered that she was showing the exact number of vertebrae that the occasion demanded. One less would be incorrect; one more would be over-modern. She thanked Providence that at forty-five she still kept her figure—as indeed, she did, having been remarkably flat on both aspects the whole of her life.

She was just raising a well-earned glass of champagne to her lips when she paused, and set it down again. Something was wrong. She glanced hurriedly round for her husband. He was not there, but a few paces off an elegant black back and smooth, straw-coloured head of hair announced the presence of her brother-in-law, Wimsey. Hastily excusing herself to Lady Mendip, with whom she had been discussing the latest enormities of the Government, she edged her way through the crowd and caught Wimsey's arm.

"Peter! Look over there. Who are those people?"

Wimsey turned and stared in the direction pointed by the Duchess' fan.

"Good God, Helen! You've caught a pair of ripe ones this time! That's the de Momerie girl and her tame dope-merchant."

The Duchess shuddered.

"How horrible! Disgusting woman! How in the world did they get in?... Do you know them?"

"Not officially, no."

"Thank goodness! I was afraid you'd let them in. I never know what you're going to do next; you know so many impossible people."

"Not guilty this time, Helen."

"Ask Bracket how he came to let them in."

"I fly," said Wimsey, "to obey your behest."

He finished the drink he had in his hand, and set off in a leisurely manner in pursuit of the footman. Presently he returned.

"Bracket says they came with Freddy Arbuthnot."

"Find Freddy."

The Hon. Freddy Arbuthnot, when found, denied all knowledge of the intruders. "But there was a bit of a scrum at the gate, you know," he admitted, ingenuously, "and I daresay they barged in with the crowd. The de Momerie girl, eh, what? Where is she? I must have a look at her. Hot stuff and all that, what?"

"You will do nothing of the sort, Freddy. Where in the world is Gerald? Not here. He never is when he's wanted. You'll have to go and turn them out, Peter."

Wimsey, who had had time for a careful calculation, asked nothing better.

"I will turn them out," he announced, "like one John Smith. Where are they?"

The Duchess, who had kept a glassy eye upon them, waved a stern hand in the direction of the terrace. Wimsey ambled off amiably.

"Forgive me, dear Lady Mendip," said the Duchess, returning to her guest, "I had a little commission to give to my brother-in-law."

Up the dimly-lit terrace steps went Wimsey. The shadow of a tall pillar-rose fell across his face and chequered his white shirt-front with dancing black: and as he went he whistled softly: "Tom, Tom, the piper's son."

Dian de Momerie clutched Milligan's arm as she turned.

Wimsey stopped whistling.

"Er—good evening," he said, "excuse me. Miss de Momerie, I think."

"Harlequin!" cried Dian.

"I beg your pardon?"

"Harlequin. So here you are. I've got you this time. And I'm going to see your face properly if I die for it."

"I'm afraid there is some mistake," said Wimsey.

Milligan thought it time to interfere.

"Ah!" said he, "the mysterious stranger. I think it's time you and I had a word, young man. May I ask why you have been tagging round after this lady in a mountebank get-up?"

"I fear," said Wimsey, more elaborately, "that you are labouring under a misapprehension, sir, whoever you are. I have been dispatched by the Duchess on a—forgive me—somewhat distasteful errand. She regrets that she has not the honour of this lady's acquaintance, nor, sir, of yours, and wishes me to ask you by whose invitation you are here."

Dian laughed, rather noisily.

"You do it marvellously, darling," she said. "We gate-crashed on the dear old bird—same as you did, I expect."

"So the Duchess inferred," replied Wimsey. "I am sorry. I'm afraid I must ask you to leave at once."

"That's pretty good," said Milligan, insolently. "I'm afraid it won't work. It may be a fact that we weren't invited here, but we aren't going to turn out for a nameless acrobat who's afraid to show his face."

"You must be mistaking me for a friend of yours," said Wimsey. "Allow me." He stepped across to the nearest pillar and pressed a switch, flooding that end of the terrace with light. "My name is Peter Wimsey; I am Denver's brother, and my face—such as it is, is entirely at your service."

He fixed his monocle in his eye and stared unpleasantly at Milligan.

"But aren't you my Harlequin?" protested Dian. "Don't be such an ass—I know you are. I know your voice perfectly well—and your mouth and chin. Besides, you were whistling that tune."

"This is very interesting," said Wimsey. "Is it possible—I fear it is—I think you must have encountered my unfortunate cousin Bredon."

"That was the name——" began Dian, uncertainly, and stopped.

"I am glad to hear it," replied Wimsey. "Sometimes he gives mine, which makes it very awkward."

"See here, Dian," broke in Milligan, "you seem to have dropped a brick. You'd better apologise and then we'll clear. Sorry we crashed in, and all that——"

"One moment," said Wimsey. "I should like to hear more about this. Be good enough to come into the house for a moment. This way."

He ushered them courteously round the corner of the terrace, up a side path and by way of a French window into a small ante-room, laid out with tables and a cocktail bar.

"What will you drink? Whiskies? I might have known it. The abominable practice of putting whisky on top of mixed drinks late at night is responsible for more ruined complexions and reputations than any other single cause. There is many a woman now walking the streets of London through putting whisky on top of gin cocktails. Two stiff whiskies, Tomlin, and a liqueur brandy."

"Very good, my lord."

"You perceive," said Wimsey, returning with the drinks, "the true object of this hospitable gesture. I have established my identity, by the evidence of the reliable Tomlin. Let us now seek a spot less open to interruption. I suggest the library. This way. My brother, being an English gentleman, possesses a library in all his houses, though he never opens a book. This is called fidelity to ancient tradition. The chairs, however, are comfortable. Pray be seated. And now, tell me all about your encounter with my scandalous cousin."

"One moment," said Milligan, before Dian could speak. "I think I know the stud-book pretty well. I was not aware that you had a cousin Bredon."

"It is not every puppy that appears in the kennel-book," replied Wimsey carelessly, "and it is a wise man that knows all his own cousins. But what matter? Family is family, though indicated by the border compony (or gobony if you prefer that form of the word) or by the bend or baton sinister, called by most writers of fiction the bar sinister, for reasons which I am unable to determine. My regrettable cousin Bredon, having no particular right to one family name more than another, makes it his practice to employ them all in turn, thus displaying a happy absence of favouritism. Please help yourselves to smokes. You will find the cigars passable, Mr.—er——"

"Milligan."

"Ah! the notor—the well-known Major Milligan? You have a residence on the river, I fancy. Charming, charming. Its fame has reached me from time to time through my good brother-in-law, Chief Inspector Parker of Scotland Yard. A beautiful, retired spot, I believe?"

"Just so," said Milligan. "I had the pleasure of entertaining your cousin there one night."

"Did he gate-crash on you? That is exactly what he would do. And you have retorted upon my dear sister-in-law. Poetic justice, of course. I appreciate it—though possibly the Duchess will take a different view of the matter."

"No; he was brought by a lady of my acquaintance."

"He is improving. Major Milligan, painful though it may be to me, I feel that I ought to warn you against that cousin of mine. He is definitely not nice to know. If he has been thrusting his attentions upon Miss de Momerie, it is probably with some ulterior object. Not," added Wimsey, "that any man would need an ulterior object for such attentions. Miss de Momerie is an object in herself——"

His eye wandered over Dian, scantily clothed and slightly intoxicated, with a cold appraisement which rendered the words almost impertinent.

"But," he resumed, "I know my cousin Bredon—too well. Few people know him better. And I must confess that he is the last man to whom I should look for a disinterested attachment. I am unhappily obliged, in self-defence, to keep an eye on Cousin Bredon's movements, and I should be deeply grateful to be informed of the details of his latest escapade."

"All right, I'll tell you," said Dian. The whisky had strung her up to recklessness, and she became suddenly voluble, disregarding Milligan's scowls. She poured out the tale of her adventures. The incident of the fountain-dive seemed to cause Lord Peter Wimsey acute distress.

"Vulgar ostentation!" he said, shaking his head. "How many times have I implored Bredon to conduct himself in a quiet and reasonable manner."

"I thought he was too marvellous," said Dian, and proceeded to relate the encounter in the wood.

"He always plays 'Tom, Tom, the piper's son', so of course, when you came along whistling it, I thought it was him."

Wimsey's face darkened in a most convincing manner.

"Disgusting," he said.

"Besides, you are so much alike—the same voice and the same face as far as one can see it, you know. But of course he never took off his mask——"

"No wonder," said Wimsey, "no wonder." He heaved a deep sigh. "The police are interested in my cousin Bredon."

"How thrilling!"

"What for?" demanded Milligan.

"For impersonating me, among other things," said Wimsey, now happily launched and well away. "I cannot tell you in the brief time at our disposal, the distress and humiliation I have been put to on Bredon's account. Bailing him out at police stations—honouring cheques drawn in my name—rescuing him from haunts of infamy—I am telling you all these distressing details in confidence, of course."

"We won't split," said Dian.

"He trades upon our unfortunate resemblance," went on Wimsey. "He copies my habits, smokes my favourite brand of cigarettes, drives a car like mine, even whistles my favourite air—one, I may say, peculiarly well adapted for performance upon the penny whistle."

"He must be pretty well off," said Dian, "to drive a car like that."

"*That*," said Wimsey, "is the most melancholy thing of all. I suspect him—but perhaps I had better not say anything about that."

"Oh, do tell," urged Dian, her eyes dancing with excitement. "It sounds too terribly breath-taking."

"I suspect him," said Wimsey, in solemn and awful tones, "of having to do with—*smug-druggling*—I mean, dash it all—drug-smuggling."

"You don't say so," said Milligan.

"Well, I can't prove it. But I have received warnings from a certain quarter. You understand me." Wimsey selected a fresh cigarette and tapped it, with the air of one who has closed the coffin-lid upon a dead secret and is nailing it down securely. "I don't want to interfere in your affairs in any way at all, Major Milligan. I trust that I shall never be called upon to do so." Here he transfixed Milligan with another hard stare. "But you will perhaps allow me to give you, and this lady, a word of warning. Do not have too much to do with my cousin Bredon."

"I think you're talking rot," said Dian. "Why, you can't even get him to——"

"Cigarette, Dian?" interrupted Milligan, rather sharply.

"I do not say," resumed Wimsey, raking Dian slowly with his eyes, and then turning again to Milligan, "that my deplorable cousin is himself an addict to cocaine or heroin or anything of that description. In some ways, it would be almost more respectable if he were. The man or woman who can batten on the weaknesses of his fellow-creatures without sharing them is, I admit, to me a singularly disgusting object. I may be old-fashioned, but there it is."

"Quite so," said Milligan.

"I do not know, and do not wish to know," went on Wimsey, "how you came to allow my cousin Bredon into your house, nor what, on his side, can have brought him there. I prefer not to suppose that he found there any other attraction than good drinks and good company. You may think, Major Milligan, that because I have interested myself in certain police cases, I am a consistent busybody. That is not the case. Unless I am forced to take an interest in another man's business, I greatly prefer to let him alone. But I think it only fair to tell you that I *am* forced to take an interest in my cousin Bredon and that he is a person whose acquaintance might prove—shall I say, embarrassing?—to anyone who preferred to live a quiet life. I don't think I need say any more, need I?"

"Not at all," said Milligan. "I am much obliged to you for the warning, and so, I am sure, is Miss de Momerie."

"Of course, I'm frightfully glad to know all about it," said Dian. "Your cousin sounds a perfect lamb. I like 'em dangerous. Pompous people are too terribly moribund, aren't they?"

Wimsey bowed.

"My dear lady, your choice of friends is entirely at your own discretion."

"I'm glad to hear it. I got the impression that the Duchess wasn't too fearfully anxious to have both arms round my neck."

"Ah! the Duchess—no. There, I fear, all the discretion is on the other side, what? Which reminds me——"

"Quite right," said Milligan. "We have trespassed on your hospitality too long. We must really apologise and remove ourselves. By the way, there were some other members of our party——"

"I expect my sister-in-law will have dealt with them by now," said Wimsey with a grin. "If not, I will make a point of seeing them and telling them that you have gone on to—where shall I say?"

Dian gave her own address.

"You'd better come round and have a drink, too," she suggested.

"Alas!" said Wimsey, "duty and all that sort of thing, what? Can't leave my sister-in-law in the lurch, greatly as I should enjoy the entertainment." He rang the bell. "You will excuse me now, I trust. I must see to our other guests. Porlock, show this lady and gentleman out."

He returned to the garden by way of the terrace, whistling a passage of Bach, as was his way when pleased.

"Nun gehn wir wo der Tudelsack, der Tudel, tudel, tudel, tudel, tudelsack . . ."

"I wonder, was the fly too big and gaudy? Will he rise to it? We shall see."

"My dear Peter," said the Duchess, fretfully, "what a terrible time you have been. Please go and fetch Mme. de Framboise-Douillet an ice. And tell your brother I want him."

CHAPTER XII

Surprising Acquisition of a Junior Reporter

VERY EARLY ONE morning, a junior reporter on the *Morning Star*, of no importance to anybody except himself and his widowed mother, walked out of that great newspaper's palatial new offices and into the affairs of Chief Inspector Parker. This nonentity's name was Hector Puncheon, and he was in Fleet Street at that time because a fire had broken out the previous night in a large City warehouse, destroying a great deal of valuable property and involving the spectacular escapes of three night-watchmen and a cat from the roofs of the adjacent buildings. Hector Puncheon, summoned to the scene for the excellent reason that he had lodgings in the West Central district and could be transported to the scene of action in a comparatively brief time, had written a short stop-press notice of the disaster for the early country editions, a longer and more exciting account for the London edition, and then a still longer and more detailed report, complete with the night-watchmen's and eye-witnesses' stories and a personal interview with the cat, for the early editions of the *Evening Comet*, twin-organ to the *Morning Star* and housed in the same building.

After completing all this toil, he was wakeful and hungry. He sought an all-night restaurant in Fleet Street, accustomed to catering for the untimely needs of pressmen, and, having previously armed himself with a copy of the *Morning Star* as it poured out damp from the machines, sat down to a 3 a.m. breakfast of grilled sausages, coffee and rolls.

He ate with leisurely zest, pleased with himself and his good fortune, and persuaded that not even the most distinguished of the senior men could have turned in a column more full of snap, pep and human interest than his own. The interview with the cat had been particularly full of appeal. The animal was, it seemed, an illustrious rat-catcher, with many famous deeds to her credit. Not only that, but she had been the first to notice the smell of fire and had, by her anguished and intelligent mewings, attracted the attention of night-watchman number one, who had been in the act of brewing a cup of tea when the outbreak took place. Thirdly, the cat, an ugly black-and-white creature with a spotted face, was about to become a mother for the tenth time, and Hector Puncheon, by a brilliant inspiration, had secured the reversion of the expected family for the *Morning Star*, so that half a dozen or so fortunate readers might, by applying to their favourite paper and enclosing a small donation for the Animals' Hospital, become the happy owners of kittens with a prenatal reputation and a magnificent rat-catching pedigree. Hector Puncheon felt that he had done well. He had been alert and courageous, offering the night-watchman ten shillings on his own responsibility the very moment the big idea occurred to him, and the night-editor had okayed the stunt and even remarked that it would do quite well.

Filled with sausages and contentment, Hector Puncheon lingered over his paper, reading the Special Friday Feature with approval and appreciating the political cartoon. At length, he folded the sheet, stuffed it in his pocket, tipped the waiter extravagantly with sixpence and emerged into Fleet Street.

The morning was fine, though chilly, and he felt that after his night's labours, a little walk would do him good. He strolled happily along, past the Griffin at Temple Bar and the Law Courts and the churches of St. Clement Danes and St. Mary-le-Strand, and made his way up Kingsway. It was only when he got to the turning into Great Queen Street that he became aware of something lacking in an otherwise satisfactory universe. Great Queen Street led into Long Acre; off Long Acre lay Covent Garden; already the vans and lorries laden with fruit and flowers were rumbling in from all over the country and rumbling out again. Already the porters were unloading their stout sacks, huge crates, round baskets, frail punnets and long flat boxes filled with living scent and colour, sweating and grumbling over their labours as though their exquisite burdens were so much fish or pig-iron. And for the benefit of these men the pubs would be open, for Covent Garden interprets the London licensing regulations to suit its own topsy-turvy hours of labour. Hector Puncheon had had a successful night and had celebrated his success with sausages and coffee; but there are, dash it all! more suitable methods of celebration.

Hector Puncheon, swinging blithely along in his serviceable grey flannel bags and tweed jacket, covered by an old burberry, suddenly realised that he owned the world, including all the beer in Covent Garden Market. He turned into Great Queen Street, traversed half the length of Long Acre, dodged under the nose of a van horse at the entrance to the Underground Station, and set his face towards the market, picking his way cheerfully between the boxes and baskets and carts and straw that littered the pavement. Humming a lively tune, he turned in through the swing doors of the White Swan.

Although it was only a quarter past four, the Swan was already doing a brisk trade. Hector Puncheon edged his way up to the bar between two enormous carters and waited modestly for the landlord to finish serving his habitual customers before calling attention to himself. A lively discussion was going on about the merits of a dog named Forked Lightning. Hector, always ready to pick up a hint about anything that was, or might conceivably be turned into news, pulled his early *Morning Star* from his pocket and pretended to read it, while keeping his ears open.

"And what I say is," said Carter the First, "—same again, Joe—what I say is, when a dawg that's fancied like that dawg is, stops dead 'arf way round the course like as if 'e'd a-bin shot, wot I say is, I likes to know wot's at the back of it."

"Ar," said Carter the Second.

"Mind you," went on Carter the First, "I ain't sayin' as animals is always to be relied on. They 'as their off-days, same as you an' me, but wot I says is——"

"That's a fact," put in a smaller man, from the other side of Carter the Second, "that's a fact, that is. An' wot's more, they 'as their fancies. I 'ad a dawg once as couldn't abide the sight of a goat. Or maybe it was the smell. I dunno. But show 'im a goat any time, and 'e got a fit of the trembles. Couldn't run all day. I remember one time when I was bringing 'im up to run at the White City, there was a bloke in the street leadin' two goats on a string——"

"Wot did a bloke want with two goats?" demanded Carter the Second, suspiciously.

" 'Ow should I know wot 'e wanted with goats?" retorted the little man, indignantly. "They wasn't my goats, was they? Well, that there dawg——"

"That's different," said Carter the First. "Nerves is nerves, and a thing like a goat might 'appen to anybody, but wot I says is——"

"What's yours, sir?" inquired the landlord.

"Oh, I think I'll have a Guinness," said Hector. "Guinness is good for you—particularly on a chilly morning. Perhaps," he added, feeling pleased with himself and the world, "these gentlemen will join me."

The two carters and the little man expressed their gratification, and ordered beer.

"It's a queer thing, this business of nerves," said the little man. "Talking of Guinness, now, my old aunt had a parrot. Some bird it was, too. Learnt to speak from a sailor. Fortunately the old lady couldn't 'ear 'alf of wot it said, and didn't understand the other 'alf. Now, that there bird——"

"You seem to have had a wide experience with live-stock," observed Hector Puncheon.

"I 'ave that," said the little man. "That there bird, as I was going to say, got fits of nerves as would surprise you. 'Unched 'isself up on 'is perch like, and shivered fit to shake 'isself to pieces. And wot was the reason of that, do you think?"

"Beggared if I know," said Carter the Second. "Your 'ealth, sir."

"Mice," said the little man, triumphantly. "Couldn't stand the sight of a mouse. And wot do you think we 'ad to give it to pull it round, like?"

"Brandy," suggested Carter the First. "Nothing like brandy for parrots. We got one at 'ome—one o' them green sort. My wife's brother brought it 'ome with 'im——"

"They ain't such good talkers as the grey ones," said Carter the Second. "There was a parrot at the old Rose & Crown dahn Seven Dials way——"

"Brandy?" scoffed the little man, "not 'im. 'E wouldn't look at brandy."

"Wouldn't 'e now?" said Carter the First. "Now, you show our old bird brandy, an' 'e'll 'op right out of 'is cage for it same as a Christian. Not too much, mind you, but give it 'im neat in a teaspoon——"

"Well, it wasn't brandy," persisted the little man. "Aunt's was a teetotal bird, 'e was. Now, I'll give you three guesses, an' if you gets it right, I'll stand drinks all round, and I can't say fairer 'an that."

"Aspirin?" suggested the landlord, anxious that the round of drinks should be stood by somebody.

The little man shook his head.

"Ginger," said Carter the Second. "Birds is sometimes wonderful fond o' ginger. Stimulates the innards. Though, mind you, some says it's too 'eatin', an' brings their fevvers aht."

"Nutrax for Nerves," suggested Hector Puncheon, a little wildly, his eye having been caught by that morning's half-double, which carried the intriguing headline: "WHY BLAME THE WOMAN?"

"Nutrax nothing," snorted the little man, "nor none o' yer patent slops. No. Strong coffee wiv' cayenne pepper in it—that's wot that bird liked. Put 'im right in a jiff, it did. Well, seein' as the drinks ain't on me this time——"

He looked wistful, and Hector obliged again with the same all round. Carter the Second, jerking his beer off at one gulp and offering a general salute to the company, shouldered his way out, and the little man moved up closer to Hector Puncheon to make way for a florid person in evening dress, who had just shot his way in through the door and now stood swaying a little uncertainly against the bar.

"Scotch-and-soda," said this person, without preface, "double Scotch and not too bloodymuch soda."

The landlord looked at him keenly.

"Thass all right," said the newcomer, "I know what you're thinking, my boy, but I'm not drunk. Norra bittovit. Nerves a liddleoutavorder, 'tsall." He paused, evidently conscious that his speech was getting a little ahead of itself. "Been sittin' up with a sick friend," he explained, carefully. "Very trying to the system, sittin' up all night. Very hard on the conshi-conshishushion—excuse me—slight acshident to my dental plate, mush gettisheento."

He leaned one elbow on the bar, pawed vaguely with his foot for the brass rail, pushed his silk hat well to the back of his head and beamed pleasantly upon the company.

The landlord of the Swan looked at him again with a practised eye, calculated that his customer could probably carry one more Scotch-and-soda without actual disaster, and fulfilled his order.

"Thanks verrimush, old feller," said the stranger. "Well, goo' luck, all. What are these gentlemen taking?"

Hector Puncheon excused himself politely, explaining that he had really had all he wanted and must now be going home.

"No, no," said the other, hurt. "Mustn't say that. Nottime to gome yet. Night yet young." He flung an affectionate arm round Hector's neck. "I like your face. You're the sortafeller I like. You must come along one day 'n see my little place. Roses roun' the porch an' all that. Give you my card." He hunted in his pockets and produced a note-case, which he flapped open on the bar-counter. A quantity of small pieces of paper flew out right and left.

"Dashitall," said the gentleman in dress clothes, "what I mean, dashit." Hector stooped to pick up some of the scattered oddments, but the little man was before him.

"Thanks, thanks," said the gentleman. "Wheresh card? Thatsh not card, thatsh my wife's shopping-list—you gorrawife?"

"Not yet," admitted Hector.

"Lucky devil," replied the stranger with emphasis. "No wife, no damned shopping-list." His vagrant attention was caught and held by the shopping-list, which he held up in one hand and tried, unsuccessfully, to focus with a slightly squinting gaze. "Alwaysh bringing home parcels like a blurry errand-boy. Where'd I put that parcel now?"

"You 'adn't no parcel when you come in 'ere, guv'nor," said Carter the First. The question of drinks seemed to have been shelved, and the worthy man no doubt felt it was time to remind the gentleman that there were others in the bar, besides the abstemious Mr. Puncheon. "Dry work," he added, "cartin' parcels round."

"Damn dry," said the married gentleman. "Mine's a Scotch-and-Soda. Whaddid you say you'd have ol' boy?" He again embraced Hector Puncheon, who gently disentangled himself.

"I really don't want——" he began; but, seeing that this reiterated refusal might give offence, he gave way and asked for a half-tankard of bitter.

"Talking about parrots," said a thin voice behind them. Hector started and, looking round, observed a dried-up old man seated at a small table in the corner of the bar absorbing a gin-and-potash. He must have been there all the time, thought Hector.

The gentleman in dress clothes swung round upon him so sharply that he lost his balance and had to cling to the little man to save himself.

"I never mentioned parrots," he said, enunciating the words very distinctly. "I shouldn't think of talking about parrots."

"I once knowed a parson wot 'ad a parrot," continued the old man. "Joey, they called 'im."

"Wot, the parson?" asked the little man.

"No, the parrot," said the old fellow, mildly, "and that there parrot hadn't ever been out of the parson's family. Joined in family prayers, he did and said 'Amen' like a Christian. Well, one day this here parson——"

A rush of customers entering from the market drew the landlord's attention away and drowned the next sentence or so of the story. The carter hailed some acquaintances and joined them in a fresh round of beer. Hector, shaking off the intoxicated gentleman, who seemed now to be inviting him to join a cosy little fishing party in Scotland, turned to go, but found himself caught and held by the old man.

"—and old parson found the bishop sitting over the cage with a lump of sugar in his fingers, saying, 'Come on, Joey, say it! B . . . b . . . b . . .'! And that, mind you," said the old man, "was a Church of England bishop. And what do you think the bishop did then?"

"I can't imagine," said Hector.

"Made the parson a canon," said the old man, triumphantly.

"Never!" said Hector.

"But that's nothing," pursued the old man. "There was a parrot I knew down in Somerset——"

Hector felt he really could not bear to hear about the parrot down in Somerset. He extricated himself politely and fled.

His next activity was to go home and have a bath, after which he coiled himself up on his bed and slept placidly till his normal breakfast-time at nine.

He breakfasted in his dressing-gown, and it was when he was transferring his various possessions from his grey flannels to his navy lounge suit that he came upon the little packet. It was neatly done up with sealing-wax in white paper, and bore the innocent label "Bicarbonate of Soda". He stared at it in surprise.

Hector Puncheon was a young man with a hearty and healthy digestion. He had heard, of course, of sodium bicarb, and its virtues, but only as a wealthy man hears of hire-purchase. For the moment he thought he must have accidentally picked the little package up in the bathroom and slipped it into his pocket unaware. Then he remembered that he had not taken his coat into the bathroom that morning, and that he had emptied out the pockets the previous night. He distinctly recollected that, when the summons to the fire had reached him, he had had to tumble hurriedly into them the few odds and ends he habitually carried about him—handkerchief, keys, loose cash, pencils and what-not, taken from his dressing-table. It was quite inconceivable that there should have been any bicarbonate on his dressing-table.

Hector Puncheon was puzzled. A glance at the clock, however, reminded him that he had no time for puzzlement just then. He had to get down to St. Margaret's, Westminster, by 10.30 to report the wedding of a fashionable beauty who was being married in the strictest secrecy at that unfashionable hour. He had then to hasten back to report a political meeting in Kingsway Hall, and thence he must gallop round the corner to attend a luncheon given to a distinguished airman in the Connaught Rooms. If the speeches were over by 3 o'clock, he could then make a dash for a train and get out to Esher, where a royalty was opening a new school and inaugurating it with a children's tea-party. After which, if he were still alive, and had contrived to get his copy written up in the train, he could turn it in at the office and find time to think.

This strenuous programme was carried out without more than the usual number of exasperating hitches, and not until he had pushed the last sheet of copy over to the sub-editor, and was sitting, tired but conscious of work well done, in the Cock Tavern, tackling a beef-steak, did he give another thought to the mysterious packet of sodium bicarb. And now, the more he thought about it, the odder the incident became.

He ran over in his mind the various activities of the previous night. At the fire, he remembered now quite distinctly, he had put on his burberry and buttoned it up, by way of protecting his light grey flannels against showers of smuts and the spray of the firemen's hoses. The mysterious package could hardly have been placed in his jacket-pocket then. After that, there had been interviews with various people—including the cat—the writing of his copy in the *Morning Star* offices and his breakfast in the Fleet Street eating-house. To suppose that he had accidentally found and pocketed four ounces of bicarbonate on any of these occasions seemed to him fantastic. Unless, of course, one of his newspaper colleagues had put the thing there for a joke. But who? And why?

He went on to consider the walk home and the conversation in the White Swan. His exhilarated acquaintance in dress clothes was the kind of man, he thought, who might from time to time require the assistance of a mild digestive and carminative. Possibly in one of his more affectionate moments he might have slipped the packet into Hector's coat-pocket by mistake for his own. The two carters would not, Mr. Puncheon felt sure, be carrying drugs round with them. . . .

Drugs. As the word shaped itself in his mind—for Hector Puncheon usually thought articulately, and often, indeed, conversed quite sensibly aloud with his own soul—an enormous query shot up in his brain. Bicarbonate of soda, hell! He was ready to stake his journalistic reputation it was nothing of the sort. His fingers sought the packet, which he had thrust back into the pocket where he had found it, and he was on the point of opening it and investigating the contents when a better idea struck him. Leaving his rump-steak half finished, and muttering to the astonished waiter that he would be back in a minute, he ran out hatless to the establishment of the nearest chemist, one Mr. Tweedle, who knew him well.

Mr. Tweedle's shop was shut, but a light still burned within, and Hector hammered violently until the door was opened by an assistant. Was Mr. Tweedle in? Yes, he was in, but he was just going. On being assured that Mr. Puncheon wanted to see Mr. Tweedle personally, the assistant volunteered to see what could be done.

Mr. Tweedle, hatted and coated, appeared from the inner recesses of the shop with just enough delay to make Hector feel that he had acted with some precipitation and had probably started out upon a wild-goose chase. Once started, however, he had to go through with it.

"Look here, Tweedle," he said, "I'm sorry to bother you, and there's probably nothing in it, but I wish you'd have a look at this for me. It came into my hands in rather a curious way."

The chemist received the packet and held it balanced in his hand for a moment.

"What's wrong with it?"

"I don't know that anything's wrong with it. I want you to tell me."

"Bicarbonate of soda," said Mr. Tweedle, glancing at the label and at the sealed flaps of the package. "No chemist's name—the ordinary printed label. You don't seem to have opened it."

"No, I haven't, and I want you to bear witness to that, if necessary. It appears to be just as it came from the chemist, doesn't it?"

"It appears to be, certainly," rejoined Mr. Tweedle in some surprise. "The label seems to be the original label and the ends have apparently only been sealed once, if that is what you want to know."

"Yes, and I couldn't have sealed it up like that, could I? I mean, it looks professional."

"Quite."

"Well, now, if you're quite satisfied about that, open it."

Mr. Tweedle carefully inserted a penknife beneath one flap, broke the wax and opened the paper. The packet was, as might have been expected, filled with a fine white powder.

"What next?" inquired Mr. Tweedle.

"Well, is it bicarbonate of soda?"

Mr. Tweedle shook some of the powder out into the palm of his hand, looked closely at it, smelt it, moistened his finger and took up a few grains, and then carried them to his tongue. Then his face changed. He took out his handkerchief, wiped his mouth, poured the powder from his palm carefully back into the paper and asked:

"How did you get hold of this?"

"I'll tell you in a moment," said Hector. "What is it?"

"Cocaine," said Mr. Tweedle.

"Are you sure?"

"Positive."

"My God!" cried Hector, jubilantly. "I'm on to something! What a day! Here, Tweedle, can you spare a moment? I want you to come round to our place and tell Hawkins about this."

"Where? What?" demanded Mr. Tweedle.

Hector Puncheon wasted no more words, but grabbed him by the arms. Thus, on Mr. Hawkins, news-editor of the *Morning Star*, there burst an agitated member of his own staff, with a breathless witness in tow, and an exhibit of cocaine.

Mr. Hawkins was a keen newspaper man and rejoiced in a stunt. He had, nevertheless, a certain conscience in such matters, so far as giving information to the police was concerned. For one thing, it does a newspaper no good to be on bad terms with the police, and, for another, there had only recently been trouble about another case in which information had been held up. Having, therefore, heard Hector Puncheon's story and scolded him soundly for having waited so long before examining the mysterious package, he telephoned to Scotland Yard.

Chief Inspector Parker, with his arm in a sling and his nerves very much on edge, received the information in his own home, just as he thought his day's work was happily done with. He grumbled horribly; but there had been a good deal of fuss made lately at the Yard about dope-gangs, and things had been said which he resented. He irritably called a taxi and trundled down to the *Morning Star* offices, accompanied by a morose person called Sergeant Lumley, who disliked him, and whom he disliked, but who happened to be the only sergeant available.

By this time, Hector Puncheon's excitement had rather worn off. He was getting sleepy and stupid after a broken night and a hard day's work. He could not control his yawns, and the Chief Inspector snapped at him. In answer to questions he managed, however, to give a fairly complete account of his movements during the night and early morning.

"Actually, then," said Parker, when the tale was finished, "you can't say with any certainty when you received this packet?"

"No, I can't," said Hector, resentfully. He could not help feeling that it was very clever of him to have received the packet at all, and that everybody ought, somehow, to be grateful to him. Instead of which, they almost seemed to think he was to blame for something.

"You say you found it in your right hand coat-pocket. Did you at no time previously to that put your hand in that pocket for anything?"

"I should think I must have," said Hector. He yawned. "But I can't exactly remember." He yawned again, uncontrollably.

"What do you keep in that pocket?"

"Odds and ends," said Hector. He dipped into the pocket and drew out a mixed collection—a pencil, a box of matches, a pair of nail-scissors, some string, a thing for opening beer-bottles with patent caps, a corkscrew for opening ordinary beer-bottles, a very dirty handkerchief and some crumbs.

"If you could remember using any of those things during the night——" suggested Parker.

"I must have used the handkerchief," said Hector, gazing at it in some dismay. "I meant to take a clean one out this morning. I did, too. Where is it? Oh, in my trousers-pocket. Here it is. But of course," he added, helpfully, "this isn't the suit I wore last night. I had my old tweed jacket on then. I must have put the dirty handkerchief in this pocket with the other things instead of into the clothes-basket. I know it's the one I had at the fire. Look at the soot on it."

"Quite so," said Parker, "but can you remember *when* you used this handkerchief last night? Surely, if you had felt in your pocket at any time, you couldn't have failed to come on the packet if it was there."

"Oh, yes, I could," said Hector, brightly. "I shouldn't notice. I'm so accustomed to having a lot of junk in my pocket. I can't help you there, I'm afraid."

Another frightful yawn attacked him. He stifled it manfully, and it forced itself painfully out at his nose, nearly breaking his ear-drums on the way. Parker gazed crossly at his grimacing countenance.

"Do try to keep your mind on what I am asking you, Mr. Firkin," he said. "If only——"

"Puncheon," said Hector, annoyed.

"Puncheon," said Parker, "I beg your pardon. Did you at any time, Mr. Puncheon——?"

"I don't know," interrupted Hector. "I honestly don't know. It's no good asking. I can't tell you. I would if I could, but I simply can't."

Mr. Hawkins, looking from one to the other, discovered in himself a little elementary knowledge of human nature.

"I think," he said, "a small drink is indicated."

He fetched a bottle of Johnnie Walker and some glasses from a locker and set them on the desk, together with a siphon. Parker thanked him and, suddenly ashamed of himself and his bad temper, apologised.

"I'm sorry," he said. "I'm afraid I was a bit curt. I got my collar-bone broken a little time ago and it still aches a bit and makes me abominably peevish. Let's go about this business another way. Why do you suppose, Mr. Puncheon, that anybody should have picked you out to take charge of this hefty dose of dope?"

"I thought whoever it was must have mistaken me for someone else."

"So I should imagine. And you think that's more likely to have happened at the pub than anywhere else?"

"Yes; unless it was in the crowd at the fire. Because in the other places—I mean in this office and when I was interviewing people, everyone knew me, or at least they knew what I was there for."

"That seems sound," agreed Parker. "How about this restaurant where you had your sausages?"

"There's that, of course. But I can't recollect anybody coming near enough to me to shove things in my pocket. And it couldn't have been during the fire either, because I had my burberry on, buttoned up. But in the pub, I had my burberry open, and there were at least four people barging up against me—one of the two carters who were there before me, and a little man who looked like a bookmaker's tout or something, and the drunken chap in dress clothes and the old boy sitting in the corner. I don't think it can have been the carter, though; he looked quite genuine."

"Had you ever been to the White Swan before?"

"Once, I think, ages ago. Certainly not often. And I think there's a new landlord since then."

"Well, then," said Parker, "what is there about you, Mr. Puncheon, that induces people to hand you out valuable cargoes of dope on sight and without payment?"

"Goodness knows," said Hector.

The desk telephone buzzed furiously, and Mr. Hawkins, snatching the receiver, plunged into a long conversation with some unknown person. The two policemen with their witness retired into a distant corner and carried on the inquiry in low tones.

"Either," said Parker, "you must be the dead spit of some habitual dope-peddler, or you must have led them in some way to imagine that you were the person they expected to see. What did you talk about?"

Hector Puncheon racked his brains.

"Greyhounds," he said at last, "and parrots. Chiefly parrots. Oh, yes—and goats."

"Greyhounds, parrots and goats?"

"We were swapping stories about parrots," said Hector Puncheon. "No, wait, we began about dogs. The little tout person said he'd had a dog that couldn't abide goats and that led on to parrots and mice (I'd forgotten the mice)—and doping parrots with coffee and cayenne."

"Doping?" said Parker, quickly. "Was that word used?"

"No, I don't know that it was. The parrot was frightened of mice, and they had to cure it of shock by giving it coffee."

"Whose parrot?"

"The little fellow's aunt's, I think. The old boy knew a parrot, too, but that belonged to a clergyman, and the bishop tried to teach it to swear and promoted the parson. I don't know whether it was blackmail, or just that he liked the parrot."

"But what did you contribute to the conversation?"

"Hardly anything. I just listened and paid for the drinks."

"And the man in dress clothes?"

"Oh, he talked about his wife's shopping-list and a parcel—yes, there was something about a parcel he ought to have brought with him."

"Was the parcel produced?"

"No, he never had a parcel."

"All right," said Parker, after a little more of this unsatisfactory conversation. "We'll go into the matter, Mr. Puncheon. We're very much obliged to you and Mr.—er—Hawkins for having called our attention to the matter. We will take charge of the packet, and if we want you again, we'll let you know."

He rose to his feet. Mr. Hawkins shot across from his desk.

"Got all you want? You don't want this story to go in, I suppose?" he added, wistfully.

"No; you mustn't say anything about it at present," said Parker, firmly. "But we're very much indebted to you, and if anything comes of it, you shall have the story first with all the details we can give you. I can't say fairer than that."

He left the office with Sergeant Lumley, mournful and silent, at his heels.

"It's a thousand pities, Lumley, that we didn't get this information earlier. We could have put a man in at that pub for the rest of the day. It's too late to do anything now."

"Yes, sir, it is," said Sergeant Lumley.

"The pub's the place, I fancy."

"Very likely, sir."

"The cargo of dope was a pretty large one. That means that it was meant for someone who distributes the stuff on a fairly extensive scale. And it didn't have to be paid for. That suggests to me that the man they expected to see was only a messenger for this distributor, who, no doubt, settles up direct with the top man by some other route."

"Very possibly, sir," said Sergeant Lumley, in an unbelieving tone.

"The thing is, what are we to do? We could raid the place, of course, but I don't think that would be advisable. We probably shouldn't find anything, and we should merely give the alarm to no purpose."

"That wouldn't be anything unusual," grunted the Sergeant, disagreeably.

"Too true. We haven't anything against the White Swan so far, have we?"

"Not that I know of, sir."

"We shall have to make certain about it first. The landlord may or may not be concerned in the business. Quite possibly he isn't, but we shall have to make sure. You had better arrange for at least two men to investigate the Swan. They mustn't make themselves conspicuous. They can drop in from time to time and talk about parrots and goats and see if anything peculiar happens to them. And they can try and get a line on those people—the little chap, and the old man, and the fellow in the boiled shirt. It ought not to be difficult. Put on two sensible, tactful men who are not teetotallers, and if they don't get anything in the course of a day or two, change them for two others. And see that they look like what they're supposed to be and don't wear regulation boots or anything foolish."

"Very well, sir."

"And for God's sake, Lumley, look a little more cheerful about it," said the Chief Inspector. "I like to see duties undertaken in a pleasant spirit."

"I do my best," replied Sergeant Lumley, offended.

Chief Inspector Parker went resolutely home to bed.

CHAPTER XIII

Embarrassing Entanglement of a Group-Manager

"EXCUSE ME, MISS," said Tompkin, the reception-clerk, to Miss Rossiter, "but do you happen to have seen Mr. Wedderburn anywhere? He's not in his room."

"I think I saw him in with Mr. Ingleby."

"Thank you very much, miss."

Tompkin's cheerful face looked worried; and all the more so, when he reached Mr. Ingleby's room and found nobody there but Mr. Ingleby himself and Mr. Bredon.

He repeated his inquiry.

"He's just gone down to Bream's Buildings about an insertion in some magazine or other," said Ingleby.

"Oh!" Tompkin looked so nonplussed that Ingleby added, "Why, what's up?"

"Well, sir, as a matter of fact and strictly between you and I, a rather awkward thing has happened. I don't quite know what to do about it."

"In all social difficulties," said Bredon, "ask Uncle Ugly. Do you want to know how many buttons there should be on a dress waistcoat? How to eat an orange in public? how to introduce your first-wife-that-was to your third-wife-to-be? Uncle Ugly will put you right."

"Well, sir, if you will treat the matter in confidence, you and Mr. Ingleby——"

"Say on, Tompkin. We will be silent as a pre-talkie movie. Any sum from £5 to £5,000 advanced on your note of hand alone. No embarrassing investigations. No security required—or offered. What's your trouble?"

"Not mine, sir. As a matter of fact, sir, there's a young woman here, asking for Mr. Tallboy, and he's in conference with Mr. Armstrong and Mr. Toule, and I don't like to send a message."

"Well," said Ingleby, "tell her to wait."

"That's just it, sir, I did, and she said I was only saying that to put her off, while Mr. Tallboy got out of the building, and she took on terribly and said she was going to speak to Mr. Pym. Well, sir, of course I don't know what the trouble is"—here Tompkin looked unnaturally blank and innocent—"but I don't think Mr. Tallboy would care for that, nor Mr. Pym neither. So I thought, seeing that Mr. Wedderburn is the gentleman who sees most of Mr. Tallboy, so to speak——"

"I see," said Ingleby. "Where is the young woman?"

"Well, I've put her in the Little Conference Room," said Tompkin, dubiously, with an accent on the "put", "but of course, if she was to come out again (and there's nothing to stop her) and was to go to Mr. Pym, or even to Miss Fearney—— You see, sir, when parties like Miss Fearney are in an official position, they have to take notice of things, as you may say, whether they like to or not. It isn't the same as you or me, sir." Tompkin glanced from Ingleby to Bredon, dividing the "sir" impartially between them.

Bredon, who was drawing patterns on his blotter, looked up.

"What is she like?" he asked. "I mean"—as Tompkin hesitated—"do you think she is genuinely in distress or merely out to make trouble?"

"Well, sir," said Tompkin, "since you ask me, I should say she was a tough jane."

"I'll go and keep her quiet," said Bredon. "Be sure you tell Mr. Tallboy the moment he is free."

"Very good, sir."

"And try not to let it get round the office. It may be nothing at all."

"Quite so, sir. I'm not one to talk. But there's the boy on the desk, sir——"

"Oh! Well, tell him to hold his tongue."

"Yes, sir."

Bredon went out, looking as though he did not care for his self-imposed task. By the time he arrived at the door of the Little Conference Room, however, his face bore nothing but an expression of amiable helpfulness. He entered briskly, and in the first glance his practised eye took in every detail about the young woman who sprang up to face him, from her hard eyes and shrewish mouth to her blood-red, pointed finger-nails and over-elaborate shoes.

"Good-afternoon," he said, brightly. "You want Mr. Tallboy, I think. He won't be long, but he's been called in to a conference with some clients and we can't rescue him, so they've sent me down to entertain you till he comes. Will you smoke, Miss—er—the clerk didn't mention your name?"

"It's Vavasour—Miss Ethel Vavasour. Who're you? Are you Mr. Pym?"

Bredon laughed.

"Good lord, no. I'm a very unimportant person—one of the junior copy-writers, that's all."

"Oh, I see. You a pal of Jim's?"

"Of Tallboy's? Not specially. I just happened to be there, so I came along, don't you know. They told me there was a very beautiful young lady asking for Tallboy, and I thought, What-ho! Why not buzz along and cheer her weary hours of waiting?"

"I'm sure it's frightfully good of you," said Miss Vavasour, laughing rather shrilly. "I expect what you mean is, that Jim's sent you along to see if you can talk me round. That's just like Jim. I suppose he's sneaked off the back way."

"I assure you, my dear young lady, that I haven't seen or spoken to Tallboy this afternoon. And I expect, when he hears that I've been along to have a chat with you, he'll be very fed-up with me. And no wonder. If you'd come to see me, I should loathe any other blighter who came and barged in."

"You can can that stuff," retorted Miss Vavasour. "I know your sort. You'd talk the hind leg off a donkey. But I can tell you this: if Jim Tallboy thinks he's going to get round me by sending his flash friends to shoot off a lot of hot air, he's mistaken."

"My dear Miss Vavasour, will nothing rid you of this misapprehension? In other words, you got me all wrong. I'm not here to forward Tallboy's interests in any way—except, perhaps, by offering the suggestion that this office is possibly not the most suitable spot for interviews of a personal and confidential kind. If I might presume to advise you, would not an appointment for some other place and time——?"

"Ah!" said Miss Vavasour. "I dare say. But if a fellow won't answer your letters or come and see you, and you don't even know where he lives, what is a girl to do? I'm sure I don't want to make trouble."

Here Miss Vavasour sniffed and applied a small handkerchief carefully to her made-up eye-lashes.

"Good heavens!" said Bredon. "How unkind and abominable!"

"You may well say so," said Miss Vavasour. "It's not what anybody would expect of a gentleman, is it? But there! When a fellow's telling the tale to a girl it's one thing, and when he's got her into trouble it's another. A girl doesn't hear so much about him marrying her then. Well, you tell him he's got to do it, see? Or I'll scream my way into old Pym's office and make him. A girl's got to look after herself these days. I'm sure I only wish I had somebody to do it for me, and now poor Auntie's dead, I haven't got a soul to stick up for me."

The handkerchief came into play again.

"But, my dear girl," said Bredon, "even Mr. Pym, great autocrat as he is, couldn't make Tallboy marry you. He's married already."

"Married?" Miss Vavasour took away the handkerchief revealing a pair of perfectly dry and very angry eyes, "the dirty beast! So *that's* why he never asked me to his home. Talking a lot of eye-wash about only one room and his landlady being very particular. I don't care, though. He's got to do it. His wife can divorce him. Goodness knows she's got cause. I've got his letters."

Her eyes turned, irresistibly, to her large and ornate handbag. It was a false move and she realised it instantly and gazed appealingly at Bredon, but he knew where he was now.

"So you've got them there with you. That was very—farsighted of you. See here, Miss Vavasour, what's the use of talking like this? You may just as well be frank with me. Your idea was to threaten to show those letters to Mr. Pym if Tallboy didn't pay up, wasn't it?"

"No, of course it wasn't."

"You're so devoted to Tallboy that you always carry his correspondence about with you?"

"Yes—no. I never said I'd got the letters with me."

"No? But you've admitted it now, you know. Now, you take the advice of a man double your age." (This was a generous estimate, for Miss Vavasour was an easy twenty-eight.) "If you make a disturbance here, nothing will happen, except that Tallboy will possibly lose his job and have no money at all for you or anybody. And if you try to sell him those letters—there's a name for that, and it's not a pretty one."

"That's all very well," said Miss Vavasour, sullenly, "but how about this trouble he's got me into? I'm a mannequin, see? And if a girl's got to chuck her job, and her figure ruined for life——"

"Are you sure you're not mistaken about that?"

"'Course I'm sure. What do you take me for? An innocent?"

"Surely not," said Bredon. "No doubt Tallboy will be ready to come to a suitable arrangement. But—if I may presume to advise you—no threats and no disturbance. And—forgive me—there are other people in the world."

"Yes, there are," said Miss Vavasour, frankly, "but they're not so keen to take over a girl with encumbrances, if you know what I mean. You wouldn't yourself now, would you?"

"Oh, me? I'm not in the running," said Bredon, with perhaps more promptness and emphasis than was quite complimentary. "But, speaking generally, I'm sure you'll find it better not to make an explosion—not here, at any rate. I mean to say, you know, that's the point. Because this is one of those old-fashioned firms that don't like anything unpleasant or—er—undesirable to happen on their premises."

"You bet they don't," said Miss Vavasour, shrewdly, "that's why I'm here."

"Yes, but take it from me, you'll do no good by making a fuss. Really not. And—ah! here is the missing gentleman. I'll be pushing along. Hullo, Tallboy—I've just been entertaining the lady in your absence."

Tallboy, his eyes burning in a very white face and his lips twitching, looked at Bredon for a moment or two in silence. Then:

"Thanks very much," he said, in a stifled tone.

"No, don't thank me," said Bredon. "The gratification is entirely on my side."

He went out and shut the door upon the pair of them.

"Now, I wonder," said Mr. Bredon, reverting to his own detective personality as he went slowly upstairs to his room, "I wonder if it's possible that I'm all wrong about our friend Victor Dean. Can it be that he was merely a common or garden blackmailer, intent on turning his colleague's human weaknesses to his own advantage? Would that be worth cracking a fellow's skull for him and hurling him down a staircase, iron, one, murderers for the use of? The chap who could probably tell me is Willis, but somehow the good Willis is deaf as an adder to my well-known charm of speech. Is it any use sounding him again? If only I could be sure that he was not the gentleman who sandbagged my poor brother-in-law Charles and that he was not still harbouring designs upon my unworthy carcase. Not that I mind having designs harboured on me, but I don't want to make a confidant of the fellow I'm after, like the fat-headed hero in one of those detective stories where the detective turns out to be the villain. If only I had ever seen Willis engaged in any game or sport, I should know better where I stood, but he seems to despise the open-air life—and that in itself, if you come to think of it, is sinister."

After a little more thought, he went along to Willis' room.

"Oh, I say, Willis," he said, "am I disturbing you?"

"No. Come in."

Willis looked up from a sheet of paper which bore the engaging headlines: "MAGNOLIA-WHITE, MAGNOLIA-SOFT—that's what they'll say of your hands." He looked depressed and ill.

"See here, Willis," said Bredon, "I want your advice. I know we don't seem to hit it off very well——"

"No—it's my fault," said Willis. He seemed to struggle with himself for a moment, and then brought his words out with a rush, as though they had been violently forced from him: "I fancy I owe you some sort of apology. I appear to have been mistaken."

"What exactly did you have against me? I never could make out what it was, to tell you the truth."

"I thought you belonged to Victor Dean's beastly doping and drinking crowd, and thought you were trying to get Pamela—Miss Dean—in among them again. She tells me that's not the case. But I saw you there with her, and now she tells me it's my fault that you—that you—oh, hell!"

"What *is* the matter?"

"I'll tell you what's the matter," said Willis, violently. "You went and forced yourself on Miss Dean—God knows what you told her, and she won't tell me. You made out you were a friend of her brother's, or something—was that true, to start with?"

"Not quite, as you put it. I made Miss Dean's acquaintance over a matter connected with her brother, but I had never met him, and she knows that."

"What had it got to do with him, then?"

"I'm afraid I can't tell you that."

"It sounds damned queer to me," said Willis, his face darkening with suspicion. Then he seemed to recollect that he was supposed to be making an apology, and went on:

"Well, anyway, you took her to that disgusting place down there by the river."

"That's not altogether true, either. I asked her to take me, because I couldn't very well have got in without an introduction."

"That's a lie; I got in all right."

"Miss Dean told them to let you in."

"Oh!" Willis was disconcerted for a moment. "Well, in any case, you had no business to ask a decent girl to do anything of the kind. That was exactly what Dean and I had trouble about. A house like that is no fit place for her, and you know it."

"I do; and I regretted the necessity which compelled me to ask her to go there. You may have noticed that I took care nothing should happen to her."

"I don't know that," grumbled Willis.

"You aren't a very good detective," said Bredon with a smile. "You must take my word for it that she was quite safe."

"I won't take your word, but I'd take hers. She says so, and I suppose I've got to believe it. But if you're not an out-and-out rotter yourself, why did you want to be taken there?"

"That's another thing I can't tell you. But I can offer you one or two reasonable explanations that might fit the case. I might be a journalist, commissioned to write an inside story about the newest kind of night-club. Or I might be a detective, engaged in tracking down dope-smugglers. Or I might be a zealot with a new brand of religion, trying to save the souls of post-war society sinners. Or I might be in love with somebody—say, if you like, the notorious Dian de Momerie—and threatening to commit suicide unless I got an introduction to her. I present you with those four solutions on the spur of the moment, and I dare say I could think of others, if I was put to it."

"You might be a dope-merchant yourself," said Willis.

"I hadn't thought of that. But if I were, I doubt if I should need Miss Dean's introduction to that particular crowd."

Willis muttered something unintelligible.

"But I gather," said Bredon, "that Miss Dean has more or less absolved me of being anything hopelessly corrupt. So what's the trouble?"

"The trouble is," groaned Willis, "that you've—my God! you swine—you've thrown her over and she says it's my fault."

"You oughtn't to say a thing like that, old son," said Bredon, really distressed. "It's not done."

"No—I daresay I'm not quite a gentleman. I've never been——"

"If you tell me you've never been to a public school," said Bredon, "I shall scream. What with Copley and Smayle, and all the other pathetic idiots who go about fostering inferiority complexes, and weighing up the rival merits of this place and that place, when it doesn't matter a damn anyway, I'm fed up. Pull yourself together. Anybody, wherever he's been educated, ought to know better than to say a thing like that about any girl. Particularly when there isn't the slightest foundation for it."

"Ah, but there is," said Willis. "You don't realise it, but I do. I know a man's a man for a' that and all the rest of it, but people like you have a sort of glamour about them and women fall for it, every time. I know I'm as good a man as you are, but I don't look it, and that's where it is."

"I can only assure you, Willis——"

"I know, I know. You've never made love to Miss Dean—that's what you're going to say—never by word, look or deed and so forth and so on, given her the slightest ground—bah! I know it. She admits it. It makes it all the worse."

"I am afraid," said Mr. Bredon, "that you are a very foolish pair of people. And I really think you must be quite mistaken in Miss Dean's feelings."

"That's damned likely."

"I think so. In any case, you oughtn't to have said anything to me about it. And in any case, there's nothing I can do."

"She asked me," said Willis, miserably, "to apologise to you and bring you—and ask you—and put the matter right."

"There's nothing to put right. Miss Dean knows quite well that my interviews with her were merely a matter of business. And all I can say is, Willis, if you accepted any such commission, she must think you as soft as a pancake. Why on earth didn't you tell her you'd see me at the devil first? That's probably what she expected you to do."

"Do you think so?"

"Sure of it," said Bredon, who was not sure at all, but thought it best to appear so. "You mustn't go about creating intolerable situations, you know. It's very awkward for me, and I'm sure Miss Dean would be horribly upset if she knew what you'd been saying about her. All she meant was, I expect, that you'd taken quite a wrong view of a perfectly ordinary business acquaintanceship and been unnecessarily antagonistic and so on, and that she wanted you to put the thing straight, so that, if I needed her help again, there wouldn't be any awkwardness about it. Isn't that, in other words, what she said to you?"

"Yes," said Willis. It was a lie, and he knew that Bredon knew that it was a lie, but he lied manfully. "Of course that was what she actually said. But I'm afraid I put another interpretation on it."

"All right," said Bredon, "that's settled. Tell Miss Dean that my business is progressing very well, and that when I need her kind help again I shall have no hesitation in calling her to my assistance. Now, is that all?"

"Yes, that's all."

"You're sure—while you are about it—that there's nothing else you want to get off your chest?"

"N-no."

"You don't sound very sure about it. You've been trying to say all this to me for some time, I dare say."

"No, not very long. A few days."

"Since the day of the monthly tea-party, shall we say?"

Willis started violently. Bredon, with a wary eye on him, followed up his advantage.

"Was that what you came round to Great Ormond Street that night to tell me?"

"How do you know about that?"

"I didn't know, I guessed. As I have said before, you would not make a good detective. You lost a pencil on that occasion, I believe?"

He drew the pencil from his pocket and held it out.

"A pencil? Not that I know of. Where did you find that?"

"In Great Ormond Street."

"I don't think it's mine. I don't know. I think I've still got mine."

"Well, never mind. You came round that night intending to apologise?"

"No—I didn't. I came round to have an explanation with you. I wanted to bash your face in, if you must know. I went round there just before ten——"

"Did you ring the bell of my flat?"

"No, I didn't. I'll tell you why. I looked in your letter-box, and I saw a letter there from Miss Dean, and I—I didn't dare go upstairs. I was afraid I might let myself go. I felt like murdering you. So I went off and wandered about till I was too done-up to think."

"I see. You didn't make any attempt to get hold of me at all?"

"No."

"Oh, well, that's that." Bredon dismissed the matter with a wave of the hand. "It's quite all right. It doesn't matter. I was only a little bit puzzled about the pencil."

"The pencil?"

"Yes. I found it on the top landing, you see, just outside my door. I couldn't quite understand how it got there, that's all."

"It wasn't me. I didn't go upstairs."

"How long did you stay in the house?"

"Only a few minutes."

"In the front hall downstairs all the time?"

"Yes."

"Oh, well then, it can't have been your pencil. It's very odd, because those pencils aren't on the market, as you know."

"Perhaps you dropped it yourself."

"Well, perhaps I did. That seems the likeliest explanation, doesn't it. It's not of any importance."

There was a short and rather uncomfortable pause. Willis broke it by asking in a constrained tone:

"What did you want to ask my advice about?"

"About the old subject," said Bredon; "perhaps, now that we've had this little explanation, you may find it easier to tell me what I want to know. Circumstances have brought me up against the Dean family, and I feel a certain amount of curiosity about the late lamented Victor. From his sister I gather that he was a good kind brother, but unfortunately a little wild in his morals—which means, I take it, that he became infatuated with Dian de Momerie. According to her, he took his sister to various places to meet the fair Dian; you interfered; Miss Dean then realised what the situation was, and withdrew from the association, while quite naturally and illogically resenting your interference; and finally Dian de Momerie shut down on Victor and sent him off home. That's true, as far as it goes, I imagine?"

"Yes," said Willis, "except that I don't believe Dean ever was really infatuated with the de Momerie woman. I think he was flattered, and I think he thought he could make something out of her. As a matter of fact, he was a mean little beast."

"Did she give him money?"

"Yes, she did; but he didn't get much out of that, because he found that crowd so expensive to run with. He wasn't naturally one of that sort. He didn't enjoy gambling, though he had to do it, to keep in with them; and he wasn't a drinker. In some ways, I'd have liked him better if he had been. He wouldn't dope, either. I expect that's why Miss de Momerie got tired of him. The worst of that crowd, you know, is that they can't rest till they've made everybody they have to do with as bad as themselves. If they'd only drug themselves into their graves and have done with it, the sooner they did it the better it would be for everyone. I'd cheerfully hand the stuff over to them by the cartload. But they get hold of quite decent people and ruin them for life. That's why I got so worried about Pamela."

"But you say that Victor managed to remain undefiled."

"Yes, but Pamela's different. She's rather impulsive and easily—no, not easily led, but easily excited about things. She's high-spirited and likes to try everything once. If she once gets a sort of enthusiasm for a person, she wants to do the same as they do. She needs somebody—well, never mind that. I don't want to discuss Pamela. I only mean that Victor was just the opposite. He was very careful of himself, and he had a very good eye for the main chance."

"Do you mean that he was the sort of man who makes what he can out of his friends?"

"He was the kind of man who never has his own cigarettes, and never happens to be there, if he can help it, when it's his turn to stand the drinks. And he'd pick your brains everytime."

"He must have had a pretty good reason, then, for going round with Dian de Momerie's lot. As you say, they're expensive."

"Yes; he must have seen something remunerative in the distance. And when it came to sacrificing his sister——"

"Exactly. Well, that's all rather by the way. What I wanted to know from you was this: supposing he found out that somebody—say somebody in this office—as it might be yourself—had a skeleton in the closet, to use the pretty old metaphor, was Victor Dean the kind of fellow to—er—to dispose of that skeleton to an anatomist?"

"Blackmail, do you mean?" asked Willis, bluntly.

"That's a strong word. But call it that."

"I don't quite know," said Willis, after a few moments' consideration. "It's a devil of a thing to suggest about anybody, isn't it? But I can only say that the question gives me no shock. If you were to tell me that he had blackmailed somebody, it wouldn't surprise me very much. Only, as it's a pretty serious offence, it would have to be a very safe kind of blackmail, with the sort of victim who couldn't possibly afford to face a court of law. Mind you, I haven't the least reason to suppose he ever did anything of the kind. And he certainly never seemed to be particularly flush of cash. Not that that's much to go by, with a careful fellow like him. *He* wouldn't have let wads of bank-notes come tumbling out of his desk."

"You think the tumbling about of notes affords a presumption of innocence?"

"Not a bit. Only of carelessness, and Dean certainly wasn't careless."

"Well, thanks for speaking so frankly."

"That's all right. Only, for goodness' sake, don't let Pamela know what I've been saying about Victor. I've had trouble enough about that."

Bredon assured him that he need not fear any such fantastic indiscretion, and took his leave, polite but still puzzled.

Mr. Tallboy was lying in wait for him at the end of the passage.

"Oh, Bredon, I'm very much obliged to you, of course. I'm sure I can rely on you not to spread the thing any further than it's gone already. All quite absurd, of course. That fool Tompkin seems to have lost his head completely. I've ticked him off properly."

"Oh, yes, absolutely," replied Bredon. "Just so. Much ado about nothing. No real necessity for me to have butted in at all. But you never know. I mean to say, if you'd been detained and Miss Vavasour had got tired of waiting or —well, you know what I mean."

"Yes." Tallboy licked his dry lips. "It might have been very awkward. When girls get hysterical and so on, they sometimes say more than they mean. I've been a bit of a fool, as I dare say you've gathered. I'm cutting it all out now. I've settled everything all right. Worrying, of course, but nothing really desperate." He laughed uncomfortably.

"You're looking a bit over-done."

"I feel it. The fact is, I was up all night. My wife—well, the fact is, my wife had a baby last night. That was partly why—oh, hell, what's it matter, anyhow?"

"I quite understand," said Bredon. "Very wearing business. Why didn't you take the day off?"

"I didn't want to do that. It's my busy day. Much better to occupy one's mind. Besides, there wasn't any necessity. Everything went all right. I suppose you think I'm an awful swine."

"You're not the first, by any means," said Bredon.

"No—it's rather usual, I believe. It's not going to happen again, I can tell you."

"It must have put you in a hell of a hole—all this."

"Yes—at least—not so bad. As you say, I'm not the only man it's ever happened to. It doesn't do to let one's self be upset, does it? Well, as I said, thanks very much and—that's all, isn't it?"

"Absolutely. There's nothing whatever to thank me about. Well, sonny, what do you want?"

"Any letters to go, sir?"

"No, thanks," said Bredon.

"Oh, stop a minute," said Tallboy. "Yes, I've got one." He searched in his breast-pocket and pulled out an envelope, all ready sealed. "Lend me a pen one moment, Bredon. Here, boy, take this penny-halfpenny and run along to Miss Rossiter and ask her for a stamp."

He took the pen Bredon held out, and bending over the desk addressed the envelope hurriedly to "T. Smith, Esq." Bredon, idly watching him, was caught by his eye in the act, and apologised.

"I beg your pardon; I was snooping. Beastly habit. One catches it in the typists' room."

"All right—it's only a note to a stockbroker."

"Lucky man to have anything to stockbroke."

Tallboy laughed, stamped the letter and tossed it to the waiting boy.

"And so ends an exhausting day," he observed.

"Toule very tiresome?"

"Not more so than usual. He turned down. 'Like Niobe, all Tears'. Said he didn't know who Niobe was and he didn't suppose anybody else did either. But he passed this week's 'Tears, Idle Tears', because when he was a boy his father used to read Tennyson aloud to the family circle."

"That's one saved from the wreck, anyhow."

"Oh, yes. He liked the general idea of the poetical quotations. Said he thought they gave his advertisements class. You'll have to think up some more. He likes the ones that illustrate well."

"All right. 'Like Summer Tempest came her Tears.' That's Tennyson, too. Picture of the nurse of ninety years setting his babe upon her knee. Babies always go well. (Sorry, we don't seem able to get off babies.) Start the copy, 'Tears are often a relief to overwrought nerves, but when they flow too often, too easily, it is a sign that you need Nutrax.' I'll do that one. Bassanio and

Antonio: 'I know not Why I am so Sad.' Carry the quote on into the copy. 'Causeless depression, like Antonio's, wearies both the sufferer and his friends. Go to the root of the matter and tone up the overstrung Nerves with Nutrax.' I can do that sort of thing by the hour."

Mr. Tallboy smiled wanly.

"It's a pity we can't cure ourselves with our own nostrums, isn't it?"

Mr. Bredon surveyed him critically.

"What *you* need," he said, "is a good dinner and a bottle of fizz.'

CHAPTER XIV

Hopeful Conspiracy of Two Black Sheep

THE GENTLEMAN IN the harlequin costume removed his mask with quiet deliberation, and laid it on the table.

"Since," he said, "my virtuous cousin Wimsey has let the cat out of the bag, I may as well take this off. I am afraid"—he turned to Dian—"my appearance will disappoint you. Except that I am handsomer and less rabbity-looking, the woman who has seen Wimsey has seen me. It is a heavy handicap to carry, but I can't help it. The resemblance, I am happy to say, is only skin-deep."

"It's almost incredible," said Major Milligan. He bent forward to examine the other's face more closely, but Mr. Bredon extended a languid arm and, without apparently using any force at all, pushed him back into his seat.

"You needn't come too close," he observed, insolently. "Even a face like Wimsey's is better than yours. Yours is spotty. You eat and drink too much."

Major Milligan, who had, indeed, been distressed that morning by the discovery of a few small pimples on his forehead, but had hoped they were not noticeable, grunted angrily. Dian laughed.

"I take it," pursued Mr. Bredon, "that you want to get something out of me. People of your sort always do. What is it?"

"I've no objection to being frank with you," replied Major Milligan.

"How nice it is to hear anybody say that. It always prepares one for a lie to follow. Fore-warned is fore-armed, isn't it?"

"If you choose to think so. But I think you'll find it to your advantage to listen."

"Financial advantage?"

"What other kind is there?"

"What indeed? I begin to like your face a trifle better."

"Oh, do you? Perhaps you may like it well enough to answer a few questions?"

"Possibly."

"How do you come to know Pamela Dean?"

"Pamela? A charming girl, isn't she? I obtained an introduction to her through what the great public—seduced by the unfortunate example of that incomparable *vulgarisateur,* Charles Dickens—abominably calls a mutual friend. I admit that my object in obtaining the introduction was a purely business one; I can only say that I wish all business acquaintances were so agreeable."

"What was the business?"

"The business, my dear fellow, was concerned with another mutual friend of us all—with the late Victor Dean, who died, deeply regretted, upon a staircase. A remarkable young man, was he not?"

"In what way?" asked Milligan, quickly.

"Don't you know? I thought you did. Otherwise, why am I here?"

"You two idiots make me tired," broke in Dian. "Where's the sense of going round and round each other like this? Your pompous cousin told us all about you, Mr. Bredon—I suppose you've got a Christian name, by the way?"

"I have. It's spelt Death. Pronounce it any way you like. Most of the people who are plagued with it make it rhyme with teeth, but personally I think it sounds more picturesque when rhymed with breath. What did my amiable cousin say about me?"

"He said you were a dope-runner."

"Where my cousin Wimsey gets his information from, I am damned if I know. Sometimes he is correct."

"And you know perfectly well that one can get what one wants at Tod's place. So why not come to the point?"

"As you say, why not? Is that the particular facet of my brilliant personality that interests you, Milligan?"

"Is that the particular facet of Victor Dean's personality that interests *you*?"

"One point to me," said Mr. Bredon. "Till this moment, I was not sure that it was a facet of his personality. Now I do. Dear me! How interesting it all is, to be sure."

"If you can find out exactly how Victor Dean was involved in that show," said Mr. Milligan, "it might be worth something to you and to me."

"Say on."

Major Milligan reflected a little and seemed to make up his mind to lay his cards on the table.

"Did you learn from Pamela Dean what her brother's job was?"

"Yes, of course. He wrote advertising copy at a place called Pym's. There's no secret about that."

"That's just what there is. And if that infernal young fool hadn't gone and got killed, we might have found out what it was and done ourselves a lot of good. As it is——"

"But look here, Tod," said Dian. "I thought it was the other way round. I thought you were afraid of *his* finding out too much."

"That's true," said Milligan, scowling. "What would be the use of it if he found out first?"

"I don't follow all this," said Bredon. "Wasn't it his secret? Why not stop talking like a sensation novel and give us the dope straight?"

"Because I don't believe you know even as much as I do about the fellow."

"I don't. I never met him in my life. But I know a good deal about Pym's Publicity, Ltd."

"How?"

"I work there."

"What?"

"I work there."

"Since when?"

"Since Dean's death."

"Because of Dean's death, do you mean?"

"Yes."

"How did that happen?"

"I received information, as my dear cousin Wimsey's police pals would say, that Dean was on to something fishy about Pym's. So, since most fish have gold in their mouths like St. Peter's, I thought it wouldn't do any harm to try a cast or two over that particular pool."

"And what did you find?"

"My dear Milligan, you would make a cat laugh. I don't give away information. I dispose of it—advantageously."

"So do I."

"As you like. You invited me here to-night. I wasn't looking for you. But there's one thing I don't mind telling you, because I've already told Miss de Momerie, and that is, that Victor Dean was bumped off deliberately to prevent him from talking. So far, the only person I can discover who wanted him out of the way was yourself. The police might be interested to know that fact."

"The police?"

"Oh! I quite agree. I don't like the police. They pay very badly and ask a hell of a lot of questions. But it might be useful, for once, to get on the right side of them."

"That's all punk," said Milligan. "You're barking up the wrong tree. I didn't kill the fellow. I didn't want him killed."

"Prove that," said the other, coolly.

He watched Milligan's impassive face, and Milligan watched his.

"Give it up," suggested Bredon, after a few minutes of this mutual scrutiny. "I can play poker just as well as you. But this time I fancy I hold a straight flush."

"Well, what do you want to know?"

"I want to know what you think Dean was in a position to find out."

"I can tell you that. He was trying to find out——"

"Had found out."

"How do you know?"

"If you want instruction in detective methods, you must pay extra. I say he had found out."

"Well, then, he had found out who was running the show from Pym's end."

"The dope-show?"

"Yes. And he may have found out, too, the way it's worked."

"*Is* worked?"

"Yes."

"It's still being worked the same way, then?"

"So far as I know."

"So far as you know? You don't seem to know much."

"Well, how much do you know about the way your own gang run the show?"

"Nothing whatever. Instructions are issued——"

"By the way, how did you get into it?"

"Sorry. Can't tell you that. Not even if you pay extra."

"How do I know I can trust you, then?"

Bredon laughed.

"Perhaps you'd like me to supply you," he said. "If you're not satisfied with your distribution, you can inscribe yourself upon the roll of my customers. Deliveries Sunday and Thursday. Meanwhile—and as a sample—you may be interested in the collar of my cloak. It is handsome, is it not? A rich velvet. A little ostentatious, perhaps you think—a little over-much buckram? Possibly you are right. But very well made. The opening is almost invisible. We delicately insert the forefinger and thumb, pull the tab gently, and produce this dainty bag of oiled silk—fine as an onion-skin, but remarkably tough. Within it, you will discover sufficient inspiration for quite a number of enthusiasts. A magician's cloak. Such stuff as dreams are made on."

Milligan examined the contents of the little bag in silence. They were, in fact, a portion of the famous packet obtained by Mr. Hector Puncheon at the White Swan.

"All right, so far. Where do you get it from?"

"I got it in Covent Garden."

"Not at Pym's?"

"No."

Milligan looked disappointed.

"What day did you get it?"

"Friday morning. Like yourself, I get it on a Friday."

"Look here," said Milligan, "you and I have got to be together on this. Dian, my child, run away and play. I'm going to talk business with your friend."

"That's a nice way to treat me in my own house," grumbled Miss de Momerie, but, seeing that Milligan meant what he said, she gathered up herself and her wraps and retreated into the bedroom. Milligan leaned forwards over the table.

"I'm going to tell you what I know," he said. "If you double-cross me, it's at your own risk. I don't want any funny business with that damned cousin of yours."

Mr. Bredon expressed his opinion of Lord Peter Wimsey in a few well-chosen words.

"All right," said Milligan. "You have been warned. Now, see here. If we can find out who works this thing and how it's worked, we can get in at the top. It pays fairly well as it is, in one way, but it's a devil of a risk and a lot of trouble, and it's expensive. Look at that place I have to keep up. It's the man in the centre of the ring that makes the big profits. I know, and you know, what we pay for the stuff, and then there's the bore of handing it out to all these fools and collecting the cash. Now, here's what I know. The whole stunt is worked from that advertising place of yours—Pym's. I found that out from a man who's dead now. I won't tell you how I fell in with him—it's a long story. But I'll tell you what he told me. I was dining with him one night at the Carlton, and he was a bit lit-up. A chap came in with a party, and this man said to me: 'Know who that is?'—'Not from Adam,' I said. He said: 'Well, it's old Pym, the publicity agent.' And then he laughed and said: 'If he only knew what his precious agency was doing, he'd have a fit.' 'How's that?' I said. 'Why,' said he, 'didn't you know? All this dope-traffic is worked from there.' Naturally, I started to ask him how he knew and all about it, but he suddenly got an attack of caution and started to be mysterious, and I couldn't get another word out of him."

"I know that brand of drunkenness," said Bredon. "Do you think he really knew what he was talking about?"

"Yes, I think so. I saw him next day, but he was sober then, and got the shock of his life when I told him what he'd said. But he admitted it was true, and implored me to keep quiet about it. That was all I could get out of him, and the same evening he was run over by a lorry."

"Was he? How remarkably well-timed."

"I thought so myself," said Milligan. "It made me rather nervous."

"But how does Victor Dean come into it?"

"There," admitted Milligan, "I dropped a bad brick. Dian brought him along one evening——"

"Just a minute. When did this conversation with your indiscreet friend take place?"

"Nearly a year ago. Naturally, I'd been trying to follow the matter up, and when Dian introduced Dean and said he worked at Pym's, I thought he must be the man. Apparently he wasn't. But I'm afraid he got an idea about the thing from me. After a bit, I found out he was trying to horn in on my show, and I told Dian to shut down on him."

"In fact," said Mr. Bredon, "you tried to pump him, just as you are trying to pump me, and you found out that he was pumping you instead."

"Something like that," confessed Milligan.

"And shortly after that he fell down a staircase."

"Yes; but I didn't push him down it. You needn't think that. I didn't want him snuffed out. I only wanted him kept out of the way. Dian's too much of a chatterer, especially when she's ginned up. The trouble is, you're never safe with these people. You'd think common sense would tell them to keep quiet in their own interests, but they've got no more sense than a cageful of monkeys."

"Well," said Bredon, "if we fill them up with stuff that notoriously saps their self-control, I suppose we can't grumble at the consequences."

"I suppose not, but it's a damned nuisance sometimes. They're as cunning as weasels in one way, and sheer idiots in another. Spiteful, too."

"Yes. Dean never became an addict, did he?"

"No. If he had, we'd have had more control over him; but unfortunately, his head was screwed on the right way. All the same, he knew pretty well that he'd have been well paid for any information."

"Very likely. The trouble is that he was taking money from the other side as well—at least, I think he was."

"Don't you try that game," said Milligan.

"I've no wish to fall down staircases. What you want, I take it, is the way the trick's worked and the name of the man who works it. I daresay I can find that out for you. How about terms?"

"My idea is, that we use the information to get into the inside ring ourselves, and each strike our own bargain."

"Just so. Alternatively, I suppose, we put the screw on the gentleman at Pym's, when we've got him, and divide the spoil. In which case, as I'm doing most of the work and taking the biggest risk, I suggest I take 75 per cent."

"Not on your life. Fifty-fifty. I shall conduct the negotiations."

"Will you? That's pretty good. Why should I bring you into it at all? You can't negotiate till I tell you whom to negotiate with. You don't think I was born yesterday."

"No. But knowing what I do, I could get you shifted from Pym's to-morrow, couldn't I? If Pym knew who you were, do you suppose he'd keep you on his virtuous premises for another day?"

"Well, look here. We conduct the negotiations together, and I take 60 per cent."

Milligan shrugged his shoulders.

"Well, leave it at that for the moment. I'm hoping it won't pan out that way. What we want to aim at is getting the reins into our own hands."

"As you say. When we've done that, it will be time enough to decide which of us is going to crack the whip."

When he had gone, Tod Milligan went into the bedroom, and found Dian kneeling on the window-seat, staring down into the street.

"Have you fixed things up with him?"

"Yes. He's a twister, but I'll be able to make him see that it'll pay him to be straight with me."

"You had much better leave him alone."

"You're talking rubbish," said Milligan, using a coarser term.

Dian turned round and faced him.

"I've warned you," she said. "Not that I care a damn what happens to you. You're getting on my nerves, Tod. It's going to be great fun to see you come to smash. But you'd better keep off that man."

"Thinking of selling me, are you?"

"I shan't need to."

"You'd better not. Lost your head over this theatrical gentleman in tights, haven't you?"

"Why do you have to be so vulgar?" she asked, contemptuously.

"What's the matter with you, then?"

"I'm frightened, that's all. Unlike me, isn't it?"

"Frightened of that advertising crook?"

"Really, Tod, you're a fool sometimes. You can't see a thing when it's under your nose. It's written too big for you to see, I suppose."

"You're drunk," said Milligan. "Just because you haven't quite managed to get off with this joker of yours——"

"Shut up," said Dian. "Get off with him? I'd as soon get off with the public hangman."

"I dare say you would. Any new sensation would do for you. What do you want? A row? Because, if so, I'm afraid I can't be bothered to oblige you."

There is a dreary convention which decrees that the final collapse of a sordid liaison shall be preceded by a series of no less sordid squabbles. But on this occasion, Miss de Momerie seemed ready to dispense with convention.

"No. I'm through with you, that's all. I'm cold. I'm going to bed.... Tod, *did* you kill Victor Dean?"

"I did not."

Major Milligan dreamed that night that Death Bredon, in his harlequin dress, was hanging him for the murder of Lord Peter Wimsey.

CHAPTER XV

Sudden Decease of a Man in Dress Clothes

CHIEF INSPECTOR PARKER continued to be disturbed in his mind. There had been another fiasco in Essex. A private motor-boat, suspected of being concerned in the drug-traffic, had been seized and searched without result—except, of course, the undesired result of giving the alarm to the parties concerned, if they were concerned. Further, a fast car, which had attracted attention by its frequent midnight excursions from the coast to the capital, had been laboriously tracked to its destination, and proved to belong to a distinguished member of the diplomatic corps, engaged on extremely incognito visits to a lady established in a popular seaside resort. Mr. Parker, still incapacitated from personal attendance upon midnight expeditions, was left with the gloomy satisfaction of saying that everything always went wrong when he wasn't there himself. He was also unreasonably annoyed with Wimsey, as the original cause of his incapacity.

Nor had the investigation at the White Swan so far borne very much fruit. For a week in succession, tactful and experienced policemen had draped themselves over its bar, chatting to all and sundry about greyhounds, goats, parrots and other dumb friends of man, without receiving any return in the shape of mysterious packets.

The old man with the parrot-story had been traced easily enough. He was an habitué. He sat there every morning and every afternoon, and had a fund of such stories. The patient police made a collection of them. The proprietor—against whose character nothing could be proved—knew this customer well. He was a superannuated Covent Garden porter, who lived on an old-age pension, and every corner of his inoffensive life was open to the day. This excellent old gentleman, when questioned, recalled the conversation with Mr. Hector Puncheon, but was positive that he had never seen any of the party before, except the two carters, whom he knew well enough. These men also agreed that the gentleman in dress clothes and the little man who had talked about greyhounds were equally unknown to them. It was not, however, unusual for a gentleman in dress clothes to drop in at the Swan by way of a good finish to a lively night—or for gentlemen without dress clothes, either. Nothing threw any light on the mystery of the packet of cocaine.

Parker was, however, roused to some enthusiasm by Wimsey's report of his conversations with Milligan.

"What incredible luck you do have, Peter. People who, in the ordinary way, would avoid you like the plague, gate-crash into your parties at the psychological moment and offer you their noses to lead them by."

"Not so much luck, old man," said Wimsey. "Good guidance, that's all. I sent the fair Dian an anonymous letter, solemnly warning her against myself and informing her that if she wanted to know the worst about me, she had only to inquire at my brother's address. It's a curious thing, but people *cannot* resist anonymous letters. It's like free sample offers. They appeal to all one's lower instincts."

"You are a devil," said Parker. "One of these days you'll get into trouble. Suppose Milligan had recognised you."

"I prepared his mind to accept a striking resemblance."

"I wonder he didn't see through it. Family resemblances don't usually extend to details of teeth and so on."

"I never let him get close enough to study details."

"That ought to have made him suspicious."

"No, because I was rude to him about it. He believed me all the time, simply because I was rude. Everybody suspects an eager desire to curry favour, but rudeness, for some reason, is always accepted as a guarantee of good faith. The only man who ever managed to see through rudeness was St. Augustine, and I don't suppose Milligan reads the *Confessions*. Besides, he wanted to believe in me. He's greedy."

"Well, no doubt you know your own business. But about this Victor Dean affair. Do you really believe that the head of this particular dope-gang is on Pym's staff? It sounds quite incredible."

"That's an excellent reason for believing it. I don't mean in a *credo quia impossibile* sense, but merely because the staff of a respectable advertising agency would be such an excellent hiding-place for a big crook. The particular crookedness of advertising is so very far removed from the crookedness of dope-trafficking."

"Why? As far as I can make out, all advertisers are dope-merchants."

"So they are. Yes, now I come to think of it, there is a subtle symmetry about the thing which is extremely artistic. All the same, Charles, I must admit that I find it difficult to go the whole way with Milligan. I have carefully reviewed the staff of Pym's, and I have so far failed to find anyone who looks in the least like a Napoleon of crime."

"But you seem convinced that the murder of Victor Dean was an inside job. Or do you now think that some stranger was hiding on the roof and did away with Dean because he was on the point of splitting on the gang? I suppose an outsider could get access to Pym's roof?"

"Oh, easily. But that wouldn't explain the catapult in Mrs. Johnson's desk."

"Nor the attack on me."

"Not if the same person that killed Dean attacked you too."

"Meaning that it might have been Willis? I take it that Willis is not the Napoleon of crime, anyhow."

"Willis isn't a Napoleon of anything. Nor, I fancy, is the chap with the catapult. If he had been, he'd have had the common sense to use his own catapult and burn it afterwards. As I see him, he is a person of considerable ingenuity but limited foresight; a person who snatches at the first thing that is offered him and does his best with it, but lacks just that little extra bit of consideration that would make the thing a real success. He lives from hand to mouth, as you may say. I dare say I could spot him without much difficulty—but that's not what you want, is it? You'd rather have the Napoleon of the dope-traffic, wouldn't you? If he exists, that is."

"Certainly I should," said Parker, emphatically.

"That's what I thought. What, if you come to think of it, is a trifle like an odd murder or assault, compared with a method of dope-running that baffles Scotland Yard? Nothing at all."

"It isn't, really," replied Parker, seriously. "Dope-runners are murderers, fifty times over. They slay hundreds of people, soul and body, besides indirectly causing all sorts of crimes among the victims. Compared with that, slugging one inconsiderable pip-squeak over the head is almost meritorious."

"Really, Charles! for a man of your religious upbringing, your outlook is positively enlightened."

"Not so irreligious, either. Fear not him that killeth, but him that hath power to cast into hell. How about it?"

"How indeed? Hang the one and give the other a few weeks in jail—or, if of good social position, bind him over or put him on remand for six months under promise of good behaviour."

Parker made a wry mouth.

"I know, old man, I know. But where would be the good of hanging the wretched victims or the smaller fry? There would always be others. We want the top people. Take even this man, Milligan, who's a pest of the first water—with no excuse for it, because he isn't an addict himself—but suppose we punish him here and now. They'd only start again, with a new distributor and a new house for him to run his show in, and what would anybody gain by that?"

"Exactly," said Wimsey. "And how much better off will you be, even if you catch the man above Milligan? The same thing will apply."

Parker made a hopeless gesture.

"I don't know, Peter. It's no good worrying about it. My job is to catch the heads of the gangs if I can, and, after that, as many as possible of the little people. I can't overthrow cities and burn the population."

" 'Tis the Last Judgment's fire must cure this place," said Wimsey, "calcine its clods and set its prisoners free. There are times, Charles, when even the unimaginative decency of my brother and the malignant virtue of his wife appear to be admirable. I could hardly say more."

"You have a certain decency of your own, Peter," replied Parker, "which I like better, because it is not negative." Having given voice to this atrocious outburst of sentiment, he became extremely red in the face, and hastened to cover up his lapse from good taste. "But at the present moment I must say you are not being very helpful. You have been investigating a crime—if it is a crime—for some weeks now. If you could confine yourself to breaking your own collar-bone——"

"It has been broken before now," said Wimsey, "and in no less good a cause. You shouldn't shove your beastly collar-bone into my affairs."

At this moment, the telephone-bell rang.

It was half-past eight in the morning, and Wimsey had been consuming an early breakfast with his brother-in-law, prior to their departure each to his own place of business. Lady Mary, who had been supplying their bodily necessities and leaving them to their argument, took up the receiver.

"It's from the Yard, darling. Something about that man Puncheon."

Parker took the instrument and plunged into an animated discussion, which ended with his saying:

"Send Lumley and Eagles along at once, and tell Puncheon to keep in touch with you. I'm coming."

"What's up?" inquired Wimsey.

"Our little friend Puncheon has seen his bloke in dress clothes again," said Parker, cursing as he tried to get his coat over his damaged shoulder. "Saw him hanging about the *Morning Star* offices this morning, buying an early paper or something. Been chasing him ever since, apparently. Landed out at Finchley, of all places. Says he couldn't get on to the 'phone before. I must push off. See you later. Cheerio, Mary dear. Bung-ho, Peter."

He bounced out in a hurry.

"Well, well," said Wimsey. He pushed back his chair and sat staring vacantly at the wall opposite, on which hung a calendar. Then, emptying the sugar-bowl on the table-cloth with a jerk, he began, frowning hideously, to build a lofty tower with its contents. Mary recognised the signs of inspiration and stole quietly away to her household duties.

Forty-five minutes afterwards she returned. Her brother had gone, and the banging of the flat-door after him had flung his column of sugar-lumps in disorder across the table, but she could see that it had been a tall one. Mary sighed.

"Being Peter's sister is rather like being related to the public hangman," she thought, echoing the words of a lady with whom she had otherwise little in common. "And being married to a policeman is almost worse. I suppose the hangman's relatives are delighted when business is looking up. Still," she thought, being not without humour, "one might be connected with an undertaker, and rejoice over the deaths of the righteous, which would be infinitely worse."

Sergeant Lumley and P.C. Eagles found no Hector Puncheon at the small eating-house in Finchley from which he had telephoned. They did, however, find a message.

"He has had breakfast and is off again," said the note, written hurriedly on a page torn from the reporter's note-book. "I will telephone to you here as soon as I can. I'm afraid he knows I am following him."

"There," said Sergeant Lumley, gloomily. "That's an amachoor all over. 'Course 'e lets the bloke know 'e's bein' followed. If one of these newspaper fellows was a bluebottle and 'ad to follow an elephant, 'e'd get buzzin' in the elephant's ear, same as 'e'd know what 'e was up to."

P.C. Eagles was struck with admiration at this flight of fancy, and laughed heartily.

"Ten to one 'e'll lose 'im for keeps, now," pursued Sergeant Lumley. "Gettin' us pushed off 'ere without our breakfusses."

"There ain't no reason why we shouldn't have our breakfusses, seein' as we are here," said his subordinate, who was of that happy disposition that makes the best of things. "'Ow about a nice pair o' kippers?"

"I don't mind if I do," said the sergeant, "if only we're allowed to eat 'em in peace. But you mark my words, 'e'll start ringin' up again afore we 'as time to swallow a bite. Which reminds me. I better ring up the Yard and stop me lord Parker from traipsin' up 'ere. 'E mustn't be put out. Oh, no!"

P.C. Eagles ordered the kippers and a pot of tea. He used his jaws more readily for eating than for talking. The sergeant got his call, and returned, just as the eatables were placed on the table.

"Says, if 'e rings up from anywhere else we better take a taxi," he announced. "Save time, 'e says. 'Ow's 'e think we're goin' to pick up a taxi 'ere. Nothing but blinkin' trams."

"Order the taxi now," suggested Mr. Eagles, with his mouth full, "so's to be in readiness, like."

"And 'ave it tickin' up the thruppences for nothing? Think they'll call that legitimate expenses? Not 'arf. 'You pay that out of your own pocket, my man,' that's what they'll say, the lousy skin-flints."

"Well, 'ave yer grub," suggested Mr. Eagles, pacifically.

Sergeant Lumley inspected his kipper narrowly.

"'Ope it's a good one, that's all," he muttered. "Looks oily, it do. 'Ope it's cooked. Eat a kipper what ain't properly cooked through and you gets kipper on your breath for the rest of the day." He forked a large portion into his mouth without pausing to remove the bones, and was obliged to expend a painful minute rescuing them with his fingers. "Tcha! it beats me why Godamighty wanted to put such a lot of bones into them things."

P.C. Eagles was shocked.

"You didn't oughter question the ways of Godamighty," he said, reprovingly.

"You keep a civil tongue in your 'ed, my lad," retorted Sergeant Lumley, unfairly intruding his official superiority into this theological discussion, "and don't go forgettin' what's due to my position."

"There ain't no position in the eyes of Godamighty," said P.C. Eagles, stoutly. His father and his sister happened to be noted lights in the Salvation

Army, and he felt himself to be on his own ground here. "If it pleases 'Im to make you a sergeant, that's one thing, but it won't do you no good when you comes before 'Im to answer to the charge of questionin' 'Is ways with kippers. Come to think of it, in 'Is sight you an' me is just the same as worms, with no bones at all."

"Not so much about worms," said Sergeant Lumley. "You oughter know better than to talk about worms when a man's eating his breakfuss. It's enough to take anyone's appetite away. And let me tell you, Eagles, worm or no worm, if I have any more lip from you—Drat that telephone! What did I tell you?"

He pounded heavily across to the insanitary little cupboard that held the instrument, and emerged in a minute or two, dismally triumphant.

"That's 'im. Kensington, this time. You 'op out an' get that taxi, while I settle up 'ere."

"Wouldn't the Underground be quicker?"

"They said taxi, so you damn well make it taxi," said Sergeant Lumley. While Eagles fetched the taxi, the sergeant took the opportunity to finish his kipper, thus avenging his defeat in religious controversy. This cheered him so much that he consented to take the Underground at the nearest suitable point, and they journeyed in comparative amity as far as South Kensington Station, and thence to the point indicated by Hector Puncheon, which was, in fact, the entrance to the Natural History Museum.

There was nobody in the entrance-hall who resembled Hector Puncheon in the least.

"Suppose 'e's gone on already?" Suggested P.C. Eagles.

"Suppose 'e 'as," retorted the sergeant. "I can't 'elp that. I told 'im to telephone 'ere if 'e did or to let them know at the Yard. I can't do no more, can I? I better take a walk round, and you sit 'ere to see as they don't come out. If they do, you be ready to take up this other bird's trail and tell Puncheon to set 'ere till I come. An' don't let your bird see you talking to Puncheon, neether. And if they comes out and you see me a-follerin' of them, then you foller on be'ind an' keep ourself outer sight, see?"

Mr. Eagles saw clearly—as indeed he well might, for he knew quite as much about his duties as Sergeant Lumley. But the worm still rankled in the sergeant's breast. Mr. Eagles strolled over to a case of humming-birds and gazed at it with absorbed interest, while Mr. Lumley went heavily up the steps, looking as much as possible like a country cousin bent on seeing the sights.

He had been in the entrance-hall about ten minutes, and had almost exhausted the humming-birds, when he saw something reflected in the glass case which made him sidle softly round so as to command a view of the staircase. A portly person in an overcoat and a top-hat was coming slowly down, one hand thrust deep into his overcoat pocket, the other swinging carelessly at his side. P.C. Eagles looked past him up the stair; there was no sign, either of Hector Puncheon or of Sergeant Lumley, and for a moment the constable hesitated. Then something caught his eye. In the gentleman's left-hand overcoat pocket was a folded copy of the *Morning Star*.

There is nothing unusual about seeing a gentleman with a copy of the *Morning Star*. The readers of that great organ periodically write to the editor, giving statistics of the number of passengers on the 8.15 who read the *Morning Star* in preference to any other paper, and their letters are printed for all to read. Nevertheless, P.C. Eagles determined to take the risk. He scribbled a hasty note on the back of an envelope and walked across to the doorkeeper.

"If you see my friend that came in with me," he said, "you might give him that and tell him I can't wait any longer. I got to get along to my work."

Out of the corner of his eye, he saw the gentleman in the overcoat pass out through the swing-door. Unobtrusively, he followed him.

Upstairs, at the top of a dark staircase barred by a trestle bearing the words "No Entrance", Sergeant Lumley was bending anxiously over the inanimate form of Hector Puncheon. The reporter was breathing heavily in a way the sergeant did not like, and there was a nasty contused wound on his temple.

"Trust your amachoors to make a mess of it," reflected Sergeant Lumley, bitterly. "I only 'ope as that Eagles 'as got 'is 'ead screwed on the right way. But there you are. I can't be in two places at once."

The man in the overcoat walked quietly down the street towards the Underground Station. He did not look back. A few yards behind him, P.C. Eagles sauntered casually along in his wake. His eyes were on his quarry. Neither of them saw a third man, who emerged from nowhere in particular and followed a few yards behind P.C. Eagles. No passer-by gave so much as a second glance to the little procession as it crossed Cromwell Road and debouched upon the station.

The man in the overcoat glanced at the taxi-rank; then he seemed to change his mind. For the first time, he looked back. All he saw was P.C. Eagles purchasing a newspaper, and in this sight there was nothing alarming. The other follower he could not have seen, because like the Spanish Fleet, he was not yet in sight, though P.C. Eagles might have seen him, had he been looking in his direction. The gentleman appeared to reject the notion of a taxi and turned into the station entrance. Mr. Eagles, his eyes apparently intent upon a headline about Food Taxes, wandered in after him, and was in time to follow his example in taking a ticket for Charing Cross. Pursued and pursuer entered the lift together, the gentleman walking across to the further gate, Eagles remaining modestly on the hither side. There were already about half a dozen people, mostly women, in the lift, and just as the gate was shutting, another man came in hurriedly. He passed Eagles and took up a central position among the group of women. At the bottom of the shaft, they all emerged in a bunch, the strange man pressing rather hastily past the man in the overcoat, and leading the way towards the platform, where an eastward-bound train was just running in.

What exactly happened then, P.C. Eagles was not quite clear about at the time, though in the light of after events he saw plainly one or two things that were not obvious to him then. He saw the third man standing close to the edge of the platform, carrying a thin walking-stick. He saw the man in the overcoat walk past him and then suddenly stop and stagger in his walk. He saw the man with the stick fling out his hand and grasp the other by the arm, saw the two waver together on the edge and heard a shriek from a woman. Then both toppled together under the advancing train.

Through the uproar, Eagles shouldered his way.

" 'Ere," he said, "I'm an officer of the law. Stand aside, please."

They stood aside, with the exception of a porter and another man, who were hauling out something between the train and the platform. An arm came up, and then a head—then the battered body of the third man, the one who had had the walking-stick. They laid him down on the platform bruised and bloody.

"Where's the other?"

"Gone, poor chap."

"Is that one dead?"

"Yes."

"No, he ain't."

"Oh, Betty, I'm going to faint."

"He's all right—see! He's opening his eyes."

"Yes, but how about the other?"

"Do stop shoving."

"Look out, that's a policeman."

"That's the live rail down there."

"Where's a doctor? Send for a doctor."

"Stand back, please. Stand right back."

"Why don't they shut off the electricity?"

"They have. That feller ran off to do it."

"How'll they get 'im out without moving the train?"

"Expect he's all in little bits, pore chap."

"That one tried to save 'im."

"Looked as if he was took ill, or drunk-like."

"Drunk, this time in the morning?"

"They ought to give 'im brandy."

"Clear all this lot out," said Eagles. "This one'll do all right. The other's done for, I suppose."

"Smashed all to blazes. 'Orrible."

"Then you can't do him any good. Clear the station and get an ambulance and another police officer."

"Right you are."

"This one's coming round," put in the man who had helped to haul the victim up. "How are you feeling now, sir?"

"Bloody," said the rescued man, faintly. Then, seeming to realise where he was, he added:

"What happened?"

"Why, sir, a poor gentleman fell off the platform and took you over with him."

"Yes, of course. Is he all right?"

"Afraid he's badly knocked about, sir. Ah!" as somebody ran up with a flask. "Take a pull at this, sir. Gently, you. Lift his head up. Don't jerk him. Now then."

"Ah!" said the man. "That's better. All right. Don't fuss. My spine's all right and I don't think anything's broken to speak of." He moved his arms and legs experimentally.

"Doctor'll be here in a minute, sir."

"Doctor be damned. I'm a doctor myself. Limbs all correct. Head apparently sound, though it aches like hell. Ribs—not so sure about those. Something gone there, I'm afraid. Pelvis intact, thank goodness."

"Very glad to hear that," said Eagles.

"It's the footboard of the train that got me, I fancy. I remember being rolled round and round like a pat of butter between two whatsinames," said the stranger, whose damaged ribs did not seem to impede his breathing altogether. "And I saw the wheels of the train get slower and stop, and I said to myself: 'This is it. You're for it, my lad. Time's stopped and this is Eternity.' But I see I was mistaken."

"Happily so, sir," said Eagles.

"Wish I'd been able to stop that other poor devil, though."

"I'm sure you did your best, sir." Eagles produced his note-book. "Excuse me, sir, but I'm a police officer, and if you could manage to tell me just how it occurred——"

"Damned if I know myself," replied the other. "All I know is, I was standing just about here when the fellow passed me." He paused, catching his breath a little. "I noticed he was looking rather queer. Heart subject, I should think. He suddenly stopped and staggered and then came towards me. I caught hold of his arm and then he lurched over with all his weight and dragged me over with him. And then I can't remember anything but the noise of the train and the tremendous size of its wheels and the feeling of having the breath squeezed out of me. I must have dropped him, I suppose."

"And no wonder," said Eagles, sympathetically.

"My name's Garfield," went on the rescuer. "Dr. Herbert Garfield." He gave an address in Kensington and another in Harley Street. "I think I see one of my professional brethren arriving, and he'll probably say I'm not to talk." He grinned faintly. "Anyhow, I shall be filed for reference for the next few weeks, if you want more information."

P.C. Eagles thanked Dr. Garfield, and then turned to the body of the man in the overcoat, which had by now been disentangled from between the wheels of the train and laid upon the platform. It was an unpleasant sight. Even Eagles, accustomed as he was to casualties, felt a violent distaste for the necessary job of searching the dead man's pockets for evidence of identity. Curiously enough, he found none in the shape of visiting cards or papers. There was a note-case with a few pound-notes, a silver cigarette-case filled with a popular brand of Turks, a little loose change, an unmarked handkerchief, and an H.T. & V. latch-key. Moreover—and this pleased him very much—in the overcoat pocket was a little rubber cosh, such as is sold for use against motor-bandits. He was in the act of hunting over the suit for the tailor's tab, when he was hailed by a local inspector of police, who had arrived with the ambulance.

Eagles was relieved to have the support of a colleague. He knew that he ought to get in touch with Sergeant Lumley and with Scotland Yard. An hour's energetic action on the part of all resulted in a happy reunion at the nearest police-station, where, in fact, Lumley had already arrived, after depositing the unconscious Mr. Puncheon in hospital. Chief Inspector Parker came hot-foot to Kensington, heard the statements of Lumley and Eagles, reviewed the scene of the disaster and the remains of the mysterious man in dress clothes, and was annoyed. When a man whom you have been elaborately chasing all over London has the impudence to be killed just as you are on the point of catching him, and turns out to have no tailor's name on his clothes and nothing to identify him by; when, moreover, he has thoughtlessly permitted his face to be smashed into pulp by an electric train, so that you cannot usefully circulate his photograph for recognition, your satisfaction in feeling that there is something wrong about him is cancelled by the thought of the weary work that his identification is going to involve.

"There's nothing for it," said Chief Inspector Parker, "but his laundry-mark, I suppose. And of course, his dentistry, if any."

Irritatingly enough, the deceased turned out to have an excellent set of teeth and at least three laundry-marks. Nor were his shoes helpful, being ready-made, though by an excellent and much-advertised firm. In fact, the wretched man had gone to meet his Maker in Farley's Footwear, thus upholding to the last the brave assertion that, however distinguished the occasion, Farley's Footwear will carry you through.

In this extremity, Mr. Parker—perhaps stimulated by the thought of Messrs. Farley's advertising—rang up Pym's Publicity and desired to speak with Mr. Bredon.

That gentleman was closeted with Mr. Armstrong when the call came through. Whifflets were causing trouble. The sales of Whifflets had been considerably affected by the publicity methods of a rival brand, Puffin Cigarettes. The manufacturers of Puffins had had a brain-wave. They were giving away aeroplanes. In every packet of Puffins they enclosed a coupon, bearing the name of a component part of a popular little touring 'plane, suitable for amateur use. When you had collected your complete set of parts (numbering one hundred) you sent up your coupons, together with a brief essay on the importance of air-mindedness for British boys. The writer of the best essay each day became the recipient of a private 'plane, and a course of free instruction enabling him or her to take out an air-pilot's certificate. This happy scheme was supported by heavy advertising of a modern and stimulating kind: "The Future is with the Air-Minded"—"The Highest Flight in Modern Cigarette Manufacture"—"Puff Puffins, and Reach the Height of your Ambition"—and so forth. If you were incapacitated, by reason of age or infirmity, from enjoying the ownership of an aeroplane, you received instead a number of shares in the new issue of the Aeroplane Company involved. The scheme had the support of several notable airmen, whose faces, adorned with flying helmets, stared and grinned from every page of the press in conjunction with their considered opinions that Puffins were doing a valuable work in helping to establish British Supremacy in the Air.

Whifflets were upset. They demanded, with some annoyance, why Pym's had not had this brilliant idea first. They clamoured for an aeroplane scheme of their own, with a larger plane and a hangar to keep it in. Mr. Armstrong pointed out to them that the sole result of this would be to confuse the public mind between Whifflets and Puffins, which were already quite sufficiently similar in quality and appearance to confuse anybody.

"They're all alike," he said to Bredon, not meaning the cigarettes, but the manufacturers. "They follow each other like sheep. If Whifflets use large heads of film-stars, Puffin's want to come out with still larger heads of still more important stars. If Gasperettes give away timepieces, Puffins follow on with grandfather clocks and Whifflets with chronometers. If Whifflets announce that they don't damage the lungs, Puffins claim that they strengthen the pulmonary system and Gasperettes quote doctors who recommend them in cases of tuberculosis. They will try to snatch each other's thunder—and what happens? The public smoke them all in turn, just as they did before."

"Isn't that a good thing for trade?" asked Mr. Bredon, innocently. "If one of them got all the sales, the others would go bankrupt."

"Oh, no, they wouldn't," said Mr. Armstrong. "They'd merely amalgamate. But it would be bad for us, because then they'd all use the same agency."

"Well, what about it, then?" queried Bredon.

"We've got to cope. We must head them off aeroplanes. For one thing, the boom won't last. The country isn't ready to be cluttered up with aeroplanes, and fathers of families are beginning to complain about it. Even to-day, few fathers care about having private aeroplanes delivered to their daughters in quiet suburban areas. What we want is a new scheme, on similar lines but with more family appeal. But it must boost Britain. We've got to have the patriotic note."

It was in that moment, and while Chief Inspector Parker was arguing over the line with the office telephonist, that Mr. Death Bredon conceived that magnificent idea that everybody remembers and talks about to-day—the scheme that achieved renown as "Whiffling Round Britain"—the scheme that sent up the sales of Whifflets by five hundred per cent in three months and brought so much prosperity to British Hotel-keepers and Road and Rail Transport. It is not necessary to go into details. You have probably Whiffled yourself. You recollect how it was done. You collected coupons for everything—railway fares, charabancs, hotel-bills, theatre-tickets—every imaginable item in a holiday programme. When you had collected enough to cover the period of time you wished to spend in travelling, you took your coupons with you (no sending up to Whifflets, nothing to post or fill in) and started on your tour. At the railway station you presented coupons entitling you to so many miles of first-class travel and received your ticket to the selected town. You sought your hotel (practically all the hotels in Britain fell eagerly in with the scheme) and there presented coupons entitling you to so many nights' board and lodging on special Whifflet terms. For your charabanc outings, your sea-bathing, your amusements, you paid in Whifflet coupons. It was all exceedingly simple and trouble-free. And it made for that happy gregariousness which is the joy of the travelling middle-class. When you asked for your packet of Whifflets in the bar, your next-door neighbour was almost sure to ask, "Are you Whiffling too?" Whiffling parties arranged to Whiffle together, and exchanged Whifflet coupons on the spot. The great Whifflers' Club practically founded itself, and Whifflers who had formed attachments while Whiffling in company, secured special Whifflet coupons entitling them to a Whifflet wedding with a Whifflet cake and their photographs in the papers. When this had happened several times, arrangements were made by which Whiffler couples could collect for a Whifflet house, whose Whifflet furniture included a handsome presentation smoking cabinet, free from advertising matter and crammed with unnecessary gadgets. After this, it was only a step to a Whifflet Baby. In fact, the Whifflet Campaign is and remains the outstanding example of Thinking Big in Advertising. The only thing that you cannot get by Whiffling is a coffin; it is not admitted that any Whiffler could ever require such an article.

It is not to be supposed that the great Whiffle-Way, in all its comprehensive perfection, sprang fully armed from Mr. Bredon's brain when Mr. Armstrong uttered the words, Family Appeal. All that then happened was a mental association with the phrase Family Hotel, coupled with a faint consciousness of inner illumination. He replied, humbly, "Yes, I see; I'll try to work out something," gathered up some sheets of paper on which Mr. Armstrong had scribbled a few illegible notes and a thing that looked like a hedgehog, and made his way out. He had taken six steps down the passage when the idiotic slogan: "If that's what you want, you can Whiffle for it" took possession of his brain; two steps further on, this repellent sentence had recast itself as: "All you Want by Whiffling", and on the threshold of his own room, the first practical possibility of Whiffledom struck him like a sledge-hammer. Fired with excitement, he hurled himself at his desk, snatched a scribbling-block, and had written the word "WHIFFLE" in capitals an inch high, when Miss Rossiter arrived with the message that Mr. Parker urgently requested Mr. Bredon to ring him up on the Whitehall number. Lord Peter Wimsey was so intimately in the skin of Mr. Death Bredon that he said: "Damn!" loudly and heartily.

Nevertheless, he obeyed the call, presented himself with leave of absence on urgent private business, and went down to Scotland Yard, where he surveyed the clothes and effects of the man in the dress suit.

"No doubt we shall end by having to circularise the laundries," said Parker. "Perhaps a photograph in some of the London and provincial papers would be as well. I loathe newspapers, but they do advertise one's requirements, and some of these laundry-marks may come from outside London. . . ."

Wimsey looked at him.

"Advertisement, my dear Charles, may be desirable in the case of laundries, but for people like ourselves it does not exist. A gentleman whose clothes are so well cut, and who yet deprives his tailor of the credit for them is, like ourselves, not of the advertising sort. This, I see, is his top-hat, mysteriously uninjured."

"It had rolled beyond the train, on to the further line."

"Quite. Here again the maker's golden imprint has been removed. How absurd, Charles! One does not—at least, you and I and this gentleman do not—consider the brand to be the guarantee of quality. For us, the quality guarantees the brand. There are two hatters in London who could have made this hat, and you have doubtless already observed that the crown is markedly dolicephalic, while the curve of the brim is also characteristic. It is a thought behind the present fashion; yet the article is undoubtedly of recent manufacture. Send one of your sleuths to each of these two establishments and ask for the customer with the elongated head who has a fancy for this type of brim. Do not waste your time on laundry-marks, which are, at best, tedious and, at worst, deceptive."

"Thanks," said Parker. "I thought you might be able to put your finger either on the hatter or the tailor."

The first hatter they visited proved to be the right man. He directed their researches to the flat of a Mr. Horace Mountjoy, who lived in Kensington. They armed themselves with a search-warrant and visited the flat.

Mr. Mountjoy, they ascertained from the commissionaire, was a bachelor of quiet habits, except that he was frequently out rather late at night. He lived alone, and was waited upon and valetted by the staff belonging to the block of flats.

The commissionaire came on duty at 9 o'clock. There was no night porter. Between 11 p.m. and 9 a.m. the outer door was locked and could be opened by the tenants with their own keys, without disturbing him in his basement flat. He had seen Mr. Mountjoy go out the previous evening at about 7.45, in evening dress. He had not seen him return. Withers, the valet, would probably be able to say whether Mr. Mountjoy had been in that night.

Withers was able to say positively that he had not. Nobody had entered Mr. Mountjoy's flat but himself, and the chambermaid who did the rooms. The bed had not been slept in. That was nothing unusual with Mr. Mountjoy. He was frequently out all night, though he generally returned to breakfast at 9.30.

Parker displayed his official card, and they went upstairs to a flat on the third floor. Withers was about to open the door with his pass-key, which, as he explained, he was accustomed to use in the mornings, to avoid disturbing the tenants, but Parker stopped him and produced the two keys which had been taken from the corpse. One of them fitted the lock and established, without much doubt, that they had come to the right place.

Everything in the flat was in perfect order. There was a desk in the sitting-room, containing a few bills and some notepaper, but its drawers were all unlocked and it appeared to hold no secrets. Nor was there anything remarkable about the bedroom or the small dining-room. In the bathroom was a little cupboard containing the usual toilet articles and household medicines. Parker made a rapid inventory of these, pausing for a few minutes over a packet labelled "Bicarbonate of Soda", but touch and taste soon assured him that this contained exactly what it purported to contain. The only thing that could be considered in the slightest degree out of the ordinary in the whole establishment was the presence (also in the bathroom cupboard) of several packets of cigarette-papers.

"Did Mr. Mountjoy roll his own cigarettes?"

"I never saw him do so," replied Withers. "He smoked Turkish Abdullas as a rule."

Parker nodded and impounded the cigarette-papers. A further search disclosed no loose tobacco. A number of boxes of cigars and cigarettes were retrieved from the dining-room sideboard. They looked innocent and a few, which Parker promptly slit open, proved to contain excellent tobacco and nothing else. Parker shook his head.

"You'll have to go through everything very carefully, Lumley."

"Yes, sir."

"Any letters by the first post?"

There were none.

"Any visitors to-day?"

"No, sir. Not unless you count the man from the post-office."

"Oh? What did *he* want?"

"Nothing," replied Withers, "except to bring the new telephone directory." He indicated the two clean volumes which lay upon the sitting-room desk.

"Oh!" said Parker. This did not sound promising. "Did he come into the room?"

"No, sir. He knocked at the door when Mrs. Trabbs and I were both here. Mrs. Trabbs was sweeping, sir, and I was brushing Mr. Mountjoy's lounge suit. I took the books in, sir, and handed him out the old ones."

"I see. All right. And beyond sweeping and brushing and so on, you disturbed nothing?"

"No, sir."

"Anything in the waste-paper basket?"

"I could not say, sir. Mrs. Trabbs would know."

Mrs. Trabbs, produced, said there had been nothing in the waste-paper basket except a wine-merchant's circular. Mr. Mountjoy wrote very little and did not receive many letters.

Satisfied that there had been no interference with the flat since the occupant had left the night before, Parker turned his attention to the wardrobe and chest of drawers, where he found various garments, all properly marked with the names of the tailor or shirt-maker responsible for them. He noticed that all were by first-class artists in their own line. Another silk hat, similar to the one now resting at Scotland Yard, but with sweat-band and crown undisfigured, was found in a hat-box; there were also several felt hats and a bowler, all by first-class makers.

"Mr Mountjoy was a rich man?"

"He appeared to be in very easy circumstances, sir. He did himself well; the best of everything. Especially during the last year or so."

"What was his profession?"

"I think he was a gentleman of independent means. I never heard of him being engaged in any business."

"Did you know that he had a silk hat from which the makers' name had been removed?"

"Yes, sir. He was very angry about it. Said that some friend of his had damaged the hat for a rag. I offered several times to get it put right, sir, but when he had cooled down he said it didn't matter. It wasn't a hat he very often used, sir. And besides, he said, why should he be a walking advertisement for his hatter?"

"Did you know that his dress suit had also lost the tailor's tab?"

"Had it indeed, sir? No, I can't say I noticed it."

"What sort of man was Mr. Mountjoy?"

"A very pleasant gentleman, sir. I'm very sorry to hear he has met with such a sad accident."

"How long has he lived here?"

"Six or seven years, I believe, sir. I've been here four years myself."

"When was the practical joke played on his silk hat?"

"About eighteen months ago, sir, if I remember rightly."

"As long ago as that? I fancied the hat looked newer."

"Well, sir, as I say, he didn't wear it above once or twice a week, sir. And Mr. Mountjoy didn't trouble about the fashion of his hats. There was one particular shape he fancied, and he had all his hats specially made to that pattern."

Parker nodded. He knew this already from the hatter and from Wimsey, but it was well to check matters up. He reflected that he had never yet caught Wimsey tripping in any fact pertaining to dress.

"Well," he said, "as you may have guessed, Withers, there will have to be an inquiry about Mr. Mountjoy's death. You had better say as little as possible to any outside person. You will give me all the keys of the flat, and I shall be leaving the police in charge here for a day or two."

"Very good, sir."

Parker waited to ascertain the name and address of the proprietor of the flats, and left Lumley to his investigations. From the proprietor he gained very little information. Mr. Mountjoy, of no profession, had taken the flat six years previously. He had paid his rent regularly. There had been no complaints. Nothing was known of Mr. Mountjoy's friends or relations. It was regrettable that so good a tenant should have come to so sudden and sad an end. It was much to be hoped that nothing would transpire of a scandalous nature as those flats had always been extremely respectable.

Parker's next visit was to Mr. Mountjoy's bank. Here he encountered the usual obstructive attitude, but eventually succeeded in getting access to the books. There was a regular income of about a thousand a year derived from sound investments. No irregularities. No mysterious fluctuations. Parker came away with an uneasy impression that Mr. Hector Puncheon had discovered a mare's nest.

CHAPTER XVI

Eccentric Behaviour of a Post Office Department

THE CHIEF INSPECTOR voiced this opinion to Wimsey the same evening. His lordship, whose mind was still divided between detection and the new Whifflet campaign, which had taken clear shape during the afternoon, was curt with him:

"Mare's nest? Then what knocked Puncheon out? A kick from the mare's heel?"

"Perhaps Mountjoy merely got fed up with him. You'd get fed up yourself if you were pursued all over London by a Puncheon."

"Possibly. But I shouldn't knock him out and leave him to his fate. I should give him in charge. How is Puncheon?"

"Still unconscious. Concussion. He seems to have got a violent blow on the temple and a nasty crack on the back of the head."

"Um. Knocked up against the wall, probably, when Mountjoy got him with the cosh."

"No doubt you're right."

"I am always right. I hope you are keeping an eye on the man Garfield."

"He won't move for a bit. Why?"

"Well—it's odd that Mountjoy should have been snuffed out so inconveniently for you."

"You don't suppose that Garfield had anything to do with it? Why, the man was nearly killed himself. Besides, we've looked into him. He's a well-known Harley Street man, with a large West End practice."

"Among the dope-maniacs, perhaps?"

"He specialises in nervous complaints."

"Exactly."

Parker whistled.

"That's what you think, is it?"

"See here," said Wimsey, "your grey matter isn't functioning as it ought. Are you tired at the end of the day? Do you suffer from torpor and lethargy after meals? Try Sparkletone, the invigorating vegetable saline that stimulates while it cleanses. Some accidents are too accidental to be true. When a gentleman removes his tailor's tab and takes the trouble to slice his hatter's imprint away with a razor, and goes skipping, for no reason at all, from Finchley to South Kensington Museum in his dress suit at unearthly hours in the morning, it's because he has something to hide. If he tops up his odd behaviour by falling under a train without the smallest apparent provocation, it's because somebody else is interested in getting the things hidden, too. And the more risks somebody else takes in the process, the more certain it is that the thing is worth hiding."

Parker looked at him and grinned quietly.

"You're a great guesser, Peter. Would you be surprised to hear that you're not the only one?"

"No, I shouldn't. You're holding something out on me. What is it? A witness to the assault, what? Somebody who was on the platform? Somebody you weren't inclined to pay much attention to? You old leg-puller, I can see it in your face. Out with it now—who was it? A woman. A hysterical woman. A middle-aged, hysterical spinster. Am I right?"

"Curse you, yes."

"Go on, then. Tell me all about it."

"Well, when Eagles took the depositions of the witnesses at the station, they all agreed that Mountjoy had walked several paces past Garfield and then suddenly staggered; that Garfield had caught him by the arm and that both had fallen together. But this female, Miss Eliza Tebbutt by name, fifty-two, unmarried, housekeeper, living in Kensington, says that she was standing a little way beyond them both and that she distinctly heard what she describes as a 'dreadful voice' say, 'Punch away, you're *for* it!' That Mountjoy immediately stopped as though he had been shot, and that Garfield 'with a terrible face', took him by the arm and tripped him up. It may increase your confidence in this good lady when you hear that she is subject to nervous disorders, has once been confined in a mental home and is persuaded that Garfield is a prominent member of a gang whose object is to murder all persons of British birth and establish the supremacy of the Jews in England."

"Jews in England be damned. Because a person has a monomania she need not be wrong about her facts. She might have imagined or invented a good deal, but she couldn't possibily imagine or invent anything so fantastic as 'Punch away', which is obviously her mishearing of the name 'Mountjoy'. Garfield's your man—though I admit that you're going to have some difficulty in fixing anything on him. But if I were you, I'd have his premises searched—if it isn't too late by now."

"I'm afraid it probably is too late. We didn't get any sense out of Miss Tebbutt for an hour or so; by which time the heroic Dr. Garfield had, naturally, telephoned both to his home and to his consulting-room to explain what had happened to him. Still, we'll keep an eye on him. The immediate matter of importance is Mountjoy. Who was he? What was he up to? Why did he have to be suppressed?"

"It's pretty clear what he was up to. He was engaged in the dope traffic and he was suppressed because he had been fool enough to let Puncheon recognise and follow him. Somebody must have been on the watch; this gang apparently keeps tabs on all its members. Or the wretched Mountjoy may have asked for help and been helped out of the world as the speediest method of disposing of the difficulty. It's a pity Puncheon can't talk—he could tell us whether Mountjoy had telephoned or spoken to anybody during his dash round town. Anyhow, he made a mistake, and people who make mistakes are not permitted to survive. The odd thing, to my mind, is that you heard nothing of any visit to the flat. You'd rather expect the gang to have made some sort of investigation there, just to make sure. I suppose those servants are to be trusted?"

"I think so. We've made inquiries. They've all got good histories. The commissionaire has an army pension and an excellent record. The valet and chambermaid are highly respectable—nothing whatever against them."

"H'm. And you've found nothing but a packet of cigarette-papers. Handy, of course, for wrapping up a grain or so of cocaine but, in themselves, no proof of anything."

"I thought you'd see the significance of the cigarette-papers."

"I am not yet blind or mentally deficient."

"But where is the dope?"

"The dope? Really, Charles! He was going to fetch the dope when friend Puncheon butted in. Haven't you yet grasped that this is part of the Milligan crowd and that Friday is their day for distributing dope? The Milligans get it on Friday and give house-parties on Friday night and Saturday, when it goes into the hands of the actual addicts. Dian de Momerie told me so."

"I wonder," said Parker, "why they stick to one day? It must add to the risk."

"It's obviously an integral part of the system. The stuff comes into the country—say on Thursdays. That's your part of the story. You don't seem to have done much about that, by the way. It is taken to—somewhere or the other—that night. Next day it is called for by the Mountjoys and sent on to the Milligans, none of whom probably knows any of the others by sight. And by Saturday the whole lot is pushed out and everybody has a happy weekend."

"That sounds plausible. It certainly explains why we found no trace of anything either in the flat or on Mountjoy's body. Except cigarette-papers. By the way, is that right? If Mountjoy has the cigarette-papers, he ought to be the one who distributes to the addicts."

"Not necessarily. He gets it himself in bulk—done up as bicarbonate of soda or what not. He divides it into small packets and parcels them out—so many to Milligan, so many to the next retailer and so forth; when, or how, I don't know. Nor do I know how the payments are worked."

"Glad to hear there's something you don't know."

"I said I didn't know; not that I couldn't guess. But I won't bother you with guesses. All the same, it's rather surprising that Garfield & Co. left that flat alone."

"Perhaps Garfield meant to go there afterwards, if he hadn't got knocked out."

"No; he'd not leave it so late. Tell me again about the flat."

Parker patiently repeated the account of his visit and the interviews with the servants. Before he was half-way through, Wimsey had sat up in his chair and was listening with fascinated attention.

"Charles! What imbeciles we are! Of course, that's it!"

"What's what?"

"The telephone directory, of course. The man who brought the new volumes and took the old away. Since when has the Post Office taken to getting *both* new volumes out at once?"

"By Jove!" exclaimed Parker.

"I should think it was, by Jove. Ring up now and find out whether two new volumes were sent round to Mountjoy's address to-day."

"It'll be a job to get hold of O.C. Directories at this time of night."

"So it will. Wait a moment. Ring up the flats and ask if anybody else received any directories this morning. My experience is that even Government departments do these things in batches, and don't make a special journey to every subscriber."

Parker acted on this suggestion. After a little trouble, he succeeded in getting into touch with three other occupants in the same block as Mountjoy's flat. All three gave the same answer. They had received a new L–Z volume about a fortnight previously. The new A–K volume was not yet due to be issued. One man went further. His name was Barrington, and he had only recently moved in. He had inquired when the new A–K volume would be out with his new 'phone number, and had been told that it would probably be issued in October.

"That settles it," said Wimsey. "Our friend Mountjoy kept his secrets in the telephone directory. That great work contains advertisements, post office regulations and names and addresses, but particularly names and addresses. May we conclude that the secret nestled among the names and addresses? I think we may."

"It seems reasonable."

"Very reasonable. Now, how do we set about discovering those names and addresses?"

"Bit of a job. We can probably get a description of the man who called for the books this morning——"

"And comb London's teeming millions for him? Had we but world enough and time. Where do good telephone directories go when they die?"

"The pulping-mills, probably."

"And the last exchange of the L–Z volume was made a fortnight ago. There's a chance that it hasn't been pulped yet. Get on to it, Charles. There's more than a chance that it, too, was marked, and that the markings were transferred at each exchange from the old book to the new one."

"Why? Mountjoy might easily have kept the old marked set by him."

"I fancy not, or we should have either found it or heard about it from the manservant. The stranger came; the two current volumes were handed to him and he went away satisfied. As I see the plan, the whole idea would be to use the current volume, so as to rouse no suspicion, have nothing to conceal and provide a convenient mechanism for getting rid of the evidence at short notice."

"You may be right. It's a chance, as you say. I'll get on to the telephone people first thing in the morning."

The tide of luck seemed to have turned. A morning's strenuous work revealed that the old directories had already been dispatched by the sackful to the pulping-mills, but had not, so far, been pulped. Six workers, toiling over the week-end among L–Z volumes collected from the Kensington district, brought to light the pleasing fact that nine people out of ten marked their directories in some way or another. Reports came pouring in. Wimsey sat with Parker in the latter's office at Scotland Yard and considered these reports.

Late on Sunday night, Wimsey raised his head from a sheaf of papers.

"I think this is it, Charles."

"What is it?" Parker was weary and his eyes blood-shot with strain, but a note of hope was in his voice.

"This one. A whole list of public-houses in Central London have been ticked off—three in the middle of the L's, two near the end of the M's, one in the N's, one in the O's, and so forth and so on, including two in the middle of the W's. The two in the W's are the White Stag in Wapping and the White Stoat off Oxford Street. The next W after that is the White Swan in Covent Garden. I would bet any money that in the new volume that was carried away, the White Swan was duly ticked off in its turn."

"I'm not quite sure what you're driving at."

"I'm making rather a long cast, but I suggest this. When the stuff comes up to London of a Thursday, I think it is taken to whichever pub stands next on the list in the directory. One week it will be a pub with a name in A—say the Anchor. Next week it will be a B—the Bull & Dog, or the Brickmaker's Arms. The week after that, it will be a C, and so on to W, X, Y, Z—if there are any. The people who have to call for their dope wander into the pub indicated, where it is slipped to them by the head distributor and his agents, probably quite without the knowledge of the proprietor. And since it never comes twice to the same place, your pretty policeman can go and talk parrots and goats in the White Swan till they are blue in the face. They ought to have been at the Yellow Peril or the York & Lancaster."

"That's an idea, Peter. Let's look at that list again."

Wimsey handed it over.

"If you're right, then this week was W week, and next week will be X week. That's unlikely. Say Y week. The next Y after the last one ticked is the Yelverton Arms in Soho. Wait a minute, though. If they have been taking them in alphabetical order, why have they got right down to the end of the M's in one case and only to WH in the other?"

"They must have been through the W's once, and be starting again."

"Yes—I suppose there are quite a lot of M's. But then there are hundreds of W's. Still, we'll try it, Peter, any way. What is it, Lumley?"

"Report from the hospital, sir. Puncheon has come round."

Parker glanced through the report.

"Much what we expected," he said, handing the paper to Wimsey. "Mountjoy evidently knew he was being followed. He put through a telephone call at Piccadilly Tube Station, and started off on a wild scamper across London."

"That was how the gang came to be ready for him."

"Yes. Finding he couldn't shake Puncheon off, he lured him into the museum, got him into a quiet corner and laid him out. Puncheon thinks he was slugged with a weapon of some kind. So he was. He did not speak to Mountjoy. In fact, this report tells us nothing we didn't know, except that, when Puncheon first saw him, Mountjoy was buying an early copy of the *Morning Star* from a man outside the office."

"Was he? That's interesting. Well, keep your eye on the Yelverton Arms."

"And you keep your eye on Pym's. Do remember that what we want is the man at the top."

"So does Major Milligan. The man at the top is very much sought after. Well, cheerio! If I can't do anything more for you, I think I'll tootle off to bed. I've got my Whifflets scheme to get out to-morrow."

"I like this scheme, Mr. Bredon," said Mr. Pym, tapping his finger on the drafts submitted to him. "It has Breadth. It has Vision. More than anything else, Advertising needs Vision and Breadth. That is what determines Appeal. In my opinion, this scheme of yours has Appeal. It is going to be expensive, of course, and needs some working out. For instance, if all these vouchers were cashed in at once, it would send up the cost per packet issued to a figure that the profits could not possibly cover. But I think that can be got over."

"They won't all be cashed in at once," said Mr. Armstrong. "Not if we mix them up sufficiently. People will want time to collect and exchange. That will give us a start. They've got to look on the cost of the thing as so much advertising expenditure. We shall want a big press splash to start it, and after that, it will run itself quite happily in small spaces."

"That's all very well, Armstrong, but we've got to think of ourselves."

"That's all right. We make all the arrangements with the hotels and railways and so forth and charge our fee or commission on the work. All we've got to do is to average the thing out so that the claims won't amount to more than their estimated appropriation for the month. If the thing goes big they'll be willing enough to increase the appropriation. The other thing we've got to do is to see that each coupon bears more or less the same actual cash value, so as not to get into trouble with the Lottery Act. The whole thing comes down to this. How much of the profit on each shilling packet are they prepared to spend in advertising? Remembering that this scheme, if properly put through, is going to sweep every other fag off the market for the time being. Then we make our coupons up to that value minus an appropriation for the opening press campaign. At present their appropriation is sixty thousand and their sales . . . have we got that report on sales?"

The two directors plunged into a maze of facts and figures. Mr. Bredon's attention wandered.

"Printing costs . . . see that they have a sufficient distribution . . . bonus to the tobacconists . . . . free displays . . . tackle the hotels first . . . news-value . . . get the *Morning Star* to give it a show . . . no, I know, but there's the Boost Britain side of it . . . I can wangle Jenks . . . reduce overheads by . . . call it £200 a day . . . Puffin's aeroplanes must be costing them that . . . front-page splash and five free coupons . . . well, that's a matter of detail. . . ."

"In any case, we've got to do *something*." Mr. Armstrong emerged from the argument with a slightly flushed face. "It's no use telling people that the cost of the advertising has to come out of the quality of the goods. They don't care. All they want is something for nothing. Pay? Yes, of course they pay in the end, but somebody's got to pay. You can't fight free gifts with solemn assertions about Value. Besides, if Whifflets lose their market they'll soon lose their quality too—or what are we here for?"

"You needn't tell me that, Armstrong," said Mr. Pym. "Whether people like it or not, the fact remains that unless you continually increase sales you must either lose money or cut down quality. I hope we've learnt that by this time."

"What happens," asked Mr. Bredon, "when you've increased sales to saturation point?"

"You mustn't ask those questions, Bredon," said Mr. Armstrong, amused.

"No, but really. Suppose you push up the smoking of every man and woman in the Empire till they must either stop or die of nicotine poisoning?"

"We're a long way off that," replied Mr. Pym, seriously. "And that reminds me. This scheme should carry a strong appeal to women. 'Give your children that seaside holiday by smoking Whifflets.' That sort of thing. We want to get women down to serious smoking. Too many of them play about with it. Take them off scented stuff and put them on to the straightforward Virginia cigarette——"

"The gasper, in fact."

"Whifflets," said Mr. Pym. "You can smoke a lot more of them in the day without killing yourself. And they're cheaper. If we increase women's smokes by 500 per cent—there's plenty of room for it——"

Mr. Bredon's attention wandered again.

"——all right, date the coupons. Let them run for three months only. That will give us plenty of duds to play with. And they'll have to see that their stockists are kept up to date with fresh goods. By the way, that makes a selling point——"

Mr. Bredon fell into a dream.

"——but you must have a good press campaign as well. Posters are good and cheap, but if you really want to tell people something, you've got to have a press campaign. Not a big one, necessarily, after the first big bang. But a good, short, snappy reminder week by week——"

"Very well, Mr. Bredon." The creator of the Whifflet scheme came out of his doze with a start. "We'll put this up to Whifflets. Will you see if you can get out some copy? And you'd better put a few other people on to it as well, Armstrong. Ingleby—it's rather his line. And Miss Meteyard. We want to get something out by the end of the week. Tell Mr. Barrow to put everything else aside and rough out some really striking displays." Mr. Pym gave the signal of dismissal, and then, as a thought struck him, called Bredon back.

"I want a word with you, Bredon. I'd almost forgotten what you were really here for. Has any progress been made in that matter?"

"Yes." The Whifflets campaign receded from Lord Peter Wimsey, dying along the distance of his mind. "In fact, the investigation is turning out to be of so much importance that I don't quite know how I can take even you into my confidence."

"That's nonsense," said Mr. Pym. "I am employing you——"

"No. There's no question of employment. I'm afraid it's a police job."

The shadows of disquiet gathered and deepened in Mr. Pym's eyes.

"Do you mean that those earlier suspicions you mentioned to me were actually justified?"

"Oh, yes. But it's a bigger thing than that."

"I don't want any scandal."

"Possibly not. But I don't quite see how it's to be avoided, if the thing comes to trial."

"Look here, Bredon," said Mr. Pym, "I don't like your behaviour. I put you in here as my private inquiry agent. I admit that you have made yourself very useful in other capacities, but you are not indispensable. If you insist on going beyond your authority——"

"You can sack me. Of course. But would that be wise?"

Mr. Pym mopped his forehead.

"Can you tell me this," he inquired anxiously, after a silence in which he seemed to be digesting the meaning of his employee's question. "Do your suspicions point to any particular person? Is it possible to remove that person promptly from our staff? You see my point. If, before this scandal breaks—whatever it is—and I really think I ought to be told—but so long as we can say that the person is no longer on the staff, it makes a difference. The firm's name might even be kept out of it—mightn't it? The good name of Pym's means a great deal to me, Mr. Bredon——"

"I can't tell you," said Wimsey; "a few days ago, I thought I knew, but just lately, other facts have come to my knowledge which suggest that the man I originally suspected may not be the right one. And until I know definitely, I can't do or say anything. At the moment it might be anybody. It might even be yourself."

"This is outrageous," cried Mr. Pym. "You can take your money and go."

Wimsey shook his head.

"If you get rid of me, the police will probably want to put somebody in my place."

"If I had the police here," retorted Mr. Pym, "I should at least know where I was. I know nothing about you, except that Mrs. Arbuthnot recommended you. I never cared for the idea of a private detective, though I certainly thought at first that you were of a somewhat superior type to the usual inquiry agent. But insolence I cannot and will not put up with. I shall communicate at once with Scotland Yard, and they will, I imagine, require you to state plainly what you imagine yourself to have discovered."

"They know it."

"Do they? You do not seem to be a model of discretion, Mr. Bredon." He pressed his buzzer. "Miss Hartley, will you please get Scotland Yard on the 'phone, and ask them to send up a reliable detective."

"Very well, Mr. Pym."

Miss Hartley danced away. This was meat and drink. She had always said there was something funny about Mr. Bredon, and now he had been caught. Pinching the cash, perhaps. She dialled the switch-board and asked for Whitehall 1212.

"Just one moment," said Wimsey, when the door had closed upon her. "If you really want Scotland Yard, tell her to ask for Chief Inspector Parker and say that Lord Peter Wimsey would like to speak to him. Then he'll know what it's about."

"You are——? Why didn't you tell me?"

"I thought it might raise difficulties about the salary and prove embarrassing. I took the job on because I thought advertising might be rather good fun. So it is," added Wimsey, pleasantly, "so it is."

Mr. Pym put his head into Miss Hartley's room.

"I'll take that call in here," he said, briefly.

They sat mute till the call came through. Mr. Pym asked for Chief Inspector Parker.

"There is a man on my staff, calling himself——"

The conversation was a brief one. Mr. Pym handed the receiver to Wimsey.

"They want to speak to you."

"Hullo, Charles! That you? Have you established my credit? All right.... No, no trouble, only Mr. Pym feels he ought to know what it's all about.... Shall I tell him? ... Not wise? ... Honestly, Charles, I don't think he's our man.... Well, that's a different question.... The Chief Inspector wants to know whether you can hold your tongue, Mr. Pym."

"I only wish to God everybody could hold his tongue," groaned Mr. Pym.

Wimsey passed on the reply. "I think I'll risk it, Charles. If anybody is going to be slugged in the dark after this, it won't be you, and I can look after myself."

He rang off and turned to Mr. Pym.

"Here's the brutal fact," he said. "Somebody's running an enormous dope-traffic from this office. Who is there that has far more money than he ought to have, Mr. Pym? We're looking for a very rich man. Can you help us?"

But Mr. Pym was past helping anybody. He was chalk-white.

"Dope? From this office? What on earth will our clients say? How shall I face the Board? The publicity ..."

"Pym's Publicity," said Lord Peter Wimsey, and laughed.

CHAPTER XVII

Lachrymose Outburst of a Nobleman's Nephew

THAT WEEK PASSED quietly. On Tuesday, Mr. Jollop passed, quite amiably, another of the new "Quotations" series for Nutrax "——And Kissed Again with Tears" ("But Tears, and Fallings-Out, however poetical, are nearly always a sign of Nerve-Strain"); on Wednesday, Green Pastures Margarine was Reduced in Price though Improved in Quality ("It might seem impossible to improve on Perfection, but we have done it!"); Sopo adopted a new advertising figure ("Let Susan Sopo do the Dirty Work"); Tomboy Toffee finished up its Cricket Campaign with a huge display containing the portraits of a complete Eleven of Famous Cricketers all eating Tomboy; five people went on holiday; Mr. Prout created a sensation by coming to the office in a black shirt; Miss Rossiter lost a handbag containing her bonus money and recovered it from the Lost Property Office, and a flea was found in the ladies' cloak-room, causing dire upheaval, some ill-founded accusations and much heart-burning. In the typists' room, the subject of the flea almost ousted for the moment the juicier and more speculative topic of Mr. Tallboy's visitor. For, whether by the indiscretion of Tompkin or of the boy at the desk, or of some other person (though not of Mr. Ingleby or Mr. Bredon, who surely knew better) the tale had somehow seeped through.

"And how he does it on his salary I don't know," observed Miss Parton. "I do think it's a shame. His wife's a nice little woman. You remember, we met her last year at the Garden Party."

"Men are all alike," said Miss Rossiter, scornfully. "Even your Mr. Tallboy. I told you, Parton, that I didn't think old Copley was so much to blame as you thought in the other business, and now, perhaps, you'll believe me. What I say is, if a man does one ungentlemanly thing, he'll do another. And as for doing it on his salary, how about that fifty pounds in an envelope? It's pretty obvious where *that* went to."

"It's always obvious where money goes to," said Miss Meteyard, sardonically. "The point is, where does it come from?"

"That's what Mr. Dean used to say," said Miss Rossiter. "You remember how he used to chip Mr. Tallboy about his stockbrokers?"

"The famous firm of Smith," said Mr. Garrett. "Smith, Smith, Smith, Smith, Smith & Smith Unlimited."

"Money-lenders, if you ask me," said Miss Rossiter. "Are you going to the cricket-match, Miss Meteyard? In *my* opinion, Mr. Tallboy ought to resign and leave somebody else to captain it. You can't wonder that people aren't keen to play under him, with all these stories going about. Don't you feel the same, Mr. Bredon?"

"Not a bit of it," said Mr. Bredon. "Provided the man can captain, I don't care a bit if he has as many wives as Solomon, and is a forger and swindler into the bargain. What's it matter?"

"It would matter to me," said Miss Rossiter.

"How feminine she is," said Mr. Bredon, plaintively, to the world at large. "She *will* let the personal element come into business."

"I dare say," said Miss Rossiter, "but you bet, if Hankie or Pymmy knew, there'd soon be an end of Mr. Tallboy."

"Directors are the last people to hear anything about the staff. Otherwise," said Miss Meteyard, "they wouldn't be able to stand on their hind legs at the Staff Dinner and shoot off the speeches about co-operation, and all being one happy family."

"Family quarrels, family quarrels." Mr. Ingleby waved his hand. "Little children, love one another and don't be such little nosey-parkers. What's Hecuba's bank-balance to you, or yours to Hecuba?"

"Bank-balance? Oh, you mean Mr. Tallboy's. Well, *I* don't know anything, except what little Dean used to say."

"And how did Dean know so much about it?"

"He was in Mr. Tallboy's office for a few weeks. Learning the work of other departments, they call it. I expect you'll be pushed round the office before long, Mr. Bredon. You'll have to mind your P's and Q's in the Printing. Mr. Thrale's a perfect tartar. Won't even allow you to slip out for coffee."

"I shall have to come to you for it."

"They won't let Mr. Bredon out of this department for a bit," said Miss Meteyard. "They're all up in the air about his Whifflets stunt. Everybody always hoped Dean would do better somewhere else. He was like a favourite book—you liked him so well that you were always yearning to lend him to somebody else."

"What a savage woman you are," observed Ingleby, coolly amused. "It's that kind of remark that gets the university woman a bad name." He glanced at Willis, who said:

"It isn't the savagery. It's the fact that there's no animosity behind it. You are all like that."

"You agree with Shaw—whenever you beat your child, be sure that you do it in anger."

"Shaw's Irish," said Bredon. "Willis has put his finger on the real offensiveness of the educated Englishman—that he will not even trouble to be angry."

"That's right," said Willis. "It's that awful, bleak, blank——" he waved his hands helplessly—"the façade."

"Meaning Bredon's face?" suggested Ingleby, mischievously.

"Icily regular, splendidly null," said Bredon, squinting into Miss Rossiter's mirror. "Strange, to think that a whole Whifflets campaign seethes and burgeons behind this solid ivory brow."

"Mixed metaphor," said Miss Meteyard. "Pots seethe, plants burgeon."

"Of course; it is a flower of rhetoric culled from the kitchen-garden."

"It's no use, Miss Meteyard," said Ingleby, "you might as well argue with an eel."

"Talking of eels," said Miss Meteyard, abandoning the position, "what's the matter with Miss Hartley?"

"The hipless wonder? Why?"

"She came up the other day to inform the world that the police were coming to arrest somebody."

"What?" said Willis.

"You mean, whom?"

"Whom, then?"

"Bredon."

"Mr. Bredon?" said Miss Parton. "What next, I wonder."

"You mean, what for? Why don't you people say what you do mean?"

Miss Rossiter turned on her chair and gazed at Mr. Bredon's gently twitching mouth.

"That's funny," she said. "Do you know, Mr. Bredon, we never told you, but Parton and I thought we saw you actually being arrested one evening, in Piccadilly Circus."

"Did you?"

"It wasn't you, of course."

"Well, as a matter of fact, it wasn't. Still, cheer up—it may happen yet. Only I suppose Pymmy doesn't keep his millions in the office safe."

"Nor yet in registered envelopes," said Miss Meteyard, casually.

"Don't say they're after our Mr. Copley!"

"I hope not. Bread-and-skilly wouldn't suit him at all."

"But what was Bredon being arrested for?"

"Loitering, perhaps," said a mild voice in the doorway. Mr. Hankin poked his head round the corner and smiled sarcastically. "I am sorry to interrupt you, but if Mr. Bredon could favour me with his attention for a moment on the subject of Twentyman's Teas——"

"I beg your pardon, sir," said Mr. Bredon, springing to attention and allowing himself to be marched off.

Miss Rossiter shook her head.

"You mark my words, there's a mystery about Mr. Bredon."

"He's a darling," objected Miss Parton, warmly.

"Oh, Bredon's all right," said Ingleby.

Miss Meteyard said nothing. She went downstairs to the Executive and borrowed the current volume of *Who's Who.* She ran her finger through the W's, till she came to the entry beginning: "WIMSEY, Peter Death Bredon (Lord), D.S.O., born 1890; second *s.* of Mortimer Gerald Bredon Wimsey, 15th. Duke of Denver, and Honoria Lucasta, *d.* of Francis Delagardie of Bellingham Manor, Bucks. *Educ.* Eton College and Balliol." She read it through.

"So that's it," said Miss Meteyard to herself. "I thought so. And now what? Does one do anything? I think not. Better leave it alone. But there's no harm in putting out feelers for another job. One's got to look after one's self."

Mr. Bredon, unaware that his disguise had been penetrated, gave but a superficial consideration to the interests of Twentyman's Teas. He meekly accepted the instruction to prepare a window-bill with two streamers on the subject of a richer infusion with fewer spoonfuls, and a gentle rebuke in the matter of wasting time in the typists' room. His mind was in Old Broad Street.

"You are playing for us on Saturday, I see," said Mr. Hankin, at the conclusion of the interview.

"Yes, sir."

"I hope the weather will hold. You have played in first-class cricket, I believe?"

"A long time ago."

"You will be able to show them a bit of style," said Mr. Hankin, happily. "Style—one sees so little of it nowadays. I am afraid you will find us a scratch lot, and for some reason, several of our best players seem unable to attend this match. A pity. But you will find Mr. Tallboy very good. An excellent all-round man, and quite remarkable in the field."

Mr. Bredon said that it was all too rare to find proper attention given to fielding. Mr. Hankin agreed with him.

"Mr. Tallboy is excellent at all games; it's a pity he can't give more time to them. Personally, I should like to see more organisation of the athletic side of our social functions here. But Mr. Pym thinks it would perhaps be too absorbing, and I dare say he is right. Still, I can't help feeling that the cultivation of the team-spirit would do this office good. I don't know whether you, as a newcomer, have noticed a certain tension from time to time——"

Bredon admitted that he had noticed something of the sort.

"You know, Mr. Bredon," said Mr. Hankin, a little wistfully, "it is sometimes difficult for the directors to get the atmosphere of situations in the office. You people keep us rather in cotton-wool, don't you? It can't be helped, naturally, but I sometimes fancy that there are currents beneath the surface. . . ."

Evidently, thought Bredon, Mr. Hankin had realised that something was on the point of breaking. He felt suddenly sorry for him. His eyes strayed to a strip poster, printed in violent colours and secured by drawing-pins to Mr. Hankin's notice-board:

EVERYONE EVERYWHERE ALWAYS AGREES
ON THE FLAVOUR AND VALUE OF TWENTYMAN'S TEAS.

No doubt it was because agreement on any point was so rare in a quarrelsome world that the fantastical announcements of advertisers asserted it so strongly and so absurdly. Actually, there was no agreement, either on trivialities like tea or on greater issues. In this place, where from morning till night a staff of over a hundred people hymned the praises of thrift, virtue, harmony, eupepsia and domestic contentment, the spiritual atmosphere was clamorous with financial storm, intrigue, dissension, indigestion and marital infidelity. And with worse things—with murder wholesale and retail, of soul and body, murder by weapon and by poison. These things did not advertise, or, if they did, they called themselves by other names.

He made some vague answer to Mr. Hankin.

At one o'clock he left the office and took a taxi citywards. He was suddenly filled with curiosity to visit Mr. Tallboy's stockbroker.

At twenty minutes past one, he was standing on the pavement in Old Broad Street, and his blood was leaping with the excitement which always accompanies discovery.

Mr. Tallboy's stockbroker inhabited a small tobacconist's shop, the name over which was not Smith but Cummings.

"An accommodation address," observed Lord Peter Wimsey. "Most unusual for a stockbroker. Let us probe this matter further."

He entered the shop, which was narrow, confined and exceedingly dark. An elderly man stepped forward to serve him. Wimsey went immediately to the point.

"Can I see Mr. Smith?"

"Mr. Smith doesn't live here."

"Then perhaps you would kindly let me leave a note for him."

The elderly man slapped his hand on the counter.

"If I've said it once, I've said it five hundred times," he snapped irritably. "There's no Mr. Smith here, and never was, to my knowledge. And if you're the gentleman that addresses his letters here, I'd be glad if you'd take that for an answer. I'm sick and tired of handing his letters back to the postman."

"You surprise me. I don't know Mr. Smith myself, but I was asked by a friend to leave a message for him."

"Then tell your friend what I say. It's no good sending letters here. None whatever. Never has been. People seem to think I've got nothing better to do than hand out letters to postmen. If I wasn't a conscientious man, I'd burn the lot of them. That's what I'd do. Burn 'em. And I will, if it goes on any longer. You can tell your friend that from me."

"I'm very sorry," said Wimsey. "There seems to be some mistake."

"Mistake?" said Mr. Cummings, angrily. "I don't believe it's a mistake at all. It's a stupid practical joke, that's what it is. And I'm fed up with it, I can tell you."

"If it is," said Wimsey, "I'm the victim of it. I've been sent right out of my way to deliver a message to somebody who doesn't exist. I shall speak to my friend about it."

"I should, if I were you," said Mr. Cummings. "A silly, tom-fool trick. You tell your friend to come here himself, that's all. I'll know what to say to him."

"That's a good idea," said Wimsey. "And you tell him off."

"You can lay your last penny I shall, sir." Mr. Cummings, having blown off his indignation, seemed a little appeased. "If your friend should turn up, what name will he give, sir?"

Wimsey, on the point of leaving the shop, pulled up short. Mr. Cummings, he noticed, had a pair of very sharp eyes behind his glasses. A thought struck him.

"Look here," he said, leaning confidentially over the counter. "My friend's name is Milligan. That mean anything to you? He told me to come to you for a spot of the doings. See what I mean?"

That got home; a red glint in Mr. Cummings' eye told Wimsey as much.

"I don't know what you are talking about," was what Mr. Cummings actually said. "I never heard of a Mr. Milligan, and I don't want to. And I don't want any of your sauce, neither."

"Sorry, old thing, sorry," said Wimsey.

"And what's more," said Mr. Cummings, "I don't want you. See?"

"I see," said Wimsey. "I see perfectly. Good-morning."

"That's torn it," he thought. "I'll have to work quickly now. St. Martin's-le-Grand comes next, I fancy."

A little pressure at headquarters produced what was required. The postmen who carried letters to Old Broad Street were found and interrogated. It was quite true that they frequently delivered letters for a Mr. Smith to Mr. Cummings' shop, and that these letters invariably were returned, and marked "Not known". Where did they go then? To the Returned Letter Office. Wimsey rang up Pym's, explained that he was unavoidably detained, and sought the Returned Letter Office. After a little delay, he found the official who knew all about it.

The letters for Mr. Smith came regularly every week. They were never returned to the sender in the ordinary course. Why? Because they bore no sender's name. In fact, they never contained anything but a sheet of blank paper.

"Had they last Tuesday's letter there?" No; it had already been opened and destroyed. Would they keep the next one that arrived and send it on to him? Seeing that Lord Peter Wimsey had Scotland Yard behind him, they would. Wimsey thanked the official, and went his way, pondering.

On leaving the office at 5.30, he walked down Southampton Row to Theobald's Road. There was a newsvendor at the corner. Wimsey purchased an *Evening Comet* and glanced carelessly through the news. A brief paragraph in the Stop Press caught his eye.

CLUBMAN KILLED IN PICCADILLY

At 3 o'clock this afternoon a heavy lorry skidded and mounted the pavement in Piccadilly, fatally injuring Major "Tod" Milligan, the well-known clubman, who was standing on the kerb.

"They work quickly," he thought with a shudder. "Why, in God's name, am I still at large?" He cursed his own recklessness. He had betrayed himself to Cummings; he had gone into the shop undisguised; by now they knew who he was. Worse, they must have followed him to the General Post Office and to Pym's. Probably they were following him now. From behind the newspaper he cast a swift glance about the crowded streets. Any one of these loitering men might be *the* man. Absurd and romantic plans flitted through his mind. He would lure his assassins into some secluded spot, such as the Blackfriars subway or the steps beneath Cleopatra's Needle, and face them there and kill them with his hands. He would ring up Scotland Yard and get a guard of detectives. He would go straight home to his own flat in a taxi ("not the first nor the second that presents itself", he thought, with a fleeting recollection of professor Moriarty, barricade himself in and wait—for what? For air-guns? . . . In this perplexity he suddenly caught sight of a familiar figure—Chief Inspector Parker himself, apparently taking his early way home, and carrying a fishmonger's bag in one hand and an attaché case in the other.

He lowered the paper and said, "Hullo!'

Parker stopped. "Hullo!" he replied, tentatively. He was obviously not quite certain whether he was being hailed by Lord Peter Wimsey or by Mr. Death Bredon. Wimsey strode forward and relieved him of the fish-bag.

"Well met. You come most carefully upon your cue, to prevent me from being murdered. What's this, lobster?"

"No, turbot," said Parker, placidly.

"I'm coming to eat it with you. They will hardly attack both of us. I've made a fool of myself and given the game away, so we may as well be open and cheerful about it."

"Good. I'd like to feel cheerful."

"What's wrong? Why so early home?"

"Fed-up. The Yelverton Arms is a wash-out, I'm afraid."

"Did you raid it?"

"Not yet. Nothing happened during the morning, but during the lunch-hour crush, Lumley saw something being smuggled into a fellow's hands by a chap who looked like a tout. They stopped the fellow and searched him. All they found was some betting-slips. It's quite possible that nothing is timed to happen before this evening. If nothing turns up, I'll have the place searched. Just before closing-time will be best. I'm going down there myself. Thought I'd step home for an early supper."

"Right. I've got something to tell you."

They walked to Great Ormond Street in silence.

"Cummings?" said Parker, when Wimsey had told his tale. "Don't know anything about him. But you say he knew Milligan's name?"

"He certainly did. Besides, here's the proof of it."

He showed Parker the stop-press item.

"But this fellow, Tallboy—is he the bird you're after?"

"Frankly, Charles, I don't understand it. I can't see him as the Big Bug in all this business. If he were, he'd be too well-off to get into difficulties with a cheap mistress. And his money wouldn't be coming to him in fifty-pound instalments. But there's a connection. There must be."

"Possibly he's only a small item in the account."

"Possibly. But I can't get over Milligan. According to his information, the whole show was run from Pym's."

"Perhaps it is. Tallboy may be merely the cat's paw for one of the others. Pym himself—he's rich enough, isn't he?"

"I don't think it's Pym. Armstrong, possibly, or even quiet little Hankie. Of course, Pym's calling me in may have been a pure blind, but I don't somehow think he has quite that kind of brain. It was so unnecessary. Unless he wanted to find out, through me, how much Victor Dean really knew. In which case, he's succeeded," added Wimsey, ruefully. "But I can't believe that any man would be such a fool as to put himself in the power of one of his own staff. Look at the opportunities for blackmail! Twelve years' penal servitude is a jolly threat to hold over a man. Still—blackmail. Somebody was being blackmailed, that's almost a certainty. But Pym can't have slugged Dean; he was in conference at the time. No, I think we must acquit Pym."

"What I don't quite see," said Lady Mary, "is why Pym's is brought into it at all. Somebody *at* Pym's is one thing, but if you say that the show is 'run from Pym's', it suggests something quite different—to me, anyhow. It sounds to me as though they were using Pym's organisation for something—doesn't it to you?"

"Well, it does," agreed her husband. "But how? And why? What has advertising got to do with it? Crime doesn't want to advertise, far from it."

"I don't know," said Wimsey, suddenly and softly. "I don't know." His nose twitched, rabbit-fashion. "Pymmy was saying only this morning that to reach the largest number of people all over the country in the shortest possible time, there was nothing like a press campaign. Wait a second, Polly—I'm not sure that you haven't said something useful and important."

"Everything I say is useful and important. Think it over while I go and tell Mrs. Gunner how to cook turbot."

"And the funny thing is," said Parker, "she seems to like telling Mrs. Gunner how to cook turbot. We could perfectly well afford more servants——"

"My dear old boy," said Wimsey. "Servants are the devil. I don't count my man Bunter, because he's exceptional, but it's a treat to Polly to kick the whole boiling out of the house at night. Don't you worry. When she wants servants, she'll ask for them."

"I admit," said Parker, "I was glad myself when the kids were old enough to dispense with a resident nurse. But look here, Peter, it seems to me you'll be wanting a resident nurse yourself, if you want to avoid nasty accidents."

"That's just it. Here I am. Why? What are they keeping me for? Something unusually nasty?"

Parker moved quietly across to the window and peered out from a little gap in the short net blind.

"He's there, I think. A repellent-looking young man in a check cap, playing with a Yo-Yo on the opposite pavement. Playing darned well, too, with a circle of admiring kids round him. What a grand excuse for loitering. There he goes. Three-leaf clover, over the falls, non-stop lift, round the world. Quite masterly. I must tell Mary to have a look at him, and take a lesson. You'd better sleep here to-night, old man."

"Thanks. I think I will."

"And stop away from the office to-morrow."

"I should, in any case. I've got to play in a cricket match at Brotherhood's. Their place is down at Romford."

"Cricket match be damned. I don't know, though. It's nice and public. Provided the fast bowler doesn't knock you out with a swift ball, it may be as safe as anywhere else. How are you going?"

"Office charabanc."

"Good. I'll see you round to the starting-point."

Wimsey nodded. Nothing further was said about dope or danger until supper was over and Parker had departed for the Yelverton Arms. Then Wimsey gathered up a calendar, the telephone directory, a copy of the official report on the volume retrieved from Mountjoy's flat, a scribbling-block and a pencil, and curled himself up on the couch with a pipe.

"You don't mind, do you, Polly? I want to brood."

Lady Mary dropped a kiss on the top of his head.

"Brood on, old thing. I won't disturb you. I'm going up to the nursery. And if the telephone rings, take care it isn't the mysterious summons to the lonely warehouse by the river, or the bogus call to Scotland Yard."

"All right. And if the door-bell rings, beware of the disguised gas-inspector and the plain-clothes cop without a warrant-card. I need scarcely warn you against the golden-haired girl in distress, the slit-eyed Chink or the distinguished grey-haired man wearing the ribbon of some foreign order."

He brooded.

He took from his pocket-book the paper he had removed, weeks earlier, from Victor Dean's desk, and compared the dates with the calendar. They were all Tuesdays. After a little further cogitation, he added the date of the previous Tuesday week, the day when Miss Vavasour called at the office and Tallboy had borrowed his pen to address a letter to Old Broad Street. To this date he appended the initial "T". Then, his mind working slowly backwards, he remembered that he had come to Pym's on a Tuesday, and that Tallboy had come into the typists' room for a stamp. Miss Rossiter had read out the name of his addressee—what had the initial been? "K", of course. He wrote this down also. Then, with rather more hesitation, he looked up the date of the Tuesday preceding Mr. Puncheon's historic adventure at the White Swan, and wrote "W?"

So far, so good. But from "K" to "T" there were nine letters—there had not been nine weeks. Nor should "W" have come between "K" and "T". What was the rule governing the letter-sequence? He drew thoughtfully at his pipe and sank into a reverie that was almost a pipe-dream, till he was aroused by a very distinct sound of yells and conflict from the floor above. Presently the door opened and his sister appeared, rather flushed.

"I'm sorry, Peter. Did you hear the row? Your young namesake was being naughty. He heard Uncle Peter's voice and refused to stay in bed. He wants to come down and see you."

"Very flattering," said Wimsey.

"But very exhausting," said Mary. "I do hate disciplining people. Why shouldn't he see his uncle? Why should uncle be busy with dull detective business when his nephew is so much more interesting?"

"Quite so," said Wimsey. "I have often asked myself the same question. I gather that you hardened your heart."

"I compromised. I said that if he was a good boy and went back to bed, Uncle Peter might come up to say good-night to him."

"And has he been a good boy?"

"Yes. In the end. That is to say, he is in bed. At least, he was when I came down."

"Very well," said Wimsey, putting down his paraphernalia. "Then I will be a good uncle."

He mounted the stairs obediently and found Peterkin, aged three, technically in bed. That is to say, he was sitting bolt upright with the blankets cast off, roaring lustily.

"Hullo!" said Wimsey, shocked.

The roaring ceased.

"What is all this?" Wimsey traced the course of a fat down-rolling drop with a reproachful finger. "Tears, idle tears? Great Scott!"

"Uncle Peter! I got a naeroplane." Peterkin tugged violently at the sleeve of a suddenly unresponsive uncle. "Look at my naeroplane, Uncle! Naeroplane, naeroplane!"

"I beg your pardon, old chap," said Wimsey, recollecting himself. "I wasn't thinking. It's a beautiful aeroplane. Does it fly? . . . Hi! you needn't get up and show me now. I'll take your word for it."

"Mummie make it fly."

It flew very competently, affecting a neat landing on the chest of drawers. Wimsey watched it with vague eyes.

"Uncle Peter!"

"Yes, son, it's splendid. Listen, would you like a speed-boat?"

"What's peed-boat?"

"A boat that will run in the water—chuff, chuff—like that."

"Will it float in my barf?"

"Yes, of course. It'll sail right across the Round Pond."

Peterkin considered.

"Could I have it in my barf wiv' me?"

"Certainly, if Mummie says so."

"I'd like a boat in my barf."

"You shall have one, old man."

"When, now?"

"To-morrow."

"Weally to-mowwow?"

"Yes, promise."

"Say thank-you, Uncle Peter."

"Fank-you, Uncle Peter. Will it be to-mowwow soon?"

"Yes, if you lie down now and go to sleep."

Peterkin, who was a practically-minded child, shut his eyes instantly, wriggled under the bed-clothes, and was promptly tucked in by a firm hand.

"Really, Peter, you shouldn't bribe him to go to sleep. How about my discipline?"

"Discipline be blowed," said Peter, at the door.

"Uncle!"

"Good-night!"

"Is it to-mowwow yet?"

"Not yet. Go to sleep. You can't have to-morrow till you've been to sleep."

"Why not?"

"It's one of the rules."

"Oh! I'm asleep now, Uncle Peter."

"Good. Stick to it." Wimsey pulled his sister out after him and shut the nursery door.

"Polly, I'll never say kids are a nuisance again."

"What's up? I can see you're simply bursting with something."

"I've got it! Tears, idle Tears. That kid deserves fifty speed-boats as a reward for howling."

"Oh, dear!"

"I couldn't tell him that, though, could I? Come downstairs, and I'll show you something."

He dragged Mary at full speed into the sitting-room, took up his list of dates and jabbed at it with a jubilant pencil.

"See that date? That's the Tuesday before the Friday on which coke was being served out at the White Swan. On that Tuesday, the Nutrax headline was finally passed for the following Friday. And what," asked Wimsey, rhetorically, "was that headline?"

"I haven't the faintest idea. I never read advertisements."

"You should have been smothered at birth. The headline was, 'Why Blame the Woman?' You will note that it begins with a 'W'. White Swan also begins with a 'W'. Got that?"

"I think so. It seems fairly simple."

"Just so. Now on this date, the Nutrax headline was 'Tears, idle Tears'—a quotation from the poets."

"I follow you so far."

"This is the date on which the headline was passed for press, you understand."

"Yes."

"Also a Tuesday."

"I have grasped that."

"On that same Tuesday, Mr. Tallboy, who is group-manager for Nutrax, wrote a letter addressed to 'T. Smith, Esq.' You get that?"

"Yes."

"Very good. That advertisement appeared on a Friday."

"Are you trying to explain that these advertisements are all passed for press on a Tuesday and all appear on a Friday?"

"Exactly."

"Then why not say so, instead of continually repeating yourself?"

"All right. But now perpend. Mr. Tallboy has a habit of sending letters on a Tuesday, addressed to a Mr. Smith—who, by the way, doesn't exist."

"I know. You told us all about that. Mr. T. Smith is Mr. Cummings; only Mr. Cummings denies it."

"He denies it, said the King. Leave out that part. The point is that Mr. Smith isn't always Mr. T. Smith. Sometimes he's other kinds of Mr. Smith. But on the day that the Nutrax headline began with a 'T', Mr. Smith was Mr. T. Smith."

"And what sort of Mr. Smith was he on the day that the Nutrax headline began with a 'W'?"

"Unfortunately I don't know. But I can guess that he was Mr. W. Smith. In any case, on this date here, which was the day I came to Pym's, the Nutrax headline was 'Kittle Cattle'. On that day, Mr. Smith——"

"Stop! I can guess this one. He was Mr. K. Smith."

"He was. Kenneth, perhaps, or Kirkpatrick, or Killarney. Killarney Smith would be a lovely name."

"And was coke distributed the next Friday from the King's Head?"

"I'm betting my boots it was. What do you think of that?"

"I think you want a little more evidence on that point. You don't seem to have any instance where you can point to the initial, the headline and the pub all together."

"That's the weak point," confessed Wimsey. "But look here. This Tuesday which I now write down is the date on which the great Nutrax row occurred, and the headline was altered at the last moment on Thursday night. On the Friday of that week, something went wrong with the supply of dope to Major Milligan. It never turned up."

"Peter, I do believe you've got hold of something."

"Do you, Polly? Well, so do I. But I wasn't sure if it would sound plausible to anybody but me. And, look here! I remember another day." Wimsey began to laugh. "I forget which date it was, but the headline was simply a blank line and an exclamation mark, and Tallboy was horribly peeved about it. I wonder what they did that week. I should think they took the initial of the sub-head. What a joke!"

"But how is it worked, Peter?"

"Well, I don't know the details, but I imagine it's done this way. On the Tuesday, as soon as the headline is decided, Tallboy sends an envelope to Cummings' shop addressed to A. Smith, Esq., or B. Smith, Esq., according to the initial of the headline. Cummings looks at it, snorts at it and hands it back to the postman. Then he informs the head distributing agent, or agents. I don't know how. Possibly he advertises too, because the great point of this scheme, as I see it, is to have as little contact as possible between the various agents. The stuff is run across on Thursday, and the agent meets it and packets it up as bicarbonate of soda, or something equally harmless. Then he gets the London telephone directory and looks up the next pub on the list whose name begins with the letter of which Cummings has advised him. As soon as the pub opens on Friday morning, he is there. The retail agents, if we may call them so, have meanwhile consulted the *Morning Star* and the telephone directory. They hasten to the pub and the packets are passed to them. The late Mr. Mountjoy must have been one of these gentry."

"How does the wholesaler recognise the retailer?"

"There must be some code or other, and our battered friend Hector Puncheon must have given the code-word by accident. We must ask about that. He's a *Morning Star* man, and it may be something to do with the *Morning Star*. Mountjoy, by the way, evidently believed in being early on the job, because he seems to have made a practice of getting his copy of the paper the second it was off the machine, which accounts for his having been in full working order at 4.30 a.m. in Covent Garden, and hanging round Fleet Street again in the small hours of the following Friday. He must have given the code-signal, whatever it was; Puncheon may remember about it. After that, he would make his supply up into smaller packets (hence his supply of cigarette-papers) and proceed with the distribution according to his own taste and fancy. Of course, there are a lot of things we don't know yet. How the payments are made, for instance. Puncheon wasn't asked for money. Tallboy seems to have got his particular share in currency notes. But that's a detail. The ingenuity of the thing is that the stuff is never distributed twice from the same place. No wonder Charles had difficulties with it. By the way, I've sent him to the wrong place to-night, poor devil. How he must be cursing me!"

Mr. Parker cursed solidly enough on his return.

"It's entirely my fault," said Wimsey, blithely. "I sent you to the Yelverton Arms. You ought to have been at the Anchor or the Antelope. But we'll pull it off next week—if we live so long."

"If," said Parker, seriously, "we live so long."

CHAPTER XVIII

Unexpected Conclusion of a Cricket Match

THE PARTY FROM Pym's filled a large charabanc; in addition, a number of people attended in their own Austins. It was a two-innings match, starting at 10 a.m., and Mr. Pym liked to see it well attended. A skeleton staff was left to hold the fort at the office during the Saturday morning, and it was expected that as many of them as possible would trundle down to Romford by the afternoon train. Mr. Death Bredon, escorted by Lady Mary and Chief Inspector Parker, was one of the last to scramble into the charabanc.

The firm of Brotherhood believed in ideal conditions for their staff. It was their pet form of practical Christianity; in addition to which, it looked very well in their advertising literature and was a formidable weapon against the trade unions. Not, of course, that Brotherhood's had the slightest objection to trade unions as such. They had merely discovered that comfortable and well-fed people are constitutionally disinclined for united action of any sort—a fact which explains the asinine meekness of the income-tax payer.

In Brotherhood's régime of bread and circuses, organised games naturally played a large part. From the pavilion overlooking the spacious cricket-field floated superbly a crimson flag, embroidered with the Brotherhood trade-mark of two clasped hands. The same device adorned the crimson blazers and caps of Brotherhood's cricket eleven. By contrast, the eleven advertising cricketers were but a poor advertisement for themselves. Mr. Bredon was, indeed, a bright spot on the landscape, for his flannels were faultless, while his Balliol blazer, though ancient, carried with it an air of authenticity. Mr. Ingleby also was correct though a trifle shabby. Mr. Hankin, beautifully laundered, had rather spoilt his general effect by a brown felt hat, while Mr. Tallboy, irreproachable in other respects, had an unfortunate tendency to come apart at the waist, for which his tailor and shirt-maker were, no doubt, jointly responsible. The dress of the remainder varied in combining white flannels with brown shoes, white shoes with the wrong sort of shirt, tweed coats with white linen hats, down to the disgraceful exhibition of Mr. Miller, who, disdaining to put himself out for a mere game, affronted the sight in grey flannel trousers, a striped shirt and braces.

The day began badly with Mr. Tallboy's having lost his lucky half-crown and with Mr. Copley's observing, offensively, that perhaps Mr. Tallboy would prefer to toss with a pound-note. This flustered Mr. Tallboy. Brotherhood's won the toss and elected to go in first. Mr. Tallboy, still flustered, arranged his field, forgetting in his agitation Mr. Hankin's preference for mid-on and placing him at cover-point. By the time this error was remedied, it was discovered that Mr. Haagedorn had omitted to bring his wicket-keeper's gloves, and a pair had to be borrowed from the pavilion. Mr. Tallboy then realised that he had put on his two fast bowlers together. He remedied this by recalling Mr. Wedderburn from the deep field to bowl his slow "spinners", and dismissing

Mr. Barrow in favour of Mr. Beeseley. This offended Mr. Barrow, who retired in dudgeon to the remotest part of the field and appeared to go to sleep.

"What's all the delay about?" demanded Mr. Copley.

Mr. Willis said he thought Mr. Tallboy must have got a little confused about the bowling order.

"Lack of organisation," said Mr. Copley. "He should make out a list and stick to it."

The first Brotherhood innings passed off rather uneventfully. Mr. Miller missed two easy catches and Mr. Barrow, to show his resentment at the placing of the field, let a really quite ordinary ball go to the boundary instead of running after it. The eldest Mr. Brotherhood, a spry old gentleman of seventy-five, came doddering cheerfully round from the pavilion and sat down to make himself agreeable to Mr. Armstrong. He did this by indulging in reminiscences of all the big cricket matches he had ever seen in a long life, and as he had been devoted to the game since his boyhood, and had never missed a game of any importance, this took him some time and was excessively wearisome to Mr. Armstrong, who thought cricket a bore and only attended the staff match out of compliment to Mr. Pym's prejudices. Mr. Pym, whose enthusiasm was only equalled by his ignorance of the game, applauded bad strokes and good strokes indifferently.

Eventually the Brotherhoods were dismissed for 155, and the Pym Eleven gathered themselves together from the four corners of the field; Messrs. Garrett and Barrow, both rather ill-tempered, to buckle on their pads, and the remainder of the team to mingle with the spectators. Mr. Bredon, languid in movement but cheerful, laid himself down at Miss Meteyard's feet, while Mr. Tallboy was collared by the aged Mr. Brotherhood, thus releasing Mr. Armstrong, who promptly accepted the invitation of a younger Brotherhood to inspect a new piece of machinery.

The innings opened briskly. Mr. Barrow, who was rather a showy bat, though temperamental, took the bowling at the factory end of the pitch and cheered the spirits of his side by producing a couple of twos in the first over. Mr. Garrett, canny and cautious, stonewalled perseveringly through five balls of the following over and then cut the leather through the slips for a useful three. A single off the next ball brought the bowling back to Mr. Barrow, who, having started favourably, exhibited a happy superiority complex and settled down to make runs. Mr. Tallboy breathed a sigh of relief. Mr. Barrow, confident and successful, could always be relied upon for some good work; Mr. Barrow, put off his stroke by a narrowly missed catch, or the sun in his eyes, or a figure crossing the screens, was apt to become defeatist and unreliable. The score mounted blithely to thirty. At this point, Brotherhood's captain, seeing that the batsmen had taken the measure of the bowling, took off the man at the factory end and substituted a short, pugnacious-looking person with a scowl, at sight of whom Mr. Tallboy quaked again.

"They're putting on Simmonds very early," he said. "I only hope nobody gets hurt."

"Is this their demon bowler?" inquired Bredon, seeing the wicket-keeper hurriedly retire to a respectful distance from the wicket.

Tallboy nodded. The ferocious Simmonds wetted his fingers greedily, pulled his cap fiercely over his eyes, set his teeth in a snarl of hatred, charged like a bull and released the ball with the velocity of a 9-inch shell in Mr. Barrow's direction.

Like most fast bowlers, Simmonds was a little erratic in the matter of length. His first missile pitched short, rocketed up like a pheasant, whizzed past Mr. Barrow's ear and was adroitly fielded by long-stop, a man with a phlegmatic countenance and hands of leather. The next two went wide. The fourth was pitched straight and with a good length. Mr. Barrow tackled it courageously. The impact affected him like an electric shock; he blinked and shook his fingers, as though not quite sure whether his bones were still intact. The fifth was more manageable; he smote it good and hard and ran.

"Again!" yelled Mr. Garrett, already half-way down the pitch for the second time. Mr. Barrow accordingly ran and once again stood ready for the onslaught. It came; it ran up his bat like a squirrel, caught him viciously on the knuckle and glanced off sharply, offering a chance to point, who, very fortunately, fumbled it. The field crossed over, and Mr. Barrow was able to stand aside and nurse his injuries.

Mr. Garrett, pursuing a policy of dogged-does-it, proceeded systematically to wear down the bowling by blocking the first four balls of the next over. The fifth produced two runs; the sixth, which was of much the same calibre, he contented himself with blocking again.

"I don't like this slow-motion cricket," complained the aged Mr. Brotherhood. "When I was a young man——"

Mr. Tallboy shook his head. He knew very well that Mr. Garrett suffered from a certain timidity when facing fast bowling. He knew, too, that Garrett had some justification, because he wore spectacles. But he knew equally well what Mr. Barrow would think about it.

Mr. Barrow, irritated, faced the redoubtable Simmonds with a sense of injury. The first ball was harmless and useless; the second was a stinger, but the third he could hit and did. He whacked it away lustily to the boundary for four, amid loud cheers. The next kept out of the wicket only by the grace of God, but the sixth he contrived to hook round to leg for a single. After which, he adopted Mr. Garrett's tactics, stonewalled through an entire over, and left Mr. Garrett to face the demon.

Mr. Garrett did his best. But the first ball rose perpendicularly under his chin and unnerved him. The second came to earth about half-way down the pitch and bumped perilously over his head. The third, pitched rather longer, seemed to shriek as it rushed for him. He stepped out, lost heart, flinched and was bowled as clean as a whistle.

"Dear, dear!" said Mr. Hankin. "It seems that it is up to me." He adjusted his pads and blinked a little. Mr. Garrett retired gloomily to the pavilion. Mr. Hankin, with exasperating slowness, minced his way to the crease. He had his own methods of dealing with demon bowlers and was not alarmed. He patted the turf lengthily, asked three times for middle and off, adjusted his hat, requested that a screen might be shifted, asked for middle and off again and faced Mr. Simmonds with an agreeable smile and a very straight bat, left elbow well forward and his feet correctly placed. The result was that Simmonds, made nervous, bowled an atrocious wide, which went to the boundary, and followed it up by two mild balls of poor length, which Mr. Hankin very properly punished. This behaviour cheered Mr. Barrow and steadied him. He hit out with confidence, and the score mounted to fifty. The applause had scarcely subsided when Mr. Hankin, stepping briskly across the wicket to a slow and inoffensive-looking ball pitched rather wide to the off, found it unaccountably twist from under his bat and strike him on the left thigh. The wicket-keeper flung up his hands in appeal.

"Out!" said the umpire.

Mr. Hankin withered him with a look and stalked very slowly and stiffly from the field, to be greeted by a chorus of: "Bad luck, indeed, sir!"

"It *was* bad luck," replied Mr. Hankin. "I am surprised at Mr. Grimbold." (Mr. Grimbold was the umpire, an elderly and impassive man from Pym's Outdoor Publicity Department.) "The ball was an atrocious wide. It could never have come anywhere near the wicket."

"It had a bit of a break on it," suggested Mr. Tallboy.

"It certainly had a break on it," admitted Mr. Hankin, "but it would have gone wide nevertheless. I don't think anybody can accuse me of being unsporting, and if I *had* been leg before, I should be the first to admit it. Did you see it, Mr. Brotherhood?"

"Oh, I saw it all right," said the old gentleman, with a chuckle.

"I put it to you," said Mr. Hankin, "whether I was l.b.w. or not."

"Of course not," said Mr. Brotherhood. "Nobody ever is. I have attended cricket matches now for sixty years, for sixty years, my dear sir, and that goes back to a time before you were born or thought of, and I've never yet known anybody to be really out l.b.w.—according to himself, that is." He chuckled again. "I remember in 1892 . . ."

"Well, sir," said Mr. Hankin, "I must defer to your experienced judgment. I think I will have a pipe." He wandered away and sat down by Mr. Pym. "Poor old Brotherhood," he said, "is getting very old and doddery. Very doddery indeed. I doubt if we shall see him here another year. That was a very unfortunate decision of Grimbold's. Of course it is easy to be deceived in these matters, but you could see for yourself that I was no more l.b.w. than he was himself. Very vexing, when I had just settled down nicely."

"Shocking luck," agreed Mr. Pym, cheerfully. "There's Ingleby going in. I always like to watch him. He puts up a very good show, doesn't he, as a rule?"

"No style," said Mr. Hankin, morosely.

"Hasn't he?" said Mr. Pym, placidly. "You know best about that, Hankin. But he always hits out. I like to see a batsman hitting out, you know. There! Good shot! Good shot! Oh, dear!"

For Mr. Ingleby, hitting out a little too vigorously, was caught at cover-point and came galloping out rather faster than he had gone in.

"Quack, quack," said Mr. Bredon.

Mr. Ingleby threw his bat at Mr. Bredon, and Mr. Tallboy, hurriedly muttering, "Bad luck!" went to take his place.

"What a nuisance," said Miss Rossiter, soothingly. "I think it was very brave of you to hit it at all. It was a frightfully fast one."

"Um!" said Mr. Ingleby.

The dismissal of Mr. Ingleby had been the redoubtable Simmonds' swan-song. Having exhausted himself by his own ferocity, he lost his pace and became more erratic than usual, and was taken off, after an expensive over, in favour of a gentleman who bowled leg-breaks. To him, Mr. Barrow fell a victim, and retired covered with glory, with a score of twenty-seven. His place was taken by Mr. Pinchley, who departed, waving a jubilant hand and declaring his intention of whacking hell out of them.

Mr. Pinchley indulged in no antics of crease-patting or taking middle. He strode vigorously to his post, raised his bat shoulder-high and stood four-square to whatever it might please Heaven to send him. Four times did he loft the ball sky-high to the boundary. Then he fell into the hands of the Philistine with the leg-break and lofted the ball into the greedy hands of the wicket-keeper.

"Short and sweet," said Mr. Pinchley, returning with his ruddy face all grins.

"Four fours are very useful," said Mr. Bredon, kindly.

"Well, that's what I say," said Mr. Pinchley. "Make 'em quick and keep things going, that's my idea of cricket. I can't stand all this pottering and poking about."

This observation was directed at Mr. Miller, whose cricket was of the pains-taking sort. A tedious period followed, during which the score slowly mounted to 83, when Mr. Tallboy, stepping back a little inconsiderately to a full-pitch, slipped on the dry turf and sat down on his wicket.

Within the next five minutes Mr. Miller, lumbering heavily down the pitch in gallant response to an impossible call by Mr. Beeseley, was run out, after compiling a laborious 12. Mr. Bredon, pacing serenely to the wicket, took counsel with himself. He reminded himself that he was still, in the eyes of Pym's and Brotherhood's at any rate, Mr. Death Bredon of Pym's. A quiet and unobtrusive mediocrity, he decided, must be his aim. Nothing that could recall the Peter Wimsey of twenty years back, making two centuries in successive innings for Oxford. No fancy cuts. Nothing remarkable. On the other hand, he had claimed to be a cricketer. He must not make a public exhibition of incompetence. He decided to make twenty runs, not more and, if possible, not less.

He might have made his mind easy; the opportunity was not vouchsafed him. Before he had collected more than two threes and a couple of demure singles, Mr. Beeseley had paid the penalty of rashness and been caught at mid-on. Mr. Haagedorn, with no pretensions to being a batsman, survived one over and was then spread-eagled without remorse or question. Mr. Wedderburn, essaying to cut a twisty one which he would have done well to leave alone, tipped the ball into the wicket-keeper's gloves and Pym's were disposed of for 99, Mr. Bredon having the satisfaction of carrying out his bat for 14.

"Well played all," said Mr. Pym. "One or two people had bad luck, but of course, that's all in the game. We must try and do better after lunch."

"There's one thing," observed Mr. Armstrong, confidently to Mr. Miller, "they always do one very well. Best part of the day, to my thinking."

Mr. Ingleby made much the same remark to Mr. Bredon. "By the way," he added, "Tallboy's looking pretty rotten."

"Yes, and he's got a flask with him," put in Mr. Garrett, who sat beside them.

"He's all right," said Ingleby. "I will say for Tallboy, he can carry his load. He's much better off with a flask than with this foul Sparkling Pompayne. All wind. For God's sake, you fellows, leave it alone."

"Something's making Tallboy bad-tempered, though," said Garrett. "I don't understand him; he seems to have gone all to pieces lately, ever since that imbecile row with Copley."

Mr. Bredon said nothing to all this. His mind was not easy. He felt as though thunder was piling up somewhere and was not quite sure whether he was fated to feel or to ride the storm. He turned to Simmonds the demon bowler, who was seated on his left, and plunged into cricket talk.

"What's the matter with our Miss Meteyard to-day?" inquired Mrs. Johnson, archly, across the visitors' table. "You're very silent."

"I've got a headache. It's very hot. I think it's going to thunder."

"Surely not," said Miss Parton. "It's a beautiful clear day."

"*I* believe," asserted Mrs. Johnson, following Miss Meteyard's gloomy gaze, "*I* believe she's more interested in the *other* table. Now, Miss Meteyard, confess, who is it? Mr. Ingleby? I hope it's not my favourite Mr. Bredon. I simply *can't* have anybody coming between us, you know."

The joke about Mr. Bredon's reputed passion for Mrs. Johnson had become a little stale, and Miss Meteyard received it coldly.

"She's offended," declared Mrs. Johnson. "I believe it *is* Mr. Bredon. She's blushing! When are we to offer our congratulations, Miss Meteyard?"

"Do you," demanded Miss Meteyard, in a suddenly harsh and resonant voice, "recollect the old lady's advice to the bright young man?"

"Why, I can't say that I do. What was it?"

"Some people can be funny without being vulgar, and some can be both funny and vulgar. I should recommend you to be either the one or the other."

"Oh, really?" said Mrs. Johnson, vaguely. After a moment's reflection she gathered the sense of the ancient gibe and said, "Oh, really!" again, with a heightened colour. "Dear me, how rude we can be when we try. I do hate a person who can't take a joke."

Brotherhood's second innings brought some balm to the feelings of the Pymmites. Whether it was the Sparkling Pompayne, or whether it was the heat ("I do believe you were right about the thunder," remarked Miss Parton), more than one of their batsmen found his eye a little out and his energy less than it had been. Only one man ever looked really dangerous, and this was a tall, dour-faced person with whipcord wrists and a Yorkshire accent, whom no bowling seemed to daunt, and who had a nasty knack of driving extremely hard through gaps in the field. This infuriating man settled down grimly and knocked up a score of fifty-eight, amid the frenzied applause of his side. It was not only his actual score that was formidable, but the extreme exhaustion induced in the field.

"I've had—too much—gas," panted Ingleby, returning past Garrett after a mad gallop to the boundary, "and this blighter looks like staying till Christmas."

"Look here, Tallboy," said Mr. Bredon, as they crossed at the next over. "Keep your eye on the little fat fellow at the other end. He's getting pumped. If this Yorkshire tyke works him like this, something will happen."

It did happen in the next over. The slogger smote a vigorous ball from the factory end, a little too high for a safe boundary, but an almost certain three. He galloped and the fat man galloped. The ball was racing over the grass, and Tallboy racing to intercept it, as they galloped back.

"Come on!" cried the Yorkshireman, already half way down the pitch for the third time. But Fatty was winded; a glance behind showed him Tallboy stooping to the ball. He gasped "No!" and abode, like Dan, in his breaches. The other saw what was happening and turned in his tracks. Tallboy, disregarding the frantic signals of Haagedorn and Garrett, became inspired. He threw from where he stood, not to Garrett, but point-blank at the open wicket. The ball sang through the air and spread-eagled the Yorkshireman's stumps while he was still a yard from the crease, while the batsman, making a frantic attempt to cover himself, flung his bat from his hand and fell prostrate.

"Oh, pretty!" exulted old Mr. Brotherhood. "Oh, well played, sir, well played!"

"He must have taken marvellous aim," said Miss Parton.

"What's the matter with you, Bredon?" asked Ingleby, as the team lolled thankfully on the pitch to await the next man in. "You're looking very white. Touch of the sun?"

"Too much light in my eyes," said Mr. Bredon.

"Well, take it easy," advised Mr. Ingleby. "We shan't have much trouble with them now. Tallboy's a hero. Good luck to him."

Mr. Bredon experienced a slight qualm of nausea.

The remainder of the Brotherhood combination achieved nothing very remarkable, and the side was eventually got out for 114. At 4 o'clock, on a fiery wicket, Mr. Tallboy again sent out his batsmen, faced with the formidable task of making 171 to win.

At 5.30, the thing still looked almost feasible, four wickets having fallen for 79. Then Mr. Tallboy, endeavouring to squeeze a run where there was no run to be got, was run out for 7, and immediately afterwards, the brawny Mr. Pinchley, disregarding his captain's frantic appeals for care, chopped his first ball neatly into the hands of point. The rot had set in. Mr. Miller, having conscientiously blocked through two overs, while Mr. Beeseley added a hard-won 6 to the score, lost his off stump to the gentleman with the leg-break. With the score at 92 by the addition of a couple of byes, and three men to bat, including the well-meaning but inadequate Mr. Haagedorn, defeat appeared to be unavoidable.

"Well," said Mr. Copley, morosely, "it's better than last year. They beat us then by about seven wickets. Am I right, Mr. Tallboy?"

"No," said Mr. Tallboy.

"I beg your pardon, I'm sure," said Mr. Copley, "perhaps it was the year before. You should know, for I believe you were the captain on both occasions."

Mr. Tallboy vouchsafed no statistics, merely saying to Mr. Bredon:

"They draw stumps at 6.30; try and stick it out till then if you can."

Mr. Bredon nodded. The advice suited him excellently. A nice, quiet, defensive game was exactly the game least characteristic of Peter Wimsey. He sauntered tediously to the crease, expended some valuable moments in arranging himself, and faced the bowling with an expression of bland expectation.

All would probably have gone according to calculation, but for the circumstance that the bowler at the garden end of the field was a man with an idiosyncrasy. He started his run from a point in the dim, blue distance, accelerated furiously to within a yard of the wicket, stopped, hopped, and with an action suggestive of a Catherine-wheel, delivered a medium-length, medium-paced, sound straight ball of uninspired but irreproachable accuracy. In executing this manoeuvre for the twenty-second time, his foot slipped round about the stop-and-hop period, he staggered, performed a sort of splits and rose, limping and massaging his leg. As a result, he was taken off, and in his place Simmonds, the fast bowler, was put on.

The pitch was by this time not only fast, but bumpy. Mr. Simmonds' third delivery rose wickedly from a patch of bare earth and smote Mr. Bredon violently upon the elbow.

Nothing makes a man see red like a sharp rap over the funny-bone, and it was at this moment that Mr. Death Bredon suddenly and regrettably forgot himself. He forgot his caution and his rôle, and Mr. Miller's braces, and saw only the green turf and the Oval on a sunny day and the squat majesty of the gas-works. The next ball was another of Simmonds' murderous short-pitched bumpers, and Lord Peter Wimsey, opening up wrathful shoulders, strode out of his crease like the spirit of vengeance and whacked it to the wide. The next he clouted to leg for three, nearly braining square-leg and so flummoxing deep-field that he flung it back wildly to the wrong end, giving the Pymmites a fourth for an overthrow. Mr. Simmonds' last ball he treated with the contempt it deserved, snicking it as it whizzed past half a yard wide to leg and running a single.

He was now faced by the merchant with the off-break. The first two balls he treated carefully, then drove the third over the boundary for six. The fourth rose awkwardly and he killed it dead, but the fifth and sixth followed number three. A shout went up, headed by a shrill shriek of admiration from Miss Parton. Lord Peter grinned amiably and settled down to hit the bowling all round the wicket.

As Mr. Haagedorn panted in full career down the pitch, his lips moved in prayer. "Oh, Lord, oh, Lord! don't let me make a fool of myself!" A four was signalled and the field crossed over. He planted his bat grimly, determined to defend his wicket if he died for it. The ball came, pitched, rose, and he hammered it down remorselessly. One. If only he could stick out the other five. He dealt with another the same way. A measure of confidence came to him. He pulled the third ball round to leg and, to his own surprise, found himself running. As the batsmen passed in mid-career, he heard his colleague call: "Good man! Leave 'em to me now."

Mr. Haagedorn asked nothing better. He would run till he burst, or stand still till he hardened into marble, if only he could keep this miracle from coming to an end. He was a poor bat, but a cricketer. Wimsey ended the over with a well-placed three, which left him still in possession of the bowling. He walked down the pitch and Haagedorn came to meet him.

"I'll take everything I can," said Wimsey, "but if anything comes to you, block it. Don't bother about runs. I'll see to them."

"Yes, sir," said Mr. Haagedorn, fervently. "I'll do anything you say. Keep it up, sir, only keep it up."

"All right," said Wimsey. "We'll beat the b——s yet. Don't be afraid of them. You're doing exactly right."

Six balls later, Mr. Simmonds, having been hit to the boundary four times running, was removed, as being too expensive a luxury. He was replaced by a gentleman who was known at Brotherhood's as "Spinner". Wimsey received him with enthusiasm, cutting him consistently and successfully to the off, till Brotherhood's captain moved up his fieldsmen and concentrated them about the off-side of the wicket. Wimsey looked at this grouping with an indulgent smile, and placed the next six balls consistently and successfully to leg. When, in despair, they drew a close net of fielders all round him, he drove everything that was drivable straight down the pitch. The score mounted to 150.

The aged Mr. Brotherhood was bouncing in his seat. He was in an ecstasy. "Oh, pretty, sir! Again! Oh, well played, indeed, sir!" His white whiskers fluttered like flags. "Why on earth, Mr. Tallboy," he asked, severely, "did you send this man in ninth? He's a cricketer. He's the only cricketer among the whole damned lot of you. Oh, well placed!" as the ball skimmed neatly between two agitated fielders who nearly knocked their heads together in the effort to retrieve it. "Look at that! I'm always telling these lads that placing is nine-tenths of the game. This man knows it. Who is he?"

"He's a new member of the staff," said Tallboy, "he's a public-school man and he said he'd done a good deal of country-house cricket, but I hadn't an idea he could play like that. Great Scott!" He paused to applaud a particularly elegant cut. "I never saw anything like it."

"Didn't you?" said the old gentleman with asperity. "Well, now, I've been watching cricket, man and boy, for sixty years, and I've seen something very like it. Let me see, now. Before the War, that would be. Dear, dear—I sometimes think my memory for names isn't what it was, but I fancy that in the 'varsity match of 1910, or it might be 1911—no, not 1910, that was the year in which——"

His tinkling voice was drowned in a yell as the 170 appeared on the scoreboard.

"One more to win!" gasped Miss Rossiter. "Oh!" For at that moment, Mr. Haagedorn, left for an unfortunate moment to face the bowling, succumbed to a really nasty and almost unplayable ball which curled round his feet like a playful kitten and skittled his leg-stump.

Mr. Haagedorn came back almost in tears, and Mr. Wedderburn, quivering with nervousness, strode forward into the breach. He had nothing to do but to survive four balls and then, except for a miracle, the game was won. The first ball rose temptingly, a little short; he stepped out, missed it, and scuttled back to his crease only just in time. "Oh, be careful! Be careful!" moaned Miss Rossiter, and old Mr. Brotherhood swore. The next ball, Mr. Wedderburn contrived to poke a little way down the pitch. He wiped his forehead. The next was a spinner and, in trying to block it, he tipped it almost perpendicularly into the air. For a moment that seemed like hours the spectators saw the spinning ball—the outstretched hand—then the ball dropped, missed by a hair.

"I'm going to scream," announced Mrs. Johnson to nobody in particular. Mr. Wedderburn, now thoroughly unnerved, wiped his forehead again. Fortunately, the bowler was also unnerved. The ball slipped in his sweating fingers and went down short and rather wide.

"Leave it alone! Leave it alone!" shrieked Mr. Brotherhood, hammering with his stick. "Leave it alone, you numbskull! You imbecile! You——"

Mr. Wedderburn, who had lost his head completely, stepped across to it, raised his bat, made a wild swipe, which missed its object altogether, heard the smack of the leather as the ball went into the wicket-keeper's gloves, and did the only possible thing. He hurled himself bodily back and sat down on the crease, and as he fell he heard the snick of the flying bails.

"How's that?"

"Not out."

"The nincompoop! The fat-headed, thick-witted booby!" yelled Mr. Brotherhood. He danced with fury. "Might have thrown the match away! Thrown it away! That man's a fool. I say he's a fool. He's a fool, I tell you."

"Well, it's all right, Mr. Brotherhood," said Mr. Hankin, soothingly. "At least, it's all wrong for your side, I'm afraid."

"Our side be damned," ejaculated Mr. Brotherhood. "I'm here to see cricket played, not tiddlywinks. I don't care who wins or who loses, sir, provided they play the game. Now, then!"

With five minutes to go, Wimsey watched the first ball of the over come skimming down towards him. It was a beauty. It was jam. He smote it as Saul smote the Philistines. It soared away in a splendid parabola, struck the pavilion roof with a noise like the crack of doom, rattled down the galvanised iron roofing, bounced into the enclosure where the scorers were sitting and broke a bottle of lemonade. The match was won.

Mr. Bredon, lolloping back to the pavilion at 6.30 with 83 runs to his credit, found himself caught and cornered by the ancient Mr. Brotherhood.

"Beautifully played, sir, beautifully played indeed," said the old gentleman. "Pardon me—the name has just come to my recollection. Aren't you Wimsey of Balliol?"

Wimsey saw Tallboy, who was just ahead of them, falter in his stride and look round, with a face like death. He shook his head.

"My name's Bredon," he said.

"Bredon?" Mr. Brotherhood was plainly puzzled. "Bredon? I don't remember ever hearing the name. But didn't I see you play for Oxford in 1911? You have a late cut which is exceedingly characteristic, and I could have taken my oath that the last time I saw you play it was at Lord's in 1911, when you made 112. But I thought the name was Wimsey—Peter Wimsey of Balliol—Lord Peter Wimsey—and, now I come to think of it——"

At this very awkward moment an interruption occurred. Two men in police uniform were seen coming across the field, led by another man in mufti. They pushed their way through the crowd of cricketers and guests, and advanced upon the little group by the pavilion fence. One of the uniformed men touched Lord Peter on the arm.

"Are you Mr. Death Bredon?"

"I am," said Wimsey, in some astonishment.

"Then you'll have to come along with us. You're wanted on a charge of murder, and it is my duty to warn you that anything you say may be taken down and used in evidence."

"Murder?" ejaculated Wimsey. The policeman had spoken in unnecessarily loud and penetrating tones, and the whole crowd had frozen into fascinated attention. "Whose murder?"

"The murder of Miss Dian de Momerie."

"Good God!" said Wimsey. He looked round and saw that the man in mufti was Chief Inspector Parker, who gave a nod of confirmation.

"All right," said Wimsey. "I'll come with you, but I don't know a thing about it. You'd better come with me while I change."

He walked away between the two officers. Mr. Brotherhood detained Parker as he was about to follow them.

"You say that man's called Bredon?"

"Yes, sir," replied Parker, with emphasis. "Bredon is his name. Mister Death Bredon."

"And you want him for murder?"

"For murder of a young woman, sir. Very brutal business."

"Well," said the old gentleman, "you surprise me. Are you sure you've got the right man?"

"Dead sure, sir. Well known to the police."

Mr. Brotherhood shook his head.

"Well," he said again, "his name may be Bredon. But he's innocent. Innocent as day, my good fellow. Did you see him play? He's a damned fine cricketer and he'd no more commit a murder than I would."

"That's as may be, sir," said Inspector Parker, stolidly.

"Just fancy that!" exclaimed Miss Rossiter. "I always *knew* there was *something*. Murder! Only think! We might all have had our throats cut! What do you think, Miss Meteyard? Were you surprised?"

"Yes, I was," said Miss Meteyard. "I was never so surprised in my life. Never!"

CHAPTER XIX

Duplicate Appearances of a Notorious Personality

"It's a fact, old man," said Parker, as the police-car sped Londonwards. "Dian de Momerie was found this morning with her throat cut in a wood near Maidenhead. Beside the body was a penny whistle and a few yards away there was a black mask caught on a bramble bush, as if someone had flung it away in a hurry. Inquiry among her friends elicited the fact that she had been going about at night with a masked harlequin, one Bredon by name. Strong suspicion was accordingly directed against the said Mr. Bredon, and Scotland Yard, acting with commendable promptitude, tracked the gentleman down to Romford and secured his person. Accused, when charged, replied——"

"I done it," said Wimsey, concluding the sentence for him. "And so, in a sense, I have, Charles. If that girl had never seen me, she'd be alive to-day."

"Well, she's no great loss," said the Chief Inspector, callously. "I'm beginning to see their game. They've not yet tumbled to the fact that you're not Death Bredon, and their idea is to put you on ice quietly till they've had time to settle up their affairs. They know you can't get bail on a murder charge."

"I see. Well, they're not quite as smart as I took them to be, or they'd have identified me long since. What happens next?"

"My idea is, that we take immediate steps to establish that Mr. Death Bredon and Lord Peter Wimsey are not one person but two. Is that chap still following us, Lumley?"

"Yes, sir."

"Take care he doesn't lose us in the traffic through Stratford. We're taking you to be questioned at Scotland Yard, and this josser shall see you safely into the building. I've arranged for some pressmen to be there, and we'll prime them with full details of the arrest and a lot about your hideous past. You, as Mr. Bredon, will then telephone to yourself, as Lord Peter Wimsey, to come and see you, with a view to arranging your defence. You will be smuggled out by the back entrance——"

"Disguised as a policeman? Oh, Charles, do let me be a policeman! I should adore it."

"Well, you're a bit under the regulation height, but we might be able to manage it; the helmet is very disguising. Anyway, you go home, or else to your club——"

"Not my club; I couldn't go to the Marlborough dressed up as a cop. Stop a bit, though—the Egotists'—I could go there. I've got a room there, and the Egotists don't care what one does. I like this. Go on."

"All right. You change there, and come down to the Yard in a temper, grumbling loudly about the trouble Mr. Bredon puts you to. You can give an interview about it if you like. Then you go home. The Sunday papers have a long bit about you, with photographs of you both."

"Splendid!"

"And on Monday you go before the magistrate and reserve your defence. It's a pity you can't be in court to hear yourself, but I'm afraid that's rather beyond our powers. Still, you can be seen immediately afterwards doing something conspicuous. You might ride in the Row and fall off——"

"No," said Wimsey. "I absolutely refuse to fall off. There are limits. I don't mind being run away with, and only saving myself by consummate horsemanship."

"Very well; I'll leave that to you. The point is that you must be in the papers."

"I will. I will advertise myself in some way. Advertising is my long suit. By the way, though, that'll mean I can't be at the office on Monday."

"Naturally."

"But that won't do. I've got to get that Whifflets campaign finished. Armstrong wants it particularly; I can't let him down. And besides, I've got interested in the thing."

Parker gazed at him in astonishment.

"Is it possible, Peter, that you are developing a kind of business morality?"

"Dash it all, Charles! You don't understand. It's a really big scheme. It'll be the biggest advertising stunt since the Mustard Club. But if that doesn't stir you, here's another thing. If I'm not at the office, you won't know the Nutrax headline next Tuesday, and won't catch the supplies being delivered."

"We can find that out without you, old man. It won't help us in the least to have you murdered, will it?"

"I suppose not. What I can't understand is, why they haven't murdered Tallboy yet."

"No; I can't understand that, either."

"I'll tell you what I think. They haven't matured their new plans yet. They're leaving him till after next Tuesday, because they've got to deliver one more consignment by the old route. They think that if I'm out of the way they can take the risk."

"Perhaps that's it. We must hope so, anyway. Well, here we are. Out you come, and try and look as much like a baffled villain as possible."

"Right-ho!" said Wimsey, distorting his face into a disagreeable sneer. The car turned into the entrance to New Scotland Yard and drew up. The sergeant got out; Wimsey followed, and, glancing round, observed three obvious newspaper men, hanging about the courtyard. Just as Parker emerged in his turn from the car, Wimsey tapped the sergeant lightly but efficiently under the chin and sent him staggering, tripped Parker neatly as he jumped from the running-board, and made for the gate like a hare. Two policemen and a reporter dived to intercept him; he dodged the bobbies, tackled the pressman and left him sprawling, swerved through the gateway and led a beautiful ding-dong chase down Whitehall. As he sped, he heard the shouts and the blowing of whistles. Foot-passengers joined in the pursuit; motorists accelerated to cut him off; people in buses crowded to the windows and stared. He slipped nimbly into the whirl of traffic, dodged three times round the Cenotaph, doubled back on the opposite side of the street and finally staged a magnificent and sensational capture in the middle of Trafalgar Square. Parker and Lumley came up panting.

" 'Ere 'e is, mister," said the man who had grabbed hold of him—a large and powerful navvy, with a bag of tools. " 'Ere 'e is. Wot's 'e done?"

"He's wanted for murder," announced Parker, briefly and loudly.

A murmur of admiration arose. Wimsey cast an offensively contemptuous glance at Sergeant Lumley.

"You ruddy bobbies are all too fat," he said. "You can't run."

"That's all right," said the sergeant, grimly. "Hold out your hands, my lad. We're taking no more chances."

"As you please, as you please. Are your hands clean? I don't want my cuffs dirtied.'"

"That's quite enough of it, my lad," said Parker, as the handcuffs snapped home, "we don't want any more trouble from you. Pass along there, please, pass along."

The little procession returned to Scotland Yard.

"Rather prettily done, I flatter myself," said Wimsey.

"Ar!" said Lumley, caressing his jaw. "You didn't need to have hit quite so hard, my lord."

"Verisimilitude," said Wimsey, "verisimilitude. You looked lovely as you went over."

"Ar!" said Sergeant Lumley.

A quarter of an hour later, a policeman whose uniform trousers were a little long for him and whose tunic was slightly too large in the waist, came out from Scotland Yard by a side-entrance, entered a car and was driven along Pall Mall to the discreet entrance of the Egotists' Club. Here he disappeared, and was never seen again, but presently an immaculately dressed gentleman, in evening dress and a silk hat, tripped out and stood on the steps to await a taxi. An elderly gentleman of military appearance stood beside him.

"You will forgive me, Colonel? I shall not be many minutes. This fellow Bredon is an abominable nuisance, but what can one do? I mean to say, one has to do something."

"Quite, quite," said the Colonel.

"I only hope this is the last time. If he's done what they say he has, it *will* be the last."

"Oh, quite," said the Colonel, "my dear Wimsey, quite."

The taxi appeared.

"Scotland Yard," said Wimsey, in very audible tones.

The taxi span away.

Miss Meteyard, skimming the papers in bed on Sunday morning, found her attention held by enormous headlines:

DE MOMERIE MURDER CASE ARREST

FAMOUS DUCAL HOUSE INVOLVED

INTERVIEW WITH LORD PETER WIMSEY

and again:

PENNY WHISTLE MURDER

ARREST OF MASKED MUMMER

CHIEF INSPECTOR PARKER INTERVIEWED

and once more:

WHISTLING HARLEQUIN CAUGHT

DESPERATE MÊLÉE IN WHITEHALL

PEER'S BROTHER VISITS SCOTLAND YARD

There followed lengthy and picturesque descriptions of the arrest; pictures of the place where the body was found; articles on Lord Peter Wimsey, on the Wimsey family, on their historic seat in Norfolk; on night-life in London and on penny whistles. The Duke of Denver had been interviewed, but refused to say anything; Lord Peter Wimsey, on the other hand, had said a good deal. Finally—and this puzzled Miss Meteyard very much—there was a photograph of Lord Peter and of Death Bredon standing side by side.

"It would be useless," said Lord Peter Wimsey in an interview, "in view of the remarkable resemblance between us, to deny that there is a relationship between this man and myself. In fact, he has on various occasions given trouble by impersonating me. If you were to see us together, you would notice that he is the darker of the two; there are also, of course, slight differences of feature; but, when we are seen separately, it is easy to mistake one of us for the other."

The Death Bredon of the photograph had certainly very much darker hair than the Peter Wimsey; his mouth was set in an unpleasing sneer, and he had that indefinable air of raffish insolence which is the hall-mark of the *chevalier d'industrie*. The newspaper article wandered on to give various unverifiable details.

"Bredon never went to a university, though he sometimes claims Oxford as his Alma Mater. He was educated at a public school in France where English sports are cultivated. He is a very fine natural cricketer, and was actually playing in a cricket match when arrested through the prompt and intelligent action of Chief Inspector Parker. Under various names he is well known in the night-clubs of London and Paris. He is said to have met the unfortunate girl, with whose murder he is charged, at the house of the late Major Milligan, who met his death two days ago by being run down by a lorry in Piccadilly. Following representations by the Wimsey family as to his mode of life, he had recently taken a post in a well-known commercial firm, and was supposed to have turned over a new leaf, but . . ."

And so on, and so forth.

Miss Meteyard sat for a long time with the papers strewn about her, smoking cigarettes, while her coffee got cold. Then she went and had a bath. She hoped it might clear her brain.

The excitement at Pym's on the Monday morning was indescribable. The Copy Department sat in the typists' room and did no work at all. Mr. Pym telephoned that he was unwell, and could not come to the office. Mr. Copley was so unnerved that he sat for three hours with a blank sheet of paper before him and then went out for a drink—a thing he had never done in his life. Mr. Willis seemed to be on the verge of nervous collapse. Mr. Ingleby laughed at his colleagues' agitation and said that it was a grand new experience for them all. Miss Parton burst into tears and Miss Rossiter proclaimed that she had always known it. Mr. Tallboy then enlivened the proceedings by fainting in Mr. Armstrong's room, thus giving Mrs. Johnson (who was hysterically inclined) useful occupation for half an hour. And Ginger Joe, of the red head and sunny temper, astonished his companions by having a fit of the sulks and then suddenly cuffing Bill's head for no reason whatever.

At 1 o'clock Miss Meteyard went out to lunch, and read in the *Evening Banner* that Mr. Death Bredon had appeared before the magistrates at 10 a.m. on the murder charge, and had reserved his defence. At 10.30, Lord Peter Wimsey (picturesquely described as "the second protagonist in this drama of dope and death") had, while riding in the Row, narrowly escaped injury, owing to his horse's having been startled by a back-fire from a racing car; the animal had bolted and only Lord Peter's consummate horsemanship had averted a nasty accident. There was a photograph of Mr. Bredon entering the court at Bow Street in a dark lounge suit and soft hat; there was also a photograph of Lord Peter Wimsey returning from his ride in neat breeches and boots and a bowler; there was, needless to say, no photograph of the metamorphosis of the one gentleman into another, behind the drawn blinds of a Daimler saloon while traversing the quiet squares north of Oxford Street.

On Monday night, Lord Peter Wimsey attended a performance of *Say When!* at the Frivolity, companioning a Royal personage.

On Tuesday morning, Mr. Willis arrived at the office late and in a great state of excited importance. He beamed at everybody, presented the typists' room with a four-pound box of chocolates and an iced cake, and informed the sympathetic Miss Parton that he was engaged to be married. At coffee-time, the name of the lady was known to be Miss Pamela Dean. At 11.30, it was divulged that the ceremony would take place at the earliest possible moment, and at 11.45 Miss Rossiter was collecting subscriptions for a wedding-present. By 2 o'clock, the subscribers were already divided into two opinionated and bitterly hostile factions, the one advocating the purchase of a handsome dining-room clock with Westminster chimes, and the other voting with passion for a silver-plated electric chafing-dish. At 4 o'clock, Mr. Jollop had turned down successively, "Sigh no more, Ladies", "O, Dry those Tears" and "Weeping Late and Weeping Early", which Mr. Toule had previously passed, and rejected with derision the proposed substitution of "If you have Tears", "O Say, What are You Weeping For?" and "A Poor Soul Sat Sighing". Mr. Ingleby, stimulated by a frantic request for new headlines, had flown into a passion because the *Dictionary of Quotations* had mysteriously disappeared. At 4.30, Miss Rossiter, feverishly typing, had completed "I Weep, I know not Why" and "In Silence and in Tears", while the distracted Mr. Ingleby was seriously contemplating "In that Deep Midnight of the Mind" (for, as he observed, "they'll never know it's Byron unless we tell them"), when Mr. Armstrong sent up word to say that he had persuaded Mr. Jollop to accept the copy of "O Say, What are you Weeping For?" combined with the headline "Flat, Stale and Unprofitable", and would Mr. Ingleby kindly verify at once whether it was "Flat, Stale" or "Stale, Flat", and get the thing re-typed and hand it to Mr. Tallboy immediately.

"Isn't Mr. Armstrong marvellous?" said Miss Rossiter. "He always finds a way out. Here you are, Mr. Ingleby—I've looked it up—it's 'Stale, Flat'. The first sentence will want altering, I suppose. You can't have this bit about 'Sometimes you are tempted to ask yourself, in the words of the old game', can you?"

"I suppose not," grunted Ingleby. "Better make it: 'Sometimes you may be tempted, like Hamlet, to exclaim'—then the whole quote—and go on, 'yet if anybody were to ask you why—' and join it up there. That'll do. Courses of the world, please, not curses."

"T'chk!" said Miss Rossiter.

"Here's Wedderburn, panting for his copy. How's Tallboy, Wedder?"

"Gone home," said Mr. Wedderburn. "He didn't want to go, but he's fagged out. He oughtn't to have come to the office at all to-day, but he would do it. Is this the thing?"

"Yes. They'll want a new sketch, of course."

"Of course," said Mr. Wedderburn, gloomily. "How they ever expect things to look right when they chop and change like this—— Oh, well! What is it? 'Picture of Hamlet'. Have the Studio got a reference for Hamlet?"

"Of course not; they never have anything. Who does these sketches? Pickering? You'd better take him my illustrated Shakespeare with my compliments, and request him not to cover it with Indian ink and rubber solution."

"All right."

"And to return it sometime before Christmas."

Wedderburn grinned and departed on his errand.

About ten minutes later, the telephone tinkled in the typists' room.

"Yes?" said Miss Rossiter, in mellifluous accents. "Who is it, please?"

"Tallboy speaking," said the telephone.

"Oh!" Miss Rossiter altered her voice from the tone reserved for clients and directors to a tarter one (for she was not too well pleased with Mr. Tallboy), modified by the sympathy due to ill-health:

"Oh, yes? Are you feeling better, Mr. Tallboy?"

"Yes, thanks. I've been trying to get Wedderburn, but he doesn't seem to be in his room."

"I expect he's in the Studio, making poor Mr. Pickering work overtime on a new Nutrax sketch."

"Oh! that's what I wanted to know. Did Jollop pass that copy?"

"No—he turned the whole lot down. It's a new one—at least, new headline with the 'What are you Weeping for?' copy."

"Oh, a new headline? What is it?"

"Stale, Flat and Unprofitable. Shakespeare, you know."

"Oh! Oh, good! Glad something managed to get through. It was worrying me."

"It's quite all right, Mr. Tallboy." Miss Rossiter rang off. "Touching devotion to business," she observed to Miss Parton. "As if the world would stop turning just because *he* wasn't here!"

"I expect he was afraid old Copley would be butting in again," said Miss Parton, with a snort.

"Oh, him!" said Miss Rossiter.

"Well, now, young man," said the policeman, "and what do *you* want?"

"I want to see Chief Inspector Parker."

"Ho!" said the policeman. "Don't want much, do you? Sure you wouldn't rather see the Lord Mayor o' London? Or Mister Ramsay MacDonald?"

"I say, are you always as funny as that? Cor lumme, don't it 'urt yer sometimes? You better buy yourself a new pair o' boots or you'll be gettin' too big for wot yer wearin'. You tell Chief Inspector Parker as Mr. Joe Potts wants ter see 'im about this 'ere 'Arlequin murder. And look snappy, 'cos I gotter git 'ome ter me supper."

"About the 'Arlequin murder, eh? And wot do you know about that?"

"Never you mind. Jest tell 'im wot I say. Tell 'im it's Joe Potts as works at Pym's Publicity and you'll 'ave 'im steppin' aht ter meet me wiv' a crimson carpet and a bokay."

"Oh! you're from Pym's. Got something to say about this Bredon, is that it?"

"That's it. Now, you 'op it, and don't waste time."

"You'd better come in here, young cocky—and be'ave yourself."

"Right-oh! it's all the same to me."

Mr. Joseph Potts wiped his boots neatly on the mat, took his seat upon a hard bench, drew out a Yo-Yo from his pocket, and began nonchalantly throwing a handsome series of loops, while the policeman retired defeated.

Presently he returned and, sternly commanding Mr. Joseph Potts to put his top away, conducted him through a series of passages to a door, upon which he knocked. A voice said "Come in," and Mr. Potts found himself in a good-sized room, furnished with two desks, a couple of comfortable arm-chairs and several other seats of penitential appearance. At the further desk sat a man in mufti, writing, with his back to the door; at the nearer, facing the door, was another man in a grey suit, with a pile of documents before him.

"The boy, sir," announced the policeman, and retired.

"Sit down," said the man in grey, briefly, indicating one of the penitential chairs. "Now then, what's all this you've got to tell us, eh?"

"Excuse me, sir, are you Chief Inspector Parker?"

"This is a very cautious witness," observed the man in grey to the world in general. "Why do you particularly want to see Chief Inspector Parker?"

" 'Cos it's important and confidential, see?" said Mr. Joseph Potts, pertly. "Information, that's wot it is. I likes ter do business with the boss, especially if there's anythink ain't bein' 'andled as it should be."

"Oh!"

"I want to tell this Parker that this case ain't bein' 'andled right. See? Mr. Bredon ain't got nothink to do with it."

"Indeed. Well, I'm Chief Inspector Parker. What do you know about Bredon?"

"This 'ere." Ginger Joe extended an inky forefinger. "You been 'ad. Mr. Bredon ain't no crook, 'e's a great detective, and I'm 'is assistant. We're 'ard on the track of a murderer, see? And this 'ere is just a mashi—macki—I men it's jest a booby-trap set by the 'ideous gang as 'e's out ter track to its lair. You been boobies ter let yerselves be took in by it, see? 'E's a sport, is Mr. Bredon, and he ain't never murdered no young woman, let alone bein' such a fool as ter leave penny whistles be'ind 'im. If you wants a murderer, Mr. Bredon's got 'is eye on one now, and you're jest playin' into the 'ands of Black Spider and 'is gang—meaning to say, 'oever done this. Wot I meantersay, the time 'as come fer me ter divulge wot I know, and I ain't agoin'—cor lumme!"

The man at the further desk had turned round and was grinning at Ginger over the back of his chair.

"That'll do, Ginger," said this person. "We know all about that here. I am obliged to you for your testimonial. I hope you haven't been divulging anything in other directions."

"Me sir? No, sir. I ain't said a word, Mr. Bredon, sir. But seein' as 'ow——"

"That's all right; I believe you. Now, Charles, I think this is just the lad we want. You can get that headline from him and save ringing up Pym's. Ginger, was the Nutrax headline passed this afternoon?"

"Yes, sir. 'Stale, Flat and Unprofitable', that's what it was. And lor', wasn't there a to-do about it! Took 'em all afternoon, it did, and Mr. Ingleby wasn't 'arf wild."

"He would be," said Wimsey. "Now, you'd better cut along home, Ginger, and not a word, mind."

"No, sir."

"We're much obliged to you for coming," added Parker, "but you see, we aren't quite such boobies as you think. We know a good deal about Mr. Bredon here. And by the way, let me introduce you to Lord Peter Wimsey."

Ginger Joe's eyes nearly popped out of his head.

"Coo! Lord Peter—where's Mr. Bredon, then? This *is* Mr. Bredon. You're pulling my leg."

"I promise," said Wimsey, "to tell you all about it this time next week. Cut along now, there's a good chap. We're busy."

On Wednesday morning, Mr. Parker received a communication from St. Martin's-le-Grand. Inside the official envelope was another, addressed in Tallboy's hand to "S. Smith, Esq." at Cummings' address in Old Broad Street.

"That settles it," said Wimsey. He consulted the marked telephone directory. "Here you are. The Stag at Bay, Drury Lane. Make no mistake this time."

It was not until Thursday evening that Miss Meteyard made up her mind to speak to Mr. Tallboy.

CHAPTER XX

Appropriate Exit of an Unskilled Murderer

"IS LORD PETER WIMSEY at home?"

The manservant raked his questioner with a swift glance, which took in everything from his hunted eyes to his respectable middle-class boots. Then he said, inclining a respectful head:

"If you will be good enough to take a seat, I will ascertain if his Lordship is at leisure. What name shall I say, sir?"

"Mr. Tallboy."

"Who, Bunter?" said Wimsey. "Mr. Tallboy? This is a little embarrassing. What does he look like?"

"He looks, my lord, if I may so poetically express myself, as though the Hound of Heaven had got him, so to say, cornered, my lord."

"You are probably right. I should not be surprised if a hound of hell or so were knocking about the neighbourhood as well. Take a squint out of the window, Bunter."

"Very good, my lord.... I can observe nobody, but I retain a distinct impression that, when I opened the door to Mr. Tallboy, I overheard a footstep on the floor below."

"Very likely. Well, it can't be helped. Show him in."

"Very good, my lord."

The young man came in and Wimsey rose to greet him.

"Good evening, Mr. Tallboy."

"I have come," began Tallboy, and then broke off. "Lord Peter—Bredon—for God's sake, which are you?"

"Both," said Wimsey, gravely. "Won't you sit down?"

"Thanks, I'd rather . . . I don't want . . . I came . . ."

"You're looking rather rotten. I really think you'd better sit down, and have a spot of something."

Tallboy's legs seemed to give way under him, and he sat down without further protest.

"And how," inquired Wimsey, pouring him out a stiff whisky, "is the Whifflets campaign getting on without me?"

"Whifflets?"

"It doesn't matter. I only asked to show you that I really was Bredon. Put that straight down. Is that better?"

"Yes. I'm sorry to have made a fool of myself. I came to you——"

"You came to find out how much I knew?"

"Yes—no. I came because I couldn't stick it out any longer. I came to tell you all about it."

"Wait a minute. There's something I must tell you first. It's all out of my hands now. You understand? As a matter of fact, I don't think there's very much you can tell me. The game's up, old man. I'm sorry—I'm really sorry, because I think you've been having a perfectly bloody time. But there it is."

Tallboy had gone very white. He accepted another drink without protest, and then said:

"Well, I'm rather glad in a way. If it wasn't for my wife and the kid—oh, God!" He hid his face in his hands, and Wimsey walked over to the window and glanced at the lights of Piccadilly, pale in the summer dusk. "I've been a bloody fool," said Tallboy.

"Most of us are," said Wimsey. "I'm damned sorry, old chap."

He came back and stood looking down at him.

"Look here," he said, "you need not tell me a thing, if you don't want to. But if you do, I want you to understand that it won't really make any difference. I mean, if you feel like getting it off your chest, I don't think it will prejudice matters for you at all."

"I'd like to tell you," said Tallboy. "I think you might understand. I realise that it's all up, anyhow." He paused. "I say, what put you on to this?"

"That letter of Victor Dean's. You remember it? The one he threatened to write to Pym. He showed it to you, I fancy."

"The little swine. Yes, he did. Didn't he destroy it?"

"No, he didn't."

"I see. Well, I'd better begin at the beginning. It all started about two years ago. I was rather hard up and I wanted to get married. I'd been losing money on horses, as well, and things were not too good. I met a man in a restaurant."

"What restaurant?"

Tallboy gave the name. "He was a middle-aged, ordinary sort of person. I've never seen him since. But we got talking about one thing and another, and how tight money was and so on, and I happened to mention where I was working. He seemed to be thinking a bit after that, and asked a good many questions about how advertisements were put together and sent to the papers, and so on, and whether I was in a position to know beforehand what the headlines were going to be. So I said, of course, that there were some accounts I knew all about, such as Nutrax, and others I didn't. So then he mentioned the *Morning Star* half-double, and asked when I knew about the headlines of that, and I said, on Tuesday afternoon. Then he suddenly asked me if I could do with an extra thousand a year, and I said, 'Couldn't I? Lead me to it.' So then he came out with his proposal. It sounded pretty innocent. At least, it was quite obviously a dirty trick, but it wasn't criminal, the way he put it. He said, if I would let him know, every Tuesday, the initial letter of the headline for the following Friday, I should be well paid for it. Of course, I made a fuss about breach of confidence and so on and he raised his terms to twelve hundred. It sounded damned tempting, and I couldn't see, for the life of me, how it was going to harm the firm in any way. So I said I'd do it, and we fixed up a code——"

"I know all about that," said Wimsey. "It was very ingenious and simple. I suppose he told you that the address was simply an accommodation address."

"Yes. Wasn't it? I went to see the place once; it was a tobacconist's."

Wimsey nodded. "I've been there. It's not exactly an accommodation address, in the sense you mean. Didn't this man give you any reason for this rather remarkable request?"

"Yes, he did, and of course I oughtn't to have had anything to do with him after that. He said he was fond of having a bit of a bet with some friends of his about one thing and another, and his idea was to bet on the initial letter of each week's headline——"

"Oh, I see. And he would be betting on a certainty as often as he liked. Plausible; not criminal, but just dirty enough to explain this insistence on secrecy. Was that it?"

"Yes. I fell for it. . . . I was damned hard up. . . . I can't excuse myself. And I suppose I ought to have guessed that there was more to it than that. But I didn't want to guess. Besides, at first I thought it was all a leg-pull, but I wasn't risking anything, so I buzzed off the first two code-letters, and at the end of the fortnight I got my fifty pounds. I was heavily in debt, and I used it. After that—well, I hadn't the courage to chuck it."

"No, it would be rather hard, I should think."

"Hard? You don't know, Bredon—Wimsey—you don't know what it means to be stuck for money. They don't pay any too well at Pym's, and there are heaps of fellows who want to get out and find something better, but they daren't. Pym's is safe—they're kind and decent, and they don't sack you if they can help it—but you live up to your income and you simply daren't cut loose. The competitition is so keen, and you marry and start paying for your house and furniture, and you must keep up the instalments, and you can't collect the capital to sit round for a month or two while you look for a new job. You've got to keep going, and it breaks your heart and takes all the stuffing out of you. So I went on. Of course, I kept hoping that I might be able to save money and get out of it, but my wife fell ill and one thing and another, and I was spending every penny of my salary and Smith's money on top of it. And then, somehow, that little devil Dean got hold of it; God knows how!"

"I can tell you that," said Wimsey, and told him.

"I see. Well, he started to put the screw on. First of all he wanted to go fifty-fifty, and then he demanded more. The devil of it was, that if he split on me, I should lose my job as well as Smith's money, and things were getting pretty awful. My wife was going to have a baby, and I was behind with the income-tax, and I think it was just because everything seemed too utterly hopeless that I got mixed up with the Vavasour girl. Naturally, that only made things worse in the long run. And then, one day, I felt I couldn't stand it any longer and told Dean I was chucking the whole show and he could do as he damn well pleased. And it wasn't till then that he told me what it was all about, and pointed out that I might easily get twelve years' penal servitude for helping to run the dope-traffic."

"Dirty," said Wimsey, "very dirty. It never occurred to you, I suppose, to turn King's Evidence and expose the whole system."

"No; not at first. I was terrified and couldn't think properly. And even if I'd done that, there'd have been awful trouble. Still, I did think of it after a bit, and told Dean that that was what I would do. And then he informed me that he was going to get his shot in first, and showed me that letter he was sending to Pym. That finished me, and I begged him to hold off for a week or two, while I thought things over. What happened about that letter exactly?"

"His sister found it among his things and sent it on to Pym, and he engaged me, through a friend, to enquire into it. He didn't know who I was. I thought there probably wasn't much in it, but I took the job on for the experience."

Tallboy nodded.

"Well, you've had your experience. I hope you haven't paid as heavily for it as I have. I could see no way out of it——"

He stopped speaking, and glanced at Wimsey.

"Perhaps I'd better tell you the next bit," said the latter. "You thought it over, and decided that Victor Dean was a wart and a scab, and would be no great loss to the world. One day, Wedderburn came along to your room, chuckling because Mrs. Johnson had caught Ginger Joe with a catapult and had confiscated it and put it in her desk. You knew you were a wonderfully good shot with any sort of missile—the kind of man who could spread-eagle a wicket from the other end of a cricket-field—and you realised how easily a man could be plugged through the skylight as he went down the iron staircase. If the blow didn't kill him, then the fall might, and it was well worth trying."

"You really do know all about it, then?"

"Nearly. You pinched the catapult, opening the drawer with Mrs. Johnson's keys during the lunch-hour, and you did a few practice shots from day to day. You left a pebble there once, you know."

"I know. Somebody came along, before I could find it."

"Yes. Well, then, the day came for putting Dean away—a nice bright day, when all the skylights were open. You dodged about the building a good bit, so that nobody should know exactly where you were at any particular minute, and then you went up on the roof. How, by the way, did you ensure that Dean would go down the iron staircase at the right moment? Oh, yes, and the scarab? It was a very good idea to use the scarab, because if anybody found it, they would naturally think it had tumbled out of his pocket as he fell."

"I'd seen the scarab on Dean's desk after lunch; I knew he often kept it there. And I had *The Times Atlas* in my room. I sent Wedderburn down to the Vouchers for something or other, and then I rang up Dean on my telephone. I said I was speaking for Mr. Hankin from the Big Conference Room, and would Mr. Dean please come down about the Crunchlets copy and bring *The Times Atlas* with him from my room. While he went for it, I pinched the scarab and slipped up on to the roof. I knew it would take him a bit of time to find the atlas, because I'd buried it under a whole heap of files, and I was pretty sure he'd go by the iron staircase, because that was the nearest way from my room to the Conference Room. As a matter of fact, it might have gone wrong at that point, because he didn't come that way at all. I think he must have gone back to his own room for something after getting the atlas, but of course, I don't know. Anyway, he came along all right and I shot him through the skylight when he was about four steps down the staircase."

"How did you know so exactly where to hit him?"

"Curiously enough, I had a young brother who was accidentally killed by being hit in just that place with a golf-ball. But I went and looked it up in a book at the British Museum to make sure. Apparently he broke his neck as well; I hadn't expected that. I stayed up on the roof till the fuss was over, and then came down quietly by the stairs. I didn't meet a soul, of course, they were all holding post-mortems and hanging round the corpse. When I knew I'd succeeded, I didn't care. I was glad. And I tell you this, if I hadn't been found out, I shouldn't care now."

"I can sympathise with that," said Wimsey.

"They asked me for a shilling for the little beast's wreath." Tallboy laughed. "I'd gladly have given twenty shillings, or twenty pounds even. . . . And then you came along. . . . I didn't suspect anything . . . till you started to talk about catapults. . . . And then I got badly frightened, and I . . . and I . . ."

"We'll draw a veil over that," said Wimsey. "You must have got a bit of a shock when you found you'd slugged the wrong man. I suppose that was when you struck a light to look for Pamela Dean's letter."

"Yes. I knew her writing—I'd seen it in Dean's room—and I knew her writing-paper, too. I really came round to find out whether you knew anything or whether you were just drawing a bow at a venture—that's rather appropriate, isn't it? Drawing a catapult at a venture would be better. When I saw that letter I felt sure there must be something in it. And Willis, too—he'd told me that you and Pamela Dean were as thick as thieves. I thought the letter might be telling you all about Dean and me. I don't know quite what I thought, to tell you the truth. Then, when I'd found out my mistake, I got frightened and thought I'd better not try again."

"I was expecting you. When nothing came of it, I began to think it hadn't been you at all, but somebody else."

"Did you know by then that the other thing was me?"

"I didn't know it was you; you were one of several possibles. But after the Nutrax row and the £50 in notes——"

Tallboy looked up with a shy, fleeting smile.

"You know," he said, "I was horribly careless and incompetent all through. Those letters—I ought never to have sent them from the office."

"No; and the catapult. You should have taken the trouble to make your own. A catapult without finger-prints is something very unusual."

"So that was it. I'm afraid I've made an awful mess of everything. Couldn't even do a simple murder. Wimsey—how much of this will have to come out? Everything, I suppose? Even that Vavasour girl . . .?"

"Ah!" said Wimsey, without replying to the question. "Don't talk about the Vavasour girl. I felt a cad about that. You know, I did tell you not to thank me."

"You did, and it frightened me badly, because you sounded as if you meant it. I knew then that it hadn't been an accident about the catapult. But I hadn't an idea who you were till that infernal cricket match."

"I was careless then. But that damned fellow Simmonds rapping me on the funny-bone got my goat. You didn't fall for my impressive arrest then?"

"Oh, yes, I did. I believed in it implicitly and put up the most heartfelt thanksgivings. I thought I'd got off."

"Then what brought you round here to-night?"

"Miss Meteyard. She got hold of me last night. She said she'd believed first of all that you and Bredon were the same person, but now she thought you couldn't be. But she said that Bredon would be dead sure to split on me by way of currying favour with the police, and I had better get out in time."

"She said that? Miss Meteyard? Do you mean to say she knew all about it?"

"Not about the Nutrax business. But she knew about Dean."

"Good God!" Wimsey's natural conceit received a shattering blow. "How in Heaven's name did *she* know?"

"Guessed. Said she'd once seen me look at Dean when I didn't know she was there—and apparently he had once let out something to her. Apparently she'd always thought there was something odd about his death. She said she'd made up her mind not to interfere either way, but after your arrest she decided you were the bigger crook of the two. She could stand Lord Peter Wimsey doing a proper investigation, but not Mr. Dirty Bredon squealing to save his skin. She's an odd woman."

"Very. I'd better forget about all this, hadn't I? She seems to have taken the whole thing very coolly."

"She did. You see, she knew Dean. He tried to blackmail her once, about some man or the other. You wouldn't think it to look at her, would you?" said Tallboy, naively. "There was nothing much in it, she said, but it was the kind of thing old Pym would have been down on like a sledge-hammer."

"And what did she do?" asked Wimsey, fascinated.

"Told him to publish and be damned. And I wish to God I'd done the same. Wimsey—how much longer is it going to hang on? I've been in torment—I've been trying to give myself up—I—my wife—why haven't I been arrested before this?"

"They've been waiting," said Wimsey, thoughtfully, for his mind was pursuing two trains of thought at the same time. "You see, you aren't really as important as this dope-gang. Once you were arrested, they would stop their little game, and we didn't want them to stop. I'm afraid you're being the tethered kid, left there to trap the tigers."

All this time, his ear was alert to catch the tinkle of the telephone, which would tell him that the raid on the Stag at Bay had succeeded. Once the arrests were made and the gang broken, the sinister watcher in the street would be harmless. He would fly for his life and Tallboy would be able to go home to whatever awaited him there. But if he were to go now——"

"When?" Tallboy was saying urgently, "when?"

"To-night."

"Wimsey—you've been frightfully decent to me—tell me—there's no way out? It isn't myself, exactly, but my wife and the kid. Pointed at all their lives. It's damnable. You couldn't give me twenty-four hours?"

"You would not pass the ports."

"If I were alone I'd give myself up. I would, honestly."

"There is an alternative."

"I know. I've thought about that. I suppose that's——" he stopped and laughed suddenly—"that's the public school way out of it. I—yes—all right.

They'll hardly make a headline of it, though, will they? 'Suicide of Old Dumbletonian' wouldn't have much news-value. Never mind, damn it! We'll show 'em that Dumbleton can achieve the Eton touch. Why not?"

"Good man!" said Wimsey. "Have a drink. Here's luck!"

He emptied his glass and stood up.

"Listen!" he said. "I think there is one other way out. It won't help you, but it may make all the difference to your wife and your child."

"How?" said Tallboy, eagerly.

"They need never know anything about all this. Nothing. Nobody need ever know anything, if you do as I tell you."

"My God, Wimsey! What do you mean? Tell me quickly. I'll do anything."

"It won't save you."

"That doesn't matter. Tell me."

"Go home now," said Wimsey. "Go on foot, and not too fast. And don't look behind you."

Tallboy stared at him; the blood drained away from his face, leaving even his lips as white as paper.

"I think I understand.... Very well."

"Quickly, then," said Wimsey. He held out his hand.

"Good-night, and good luck."

From the window, Wimsey watched him come out into Piccadilly, and walk quickly away towards Hyde Park Corner. He saw the shadow slip from a neighbouring doorway and follow him.

"—and from thence to the place of execution... and may the Lord have mercy upon your soul."

Half an hour later, the telephone rang.

"Bagged the whole crew," said Parker's cheerful voice. "We let the stuff go up to town. What do you think it went as? Traveller's samples—one of those closed cars with blinds all round."

"That's where they made it into packets, then."

"Yes. We watched our man into the Stag; then we pulled in the motor-boat and the car. Then we kept our eye on the pub and let the birds hop out into our arms, one after the other. It went off beautifully. No hitch at all. Oh, and by the way—their code-word. We ought to have thought of that. It was just anything to do with Nutrax. Some of them had the *Morning Star*, showing the ad., and some of them just mentioned Nutrax for Nerves. One chap had a bottle of the stuff in his pocket, another had it written on a shopping-list and so on. And one frightfully ingenious chap was bursting with information about some new tracks for greyhound racing. Simple as pie, wasn't it?"

"That explains Hector Puncheon."

"Hector——? Oh, the newspaper fellow. Yes. He must have had his copy of the *Morning Star* with him. We've got old Cummings, too, of course. He turns out to be the actual top-dog of the whole show, and as soon as we collared him he coughed up the whole story, the mangy little blighter. That doctor fellow who shoved Mountjoy under the train is in it—we've got definite information about him, and we've also got our hands on Mountjoy's loot. He's got a safe-deposit somewhere, and I think I know where to find the key. He kept a woman in Maida Vale, bless his heart. The whole thing is most satisfactory. Now we have only got to rake in your murderer chap, what's his name, and everything in the garden will be lovely."

"Lovely," said Wimsey, with a spice of bitterness in his tone, "simply lovely."

"What's the matter? You sound a bit peeved. Hang on a minute till I've cleared up here and we'll go round somewhere to celebrate."

"Not to-night," said Wimsey, "I don't feel quite like celebrating."

CHAPTER XXI

Death Departs from Pym's Publicity

"SO YOU SEE," said Wimsey to Mr. Pym, "the thing need never come into the papers at all, if we're careful. We've plenty of evidence against Cummings without that, and there's no need to take the public into our confidence about the details of their distributing system."

"Thank Heaven!" said Mr. Pym. "It would have been a terrible thing for Pym's Publicity. How I have lived through this last week, I really don't know. I suppose you will be leaving the advertising?"

"I'm afraid so."

"Pity. You have a natural flair for copy-writing. You will have the satisfaction of seeing your Whifflets scheme go through."

"Splendid! I shall begin to collect coupons at once."

"Just fancy!" said Miss Rossiter. "Charge withdrawn."

"I always *said* Mr. Bredon was a darling," triumphed Miss Parton. "Of course the *real* murderer was one of those horrible dope-trafficking beasts. That was far more likely. I said so at the time."

"I didn't hear you, dear," snapped Miss Rossiter. "I say, Miss Meteyard, you've seen the news? You've seen that our Mr. Bredon is discharged and never did any murder at all?"

"I've done better," replied Miss Meteyard. "I've seen Mr. Bredon."

"No, where?"

"Here."

"*No!*"

"And he isn't Mr. Bredon, he's Lord Peter Wimsey."

"What!!!"

Lord Peter poked his long nose round the door.

"Did I hear my name?"

"You did. She says you're Lord Peter Wimsey."

"Quite right."

"Then what were you doing here?"

"I came here," said his lordship, unabashed, "for a bet. A friend of mine laid me ten to one I couldn't earn my own living for a month. I did it, though, didn't I? May I have a cup of coffee?"

They would gladly have given him anything.

"By the way," said Miss Rossiter, when the first tumult had subsided, "you heard about poor Mr. Tallboy?"

"Yes, poor chap."

"Knocked down and killed on his way home—wasn't it dreadful? And poor Mrs. Tallboy with a small baby—it does seem awful! Goodness knows what they'll have to live on, because—well, you know! And that reminds me, while you're here, could I have your shilling for a wreath? At least, I suppose you'll be leaving Pym's now, but I expect you'd like to contribute."

"Yes, rather. Here you are."

"Thanks awfully. Oh, and I say! There's Mr. Willis' wedding-present. You know he's getting married?"

"No, I didn't. Everything seems to happen while I'm away. Whom is he marrying?"

"Pamela Dean."

"Oh, good work. Yes, of course. How much for Willis?"

"Well, most people are giving about two bob, if you can spare it."

"I think I can manage two bob. What are we giving him, by the way?"

"Well," said Miss Rossiter, "there's been *rather* a fuss about that. The Department was awfully keen on a clock, but Mrs. Johnson and Mr. Barrow went off on their own and bought an electric chafing-dish—such a silly thing, because I'm sure they'll never use it. And in any case, Mr. Willis did belong to the Copy Department and we ought to have had a voice in it, don't you think? So there are going to be two presents—the staff as a whole is giving the chafing-dish and the Department is giving its own present. I'm afraid we shan't be able to manage a chiming clock, though, because you can't very well ask people for more than two bob or so, though Hankie and Armstrong have been very decent and stumped up half a quid each."

"I'd better make it half a quid too."

"Oh, no," said Miss Rossiter. "You're a lamb, but it isn't fair."

"It's quite fair," said Wimsey. "There are excellent reasons why I should contribute largely to a wedding present for Mr. Willis."

"Are there? I thought you and he didn't get on very well. I expect I'm being tactless, as usual. If you're quite sure—oh, I forgot, I *am* a fool. Of course, if you're Lord Peter Wimsey, you're simply frightfully rich, aren't you?"

"Fair to middling," confessed Wimsey. "It might run to a cake for tea."

He had a word with Miss Meteyard.

"I'm sorry, you know," he said.

She shrugged her angular shoulders.

"It's not your fault. Things have to happen. You're one of the sort that pushes round and makes them happen. I prefer to leave them alone. You've got to have both kinds."

"Perhaps your way is wiser and more charitable."

"It isn't. I shirk responsibility, that's all. I just let things rip. I don't make it my business to interfere. But I don't blame the people who do interfere. In a way, I rather admire them. They do make something, even if it's only mischief. My sort make nothing. We exploit other people's folly, take the cash and sneer at the folly. It's not admirable. Never mind. You'd better run along now. I've got to get out a new series for Sopo. 'Sopo Day is Cinema Day'. 'Leave the Laundry to ruin itself while you addle your brains at the Talkies'. Muck! Dope! And they pay me £10 a week for that sort of thing. And yet, if we didn't do it, what would happen to the trade of this country? You've got to advertise."

Mr. Hankin tripped along the passage and encountered them.

"So you're leaving us, Mr. Bredon? In fact, I understand that we've been nursing a cuckoo in the nest."

"Not so bad as that, sir. I'm leaving a few of the original nestlings behind me."

Miss Meteyard evaporated quietly, and Mr. Hankin continued:

"A very sad business. Mr Pym is very grateful for the discretion you have shown. I hope you will lunch with me some day. Yes, Mr. Smayle?"

"Excuse me, sir—about this window-bill for Green Pastures?"

Wimsey made his way out, exchanging mechanical handgrips and farewells. At the foot of the lift, in the lower vestibule, he found Ginger, with his arms full of parcels.

"Well, Ginger," said Wimsey, "I'm off."

"Oh, sir!"

"By the way, I've still got your catapult."

"I'd like you to keep it, please, sir. You see, sir——" Ginger struggled with a variety of emotions—"if I was ter keep that there catapult, I might get telling some of the boys about it, not meaning to, like. Wot I meantersay, it's 'istorical, like, ain't it, sir?"

"So it is." Wimsey sympathised with the temptation. It is not every fellow whose catapult has been borrowed for the purpose of committing a murder. "Well, I'll keep it, and thank you very much for all your help. Look here, I'll tell you what. I'll give you something in exchange. Which would you rather have—a model aeroplane, or the pair of scissors with which the steward of the *Nancy Belle* stabbed the captain and the purser?"

"Ooh, sir! 'As the scissors got the marks on 'em, sir?"

"Yes, Ginger. Genuine, original bloodstains."

"Then, please, sir, I'd like the scissors."

"You shall have them."

"Thank you *very* much, sir."

"And you'll never say one word to anybody about you know what?"

"Not if you was to roast me alive, sir."

"Right you are; good-bye, Ginger."

"Good-bye, sir."

Wimsey stepped out into Southampton Row. Facing him was a long line of hoardings. Enormous in its midst stretched a kaleidoscopic poster:

NUTRAX FOR NERVES

In the adjoining space, a workman with a broom and a bucket of paste was unfolding a still more vast and emphatic display in blue and yellow:

ARE YOU A WHIFFLER?
IF NOT, WHY NOT?

A 'bus passed, bearing a long ribbon display upon its side:

WHIFFLE YOUR WAY ROUND BRITAIN!

The great campaign had begun. He contemplated his work with a kind of amazement. With a few idle words on a sheet of paper he had touched the lives of millions. Two men, passing, stopped to stare at the hoarding.

"What's this Whiffling business, Alf?"

"I dunno. Some advertising stunt or other. Cigarettes, ain't it?"

"Oh, Whifflets?"

"I suppose so."

"Wonderful how they think of it all. What's it about, anyway?"

"Gawd knows. Here, let's get a packet and see."

"All right. I don't mind."

They passed on.

Tell England. Tell the world. Eat more Oats. Take Care of your Complexion. No More War. Shine your Shoes with Shino. Ask your Grocer. Children Love Laxamalt. Prepare to meet thy God. Bung's Beer is Better. Try Dogsbody's Sausages. Whoosh the Dust Away. Give them Crunchlets. Snagsbury's Soups are Best for the Troops. *Morning Star,* best Paper by Far. Vote for Punkin and Protect your Profits. Stop that Sneeze wth Snuffo. Flush your Kidneys with Fizzlets. Flush your Drains with Sanfect. Wear Woolfleece next the Skin. Popp's Pills Pep you Up. Whiffle your Way to Fortune. . . .

Advertise, or go under.

THE NINE TAILORS

CHANGES RUNG ON

AN OLD THEME

in

Two Short Touches and

Two Full Peals

FOREWORD

From time to time complaints are made about the ringing of church bells. It seems strange that a generation which tolerates the uproar of the internal combustion engine and the wailing of the jazz band should be so sensitive to the one loud noise that is made to the glory of God. England, alone in the world, has perfected the art of change-ringing and the true ringing of bells by rope and wheel, and will not lightly surrender her unique heritage.

I have to ask the indulgence of all change-ringers for any errors I may have made in dealing with their ancient craft. The surnames used in these books are all such as I have myself encountered among the people of East Anglia, but every place and person described is wholly fictitious, as are also the sins and negligences of those entirely imaginary bodies, the Wale Conservancy Board, the Fen Drainage Board and the East Level Waterways Commission.

My grateful thanks are due to Mr. W. J. Redhead, who so kindly designed for me the noble Parish Church of Fenchurch St. Paul and set it about with cherubims.

DOROTHY L. SAYERS

Parish Church of Fenchurch St. Paul with Detail of Roof

W. J. Redhead Architect

CONTENTS

A Short Touch of Kent Treble Bob Major (*Two Courses*)

A Full Peal of Grandsire Triples (*Holt's Ten-Part Peal*)

A Short Touch of Stedman's Triples (*Five Parts*)

A Full Peal of Kent Treble Bob Major
(*Three Parts*)

I

A SHORT TOUCH OF KENT TREBLE BOB MAJOR

(Two Courses)

704

By the Course Ends

64352

23456

8th the Observation.

Call her in the middle with a double, before,
wrong and home.
Repeated once.

(TROYTE)

THE FIRST COURSE

The Bells are Rung Up

> The coil of rope which it is necessary to hold in the hand, before, and whilst raising a bell, always puzzles a learner; it gets into his face, and perhaps round his neck (in which case he may be hanged!).
>
> TROYTE *On Change-Ringing*

"THAT'S TORN IT!" said Lord Peter Wimsey.

The car lay, helpless and ridiculous, her nose deep in the ditch, her back wheels cocked absurdly up on the bank, as though she were doing her best to bolt to earth and were scraping herself a burrow beneath the drifted snow. Peering through a flurry of driving flakes, Wimsey saw how the accident had come about. The narrow, hump-backed bridge, blind as an eyeless beggar, spanned the dark drain at right angles, dropping plump down upon the narrow road that crested the dyke. Coming a trifle too fast across the bridge, blinded by the bitter easterly snowstorm, he had overshot the road and plunged down the side of the dyke into the deep ditch beyond, where the black spikes of a thorn hedge stood bleak and unwelcoming in the glare of the headlights.

Right and left, before and behind, the fen lay shrouded. It was past four o'clock and New Year's Eve; the snow that had fallen all day gave back a glimmering greyness to a sky like lead.

"I'm sorry," said Wimsey. "Whereabouts do you suppose we've got to, Bunter?"

The manservant consulted a map in the ray of an electric torch.

"I think, my lord, we must have run off the proper road at Leamholt. Unless I am much mistaken, we must be near Fenchurch St. Paul."

As he spoke, the sound of a church clock, muffled by the snow, came borne upon the wind; it chimed the first quarter.

"Thank God!" said Wimsey. "Where there is a church there is civilisation. We'll have to walk it. Never mind the suitcases; we can send somebody for them. Br'rh! it's cold. I bet that when Kingsley welcomed the wild north-easter he was sitting indoors by a good fire, eating muffins. I could do with a muffin myself. Next time I accept hospitality in the Fen-country, I'll take care that it's at mid-summer, or else I'll go by train. The church lies to windward of us, I fancy. It would."

They wrapped their coats about them and turned their faces to the wind and snow. To left of them, the drain ran straight as a rule could make it, black and sullen, with a steep bank shelving down to its slow, unforgiving waters. To their right was the broken line of the sunk hedge, with, here and there, a group of poplars or willows. They tramped on in silence, the snow beating on their eyelids. At the end of a solitary mile the gaunt shape of a windmill loomed up upon the further bank of the drain, but no bridge led to it, and no light showed.

Another half-mile, and they came to a signpost and a secondary road that turned off to the right. Bunter turned his torch upon the signpost and read upon the single arm:

"Fenchurch St. Paul."

There was no other direction; ahead, road and dyke marched on side by side into an eternity of winter.

"Fenchurch St. Paul for us," said Wimsey. He led the way into the side-road, and as he did so, they heard the clock again—nearer—chiming the third quarter.

A few hundred yards of solitude, and they came upon the first sign of life in this frozen desolation: on their left, the roofs of a farm, standing some way back from the road, and, on the right, a small, square building like a box of bricks, whose sign, creaking in the blast, proclaimed it to be the Wheatsheaf public-house. In front of it stood a small, shabby car, and from windows on the ground and first floors light shone behind red blinds.

Wimsey went up to it and tried the door. It was shut, but not locked. He called out, "Anybody about?"

A middle-aged woman emerged from an inner room.

"We're not open yet," she began, abruptly.

"I beg your pardon," said Wimsey. "Our car has come to grief. Can you direct us——?"

"Oh, I'm sorry, sir. I thought you were some of the men. Your car broke down? That's bad. Come in. I'm afraid we're all in a muddle——"

"What's the trouble, Mrs. Tebbutt?" The voice was gentle and scholarly, and, as Wimsey followed the woman into a small parlour, he saw that the speaker was an elderly parson.

"The gentlemen have had an accident with their car."

"Oh, dear," said the clergyman. "Such a terrible day, too! Can I be of any assistance?"

Wimsey explained that the car was in the ditch, and would certainly need ropes and haulage to get it back to the road again.

"Dear, dear," said the clergyman again. "That would be coming over Frog's Bridge, I expect. A most dangerous place, especially in the dark. We must see what can be done about it. Let me give you a lift into the village."

"It's very good of you, sir."

"Not at all, not at all. I am just getting back to my tea. I am sure you must be wanting something to warm you up. I trust you are not in a hurry to reach your destination. We should be delighted to put you up for the night."

Wimsey thanked him very much, but said he did not want to trespass upon his hospitality.

"It will be a great pleasure," said the clergyman, courteously. "We see so little company here that I assure you you will be doing my wife and myself a great favour."

"In that case——" said Wimsey.

"Excellent, excellent."

"I'm really most grateful. Even if we could get the car out to-night, I'm afraid the axle may be bent, and that means a blacksmith's job. But couldn't we get rooms at an inn or something? I'm really ashamed——"

"My dear sir, pray don't think twice about it. Not but what I am sure Mrs. Tebbutt here would be delighted to take you in and would make you very comfortable—very comfortable indeed; but her husband is laid up with this dreadful influenza—we are suffering from quite an epidemic of it, I am sorry to say—and I fear it would not be altogether convenient, would it, Mrs. Tebbutt?"

"Well, sir, I don't know as how we could manage very well, under the circumstances, and the Red Cow has only one room——"

"Oh, no," said the clergyman, quickly, "not the Red Cow; Mrs. Donnington has visitors already. Indeed, I will take no denial. You must positively come along to the Rectory. We have ample accommodation—too much, indeed, too much. My name, by the way, is Venables—I should have mentioned it earlier. I am, as you will have gathered, rector of the parish."

"It's extremely good of you, Mr. Venables. If we're really not putting you out, we will accept your invitation with pleasure. My name is Wimsey—here is my card—and this is my man, Bunter."

The Rector fumbled for his glasses, which, after disentangling the cord, he perched very much askew on his long nose, in order to peer at Wimsey's card.

"Lord Peter Wimsey—just so. Dear me! The name seems familiar. Have I not heard of it in connection with—ah! I have it! *Notes on the Collection of Incunabula*, of course. A very scholarly little monograph, if I may say so. Yes. Dear me. It will be charming to exchange impressions with another book-collector. My library is, I fear, limited, but I have an edition of the *Gospel of Nicodemus* that may interest you. Dear me! Yes. Delightful to have met you like this. Bless my heart, there's five o'clock striking. We must be off, or I shall get a scolding from my wife. Good afternoon, Mrs. Tebbutt. I hope your good man will be much improved by to-morrow; I really think he is looking better already."

"Thank you, sir; Tom's always so pleased to see you. I'm sure you do him a lot of good."

"Tell him to keep his spirits up. Such a nasty, depressing complaint. But he's over the worst now. I will send a little bottle of port wine as soon as he is able to take it. Tuke Holdsworth '08," added the Rector, in an aside to Wimsey; "couldn't harm a fly, you know. Yes. Dear me! Well! We really must be going. I'm afraid my car is not much to boast of, but there's more room in it than one would think. Many's the christening party we've managed to squeeze into it, eh, Mrs. Tebbutt? Will you sit beside me, Lord Peter? Your man and your—dear me! have you any luggage? . . . Ah! down at Frog's Bridge? I will send my gardener to fetch it. It will be quite safe where it is; we're all honest people about here, aren't we, Mrs. Tebbutt? That's right. You must have this rug about your legs—yes, I insist. No, no, thank you. I can start her up quite well. I am so well accustomed to do it. There, you see! A few good pulls and she comes up as brisk as a bell. All right behind, my man? Good. Excellent. *Good* afternoon, Mrs. Tebbutt!"

The ancient car, shuddering to her marrow-bones, lurched away down the straight and narrow road. They passed a cottage, and then, quite suddenly, on their right, there loomed out of the whirling snow a grey, gigantic bulk.

"Great Heavens!" exclaimed Wimsey, "is that your church?"

"Yes, indeed," said the Rector, with pride. "You find it impressive?"

"Impressive!" said Wimsey. "Why, it's like a young cathedral. I'd no idea. How big is your parish, then?"

"You'll be surprised when I tell you," said the Rector, with a chuckle. "Three hundred and forty souls—no more. Astonishing, is it not? But you find the same thing all over the Fens. East Anglia is famous for the size and splendour of its parish churches. Still, we flatter ourselves we are almost unique, even in this part of the world. It was an abbey foundation, and in the old days Fenchurch St. Paul must have been quite an important place. How high should you say our tower was?"

Wimsey gazed up at the great pile.

"It's difficult to tell in this darkness. Not less than a hundred and thirty feet, surely."

"Not a bad guess. A hundred and twenty-eight, to be exact, to the top of the pinnacles, but it looks more, because of the comparative lowness of the clerestory roof. There aren't many to beat us. St. Peter Mancroft, of course—but that's a town church. And St. Michael's, Coventry, is one hundred and thirty feet without the spire. But I would venture to back Fenchurch St. Paul against them all for beauty of proportion. You will see that better when we turn the corner. Here we are. I always blow my horn here; the wall and the trees make it so very dangerous. I sometimes think we ought to have the churchyard wall set back a little, in the public interest. Ah! now you get a little idea. Very fine, is it not, the piling of the aisle and clerestory? You will be able to judge better in daylight. Here is the Rectory—just opposite the church. I always blow my horn at the gate for fear anybody should be about. The bushes make it so very dark. Ah! safely negotiated. I'm sure you will be glad to get into the warm and have a cup of tea—or possibly something stronger. I always blow my horn at the door, so as to tell my wife I am back. She gets nervous when I am out after lighting-up time; the dykes and drains make these roads so very awkward, and I am not as young as I was. I fear I am already a little late. Ah! here is my wife. Agnes, my dear, I am sorry to be a little behind time, but I have brought a guest back with me. He has had an accident with his car and will stay the night with us. The rug! Allow me! I fear that seat is something of a *res angusta*. Pray be careful of your head. Ah! all is well. My dear—Lord Peter Wimsey."

Mrs. Venables, a plump and placid figure in the lamplight from the open door, received the invasion with competent tranquillity.

"How fortunate that my husband should have met you. An accident? I do hope you are not hurt. I always say these roads are perfect death-traps."

"Thank you," said Wimsey. "There is no harm done. We stupidly ran off the road—at Frog's Bridge, I understand."

"A very nasty place—quite a mercy you didn't go into the Thirty-foot Drain. Do come in and sit down and get yourselves warm. Your man? Yes, of course. Emily! Take this gentleman's manservant into the kitchen and make him comfortable."

"And tell Hinkins to take the car and go down to Frog's Bridge for the luggage," added the Rector. "He will find Lord Peter's car there. He had better go at once, before the weather gets worse. And, Emily! tell him to send over to Wilderspin and arrange to get the car out of the dyke."

"To-morrow morning will do for that," said Wimsey.

"To be sure. First thing to-morrow morning. Wilderspin is the blacksmith—an excellent fellow. He will see to the matter most competently. Dear me, yes! And now, come in, come in! We want our tea. Agnes, my dear, have you explained to Emily that Lord Peter will be staying the night?"

"That will be all right," said Mrs. Venables, soothingly. "I do hope, Theodore, you have not caught cold."

"No, no, my dear. I have been well wrapped up. Dear me, yes! Ha! What do I see? Muffins?"

"I was just wishing for muffins," said Wimsey.

"Sit down, sit down and make a good meal. I'm sure you must be famished. I have seldom known such bitter weather. Would you prefer a whisky-and-soda, perhaps?"

"Tea for me," said Wimsey. "How jolly all this looks! Really, Mrs. Venables, it's tremendously good of you to take pity upon us."

"I'm only so glad to be able to help," said Mrs. Venables, smiling cheerfully. "Really, I don't think there's anything to equal the dreariness of these fen roads in winter. It's most fortunate your accident landed you comparatively close to the village."

"It is indeed." Wimsey gratefully took in the cosy sitting-room, with its little tables crowded with ornaments, its fire roaring behind a chaste canopy of velvet overmantel, and the silver tea-vessel winking upon the polished tray. "I feel like Ulysses, come to port after much storm and peril."

He bit gratefully into a large and buttery muffin.

"Tom Tebbutt seems a good deal better to-day," observed the Rector. "Very unfortunate that he should be laid up just now, but we must be thankful that it is no worse. I only hope there are no further casualties. Young Pratt will manage very well, I think; he went through two long touches this morning without a single mistake, and he is extremely keen. By the way, we ought, perhaps, to warn our visitor——"

"I'm sure we ought," said Mrs. Venables. "My husband has asked you to stay the night, Lord Peter, but he ought to have mentioned that you will probably get very little sleep, being so close to the church. But perhaps you do not mind the sound of bells."

"Not at all," said Wimsey.

"My husband is a very keen change-ringer," pursued Mrs. Venables, "and, as this is New Year's Eve——"

The Rector, who seldom allowed anybody else to finish a sentence, broke in eagerly.

"We hope to accomplish a real feat to-night," he said, "or rather, I should say, to-morrow morning. We intend to ring the New Year in with—you are not, perhaps, aware that we possess here one of the finest rings in the country?"

"Indeed?" said Wimsey. "Yes, I believe I have heard of the Fenchurch bells."

"There are, perhaps, a few heavier rings," said the Rector, "but I hardly know where you would rival us for fullness and sweetness of tone. Number seven, in particular, is a most noble old bell, and so is the tenor, and the John and Jericho bells are very remarkably fine—in fact, the whole ring is most 'tuneable and sound', as the old motto has it."

"It is a full ring of eight?"

"Oh, yes. If you are interested, I should like to show you a very charming little book, written by my predecessor, giving the whole history of the bells. The tenor, Tailor Paul, was actually cast in a field next to the churchyard in the year 1614. You can still see the depression in the earth where the mould was made, and the field itself is called the Bell-Field to this day."

"And have you a good set of ringers?" inquired Wimsey politely.

"Very good indeed. Excellent fellows and most enthusiastic. That reminds me. I was about to say that we have arranged to ring the New Year in to-night with no less," said the Rector, emphatically, "no less than fifteen thousand, eight hundred and forty Kent Treble Bob Majors. What do you think of that? Not bad, eh?"

"Bless my heart!" said Wimsey. "Fifteen thousand——"

"Eight hundred and forty," said the Rector.

Wimsey made a rapid calculation.

"A good many hours' work there."

"Nine hours," said the Rector, with relish.

"Well done, sir," said Wimsey. "Why, that's equal to the great performance of the College Youths in eighteen hundred and something."

"In 1868," agreed the Rector. "That is what we aim to emulate. And, what's more, but for the little help I can give, we shall be obliged to do as well as they did, and ring the whole peal with eight ringers only. We had hoped to have twelve, but unhappily, four of our best men have been laid low by this terrible influenza, and we can get no help from Fenchurch St. Stephen (which has a ring of bells, though not equal to ours) because there they have no Treble Bob ringers and confine themselves to Grandsire Triples."

Wimsey shook his head, and helped himself to his fourth muffin.

"Grandsire Triples are most venerable," he said solemnly, "but you can never get the same music——"

"That's what I say," crowed the Rector. "You never can get the same music when the tenor is rung behind—not even with Stedman's, though we are very fond here of Stedman's and ring them, I venture to say, very well. But for interest and variety and for sweetness in the peal, give me Kent Treble Bob every time."

"Quite right, sir," said Wimsey.

"You will never beat it," said Mr. Venables, soaring away happily to the heights of the belfry, and waving his muffin in the air, so that the butter ran down his cuff. "Take even Grandsire Major—I cannot help feeling it as a defect that the blows come behind so monotonously at the bobs and singles—

particularly at the singles, and the fact that the treble and second are confined to a plain hunting course——"

The rest of the Rector's observations on the Grandsire method of change-ringing were unhappily lost, for at that moment Emily made her appearance at the door, with the ominous words:

"If you please, sir, could James Thoday speak to you for a moment?"

"*James* Thoday?" said the Rector. "Why, certainly, of course. Put him in the study, Emily, and I will come in a moment."

The Rector was not long gone, and when he returned his face was as long as a fiddle. He let himself drop into his chair in an attitude of utter discouragement.

"This," he ejaculated, dramatically, "is an irreparable disaster!"

"Good gracious, Theodore! What in the world is the matter?"

"William Thoday! Of all nights in the year! Poor fellow, I ought not to think of myself, but it is a bitter disappointment—a bitter disappointment."

"Why, what has happened to Thoday?"

"Struck down," said the Rector, "struck down by this wretched scourge of influenza. Quite helpless. Delirious. They have sent for Dr. Baines."

"T'chk, t'chk," said Mrs. Venables.

"It appears," went on the Rector, "that he felt unwell this morning, but insisted—most unwisely, poor man—on driving in to Walbeach on some business or other. Foolish fellow! I thought he looked seedy when he came in to see me last night. Most fortunately, George Ashton met him in the town and saw how bad he was and insisted on coming back with him. Poor Thoday must have taken a violent chill in all this bitter cold. He was quite collapsed when they got home and they had to put him to bed instantly, and now he is in a high fever and worrying all the time because he cannot get to the church to-night. I told his brother to make every effort to calm his mind, but I fear it will be difficult. He is so enthusiastic, and the thought that he has been incapacitated at this crisis seems to be preying on his mind."

"Dear, dear," said Mrs. Venables, "but I expect Dr. Baines will give him something to quiet him down."

"I hope so, sincerely. It *is* a disaster, of course, but it is distressing that he should take it so to heart. Well, well. What can't be cured must be endured. This is our last hope gone. We shall be reduced to ringing minors."

"Is this man one of your ringers, then, padre?"

"Unfortunately, he is, and there is no one now to take his place. Our grand scheme will have to be abandoned. Even if I were to take a bell myself, I could not possibly ring for nine hours. I am not getting younger, and besides, I have an Early Service at 8 o'clock, in addition to the New Year service which will not release me till after midnight. Ah, well! Man proposes and God disposes—unless"—the Rector turned suddenly and looked at his guest—"you were speaking just now with a good deal of feeling about Treble Bob—you are not, yourself, by any chance, a ringer?"

"Well," said Wimsey, "I used at one time to pull quite a pretty rope. But whether, at this time of day——"

"Treble Bob?" inquired the Rector, eagerly.

"Treble Bob, certainly. But it's some time since——"

"It will come back to you," cried the Rector, feverishly. "It will come back. Half an hour with the handbells—"

"My dear!" said Mrs. Venables.

"Isn't it wonderful?" cried the Rector. "Is it not really providential? That just at this moment we should be sent a guest who is actually a ringer and accustomed to ringing Kent Treble Bob?" He rang for the maid. "Hinkins must go round at once and call the lads together for a practice ring on the handbells. My dear, I am afraid we shall have to monopolise the dining-room, if you don't mind. Emily, tell Hinkins that I have here a gentleman who can ring the peal with us and I want him to go round immediately——"

"One moment, Emily. Theodore, is it quite fair to ask Lord Peter Wimsey, after a motor accident, and at the end of a tiring day, to stay up ringing bells from midnight to nine o'clock? A short peal, perhaps, if he really does not mind, but even so, are we not demanding rather a lot of his good nature?"

The Rector's mouth drooped like the mouth of a hurt child and Wimsey hastened to his support.

"Not in the least, Mrs. Venables. Nothing would please me more than to ring bells all day and all night. I am not tired at all. I really don't need rest. I would far rather ring bells. The only thing that worries me is whether I shall be able to get through the peal without making stupid mistakes."

"Of course you will, of course you will," said the Rector, hurriedly. "But as my wife says—really, I am afraid I am being very thoughtless. Nine hours is too much. We ought to confine ourselves to five thousand changes or so——"

"Not a bit of it," said Wimsey. "Nine hours or nothing. I insist upon it. Probably, once you have heard my efforts, it will be nothing."

"Pooh! nonsense!" cried the Rector. "Emily, tell Hinkins to get the ringers together here by—shall we say half-past six? I think they can all be here by then, except possibly Pratt, who lives up at Tupper's End, but I can make the eighth myself. How delightful this is! Positively, I cannot get over the amazing coincidence of your arrival. It shows the wonderful way in which Heaven provides even for our pleasures, if they be innocent. I hope, Lord Peter, you will not mind if I make a little reference to it in my sermon to-night? At least, it will hardly be a sermon—only a few thoughts appropriate to the New Year and its opportunities. May I ask where you usually ring?"

"Nowhere, nowadays; but when I was a boy I used to ring at Duke's Denver, and when I go home at Christmas and so on, I occasionally lay hand to a rope even now."

"Duke's Denver? Of course—St. John ad-Portam-Latinam—a beautiful little church; I know it quite well. But I think you will admit that our bells are finer. Well, now, if you will excuse me, I will just run and put the dining-room in readiness for our practice."

He bustled away.

"It is very good of you to indulge my husband's hobby," said Mrs. Venables; "this occasion has meant so much to him, and he has had so many disappointments about it. But it seems dreadful to offer you hospitality and then keep you hard at work all night."

Wimsey again assured her that the pleasure was entirely his.

"I shall insist on your getting a few hours' rest at least," was all Mrs. Venables could say. "Will you come up now and see your room? You will like a wash and brush-up at any rate. We will have supper at 7.30, if we can get my husband to release you by then, and after that, you really must go and lie down for a nap. I have put you in here—I see your man has everything ready for you."

"Well, Bunter," said Wimsey, when Mrs. Venables had departed, leaving him to make himself presentable by the inadequate light of a small oil-lamp and a candle, "that looks a nice bed—but I am not fated to sleep in it."

"So I understand from the young woman, my lord."

"It's a pity you can't relieve me at the rope, Bunter."

"I assure your lordship that for the first time in my existence I regret that I have made no practical study of campanology."

"I am always so delighted to find that there are things you cannot do. Did you ever try?"

"Once only, my lord, and on that occasion an accident was only narrowly averted. Owing to my unfortunate lack of manual dexterity I was very nearly hanged in the rope, my lord."

"That's enough about hanging," said Wimsey, peevishly. "We're not detecting now, and I don't want to talk shop."

"Certainly not, my lord. Does your lordship desire to be shaved?"

"Yes—let's start the New Year with a clean face."

"Very good, my lord."

Descending, clean and shaven, to the dining-room, Wimsey found the table moved aside and eight chairs set in a circle. On seven of the chairs sat seven men, varying in age from a gnarled old gnome with a long beard to an embarrassed youth with his hair plastered into a cow-lick; in the centre, the Rector stood twittering like an amiable magician.

"Ah! there you are! Splendid! excellent! Now, lads, this is Lord Peter Wimsey, who has been providentially sent to assist us out of our difficulty. He tells me he is a little out of practice, so I am sure you will not mind putting in a little time to enable him to get his hand in again. Now I must introduce you all. Lord Peter, this is Hezekiah Lavender, who has pulled the Tenor for sixty years and means to pull it for twenty years longer, don't you, Hezekiah?"

The little gnarled man grinned toothlessly and extended a knobby hand.

"Proud to meet you, my lord. Yes, I've pulled old Tailor Paul a mort o' times now. Her and me's well acquainted, and I means to go on a-pulling of her till she rings the nine tailors for me, that I do."

"I hope you will long be spared to do it, Mr. Lavender."

"Ezra Wilderspin," went on the Rector. "He's our biggest man, and he pulls the smallest bell. That's often the way of things, isn't it? He is our blacksmith, by the way, and has promised to get your car put right for you in the morning."

The blacksmith laughed sheepishly, engulfed Wimsey's fingers in an enormous hand and retired to his chair in some confusion.

"Jack Godfrey," continued the Rector. "Number Seven. How's Batty Thomas going now, Jack?"

"Going fine, thank you, sir, since we had them new gudgeons put in."

"Jack has the honour of ringing the oldest bell we have," added the Rector. "Batty Thomas was cast in 1338 by Thomas Belleyetere of Lynn; but she gets her name from Abbot Thomas who re-cast her in 1380—doesn't she, Jack?"

"So she do, sir," agreed Mr. Godfrey. Bells, it may be noted, like ships and kittens, have a way of being female, whatever names they are given.

"Mr. Donnington, the landlord of the Red Cow, our churchwarden," went on the Rector, bringing forward a long, thin man with a squint. "I ought to have mentioned him first of all, by right of his office, but then, you see, though he himself is very distinguished, his bell is not so ancient as Tailor or Batty Thomas. He takes charge of Number Six—Dimity, we call her—a comparative newcomer in her present shape, though her metal is old."

"And a sweeter bell we haven't got in the ring," averred Mr. Donnington, stoutly. "Pleased to meet you, my lord."

"Joe Hinkins, my gardener. You have already met, I think. He pulls Number Five. Harry Gotobed, Number Four; our sexton, and what better name could a sexton have? And Walter Pratt—our youngest recruit, who is going to ring Number Three and do it very well indeed. So glad you were able to get here in time, Walter. That's all of us. You, Lord Peter, will take poor William Thoday's bell, Number Two. She and Number Five were recast in the same year as Dimity—the year of the old Queen's Jubilee; her name is Sabaoth. Now, let's get to work. Here is your handbell; come and sit next to Walter Pratt. Our good old friend Hezekiah will be the conductor, and you'll find he can sing out his calls as loud and clear as the bells, for all he's seventy-five years past. Can't you, Grand-dad?"

"Ay, that I can," cried the old man, cheerfully. "Now, boys, if you be ready, we'll ring a little touch of 96, just to put this gentleman in the way of it, like. You'll remember, my lord, that you starts by making the first snapping lead with the treble and after that you goes into the slow hunt till she comes down to snap with you again."

"Right you are," said Wimsey. "And after that I make the thirds and fourths."

"That's so, my lord. And then it's three steps forward and one step back till you lay the blows behind."

"Carry on, sergeant major."

The old man nodded, adding: "And you, Wally Pratt, mind what you're about, and don't go a-follerin' your course bell beyond thirds place. I've telled yew about that time and again. Now, are you ready, lads—go!"

The art of change-ringing is peculiar to the English, and, like most English peculiarities, unintelligible to the rest of the world. To the musical Belgian, for example, it appears that the proper thing to do with a carefully-tuned ring of bells is to play a tune upon it. By the English campanologist, the playing of tunes is considered to be a childish game, only fit for foreigners; the proper use of bells is to work out mathematical permutations and combinations. When he speaks of the music of his bells, he does not mean musicians' music—still less what the ordinary man calls music. To the ordinary man, in fact, the pealing of bells is a monotonous jangle and a nuisance, tolerable only when mitigated by remote distance and sentimental association. The change-ringer does, indeed, distinguish musical differences between one method of producing his permutations and another; he avers, for instance, that where the hinder bells run 7, 5, 6, or 5, 6, 7, or 5, 7, 6, the music is always prettier, and can detect and approve, where they occur, the consecutive fifths of Tittums and the cascading thirds of the Queen's change. But what he really means is, that by the English method of ringing with rope and wheel, each several bell gives forth her fullest and her noblest note. His passion—and it is a passion—finds its satisfaction in mathematical completeness and mechanical perfection, and as his bell weaves her way rhythmically up from lead to hinder place and down again, he is filled with the solemn intoxication that comes of intricate ritual faultlessly performed. To any disinterested spectator, peeping in upon the rehearsal, there might have been something a little absurd about the eight absorbed faces; the eight tense bodies poised in a spellbound circle on the edges of eight dining-room chairs; the eight upraised right hands, decorously wagging the handbells upward and downward; but to the performers, everything was serious and important as an afternoon with the Australians at Lord's.

Mr. Hezekiah Lavender having called three successive bobs, the bells came back into rounds without mishap.

"Excellent," said the Rector. "You made no mistake about that."

"All right, so far," said Wimsey.

"The gentleman will do well enough," agreed Mr. Lavender. "Now, boys, once again. What 'ull we make it this time, sir?"

"Make it a 704," said the Rector, consulting his watch. "Call her in the middle with a double, before, wrong and home, and repeat."

"Right you are, sir. And you, Wally Pratt, keep your ears open for the treble and your eyes on your course bell, and don't go gapin' about or you'll have us all imbrangled."

The unfortunate Pratt wiped his forehead, curled his boots tightly round the legs of his chair, and took a firm hold of his bell. Whether out of nervousness or for some other cause, he found himself in trouble at the beginning of the seventh lead, "imbrangled" himself and his neighbours very successfully and broke into a severe perspiration.

"Stand!" growled Mr. Lavender, in a disgusted tone. "If that's the way you mean to set about it, Wally Pratt, we may just so well give up the ringing of this here peal. Surely you know by this time what to do at a bob?"

"Come, come," said the Rector. "You mustn't be disheartened, Wally. Try again. You forgot to make the double dodge in 7, 8, didn't you?"

"Yes, sir."

"Forgot!" exclaimed Mr. Lavender, waggling his beard. "Now, just yew take example by his lordship here. *He* didn't go forgettin' things, none the more for bein' out o' practice."

"Come, come, Hezekiah," cried the Rector again. "You mustn't be hard on Wally. We haven't all had sixty years' experience."

Mr. Lavender grunted, and started the whole touch again from the beginning. This time Mr. Pratt kept his head and his place and the ringing went successfully through to its conclusion.

"Well rung all," cried the Rector. "Our new recruit will do us credit, I think, Hezekiah?"

"I almost fell down in the second lead, though," said Wimsey, laughing. "I as nearly as possible forgot to lay the four blows in fourths place at the bob. However, nearly isn't quite."

"You'll keep your place all right, my lord," said Mr. Lavender. "As for you, Wally Pratt——"

"I think," said the Rector, hastily, "we'd better run across to the church now and let Lord Peter get the feel of his bell. You may as well all come over and ring the bells up for service. And, Jack, see to it that Lord Peter's rope is made comfortable for him. Jack Godfrey takes charge of the bells and ropes," he added in explanation, "and keeps them in apple-pie order for us."

Mr. Godfrey smiled.

"We'll need to let the tuckings down a goodish bit for his lordship," he observed, measuring Wimsey with his eye; "he's none so tall as Will Thoday, not by a long chalk."

"Never you mind," said Wimsey. "In the words of the old bell-motto: I'd have it to be understood that though I'm little, yet I'm good."

"Of course," said the Rector, "Jack didn't mean anything else. But Will Thoday is a very tall man indeed. Now where did I put my hat? Agnes, my dear! Agnes! I can't find my hat. Oh, here, to be sure. And my muffler—I'm so much obliged to you. Now, let me just get the key of the belfry and we—dear me, now! When did I have that key last?"

"It's all right, sir," said Mr. Godfrey. "I have all the keys here, sir."

"The church-key as well?"

"Yes, sir, and the key of the bell-chamber."

"Oh, good, good—excellent. Lord Peter will like to go up into the bell-chamber. To my mind, Lord Peter, the sight of the ring of good bells—I beg your pardon, my dear?"

"I said, Do remember dinner-time, and don't keep poor Lord Peter too long."

"No, no, my dear, certainly not. But he will like to look at the bells. And the church itself is worth seeing, Lord Peter. We have a very interesting twelfth-century font, and the roof is considered to be one of the finest specimens—yes, yes, my dear, we're just going."

The hall-door was opened upon a glimmering world. The snow was still falling fast; even the footprints made less than an hour earlier by the ringers were almost obliterated. They straggled down the drive and crossed the road. Ahead of them, the great bulk of the church loomed dark and gigantic. Mr. Godfrey led the way with an old-fashioned lantern through the lych-gate and along a path bordered with tombstones to the south door of the church, which he opened, with a groaning of the heavy lock. A powerful ecclesiastical odour, compounded of ancient wood, varnish, dry rot, hassocks, hymn-books, paraffin lamps, flowers and candles, all gently baking in the warmth of slow-combustion stoves, billowed out from the interior. The tiny ray of the lantern picked out here the poppy-head on a pew, here the angle of a stone pillar, here the gleam of brass from a mural tablet. Their footsteps echoed queerly in the great height of the clerestory.

"All Transitional here," whispered the Rector, "except the Late Perpendicular window at the end of the north aisle, which of course you can't see. Nothing is left of the original Norman foundation but a couple of drums at the base of the chancel arch, but you can trace the remains of the Norman apse, if you look for it, underneath the Early English sanctuary. When we have more light, you will notice——Oh, yes, Jack, by all means. Jack Godfrey is quite right, Lord Peter—we must not waste time. I am apt to be led away by my enthusiasm."

He conducted his guest westwards under the tower arch, and thence, in the wake of Jack Godfrey's lantern, up a steep and winding belfry stair, its stone treads worn shallow with the feet of countless long-dead ringers. After a turn or so, the procession halted; there was a jingling of keys and the lantern moved away to the right through a narrow door. Wimsey, following, found himself in the ringing chamber of the belfry.

It was in no way remarkable, except in being perhaps a little loftier than the average, on account of the exceptional height of the tower. By daylight, it was well lit, having a fine window of three lights on each of its three exterior sides, while low down in the eastern wall, a couple of unglazed openings, defended by iron bars against accident, gave upon the interior of the church, a little above the level of the clerestory windows. As Jack Godfrey set the lantern on the floor, and proceeded to light a paraffin lamp which hung against the wall, Wimsey could see the eight bell-ropes, their woollen sallies looped neatly to the walls, and their upper ends vanishing mysteriously into the shadows of the chamber room. Then the light streamed out and the walls took shape and colour. They were plainly plastered, with a painted motto in Gothic lettering running round below the windows: "They Have Neither Speech nor Language but their Voices are Heard Among Them, their Sound is Gone Forth into All Lands." Above this, various tablets of wood, brass and even stone, commemorated the ringing of remarkable peals in the past.

"We shall hope to put up a new tablet after to-night," said the Rector's voice in Wimsey's ear.

"I only hope I may do nothing to prevent it," said Wimsey. "I see you have the old regulations for your ringers. Ah! 'Keep stroak of time and goe not out, Or elles you forfeit out of doubt For every fault a Jugg of beer.' It doesn't say how big a jug, but there is something about the double g that suggests size and potency. 'If a bell you overthrow 'Twill cost you sixpence ere you goe.' That's cheap, considering the damage it does. On the other hand, sixpence for every swear or curse is rather on the dear side, I think, don't you, padre? Where's this bell of mine?"

"Here, my lord." Jack Godfrey had unhitched the rope of the second bell, and let down to its full length the portion of rope below the sallie.

"When you've got her raised," he said, "we'll fix them tuckings proper. Unless you'd like me to raise her for you?"

"Not on your life," said Wimsey. "It's a poor ringer that can't raise his own bell." He grasped the rope and pulled it gently downwards, gathering the slack in his left hand. Softly, tremulously, high overhead in the tower, Sabaoth began to speak, and her sisters after her as the ringers stood to their ropes. "Tin-tin-tin", cried Gaude in her silvery treble; "tan-tan", answered Sabaoth; "din-din-din", "dan-dan-dan", said John and Jericho, climbing to their places; "bim, bam, bim, bam", Jubilee and Dimity followed; "bom", said Batty Thomas; and Tailor Paul, majestically lifting up her great bronze mouth, bellowed "bo, bo, bo", as the ropes hauled upon the wheels.

Wimsey brought his bell competently up and set her at backstroke while the tuckings were finally adjusted, after which, at the Rector's suggestion, a few rounds were rung to let him "get the feel of her".

"You can leave your bells up, boys," said Mr. Hezekiah Lavender, graciously, when this last rehearsal was concluded, "but don't you go a-taking that for what they calls a preceedent, Wally Pratt. And listen here, all on you; don't make no mistake. You comes here, sharp at the quarter to eleven, see—and you rings same as usual for service, and after Rector has finished his sermon, you comes up here again quiet and decent and takes your places. Then, while they're a-singin' their 'ymn, I rings the nine tailors and the 'alf-minute passing strokes for Old Year, see. Then you takes your ropes in hand and waits for the clock to strike. When she's finished striking, I says 'Go!' and mind as you're ready to go. And when Rector's done down below, he's promised to come up and give a 'and from time to time to any man as needs a rest, and I'm sure it's very kind of him. And I take leave to suppose, Alf Donnington, as you won't forget the usual."

"Not me," said Mr. Donnington. "Well, so long, boys."

The lantern led the way from the ringing-chamber, and a great shuffling of feet followed it.

"And now," said the Rector, "and now, Lord Peter, you will like to come and see——Dear me!" he ejaculated, as they groped upon the dark spiral stair, "where in the world is Jack Godfrey? Jack! He has gone on down with the others. Ah, well, poor fellow, no doubt he wants to get home to his supper. We must not be selfish. Unfortunately he has the key of the bell-chamber, and without it we cannot conduct our researches. However, you will see much better to-morrow. Yes, Joe, yes—we are coming. Do be careful of these stairs—they are very much worn, especially on the inside. Here we are, safe and sound. Excellent! Now, before we go, Lord Peter, I should so much like to show you——"

The clock in the tower chimed the three-quarters.

"Bless my heart!" cried the Rector, conscience-stricken, "and dinner was to be at half-past! My wife—we must wait till to-night. You will get a general idea of the majesty and beauty of our church if you attend the service, though there are many most interesting details that a visitor is almost bound to miss if they are not pointed out to him. The font, for instance—Jack! bring the lantern here a moment—there is one point about our font which is most uncommon, and I should like to show it to you. Jack!"

But Jack, unaccountably deaf, was jingling the church keys in the porch, and the Rector, sighing a little, accepted defeat.

"I fear it is true," he said, as he trotted down the path, "that I am inclined to lose count of time."

"Perhaps," replied Wimsey politely, "the being continually in and about this church brings eternity too close."

"Very true," said the Rector, "very true—though there are mementoes enough to mark the passage of time. Remind me to-morrow to show you the tomb of Nathaniel Perkins—one of our local worthies and a great sportsman. He refereed once for the great Tom Sayers, and was a notable figure at all the 'mills' for miles around, and when he died—— Here we are at home. I will tell you later about Nathaniel Perkins. Well, my dear, we're back at last! Not so *very* late after all. Come along, come along. You must make a good dinner, Lord Peter, to fit you for your exertions. What have we here? Stewed oxtail? Excellent! Most sustaining! I trust, Lord Peter, you can eat stewed oxtail. For what we are about to receive . . ."

THE SECOND COURSE

The Bells in their Courses

When mirth and pleasure is on the wing we ring;
At the departure of a soul we toll.

Ringers' Rules at Southill, Bedfordshire

AFTER DINNER, MRS. VENABLES resolutely asserted her authority. She sent Lord Peter up to his room, regardless of the Rector, who was helplessly hunting through a set of untidy bookshelves in search of the Rev. Christopher Woollcott's *History of the Bells of Fenchurch St. Paul*.

"I can't imagine what has become of it," said the Rector: "I fear I'm sadly unmethodical. But perhaps you would like to look at this—a trifling contribution of my own to campanological lore. I know, my dear, I know—I must not detain Lord Peter—it is thoughtless of me."

"You must get some rest yourself, Theodore."

"Yes, yes, my dear. In a moment. I was only——"

Wimsey saw that the one way to quiet the Rector was to desert him without compunction. He retired, accordingly, and was captured at the head of the stairs by Bunter, who tucked him firmly up beneath the eiderdown with a hot-water bottle and shut the door upon him.

A roaring fire burned in the grate. Wimsey drew the lamp closer to him, opened the little brochure presented to him by the Rector, and studied the title-page:

An Inquiry into
the Mathematical Theory
of the

IN AND OUT OF COURSE

together with

Directions for

Calling Bells into Rounds

from any position
in all the recognised Methods
upon a
New and Scientific Principle

by
Theodore Venables, M.A.

Rector of Fenchurch St. Paul
sometime Scholar of Caius Coll: Camb:
author of
"Change-ringing for Country Churches",
"Fifty Short Touches of Grandsire Triples", etc.

"God is gone up with a merry noise."

MCMII

The letterpress was of a soporific tendency; so was the stewed oxtail; the room was warm; the day had been a tiring one; the lines swam before Lord Peter's eyes. He nodded; a coal tinkled from the grate; he roused himself with a jerk and read: ". . . if the 5th is in course after the 7th (says Shipway), and 7th after the 6th, they are right, when the small bells, 2, 3, 4, are brought as directed in the preceding peals; but if 6, 7 are together without the 5th, call the 5th into the hunt. . . ."

Lord Peter Wimsey nodded away into dreams.

He was roused by the pealing of bells.

For a moment, memory eluded him—then he flung the eiderdown aside and sat up, ruffled and reproachful, to encounter the calm gaze of Bunter.

"Good God! I've been asleep! Why didn't you call me? They've begun without me."

"Mrs. Venables gave orders, my lord, that you were not to be disturbed until half-past eleven, and the reverend gentleman instructed me to say, my lord, that they would content themselves with ringing six bells as a preliminary to the service."

"What time is it now?"

"Nearly five minutes to eleven, my lord."

As he spoke, the pealing ceased, and Jubilee began to ring the five-minute bell.

"Dash it all!" said Wimsey. "This will never do. Must go and hear the old boy's sermon. Give me a hair-brush. Is it still snowing?"

"Harder than ever, my lord."

Wimsey made a hasty toilet and ran downstairs, Bunter following him decorously. They let themselves out by the front door, and, guided by Bunter's electric torch, made their way through the shrubbery and across the road to the church, entering just as the organ boomed out its final notes. Choir and parson were in their places and Wimsey, blinking in the yellow lamplight, at length discovered his seven fellow-ringers seated on a row of chairs beneath the tower. He picked his way cautiously over the coconut matting towards them, while Bunter, who had apparently acquired all the necessary information beforehand, made his unperturbed way to a pew in the north aisle and sat down beside Emily from the Rectory. Old Hezekiah Lavender greeted Wimsey with a welcoming chuckle and thrust a prayer-book under his nose as he knelt down to pray.

"Dearly beloved brethren——"

Wimsey scrambled to his feet and looked round.

At the first glance he felt himself sobered and awe-stricken by the noble proportions of the church, in whose vast spaces the congregation—though a good one for so small a parish in the dead of a winter's night—seemed almost lost. The wide nave and shadowy aisles, the lofty span of the chancel arch—crossed, though not obscured, by the delicate fan-tracery and crenellated moulding of the screen—the intimate and cloistered loveliness of the chancel, with its pointed arcading, graceful ribbed vault and five narrow east lancets, led his attention on and focused it first upon the remote glow of the sanctuary. Then his gaze, returning to the nave, followed the strong yet slender shafting that sprang fountain-like from floor to foliated column-head, spraying into the light, wide arches that carried the clerestory. And there, mounting to the steep pitch of the roof, his eyes were held entranced with wonder and delight. Incredibly aloof, flinging back the light in a dusky shimmer of bright hair and gilded outspread wings, soared the ranked angels, cherubim and seraphim, choir over choir, from corbel and hammer-beam floating face to face uplifted.

"My God!" muttered Wimsey, not without reverence. And he softly repeated to himself: "He rode upon the cherubims and did fly; He came flying upon the wings of the wind."

Mr. Hezekiah Lavender poked his new colleague sharply in the ribs, and Wimsey became aware that the congregation had settled down to the General Confession, leaving him alone and agape upon his feet. Hurriedly he turned the leaves of his prayer-book and applied himself to making the proper responses. Mr. Lavender, who had obviously decided that he was either a half-wit or a heathen, assisted him by finding the Psalms for him and by bawling every verse very loudly in his ear.

". . . Praise Him in the cymbals and dances: praise Him upon the strings and pipe."

The shrill voices of the surpliced choir mounted to the roof, and seemed to find their echo in the golden mouths of the angels.

"Praise Him upon the well-tuned cymbals; praise Him upon the loud cymbals.

"Let everything that hath breath praise the Lord."

The time wore on towards midnight. The Rector, advancing to the chancel steps, delivered, in his mild and scholarly voice, a simple and moving little address, in which he spoke of praising God, not only upon the strings and pipe, but upon the beautiful bells of their beloved church, and alluded, in his gently pious way, to the presence of the passing stranger—"please do not turn round to stare at him; that would be neither courteous nor reverent"—who had been sent "by what men call chance" to assist in this work of devotion. Lord Peter blushed, the Rector pronounced the Benediction, the organ played the opening bars of a hymn and Hezekiah Lavender exclaimed sonorously: "Now, lads!" The ringers, with much subdued shuffling, extricated themselves from their chairs and wound their way up the belfry stair. Coats were pulled off and hung on nails in the ringing-chamber, and Wimsey, observing on a bench near the door an enormous brown jug and nine pewter tankards, understood, with pleasure, that the landlord of the Red Cow had, indeed, provided "the usual" for the refreshment of the ringers.

The eight men advanced to their stations, and Hezekiah consulted his watch.

"Time!" he said.

He spat upon his hands, grasped the sallie of Tailor Paul, and gently swung the great bell over the balance.

Toll-toll-toll; and a pause; toll-toll-toll; and a pause; toll-toll-toll; the nine tailors, or teller-strokes, that mark the passing of a man. The year is dead; toll him out with twelve strokes more, one for every passing month. Then silence. Then, from the faint, sweet tubular chimes of the clock overhead, the four quarters and the twelve strokes of midnight. The ringers grasped their ropes.

"Go!"

The bells gave tongue: Gaude, Sabaoth, John, Jericho, Jubilee, Dimity, Batty Thomas and Tailor Paul, rioting and exulting high up in the dark tower, wide mouths rising and falling, brazen tongues clamouring, huge wheels turning to the dance of the leaping ropes. Tin tan din dan bim bam bom bo—tan tin din dan bam bim bo bom—tin tan dan din bim bam bom bo—tan tin dan din bam bim bo bom—tan dan tin bam din bo bim bom—every bell in her place striking tuneably, hunting up, hunting down, dodging, snapping, laying her blows behind, making her thirds and fourths, working down to lead the dance again. Out over the flat, white wastes of fen, over the spear-straight, steel-dark dykes and the wind-bent, groaning poplar trees; bursting from the snow-choked louvres of the belfry, whirled away southward and westward in gusty blasts of clamour to the sleeping counties went the music of the bells—little Gaude, silver Sabaoth, strong John and Jericho, glad Jubilee, sweet Dimity and old Batty Thomas, with great Tailor Paul bawling and striding

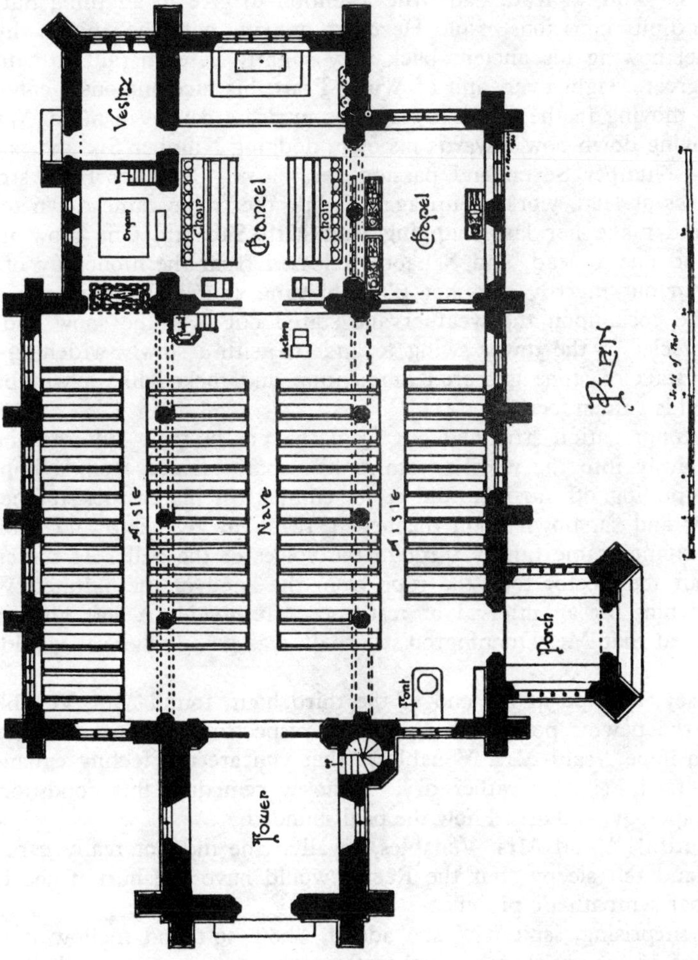
Vestry
Organ
Choir
Chancel
Choir
Chapel
Lectern
Aisle
Nave
Aisle
Porch
Font
Tower
Plan
Scale of Feet

like a giant in the midst of them. Up and down went the shadows of the ringers upon the walls, up and down went the scarlet sallies flickering roofwards and floorwards, and up and down, hunting in their courses, went the bells of Fenchurch St. Paul.

Wimsey, his eye upon the ropes and his ear pricked for the treble's shrill tongue speaking at lead, had little attention to give to anything but his task. He was dimly conscious of old Hezekiah, moving with the smooth rhythm of a machine, bowing his ancient back very slightly at each pull to bring Tailor Paul's great weight over, and of Wally Pratt, his face anxiously contorted and his lips moving in the effort to keep his intricate course in mind. Wally's bell was moving down now towards his own, dodging Number Six and passing her, dodging Number Seven and passing her, passing Number Five, striking her two blows at lead, working up again, while the treble came down to take her place and make her last snapping lead with Sabaoth. One blow in seconds place and one at lead, and Sabaoth, released from the monotony of the slow hunt, ran out merrily into her plain hunting course. High in the air above them the cock upon the weathervane stared out over the snow and watched the pinnacles of the tower swing to and fro with a slowly widening sweep as the tall stalk of stone gathered momentum and rocked like a windblown tree beneath his golden feet.

The congregation streamed out from the porch, their lanterns and torches flitting away into the whirling storm like sparks tossed from a bonfire. The Rector, pulling off surplice and stole, climbed in his cassock to the ringing-chamber and sat down upon the bench, ready to give help and counsel. The clock's chimes came faintly through the voices of the bells. At the end of the first hour the Rector took the rope from the hand of the agitated Wally and released him for an interval of rest and refreshment. A soft glugging sound proclaimed that Mr. Donnington's "usual" was going where it would do most good.

Wimsey, relieved at the end of the third hour, found Mrs. Venables seated among the pewter pots, with Bunter in respectful attendance beside her.

"I do hope," said Mrs. Venables, "that you are not feeling exhausted."

"Far from it; only rather dry." Wimsey remedied this condition without further apology, and asked how the peal sounded.

"Beautiful!" said Mrs. Venables, loyally. She did not really care for bell-music, and felt sleepy; but the Rector would have felt hurt if she had withdrawn her sympathetic presence.

"It's surprising, isn't it?" she added, "how soft and mellow it sounds in here. But of course there's another floor between us and the bell-chamber." She yawned desperately. The bells rang on. Wimsey, knowing that the Rector was well set for the next quarter of an hour, was seized with a fancy to listen to the peal from outside. He slipped down the winding stair and groped his way through the south porch. As he emerged into the night, the clamour of the bells smote on his ears like a blow. The snow was falling less heavily now. He turned to his right, knowing that it is unlucky to walk about a church widdershins, and followed the path close beneath the wall till he found himself standing by the west door. Sheltered by the towering bulk of the masonry, he lit a sacrilegious cigarette, and, thus fortified, turned right again. Beyond the foot of the tower, the pathway ended, and he stumbled among grass and tombstones for the whole length of the aisle, which, on this side, was prolonged to the extreme east end of the church. Midway between the last two buttresses on the north side he came upon a path leading to a small door; this he tried, but found it locked, and so passed on, encountering the full violence of the wind as he rounded the east end. Pausing a moment to get his breath, he looked out over the Fen. All was darkness, except for a dim stationary light which might have been shining from some cottage window. Wimsey reckoned that the cottage must lie somewhere along the solitary road by which they had reached the Rectory, and wondered why anybody should be awake at three o'clock on New Year's morning. But the night was bitter and he was wanted back at his job. He completed his circuit, re-entered by the south porch and returned to the belfry. The Rector resigned the rope to him, warning him that he had now to make his two blows behind and not to forget to dodge back into eighth's place before hunting down.

At six o'clock, the ringers were all in pretty good case. Wally Pratt's cow-lick had fallen into his eyes, and he was sweating freely, but was still moving well within himself. The blacksmith was fresh and cheerful, and looked ready to go on till next Christmas. The publican was grim but determined. Most unperturbed of all was the aged Hezekiah, working grandly as though he were part and parcel of his rope, and calling his bobs without a tremor in his clear old voice.

At a quarter to eight the Rector left them to prepare for his early service. The beer in the jug had sunk to low tide and Wally Pratt, with an hour and a half to go, was beginning to look a little strained. Through the southern window a faint reflection of the morning light came, glimmering frail and blue.

At ten minutes past nine the Rector was back in the belfry, standing watch in hand with a beaming smile on his face.

At thirteen minutes past nine the treble came shrilling triumphantly into her last lead.

Tin tan din dan bim bam bom bo.

Their long courses ended, the bells came faultlessly back into rounds, and the ringers stood.

"Magnificent, lads, magnificent!" cried Mr. Venables. "You've done it, and it couldn't have been better done."

"Eh!" admitted Mr. Lavender, "it was none so bad." A slow toothless grin overspread his countenance. "Yes, we done it. How did it sound from down below, sir?"

"Fine," said the Rector. "As firm and true as any ringing I have ever heard. Now you must all be wanting your breakfasts. It's all ready for you at the Rectory. Well now, Wally, you can call yourself a real ringer now, can't you? You came through it with very great credit—didn't he, Hezekiah?"

"Fair to middlin'," said Mr. Lavender, grudgingly. "But you takes too much out o' yourself, Wally. You've no call to be gettin' yourself all of a muck o' sweat that way. Still, you ain't made no mistakes, an' that's something, but I see you a mumblin' and countin' to yourself all the time. If I've telled yew once I've telled yew a hundred times to keep your eye on the ropes and then you don't need——"

"There, there!" said the Rector. "Never mind, Wally, you did very well indeed. Where's Lord Peter—oh! there you are. I'm sure we owe you a great deal. Not too fatigued, I hope?"

"No, no," said Wimsey, extricating himself from the congratulatory handshakes of his companions. He felt, in fact, exhausted to dropping-point. He had not rung a long peal for years, and the effort of keeping alert for so many hours had produced an almost intolerable desire to tumble down in a corner and go to sleep. "I—ah—oh—I'm perfectly all right."

He swayed as he walked and would have pitched head-long down the steep stair, but for the blacksmith's sustaining arm.

"Breakfast," said the Rector, much concerned, "breakfast is what we all want. Hot coffee. A very comforting thing. Dear me, yes, I for one am looking forward to it very much. Ha! the snow has ceased falling. Very beautiful, this white world—if only there were not a thaw to follow. This will mean a lot of water down the Thirty-foot, I expect. Are you sure you're all right? Come along, then, come along! Why, here is my wife—come to chide my tardiness, I expect. We're just coming, my dear—— Why, Johnson, what is it?"

He addressed a young man in chauffeur's livery who was standing at Mrs. Venables' side. Mrs. Venables broke in before he could reply.

"My dear Theodore—I have been saying, you can't go just yet. You must have something to eat——"

Mr. Venables put the interruption aside with an unexpected, quiet authority. "Agnes, my dear, permit me. Am I wanted, Johnson?"

"Sir Henry sent me to say, sir, that the mistress was very bad this morning, and they're afraid she's sinking, sir, and she is very anxious to receive the Sacrament if you could see your way——"

"Good Heavens!" exclaimed the Rector. "So ill as that? Sinking? I am terribly grieved to hear it. Of course, I will come immediately. I had no idea——"

"No more hadn't any of us, sir. It's this wicked influenza. I'm sure nobody ever thought yesterday——"

"Oh, dear, oh, dear! I hope it's not as bad as you fear! But I mustn't delay. You shall tell me about it as you go. I will be with you in one moment. Agnes, my dear, see that the men get their breakfast and explain to them why I cannot join them. Lord Peter, you must excuse me. I shall be with you later. Bless my heart! Lady Thorpe—what a scourge this influenza is!"

He trotted hurriedly back into the church. Mrs. Venables looked ready to cry, between anxiety and distress.

"Poor Theodore! After being up all night—of course he has to go, and we ought not to think about ourselves. Poor Sir Henry! An invalid himself! Such a bitter morning, and no breakfast! Johnson, please say to Miss Hilary how sorry I am and ask if there is anything I can do to help Mrs. Gates. The housekeeper, you know, Lord Peter—such a nice woman, and the cook away on holiday, it does seem so hard. Troubles never come singly. Dear me, you must be famished. Do come along and be looked after. You'll be sure to send round, Johnson, if you want any help. Can Sir Henry's nurse manage, I wonder? This is such an isolated place for getting any help. Theodore! are you sure you are well wrapped up?"

The Rector, who now rejoined them, carrying the Communion vessels in a wooden case, assured her that he was well protected. He was bundled into the waiting car by Johnson, and whirled away westwards towards the village.

This untoward incident cast a certain gloom over the breakfast table, though Wimsey, who felt his sides clapping together like an empty portmanteau, was only too thankful to devour his eggs and bacon and coffee in peace. Eight pairs of jaws chumped steadily, while Mrs. Venables dispensed the provisions in a somewhat distracted way, interspersing her hospitable urgings with ejaculations of sympathy for the Thorpe family and anxiety for her husband's wellbeing.

"Such a lot of trouble as the Thorpes have had, too, one way and another," she remarked. "All that dreadful business about old Sir Charles, and the loss of the necklace, and that unfortunate girl and everything, though it was a merciful thing the man died, after killing a warder and all that, though it upset the whole family very much at the time. Hezekiah, how are you getting on? A bit more bacon? Mr. Donnington? Hinkins, pass Mr. Godfrey the cold ham. And of course, Sir Henry never has been strong since the War, poor man. Are you getting enough to eat down there, Wally? I do hope the Rector won't be kept too long without his breakfast. Lord Peter, a little more coffee?"

Wimsey thanked her, and asked what, exactly, was the trouble about old Sir Charles and the necklace.

"Oh, of course, you don't know. So silly of me! Living in this solitary place, one imagines that one's little local excitements are of world-wide importance. It's rather a long story, and I shouldn't have mentioned it at all"—here the good lady lowered her voice—"if William Thoday had been here. I'll tell you after breakfast. Or ask Hinkins. He knows all about it. How is William Thoday this morning, I wonder? Has anybody heard?"

"He's mortal bad, ma'am, I'm afeard," replied Mr. Donnington, taking the question to himself. "I saw my missus after service, and she told me she'd heard from Joe Mullins as he was dreadfully delirious all night, and they couldn't hardly keep him in his bed, on account of his wanting to get up and ring."

"Dear, dear! It's a good thing for Mary that they've got James at home."

"So it is," agreed Mr. Donnington. "A sailor's wonderful handy about the house. Not but what his leave's up in a day or two, but it's to be hoped as they'll be over the worst by then."

Mrs. Venables clucked gently.

"Ah!" said Hezekiah. "'Tis a mortal bad thing, this influenza. And it do take the young and strong cruel often, and leave the old uns be. Seems like old fellers like me is too tough fer it."

"I hope so, Hezekiah, I'm sure," said Mrs. Venables. "There! Ten o'clock striking, and the Rector not back. Well, I suppose one couldn't expect—why, there's the car coming up the drive! Wally, would you please ring that bell.

We want some fresh eggs and bacon for the Rector, Emily, and you'd better take the coffee out and hot it up for him."

Emily took out the jug, but returned almost immediately.

"Oh, if you please, ma'am, the Rector says, will you all excuse him, please, and he'll take his breakfast in the study. And oh! if you please, ma'am, poor Lady Thorpe's gone, ma'am, and if Mr. Lavender's finished, he's please to go over to the church at once and ring the passing bell."

"Gone!" cried Mrs. Venables. "Why, what a terrible thing!"

"Yes, ma'am. Mr. Johnson says it was dreadful sudden. The Rector hadn't hardly left her room, ma'am, when it was all over, and they don't know how they're to tell Sir Henry."

Mr. Lavender pushed his chair back and quavered to his ancient feet.

"In the midst of life," he said solemnly, "we are in death. Terrible true that is, to be sure. If so be as you'll kindly excuse me, ma'am, I'll be leaving you now, and thank you kindly. Good mornin' to you all. That were a fine peal as we rung, none the more for that, and now I'll be gettin' to work on old Tailor Paul again."

He shuffled sturdily out, and within five minutes they heard the deep and melancholy voice of the bell ringing, first the six tailors for a woman and then the quick strokes which announce the age of the dead. Wimsey counted them up to thirty-seven. Then they ceased, and were followed by the slow tolling of single strokes at half-minute intervals. In the dining-room, the silence was only broken by the shy sound of hearty feeders trying to finish their meal inconspicuously.

The party broke up quietly. Mr. Wilderspin drew Wimsey to one side and explained that he had sent round to Mr. Ashton for a couple of farm-horses and a stout rope, and hoped to get the car out of the ditch in a very short time, and would then see what was needed in the way of repairs. If his lordship cared to step along to the smithy in an hour or so, they could go into consultation about the matter. His (Mr. Wilderspin's) son George was a great hand with motors, having had considerable experience with farm engines, not to mention his own motor-bike. Mrs. Venables retired into the study to see that her husband had everything he wanted and to administer such consolation as she might for the calamity that had befallen the parish. Wimsey, knowing that his presence at Frog's Bridge could not help and would probably only hinder the break-down team, begged his hostess not to trouble about him, and wandered out into the garden. At the back of the house, he discovered Joe Hinkins, polishing the Rector's aged car. Joe accepted a cigarette, passed a few remarks about the ringing of the peal, and thence slid into conversation about the Thorpe family.

"They live in the big red-brick house t'other side the village. A rich family they were once. They do say as they got their land through putting money into draining of the Fen long ago under the Earl of Bedford. You'd know all about that, my lord, I dare say. Anyhow, they reckon to be an old family hereabouts. Sir Charles, he was a fine, generous gentleman; did a lot of good in his time, though he wasn't what you'd call a rich man, not by no means. They do say his father lost a lot of money up in London, but I don't know how. But he farmed his land well, and it was a rare trouble to the village when he died along of the burglary."

"What burglary was that?"

"Why, that was the necklace the mistress was talking about. It was when young Mr. Henry—that's the present Sir Henry—was married. The year of the War, it was, in the spring—April 1914—I remember it very well. I was a youngster at the time, and their wedding-bells was the first long peal I ever rang. We gave them 5,040 Grandsire Triples, Holt's Ten-part Peal—you'll find the record of it in the church yonder, and there was a big supper at the Red House afterwards, and a lot of fine visitors came down for the wedding. The young lady was an orphan, you see, and some sort of connection with the family, and Mr. Henry being the heir they was married down here. Well, there was a lady come to stay in the house, and she had a wonderful fine emerald necklace—worth thousands and thousands of pounds it was—and the very night after the wedding, when Mr. Henry and his lady was just gone off for their honeymoon, the necklace was stole."

"Good lord!" said Wimsey. He sat down on the running-board of the car and looked as encouraging as he could.

"You may say so," said Mr. Hinkins, much gratified. "A big sensation it made at the time in the parish. And the worst part of it was, you see, that one of Sir Charles' own men was concerned in it. Poor gentleman, he never held up his head again. When they took this fellow Deacon and it came out what he'd done——"

"Deacon was——?"

"Deacon, he was the butler. Been with them six years, he had, and married the housemaid, Mary Russell, that's married to Will Thoday, him as rings Number Two and has got the influenzy so bad."

"Oh!" said Wimsey. "Then Deacon is dead now, I take it."

"That's right, my lord. That's what I was a-telling you. You see, it 'appened this way. Mrs. Wilbraham woke up in the night and saw a man standing by her bedroom window. So she yelled out, and the fellow jumped out into the garden and dodged into the shrubbery, like. So she screamed again, very loud, and rang her bell and made a to-do, and everybody came running out to see what was the matter. There was Sir Charles and some gentlemen that was staying in the house, and one of them had a shot-gun. And when they got downstairs, there was Deacon in his coat and trousers just running out at the back door, and the footman in pyjamas; and the chauffeur as slept over the garage, he came running out too, because the first thing as Sir Charles did, you see, was to pull the house-bell what they had for calling the gardener. The gardener, he came too, of course, and so did I, because you see, I was the gardener's boy at the time, and wouldn't never have left Sir Charles, only for him having to cut down his establishment, what with the War and paying Mrs. Wilbraham for the necklace."

"Paying for the necklace?"

"Yes, my lord. That's just where it was, you see. It wasn't insured, and though of course nobody could have held Sir Charles responsible, he had it on his conscience as he ought to pay Mrs. Wilbraham the value of it, though how anybody calling herself a lady could take the money off him I don't understand. But as I was a-saying, we all came out and then one of the gentlemen see the man a-tearing across the lawn, and Mr. Stanley loosed off the shot-gun at him and hit him, as we found out afterwards, but he got away over the wall, and there was a chap waiting for him on the other side with a motor-car, and he got clear away. And in the middle of it all, out comes Mrs. Wilbraham and her maid, a-hollering that the emerald necklace has been took."

"And didn't they catch the man?"

"Not for a bit, they didn't, my lord. The chauffeur, he gets the car out and goes off after them, but by the time he'd got started up, they was well away. They went up the road past the church, but nobody knew whether they'd gone through Fenchurch St. Peter or up on to the Bank, and even then they might have gone either by Dykesey and Walea or Walbeach way, or over the Thirty-foot to Leamholt or Holport. So the chauffeur went after the police. You see, barring the village constable at Fenchurch St. Peter there's no police nearer than Leamholt, and in those days they didn't have a car at the police-station even there, so Sir Charles said to send the car for them would be quicker than telephoning and waiting till they came."

"Ah!" said Mrs. Venables, suddenly popping her head in at the garage door. "So you've got Joe on to the Thorpe robbery. He knows a lot more about it than I do. Are you sure you aren't frozen to death in this place?"

Wimsey said he was quite warm enough, thanks, and he hoped the Rector was none the worse for his exertions.

"He doesn't seem to be," said Mrs. Venables, "but he's rather upset, naturally. You'll stay to lunch, of course. No trouble at all. Can you eat shepherd's pie? You're sure? The butcher doesn't call to-day, but there's always cold ham."

She bustled away. Joe Hinkins passed a chamois leather thoughtfully over a headlight. "Carry on," said Wimsey.

"Well, my lord, the police did come and of course they hunted round a good bit, and didn't we bless them, the way they morrised over the flower-beds, a-looking for footprints and breaking down the tulips. Anyhow, there 'twas, and they traced the car and got the fellow that had been shot in the leg. A well-known jewel thief he was, from London. But you see, they said it must have been a inside job, because it turned out as the fellow as jumped out o' the window wasn't the same as the London man, and the long and short of it was, they found out as the inside man was this here Deacon. Seems the Londoner had been keeping his eye on that necklace, like, and had got hold of Deacon and got him to go and steal the stuff and drop it out of the window to him. They was pretty sure of their ground—I think they found finger-prints and such like—and they arrested Deacon. I remember it very well, because they took him one Sunday morning, just a-coming out of church, and a terrible job it was to take him; he near killed a constable. The robbery was on the Thursday night, see? and it had took them that time to get on to it."

"Yes, I see. How did Deacon know where to find the jewels?"

"Well, that was just it, my lord. It came out as Mrs. Wilbraham's maid had let out something, stupid-like, to Mary Russell—that is, her as had married

Deacon, and she, not thinking no harm, had told her husband. Of course, they had them two women up too. All the village was in a dreadful way about it, because Mary was a very decent, respectable girl, and her father was one of our sidesmen. There's not an honester, better family in the Fenchurches than what the Russells are. This Deacon, he didn't come from these parts, he was a Kentish man by birth. Sir Charles brought him down from London. But there wasn't no way of getting him out of it, because the London thief—Cranton, he called himself, but he had other names—he blew the gaff and gave Deacon away."

"Dirty dog!"

"Ah! but you see, he said as Deacon had done him down and so, if Cranton was telling the truth, he had. Cranton said as Deacon dropped out nothing but the empty jewel-case and kept the necklace for himself. He went for Deacon 'ammer-and-tongs in the dock and tried for to throttle him. But of course, Deacon swore as it was all a pack of lies. His tale was, that he heard a noise and went to see what was the matter, and that when Mrs. Wilbraham saw him in her room, he was just going to give chase to Cranton. He couldn't deny he'd been in the room, you see, because of the finger-prints and that. But it went against him that he'd told a different story at the beginning, saying as how he'd gone out by the back door, hearing somebody in the garden. Mary supported that, and it's a fact that the back door was unbolted when the footman got to it. But the lawyer on the other side said that Deacon had unbolted the door himself beforehand, just in case he had to get out by the window, so as to leave himself a way back into the house. But as for the necklace, they never could settle that part of it, for it wasn't never found. Whether Cranton had it, and was afraid to get rid of it, like, or whether Deacon had it and hid it, I don't know and no more does nobody. It ain't never turned up to this day, nor yet the money Cranton said he'd given Deacon, though they turned the place upside-down looking for both on 'em. And the upshot was, they acquitted the two women, thinking as how they'd only been chattering silly-like, the way women do, and they sent Cranton and Deacon to prison for a good long stretch. Old Russell, he couldn't face the place after that, and he sold up and went off, taking Mary with him. But when Deacon died——"

"How was that?"

"Why, he broke prison and got away after killing a warder. A bad lot, was Deacon. That was in 1918. But he didn't get much good by it, because he fell into a quarry or some such place over Maidstone way, and they found his body two years later, still in his prison clothes. And as soon as he heard about it, young William Thoday, that had always been sweet on Mary, went after her and married her and brought her back. You see, nobody here ever believed as there was anything against Mary. That was ten year ago, and they've got two fine kids and get along first-class. This fellow Cranton got into trouble again after his time was up and was sent back to prison, but he's out again now, so I'm told, and Jack Priest—that's the bobby at Fenchurch St. Peter—he says he wouldn't wonder if we heard something about the necklace again, but I don't know. Cranton may know where it is, and again he may not, you see."

"I see. So Sir Charles compensated Mrs. Wilbraham for the loss of it."

"Not Sir Charles, my lord. That was Sir Henry. He came back at once, poor gentleman, from his honeymoon, and found Sir Charles terrible ill. He'd had a stroke from the shock, when they took Deacon, feeling responsible-like, and being over seventy at the time. After the verdict, Mr. Henry as he was then, told his father he'd see that the thing was put right, and Sir Charles seemed to understand him; and then the War came and Sir Charles never got over it. He had another stroke and passed away, but Mr. Henry didn't forget, and when the police had to confess as they'd almost give up hope of the necklace, then he paid the money, but it came very hard on the family. Sir Henry got badly wounded in the Salient and was invalided home, but he's never been the same man since, and they say he's in a pretty bad way now. Lady Thorpe dying so sudden won't do him no good, neither. She was a very nice lady and very much liked."

"Is there any family?"

"Yes, my lord; there's one daughter, Miss Hilary. She'll be fifteen this month. She's just home from school for the holidays. It's been a sad holiday for her, and no mistake."

"You're right," said Lord Peter. "Well, that's an interesting tale of yours, Hinkins. I shall look out for news of the Wilbraham emeralds. Ah! here's my friend Mr. Wilderspin. I expect he's come to say that the car's on deck again."

This proved to be the case. The big Daimler stood outside the Rectory gate, forlornly hitched to the back of a farm wagon. The two stout horses who drew it seemed, judging by their sleek complacency, to have no great opinion of it. Messrs. Wilderspin senior and junior, however, took a hopeful view of the matter. A little work on the front axle, at the point where it had come into collision with a hidden milestone, would, they thought, do wonders with it, and, if not, a message could be sent to Mr. Brownlow at Fenchurch St. Peter, who ran a garage, to come and tow it away with his lorry. Mr. Brownlow was a great expert. Of course, he might be at home or he might not. There was a wedding on at Fenchurch St. Stephen, and Mr. Brownlow might be wanted there to take the wedding-party to church, they lived a good way out along Digg's Drove, but if necessary the postmistress could be asked to telephone and find out. She would be the right party to do it, since, leaving out the post-office, there was no other telephone in the village, except at the Red House, which wouldn't be convenient at a time like the present.

Wimsey, looking dubiously at his front axle, thought it might perhaps be advisable to procure the skilled assistance of Mr. Brownlow and said he would approach the postmistress for that purpose, if Mr. Wilderspin would give him a lift into the village. He scrambled up, therefore, behind Mr. Ashton's greys, and the procession took its way past the church for the better part of a quarter of a mile, till it reached the centre of the village.

The parish church of Fenchurch St. Paul, like a good many others in that part of the country, stands completely isolated from the village itself, with only the Rectory to neighbour it. The village itself is grouped about a cross-roads, one arm of which runs southward to Fenchurch St. Stephen and northwards to join the Fenchurch St. Peter road a little south of the Thirty-foot;

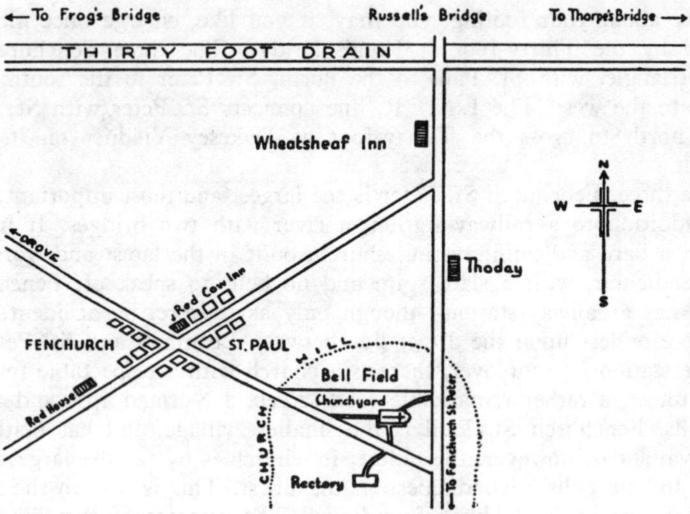
← To Frog's Bridge
Russell's Bridge
To Thorpe's Bridge →
THIRTY FOOT DRAIN
Wheatsheaf Inn
N
W
E
S
Thoday
DROVE
Red Cow Inn
FENCHURCH
ST. PAUL
MILL
Bell Field
Churchyard
Red House
CHURCH
Rectory
To Fenchurch St. Peter

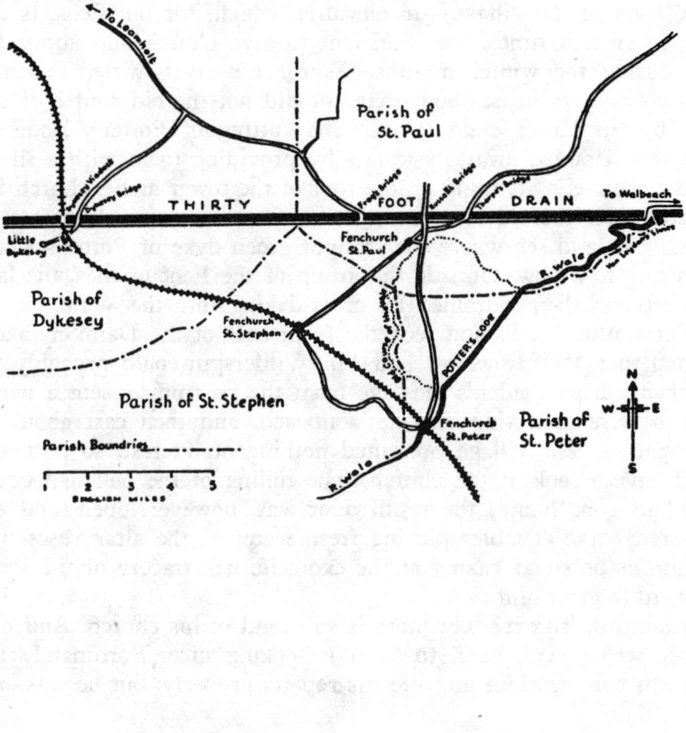
To Leamholt
Parish of St. Paul
Dykesey Viaduct
Dykesey Bridge
THIRTY
Frog's Bridge
Russell's Bridge
Thorpe's Bridge
FOOT
DRAIN
To Walbeach
Little Dykesey
Fenchurch St. Paul
R. Wale
Parish of Dykesey
Fenchurch St. Stephen
POTTER'S LODE
Old Course of Wale
Parish of St. Stephen
Fenchurch St. Peter
Parish of St. Peter
N
E
S
Parish Boundries
1 2 3 4 5
ENGLISH MILES

while the other, branching off from the same road by the church, degenerates at the western end of the village into a muddy drove by which, if you are not particular about your footing, you may, if you like, emerge once more on to the road by the Thirty-foot at Frog's Bridge. The three Fenchurches thus form a triangle, with St. Paul to the north, St. Peter to the south, and St. Stephen to the west. The L.N.E.R. line connects St. Peter with St. Stephen, passing north to cross the Thirty-foot at Dykesey Viaduct on its way to Leamholt.

Of the three, Fenchurch St. Peter is the largest and most important, possessing in addition to a railway-station, a river with two bridges. It has, however, but a bare and uninteresting church, built in the latest and worst period of Perpendicular, with a slate spire and no bells to speak of. Fenchurch St. Stephen has a railway-station—though only as it were, by accident, through lying more or less upon the direct line between Leamholt and St. Peter. Still, there the station is; moreover, there is a church with a respectable fourteenth-century tower, a rather remarkable rood-screen, a Norman apse and a ring of eight bells. Fenchurch St. Paul is the smallest village, and has neither river nor railway; it is, however, the oldest; its church is by far the largest and the noblest, and its bells beyond question the finest. This is due to the fact that St. Paul is the original abbey foundation. The remains of the first Norman church and a few stones which mark the site of the old cloisters may still be seen to east and south of the existing chancel. The church itself, with the surrounding glebe, stands on a little mound rising some ten or twelve feet above the level of the village—an elevation which, for the Fens, is considerable and, in ancient times, was sufficient to save church and abbey from inundation during the winter months. As for the river Wale, Fenchurch St. Peter has no right to boast about that, for did not the old course of the Wale run close by St. Paul's church, until the cutting of Potter's Lode in King James I's time drained away its waters by providing them with a shorter and more direct channel? Standing on the roof of the tower at Fenchurch St. Paul, you can still trace the old river bed, as it wanders circuitously across meadow and ploughland, and see where the straight green dyke of Potter's Lode spans it like a string to a bow. Outside the group of the Fenchurches, the land rises slightly all round, being drained by cross-dyking into the Wale.

Lord Peter Wimsey, having seen the front axle of the Daimler taken down and decided that Mr. Brownlow and Mr. Wilderspin could probably fix it up between them, dispatched his message from the post-office, sent a wire to the friends who were expecting him at Walbeach, and then cast about him for some occupation. The village presented nothing of interest, so he determined to go and have a look at the church. The tolling of the bell had ceased and Hezekiah had gone home; the south door was, however, open, and entering, he discovered Mrs. Venables putting fresh water in the altar vases. Catching sight of him as he stood gazing at the exquisite oak tracery of the screen, she came forward to greet him.

"It *is* beautiful, isn't it? Theodore is so proud of his church. And he's done a lot, since we've been here, to keep it looking nice. Fortunately the man before us was conscientious and did his repairs properly, but he was *very* Low and allowed all manner of things that quite shocked us. This beautiful chapel, for instance, would you *believe* that he allowed it to be used for furnace-coke? Of course, we had all that cleared out. Theodore would like a lady-altar here, but we're afraid the parishioners would think it popish. Yes—it's a magnificent window, isn't it? Later than the rest, of course, but so fortunate that it's kept its old glass. We were so afraid when the Zeppelins came over. You know, they dropped a bomb at Walbeach, only twenty miles off, and it might just as easily have been here. Isn't the parclose lovely? Like lace, I always think. The tombs belong to the Gaudy family. They lived here up to Queen Elizabeth's time, but they've all died out now. You'll find the name on the Treble bell: GAUDE, GAUDY, DOMINI IN LAUDE. There used to be a chantry on the north side, corresponding to this: Abbot Thomas' chantry, it was, and that's his tomb. Batty Thomas is named after him—a corruption of 'Abbot', of course. Some vandal in the nineteenth century tore down the screen behind the choir stall to put the organ in. It's a hideous thing, isn't it? We put in a new set of pipes a few years ago, and now the bellows want enlarging. Poor Potty has his work cut out to keep the wind-chest filled when Miss Snoot is using the full organ. They all call him Potty Peake, but he's not really potty, only a little lacking, you know. Of course, the angel roof is our great showpiece—I think myself it's even lovelier than the ones at March or Needham Market, because it has all the original colouring. At least, we had it touched up here and there about twelve years back, but we didn't add anything. It took ten years to persuade the churchwardens that we could put a little fresh gold-leaf on the angels without going straight over to Rome, but they're proud of it now. We hope to do the chancel roof too, one day. All these ribs ought to be painted, you can still see traces of colour, and the bosses ought to be gilt. The east window is Theodore's *bête noire*. That dreadful crude glass—about 1840, I think it is. Quite the worst period, Theodore says. The glass in the nave has all gone, of course—Cromwell's men. Thank goodness they left part of the clerestory. I suppose it was rather a job to get up there. The pews are modern; Theodore got them done ten years ago. He'd have preferred chairs, but the congregation wouldn't have liked it, being used to pews, and he had them copied from a nice old design that wasn't too offensive. The old ones were terrible—like bathrooms—and there was a frightful gallery along both sides, blocking the aisle windows completely and ruining the look of the pillars. We had that taken down at the same time. It wasn't needed, and the schoolchildren *would* drop hymn-books and things on people's heads. Now, the choir-stalls are different. *They* are the original monks' stalls, with misereres. Isn't the carving fine? There's a piscina in the sanctuary, but not a very exciting one."

Wimsey admitted that he was unable to feel great excitement about piscinas.

"And the altar-rails are very poor, of course—Victorian horrors. We want very much to put up something better in their place when we can find the money. I'm sorry I haven't the key to the tower. You'd like to go up. It's a wonderful view, though it's all ladders above the ringing-chamber. It makes my head swim, especially going over the bells. I think bells are rather frightening, somehow. Oh, the font! You must look at the font. That carving is supposed to be quite remarkable. I forget exactly what it is that's so special about it—stupid of me. Theodore must show you, but he's been sent for in a hurry to take a sick woman off to hospital, right away on the other side of the Thirty-foot, across Thorpe's Bridge. He rushed off almost before he'd finished his breakfast."

("And they say," thought Wimsey, "that Church of England parsons do nothing for their money.")

"Would you like to stay on and look round? Do you mind locking the door and bringing the key back? It's Mr. Godfrey's key—I can't *think* where Theodore has put his bunch. It does seem wrong to keep the church locked, but it's such a solitary place. We can't keep an eye on it from the Rectory because of the shrubbery and there are sometimes very unpleasant-looking tramps about. I saw a most horrible man go past only the other day, and not so long ago someone broke open the alms-box. That wouldn't have mattered so much, because there was very little in it, but they did a lot of wanton damage in the sanctuary—out of disappointment, I suppose, and one can't really allow that, can one?"

Wimsey said, No, one couldn't, and Yes, he would like to look round the church a little longer and would remember about the key. He spent the first few minutes after the good lady had left him in putting a suitable donation into the alms-box and in examining the font, whose carvings were certainly curious and, to his mind, suggestive of a symbolism neither altogether Christian nor altogether innocent. He noted a heavy old cope-chest beneath the tower, which, on being opened, proved to contain nothing more venerable than a quantity of worn bell-ropes, and passed on into the north aisle, noticing that the corbels supporting the principals of the angel-roof were very appropriately sculptured with cherubs' heads. He brooded for a little time over the tomb of Abbot Thomas, with its robed and mitred effigy. A stern old boy, he thought, this fourteenth-century cleric, with his strong, harsh face, a ruler rather than a shepherd of his people. Carved panels decorated the sides of the tomb, and showed various scenes in the life of the abbey; one of them depicted the casting of a bell, no doubt of "Batty Thomas", and it was evident that the Abbot had taken particular pride in his bell, for it appeared again, supporting his feet, in place of the usual cushion. Its decorations and mottoes were realistically rendered: on the shoulder: + NOLI + ESSE + INCREDVLVS + SED + FIDELIS +; on the sound-bow: + *Abbat Thomas sett mee heare* + *and bad me ringe both lovd and cleer* + 1380 +; and on the waist: O SANCTE THOMA, which inscription, being embellished with an abbot's mitre, left the spectator in a pleasing uncertainty whether the sanctity was to be attributed to the Apostle or the ecclesiastic. It was as well that Abbot Thomas had died long before the spoliation of his house by King Henry. Thomas would have made a fight for it, and his church might have suffered in the process. His successor, douce man, had meekly acquiesced in the usurpation, leaving his abbey to moulder to decay, and his church to be purified peaceably by the reformers. So, at least, the Rector informed Wimsey over the shepherd's pie at lunch.

It was only very reluctantly that the Venables consented to let their guest go; but Mr. Brownlow and Mr. Wilderspin between them had made such good progress on the car that it was ready for use by two o'clock, and Wimsey was anxious to press on to Walbeach before dusk set in. He started off, therefore, speeded by many handshakes and much earnest solicitation to come again soon and help to ring another peal. The Rector, at parting, thrust into his hands a copy of *Venables on the In and Out of Course*, while Mrs. Venables insisted on his drinking an amazingly powerful hot whisky-and-water, to keep the cold out. As the car turned right along the Thirty-foot Bank, Wimsey noticed that the wind had changed. It was hauling round to the south, and, though the snow still lay white and even over the Fen, there was a softness in the air.

"Thaw's coming, Bunter."

"Yes, my lord."

"Ever seen this part of the country when the floods are out?"

"No, my lord."

"It looks pretty desolate; especially round about the Welney and Mepal Washes, when they let the waters out between the Old and New Bedford Rivers, and across the fen between Over and Earith Bridge. Acres of water, with just a bank running across it here and there or a broken line of willows. Hereabouts I think it's rather more effectively drained. Ah! look—over to the right—that must be Van Leyden's Sluice that turns the tide up the Thirty-foot Drain—Denver Sluice again on a smaller scale. Let's look at the map. Yes, that's it. See, here's where the Drain joins the Wale, but it meets it at a higher level; if it wasn't for the sluice, all the Drain water would turn back up the Wale and flood the whole place. Bad engineering—but the seventeenth-century engineers had to work piecemeal and take things as they found 'em. That's the Wale, coming down through Potter's Lode from Fenchurch St. Peter. I shouldn't care for the sluice-keeper's job—dashed lonely, I should think."

They gazed at the ugly little brick house, which stood up quaintly on their right, like a pricked ear, between the two sides of the Sluice. On the one side a weir, with a small lock, spanned the Thirty-foot, where it ran into the Wale six feet above the course of the river. On the other, the upper course of the Wale itself was spanned by a sluice of five gates, which held the Upper Level waters from turning back up the river.

"Not another house within sight—oh, yes—one cottage about two miles further up the bank. Boo! Enough to make one drown one's self in one's own lock. Hullo! what happens to the road here? Oh, I see; over the Drain by the bridge and turn sharp right—then follow the river. I do wish everything wasn't so rectangular in this part of the world. Hoops-a-daisy, over she goes! There's the sluice-keeper running out to have a look at us. I expect we're his great event of the day. Let's wave our hats to him—Hullo-ullo! Cheerio!—I'm all for scattering sunshine as we pass. As Stevenson says, we shall pass this way but once—and I devoutly hope he's right. Now then, what's this fellow want?"

Along the bleak white road a solitary figure, plodding towards them, had stopped and extended both arms in appeal. Wimsey slowed the Daimler to a halt.

"Excuse me stopping you, sir," said the man, civilly enough. "Would you be good enough to tell me if I'm going right for Fenchurch St. Paul?"

"Quite right. Cross the bridge when you come to it and follow the Drain along in the direction you are going till you come to the signpost. You can't miss it."

"Thank you, sir. About how far would it be?"

"About five and a half miles to the signpost and then half a mile to the village."

"Thank you very much, sir."

"You've got a cold walk, I'm afraid."

"Yes, sir—not a nice part of the country. However, I'll be there before dark, that's a comfort."

He spoke rather low, and his voice had a faint London twang; his drab overcoat, though very shabby, was not ill-cut. He wore a short, dark, pointed beard and seemed to be about fifty years old, but kept his face down when talking as if evading close scrutiny.

"Like a fag?"

"Thank you very much, sir."

Wimsey shook a few cigarettes out of his case and handed them over. The palm that opened to receive them was calloused, as though by heavy manual labour, but there was nothing of the countryman about the stranger's manner or appearance.

"You don't belong to these parts?"

"No, sir."

"Looking for work?"

"Yes, sir."

"Labourer?"

"No, sir. Motor mechanic."

"Oh, I see. Well, good luck to you."

"Thank you, sir. Good afternoon, sir."

"Good afternoon."

Wimsey drove on in silence for about half a mile. Then he said:

"Motor mechanic possibly, but not recently, I think. Stone-quarrying's more about the size of it. You can always tell an old lag by his eyes, Bunter. Excellent idea to live down the past, and all that, but I hope our friend doesn't put anything across the good Rector."

II

A FULL PEAL OF GRANDSIRE TRIPLES

(Holt's Ten-Part Peal)

5,040
By the Part Ends

First Half	*Second Half*
246375	257364
267453	276543
275634	264735
253746	243657
235476	234567

2nd the Observation

Call her 1st Half) Out of the hunt, middle, in and out at 5, right, middle, wrong, right, middle and into the hunt (4 times repeated).

2nd Half) Out of the hunt, wrong, right, middle, wrong, right, in and out at 5, wrong and into the hunt (4 times repeated).

The last call in each half is a single; Holt's Single must be used in ringing this peal.

THE FIRST PART

Mr Gotobed is Called Wrong with a Double

Thou shalt pronounce this hideous thing
With cross, and candle, and bell-knelling.

JOHN MYRIC: *Instructions for Parish Priests (15th century)*

SPRING AND EASTER came late together that year to Fenchurch St. Paul. In its own limited, austere and almost grudging fashion the Fen acknowledged the return of the sun. The floods withdrew from the pastures; the wheat lifted its pale green spears more sturdily from the black soil; the stiff thorns bordering dyke and grass verge budded to a softer outline; on the willows, the yellow catkins danced like little bell-rope sallies, and the silvery pussies plumped themselves for the children to carry to church on Palm Sunday; wherever the grim banks were hedge-sheltered, the shivering dog-violets huddled from the wind.

In the Rectory garden, the daffodils were (in every sense of the word) in full blow, for in the everlasting sweep and torment of wind that sweeps across East Anglia, they tossed desperately and madly. "My poor daffodils!" Mrs. Venables would exclaim, as the long leaf-tufts streamed over like blown water, and the golden trumpets kissed the ground, "this dreadful old wind! I don't know how they stand it!" She felt both pride and remorse as she cut them—sound stock varieties, Emperor, Empress, Golden Spur—and took them away to fill the altar-vases and the two long, narrow, green-painted tin troughs that on Easter Sunday stood one on either side of the chancel screen. "The yellow looks so bright," thought Mrs. Venables, as she tried to persuade the blossoms to stand upright among the glossy green of periwinkle and St. John's Wort, "though it really seems a shame to sacrifice them."

She knelt before the screen on a long red cushion, borrowed from a pew-seat to protect her "bones" from the chill of the stone floor. The four brass altar-vases stood close beside her, in company with a trug full of flowers and a watering-can. Had she tried to fill them at the Rectory and carry them over, the sou'-wester would have blown them into ruin before she had so much as crossed the road. "Tiresome things!" muttered Mrs. Venables, as the daffodils flopped sideways, or slid down helplessly out of sight into the bottom of the trough. She sat up on her heels and reviewed her work, and then turned, hearing a step behind her.

A red-haired girl of fifteen, dressed in black, had come in, bearing a large sheaf of pheasant-eye narcissi. She was tall and thin and rather gawky, though with promise of being some day a striking-looking woman.

"Are these any use to you, Mrs. Venables? Johnson's trying to get the arums along, but the wind's so terrific, he's afraid they'll be broken all to bits in the barrow. I think he'll have to pack them into the car, and drive them down in state."

"My dear Hilary, how kind of you! Yes, indeed—I can do with all the white flowers I can get. These are beautiful, and *what* a delicious scent! Dear things! I thought of having some of our plants stood along there in front of Abbot Thomas, with some tall vases among them. And the same on the other side under old Gaudy. But I am *not*"—here she became very much determined—"I am *not* going to tie bunches of greenery on to the font and the pulpit this year. They can have that at Christmas and Harvest Festival, if they like, but at Easter it's unsuitable and absurd, and now that old Miss Mallow's gone, poor dear, there's no need to go on with it."

"I hate Harvest Festivals. It's a shame to hide up all this lovely carving with spiky bits of corn and vegetable marrows and things."

"So it is, but the village people like it, you know. Harvest Festival is *their* festival, Theodore always says. I suppose it's wrong that it should mean so much more to them than the Church seasons, but it's natural. It was much worse when we came here—before you were born or thought of, you know. They actually used to drive spikes into the pillars to hold up wreaths of evergreens. Quite wicked. Just thoughtlessness, of course. And at Christmas they had horrible texts all across the screens and along that abominable old gallery—done in cotton-wool on red flannel. Disgusting, dirty old things. We found a great bundle of them in the vestry when we came here, full of moths and mice. The Rector put his foot down about *that*."

"And I suppose half the people went over to the Chapel."

"No, dear—only two families, and one of them has come back since—the Wallaces, you know, because they had some sort of dispute with the Minister about their Good Friday beanfeast. Something to do with the tea-urns, but I forget what. Mrs. Wallace is a funny woman; she takes offence rather easily, but so far—touch wood"—(Mrs. Venables performed this ancient pagan rite placidly on the oak of the screen)—"so far, I've managed to work in quite smoothly with her over the Women's Institute. I wonder if you'd just step back a little way and tell me if these two sides match."

"You want a few more daffs. on the decani side, Mrs. Venables."

"Here? Thank you, dear. Is that better? Well, I think it will have to do. Oo-oh! my poor old bones! Yes, it'll pass in a crowd with a push, as they say. Oh, here's Hinkins with the aspidistras. People may say what they like about aspidistras, but they do go on all the year round and make a background. That's right, Hinkins. Six in front of this tomb and six the other side—and have you brought those big pickle-jars? They'll do splendidly for the narcissi, and the aspidistras will hide the jars and we can put some ivy in front of the pots. Hinkins, you might fill up my watering-can. How is your father to-day, Hilary? Better, I hope."

"I'm afraid he isn't any better, Mrs. Venables. Doctor Baines is very much afraid he won't get over it. Poor old Dad!"

"Oh, my dear! I'm terribly sorry. This has been a dreadful time for you. I'm afraid the shock of your dear mother's death coming so suddenly was too much for him."

The girl nodded.

"We'll hope and pray it isn't as bad as the doctors think. Dr. Baines always takes a pessimistic view of everything. I expect that's why he's only a country practitioner, because I think he's really very clever; but patients do like a doctor to be cheerful. Why don't you get a second opinion?"

"We're going to. There's a man called Hordell coming down on Tuesday. Dr. Baines tried to get him to-day, but he's away for Easter."

"Doctors oughtn't to go away," said Mrs Venables, rather uncharitably. The Rector never took holidays at the greater festivals, and scarcely ever at any other time, and she could not quite see that there was any necessity for the rest of the world to do so.

Hilary Thorpe laughed rather ruefully.

"I feel a little like that myself. But he's supposed to be the best man there is, and we're hoping that a couple of days won't make all that difference."

"Good gracious, no, I hope not," said the Rector's wife. "Is that Johnson with the arums? Oh, no, it's Jack Godfrey. I expect he's going up to grease the bells."

"Is he? I'd like to watch him. May I go up to the belfry, Mrs. Venables?"

"I'm sure you may, my dear. But do be careful. I never think those great high ladders are really safe."

"Oh, I'm not afraid of them. I love looking at the bells."

Hilary hastened down the church and caught Jack Godfrey up just as he emerged from the winding stair into the ringing chamber.

"I've come to watch you do the bells, Mr. Godfrey. Shall I be in your way?"

"Why, no, Miss Hilary, I'd be very pleased for you to come. You better go first up them ladders, same as I can help you if you was to slip."

"I shan't slip," said Hilary, scornfully. She climbed briskly up the thick and ancient rungs, to emerge into the chamber which formed the second storey of the tower. It was empty, except for the case which housed the chiming mechanism of the church clock, and the eight-ropes rising through the sallie-holes in the floor to vanish through the ceiling in the same way. Jack Godfrey followed her up soberly, carrying his grease and cleaning-rags.

"Be a bit careful of the floor, Miss Hilary," he urged, "it's none so good in places."

Hilary nodded. She loved this bare, sun-drenched room, whose four tall walls were four tall windows. It was like a palace of glass lifted high into the air. The shadows of the splendid tracery of the south window lay scrawled on the floor like a pattern of wrought iron on a gate of brass. Looking down through the dusty panes, she could see the green fen spread out mile upon mile.

"I'd like to go up to the top of the tower, Mr. Godfrey."

"All right, Miss Hilary; I'll take you up, if so be as there's time when I've done with the bells."

The trap-door that led to the bell-chamber was shut; a chain ran down from it, vanishing into a sort of wooden case upon the wall. Godfrey produced a key from his bunch and unlocked this case, disclosing the counter poise. He pulled it down and the trap swung open.

"Why is that kept locked, Mr. Godfrey?"

"Well, Miss Hilary, now and again it has happened as the ringers has left the belfry door open, and Rector says it ain't safe. You see, that Potty Peake might come a-traipsing round, or some of they mischeevious lads might come up here and get larking about with the bells. Or they might go up the tower and fall off and hurt theirselves. So Rector said to fix a lock the way they couldn't get the trap-door open."

"I see." Hilary grinned a little. "Hurt theirselves" was a moderate way of expressing the probable result of a hundred-and-twenty-foot fall. She led the way up the second ladder.

By contrast with the brilliance below, the bell-chamber was sombre and almost menacing. The main lights of its eight great windows were darkened throughout their height; only through the slender panelled tracery above the slanting louvres the sunlight dripped rare and chill, striping the heavy beams of the bell-cage with bars and splashes of pallid gold, and making a curious fantastic patterning on the spokes and rims of the wheels. The bells, with mute black mouths gaping downwards, brooded in their ancient places.

Mr. Godfrey, eyeing them with the cheerful familiarity born of long use, fetched a light ladder that stood against the wall, set it up carefully against one of the crossbeams, and prepared to mount.

"Let me go up first, or I shan't see what you're doing."

Mr. Godfrey paused and scratched his head. The proposal did not seem quite safe to him. He voiced an objection.

"I shall be quite all right; I can sit on the beam. I don't mind heights one bit. I'm very good at gym."

Sir Henry's daughter was accustomed to have her own way, and got it—with the stipulation that she should hold on very tightly by the timber of the cage and not let go or "morris about". The promise being given, she was assisted to her lofty perch. Mr. Godfrey, whistling a lively air between his teeth, arranged his materials methodically about him and proceeded with his task, greasing the gudgeons and trunnions, administering a spot of oil to the pulley-axle, testing the movement of the slider between the blocks and examining the rope for signs of friction where it passed over wheel and pulley.

"I've never seen Tailor Paul as close as this before. She's a big bell, isn't she?"

"Pretty fair," said Jack Godfrey, approvingly, giving the bell a friendly pat on her bronze shoulder. A shaft of sunshine touched the soundbow, lighting up a few letters of the inscription, which ran, as Hilary very well knew:

NINE+TAYLERS+MAKE+A+MANNE+IN+CHRIST+
IS+DETH+ATT+END+IN+ADAM+YAT+BEGANNE+
1614

"She've done her bit in her time, have old Tailor Paul—many a good ring have we had out of her, not to say a sight of funerals and passing-bells. And we rung her with Gaude for them there Zeppelin raids, to give the alarm like. Rector was saying the other day as she did soon ought ter be quarter-turned, but I don't know. Reckon she'll go a bit longer yet. She rings out true enough to my thinking."

"You have to ring the passing-bell for everyone that dies in the parish, don't you, whoever they are?"

"Yes, dissenter and church alike. That was laid down by old Sir Martin Thorpe, your great-great-grandfather, when he left the money for the bell-fund. 'Every Christian soul' was the words in his will. Why, we even had to ring for that woman as lived up the Long Drove, as was a Roman Catholic. Old Hezekiah was rare put out." Mr. Godfrey chuckled reminiscently. " 'What, ring old Tailor Paul for a Roman?' he says. 'You wouldn't call the like o' them Christians, would you, Rector?' he says. 'Why, Hezekiah,' says Rector, 'we was all Romans in this country once; this church was built by Romans,' he says. But Hezekiah, he wouldn't see it. He never had much education, you see. Well, now, Miss Hilary, that'll do for Tailor Paul, I'm thinking, so if you'll give me your hand I'll be helping you down."

Gaude, Sabaoth, John, Jericho, Jubilee and Dimity each in her turn was visited and anointed. When, however, it came to the turn of Batty Thomas, Mr. Godfrey displayed a sudden and unexpected obstinacy.

"I'm not taking you up to Batty Thomas, Miss Hilary. She's an unlucky bell. What I mean, she's a bell that has her fancies and I wouldn't like for to risk it."

"What *do* you mean?"

Mr. Godfrey found it difficult to express himself more plainly.

"She's my own bell," he said; "I've rung her close on fifteen years now and I've looked after her for ten, ever since Hezekiah got too old for these here ladders. Her and me knows one another and she've no quarrel with me nor I with her. But she's queer-tempered. They do say as how old Batty down below, what had her put up here, was a queer sort of man and his bell's took after him. When they turned out the monks and that—a great many years ago, that'd be—they do say as Batty Thomas tolled a whole night through on her own like, without a hand laid to the rope. And when Cromwell sent his men to break up the images an' that, there was a soldier come up here into the belfry, I don't know for what, maybe to damage the bells, but anyhow, up he come; and some of the others, not knowing he was here, began to haul on the ropes, and it seems as how the bells must have been left mouth up. Careless ringers they must have been in those days, but anyhow, that's how 'twas. And just as this soldier was leaning over to look at the bells, like, Batty Thomas came swinging down and killed him dead. That's history, that is, and Rector says as how Batty Thomas saved the church, because the soldiers took fright and ran away, thinking it was a judgment, though to my thinking, it was just carelessness, leaving the bell that fashion. Still, there it was. And then, there was a poor lad in old Rector's time learning to ring, and he tried to raise Batty Thomas and got hisself hanged in the rope. A terrible thing that was, and there again, I say it was carelessness and the lad didn't ought to have been let practise all alone, and it's a thing Mr. Venables never will allow. But you see, Miss Hilary, Batty Thomas has killed two men, and while it's quite understandable as there was carelessness both times or it wouldn't have happened—well! I wouldn't like to take any risks, like I said."

And with this as his last word on the subject, Mr. Godfrey mounted aloft to grease the gudgeons of Batty Thomas unassisted. Hilary Thorpe, dissatisfied but recognising an immovable obstacle when she met one, wandered vaguely about the belfry, scuffing up the dust of ages with her square-toed, regulation-pattern school shoes and peering at the names which bygone rustics had scrawled upon the plastered walls. Suddenly, in a remote corner, something gleamed white in a bar of sunlight. Idly she picked it up. It was a sheet of paper, flimsy and poor in quality and ruled in small, faint squares. It reminded her of the letters she occasionally received from a departed French governess and, when she examined it, she saw that it was covered with writing in the very same purple ink that she associated with "Mad'm'selle", but the hand was English—very neat, and yet somehow not the hand of a well-educated person. It had been folded in four and its under side was smeared with fine dust from the floor on which it had lain, but it was otherwise fairly clean.

"Mr. Godfrey!"

Hilary's voice was so sharp and excited that Jack Godfrey was quite startled. He very nearly fell off the ladder, adding thereby one more to Batty Thomas' tale of victims.

"Yes, Miss Hilary?"

"I've found such a funny thing here. Do come and look at it."

"In one moment, Miss Hilary."

He finished his task and descended. Hilary was standing in a splash of sunshine that touched the brazen mouth of Tailor Paul and fell all about her like Danaë's shower. She was holding the paper where the light could catch it.

"I found this on the floor. Do listen to it. It's absolutely loony. Do you think Potty Peake could have written it?"

Mr. Godfrey shook his head.

"I couldn't say, I'm sure, Miss Hilary. He's queer, is Potty, and he did use to come up here one time, before Rector locked up the trap-door chain. But that don't look to me like his writing."

"Well, I don't think anybody but a lunatic could have written it. Do read it. It's so funny." Hilary giggled, being of an age to be embarrassed by lunacy.

Mr. Godfrey set down his belongings with deliberation, scratched his head and perused the document aloud, following the lines with a somewhat grimy forefinger.

> "I thought to see the fairies in the fields, but I saw only the evil elephants with their black backs. Woe! how that sight awed me! The elves danced all around and about while I heard voices calling clearly. Ah! how I tried to see—throw off the ugly cloud—but no blind eye of a mortal was permitted to spy them. So then came minstrels, having gold trumpets, harps and drums. These played very loudly beside me, breaking that spell. So the dream vanished, whereat I thanked Heaven. I shed many tears before the thin moon rose up, frail and faint as a sickle of straw. Now though the Enchanter gnash his teeth vainly, yet shall he return as the Spring returns. Oh, wretched man! Hell gapes, Erebus now lies open. The mouths of Death wait on thy end."

"There, now," said Mr. Godfrey, astonished. "That's a funny one, that is. Potty it is, but, if you follow me, it ain't Potty neither. Potty ain't scholar. This here, now, about Ereebus—what do you take that to mean?"

"It's a kind of an old name for hell," said Hilary.

"Oh, that's what it is, is it? Chap that wrote this seems to have got that there place on his mind, like. Fairies, too, and elephants. Well, I don't know. Looks like a bit of a joke, don't it now? Perhaps" (his eye brightened with an idea), "perhaps somebody's been copying out something out of a book. Yes, I wouldn't wonder if that's what that is. One of them old-fashioned books. But it's a funny thing how it got up here. I'd show it to Rector, Miss Hilary, that's what I'd do. He knows a lot of books, and maybe he'd know where it come from."

"That's a good idea. I will. But it's awfully mysterious, isn't it? Quite creepy. Can we go up the tower now, Mr. Godfrey?"

Mr. Godfrey was quite willing, and together they climbed the last long ladder, stretching high over the bells and leading them out by way of a little shelter like a dog-kennel on to the leaded roof of the tower. Leaning against the wind was like leaning against a wall. Hilary pulled off her hat and let her thick bobbed hair blow out behind her, so that she looked like one of the floating singing angels in the church below. Mr. Godfrey had no eyes for this resemblance; he thought Miss Hilary's angular face and straight hair rather unattractive, if the truth were known. He contented himself with advising her to hold tight by the iron stays of the weathercock. Hilary paid no attention to him, but advanced to the parapet, leaning over between the pierced battlements to stare out southward over the Fen. Far away beneath her lay the churchyard, and, while she looked, a little figure, quaintly foreshortened, crawled beetle-like from the porch and went jogging down the path. Mrs. Venables, going home to lunch. Hilary watched her struggle with the wind at the gate, cross the road and enter the Rectory garden. Then she turned and moved to the east side of the tower, and looked out along the ridged roofs of the nave and chancel. A brown spot in the green churchyard caught her eye and her heart seemed to turn over in her body. Here, at the north-east angle of the church, her mother lay buried, her grave not yet turfed over; and now it looked as though, before long, the earth would have to be opened up again to let the husband join his wife. "Oh, God!" said Hilary, desperately, "don't let Dad die—You can't—You simply can't." Beyond the churchyard wall lay a green field, and in the middle of the field there was a slight hollow. She knew that hollow well. It had been there now for over three hundred years. Time had made it shallower, and in three hundred years more it might disappear altogether, but there it still was—the mark left by the great pit dug for the founding of Tailor Paul.

Jack Godfrey spoke close beside her.

"Time I was getting along now, Miss Hilary."

"Oh, yes. I'm sorry. I wasn't thinking. Are you ringing a peal to-morrow?"

"Yes, Miss Hilary. We're going to have a try at Stedman's. They're difficult to ring, are Stedman's, but very fine music when you get them going proper. Mind your head, Miss Hilary. A full peal of 5,040 we're going to give them—that's three hours. It's a fortnit thing as Will Thoday's all right again, because neither Tom Tebbutt nor young George Wilderspin is what you might call reliable in Stedman's, and of course, Wally Pratt's no good at all. Excuse me one minute, Miss Hilary, while I gathers up my traps. But to my mind, there's more interest, as you might say, in Stedman's than in any other method, though it takes a bit of thinking about to keep it all clear in one's head. Old Hezekiah don't so much care about it, of course, because he likes the tenor rung in. Triples ain't much fun for him, he says, and it ain't to be wondered at. Still, he's an old man now, and you couldn't hardly expect him to learn Stedman's at his age, and what's more, if he could, you'd never get him to leave Tailor Paul. Just a moment, Miss Hilary, while I lock up this here counterpoise. But give me a nice peal of Stedman's and I ask no better. We never had no Stedman's till Rector come, and it took him a powerful long time to learn us to ring them. Well I mind the trouble we had with them. Old John Thoday—that's Will's father, he's dead and gone now—he used to say, 'Boys,' he said, 'it's my belief the Devil himself couldn't get no sense out of this dratted method.' And Rector fined him sixpence for swearing, like it says in they old rules. Mind you don't slip on the stair, Miss Hilary, it's terrible worn. But we learned Stedman to rights, none the more for that, and to my mind it's a very pretty method of ringing. Well, good morning to you, Miss Hilary."

The peal of 5,040 Stedman's Triples was duly rung on Easter Sunday morning. Hilary Thorpe heard it from the Red House, sitting beside the great old four-poster bed, as she had sat on New Year's morning to hear the peal of Treble Bob Major. Then the noise of the bells had come full and clear; to-day, it reached her only in distant bursts, when the wind, rollicking away with it eastward, bated for a moment or veered round a little to the south.

"Hilary!"

"Yes, Dad."

"I'm afraid—if I go west this time—I'll be leaving you rottenly badly off, old girl."

"I don't care a dash about that, old thing. Not that you are going west. But if you did, I should be quite all right."

"There'll be enough to send you to Oxford, I dare say. Girls don't seem to cost much there—your uncle will see to it."

"Yes—and I'm going to get a scholarship, anyway. And I don't want money. I'd rather make my own living. Miss Bowler says she doesn't think anything of a woman who can't be independent." (Miss Bowler was the English mistress and the idol of the moment.) "I'm going to be a writer, Dad. Miss Bowler says she wouldn't wonder if I'd got it in me."

"Oh? What are you going to write? Poetry?"

"Well, perhaps. But I don't suppose that pays very well. I'll write novels. Best-sellers. The sort that everybody goes potty over. Not just bosh ones, but like *The Constant Nymph*."

"You'll want a bit of experience before you can write novels, old girl."

"Rot, Daddy. You don't want experience for writing novels. People write them at Oxford and they sell like billy-ho. All about how awful everything was at school."

"I see. And when you leave Oxford, you write one about how awful everything was at college."

"That's the idea. I can do that on my head."

"Well, dear, I hope it'll work. But all the same, I feel a damned failure, leaving you so little. If only that rotten necklace had turned up! I was a fool to pay that Wilbraham woman for it, but she as good as accused the old Governor of being an accessory, and I——"

"Oh, Dad, please—*please* don't go on about that silly necklace. Of course you couldn't do anything else about it. And I don't want the beastly money. And anyhow, you're not going to peg out yet."

But the specialist, arriving on Tuesday, looked grave and, taking Dr. Baines aside, said to him kindly:

"You have done all you could. Even if you had called me in earlier, it could have made no possible difference."

And to Hilary, still kindly:

"We must never give up hope, you know, Miss Thorpe. I can't disguise from you that your father's condition is serious, but Nature has marvellous powers of recuperation. . . ."

Which is the medical man's way of saying that, short of miraculous intervention, you may as well order the coffin.

On the following Monday afternoon, Mr. Venables was just leaving the cottage of a cantankerous and venomous-tongued old lady on the extreme outskirts of the parish, when a deep, booming sound smote his ear from afar. He stood still with his hand upon the gate.

"That's Tailor Paul," said the Rector to himself.

Three solemn notes, and a pause.

"Man or woman?"

Three notes, and then three more.

"Man," said the Rector. He still stood listening. "I wonder if poor old Merryweather has gone at last. I hope it isn't that boy of Hensman's." He counted twelve strokes, and waited. But the bell tolled on, and the Rector breathed a sigh of relief. Hensman's boy, at least, was safe. He hastily reckoned up the weaklings of his flock. Twenty strokes, thirty strokes—a man of full age. "Heaven send," thought the Rector, "it isn't Sir Henry. He seemed better when I saw him yesterday." Forty strokes, forty-one, forty-two. Surely it must be old Merryweather—a happy release for him, poor old man. Forty-three, forty-four, forty-five, forty-six. Now it must go on—it could not stop at that fatal number. Old Merryweather was eighty-four. The Rector strained his ears. He must have missed the next stroke—the wind was pretty strong, and his hearing was perhaps not as good as it had been.

But he waited full thirty seconds before Tailor Paul spoke again; and after that there was silence for another thirty seconds.

The cantankerous old lady, astonished to see the Rector stand so long bare-headed at her gate, came hobbling down the garden path to know what it was all about.

"It's the passing-bell," said Mr. Venables, "they have rung the nine tailors and forty-six strokes, and I'm afraid it must be for Sir Henry."

"Oh, dear," said the cantankerous old woman. "That's bad. Terrible bad, that is." A peevish kind of pity came into her eyes. "What's to become of Miss Hilary now, with her mother and father gone so quick, and her only fifteen, and nobody to keep her in check? I don't hold with girls being left to look arter themselves. They're troublesome at the best and they didn't ought to have their parents took away from them."

"We mustn't question the ways of Providence," said the Rector.

"Providence?" said the old woman. "Don't yew talk to me about Providence. I've had enough o' Providence. First he took my husband, and then he took my 'taters, but there's One above as'll teach him to mend his manners, if he don't look out."

The Rector was too much distressed to challenge this remarkable piece of theology.

"We can but trust in God, Mrs. Gillings," he said, and pulled up the starting-handle with a jerk.

Sir Henry's funeral was fixed for the Friday afternoon. This was an occasion of mournful importance to at least four persons in Fenchurch St. Paul. There was Mr. Russell, the undertaker, who was a cousin of that same Mary Russell who had married William Thoday. He was determined to excel himself in the matter of polished oak and brass plates, and his hammer and plane had been keeping up a dismal little harmony of their own during the early part of the week. His, also, was the delicate task of selecting the six bearers so that they might be well-matched in height and step. Mr. Hezekiah Lavender and Mr. Jack Godfrey went into conference about the proper ringing of a muffled peal—Mr. Godfrey's business being to provide and adjust the leather buffets about the clappers of the bells, and Mr. Lavender's to arrange and conduct the ringing. And Mr. Gotobed, the sexton, was concerned with the grave—so much concerned that he had declined to take part in the peal, preferring to give his whole mind to the graveside ceremonies, although his son, Dick, who assisted him with the spadework, considered himself quite capable of carrying on on his own. There was not, indeed, very much to do in the way of digging. Rather to Mr. Gotobed's disappointment, Sir Henry had expressed a wish to be buried in the same grave with his wife, so that there was little opportunity for any fine work in the way of shaping, measuring and smoothing the sides of the grave. They had only to cast out the earth—scarcely yet firm after three rainy months—make all neat and tidy and line the grave with fresh greenery. Nevertheless, liking to be well beforehand with his work, Mr. Gotobed took measures to carry this out on the Thursday afternoon.

The Rector had just come in from a round of visits, and was about to sit down to his tea, when Emily appeared at the sitting-room door.

"If you please, sir, could Harry Gotobed speak to you for a moment?"

"Yes, certainly. Where is he?"

"At the back door, sir. He wouldn't come in on account of his boots being dirty."

Mr. Venables made his way to the back door; Mr. Gotobed stood awkwardly on the step, twirling his cap in his hands.

"Well, Harry, what's the trouble?"

"Well, sir, it's about this here grave. I thought I better come and see you, being as it's a church matter, like. You see, when Dick and me come to open it up, we found a corpus a-laying inside of it, and Dick says to me——"

"A corpse? Well, of course there's a corpse. Lady Thorpe is buried there. You buried her yourself."

"Yes, sir, but this here corpus ain't Lady Thorpe's corpus. It's a man's corpus, that's what it is, and it du seem as though it didn't have no right to be there. So I says to Dick——"

"A man's corpse! What do you mean? Is it in a coffin?"

"No, sir, no coffin. Just an ordinary suit o' clothes, and he du look as though he's abeen a-laying there a goodish while. So Dick says, 'Dad,' he says, 'this looks like a police matter to me. Shall I send for Jack Priest?' he says. And I says, 'No,' I says, 'this here is church property, this is, and Rector did ought to be told about it. That's only right and respectful,' I says. 'Throw a bit o' summat over it,' I says, 'while I goes and fetches Rector, and don't let any o' they boys come into the churchyard.' So I puts on my coat and comes over, because we don't rightly know what to do about it."

"But what an extraordinary thing, Harry!" exclaimed the Rector, helplessly. "I really—I never—who is this man? Do you know him?"

"It's my belief, sir, his own mother wouldn't know him. Perhaps you'd like to step across and take a look at him?"

"Why, yes, of course, I'd better do that. Dear me, dear me! how very perplexing. Emily! Emily! have you seen my hat anywhere? Ah, thank you. Now, Harry. Oh, Emily, please tell Mrs. Venables that I am unexpectedly detained, and not to wait tea for me. Yes, Harry, I'm quite ready now."

Dick Gotobed had spread a tarpaulin over the half-open grave, but he lifted this as the Rector approached. The good gentleman gave one look and averted his eyes rather hastily. Dick replaced the tarpaulin.

"This is a very terrible thing," said Mr. Venables. He had removed his clerical felt in reverence for the horrid thing under the tarpaulin, and stood bewildered, his thin grey hair ruffled by the wind. "We must certainly send for the constable—and—and"—here his face brightened a little—"and for Dr. Baines, of course. Yes, yes—Dr. Baines will be the man. And, Harry, I think I have read that it is better in these cases to disturb things as little as possible. Er—I wonder who this poor fellow can possibly be. It's nobody belonging to the village, that's certain, because if anybody was missing we should have heard about it. I cannot imagine how he can have come here."

"No more can't we, sir. Looks like he was a proper stranger. Excuse me, sir, but didn't we ought to inform the coroner of this here?"

"The coroner? Oh, dear! yes, naturally; I suppose there will have to be an inquest. What a dreadful business this is! Why, we haven't had an inquest in the village since Mrs. Venables and I came to the Rectory, and that's close on twenty years. This will be a very shocking blow for Miss Thorpe, poor child. Her parents' grave—such a fearful desecration. Still, it can't be hushed up, of course. The inquest—well, well, we must try to keep our wits about us. I think, Dick, you had better run up to the post-office and get a call put through to Dr. Baines and ask him to come over at once and you had better ring through to St. Peter and get someone to send a message to Jack Priest. And you, Harry, had better stay here and keep an eye on—on the grave. And I will go up to the Red House myself and break the shocking news to Miss Thorpe, for fear she should hear it in an abrupt and painful way from somebody else. Yes, I think that is what I had better do. Or perhaps it would be more suitable if Mrs. Venables were to go round. I must consult her. Yes, yes, I must consult Mrs. Venables. Now, Dick, off you go, and be sure you don't say a word about this to anybody till the constable comes."

There is no doubt that Dick Gotobed did his best in the matter, but, since the post-office telephone lived in the postmistress's sitting-room, it was not altogether easy to keep any message confidential. At any rate, by the time that P.C. Priest arrived, rather blown, upon his push-cycle, a small knot of men and women had gathered in and about the churchyard, including Hezekiah Lavender, who had run as fast as his ancient legs could carry him from his cottage-garden, and was very indignant with Harry Gotobed for not letting him lift the tarpaulin.

" 'Ere!" said the constable, running his machine adroitly into the midst of a bunch of children clustered round the lych-gate and tipping himself off bodily sideways. " 'Ere! what's all this? You run along home to yer mothers, see? And don't let me catch you here again. 'Afternoon, Mr. Venables, sir. What's the trouble here?"

"There's been a body found in the churchyard," said Mr. Venables.

"Body, eh?" said the constable. "Well, it's come to the right place, ain't it? What have you done with it? Oh, you've left it where you found it. Quite right, sir. And where might that be? Oh, 'ere. *I* see. All right; let's have a look at him. Oh! ah! that's it, is it? Why, Harry, whatever have you been a-doing of? Tryin' to bury him?"

The Rector began to explain, but the constable stopped him with an upraised hand.

"One moment, sir. We'll take this here matter in the proper and correct order. Just a moment while I gets out my notebook. Now, then. Date. Call received 5.15 pee hem. Proceeded to the churchyard, arriving 5.30 pee hem. Now, who found this here body?"

"Dick and me."

"Name?" said the constable.

"Go on, Jack. You knows me well enough."

"That don't matter. I've got to do it in the proper way. Name?"

"Harry Gotobed."

"Hoccupation?"

"Sexton."

"Righto, Harry. Go ahead."

"Well, Jack, we was a-openin' this here grave, which is Lady Thorpe's grave what died last New Year's Day, for to be ready for her 'usband's body, see, what's to be buried to-morrow. We begins to shovel away the earth, one at each end, like, and we hadn't got much more than a foot or so below ground level, as you might say, when Dick drives his spade down a good spit, and he says to me, 'Dad,' he says, 'there's something in here.' And I says to him, 'What's that?' I says, 'what do you mean? Something in here?' and then I strikes my spade hard down and I feels something sort of between hard and soft, like, and I says, 'Dick,' I says, 'that's a funny thing, there *is* something here.' So I says, 'Go careful, my boy,' I says, 'because it feels funny-like to me,' I says. So we starts at one end and shovels away gentle, and arter a bit we sees something sticking up like it might be the toe of a boot. So I says, 'Dick,' I says, 'that's a boot, that is.' And he says, 'You're right, Dad, so 'tis.' So I says, 'Looks to me like we begun at the wrong end of this here, so to say.' So he says, 'Well, Dad, now we've gone so far we may so well have a look at him.' So we gets a-shovellin' again, still going very careful, and arter a bit more we sees something lookin' like 'air. So I says, 'You put that there shovel away and use your 'ands, because we don't want to spile it.' And he says, 'I don't like.' And I says, 'Don't you be a fool, my boy. You can wash your 'ands, can't you, when you've done?' So we clears away very careful, and at last we sees him plain. And I says, 'Dick, I don't know who he is nor yet how he got here, but he didn't ought to be here.' And Dick says, 'Shall I go for Jack Priest?' And I says, 'No. 'Tis Church ground and we better tell Rector.' So that's what we done."

"And I said," put in the Rector, "that we had better send at once for you and for Dr. Baines—and here he is, I see."

Dr. Baines, a peremptory-looking little man, with a shrewd Scotch face, came briskly up to them.

"Good afternoon, Rector. What's happened here? I was out when your message came, so I—— Good Lord!"

A few words put him in possession of the facts, and he knelt down by the graveside.

"He's terribly mutilated—looks as though somebody had regularly beaten his face in. How long has he been here?"

"That's what we'd like you to tell us, Doctor."

"Half a minute, half a minute, sir," interrupted the policeman. "What day was it you said you buried Lady Thorpe, Harry?"

"January 4th, it were," said Mr. Gotobed, after a short interval for reflection.

"And was this here body in the grave when you filled it up?"

"Now don't you be a fool, Jack Priest," retorted Mr. Gotobed. "'Owever can you suppose as we'd fill up a grave with this here corpus in it? It ain't a thing as a man might drop in careless like, without noticing. If it was a pocket-knife or a penny-piece, that'd be another thing, but when it comes to the corpus of a full-grown man, that there question ain't reasonable."

"Now, Harry, that ain't a proper answer to my question. I knows my duty."

"Oh, all right. Well, then, there weren't no body in that there grave when I filled it upon January 4th—leavin' out, of course, Lady Thorpe's body. That was there, I don't say it wasn't, and for all I know it's there still. Unless him as put this here corpus where it is took the other away with him, coffin and all."

"Well," said the doctor, "it can't have been here longer than three months, and so far as I can tell, it hasn't been there much less. But I'll tell you that better when you get it out."

"Three months, eh?" Mr. Hezekiah Lavender had pushed his way to the front. "That 'ud be about the time that stranger chap disappeared—him as was stayin' at Ezra Wilderspin's and wanted a job to mend up moty-cars and sich. He had a beard, too, by my recollection."

"Why, so he had," cried Mr. Gotobed. "What a head you have on you, Hezekiah! That's who it is, sure-lie. To think o' that, now! I always thought that chap was after no good. But who could have gone for to do a thing like this here?"

"Well," said the doctor. "If Jack Priest has finished with his interrogation, you may as well get the body dug out. Where are you going to put it? It won't be a very nice thing to keep hanging about."

"Mr. Ashton have a nice airy shed, sir. If we was to ask him, I dessay he could make shift to move his ploughs out for the time being. And it's got a decent-sized window and a door with a lock to it."

"That'll do well. Dick, run round and ask Mr. Ashton and get him to lend us a cart and a hurdle. How about getting hold of the coroner, Rector? It's Mr. Compline, you know, over at Leamholt. Shall I ring him up when I get back?"

"Oh, thank you, thank you. I should be very grateful."

"All right. Can they carry on now, Jack?"

The constable signified his assent, and the digging was resumed. By this time the entire village seemed to have assembled in the churchyard, and it was with the greatest difficulty that the children were prevented from crowding round the grave, since the grown-ups who should have restrained them were themselves struggling for positions of vantage. The Rector was just turning upon them with the severest rebuke he knew how to utter, when Mr. Lavender approached him.

"Excuse me, sir, but did I ought to ring Tailor Paul for that there?"

"Ring Tailor Paul? Well, really, Hezekiah, I hardly know."

"We got to ring her for every Christian soul dyin' in the parish," persisted Mr. Lavender. "That's set down for us. And seemin'ly he must a-died in the parish, else why should anybody go for to bury him here?"

"True, true, Hezekiah."

"But as for bein' a Christian soul, who's to say?"

"That, I fear, is beyond me, Hezekiah."

"As to bein' a bit behindhand with him," went on the old man, "that ain't no fault of ours. We only knowed to-day as he'd died, so it stands to reason we couldn't ring for him earlier. But Christian—well, there! that's a bit of a puzzle, that is."

"We'd better give him the benefit of the doubt, Hezekiah. Ring the bell by all means."

The old man looked dubious, and at length approached the doctor.

"How old?" said the latter, looking round in some surprise. "Why, I don't know. It's hard to say. But I should think he was between forty and fifty. Why do you want to know? The bell? Oh, I see. Well, put it at fifty."

So Tailor Paul tolled the mysterious stranger out with nine strokes and fifty and a hundred more, while Alf Donnington at the Red Cow and Tom Tebbutt at the Wheatsheaf did a roaring trade, and the Rector wrote a letter.

THE SECOND PART

Lord Peter is Called into the Hunt

> Hunting is the first part of change ringing which it is necessary to understand.
>
> TROYTE *On Change-Ringing*

"MY DEAR LORD PETER [wrote the Rector],

"Since your delightful visit to us in January, I have frequently wondered, with a sense of confusion, what you must have thought of us for not realising how distinguished an exponent of the methods of Sherlock Holmes we were entertaining beneath our roof. Living so very much out of the world, and reading only *The Times* and the *Spectator*, we are apt, I fear, to become somewhat narrow in our interests. It was only when my wife wrote to her cousin Mrs. Smith (whom you may know, perhaps, as she lives in Kensington) and mentioned your stay with us, that we were informed, by Mrs. Smith's reply, what manner of man our guest was.

"In the hope that you will pardon our lamentable ignorance, I venture to write and ask you to give us some advice out of your great experience. This afternoon we have been jerked rudely out of 'the noiseless tenor of our way' by the most mysterious and shocking occurrence. On opening the grave of the late Lady Thorpe to receive the body of her husband—whose sad death you no doubt saw in the Obituary columns of the daily press—our sexton was horrified to discover the dead body of a completely strange man, who appears to have come by his end in some violent and criminal manner. His face has been terribly mutilated, and—what seems even more shocking—the poor fellow's hands have been cut right off at the wrists! Our local police have, of course, the matter in hand, but the sad affair is of peculiar and painful interest to me (being in some sort connected with our parish church), and I am somewhat at a loss to know how I, personally, should proceed. My wife, with her usual great practical ability, suggested that we should seek your aid and advice, and Superintendent Blundell of Leamholt, with whom I have just had an interview, most obligingly says that he will give you every facility for investigation should you care to look into the matter personally. I hardly like to suggest to so busy a man that you should actually come and conduct your investigations on the spot, but, in case you thought of doing so, I need not say how heartily welcome you would be at the Rectory.

"Forgive me if this letter is somewhat meandering and confused; I am writing in some perturbation of mind. I may add that our Ringers retain a most pleasant and grateful recollection of the help you gave us with our famous peal, and would, I am sure, wish me to remember them to you.

"With kindest regards from my wife and myself,

"Most sincerely yours,

"THEODORE VENABLES."

"P.S.—My wife reminds me to tell you that the inquest is at 2 o'clock on Saturday."

This letter, dispatched on the Friday morning, reached Lord Peter by the first post on Saturday. He wired that he would start for Fenchurch St. Paul at once, joyfully cancelled a number of social engagements, and at 2 o'clock was seated in the Parish Room, in company with a larger proportion of the local population than had probably ever gathered beneath one roof since the spoliation of the Abbey.

The coroner, a florid-faced country lawyer, who seemed to be personally acquainted with everybody present, got to work with the air of an immensely busy person, every moment of whose time was of value.

"Come now, gentlemen.... No talking over there *if* you please... all the jury this way.... Sparkes, give out these Testaments to the jury... choose a foreman, please.... Oh! you have chosen Mr. Donnington... very good.... Come along, Alf... take the Book in your right hand... diligently inquire... Sovereign Lord the King... man unknown... body... view... skill and knowledge... help you God... kiss the Book... sit down... table over there ... now the rest of you... take the Book in your right hand... your *right* hand, Mr. Pratt... don't you know your left hand from your right, Wally?... No laughing, please, we've no time to waste... same oath that your foreman ... you and each of you severally to keep... help you God... kiss the Book ... on that bench by Alf Donnington.... Now then, you know what we're here for... inquire how this man came by his death... witnesses to identity ... understand no witnesses to identity.... Yes, Superintendent?... Oh, I see ... why didn't you say so? Very well... this way, please.... I beg your pardon, sir?... Lord Peter... do you mind saying that again... Whimsy? Oh, no H... just so... Wimsey with an E... quite... occupation?... what?... Well, we'd better say, Gentleman... now then, my lord, you say you can offer evidence as to identity?"

"Not exactly, but I rather think..."

"One moment, please... take the Book in your right hand... evidence... inquiry... truth, whole truth and nothing but the truth... kiss the Book... yes... name, address, occupation we've got all that.... If you can't keep that baby quiet, Mrs. Leach, you'll have to take it out.... Yes?"

"I have been taken to see the body, and, from my observation, I think it possible that I saw this man on January 1st last. I do not know who he was, but if it is the same man he stopped my car about half a mile beyond the bridge by the sluice and asked the way to Fenchurch St. Paul. I never saw him again, and had never seen him before to my knowledge."

"What makes you think it may be the same man?"

"The fact that he is dark and bearded and that the man I saw also appeared to be wearing a dark blue suit similar to that worn by deceased, I say 'appeared', because he was wearing an overcoat, and I only saw the legs of his trousers. He seemed to be about fifty years of age, spoke in a low voice with a London accent and was of fairly good address. He told me that he was a motor-mechanic and was looking for work. In my opinion, however . . ."

"One moment. You say you recognise the beard and the suit. Can you swear . . . ?"

"I cannot swear that I definitely recognise them. I say that the man I saw resembled the deceased in these respects."

"You cannot identify his features?"

"No; they are too much mutilated."

"Very well. Thank you. Are there any more witnesses to identity?"

The blacksmith rose up rather sheepishly.

"Come right up to the table, please. Take the Book . . . truth . . . truth . . . truth . . . Name Ezra Wilderspin. Well now, Ezra, what have you got to say?"

"Well, sir, if I was to say I recognised the deceased, I should be telling a lie. But it's a fact that he ain't unlike a chap that come along, same as his lordship here says, last New Year's Day a-looking for a job along of me. Said he was a motor-mechanic out o' work. Well, I told him I might do with a man as knowed somethin' about motors, so I takes him on and gives him a trial. He did his work pretty well, near as I could judge, for three days, livin' in our place, and then, all of a sudden, off he goes in the middle of the night and we never seen no more of him."

"What night was that?"

"Same day as they buried her ladyship it was . . ."

Here a chorus of voices broke in:

"January 4th, Ezra! that's when it were."

"That's right. Saturday, January 4th, so 'twere."

"What was the name of this man?"

"Stephen Driver, he called hisself. Didn't say much; only that he'd been trampin' about a goodish time, lookin' for work. Said he'd been in the Army, and in and out of work ever since."

"Did he give you any references?"

"Why, yes, sir, he did, come to think of it. He give me the name of a garridge in London where he'd been, but he said it had gone bankrupt and shut up. But he said if I was to write to the boss, he'd put in a word for him."

"Have you got the name and address he gave you?"

"Yes, sir. Leastways, I think the missus put it away in the teapot."

"Did you take up the reference?"

"No, sir. I did think of it, but being no great hand at writing I says to myself I'd wait till the Sunday, when I'd have more time, like. Well, you see, before that he was off, so I didn't think no more about it. He didn't leave nothing behind him, bar an old toothbrush. We 'ad to lend him a shirt when he came."

"You had better see if you can find that address."

"That's right, sir. Liz!" (in a stentorian bellow). "You cut off home and see if you can lay your 'and on that bit o' paper what Driver give me."

Voice from the back of the room: "I got it here, Ezra," followed by a general upheaval, as the blacksmith's stout wife forced her way to the front.

"Thanks, Liz," said the coroner. "Mr. Tasker, 103 Little James St., London, W.C. Here, Superintendent, you'd better take charge of that. Now, Ezra, is there anything more you can tell us about this man Driver?"

Mr. Wilderspin explored his stubble with a thick forefinger.

"I dunno as there is, sir."

"Ezra! Ezra! don't yew remember all them funny questions he asked?"

"There now," said the blacksmith, "the missus is quite right. That was a funny thing about them questions, that was. He said he 'adn't never been in this here village before, but he knowed a friend as had and the friend had told him to ask after Mr. Thomas. 'Mr. Thomas!' I says. 'There ain't no Mr. Thomas in this here village, nor never has been to my knowledge.' 'That's queer,' he says, 'but maybe he's got another name as well. Far as I can make out,' he says, 'this Thomas ain't quite right in his 'ead. My friend said as he was potty, like.' 'Why,' I says, 'you can't mean Potty Peake? Because Orris is his Chrissen name.' 'No,' he says, 'Thomas was the name. Batty Thomas, that's right. And another name my friend gi'n me,' he says, 'was a fellow called Paul—a tailor or some'in o' that, living next door to him, like.' 'Why,' I says to him, 'your friend's been havin' a game with you. Them ain't men's names, them's the names of bells,' I says. 'Bells?' he says. 'Yes,' I says, 'church bells, that's what they is. Batty Thomas and Tailor Paul, they call 'em.' And then he went on and asked a sight o' questions about they bells. 'Well,' I says, 'if you want to know about Batty Thomas and Tailor Paul, you better ask Rector,' I says. 'He knows all about they old bells.' I dunno if he ever went to Rector, but he come back one day—that were the Friday—and says he been in the church and see a bell carved on old Batty Thomas' tomb, like, and what did the writing on it mean. And I says to ask Rector, and he says: 'Did all bells have writing on 'em,' and I says, 'Mostly'; and arter that he didn't say no more about it."

Nobody being able to make very much sense out of Mr. Wilderspin's revelations, the Rector was called, who said that he remembered having seen the man called Stephen Driver on one occasion when he was distributing the parish magazine at the smithy, but that Driver had said nothing then, or at any other time, about bells. The Rector then added his own evidence about finding the body and sending for the police, and was dismissed in favour of the sexton.

Mr. Gotobed was very voluble, repeating, with increased circumlocutory detail and reference to what he had said to Dick and Dick to him, the account he had originally given to the police. He then explained that Lady Thorpe's grave had been dug on January 3rd and filled in on the 4th, immediately after the funeral.

"Where do you keep your tools, Harry?"

"In the coke-house, sir."

"Where's that?"

"Well, sir, it's down underneath the church—where Rector says the old cryp used to be. Makes a sight o' work, that it du, a-carryin' coke up and down they stairs and through the chancel and sweepin' up arter it. You can't 'elp it a-dribbling out o' the scuttle, do as you like."

"Is the door kept locked?"

"Oh, yes, sir, always kept locked. It's the little door under the organ, sir. You can't get to it without you have the key and the key of the west door as well. That is to say, either the key of the west door or one of the church keys, sir, if you take my meaning. I has the west door key, bein' 'andiest for me where I live, but either of the others would do as well."

"Where do you keep these keys?"

"Hanging up in my kitchen, sir."

"Has anybody else got a key to the coke-house door?"

"Yes, sir; Rector has all the keys."

"Nobody else?"

"Not as I knows on, sir. Mr. Godfrey has they all, only the key of the cryp."

"I see. When these keys are in your kitchen, I suppose any of your family has access to them?"

"Well, sir, in a manner of speaking', yes, but I 'opes as how you ain't tryin' to put anything on me and my missus, nor yet Dick, let alone the children. I been sexton in this here village twenty years follerin' on Hezekiah, and none of us ain't never yet been suspected of 'ittin' strangers over the 'ead and buryin' of them. Come to think of it, this chap Driver came round to my place one morning on a message, and 'ow do I know what he did? Not but what, if he'd a-took the keys I'd be bound to miss them; still, none the more for that..."

"Come, come, Harry! Don't talk nonsense. You don't suppose this unfortunate man dug his own grave and buried himself? Don't waste time."

(Laughter, and cries of "That's a good 'un, Harry!")

"Silence, *if* you please. Nobody's accusing you of anything. Have you in fact ever missed the keys at any time?"

"No, sir" (sulkily).

"Or ever noticed that your tools had been disturbed?"

"No, sir."

"Did you clean them after digging Lady Thorpe's grave?"

" 'Course I cleaned 'em. I always leaves my tools clean."

"When did you use them next after that?"

This puzzled Mr. Gotobed for a moment. The voice of Dick supplied helpfully: "Massey's baby."

("Don't prompt the witness, please!")

"That's right," agreed Mr. Gotobed. "Massey's baby it were, as you can see by the Register. And that 'ud be about a week later—ah! just about."

"You found the tools clean and in their right place when you dug the grave for Mrs. Massey's baby?"

"I ain't noticed nothing different."

"Not at any time since?"

"No, sir."

"Very well. That will do. Constable Priest."

The constable, taking the oath briskly, informed the court of his having been called to the scene of action, having communicated with Superintendent Blundell, having assisted at the removal of the body and of having helped to search the clothes of the deceased. He then made way for the Superintendent, who corroborated his evidence and produced a brief list of the dead man's belongings. These were: a suit of navy-blue serge of poor quality, much deteriorated by its burial in the earth, but apparently purchased fairly recently from a well-known firm of cheap outfitters; much-worn vest and pants, bearing (unexpectedly enough) the name of a French manufacturer; a khaki shirt (British army type); a pair of working-man's boots, nearly new; a cheap spotted tie. In his pockets they had found a white cotton handkerchief; a packet of woodbines; twenty-five shillings and eightpence in cash; a pocket-comb; a ten-centime piece; and a short length of stiff wire, bent at one end into a hook. The body had worn no overcoat.

The French money and underclothing and the piece of wire were the only objects which seemed to suggest any kind of clue. Ezra Wilderspin was recalled, but could not bring to mind that Driver had ever said anything about France, beyond mentioning that he had served in the War; and the Superintendent, asked whether he thought the wire could be anything in the nature of a pick-lock, shook his head, and said it didn't look like anything of that sort to *him*.

The next witness was Dr. Baines, and his evidence produced the only real sensation of the day. He said:

"I have examined the body of deceased and made an autopsy. I should judge the subject to be a man aged between forty-five and fifty. He appears to have been well-nourished and healthy. Taking into account the nature of the soil, which tends to retard putrefaction, the position of the body when found, that is, about two feet beneath the level of the churchyard and from three to four feet beneath the actual surface of the mound, I should judge the extent of decomposition found to indicate that deceased had been lying in the grave between three and four months. Decay does not proceed so rapidly in a buried body as in one exposed to the air, or in a clothed body as in a naked body. In this case, the internal organs and the soft tissues generally were all quite distinguishable and fairly well preserved. I made a careful examination and could discover no signs of external injury on any part of the body except upon the head, arms, wrists and ankles. The face had apparently been violently battered in with some blunt instrument, which had practically reduced all the anterior—that is, the front—part of the skull to splinters. I was not able to form any exact estimate of the number of blows inflicted, but they must have been numerous and heavy. On opening the abdomen——"

"One moment, Doctor. I take it we may assume that the deceased died in consequence of one or some of these blows upon the skull?"

"No; I do not think that the blows were the cause of death."

At this point an excited murmur ran round the little hall, and Lord Peter

Wimsey was distinctly observed to rub his finger-tips lightly together with a gratified smile.

"Why do you say that, Dr. Baines?"

"Because, to the best of my judgment and belief, all the blows were inflicted after death. The hands also were removed after death, apparently with a short, heavy knife, such as a jack-knife."

Further sensation; and Lord Peter Wimsey audibly observed: "Splendid!"

Dr. Baines added a number of technical reasons for his opinion, chiefly connected with the absence of any extravasation of blood and the general appearance of the skin; adding, with proper modesty, that he was, of course, not an expert and could only proffer his opinion for what it was worth.

"But why should anybody inflict such savage injuries on a dead body?"

"That," said the doctor drily, "is outside my province. I am not a specialist in lunacy or neurosis."

"That is true. Very well, then. In your opinion, what was the cause of death?"

"I do not know. On opening the abdomen I found the stomach, intestine, liver and spleen considerably decomposed, the kidneys, pancreas and oesophagus in a fairly good state of preservation." (Here the doctor wandered off into medical detail.) "I could not see," he resumed, "any superficial signs of disease or injury by poison. I, however, removed certain organs" (he enumerated them) "and placed them in sealed jars" (further technical details) "and propose dispatching them to-day for expert examination by Sir James Lubbock. I should expect to receive his report in about a fortnight's time—possibly earlier."

The coroner expressed himself satisfied with this suggestion, and then went on:

"You mentioned injuries to the arms and ankles, Doctor; what was the nature of those?"

"The skin of the ankles seemed to have been very much broken and abraded—as though the ankles had been tightly bound with cord or rope which had cut through the socks. The arms also showed the pressure marks of a rope above the elbows. These injuries were undoubtedly inflicted before death."

"You suggest that somebody tied the deceased up with ropes, and then, by some means or other, brought about his death?"

"I think that the deceased was undoubtedly tied up—either by another person or by himself. You may remember that there was a case in which a young man at one of the universities died in curcumstances which suggested that he had himself bound his own wrists and arms."

"In that case, the cause of death was suffocation, I believe?"

"I believe it was. I do not think that was the case here. I found nothing to indicate it."

"You do not, I suppose, suggest that the deceased went so far as to bury himself?"

"No; I do not suggest that."

"I am glad to hear it," said the coroner, sarcastically. "Can you suggest any reason why, if a man had accidentally or intentionally killed himself by tying himself up——?"

"After tying himself up; the tying of the arms and ankles would not in themselves be likely to cause death."

"After tying himself up—why somebody else should then come along, smash his face in and then bury him secretly?"

"I could suggest a variety of reasons; but I do not think that is my province."

"You are very correct, Doctor."

Dr. Baines bowed.

"He might, I suppose, have perished of starvation, if he had tied himself up and been unable to free himself?"

"No doubt. Sir James Lubbock's report will tell us that."

"Have *you* anything further to tell us?"

"Only that, as a possible aid to identification, I have made as careful a note as I can—in view of the extensive mutilation of the jaws—of the number and condition of deceased's teeth, and of the dental work done upon them at various times. I have handed this note over to Superintendent Blundell in order that he may issue an inquiry."

"Thank you, Doctor; that will no doubt be very helpful."

The coroner paused, glanced through his notes and then turned to the Superintendent.

"In the circumstances, Superintendent, it seems to me advisable to adjourn the inquest until you have completed your investigations. Shall we say, till to-day fortnight? Then, if you should see your way to making any charge against anybody in connection with this crime, or accident, or whatever it is, we may if you like adjourn the inquiry *sine die*."

"I think that would be the best way, Mr. Compline."

"Very well. Gentlemen, we will adjourn until to-day fortnight."

The jury, a little puzzled and disappointed at not being asked for any opinion, filed slowly out from behind the long trestle table at which they had been seated—a table dedicated, under happier circumstances, chiefly to parish teas.

"A beautiful case," said Lord Peter, enthusiastically, to Mr. Venables. "Quite charming. I am uncommonly grateful to you for drawing my attention to it. I wouldn't have missed it for the world. I liked your doctor."

"We consider him a very able man."

"You must introduce me to him; I feel that we should get on well together. The coroner doesn't like him. Some trifling personal antagonism, no doubt. Why, here is my old friend Hezekiah! How do you do, Mr. Lavender? How's Tailor Paul?"

There was general greeting. The Rector caught the arm of a tall, thin man hurrying past their little group.

"Just a moment, Will. I want to introduce you to Lord Peter Wimsey. Lord Peter, this is Will Thoday, whose bell you rang on your last visit."

Hands were shaken.

"Very sorry I was to miss that peal," said Thoday. "But I was pretty bad, wasn't I, Rector?"

"You were indeed. You don't look to have quite got over it yet."

"I'm all right, sir, except for being troubled by a bit of a cough. But that'll pass away with the spring weather coming."

"Well, you must take care of yourself. How's Mary?"

"Fine, sir, thank you. She was for coming to this here inquest, but I said as it wasn't no place for a woman. I'm thankful I got her to stop at home."

"Yes; the doctor's evidence was very disagreeable. Children all right? That's splendid. Tell your wife Mrs. Venables will be coming round to see her in a day or two. Yes, she's very well, thank you—distressed, naturally, by all this sad business. Ah! There's Dr. Baines. Doctor! Lord Peter Wimsey wants very much to make your acquaintance. You'd better come and have a cup of tea at the Rectory. Good day, Will, good day! . . . I don't like the looks of that fellow," added the Rector, as they turned towards the Rectory. "What do you think of him, Doctor?'

"He's looking a bit white and strained to-day. Last week I thought he was a lot better, but he had a bad bout of it and he's rather a nervous subject. You don't expect farm-labourers to have nerves, do you, Lord Peter? But they're human, like the rest of us."

"And Thoday is a very superior man," said the Rector, as though superiority conveyed a licence to keep a nervous system. "He used to farm his own land till these bad times set in. Now he works for Sir Henry—that is to say, he did. I'm sure I don't know what will happen now, with only that poor child left at the Red House. I suppose the trustee will let the place, or put in a steward to run it for her. It doesn't bring in very much these days, I fear."

At this point a car overtook them and stopped a little way ahead. It proved to contain Superintendent Blundell and his assistants, and the Rector, apologising fussily for his remissness, made him and Wimsey acquainted with one another.

"Pleased to meet you, my lord. I've heard of you through my old friend Inspector Sugg. He's retired now—did you know?—and got a nice little place the other side of Leamholt. He often talks about you. Says you used to pull his leg something cruel. This is a bad job, this is. Between you and me, my lord, what was it you were going to say when the coroner interrupted you—about this chap Driver's not being a motor-mechanic?"

"I was going to say that he gave me the impression of having done most of his manual labour lately at Princetown or somewhere like that."

"Ah!" said the Superintendent, thoughtfully. "Struck you that way, did he? How was that?"

"Eyes, voice, attitude—all characteristic, what?"

"Ah!" said the Superintendent again. "Ever heard of the Wilbraham emeralds, my lord?"

"Yes."

"You know that Nobby Cranton's out again? And it seems he ain't reported himself lately, neither. Last heard of six months ago in London. They've been looking for him. Maybe we've found him. In any case, I wouldn't be surprised if we was to hear of those emeralds again before very long."

"Loud cheers!" said Wimsey. "I'm all for a treasure-hunt. This is confidential, of course?"

"If you please, my lord. You see, if somebody thought it worth while to kill Cranton and smash him up and bury him, *and* cut off his hands, where he keeps his finger-prints, there's somebody in this village that knows something. And the less they think we guess, the more free they'll act and speak. And that's why, my lord, I was rather glad when the reverend gentleman suggested you coming down here. They'll talk freer to you than to me—see?"

"Perfectly. I'm a terrific success at pottering round asking sloppy questions. And I can put away quite a lot of beer in a good cause."

The Superintendent grinned, begged Wimsey to come and see him at any time, clambered into his car and drove off.

The great difficulty about any detective inquiry is knowing where to start. After some thought, Lord Peter made out the following list of queries:

A. *Identity of the Corpse*

1. Was it Cranton?—Wait for report on teeth and police report.
2. Consider the question of the ten-centime piece and the French underclothing. Has Cranton been in France? When? If not Cranton, is anyone known in the village also known to have been in France at any period since the War?
3. The destruction of the hands and features after death suggests that the murderer had an interest in making recognition impossible. If the body is Cranton, who knew Cranton (a) by sight? (b) personally? (Note: Deacon knew him; but Deacon is dead. Did Mary Thoday know him?) Many people must have seen him at the trial.

B. *The Wilbraham Emeralds*

1. Resulting from the above: Was Mary Thoday (formerly Mary Deacon, née Russell) really after all concerned in the theft?
2. Who really had the emeralds—Deacon or Cranton?
3. Where are the emeralds now? Did Cranton (if it was Cranton) come to Fenchurch St. Paul to look for them?
4. If the answer to 3 is "Yes", why did Cranton wait till now to make his search? Because some fresh information had lately reached him? Or merely because he was continuously in prison till just lately? (Ask the Superintendent.)
5. What is the meaning of "Driver's" interest in Batty Thomas and Tailor Paul? Is anything to be gained from a study of the bells and/or their mottoes?

C. *The Crime*

1. What did deceased die of? (Wait for experts' report.)
2. Who buried (and presumably also killed) him?
3. Can any clue to the time of the burial be gained by looking up the weather reports? (Snow? rain? foot-prints?)
4. Whereabouts did the murder take place? The churchyard? the church? somewhere in the village?

5. If the sexton's tools were used, who had access to them? ("Driver", apparently, but who else?)

Quite a lot of questions, thought his lordship, and some of them unanswerable till outside reports came in. The matter of the bell-mottoes could, of course, be looked into at once. He sought the Rector and asked whether he could, without too much trouble, lay his hand on Woollcott's *History of the Bells of Fenchurch St. Paul*, which he had once spoken about. The Rector thought he could, and after he had hunted through all his study shelves and enlisted the aid of Mrs. Venables and Emily, the book was in fact discovered in a small room devoted to the activities of the Clothing Club ("and how it could have got there, I cannot imagine!"). From this work Wimsey distilled the following facts, interesting to archaeologists, but not immediately suggestive of anything in the way of corpses or emeralds:

Batty Thomas (No. 7. Weight 30½ cwt. Note: D). The oldest bell in the ring in her present form, and older still in her original metal. First cast by Thomas Belleyetere of Lynn in 1338. Re-cast, with additional metal by Abbot Thomas of Fenchurch (fl. 1356–1392) in 1380. (This abbot also built the tower and the greater part of the existing nave, though the aisle windows were enlarged in Perpendicular style by Abbot Martin circ. 1423.)

Inscriptions:

Shoulder —NOLI + ESSE + INCREDVLVS + SED + FIDELIS +
Waist —O SANCTE THOMA.
Soundbow—ABBAT . THOMAS . SETT . MEE . HEARE . AND . BAD . MEE . RINGE . BOTH . LOVD . AND . CLEER . 1380 .

No record of any other bells at this time, though there was probably at least one other. We know, however, that in the reign of Elizabeth there was a ring of five bells in D of which

John (No. 3. Weight 8 cwt. Note: A) was the original treble. She bears the name of her founder, John Cole, an itinerant founder of the period.

Inscription:

Soundbow—JHON . COLE . MAD . MEE . JHON PRESBYTER . PAYD . MEE . JHON . EVÃGELIST . AID . MEE . MDLVII .

Jericho (No. 4. Weight 8½ cwt. Note: G) was the No. 2 of the old peal, and her maker seems to have thought aggressively well of her.

Inscription:

Shoulder—FROM . IERICHO . TO IOHN . AGROAT . YR . IS . NOE . BELLE . CAN . BETTER . MY . NOTE . 1559 .

Of the original No. 4, nothing is known. The original No. 3 (F♯) was a poor bell, flat in pitch and weak in quality. In James I's reign, this bell was further flattened by the grinding away of its inner surface so as to produce some sort of approximation to F♮, and the great tenor bell was added to make a ring of six in C.

Tailor Paul (No. 8. Weight 41 cwt. Note: C). A very noble bell of superb truth and tone. She was cast in the Bellfield by the church. (See parish records.)

Inscriptions:

Shoulder —PAVLE + IS + MY + NAME + HONOVR + THAT + SAME +

Soundbow—NINE + TAYLERS + MAKE + A + MANNE + IN + CHRIST + IS + DETH + ATT + END + IN + ADAM + YAT + BEGANNE + 1614

The bells survived the tumults of the Great Rebellion, and in the later part of the century, when the fashion for change-ringing set in, a new treble and second were added to bring the number up to eight.

Gaude (Treble. Weight 7 cwt. Note: C). The gift of the Gaudy family, she bears a "canting" motto.

Inscription:

Soundbow—GAVDE . GAUDY . DÑI . IN . LAVDE . MDCLXVI .

The No. 2 of that period was known as *Carolus* having been given in honour of the King's Restoration. This bell, however, was cracked in the 18th century, as a result of the abominable practice of "clappering" the two smallest bells for occasional services, so that the ring was again reduced to six, of which No. 5 (F ♮) had always been unsatisfactory. In the first half of the 19th century (that period of ecclesiastical apathy) the worm was allowed to get into the timbers of the bell-cage, as a result of which No. 6 (the Elizabethan No. 4) fell and was broken. Nothing was done until the 'eighties, when an energetic High-Church rector called public attention to the bad state of the bells. Subscriptions were raised, the framework of the bell-cage was repaired and put in order, and three bells were re-cast:

Sabaoth (No. 2. Weight 7¼ cwt. Note: B) was the gift of the Rector.

Inscriptions:

Shoulder —SANCTUS . SANCTUS . SANCTUS . DOMINUS . DEUS . SABAOTH .

Soundbow—RECAST BY JOHN TAYLOR OF LOUGHBOROUGH 1887.

Dimity (No. 6. Weight 14 cwt. Note: E) was given in memory of Sir Richard Thorpe, who died in 1883.

Inscriptions:

Shoulder —RECAST BY JOHN TAYLOR OF LOUGHBOROUGH 1887.
Soundbow—IN . PIAM . MEMORIAM . RICARDI . THORPE . ARMIGERI . NUNC . DIMITTIS . DOMINE . SERVUM . TUUM . IN . PACE.

Jubilee (No. 5. Weight 9½ cwt. Note: F ♮). The funds for this bell were raised by public subscription in commemoration of the Queen's Jubilee.

Inscriptions:

Shoulder —JUBILATE . DEO . OMNIS . TERRA .
Waist —RECAST . IN . THE . YEAR . OF . THE . QUEEN'S . JUBILEE . BY . JOHN . TAYLOR . AND . CO . E. HINKINS . AND . B. DONNINGTON . CHURCHWARDENS.

Wimsey puzzled his head for some time over this information, but without very much result. The dates, the weights and the mottoes—was there anything here that could serve as a guide to buried treasure? Batty Thomas and Tailor Paul had been particularly mentioned, but try as he would, for him they had neither speech nor language. After a time he gave up his calculations. Possibly there was something about the bells themselves that did not appear in Mr. Woollcott's work. Something written or carved on the timbers, possibly. He must go up and look some time.

It was Sunday morning. As he lifted his head from his calculations, he heard the bells begin to ring for matins. He hastened out in the hall, where he found his host winding the grandfather clock.

"I always wind it when the bells begin on a Sunday morning," explained Mr. Venables, "otherwise I might forget. I fear I am none too methodical. I hope you will not feel obliged to come to church, merely because you are our guest. I always make a point of telling our visitors that they are quite free to do as they wish. What time do *you* make it? Ten thirty-seven—we will put the hands at 10.45. He always loses about a quarter of an hour during the week, you see, and by putting him a little forward each time he is wound, we strike a happy mean. If you will just remember that he is always *fast* on Sundays, Mondays and Tuesdays, *right* on Wednesdays, and *slow* on Thursdays, Fridays and Saturdays, you will find him a very reliable guide."

Wimsey said he was sure of it, and turned to find Bunter at his elbow, offering him with one hand his hat and with the other two leather-bound volumes on a small salver.

"You see, padre, we have every intention of going to Church; we have, in fact, come prepared. Hymns A & M—I suppose that is the right work?"

"I took the liberty of ascertaining as much beforehand, my lord."

"Of course you did, Bunter. You always ascertain everything. Why, padre, what's the trouble? Have you lost anything?"

"I—er—it's very odd—I could have declared that I laid them down just here. Agnes! Agnes, my dear! Have you seen those banns anywhere?"

"What is it, Theodore?"

"The banns, my dear. Young Flavel's banns. I know I had them with me. I always write them out on a slip of paper, you see, Lord Peter; it is so very inconvenient to carry the register to the lectern. Now what in the world——?"

"Are they on top of the clock, Theodore?"

"My dear, what a——! Bless me, though, you are quite right. How did that come about, I wonder? I must have put them up there unconsciously when I was picking up the key. Very strange indeed, but the little mishap is now remedied, thanks to my wife. She always knows where I have put things. I believe she knows the workings of my mind better than I do myself. Well, I must go across to the church now. I go early, because of the choir-boys. My wife will show you the Rectory pew."

The pew was conveniently situated for observation, towards the rear of the nave on the north side. From it, Mrs. Venables was able to survey the south porch, by which the congregation entered, and also to keep an admonitory eye on the school-children who occupied the north aisle, and to frown at those who turned round to stare or make faces. Lord Peter, presenting a placid front to the inquisitive glances of his fellow-worshippers, also watched the south porch. There was a face he was particularly anxious to see. Presently he saw it. William Thoday came in, and with him a thin, quietly dressed woman accompanied by two little girls. He guessed her to be about forty, though, as is frequently the case with country women, she had lost most of her front teeth and looked older. But he could still see in her the shadow of the smart and pretty parlour-maid that she must have been sixteen years before. It was, he thought, an honest face, but its expression was anxious and almost apprehensive—the face of a woman who had been through trouble and awaited, with nervous anticipation, the next shock which fate might hold in store for her. Probably, thought Wimsey, she was worried about her husband. He did not look well; he, too, had the air of being braced in self-defence. His uneasy eyes wandered about the church and then returned, with a curious mingling of wariness and protective affection, to his wife. They took their seats almost immediately opposite the Rectory pew, so that Wimsey, from his corner seat, was able to watch them without any appearance of particularity. He gained the impression, however, that Thoday felt his scrutiny and resented it. He turned his eyes away, therefore, and fixed them on the splendours of the angel roof, lovelier than ever in the soft spring sunshine that streamed through the rich reds and blues of the clerestory windows.

The pew which belonged to the Thorpe family was empty, except for an upright middle-aged gentleman who was pointed out in a whisper by Mrs. Venables as being Hilary Thorpe's uncle from London. The housekeeper, Mrs. Gates, and the Red House servants sat in the south aisle. In the pew immediately in front of Wimsey was a stout little man in a neat black suit, who, Mrs. Venables further informed him, was Mr. Russell, the village undertaker, and a cousin of Mary Thoday. Mrs. West, the postmistress, arrived with her daughter, and greeted Wimsey, whom she remembered from his last visit, with a smile and something between a nod and a bob. Presently, the bells ceased, with the exception of the five-minutes bell, and the ringers came clattering up to their places. Miss Snoot, the schoolmistress, struck into a voluntary, the choir came in from the vestry with much noise of hobnailed boots, and the Rector entered his stall.

The service was devoid of incident, except that Mr. Venables again mislaid the banns, which had to be fetched from the vestry by the tenor on the cantoris side, and that, in his sermon, he made a solemn little allusion to the unfortunate stranger whose funeral was to take place on the morrow, whereat Mr. Russell nodded, with an air of importance and approbation. The Rector's progress to the pulpit was marked by a loud and gritty crunching, which caused Mrs. Venables to mutter in an exasperated tone, "That's the coke again—Gotobed *will* be so careless with it." At the conclusion, Wimsey found himself stranded with Mrs. Venables in the porch, while handshakings and inquiries passed.

Mr. Russell and Mr. Gotobed came out together, busily talking, and the former was introduced to Lord Peter.

"Where are they a-putting of him, Harry?" asked Mr. Russell, eagerly turning from ceremony to business.

"Over on north side, next to old Susan Edwards," replied the sexton. "We got him dug last night, all very fit and proper. Maybe his lordship would like to come and see."

Wimsey expressed suitable interest, and they made their way round to the other side of the church.

"We're giving him a nice bit of elm," said Mr. Russell, with some satisfaction, when the handsome proportions of the grave had been duly admired. "He did ought by rights to have come on the parish, and that means deal, as you know, but Rector says to me, 'Poor fellow,' he says, 'Let's put him away nice and seemly, and I'll pay for it,' he says. And I've trued up the boards good and tight, so there won't be no unpleasantness. Of course, lead would be the right thing for him, but it ain't a thing as I'm often asked for, and I didn't think as I could get it in time, and the fact is, the sooner he's underground again, the better. Besides, lead is cruel 'ard work on the bearers. Six of them we're giving him—I wouldn't want to be thought lacking in respect for the dead, however come by, so I says to Rector, 'No, sir,' I says, 'not that old handcart,' I says, 'but six bearers just the same as if he was one of ourselves.' And Rector, he quite agreed with me. Ah! I daresay there's be a sight of folk come in from round about, and I wouldn't like them to see the thing done mean or careless like."

"That's right," said Mr. Gotobed. "I've heerd as there's a reglar party comin' from St. Stephen in Jack Brownlow's sharrer. It'll be a rare frolic for 'em."

"Rector's giving a wreath, too," pursued Mr. Russell, "and Miss Thorpe's sending another. And there'll be a nice bunch o' flowers from the schoolchildren and a wreath from the Women's Institute. My missus was round collecting the pennies just as soon as we knowed we'd have the buryin' of him."

"Ah! she's a quick worker and no mistake," said the sexton, admiringly.

"Ah! and Mrs. Venables, she made the money up to a guinea, so it'll be a real good one. I like to see a nice lot of flowers at a funeral. Gives it tone, like."

"Is it to be choral?"

"Well, not what you might call fully choral, but just a 'ymn at the graveside. Rector says, 'Not too much about parted friends,' he says, ''Twouldn't be suitable, seeing we don't know who his friends was.' So I says, 'What about *God moves in a myster'ous way*?' I says. 'That's a good solemn-like, mournful 'ymn, as we all knows the tune on, and if anything can be said to be myster'ous, it's this here death,' I says. So that's what was settled."

"Ah!" said the voice of Mr. Lavender, "you're right there, Bob Russell. When I was a lad, there wasn't none o' this myster'ousness about. Everything was straightforward an' proper. But ever since eddication come in, it's been nothing but puzzlement, and fillin' up forms and 'ospital papers and sustificates and such, before you can even get as much as your Lord George pension."

"That may be, Hezekiah," replied the sexton, "but to my mind it all started with that business of Jeff Deacon at the Red House, bringin' strangers into the place. First thing as 'appened arter that was the War, and since then we been all topsy-turvy, like."

"As to the War," said Mr. Russell. "I daresay we'd a-had that anyhow, Jeff Deacon or no Jeff Deacon. But in a general way you're quite right. He was a bad 'un, was Jeff, though even now, poor Mary won't hear a word again him."

"That's the way with women," said Mr. Lavender, sourly. "The wusser a man is, the more they dotes on him. Too soft-spoken he were, to my liking, were that Deacon. I don't trust these London folk, if you'll excuse me, sir."

"Don't mention it," said Wimsey.

"Why, Hezekiah," remonstrated Mr. Russell, "you thought a sight o' Jeff Deacon yourself at one time. Said he was the quickest chap at learning Kent Treble Bob as you ever had to do with."

"That's a different thing," retorted the old gentleman. "Quick he was, there ain't no denyin', and he pulled a very good rope. But quickness in the 'ed don't mean a good 'eart. There's many evil men is as quick as monkeys. Didn't the good Lord say as much? The children o' this world is wiser in their generation than the children o' light. He commended the unjust steward, no doubt, but he give the fellow the sack just the same, none the more for that."

"Ah, well," said the sexton, "Jeff Deacon 'ull be put in his proper place where he've gone, and the same with this poor chap, whoever he be. We ain't got nothing to meddle wi' that, only to do our dooties in the station whereto we are called. That's Scripture, that is, and so I says, Give him a proper funeral, for we don't know when it may be our turn next."

"That's very true, Harry; very true, that is. It may be you or me to be 'it on the 'ed one o' these days—though who can be going about to do such things beats me. Now then, Potty, what do you want here?"

"Nothing, nothing, Bob. Only to see where you was a-putting of the dead 'un. Ah! he were reglar smashed up, he were, weren't he? Beat all to a pulp, eh? Whack! whack! I a-liked to a-seen that, I would."

"Clear off," said the undertaker. "I'm disgusted wi' you, Potty. Fair disgusted. Don't you get talkin' that a-way, or I'll tell Rector on you, and he won't let you blow the organ no more. See? What you mean by it?"

"Nothing, Bob, nothing."

"That's a good thing."

Mr. Russell watched the imbecile uneasily as he shuffled away, his big head rolling and his hands swinging loosely at his sides.

"He's getting very queer, is Potty," said he. "I 'ope as he's safe. I reckon he did ought to be shut up."

"No, no," said the sexton. "Potty's safe enough. I don't 'old with these 'ere asylums."

At this point Mrs. Venables joined them to take possession of her guest.

"Poor little Hilary Thorpe wasn't in church," she observed. "Such a nice child. I should have liked you to see her. But she's quite prostrated, poor child, so Mrs. Gates tell me. And you know, the village people do stare so at anybody who's in trouble, and they will want to talk and condole. They mean well, but it's a terrible ordeal. I'll take you along to the Red House one day. Come along now—I'm sure you want your dinner."

THE THIRD PART

Lord Peter is Taken from Lead and Makes Thirds Place

> The bell that the treble takes from lead makes thirds place and returns to lead again; while the bells in 4, 5 and 6, 7 dodge when the place is made.
>
> *Rules for Ringing Grandsire Triples*

LORD PETER WATCHED the coffin borne up the road.

"Here comes my problem," said he to himself, "going to earth on the shoulders of six stout fellows. Finally, this time, I suppose, and I don't seem to have got very much out of it. What a gathering of the local worthies—and how we are all enjoying it! Except dear old Venables—he's honestly distressed. ... This everlasting tolling makes your bones move in your body. ... Tailor Paul ... Tailor Paul ... two mortal tons of bawling bronze. ... 'I am the Resurrection and the Life ...' that's all rather sobering. This chap's first resurrection was ghastly enough—let's hope there won't be another this side of Doomsday. ... Silence that dreadful bell! ... Tailor Paul ... though even that might happen, if Lubbock finds anything funny. ... 'Though after my skin worms destroy this body. ...' How queer that fellow Thoday looks ... something wrong there, I shouldn't wonder. ... Tailor Paul ... 'We brought nothing into this world and it is certain we can carry nothing out ...' except our secrets, old Patriarch; we take those with us all right." The deep shadows of the porch swallowed up priest, corpse and bearers, and Wimsey, following with Mrs. Venables, felt how strange it was that he and she should follow that strange corpse as sole and unexpected mourners.

"And people may say what they like," thought Wimsey again, "about the services of the Church of England, but there was genius in the choosing of these psalms. 'That I may be certified how long I have to live'—what a terrifying prayer! Lord, let me never be certified of anything of the kind. 'A stranger with Thee and a sojourner'—that's a fact, God knows.... 'Thou hast set our misdeeds before Thee'... very likely, and why should I, Peter Wimsey, busy myself with digging them up? I haven't got so very much to boast about myself, if it comes to that.... Oh, well!... 'world without end, Amen.' Now the lesson. I suppose we sit down for this—I'm not very well up in the book of the words.... Yes.... This is the place where the friends and relations usually begin to cry—but there's nobody here to do it—not a friend, nor a—— How do I know that? I don't know it. Where's the man or woman who would have recognised that face, if the murderer hadn't taken all those pains to disfigure it?... That red-haired kid must be Hilary Thorpe... decent of her to come... interesting type... I can see her making a bit of a splash in five years' time.... 'I have fought with beasts at Ephesus'... what on earth has that got to do with it?... 'raised a spiritual body'—what does old Donne say? 'God knows in what part of the world every grain of every man's dust lies.... He whispers, he hisses, he beckons for the bodies of his saints'... do all these people believe that? Do I? Does anybody? We all take it pretty placidly, don't we? 'In a flash, at a trumpet crash, this Jack, joke, poor potsherd, patch, matchwood, immortal diamond is—immortal diamond.' Did the old boys who made that amazing roof believe? Or did they just make those wide wings and adoring hands for fun, because they liked the pattern? At any rate, they made them *look* as though they believed something, and that's where they have us beat. What next? Oh, yes, out again to the grave, of course. Hymn 373... there must be some touch of imagination in the good Mr. Russell to have suggested this, though he looks as if he thought of nothing but having tinned salmon to his tea.... 'Man that is born of a woman...' not very much further to go now; we're coming into the straight.... 'Thou knowest, Lord, the secrets of our hearts....' I knew it, I knew it! Will Thoday's going to faint.... No, he's got hold of himself again. I shall have to have a word with that gentleman before long... 'for any pains of death, to fall from Thee.' Damn it! that goes home. Why? Mere splendour of rhythm, I expect—there are plenty of worse pains.... 'Our dear brother here departed'... *brother*... we're all dear when we're dead, even if beforehand somebody hated us enough to tie us up and... Great Scott, yes! What about that rope?"

The problem of the rope—absurdly overlooked and now absurdly insistent—took such possession of Wimsey that he forgot to join in the Lord's Prayer; nor had he even wits to spare for a sardonic commentary on the means used by providence to deliver this our brother out of the miseries of this sinful world. He was amazed that he had not earlier seized upon the rope as a clue to the labyrinth. For the tying-up of the dead man implied so much.

Where had the rope come from? How had it happened to be handy for the tying-up, and where had that tying taken place? You might kill a man in hot blood, but you did not first tie him. The death of a bound man meant premeditation—a calf roped for the shambles. The rope had been removed before burial; there was a horrid thrift about that.... At this point Wimsey shook himself. There was no need to fancy things; there were plenty of other reasons for the removal of the rope. It had been removed before death. It had been removed and replaced where it came from, lest its absence should arouse suspicion. It had been removed for the same reason that the face had been mutilated—lest anyone finding the body should recognise it. Finally, it had been removed because it had tied the body *to* something—and that, perhaps, was the likeliest reason. For the body must have been brought from somewhere —how? Car, lorry, cart, wagon, wheelbarrow, truck...? It reminded one of "Tinker, tailor..."

"Everything *very* nicely done, Mr. Russell," said Mrs. Venables.

"Yes'm?" said Mr. Russell. "Very glad you think so, 'm. We done what we could to the best of our ability."

"I'm sure," said Mrs. Venables, "that if his own people had been here, they couldn't have wished for anything *nicer*."

"No,'m," agreed Mr. Russell, much gratified, "and it's a pity they couldn't a-been present, for there's no doubt a handsome funeral is a great comfort to them as is left. Of course, it ain't so grand as a London funeral would be——" He glanced wistfully at Wimsey.

"But much nicer," said Wimsey, in a ridiculous echo of Mrs. Venables. "You see, it has so much more of the personal touch."

"That's very true," said the undertaker, much encouraged. "Why, I dessay these London men get as much as three or four funerals every week, and it stands to reason as they can't put the same 'eart into it—let alone not knowing the parties. Well, I'll be getting along now. There's someone wants to speak to you, my lord."

"No," said Wimsey, firmly, to a gentleman in well-worn tweeds, who approached briskly. "I have no story for the *Morning Star*. Nor for any other paper. Hop it. I have other things to do."

"Yes," added Mrs. Venables, addressing the reporter as though he were an importunate child at a school treat, "run away now, the gentleman's busy. How tiresome these newspapers are! You must get sick to death of them. Come along. I want to introduce you to Hilary Thorpe. Hilary, my dear, how are you? Very sweet of you to come—so trying for you. How is your uncle? This is Lord Peter Wimsey."

"I'm ever so glad to meet you, Lord Peter. Dad used to read all about your cases—he'd have loved to have a talk with you. You know, I think he'd have been frightfully amused to think of being mixed up in one himself—if only it hadn't been Mother's grave. I'm glad he didn't know about that. But it is a mystery, isn't it? And he was—well, quite a kid about mysteries and things."

"Was he? I should have thought he'd had about enough of them."

"You mean about the necklace? That was pretty awful for him, poor dear. Of course, it all happened before I was born, but he often used to talk about it. He always used to say he believed Deacon was the worst of the two men, and that Grand-dad ought never to have had him in the house. It was funny, but I believe he rather took a liking to the other man—the London thief. He only saw him at the trial, of course, but he said he was an amusing beggar and he believed he was telling the truth."

"That's dashed interesting." Lord Peter turned suddenly and savagely on the young man from the *Morning Star*, who still hovered at a little distance. "See here, my lad, if you don't make a noise like a hoop and roll away, I shall have something to say to your editor. I will not have this young lady followed about and bothered by you. Go right away, and if you're good I'll see you later and tell you any lies you like. See? Now vanish! .... Curse the Press!"

"That lad's a sticker," said Miss Thorpe. "He badgered poor Uncle nearly out of his senses this morning. That's Uncle, talking to the Rector. He's a Civil Servant, and he disapproves of the Press altogether. He disapproves of mysteries, too. It's rotten for Uncle."

"I expect he'll disapprove of me."

"Yes, he does. He thinks your hobby unsuited to your position in life. That's why he's rather carefully avoiding an introduction. Uncle's a comic old bird, but he isn't a snob and he's rather decent, really. Only he's not a bit like Dad. You and Dad would have got on splendidly. Oh, by the way—you know where Dad and Mother are buried, don't you? I expect that was the first place you looked at."

"Well, it was; but I'd rather like to look at it again. You see, I'm wondering just exactly how the—the—"

"How they got the body there? Yes, I thought you'd be wondering that. I've been wondering, too. Uncle doesn't think it's nice of me to wonder anything of the sort. But it really makes things easier to do a little wondering, I mean, if you're once interested in a thing it makes it seem less real. That's not the right word, though."

"Less personal?"

"Yes; that's what I mean. You begin to imagine how it all happened, and gradually it gets to feel more like something you've made up."

"H'm!" said Wimsey. "If that's the way your mind works, you'll be a writer one day."

"Do you think so? How funny! That's what I want to be. But why?"

"Because you have the creative imagination, which works outwards, till finally you will be able to stand outside your own experience and see it as something you have made, existing independently of yourself. You're lucky."

"Do you really think so?" Hilary looked excited.

"Yes—but your luck will come more at the end of life than at the beginning, because the other sort of people won't understand the way your mind works. They will start by thinking you dreamy and romantic, and then they'll be surprised to discover that you are really hard and heartless. They'll be quite wrong both times—but they won't ever know it, and *you* won't know it at first, and it'll worry you."

"But that's just what the girls say at school. How did you know? . . . Though they're all idiots—mostly, that is."

"Most people are," said Wimsey, gravely, "but it isn't kind to tell them so. I expect you do tell them so. Have a heart; they can't help it. . . . Yes, this is the place. Well, you know, it isn't very much overlooked, is it? That cottage is the nearest—whose is that?"

"Will Thoday's."

"Oh, is it? . . . And after that, there's only the Wheatsheaf and a farm. Whose is the farm?"

"That's Mr. Ashton's place. He's quite a well-to-do kind of man, one of the churchwardens. I liked him very much when I was a kid; he used to let me ride on the farm-horses."

"I've heard of him: he pulled my car out of the ditch one day—which reminds me. I ought to call and thank him personally."

"That means you want to ask him questions."

"If you *do* see through people as clearly as that, you oughtn't to make it so brutally plain to them."

"That's what Uncle calls my unfeminine lack of tact. He says it comes of going to school and playing hockey."

"He may be right. But why worry?"

"I'm not worrying—only, you see, Uncle Edward will have to look after me now, and he thinks it's all wrong for me to be going to Oxford. . . . What are you looking at? The distance from the South gateway?"

"Uncomfortably discerning woman—yes, I was. You could bring the body in a car and carry it round without too much difficulty. What's that, there, close up by the north wall of the churchyard? A well?"

"Yes; that's the well where Gotobed gets the water for washing out the porch and scrubbing the chancel and all that. I think it's rather deep. There used to be a pump there at one time, but the village people used to come and use it for drinking water, when the village well ran dry, and Mr. Venables had to stop it, because he said it wasn't sanitary, drinking water out of a graveyard; so he took the pump away, and paid for having the village well dug deeper and put in order. He's a frightfully good old sort. When Gotobed wants water he has to haul it up as best he can in a bucket. He grumbles a lot about it. The well's a great nuisance, anyway, because it makes the graves on that side very damp, and sometimes in the winter you can't dig them properly. It was worse before Mr. Venables had the churchyard drained."

"Mr. Venables seems to do a lot for the parish."

"He does. Dad used to subscribe to things, of course, but Mr. Venables generally starts things, when it's anything to do with the church. At least, when it's things like drains, it's probably Mrs. Venables. Why did you want to know about the well?"

"I wanted to know whether it was used or disused. As it's used, of course nobody would think of hiding anything large in it."

"Oh, you mean the body? No, that wouldn't have done."

"All the same," said Wimsey. . . . "Look here! forgive me asking, but, supposing your father hadn't died when he did, what sort of tombstone would he have been likely to put up to your mother? Any idea?"

"None at all. He hated tombstones and wouldn't discuss them, poor darling. It's horrid to think that he's got to have one."

"Quite. So that for all anybody knew, he might have had a flat stone put down, or one of those things with a marble kerb round and chips in the middle."

"A thing like a fender? Oh, no! he'd never have had *that*. And certainly not chips. They always reminded him of that fearfully genteel kind of coffee-sugar you get at the sort of places where everything's served on mats and all the wine-glasses are coloured."

"Ah! but did the murderer know your father's feelings about coffee-sugar and wine-glasses?"

"Sorry—I don't know what you're driving at."

"My fault; I'm always so incoherent. I mean—when there are such lots of good places for putting bodies in—dykes and drains and so on, why cart one at great risk and trouble to a churchyard to plant it where it might quite easily be dug up by a stonemason smoothing away the earth for a fenderful of marble chips? I know the body was a good two feet below ground-level, but I suppose they have to dig a bit when they set up gravestones. It all seems so odd and so rash. And yet, of course, I can see the fascination of the idea. You'd think a grave was about the last place where anyone would look for a stray body. It was sheer bad luck that it should have to be opened up again so soon. All the same—when you think of the job of getting it here, and digging away at night in secret——! But it looks as though it must have been done that way, because of the rope-marks, which show that the man was tied up somewhere first. It must, I mean, all have been deliberate and thought-out beforehand."

"Then the murderer couldn't have thought about it earlier than New Year's Day when Mother died. I mean, he couldn't have counted on having a grave handy."

"Of course he couldn't; but it may have happened at any time since."

"Surely not at *any* time. Only within a week or so after Mother died."

"Why?" asked Wimsey, quickly.

"Why, because old Gotobed would be certain to notice if anybody had been digging his grave about after the earth had been firmed up properly. Don't you think it must have happened quite soon—probably while the wreaths were still on the grave? They stayed there for a week, and then they looked dead and beastly, and I told Gotobed to chuck them away."

"That's an idea," said Wimsey. "I never thought about that—not having had very much to do with the digging of graves. I must ask Gotobed about it. I say! Can you remember how long the snow lay after your mother died?"

"Let me see. It stopped snowing on New Year's Day, and they swept the path up to the south door. But it didn't start to thaw till—wait! I know! It was during the night of the second, though it had been getting sort of warmer for two days, and the snow was kind of damp. I remember quite well now. They dug the grave on the third, and everything was all sloshy. And on the day of the funeral it rained like billy-oh! It was dreadful. I don't think I shall ever forget it."

"And that took all the snow away, of course."

"Oh, yes."

"So it would have been easy enough for anybody to get to the grave without leaving foot-prints. Yes. I suppose you never noticed yourself that the wreaths had been moved, or anything?"

"Oh, no! As a matter of fact, I didn't come here much. Dad was so ill, I had to be with him—and anyway, I didn't think of Mother as being *here*, you know. Lord Peter, I think all this business about graves is hateful, don't you? But I'll tell you who would have noticed anything, and that's Mrs. Gates —our housekeeper, you know. She came down every day. She's a perfect ghoul. She kept on trying to talk to me about it, and I wouldn't listen to her. She's quite nice, really, but she ought to live in a Victorian novel, where people wear crape and weep into the tea-cups. . . . Oh, dear! there's Uncle Edward looking for me. He looks quite dyspeptic with disapproval. I'm going to introduce you to him, just to embarrass the poor dear. . . . Uncle Edward! This is Lord Peter Wimsey. He's been so kind. He says I have a creative imagination, and ought to be a writer."

"Ah! how do you do?" Mr. Edward Thorpe, forty-four, very correct and formal, presented a bland Civil Service front to the impact of Wimsey's personality. "I believe I have met your brother, the Duke of Denver. I hope he is quite well . . . Quite . . . quite so. . . . It is very good of you to take an interest in my niece's young ambitions. All these young women mean to do great things, don't they? But I tell her, authorship is a good stick, but a bad crutch. Very distressing business, this. I am so sorry she should be dragged into it, but of course, in her position, the village people expect her to—ah!—enter into their —ah!—their—um——"

"Amusements?" suggested Wimsey. It came upon him with a shock that Uncle Edward could not be many years older than himself. He felt for him the apprehensive reverence which one feels for a quaint and brittle piece of antiquity.

"For anything which touches them nearly," said Mr. Thorpe. Gallant fellow! Deeply disapproving, he yet sought to defend his niece against criticism. "But I am taking her away for a little peace and quietness," he added. "Her aunt, unhappily, was unable to come to Fenchurch—she suffers sadly from rheumatoid arthritis—but she is looking forward to seeing Hilary at home."

Wimsey, glancing at Hilary's sullen face, saw rebellion rising; he knew exactly the kind of woman who would have married Uncle Edward.

"In fact," said Mr. Thorpe, "we are leaving to-morrow. I am so sorry we cannot ask you to dine, but under the circumstances——"

"Not at all," said Wimsey.

"So I fear it must be a case of Hail and Farewell," continued Mr. Thorpe, firmly. "Delighted to have met you. I could wish that it were under happier circumstances. Ah—good afternoon. Please remember me to your brother when you see him."

"Warned off!" said Wimsey, when he had shaken hands with Uncle Edward and bestowed on Hilary Thorpe a grin of understanding sympathy. "Why? Corrupting the morals of youth? Or showing too much zeal about digging up the family mystery? Is Uncle Edward a dark horse or a plain ass, I wonder? Did he go to his brother's wedding? I must ask Blundell. Where is Blundell? I wonder if he is free to-night?"

He hastened to catch the Superintendent, who had dutifully attended the funeral, and arranged to run over to Leamholt after dinner. Gradually the congregation melted away. Mr. Gotobed and his son Dick removed their official "blacks" and fetched the spades that leaned against the wall near the covered well.

As the earth thudded heavily upon the coffin lid, Wimsey joined the small group that had gathered to discuss the ceremony and read the cards upon the wreaths He stooped idly to examine an exceptionally handsome and exotic floral tribute of pink and purple hothouse exhibits, wondering who could have gone to so much expense for the unknown victim. With a slight shock he read, on a visiting card: "With reverent sympathy. Lord Peter Wimsey. St. Luke xii. 6."

"Very appropriate," said his lordship, identifying the text after a little thought (for he had been carefully brought up). "Bunter, you are a great man."

"What I really want to know," said Lord Peter, as he stretched comfortable legs upon the Superintendent's hearth, "is the relation between Deacon and Cranton. How did they get into touch? Because a lot seems to turn on that?"

"So it does," agreed Mr. Blundell; "but the trouble is, we have only got their words to go on, and which was the biggest liar, the Lord God only knows, though Mr. Justice Bramhill made a guess. There's no doubt of one thing, and that is that they knew each other in London. Cranton was one of those smooth-spoken, gentlemanly sort of crooks that you meet hanging about the lounge in cheap-smart restaurants—you know the type. He'd been in trouble before, but he gave out he was a reformed character, and made quite a spot of money writing a book. At least, I suppose somebody wrote it for him, but he had his name put on the cover, and all that. There've been several of that sort since the War, but this chap was a smart lad—a bit ahead of his time, really. He was thirty-five in 1914; not educated anything to speak of, but with a kind of natural wit, sharpened by having had to look out for himself, if you take my meaning."

"Just so. A graduate in the university of the world."

"That's very well put," said Mr. Blundell, welcoming the cliché as an inspiration. "Very cleverly put indeed. Yes—that's just what he was. Deacon, now, he was different. A very superior man indeed, he was, and a great reader. In fact, the chaplain down at Maidstone said he was quite a remarkable scholar in his way, with a poetic imagination, whatever that may be exactly. Sir Charles Thorpe took quite a fancy to the fellow, treated him friendly and all that, and gave him the run of the library. Well, these two met in some dance place or other, some time in 1912, when Sir Charles was staying in London. Cranton's story is that some girl that Deacon had picked up—Deacon was always after a skirt—pointed him out to Deacon as the author of this book I was telling you about, and that Deacon made out to be tremendously interested in the book and pumped him a lot about crooks and their doings and the way they worked their little games and all that. He said Deacon made a dead set at him and wouldn't leave him alone, and was always kind of hinting that he was bound to go back to the old life in the end. Deacon said different. He said that what interested him was the literary side of the business, as he called it. Says he thought, if a crook could write a book and make money, why not a butler? According to him, it was Cranton made a dead set at *him*, and started pumping him about what sort of place he'd got, and suggesting if there was anything to be pinched, they should pinch it together and go shares, Deacon working the inside part of the job and Cranton seeing to the rest—finding a fence and settling the terms and so on. I daresay it was six of one and half-a-dozen of the other, if you ask me. A pretty pair they were, and no mistake."

The Superintendent paused to take a long draught of beer from a pewter mug and then resumed.

"You understand," he said, "this was the story they told after we'd got hold of 'em both for the robbery. At first, naturally, they both lied like Ananias and swore they'd never seen each other before in their lives, but when they found what the prosecution had up against them, they changed their tune. But there was this about it. As soon as Cranton realised that the game was up, he adopted this story and stuck to it. In fact, he pleaded guilty at the trial and his one idea seemed to be to get Deacon into trouble and have him gaoled good and hard. He said Deacon had double-crossed him and he was out to get his own back—though whether there was any truth in that, or whether he thought he would get off easy by making himself out to be the poor unfortunate victim of temptation, or whether it was all pure malice, I don't know. The jury had their own idea about it, and so had the judge.

"Well, now. In April 1914 this wedding of Mr. Henry Thorpe's came along, and it was pretty well known that Mrs. Wilbraham was going to be there with her emerald necklace. There wasn't a thief in London that didn't know all about Mrs. Wilbraham. She's a sort of cousin of the Thorpes, a lot of times removed, and long way back, and she's got a stack of money and the meanness of fifty thousand Scotch Jews rolled into one. She'll be about eighty-six or seven now and getting childish, so I'm told; but in those days she was just eccentric. Funny old lady, stiff as a ramrod, and always dressed in black silks and satins—very old-fashioned—with jewels and bangles and brooches and God knows what stuck all over her. That was one of her crazes, you understand. And another was, that she didn't believe in insurance and she didn't believe a lot in safes, neither. She had a safe in her town house, naturally, and kept her stuff locked up in it, but I don't suppose she'd have done that if the safe hadn't been put in by her husband when he was alive. She was too mean to buy as much as a strong-box for herself, and when she went away on a visit, she preferred to trust to her own wits. Mad as a March hare, she must have been," said the Superintendent, thoughtfully, "but there! you'd be surprised what a lot of these funny old ladies there are going about loose in the world. And of course, nobody ever liked to say anything to her, because she was disgustingly rich and had the full disposal of her own property. The Thorpes were about the only relations she had in the world, so they invited her to Mr.

Henry's wedding, though it's my belief they all hated the sight of her. If they hadn't have asked her, she'd have taken offence, and—well, there! You can't offend your rich relations, can you?"

Lord Peter thoughtfully refilled his own beer-mug and said, "Not on any account."

"Well, then," pursued the Superintendent, "here's where Cranton and Deacon tell different tales again. According to Deacon, he got a letter from Cranton as soon as the wedding-day was announced, asking him to come and meet him at Leamholt and discuss some plan for getting hold of the emeralds. According to Cranton, it was Deacon wrote to him. Neither of 'em could produce a scrap of evidence about it, one way or the other, so, there again, you paid your money and you took your choice. But it was proved that they did meet in Leamholt and that Cranton came along the same day to have a look at the house.

"Very good. Now Mrs. Wilbraham had a lady's maid, and if it hadn't been for her and Mary Thoday, the whole thing might have come to nothing. You'll remember that Mary Thoday was Mary Deacon then. She was housemaid at the Red House, and she'd got married to Deacon at the end of 1913. Sir Charles was very kind to the young couple. He gave them a nice bedroom to themselves away from the other servants, just off a little back stair that runs up by the butler's pantry, so that it was quite like a little private home for them. The plate was all kept in the pantry, of course, and it was supposed to be Deacon's job to look after it.

"Now, this maid of Mrs. Wilbraham's—Elsie Bryant was her name—was a quick, smart sort of girl, full of fun and high spirits, and it so happened that she'd found out what Mrs. Wilbraham did with her jewels when she was staying away from home. It seems the old girl wanted to be too clever by half. I think she must have been reading too many detective stories, if you ask me, but anyway, she got it into her head that the best place to keep valuables wasn't a jewel case or a strong-box or anything of that kind, that would be the first thing a burglar would go for, but some fancy place where nobody would think of looking, and to cut a long story short, the spot she pitched upon was—if you'll excuse me mentioning it—underneath one of the bedroom utensils. You may well laugh—so did everybody in court, except the judge, and he happened to get a fit of coughing at the time and his handkerchief was over his face, so nobody could see how he took it. Well, this Elsie, she was a bit inquisitive, as girls are, and one day—not very long before the wedding—she managed to take a peep through a keyhole or something of that kind, and caught the old lady just in the act of putting the stuff away. Naturally, she couldn't keep a thing like that to herself, and when she and her mistress got to Fenchurch—which they did a couple of days before the wedding—the first thing she had to do was to strike up a bosom friendship with Mary Deacon (as she was then) for the express purpose, as it seems to me, of telling her all about it in confidence. And of course, Mary, being a devoted wife and all that, had to share the joke with her husband. I dare say it's natural. Anyhow, counsel for the defence made a big point of it, and there's no doubt it was that utensil kept Elsie and Mary out of quod. 'Gentlemen,' he said to the jury, in his speech, 'I see you all smiling over Mrs. Wilbraham's novel idea of a safe-deposit, and I've no doubt you're looking forward to passing the whole story on to your wives when you get home. And that being so, you can very well enter into the feelings of my client Mary Deacon and her friend, and see how—in the most innocent manner in the world—the secret was disclosed to the one man who might have been expected to keep it quiet.' He was a clever lawyer, he was, and had the jury eating out of his hand by the time he'd done with them.

"Now we've got to guess again. There was a telegram sent off to Cranton from Leamholt—no doubt about that, for we traced it. He said it came from Deacon, but Deacon said that if anybody sent it, it must have been Elsie Bryant. She and Deacon were both in Leamholt that afternoon, but we couldn't get the girl at the post-office to recognise either of them, and the telegram was written in block letters. To my mind, that points to Deacon, because I doubt if the girl would have thought of such a thing, but needless to say, when the two of them were told to show a specimen of their printing, it wasn't a mite like the writing on the form. Whichever of them it was, either they were pretty clever, or they got somebody else to do it for them.

"You say you've heard already about what happened that night. What you want to know is the stories Cranton and Deacon told about it. Here's where Cranton, to my mind, shows up better than Deacon, unless he was very deep indeed. He told a perfectly consistent tale from start to finish. It was Deacon's plan first and last. Cranton was to come down in a car and be under Mrs. Wilbraham's window at the time mentioned in the telegram. Deacon would then throw out the emerald necklace, and Cranton would go straight off with it to London and get it broken up and sold, dividing the loot fifty-fifty with Deacon, less £50 he'd given him on account. Only he said that what came out of the window was only the jewel-case and not the emeralds, and he accused Deacon of taking the stuff himself and rousing the house on purpose to put the blame on him—on Cranton, that is. And of course, if that was Deacon's plan, it was a very good one. He would get the stuff and the kudos as well.

"The trouble was, of course, that none of this came out till some time after Cranton had been arrested, so that when Deacon was taken and made his first statement to the police, he didn't know what story he'd got to meet. The first account he gave was very straightforward and simple, and the only trouble about it was that it obviously wasn't true. He said he woke up in the night and heard somebody moving about in the garden, and at once said to his wife: 'I believe there's somebody after the plate.' Then, he said, he went downstairs, opened the back door and looked out, in time to see somebody on the terrace under Mrs. Wilbraham's window. Then (according to him) he rushed back indoors and upstairs, just quick enough to catch a fellow making off through Mrs. Wilbraham's window."

"Hadn't Mrs. Wilbraham locked her door?"

"No. She never did, on principle—afraid of fire, or something. He said he shouted loudly to alarm the house, and then the old lady woke up and saw him at the window. In the meantime the thief had climbed down by the ivy and got away. So he rushed off downstairs and found the footman just coming out of the back door. There was a bit of confusion about the back door part of the story, because Deacon didn't explain, first go-off, how he happened to be in Mrs. Wilbraham's bedroom at all. His very first tale, to Sir Charles, had been that he went straight out when he heard the noise in the garden, but by the time the police got him, he'd managed to fit the two accounts together, and said that he'd either been too upset at the time to explain himself clearly or else that everybody else had been too upset to understand what he said. Well, that was all right, until they started to unearth all the history of his having met Cranton before, and the telegram and so on. Then Cranton, seeing that the game was up, told his tale in full, and of course, that made it pretty awkward for Deacon. He couldn't deny it altogether, so he now admitted knowing Cranton, but said it was Cranton who had tried to tempt him into stealing the emeralds, while he had been perfectly sea-green incorruptible. As for the telegram, he denied that altogether, and put it on Elsie. And he denied the £50 altogether, and it's a fact that they never traced it to him.

"Of course, they cross-examined him pretty fiercely. They wanted to know, first, why he hadn't warned Sir Charles about Cranton and secondly, why he'd told a different tale at first. He declared that he thought Cranton had given up all idea of the theft, and he didn't want to frighten anybody; but that when he heard noises in the garden, he guessed what was happening. He also said that afterwards he was afraid to own up to knowing Cranton for fear he should be accused of complicity. But it sounded a pretty thin story, and neither the judge nor the jury believed a word of it. Lord Bramhill spoke very severely to him after the verdict, and said that if it hadn't been his first offence, he'd have given him the heaviest sentence it was in his power to bestow. He called it aggravated larceny of the very worst type, being committed by a servant in a position of trust, in a dwelling-house and his master's dwelling-house at that, and accompanied by the opening of a window, which made it into burglary, and then he had violently resisted arrest, and so forth and so on; and in the end he gave Deacon eight years' penal servitude and told him he was lucky to get off with that. Cranton was an old offender and might have got a lot more, but the judge said he was unwilling to punish him much more heavily than Deacon, and gave him ten years. So that was that. Cranton went to Dartmoor, and served his full time as a perfectly good old lag, without giving much trouble to anybody. Deacon, being a first offender, went to Maidstone, where he set up to be one of those model prisoners—which is a kind you always want to look out for, because they are always up to some mischief or other. After nearly four years—early in 1918, it was—this nice, refined, well-conducted convict made a brutal attack on a warder and broke prison. The warder died, and of course the whole place was scoured for Deacon, without any success. I daresay, what with the War and one thing and another, they hadn't as many men to carry on the job as they ought to have had. Anyhow, they didn't find him, and for two years he enjoyed the reputation of being about the only man who had ever broken prison successfully. Then his bones turned up in one of those holes—dene-holes, I think they call them, in a wood in North Kent, so they found it was one up to the prison system after all. He was still in his convict clothes and his skull was all smashed in, so he must have tumbled over during the night—probably within a day or two of his escape. And that was the end of *him*."

"I suppose there's no doubt he was guilty."

"Not the slightest. He was a liar from beginning to end, and a clumsy liar at that. For one thing, the ivy on the Red House showed clearly enough that nobody had climbed down by it that night—and in any case, his final story was as full of holes as a sieve. He was a bad lot, and a murderer as well, and the country was well rid of him. As for Cranton, he behaved pretty well for a bit after he came out. Then he got into trouble again for receiving stolen goods, or goods got by false pretences or something, and back he went into quod. He came out again last June, and they kept tabs on him till the beginning of September. Then he disappeared, and they're still looking for him. Last seen in London—but I shouldn't be surprised if we'd seen the last of him to-day. It's my belief, and always was, that Deacon had the necklace, but what he did with it, I'm damned if I know. Have another spot of beer, my lord. It won't do you any harm."

"Where do you think Cranton was, then, between September and January?"

"Goodness knows. But if he's the corpse, I should say France, at a guess. He knew all the crooks in London, and if anybody could wangle a forged passport, he could."

"Have you got a photograph of Cranton?"

"Yes, my lord, I have. It's just come. Like to have a look at it?"

"Rather!"

The Superintendent brought out an official photograph from a bureau which stood, stacked neatly with documents, in a corner of the room. Wimsey studied it carefully.

"When was this taken?"

"About four years ago, my lord, when he went up for his last sentence. That's the latest we have."

"He had no beard then. Had he one in September?"

"No, my lord. But he'd have plenty of time to grow one in four months."

"Perhaps that's what he went to France for."

"Very likely indeed, my lord."

"Yes—well—I can't be dead positive, but I think this is the man I saw on New Year's Day."

"That's very interesting," said the Superintendent.

"Have you shown the photograph to any of the people in the village?"

Mr. Blundell grinned ruefully.

"I tried it on the Wilderspins this afternoon, but there! Missus said it was him, Ezra said 'twas nothing like him—and a bunch of neighbours agreed heartily with both of them. The only thing is to get a beard faked on to it and try 'em again. There's not one person in a hundred can swear to a likeness between a bearded face and one that's clean-shaven."

"H'm, too true. Defeat thy favour with an usurped beard. . . . And of course you couldn't take the body's finger-prints, since he had no hands."

"No, my lord, and that's a sort of an argument, in a way, for it's being Cranton."

"If it *is* Cranton, I suppose he came here to look for the necklace, and grew a beard so that he shouldn't be recognised by the people that had seen him in court."

"That's about it, my lord."

"And he didn't come earlier simply because he had to let his beard grow. So much for my bright notion that he might have received some message within the last few months. What I can't understand is that stuff about Batty Thomas and Tailor Paul. I've been trying to make out something from the inscriptions on the bells, but I might as well have left it alone. Hear the tolling of the bells, iron bells—though I'd like to know when church bells were ever made of iron—what a world of solemn thought their monody compels! Was Mr. Edward Thorpe at his brother's wedding, do you know?"

"Oh, yes, my lord. He was there, and a terrible row he made with Mrs. Wilbraham after the theft. It upset poor Sir Charles very much. Mr. Edward as good as told the old lady that it was all her fault, and he wouldn't hear a word against Deacon. He was certain Elsie Bryant and Cranton had fixed it all up between them. I don't believe myself that Mrs. Wilbraham would ever have cut up so rough if it weren't for the things Mr. Edward said to her, but she was—is—a damned obstinate old girl, and the more he swore it was Elsie, the more *she* swore it was Deacon. You see, Mr. Edward had recommended Deacon to his father——"

"Oh, had he?"

"Why, yes. Mr. Edward was working in London at the time—quite a lad, he was, only twenty-three—and hearing that Sir Charles was wanting a butler, he sent Deacon down to see him."

"What did he know about Deacon?"

"Well, only that he did his work well and looked smart. Deacon was a waiter in some club that Mr. Edward belonged to, and it seems he mentioned that he wanted to try private service, and that's how Mr. Edward came to think of him. And, naturally, having recommended the fellow, he had to stick up for him. I don't know if you've met Mr. Edward Thorpe, but if you have, my lord, you'll know that anything that belongs to him is always perfect. He's never been known to make a mistake, Mr. Edward hasn't—and so, you see, he couldn't possibly have made a mistake about Deacon."

"Oh, yes?" said Wimsey. "Yes, I've met him, Frightful blithering ass. Handy thing to be, sometimes. Easily cultivated. Five minutes' practice before the glass every day, and you will soon acquire that vacant look so desirable for all rogues, detectives and Government officials. However, we will not dwell on Uncle Edward. Let us return to our corpse. Because, Blundell, after all, even if it is Cranton, come to look for emeralds—who killed him, and why?"

"Why," returned the policeman, "supposing he found the emeralds all right and somebody lammed him on the head and took them off him. What's wrong with that?"

"Only that he doesn't seem to have been lammed on the head."

"That's what Dr. Baines says; but we don't know that he's right."

"No—but anyway, the man was killed somehow. Why kill him, when you'd already got him tied up and could take the emeralds without any killing at all?"

"To prevent him squealing. Stop! I know what you're going to say—Cranton wasn't in a position to squeal. But he was, don't you see. He'd already been punished for the theft—they couldn't do anything more to him for that, and he'd only to come and tell us where the stuff was to do himself quite a lot of good. You see his game. He could have done the sweet injured innocence stunt. He'd say: 'I always told you Deacon had the stuff, so the minute I could manage it, I went down to Fenchurch to find it, and I did find it—and of course I was going to take it straight along to the police-station like a good boy, when Tom, Dick or Harry came along and took it off me. So I've come and told you all about it, and when you lay your hands on Tom, Dick or Harry and get the goods you'll remember it was me gave you the office.' Oh, yes—that's what he could have done, and the only thing we'd have been able to put on him would be failing to report himself, and if he'd put us on to getting the emeralds, he'd be let off light enough, you bet. No! anybody as wanted those emeralds would have to put Cranton where he couldn't tell any tales. That's clear enough. But as to who it was, that's a different thing."

"But how was this person to know that Cranton knew where the necklace was? And how did he know, if it comes to that? Unless it really was he who had them after all, and he hid them somewhere in Fenchurch instead of taking them to London. It looks to me as though this line of argument was going to make Cranton the black sheep after all."

"That's true. How'd he come to know? He can't have got the tip from anybody down here, or they'd have got the stuff for themselves, and not waited for him. They've had long enough to do it, goodness knows. But why should Cranton have left the stuff behind him?"

"Hue and cry. Didn't want to be caught with it on him. He may have parked it somewhere when he drove off, meaning to come back and fetch it later. You never know. But the longer I look at these photographs, the more positive I feel that the man I met was Cranton. The official description agrees, too—colour of eyes and all that. And if the corpse isn't Cranton, what's become of him?"

"There you are," said Mr. Blundell. "I don't see as we can do much more till we get the reports from London. Except, of course, as regards the burying. We ought to be able to get a line on that. And what you say about Miss Thorpe's notion—I mean, as to the wreaths and that—may have something in it. Will you have a chat with this Mrs. Gates, or shall I? I think you'd better tackle Mr. Ashton. You've got a good excuse for seeing him, and if I went there officially, it might put somebody on his guard. It's a nuisance, the churchyard being so far from the village. Even the Rectory doesn't overlook it properly, on account of the shrubbery."

"No doubt that circumstance was in the mind of the murderer. You mustn't quarrel with your bread and butter, Superintendent. No difficulty, no fun."

"Fun?" said the Superintendent. "Well, my lord, it's nice to be you. How about Gates?"

"You'd better do Gates. If Miss Thorpe's leaving to-morrow, I can't very well call without looking a nosey parker. And Mr. Thorpe doesn't approve of me. I daresay he's issued an order: No information. But *you* can invoke all the terrors of the law."

"Not much, I can't. Judges' rules and be damned. But I'll have a try. And then there's——"

"Yes, there's Will Thoday."

"Ah! . . . but if Miss Thorpe's right, he's out of it. He was laid up in bed from New Year's Eve till January 14th. I know that for certain. But somebody in his house may have noticed something. It'll be a bit of a job getting anything out of them, though. They've had a taste of the dock once, and they'll get frightened, ten to one, the minute they see me."

"You needn't worry about that. You can't very well frighten them worse than they're frightened already. Go and read the Burial Service to them and watch their reactions."

"Oh!" said the Superintendent. "Religion's a bit out of my line, except on Sundays. All right—I'll take on that part of it. Maybe, if I don't mention that dratted necklace . . . but there, my mind's that full of it, it'll be a mercy if it don't slip out."

Which shows that policemen, like other people, are at the mercy of their sub-conscious preoccupations.

THE FOURTH PART

Lord Peter Dodges with Mr. Blundell and Passes Him

> "Dodging" is taking a retrograde movement, or moving a place backwards out of the ordinary hunting course. . . . She will be seen to dodge with a bell, and pass a bell alternately throughout her whole work.
>
> TROYTE

"WELL NOW, MA'AM,'' said Superintendent Blundell.

"Well, officer?" retorted Mrs. Gates.

It is said, I do not know with how much reason, that the plain bobby considers "officer" a more complimentary form of address than "my man" or even "constable"; while some people, of the Disraelian school of thought, affirm that an unmerited "Sergeant" is not taken amiss. But when a highly-refined lady, with a grey glacé gown and a grey glacé eye, addresses a full-blown Superintendent in plain clothes as "officer", the effect is not soothing, and is not meant to be so. At this rate, thought Mr. Blundell, he might just as well have sent a uniformed inspector, and had done with it.

"We should be greatly obliged, ma'am," pursued Mr. Blundell, "for your kind assistance in this little matter."

"A little matter?" said Mrs. Gates. "Since when have murder and sacrilege been considered little matters in Leamholt? Considering that you have had nothing to do for the last twenty years but run in a few drunken labourers on market days, you seem to take your new responsibilities very coolly. In my opinion, you ought to call in the assistance of Scotland Yard. But I suppose, since being patronised by the aristocracy, you consider yourself quite competent to deal with any description of crime."

"It does not lie with me, ma'am, to refer anything to Scotland Yard. That is a matter for the Chief Constable."

"Indeed?" said Mrs. Gates, not in the least disconcerted. "Then why does the Chief Constable not attend to the business himself? I should prefer to deal directly with him."

The Superintendent explained patiently that the interrogation of witnesses was not, properly speaking, the duty of the Chief Constable.

"And why should I be supposed to be a witness? I know nothing about these disgraceful proceedings."

"Certainly not, ma'am. But we require a little information about the late Lady Thorpe's grave, and we thought that a lady with your powers of observation would be in a position to assist us."

"In what way?"

"From information received, ma'am, it appears probable that the outrage may have been committed within a very short period after Lady Thorpe's funeral. I understand that you were a frequent visitor at the graveside after the melancholy event——"

"Indeed? And who told you that?'

"We have received information to that effect, ma'am."

"Quite so. But from whom?"

"That is the formula we usually employ, ma'am," said Mr. Blundell, with a dim instinct that the mention of Hilary would only make bad worse. "I take it, that is a fact, is it not?"

"Why should it not be a fact? Even in these days, some respect may be paid to the dead, I trust."

"Very proper indeed, ma'am. Now can you tell me whether, on any occasion when you visited the grave, the wreaths presented the appearance of having been disturbed, or the earth shifted about, or anything of that kind?"

"Not," said Mrs. Gates, "unless you refer to the extremely rude and vulgar behaviour of that Mrs. Coppins. Considering that she is a Nonconformist, you would think she would have more delicacy than to come into the churchyard at all. And the wreath itself was in the worst possible taste. I suppose she was entitled to send one if she liked, considering the great and many favours she had always received from Sir Charles' family. But there was no necessity whatever for anything so large and ostentatious. Pink hot-house lilies in January were entirely out of place. For a person in her position, a simple bunch of chrysanthemums would have been ample to show respect, without going out of her way to draw attention to herself."

"Just so, ma'am," said the Superintendent.

"Merely because," pursued Mrs. Gates, "I am here in a dependent position, that does not mean that I could not have afforded a floral tribute quite as large and expensive as Mrs. Coppins'. But although Sir Charles and his lady, and Sir Henry and the late Lady Thorpe after them, were always good enough to treat me rather as a friend than a servant, I know what is due to my position, and should never have dreamed of allowing my modest offering to compete in any way with those of the Family."

"Certainly not, ma'am," agreed the Superintendent, heartily.

"I don't know what you mean by 'Certainly not,'" retorted Mrs. Gates. "The Family themselves would have raised no objection, for I may say that they have always looked on me as one of themselves, and seeing that I have been housekeeper here thirty years, it is is scarcely surprising that they should."

"Very natural indeed, ma'am. I only meant that a lady like yourself would, of course, take the lead in setting an example of good taste and propriety, and so forth. My wife," added Mr. Blundell, lying with great determination and an appearance of the utmost good faith, "my wife is always accustomed to say to our girls, that for an example of ladylike behaviour, they cannot do better than look up to Mrs. Gates of the Red House at Fenchurch. Not"—— (for Mrs. Gates looked a little offended)—"that Mrs. Blundell would presume to think our Betty and Ann in any way equal to *you*, ma'am, being only one of them in the post-office and the other a clerk in Mr. Compline's office, but it does young people no harm to look well above themselves, ma'am, and my wife always says that if they will model themselves upon Queen Mary, or—since they cannot have very much opportunity of studying her Gracious Majesty's behaviour—upon Mrs. Gates of the Red House, they can't fail to grow up a credit to their parents, ma'am."

Here Mr. Blundell—a convinced Disraelian—coughed. He thought he had done that rather well on the spur of the moment, though, now he came to think of it, "deportment" would have been a better word than "behaviour".

Mrs. Gates unbent slightly, and the Superintendent perceived that he would have no further trouble with her. He looked forward to telling his wife and family about this interview. Lord Peter would enjoy it, too. A decent sort of bloke, his lordship, who would like a bit of a joke.

"About the wreath, ma'am," he ventured to prompt.

"I am telling you about it. I was disgusted—really *disgusted*, officer, when I found that Mrs. Coppins had had the *impertinence* to remove my wreath and put her own in its place. There were, of course, a great many wreaths at Lady Thorpe's funeral, some of them extremely handsome, and I should have been quite content if my little tribute had been placed on the roof of the hearse, with those of the village people. But Miss Thorpe would not hear of it. Miss Thorpe is always very thoughtful."

"A very nice young lady," said Mr. Blundell.

"Miss Thorpe is one of the Family," said Mrs. Gates, "and the Family are always considerate of other people's feelings. True gentlefolk always are. Upstarts are not."

"That's very true indeed, ma'am," said the Superintendent, with so much earnestness that a critical listener might almost have supposed the remark to have a personal application.

"My wreath was placed upon the coffin itself," went on Mrs. Gates, "with the wreaths of the Family. There was Miss Thorpe's wreath, and Sir Henry's, of course, and Mr. Edward Thorpe's and Mrs. Wilbraham's and mine. There was quite a difficulty to get them all upon the coffin, and I was quite willing that mine should be placed elsewhere, but Miss Thorpe insisted. So Mrs. Wilbraham's was set up against the head of the coffin, and Sir Henry's and Miss Thorpe's and Mr. Edward's *on* the coffin, and mine was given a position at the foot—which was practically the same thing as being on the coffin itself. And the wreaths from the Servants' Hall and the Women's Institute were on one side and the Rector's wreath and Lord Kenilworth's wreath were on the other side. And the rest of the flowers were placed, naturally, on top of the hearse."

"Very proper, I'm sure, ma'am."

"And consequently," said Mrs. Gates, "after the funeral, when the grave was filled in, Harry Gotobed took particular notice that the Family's wreaths (among which I include mine) were placed in suitable positions on the grave itself. I directed Johnson the chauffeur to attend to this—for it was a very rainy day, and it would not have been considerate to ask one of the maids to go—and he assured me that this was done. I have always found Johnson sober and conscientious in his work, and I believe him to be a perfectly truthful man, as such people go. He described to me exactly where he placed the wreaths, and I have no doubt that he carried out his duty properly. And in any case, I interrogated Gotobed the next day, and he told me the same thing."

"I daresay he did," thought Mr. Blundell, "and in his place I'd have done the same. I wouldn't get a fellow into trouble with this old cat, not if I knew it." But he merely bowed and said nothing.

"You may judge of my surprise," went on the lady, "when, on going down the next day after Early Service to see that everything was in order, I found Mrs. Coppins' wreath—not at the side, where it should have been—but *on* the grave, as if she were somebody of importance, and *mine* pushed away into an obscure place and actually covered up, so that nobody could see the card at all. I was extremely angry, as you may suppose. Not that I minded in the least where my poor little remembrance was placed, for that can make no difference to anybody, and it is the thought that counts. But I was so much incensed by the woman's insolence—merely because I had felt it necessary to speak to her one day about the way in which her children behaved in the post-office. Needless to say, I got nothing from her but impertinence."

"That was on January 5th, then?"

"It was the morning after the funeral. That, as you say, would be Sunday the 5th. I did not accuse the woman without proof. I had spoken to Johnson again, and made careful inquiries of Gotobed, and they were both positive of the position in which the wreaths had been left the night before."

"Mightn't it have been some of the school-children larking about, ma'am?"

"I could well believe anything of *them*," said Mrs. Gates, "they are always ill-behaved, and I have frequently had to complain to Miss Snoot about them, but in this case the insult was too pointed. It was quite obviously and definitely aimed at myself, by that vulgar woman. Why a small farmer's wife should give herself such airs, I do not know. When I was a girl, village people knew their place, and kept it."

"Certainly," replied Mr. Blundell, "and I'm sure we were all much happier in those days. And so, ma'am, you never noticed any disturbance except on that one occasion?"

"And I should think that was quite enough," replied Mrs. Gates. "I kept a very good look-out after that, and if anything of a similar kind had occurred again, I should have complained to the police."

"Ah, well," said the Superintendent, as he rose to go, "you see, it's come round to us in the end, and I'll have a word with Mrs. Coppins, ma'am, and you may be assured it won't happen again. Whew! What an old catamaran!" (this to himself, as he padded down the rather neglected avenue beneath the budding horse-chestnuts). "I suppose I had better see Mrs. Coppins."

Mrs. Coppins was easily found. She was a small, shrewish woman with light hair and eyes which boded temper.

"Oh, yes," she said, "Mrs. Gates did have the cheek to say it was me. As if I'd have touched her mean little wreath with a hay-fork. Thinks she's a lady. No real lady would think twice about where her wreath was or where it wasn't. Talking that way to me, as if I was dirt! Why shouldn't we give Lady Thorpe as good a wreath as we could get? Ah! she was a sweet lady—a *real* lady, she was—and her and Sir Henry were that kind to us when we were a bit put about, like, the year we took this farm. Not that we were in any real difficulty—Mr. Coppins has always been a careful man. But being a question of capital at the right moment, you see, we couldn't just have laid our hand on it at the moment, if it hadn't been for Sir Henry. Naturally, it was all paid back—with the proper interest. Sir Henry said he didn't want interest, but that isn't Mr. Coppins' way. Yes—January 5th, it would be—and I'm quite sure none of the children had anything to do with it, for I asked them. Not that my children would go to do such a thing, but you know what children are. And it's quite true that her wreath was where she said it was, last thing on the evening of the funeral, for I saw Harry Gotobed and the chauffeur put it there with my own eyes, and they'll tell you the same."

They did tell the Superintendent so, at some considerable length; after which, the only remaining possibility seemed to be the school-children. Here, Mr. Blundell enlisted the aid of Miss Snoot. Fortunately, Miss Snoot was not only able to reassure him that none of her scholars was in fault ("for I asked them all very carefully at the time, Superintendent, and they assured me they had not, and the only one I might be doubtful of is Tommy West, and he had a broken arm at the time, through falling off a gate"); she was also able to give valuable and unexpected help as regards the time at which the misdemeanour was committed.

"We had a choir-practice that night, and when it was over—that would be about half-past seven—the rain had cleared up a little, and I thought I would just go and give another little look at dear Lady Thorpe's resting-place; so I went round with my torch, and I quite well remember seeing Mrs. Coppins' wreath standing up against the side of the grave next the church, and thinking what a beautiful one it was and what a pity the rain should spoil it."

The Superintendent felt pleased. He found it difficult to believe that Mrs. Coppins or anybody else had gone out to the churchyard on a dark, wet Saturday night to remove Mrs. Gates' wreath. It was surely much more reasonable to suppose that the burying of the corpse had been the disturbing factor, and that brought the time of the crime down to some hour between 7.30 p.m. on the Saturday and, say, 8.30 on the Sunday morning. He thanked Miss Snoot very much and, looking at his watch, decided that he had just about time to go along to Will Thoday's. He was pretty sure to find Mary at home, and, with luck, might catch Will himself when he came home to dinner. His way led him past the churchyard. He drove slowly, and, glancing over the churchyard wall as he went, observed Lord Peter Wimsey, seated in a reflective manner and apparently meditating among the tombs.

"'Morning!" cried the Superintendent cheerfully, "'Morning, my lord!"

"Oy!" responded his lordship. "Come along here a minute. You're just the man I wanted to see."

Mr. Blundell stopped his car at the lych-gate, clambered out, grunting (for he was growing rather stout) and made his way up the path.

Wimsey was sitting on a large, flat tombstone, and in his hands was about the last thing the Superintendent might have expected to see, namely, a large reel of line, to which, in the curious, clumsy-looking but neat and methodical manner of the fisherman, his lordship was affixing a strong cast adorned with three salmon-hooks.

"Hullo!" said Mr. Blundell. "Bit of an optimist, aren't you? Nothing but coarse fishing about here."

"Very coarse," said Wimsey. "Hush! While you were interviewing Mrs. Gates, where do you think I was? In the garage, inciting our friend Johnson to theft. From Sir Henry's study. Hist! not a word!"

"A good many years since he went fishing, poor soul," said Mr. Blundell, sympathetically.

"Well, he kept his tackle in good order all the same," said Wimsey, making a complicated knot and pulling it tight with his teeth. "Are you busy, or have you got time to look at something?"

"I was going along to Thoday's, but there's no great hurry. And, by the way, I've got a bit of news."

Wimsey listened to the story of the wreath.

"Sounds all right," he said. He searched in his pocket, and produced a handful of lead sinkers, some of which he proceeded to affix to his cast.

"What in the world are you thinking of catching with that?" demanded Mr. Blundell. "A whale?"

"Eels," replied his lordship. He weighed the line in his hand and gravely added another piece of lead.

Mr. Blundell, suspecting some kind of mystification, watched him in discreet silence.

"That will do," said Wimsey, "unless eels swim deeper than ever plummet sounded. Now come along. I've borrowed the keys of the church from the Rector. He had mislaid them, of course, but they turned up eventually among the Clothing Club accounts."

He led the way to the cope-chest beneath the tower, and threw it open.

"I have been chattin' with our friend Mr. Jack Godfrey. Very pleasant fellow. He tells me that a complete set of new ropes was put in last December. One or two were a little dicky, and they didn't want to take any chances over the New Year peal, so they renewed the lot while they were about it. These are the old ones, kept handy in case of sudden catastrophe. Very neatly coiled and stowed. This whopper belong to Tailor Paul. Lift 'em out carefully—eighty feet or so of rope is apt to be a bit entanglin' if let loose on the world. Batty Thomas. Dimity. Jubilee. John. Jericho. Sabaoth. But where is little Gaude? Where and oh where is she? With her sallie cut short and her rope cut long, where and oh where can she be? No—there's nothing else in the chest but the leather buffets and a few rags and oilcans. No rope for Gaude. *Gaudeamus igitur, juvenes dum sumus.* The mystery of the missing bell-rope. *Et responsum est ab omnibus: Non est inventus— -a* or *-um.*"

The Superintendent scratched his head and gazed vaguely about the church.

"Not in the stove," said Wimsey. "My first thought, of course. If the burying was done on Saturday, the stoves would be alight, but they'd be banked down for the night, and it would have been awkward if our Mr. Gotobed had raked out anything unusual on Sunday morning with his little scraper. As a matter of fact, he tells me that one of the first things he does on Sunday morning is to open the top thingumajig on the stove and take a look inside to see that the flue-pipe is clear. Then he stirs it up a-top, rakes it out at the bottom door and sets it drawing for the day. I don't *think* that was where the rope went. I hope not, anyway. I think the murderer used the rope to carry the body by, and didn't remove it till he got to the graveside. Hence these salmon-hooks."

"The well?" said Mr. Blundell, enlightened.

"The well," replied Wimsey. "What shall we do—go fishing?"

"I'm on; we can but try."

"There's a ladder in the vestry," said Wimsey. "Bear a hand. Along this way—out through the vestry-door—and here we are. Away, my jolly boys, we're all bound away. Sorry! forgot this was consecrated ground. Now then—up with the cover. Half a jiff. We'll sacrifice half a brick to the water-gods. Splosh!—it's not so very deep. If we lay the ladder over the mouth of the well, we shall get a straight pull."

He extended himself on his stomach, took the reel in his left hand and began to pay the line cautiously out over the edge of the ladder, while the Superintendent illumined the proceedings with a torch.

The air came up cold and dank from the surface of the water. Far below a circle of light reflected the pale sky and the beam of the torch showed hooks and line working steadily downwards. Then a tiny break in the reflection marked the moment when the hooks touched the water.

A pause. Then the whirr of the reel as Wimsey rewound the line.

"More water than I thought. Where are those leads? Now then, we'll try again."

Another pause. Then:

"A bite, Super, a bite! What's the betting it's an old boot? It's not heavy enough to be the rope. Never mind. Up she comes. Ahoy! up she rises! Sorry! I forgot again. Hullo, ullo, ullo! What's this? Not a boot, but the next thing to it. A hat! Now then, Super! Did you measure the head of the corpse? You did? Good! then we shan't need to dig him up again to see if his hat fits. Stand by with the gaff. Got him! Soft felt, rather the worse for wear and water. Mass production. London maker. Exhibit One. Put it aside to dry. Down she goes again.... *And* up she comes. Another tiddler. Golly! what's this? Looks like a German sausage. No, it isn't. No, it isn't. It's a sallie. Sallie in our alley. She is the darling of my heart. Little Gaude's sallie. Take her up tenderly, lift her with care. Where the sallie is, the rest will be.... Hoops-a-daisy! ... I've got it.... It's caught somewhere.... No, don't pull too hard, or the hook may come adrift. Ease her. Hold her.... Damn! ... Sorry, un-damn! I mean, how very provoking, it's got away.... *Now* I've got it.... Was that the ladder cracking on my breastbone, I wonder? Surprisin'ly sharp edge a ladder has.... There now, there now! there's your eel—all of a tangle. Catch hold. Hurray!"

"It's not all here," said the Superintendent, as the slimy mass of rope was hauled over the edge of the well.

"Probably not," said Wimsey, "but this is one of the bits that were used to do the tying. He's cut it loose and left the knots in."

"Yes. Better not touch the knots, my lord. They might tell us something about who tied 'em."

"Take care of the knots and the noose will take care of itself. Right you are. Here we go again."

In process of time, the whole length of the rope—as far as they could judge—lay before them in five sections, including the sallie.

"Arms and ankles tied separately. Then body tied up to something or other and the slack cut off. And he removed the sallie because it got in the way of his knots. H'm!" said Mr. Blundell. "Not very expert work, but effective, I dare say. Well, my lord, this is a very interesting discovery of yours. But—it's a bit of a facer, isn't it? Puts rather a different complexion on the crime, eh?"

"You're right, Super. Well, one must face up to things, as the lady said when she went to have hers lifted. Hullo! what the——"

A face, perched in a bodiless sort of way on the churchyard wall, bobbed suddenly out of sight as he turned, and then bobbed up again.

"What the devil do you want, Potty?" demanded the Superintendent.

"Oh, nothing," replied Potty. "I don't want nothing. Who're you goin' to hang with that there, mister? That's a rope, that is. They've got eight on 'em hanging up the tower there," he added, confidentially. "Rector don't let me go up there no more, because they don't want nobody to know. But Potty Peake knows. One, two, three, four, five, six, seven, eight—all hung up by the neck. Old Paul, he's the biggest—Tailor Paul—but there did ought to be nine tailors by rights. I can count, you see; Potty can count. I've counted 'em over time and again on my fingers. Eight. And one is nine. And one is ten—but I ain't telling you *his* name. Oh, no. He's waiting for the nine tailors—one, two, three, four——"

"Here, you, hop it!" cried the Superintendent, exasperated. "And don't let me catch you hanging round here again."

"Who's a-hanging? Listen—you tell me, and I'll tell you. There's Number Nine a-coming, and that's a rope to hang him, ain't it, mister? Nine of 'em, and eight's there already. Potty knows. Potty can say. But he won't. Oh, no! Somebody might be listening." His face changed to its usual vacant look and he touched his cap.

"Good-day, sir. Good-day, mister. I got to feed the pigs, that's Potty's work. Yes, that's right. They pigs did ought to be fed. 'Morning, sir; 'morning, mister."

He slouched away across the fields towards a group of out-houses some distance away.

"There!" said Mr. Blundell, much vexed. "He'll go telling everybody about this rope. He's got hanging on the brain, ever since he found his mother hanging in the cow-house when he was a kid. Over at Little Dykesey, that was, a matter of thirty years back. Well, it can't be helped. I'll get these things taken along to the station, and come back later on for Will Thoday. It'll be past his lunch-time now."

"It's past mine, too," said Wimsey, as the clock chimed the quarter past one. "I shall have to apologise to Mrs. Venables."

"So you see, Mrs. Thoday," said Superintendent Blundell, pleasantly, "if anybody can help us over this awkward business it's you."

Mary Thoday shook her head.

"I'm sure I would if I could, Mr. Blundell, but there! how can I? It's right enough to say I was up all night with Will. I hardly had my clothes off for a week, he was that bad, and the night after they laid poor Lady Thorpe to rest, he was just as bad as could be. It turned to pneumonia, you know, and we didn't think as we should ever pull him through. I'm not likely to forget that night, nor the day neither. Sitting here, listening to old Tailor Paul and wondering if he was going to ring for Will before the night was out."

"There, there!" said her husband, embarrassed, and sprinkling a great quantity of vinegar on his tinned salmon, "it's all over now, and there's no call to get talking that way."

"Of course not," said the Superintendent. "Not but what you had a pretty stiff time of it, didn't you, Will? Delirious and all that kind of thing, I'll lay. I know what pneumonia is, for it carried off my old mother-in-law in 1922. It's a very trying thing to nurse, is pneumonia."

"So 'tis," agreed Mrs. Thoday. "Very bad he was, that night. Kept on trying to get out of his bed and go to church. He thought they were ringing the peal without him, though I kept on telling him that was all rung and finished with New Year's Day. A terrible job I had with him, and nobody to help me, Jim having left us that very morning. Jim was a great help while he was here, but he had to go back to his ship. He stayed as long as he could, but of course he's not his own master."

"No," said Mr. Blundell. "Mate on a merchantman, isn't he? How's he getting along? Have you heard from him lately?"

"We had a postcard last week from Hong Kong," said Mary, "but he didn't say much. Only that he was well and love to the children. He hasn't sent nothing but postcards this voyage, and he must be terrible busy, for he's such a man for writing letters as a rule."

"They'll be a bit shorthanded, maybe," said Will. "And it's an anxious time for men in his line of business, freights being very scarce and hard to come by. It'll be all this depression, I suppose."

"Yes, of course. When do you expect him back?"

"Not for I don't know when," replied Will. The Superintendent looked sharply at him, for he seemed to detect a note almost of satisfaction in the tone. "Not if trade's decent, that is. You see, his ship don't make regular trips. She follows cargo, as they call it, tramping round from port to port wherever there's anything to be picked up."

"Ah, yes, of course. What's the name of the ship, again?"

"The *Hannah Brown*. She belongs to Lampson & Blake of Hull. Jim is doing very well, I'm told, and they set great store by him. If anything happened to Captain Woods, they'd give the ship to Jim. Would't they, Will?"

"So he says," replied Thoday uneasily. "But it don't do to count on anything these days."

The contrast between the wife's enthusiasm and the husband's lack of it was so marked, that Mr. Blundell drew his own conclusions.

"So Jim's been making trouble between 'em, has he?" was his unspoken comment. "That explains a lot. But it doesn't help me much. Better change the subject."

"Then you didn't happen to see anything going on at the church that night?" he said. "No lights moving about? Nothing of that kind?"

"I didn't move from Will's bedside all night," replied Mrs. Thoday, with a hesitating glance at her husband. "You see, he was so ill, and if I left him a minute, he'd be throwing the clothes off and trying to get up. When it wasn't the peal that was in his mind, it was the old trouble—you know."

"The old Wilbraham affair?"

"Yes. He was all muddled up in his head, thinking the—the—that dreadful trial was on and he had to stand by me."

"That'll *do*!" cried Thoday, suddenly, pushing his plate away so violently that the knife and fork clattered from the plate upon the table. "I won't have you fretting yourself about that old business no more. All that's dead and buried. If it come up in my mind when I wasn't rightly in my senses, I can't help that. God knows, I'd be the last to put you in mind of it if I'd been able to help myself. You did ought to know that."

"I'm not blaming you, Will."

"And I won't have nothing more said about it in my house. What do you want to come worrying her this way, Mr. Blundell? She's told you as she don't know a thing about this chap that was buried, and that's all there is to it. What I may have said and done, when I was ill, don't matter a hill of beans."

"Not a scrap," admitted the Superintendent, "and I'm very sorry such an allusion should have come up, I'm sure. Well, I won't keep you any longer.

You can't assist me and that's all there is to it. I'm not saying it isn't a disappointment, but a policeman's job's all disappointments, and one must take the rough with the smooth. Now I'll be off and let the youngsters come back to their tea. By the way, what's gone with the parrot?"

"We've put him in the other room," said Will, with a scowl. "He's taken to shrieking fit to split your head."

"That's the worst of parrots," said Mr. Blundell. "He's a good talker, though. I've never heard a better."

He bade them a cheerful good evening and went out. The two Thoday children—who had been banished to the woodshed during the discussion of murders and buryings, unsuited to their sex and tender years—ran down to open the gate for him.

"Evening, Rosie," said Mr. Blundell, who never forgot anybody's name, "evening, Evvie. Are you being good girls at school?"

But, the voice of Mrs. Thoday calling them at that moment to their tea, the Superintendent received but a brief answer to his question.

Mr. Ashton was a farmer of the old school. He might have been fifty years old, or sixty or seventy, or any age. He spoke in a series of gruff barks, and held himself so rigidly that if he had swallowed a poker it could only have produced unseemly curves and flexions in his figure. Wimsey, casting a thoughtful eye upon his hands, with their gnarled and chalky joints, concluded, however, that his unbending aspect was due less to austerity than to chronic arthritis. His wife was considerably younger than himself; plump where he was spare, bounce-about where he was stately, merry where he was grave, and talkative where he was monosyllabic. They made his lordship extremely welcome and offered him a glass of home-made cowslip wine.

"It's not many that makes it now," said Mrs. Ashton. "But it was my mother's recipe, and I say, as long as there's peggles to be got, I'll make my peggle wine. I don't hold by all this nasty stuff you get at the shops. It's good for nothing but to blow out the stomach and give you gas."

"Ugh!" said Mr. Ashton, approvingly.

"I quite agree with you, Mrs. Ashton," said his lordship. "This is excellent." And so it was. "It is another kindness I have to thank you for." And he expressed his gratitude for the first-aid given to his car the previous January.

"Ugh!" said Mr. Ashton. "Pleased, I'm sure."

"But I always hear of Mr. Ashton engaged in some good work or other," went on his lordship. "I believe he was the good samaritan who brought poor William Thoday back from Walbeach the day he was taken ill."

"Ugh!" repeated Mr. Ashton. "Very fortunate we happened to see him. Ugh! Very bad weather for a sick man. Ugh! Dangerous thing, influenza."

"Dreadful!" said his wife. "Poor man—he was quite reeling with it as he came out of the bank. I said to Mr. Ashton, 'How terrible bad poor Will do look, to be sure! I'm sure he's not fit to go home.' And sure enough, we hadn't got but a mile or so out of the town when we saw his car drawn up by the side of the road, and him quite helpless. It was God's mercy he didn't drive into the Drain and kill himself. And with all that money on him, too! Dear,

dear! What a terrible loss it would have been. Quite helpless and out of his head he was, counting them notes over and dropping of them all over the place. 'Now, Will,' I said, 'you just put them notes back in your pocket and keep quiet and we'll drive you home. And you've no call to worry about the car,' I said, 'for we'll stop at Turner's on the way and get him to bring it over next time he comes to Fenchurch. He'll do it gladly, and he can go back on the 'bus.' So he listened to me and we got him into our car and brought him home. And a hard time he had, dear, dear! He was prayed for in church two weeks running."

"Ugh!" said Mr. Ashton.

"What he ever wanted to come out for in such weather I can't think," went on Mrs. Ashton, "for it wasn't market day, and we wouldn't have been there ourselves, only for Mr. Ashton having to see his lawyer about Giddings' lease, and I'm sure if Will had wanted any business done, we'd have been ready to do it for him. Even if it was the bank, he could have trusted us with it, I should think. It's not as though Mr. Ashton couldn't have taken care of two hundred pounds, or two thousand, for that matter. But Will Thoday was always very close about his business."

"My dear!" said Mr. Ashton, "ugh! It may have been Sir Henry's business. You wouldn't have him anything but close about what's not, rightly speaking, his affair."

"And since when, Mr. Ashton," demanded his lady, "has Sir Henry's family banked at the London and East Anglia? Let alone that Sir Henry was always a deal too considerate to send a sick man out to do business for him in a snowstorm? I've told you before that I don't believe that two hundred pounds had anything to do with Sir Henry, and you'll find out one of these days I'm right, as I always am. Aren't I, now?"

"Ugh!" said Mr. Ashton. "You make a lot of talk, Maria, and some of it's bound to be right. Funny if it wasn't, now and again. Ugh! But you've no call to be interfering with Will's money. You leave that to him."

"That's true enough," admitted Mrs. Ashton, amiably. "I do let my tongue run on a bit, I'll allow. His lordship must exuse me."

"Not at all," said Wimsey. "In a quiet place like this, if one doesn't talk about one's neighbours, what is there to talk about? And the Thodays are really your only near neighbours, aren't they? They're very lucky. I'll be bound, when Will was laid up, you did a good bit of the nursing, Mrs. Ashton."

"Not as much as I'd have liked," said Mrs. Ashton. "My daughter was took ill at the same time—half the village was down with it, if it comes to that. I managed to run in now and again, of course—'twouldn't be friendly else—and our girl helped Mary with the cooking. But what with being up half the night——"

This gave Wimsey his opportunity. In a series of tactful inquiries he led the conversation to the matter of lights in the churchyard.

"There, now!" exclaimed Mrs. Ashton. "I always thought as there might be something in that tale as little Rosie Thoday told our Polly. But children do have so many fancies, you never know."

"Why, what tale was that?" asked Wimsey.

"Ugh! foolish nonsense, foolish nonsense," said Mr. Ashton. "Ghosts and what not."

"Oh, *that's* foolish enough, I dare say," retorted his lady, "but you know well enough, Luke Ashton, that the child might be telling the truth, ghost or no ghost. You see, your lordship, it's this way. My girl Polly—she's sixteen now and going out to service next autumn, for whatever people may say and whatever airs they may give themselves, I will maintain there's nothing like good service to train a girl up to be a good wife, and so I told Mrs. Wallace only last week. It's not standing behind a counter all day selling ribbons and bathing-dresses (if they call them dresses, with no legs and no backs and next to no fronts neither) will teach you how to cook a floury potato, let alone the tendency to fallen arches and varicose veins. Which," added Mrs. Ashton triumphantly, "she couldn't hardly deny, suffering sadly from her legs as she do."

Lord Peter expressed his warm appreciation of Mrs. Ashton's point of view and hinted that she had been about to say that Polly——

"Yes, of course. My tongue do run on and no mistake, but Polly's a good girl, though I say it, and Rosie Thoday's always been a pet of Polly's, like, ever since she was quite a baby and Polly only seven. Well, then, it was a good time ago, now—when would it be, Luke? End of January, maybe, near enough—it was pretty near dark at six o'clock, so it couldn't be much later—well, call it end of January—Polly comes on Rosie and Evvie sitting together under the hedge just outside their place, both of them crying. 'Why, Rosie,' says Polly, 'what's the matter?' And Rosie says, Nothing, now that Polly's come and can they walk with her to the Rectory, because their Dad has a message for Rector. Of course, Polly was willin' enough, but she couldn't understand what they was cryin' about, and then, after a bit—for you know how difficult it is to get children to tell you what they're frightened on—it comes out that they're afraid to go past the churchyard in the dark. Well, Polly being a good girl, she tells 'em there's no call to be frighted, the dead being in the arms of our Saviour and not having the power to come out o' their graves nor to do no harm to nobody. But that don't comfort Rosie, none the more for that, and in the end Polly makes out that Rosie's seen what she took to be the spirit of Lady Thorpe a-flittin' about her grave. And it seems the night she see her was the night of the funeral."

"Dear me," said Wimsey. "What exactly did she see?"

"No more than a light, by what Polly could make out. That was one of the nights Will Thoday was very bad, and it seems Rosie was up and about helping her mother—for she's a good, handy child, is Rosie—and she looks out o' the window and sees the light just a-rising out of where the grave would be."

"Did she tell her mother and father?"

"Not then, she didn't. She didn't like too, and I remember well, as a child I was just the same, only with me it was a funny sort of thing that used to groan in the wash-house, which I took to be bears—but as to telling anybody, I'd ha' died first. And so would Rosie, only that night her father wanted her to go a message to the Rectory and she tried everything to get off doing it, and at last he got angry and threatened to take a slipper to her. Not that he meant it, I don't suppose," said Mrs. Ashton, "for he's a kind man as a rule, but he hadn't hardly got over his illness and he was fratchety, like, as sick people will be. So then Rosie made up her mind to tell him what she seen. Only that made him angrier still, and he said she was to go and no more nonsense, and never to speak about ghosts, and such like to him again. If Mary had been there, she'd a-gone, but she was out getting his medicine from Dr. Baines, and the 'bus don't come back till half-past seven and Will wanted the message sent particular, though I forget now what it were. So Polly told Rosie it couldn't have been Lady Thorpe's spirit, for that was at rest, and if it had been, Lady Thorpe wouldn't do harm to a living soul; and she said Rosie must a-seen Harry Gotobed's lantern. But it couldn't well a-been that, for by what the child said it was one o'clock in the morning past that Rosie see the light. Dear me an' all! I'm sure if I'd a-known then what I know now, I'd a-paid more attention to it."

Superintendent Blundell was not best pleased when this conversation was repeated to him.

"Thoday and his wife had better be careful," he observed.

"They told you the exact truth, you know," said Wimsey.

"Ah!" said Mr. Blundell. "I don't like witnesses to be so damned particular about exact truth. They get away with it as often as not, and then where are you? Not but what I did think of speaking to Rosie, but her mother called her away double quick—and no wonder! Besides, I don't care, somehow, for pumping kids about their parents. I can't help thinking of my own Betty and Ann."

And if that was not quite the exact truth, there was a good deal of truth in it; for Mr. Blundell was a kindly man.

THE FIFTH PART

Tailor Paul is Called Before with a Single

> The canal has been dangerously ignored. Each year of the Republic, our family have reported to the Capital that there were silted channels and weakened dykes in our neighbourhood. My husband and Mai-da's father have just interviewed the present President. They were received politely, but their conclusion is that nothing will be done.
>
> NORA WALN: *The House of Exile*

LORD PETER WIMSEY sat in the schoolroom at the Rectory, brooding over a set of underclothing. The schoolroom was, in fact, no longer the schoolroom, and had not been so for nearly twenty years. It had retained its name from the time when the Rector's daughters departed to a real boarding-school. It was now devoted to Parish Business, but a fragrance of long-vanished governesses still clung about it—governesses with straight-fronted corsets and high-necked frocks with bell sleeves, who wore their hair *à la* Pompadour. There was a shelf of battered lesson-books, ranging from *Little Arthur's England* to Hall & Knight's *Algebra*, and a bleached-looking Map of Europe still adorned one wall. Of this room, Lord Peter had been made free, "except", as Mrs. Venables, explained, "on Clothing-Club nights, when I am afraid we shall have to turn you out."

The vest and pants were spread upon the table, as though the Clothing Club, in retiring, had left some forlorn flotsam and jetsam behind. They had been washed, but there were still faint discolorations upon them, like the shadow of corruption, and here and there the fabric had rotted away, as the garments of mortality will, when the grave has had its way with them. Wafted in through the open window came the funeral scent of jonquils.

Wimsey whistled gently as he examined the underclothes, which had been mended with scrupulous and economical care. It puzzled him that Cranton, last seen in London in September, should possess a French vest and pants so much worn and so carefully repaired. His shirt and outer garments—now also clean and folded—lay on a chair close at hand. They, too, were well-worn, but they were English. Why should Cranton be wearing second-hand French underclothes?

Wimsey knew that it would be hopeless to try tracing the garments through the makers. Underwear of this mark and quality was sold by the hundred thousand in Paris and throughout the provinces. It lay stacked up outside the great linen-drapers' shops, marked "Occasions", and thrifty housewives bought it there for cash. There was no laundry-mark; the washing had doubtless been done at home by the housewife herself or the *bonne à tout faire*. Holes here and there had been carefully darned; under the arm-pits, patches of a different material had been neatly let in; the wrists of the vest, frayed with use, had been over-sewn; buttons had been renewed upon the pants. Why not? One must make economies. But they were not garments that anyone would have gone out of his way to purchase, even at a second-hand dealer's. And it would be hard for even the most active man to reduce his clothes to such a state of senility in four months' wear.

Lord Peter thrust his fingers into his hair till the sleek yellow locks stood upright. "Bless his heart!" thought Mrs. Venables, looking in upon him through the window. She had conceived a warm maternal affection for her guest. "Would you like a glass of milk, or a whisky-and-soda, or a cup of beef-tea?" she suggested, hospitably. Wimsey laughed and thanked her, but declined.

"I hope you won't catch anything from those dreadful old clothes," said Mrs. Venables. "I'm sure they can't be healthy."

"Oh, I don't expect to get anything worse than brain-fever," said Wimsey. "I mean"—seeing Mrs. Venables look concerned—"I can't quite make out about these underthings. Perhaps you can suggest something." Mrs. Venables came in, and he laid his problem before her.

"I'm sure I don't know," said Mrs. Venables, gingerly examining the objects before her. "I'm afraid I'm not a Sherlock Holmes. I should think the man must have had a very good, hard-working wife, but I can't say more."

"Yes, but that doesn't explain why he should get his things in France. Especially as everything else is English. Except, of course, the ten-centime piece, and they're common enough in this country."

Mrs. Venables, who had been gardening and was rather hot, sat down to consider the question.

"The only thing I can think of," she said, "is that he got his English clothes as a disguise—you said he came here in disguise, didn't you? But, of course, as nobody would see his underneaths, he didn't bother to change them."

"But that would mean that he came from France."

"Perhaps he did. Perhaps he was a Frenchman. They often wear beards, don't they?"

"Yes; but the man I met wasn't a Frenchman."

"But you don't know he was the man you met. He may be somebody quite different."

"Well, he *may*," said Wimsey, dubiously.

"He didn't bring any other clothes with him, I suppose?"

"No; not a thing. He was just a tramping out-of-work. Or he said he was. All he brought was an old British trench-coat, which he took with him, and a toothbrush. He left that behind him. Can we wangle a bit of evidence out of that? Can we say that he must have been murdered because, if he had merely wandered away, he would have taken his toothbrush with him? And if he was the corpse, where is his coat? For the corpse had no coat."

"I can't imagine," replied Mrs. Venables, "and that reminds me, do be careful when you go down the bottom of the garden. The rooks are building and they *are* so messy. I should wear a hat if I were you. Or there's always an old umbrella in the summer-house. Did he leave his hat behind too?"

"In a sense he did," said Wimsey. "We've found that, in rather a queer place. But it doesn't help us much."

"Oh!" said Mrs. Venables, "how tiresome it all is. I'm sure you'll wear your brains right out with all these problems. You mustn't overdo yourself. And the butcher says he has some nice calf's liver to-day, only I don't know if you can eat it. Theodore is very fond of liver-and-bacon, though I always think it's rather rich. And I've been meaning to say, it's very good of that nice manservant of yours to clean the silver and brass so beautifully, but he really shouldn't have troubled. I'm quite used to giving Emily a hand with it. I hope it isn't very dull for him here. I understand he's a great acquisition in the kitchen and extraordinarily good at music-hall imitations. Twice as good as the talkies, Cook says."

"Is he indeed?" said Wimsey. "I had no idea of it. But what I don't know about Bunter would fill a book."

Mrs. Venables bustled away, but her remarks remained in Wimsey's mind. He put aside the vest and pants, filled a pipe and wandered down the garden, pursued by Mrs. Venables with an ancient and rook-proof linen hat, belonging to the Rector. The hat was considerably too small for him, and the fact that he immediately put it on, with expressions of gratitude, may attest the kind heart which, despite the poet, is frequently found in close alliance with coronets; though the shock to Bunter's system was severe when his master suddenly appeared before him, wearing this grotesque headgear, and told him to get the car out and accompany him on a short journey.

"Very good, my lord," said Bunter. "Ahem! there is a fresh breeze, my lord."

"All the better."

"Certainly, my lord. If I may venture to say so, the tweed cap or the grey felt would possibly be better suited to the climatic conditions."

"Eh? Oh! Possibly you are right, Bunter. Pray restore this excellent hat to its proper place, and, if you should see Mrs. Venables, give her my compliments and say that I found its protection invaluable. And, Bunter, I rely upon you to keep a check upon your Don Juan fascinations and not strew the threshold of friendship with the wreckage of broken hearts."

"Very good, my lord."

On returning with the grey felt, Bunter found the car already out and his lordship in the driving-seat.

"We are going to try a long shot, Bunter, and we will begin with Leamholt."

"By all means, my lord."

They sped away up the Fenchurch Road, turned left along the Drain, switchbacked over Frog's Bridge without mishap and ran the twelve or thirteen miles to the little town of Leamholt. It was market day, and the Daimler had to push her way decorously through droves of sheep and pigs and through groups of farmers, who stood carelessly in the middle of the street, disdaining to move till the mudguards brushed their thighs. In the centre of one side of the market-place stood the post-office.

"Go in here, Bunter, and ask if there is any letter here for Mr. Stephen Driver, to be left till called for."

Lord Peter waited for some time, as one always waits when transacting business in rural post-offices, while pigs lurched against his bumpers and bullocks blew down his neck. Presently, Bunter returned, having drawn a blank despite a careful search conducted by three young ladies and the postmaster in person.

"Well, never mind," said Wimsey. "Leamholt is the post town, so I thought we ought to give it the first chance. The other possibilities are Holport and Walbeach, on this side of the Drain. Holport is a long way off and rather unlikely. I think we will try Walbeach. There's a direct road from here—at least, as direct as any fen road ever is. . . . I suppose God could have made a sillier animal than a sheep, but it is very certain that He never did. . . . Unless it's cows. Hoop, there, hup! hup! get along with you, Jemima!"

Mile after mile the flat road reeled away behind them. Here a windmill, there a solitary farm-house, there a row of poplars strung along the edge of a reed-grown dyke. Wheat, potatoes, beet, mustard and wheat again, grassland, potatoes, lucerne, wheat, beet and mustard. A long village street with a grey and ancient church tower, a red-brick chapel, and the Vicarage set in a little oasis of elm and horse-chestnut, and then once more dyke and windmill, wheat, mustard and grassland. And as they went, the land flattened more and more, if a flatter flatness were possible, and the windmills became more numerous, and on the right hand the silver streak of the Wale River came back into view, broader now, swollen with the water of the Thirty-foot and of Harper's Cut and St. Simon's Eau, and winding and spreading here and there, with a remembrance of its ancient leisure. Then, ahead of the great circle of the horizon, a little bunch of spires and roofs and a tall tree or so, and beyond them the thin masts of shipping. And so, by bridge and bridge the travellers came to Walbeach, once a great port, but stranded now far inland with the silting of the marshes and the choking of the Wale outfall; yet with her maritime tradition written unerringly upon her grey stones and timber warehouses, and the long lines of her half-deserted quays.

Here, at the post-office in the little square, Lord Peter waited in the pleasant hush that falls on country towns where all days but market days are endless sabbaths. Bunter was absent for some time, and, when he emerged, did so with a trifle less than his usual sedateness, while his usually colourless face was very slightly flushed about the cheek-bones.

"What luck?" inquired Wimsey, genially.

To his surprise, Bunter replied by a hasty gesture enjoining silence and caution. Wimsey waited till he had taken his place in the car and altered his question to:

"What's up?"

"Better move on quickly, my lord," said Bunter, "because, while the manoeuvre has been attended with a measure of success, it is possible that I have robbed His Majesty's Mails by obtaining a postal packet under false pretences."

Long before this handsome period had thundered to its close, the Daimler was running down a quiet street behind the church.

"What *have* you been doing, Bunter?"

"Well, my lord, I inquired, as instructed, for a letter addressed to Mr. Stephen Driver, poste restante, which might have been lying here some time. When the young person inquired how long a time, I replied, according to our previous arrangement, that I had intended to visit Walbeach a few weeks ago, but had been prevented from doing so, and that I understood that an important letter had been forwarded to me at this address under a misapprehension."

"Very good," said Wimsey. "All according to Cocker."

"The young person, my lord, then opened a species of safe or locker, and searched in it, and after the expiration of a considerable period, turned round with a letter in her hand and inquired what name I had said."

"Yes? These girls are very bird-witted. It would have been more surprising if she hadn't asked you to repeat the name."

"Quite so, my lord. I said, as before, that the name was Stephen or Steve Driver, but at the same time I observed from where I was standing that the letter in her hand bore a blue stamp. There was only the counter between us, and, as you are aware, my lord, I am favoured with excellent sight."

"Let us always be thankful for blessings."

"I hope I may say that I always am, my lord. On seeing the blue stamp, I added quickly (calling to mind the circumstances of the case) that the letter had been posted in France."

"Very good, indeed," said Wimsey, nodding approval.

"The young person, my lord, appeared to be puzzled by this remark. She said, in a doubtful tone, that there was a letter from France which had been lying in the post-office for three weeks, but that it was addressed to another person."

"Oh, hell!" said Wimsey.

"Yes, my lord; that thought passed through my own mind. I said, 'Are you quite sure, miss, that you have not mistaken the handwriting?' I am happy to say, my lord, that the young person—being young, and, no doubt, inexperienced—succumbed to this somewhat elementary strategy. She answered immediately, 'Oh, no—it's as plain as print: M. Paul Taylor.' At that point——"

"Paul Taylor!" cried Wimsey, in sudden excitement, "Why, that was the name——"

"Precisely, my lord. As I was about to say, at that point it was necessary to act promptly. I said at once: 'Paul Taylor? Why, that is the name of my chauffeur.' You will excuse me, my lord, if the remark should appear to carry any disrespectful implication, seeing that you were at that moment in the car and might conceivably be supposed to be the person alluded to, but in the momentary agitation of my spirits, my lord, I was not in a position to think as quickly or as clearly as I should have wished."

"Bunter," said his lordship, "I warn you that I am growing dangerous. Will you say at once, yes or no, did you get that letter?"

"Yes, my lord, I did. I said, of course, that since the letter for my chauffeur was there, I would take it to him, adding some facetious observations to the effect that he must have made a conquest while we were travelling abroad and that he was a great man for the ladies. We were quite merry on the subject, my lord."

"Oh, were you?"

"Yes, my lord. At the same time, I said, it was exceedingly vexatious that my own letter should have gone astray, and I requested the young person to institute another search. She did so, with some reluctance, and in the end I went away, after remarking that the postal system in this country was very undependable and that I should certainly write to *The Times* about it."

"Excellent. Well, it's all very illegal, either way, but we'll get Blundell to put it right for us—I'd have suggested his doing it himself, but it was such a shot at a venture that I didn't think he'd cotton to it, and I hadn't a devil of a lot of faith in it myself. And anyway"—here Wimsey was seized with an uprush of candour to the lips—"anyway, it was *my* jolly old idea and I wanted us to have the fun of it ourselves. Now, don't start apologising any more. You were perfectly brilliant in two places and I'm as bucked as hell. What's that? It mayn't be the right letter? Rot! It *is* the right letter. It's damn well got to be the right letter, and we're going to go straight along to the Cat and Fiddle, where the port is remarkable and the claret not to be despised, to celebrate our deed of darkness and derring-do."

Accordingly, within a very short time, Wimsey and his follower found themselves established in a dark old upper room, facing away from the square and looking out upon the squat, square church tower, with the rooks wheeling over it and the seagulls swooping and dipping among the gravestones. Wimsey ordered roast lamb and a bottle of the far-from-despicable claret and was soon in conversation with the waiter, who agreed with him that things were very quiet.

"But not so quiet as they used to be, sir. The men working on the Wash Cut make a difference to the town. Oh, yes, sir—the Cut's nearly finished now, and they say it will be opened in June. It will be a good thing, so they say, and improve the draining very much. It's hoped as it will scour the river out ten feet or more and take the tide up again to the head of the Thirty-foot Drain, like it was in the old days, by what they tell us. Of course, I don't know about that, sir, for it seems that was in Oliver Cromwell's time, and I've only been here twenty year, but that's what the Chief Engineer says. They've brought the Cut to within a mile of the town now, sir, and there's to be a great opening in June, with a gala and a cricket match and sports for the young people, sir. And they say as they're asking the Duke of Denver to come down and open the Cut, but we haven't heard yet if he'll come."

"He'll come all right," said Wimsey. "Dash it, he shall come. He does no work and it will do him good."

"Indeed, sir?" said the waiter, a little dubiously, not knowing the cause of this certainty, but unwilling to offend. "Yes, sir, it would be much appreciated in the town if he was to come. Will you take another potato, sir?"

"Yes, please," said Wimsey. "I'll make a point of jogging old Denver up to do his duty. We'll all come. Great fun. Denver shall present gold cups to all the winners and I will present silver rabbits to all the losers, and with luck somebody will fall into the river."

"That," said the waiter, seriously, "will be very gratifying."

Not till the port (Tuke Holdsworth '08) was set upon the table did Wimsey draw the letter from his pocket and gloat upon it. It was addressed in a foreign hand to "M. Paul Taylor, Poste Restante, Walbeach, Lincolnshire, Angleterre".

"My family," observed Lord Peter, "have frequently accused me of being unrestrained and wanting in self-control. They little know me. Instead of opening this letter at once, I reserve it for Superintendent Blundell. Instead of rushing off at once to Superintendent Blundell, I remain quietly at Walbeach and eat roast mutton. It is true that the good Blundell is not at Leamholt to-day, so that nothing would be gained if I did rush back, but still—it just shows you. The envelope bears a post-mark which is only half-decipherable, but which I make out to be something ending in y in the department of either Marne or Seine-et-Marne—a district endeared to many by the recollection of mud, blood, shell-holes and trench-feet. The envelope is of slightly worse quality than even the majority of French envelopes, and the writing suggests that it was carried out with what may be called a post-office pen and ink to match, by a hand unaccustomed to the exercise. The ink and pen mean little, for I have never yet encountered in any part of France a pen and ink with which any normal person could write comfortably. But the handwriting is suggestive, because, owing to the system of State education in that country, though all the French write vilely, it is rare to find one who writes very much more vilely than the rest. The date is obscure, but, since we know the time of arrival, we may guess the time of dispatch. Can we deduce anything further from the envelope?"

"If I may be allowed to say so, my lord, it is possibly a little remarkable that the name and address of the sender does not appear on the back."

"That is well observed. Yes, Bunter, you may have full marks for that. The French, as you have no doubt often noticed, seldom head their letters with an address as we do in England, though they occasionally write at the foot some such useless indication as 'Paris' or 'Lyon', without adding the number of the house and the name of the street. They do, however, frequently place these necessary indications on the flap of the envelope, in the hope that they may be thrown into the fire and irrecoverably lost before the letter is answered or even read."

"It has sometimes occurred to me, my lord, to be surprised at that habit."

"Not at all, Bunter. It is quite logical. To begin with, it is a fixed idea with the French that the majority of letters tend to be lost in the post. They put no faith in Government departments, and I think they are perfectly right. They hope, however, that, if the post-office fails to deliver the letter to the addressee it may, in time, return it to the sender. It seems a forlorn hope, but they are again perfectly right. One must explore every stone and leave no avenue unturned. The Englishman, in his bluff, hearty way, is content that under such circumstances the post-office should violate his seals, peruse his correspondence, extract his signature and address from the surrounding verbiage, supply a fresh envelope and return the whole to him under the blushing pseudonym of 'Hubbykins' or 'Dogsbody' for the entertainment of his local postman. But the Frenchman, being decorous, not to say secretive, by nature, thinks it better to preserve his privacy by providing, on the exterior of the missive, all the necessary details for the proper functioning of this transaction. I do not say he is wrong, though I do think it would be better if he wrote the address in both places. But the fact that this particular letter provides no address for return does perhaps suggest that the sender was not precisely out for publicity. And the devil of it is, Bunter, that ten to one there will be no address on the inside, either. No matter. This is very excellent port. Be good enough to finish the bottle, Bunter, because it would be a pity to waste it and if I have any more I shall be too sleepy to drive."

They took the direct road back from Walbeach to Fenchurch, following the bank of the river.

"If this country had been drained intelligently and all of a piece," remarked Wimsey, "by running all the canals into the rivers instead of the rivers into the canals, so as to get a good scour of water, Walbeach might still be a port and the landscape would look rather less like a crazy quilt. But what with seven hundred years of greed and graft and laziness, and perpetual quarrelling between one parish and the next, and the mistaken impression that what suits Holland must suit the Fens, the thing's a mess. It answers the purpose, but it might have been a lot better. Here's the place where we met Cranton—if it was Cranton. By the way, I wonder if that fellow at the sluice saw anything of him. Let's stop and find out. I love dawdling round locks."

He twisted the car across the bridge and brought it to a standstill close beside the sluice-keeper's cottage. The man came out to see what was wanted and was lured, without difficulty, into a desultory conversation, beginning with the weather and the crops and going on to the Wash Cut, the tides and the river. Before very long, Wimsey was standing on the narrow wooden foot-bridge that ran across the sluice, gazing down thoughtfully into the green water. The tide was on the ebb and the gates partly open, so that a slow trickle ran through them as the Wale water discharged itself sluggishly towards the sea.

"Very picturesque and pretty," said Wimsey. "Do you ever get artists and people along here to paint it?"

The sluice-keeper didn't know as he did.

"Some of those piers would be none the wore for a bit of stone and mortar," went on Wimsey; "and the gates look pretty ancient."

"Ah!" said the sluice-keeper. "I believe you." He spat into the river. "This here sluice has been needing repairs—oh! a matter of twenty years, now. And more."

"Then why don't they do it?"

"Ah!" said the sluice-keeper.

He remained lost in melancholy thought for some minutes, and Wimsey did not interrupt him. Then he spoke, weightily, and with long years of endurance in his voice.

"Nobody knows whose job this here sluice is, seemin'ly. The Fen Drainage Board, now—they say as it did oughter be done by the Wale Conservancy Board. And *they* say the Fen Drainage Board did oughter see to it. And now they've agreed to refer it, like, to the East Level Waterways Commission. But they ain't made their report yet." He spat again and was silent.

"But," said Wimsey, "suppose you got a lot of water up this way, would the gates stand it?"

"Well, they might and they mightn't," replied the sluice-keeper. "But we don't get much water up here these days. I have heard tell as it was different in Oliver Cromwell's time, but we don't get a great lot now."

Wimsey was well used to the continual intrusion of the Lord Protector upon the affairs of the Fen, but he felt it to be a little unjustified in the present case.

"It was the Dutchmen built this sluice, wasn't it?" he said.

"Ah!" agreed the sluice-keeper. "Yes, that's who built this sluice. To keep the water out. In Oliver Cromwell's time this country was all drowned every winter, so they say. So they built this sluice. But we don't get much water up nowadays."

"You will, though, when they've finished the New Wash Cut."

"Ah! so they say. But I don't know. Some says it won't be no different. And some says as it'll drown the land round about Walbeach. All I know, they've spent a sight of money, and where's it coming from? To my mind, things was all very well as they was."

"Who's responsible for the Wash Cut? The Fen Drainage Board?"

"No, that's the Wale Conservancy, that is."

"But it must have occurred to them that it might make a difference to this sluice. Why couldn't they do it all at the same time?"

The fenman gazed at Wimsey with a slow pity for his bird-witted feebleness of mind.

"Ain't I telling yew? They don't rightly know if it did oughter be paid for by the Fen Drainage or the Wale Conservancy. Why," and a note of pride crept into his tone, "they've had five law actions about this here sluice. Ah! they took one on 'em up to Parliament, they did. Cost a heap of money, so they say."

"Well, it seems ridiculous," said Wimsey. "And with all this unemployment about, too. Do you get many of the unemployed tramping round this way?"

"Times we do, times we don't."

"I remember meeting a chap along the Bank last time I was down here—on New Year's Day. I thought he looked a bit of a tough nut."

"Oh, him? Yes. He got took on at Ezra Wilderspin's place, but he soon had enough o' that. Didn't want to do no work. Half on 'em don't. He came along askin' for a cup o' tea, but I told him to get out. It wasn't tea he was lookin' for. Not him. I know his sort."

"I suppose he'd come from Walbeach."

"I suppose he had. He said so, anyhow. Said he'd been trying to get work on the Wash Cut."

"Oh? He told me he was a motor mechanic."

"Ah!" The sluice-keeper spat once more into the tumbling water. "They'd say anything."

"He looked to me as though he'd worked a good bit with his hands. Why shouldn't there be work for men on the Cut? That's what I was saying."

"Yes, sir, it's easy to say them things. But with plenty o' skilled men out of a job, they don't need to go taking on the like of him. That's where it is, you see."

"Well," said Wimsey, "I still think that the Drainage Board and the Conservancy Board and the Commission between them ought to be able to absorb some of these men and give you a fresh set of gates. However, it's not my business, and I'll have to be pushing along."

"Ah!" said the sluice-keeper. "New gates? Ah!"

He remained hanging on the rail and spitting thoughtfully into the water till Wimsey and Bunter had regained the car. Then he came hobbling after them.

"What I says is," he observed, leaning so earnestly over the door of the Daimler that Wimsey hurriedly drew back his feet, thinking that the usual expectoration was about to follow, "what I says is, Why don't they refer it to Geneva? See? Why don't they refer it to Geneva? Then we might get it, same time as they gets disarmament, see?"

"Ha, ha!" said Wimsey, rightly supposing this to be irony. "Very good! I must tell my friends about that. Good work, what? Why don't they refer it to Geneva? Ha, ha!"

"That's right," said the sluice-keeper, anxious that the point of the jest should not be lost. "Why don't they refer it to Geneva? See?"

"Splendid!" said Wimsey. "I won't forget that. Ha, ha, ha!"

He gently released the clutch. As they moved away, he glanced back and saw the sluice-keeper convulsed by the remembrance of his own wit.

Lord Peter's misgivings about the letter were duly confirmed. He honourably submitted it, unopened, to Superintendent Blundell, as soon as the latter returned from attendance at the Quarter Sessions where he had been engaged all day. The Superintendent was alarmed by Wimsey's unorthodox raid on the post-office, but pleased by his subsequent discretion, and readily allowed him full credit for zeal and intelligence. Together they opened the envelope. The letter, which bore no address, was written on thin paper of the same poor quality as the envelope, and began:

"*Mon cher mari*——"

"Hey!" said Mr. Blundell. "What's that mean? I'm not much of a French scholar, but doesn't *mari* mean 'husband'?"

"Yes. 'My dear husband,' it begins."

"I never knew that Cranton—dash it!" exclaimed Mr. Blundell. "Where does Cranton come into this? I never heard of his having any wife at all, let alone a French one."

"We don't know that Cranton comes into it at all. He came to St. Paul and asked for a Mr. Paul Taylor. This, presumably, is addressed to the Paul Taylor he asked for."

"But they said Paul Taylor was a bell."

"Tailor Paul is a bell, but Paul Taylor may be a person."

"Who is he, then?"

"God knows. Somebody with a wife in France."

"And the other chap, Batty Something—is he a person?"

"No, he's a bell. But he may be a person, too."

"They can't both be persons," said Mr. Blundell, "it's not reasonable. And where is this Paul Taylor, anyhow?"

"Perhaps he was the corpse."

"Then where's Cranton? They can't," added the Superintendent, "both be the corpse. That's not reasonable, either."

"Possibly Cranton gave one name to Wilderspin and another to his correspondent."

"Then what did he mean by asking for Paul Taylor at Fenchurch St. Paul?"

"Perhaps that was the bell, after all."

"See here," said Mr. Blundell, "it doesn't seem reasonable to me. This Paul Taylor, or Tailor Paul, can't be both a bell and a person. At least, not both at once. It sounds kind of, well, kind of batty to me."

"Why bring Batty into it? Batty is a bell. Tailor Paul is a bell. Paul Taylor is a person, because he gets letters. You can't send letters to a bell. If you did you'd be batty. Oh, bother!"

"Well, I don't understand it," said Mr. Blundell. "Stephen Driver, he's a person, too. You don't say he's a bell, do you? What I want to know is, which of 'em all is Cranton. If he's been and fixed himself up with a wife in France between this last September—I mean, between this and January—no, I mean between September and January—I mean—here, dash it all, my lord, let's read the blooming letter. You might read it out in English, would you? My French is a bit off, these days."

> "My dear husband" [Wimsey translated], You told me not to write to you, without great urgency, but three months are past and I have no news of you. I am very anxious, asking myself if you have not been taken by the military authorities. You have assured me that they could not now have you shot, the War being over so long ago, but it is known that the English are very strict. Write, I beseech you, a little word to say that you are safe. It begins to be very difficult to do the work of the farm alone, and we have had great trouble with the spring sowing. Also the red cow is dead. I am obliged to carry the fowls to market myself, because Jean is too exigent, and prices are very low. Little Pierre helps me as much as he can, but he is only nine. Little Marie has had the whooping-cough and the Baby also. I beg your pardon if I am indiscreet to write to you, but I am very much troubled. Pierre and Marie send kisses to their papa.
>
> "Your loving wife,
>
> "SUZANNE."

Superintendent Blundell listened aghast; then snatched the paper from Wimsey, as though he mistrusted his translation and thought to tear out some better meaning from the words by mere force of staring at them.

"Little Pierre—nine years old—kisses to their papa—and the red cow's dead—t'cha!" He did a little arithmetic on his fingers. "Nine years ago, Cranton was in gaol."

"Step-father, perhaps?" suggested Wimsey.

Mr. Blundell paid no heed. "Spring sowing—since when has Cranton turned farmer? And what's all that about military authorities? And the War. Cranton never was in the War. There's something here I can't make head or tail of. See here, my lord—this can't be Cranton. It's silly, that's what it is. It can't be Cranton."

"It begins to look as if it wasn't," said Wimsey. "But I still think it was Cranton I met on New Year's Day."

"I'd better get on the telephone to London," said Mr. Blundell. "And then I'll have to be seeing the Chief Constable about this. Whatever it is, it's got to be followed up. Driver's disappeared and we've found a body that looks like his and we've got to do something about it. But France—well, there! How we're to find this Suzanne I don't know, and it'll cost a mint of money."

THE SIXTH PART

Monsieur Rozier Hunts the Treble Down

The remaining bell . . . does nothing but plain hunting, and is therefore said to be "in the hunt with the Treble".

TROYTE *On Change-Ringing*

THERE ARE HARDER jobs in detective work than searching a couple of French departments for a village ending in "y", containing a farmer's wife whose first name is Suzanne, whose children are Pierre, aged nine, Marie and a baby of unknown age and sex, and whose husband is an Englishman. All the villages in the Marne district end, indeed, in "y", and Suzanne, Pierre and Marie are all common names enough, but a foreign husband is rarer. A husband named Paul Taylor would, of course, be easily traced, but both Superintendent Blundell and Lord Peter were pretty sure that "Paul Taylor" would prove to be an alias.

It was about the middle of May when a report came in from the French police which looked more hopeful than anything previously received. It came through the Sûreté, and originated with M. le commissaire Rozier of Château-Thierry in the department of Marne.

It was so exceedingly promising that even the Chief Constable, who was a worried gentleman with an itch for economy, agreed that it ought to be investigated on the spot.

"But I don't know whom to send," he grumbled. "Dashed expensive business, anyhow. And then there's the language. Do you speak French, Blundell?"

The Superintendent grinned sheepishly. "Well, sir, not to say speak it. I could ask for a spot of grub in an *estaminet*, and maybe swear at the garsong a bit. But examining witnesses—that's a different question."

"I can't go myself," said the Chief Constable, sharply and hastily, as though anticipating a suggestion that nobody had had the courage to make. "Out of the question." He tapped his fingers on his study table and stared vaguely over the Superintendent's head at the rooks wheeling high over the elms at the end of the garden. "You've done your best, Blundell, but I think we had better hand the thing over, lock, stock and barrel to Scotland Yard. Perhaps we ought to have done so earlier."

Mr. Blundell looked chagrined. Lord Peter Wimsey, who had come with him, ostensibly in case help should be needed to translate the commissaire's letter, but actually because he was determined not to be left out of anything, coughed gently.

"If you would entrust the inquiry to me, sir," he murmured, "I could pop over in two ticks—at my own expense, of course," he added, insinuatingly.

"I'm afraid it would be rather irreguluar," said the Chief Constable, with the air of one who only needs to be persuaded.

"I'm more reliable than I look, really I am," said his lordship. "And my

French is my one strong point. Couldn't you swear me in as a special constable, or something? with a natty little armlet and a truncheon? Or isn't interrogation part of a special constable's duties?"

"It is not," said the Chief Constable. "Still," he went on, "still—I suppose I might stretch a point. And I suppose"—he looked hard at Wimsey—"I suppose you'll go in any case."

"Nothing to prevent me from making a private tour of the battle-fields," said Wimsey, "and, of course, if I met one of my old Scotland Yard pals knocking round there, I might join up with him. But I really think that, in these hard times, we ought to consider the public purse, don't you, sir?"

The Chief Constable was thoughtful. He had no real wish to call in Scotland Yard. He had an idea that a Yard man might make himself an officious nuisance. He gave way. Within two days, Wimsey was being cordially received by M. le commissaire Rozier. A gentleman who has "*des relations intimes*" with the Paris Sûreté, and who speaks perfect French, is likely to be well received by country *commissaires de police.* M. Rozier produced a bottle of very excellent wine, entreated his visitor to make himself at home, and embarked upon his story.

"It does not in any way astonish me, milord, to receive an inquiry concerning the husband of Suzanne Legros. It is evident that there is there a formidable mystery. For ten years I have said to myself, 'Aristide Rozier, the day will come when your premonitions concerning the so-called Jean Legros will be justified.' I perceive that the day is at hand, and I congratulate myself upon my foresight."

"Evidently," said Wimsey, "M. le commissaire possesses a penetrating intelligence."

"To lay the matter clearly before you, I am obliged to go back to the summer of 1918. Milord served in the British Army? Ah! then milord will remember the retreat over the Marne in July. *Quelle histoire sanglante!* On that occasion the retreating armies were swept back across the Marne pell-mell and passed in disorder through the little village of C——y, situated upon the left bank of the river. The village itself, you understand, milord, escaped any violent bombardment, for it was behind the front-line trenches. In that village lived the aged Pierre Legros and his grand-daughter Suzanne. The old man was eighty years of age and refused to leave his home. His grandchild, then aged twenty-seven, was a vigorous and industrious girl, who, single-handed, kept the farm in a sort of order throughout the years of conflict. Her father, her brother, her affianced husband had all been killed.

"About ten days after the retreat, it was reported that Suzanne Legros and her grandfather had a visitor at the farm. The neighbours had begun to talk, you understand, and the curé, the reverend Abbé Latouche, now in paradise, thought it his duty to inform the authorities here. I myself, you comprehend, was not here at that time; I was in the Army; but my predecessor, M. Dubois, took steps to investigate the matter. He found that there was a sick and wounded man being kept at the farm. He had suffered a severe blow upon the head and various other injuries. Suzanne Legros, and her grandfather, being interrogated, told a singular story.

"She said that, on the second night after the retreat had passed through the village, she went to a distant outhouse and there found this man lying sick and burning with fever, stripped to his underclothing, with his head roughly bandaged. He was dirty and bloodstained and his clothes were bedaubed with mud and weeds as though he had been in the river. She contrived to carry him home with the old man's help, washed his wounds and nursed him as best she might. The farm is a couple of kilometres distant from the village itself, and she had no one whom she could send for assistance. At first, she said, the man had raved in French about the incidents of the battle, but afterwards he had fallen into a heavy stupor, from which she could not rouse him. When seen by the curé and by the commissaire he lay inert, breathing heavily and unconscious.

"She showed the clothing in which she had found him—a vest, under-pants, socks, and shirt of regulation army pattern, very much stained and torn. No uniform; no boots; no identity disc; no papers. It seemed evident that he had been in the retreat and had been obliged to swim across the river in making his way back from the front line—this would account for the abandoning of his boots, uniform and kit. He seemed to be a man of some thirty-five or forty years of age, and when first seen by the authorities, he had a dark beard of about a week's growth."

"Then he had been clean-shaven?"

"It would seem so, milord. A doctor from the town was found to go out and see him, but he could only say that it appeared to be a severe case of injury to the brain from the wound in the head. He advised ameliorative measures. He was only a young student of small experience, incapacitated from the Army by reason of frail health. He has since died.

"It was at first supposed that they had only to wait till the man came to himself to learn who he was. But when, after three more weeks of coma, he slowly regained consciousness, it was found that his memory, and, for some time, his speech also, was gone. Gradually, the speech was regained, though for some time he could express himself only in a thick and mumbling manner, with many hesitations. It seemed that there were injuries to the locutory centres in the brain. When he was well enough to understand and make himself understood, he was, naturally, interrogated. His replies were simply that his mind was a blank. He remembered nothing of his past—but nothing. He did not know his name, or his place of origin; he had no recollection of the War. For him, his life began in the farm-house at C——y."

M. Rozier paused impressively, while Wimsey registered amazement.

"Well, milord, you will understand that it was necessary to report the case at once to the Army authorities. He was seen by a number of officers, none of whom could recognise him, and his portrait and measurements were circulated without result. It was thought at first that he might be an Englishman —or even a Boche—and that, you understand, was not agreeable. It was stated, however, that when Suzanne first found him, he had deliriously muttered in French, and the clothes found upon him were undoubtedly French also. Nevertheless, his description was issued to the British Army, again without result, and, when the Armistice was signed, inquiries were extended to Germany. But they knew nothing of him there. Naturally, these inquiries took some time, for the Germans had a revolution, as you know, and everything was much disordered. In the meanwhile, the man had to live somewhere. He was taken to hospital—to several hospitals—and examined by psychologists, but they could make nothing of him. They tried—you understand, milord—to set traps for him. They suddenly shouted words of command at him in English, French and German, thinking that he might display an automatic reaction. But it was to no purpose. He seemed to have forgotten the War."

"Lucky devil!" said Wimsey, with feeling.

"*Je suis de votre avis.* Nevertheless, a reaction of some kind would have been satisfying. Time passed, and he became no better. They sent him back to us. Now you know, milord, that it is impossible to repatriate a man who has no nationality. No country will receive him. Nobody wanted this unfortunate man except Suzanne Legros and her *bon-papa.* They needed a man to work on the farm and this fellow, though he had lost his memory, had recovered his physical strength and was well suited for manual labour. Moreover, the girl had taken a fancy to him. You know how it is with women. When they have nursed a man, he is to them in a manner their child. Old Pierre Legros asked leave to adopt this man as his son. There were difficulties—*que voulez-vous?* But, *enfin,* since something had to be done with the man, and he was quiet and well-behaved and gave no trouble, the consent was obtained. He was adopted under the name of Jean Legros and papers of identity were made out for him. The neighbours began to be accustomed to him. There was a man—a fellow who had thought of marrying Suzanne—who was his enemy and called him *sale Boche*—but Jean knocked him down one evening in the *estaminet* and after that there was no more heard of the word *Boche.* Then, after a few years, it became known that Suzanne had the wish to marry him. The old curé opposed the match—he said it was not known but that the man was married already. But the old curé died. The new one knew little of the circumstances. Besides, Suzanne had already thrown her bonnet over the windmill. Human nature, milord, is human nature. The civil authorities washed their hands of the matter; it was better to regularise the position. So Suzanne Legros wedded this Jean, and their eldest son is now nine years of age. Since that time there has been no trouble—only Jean still remembers nothing of his origin."

"You said in your letter," said Wimsey, "that Jean had now disappeared."

"Since five months, milord. It is said that he is in Belgium, buying pigs, cattle, or I know not what. But he has not written, and his wife is concerned about him. You think you have some information about him?"

"Well," said Wimsey, "we have a corpse. And we have a name. But if this Jean Legros has conducted himself in the manner you describe, then the name is not his, though the corpse may be. For the man whose name we have was in prison in 1918 and for some years afterwards."

"Ah! then you have no further interest in Jean Legros?"

"On the contrary. An interest of the most profound. We still have the corpse."

"*A la bonne heure,*" said M. Rozier cheerfully. "A corpse is always something. Have you any photograph? any measurements? any marks of identification?"

"The photograph will assuredly be of little use, since the corpse when found was four months old and the face had been much battered. Moreover, his hands had been removed at the wrists. But we have measurements and two medical reports. From the latest of these, recently received from a London expert, it appears that the scalp bears the mark of an old scar, in addition to those recently inflicted."

"Aha! that is perhaps some confirmation. He was, then, killed by being beaten on the head, your unknown?"

"No," said Wimsey. "All the head injuries were inflicted after death. The expert opinion confirms that of the police-surgeon on this point."

"He died, then, of what?"

"There is the mystery. There is no sign of fatal wound, or of poison, or of strangling, nor yet of disease. The heart was sound; the intestines show that he had not died of starvation—indeed, he was well-nourished, and had eaten a few hours before his death."

"*Tiens!* an apoplexy, then?"

"It is possible. The brain, you understand, was in a somewhat putrefied condition. It is difficult to say with certainty, though there are certain signs that there had been an effusion of blood into the cortex. But you comprehend that, if a thundering apoplexy killed this man, it was not so obliging as to bury him also."

"Perfectly. You are quite right. Forward, then, to the farm of Jean Legros."

The farm was a small one, and did not seem to be in too flourishing a state. Broken fences, dilapidated outhouses and ill-weeded fields spoke of straitened means and a lack of the necessary labour. The mistress of the house received them. She was a sturdy, well-muscled woman of some forty years of age, and carried in her arms a nine-month-old child. At the sight of the commissaire and his attendant gendarme a look of alarm came unmistakably into her eyes. Another moment, and it had given place to that expression of mulish obstinacy which no one can better assume at will than the French peasant.

"M. le commissaire Rozier?"

"Himself, madame. This gentleman is milord Vainsé, who has voyaged from England to make certain inquiries. It is permitted to enter?"

It was permitted, but at the word "England" the look of alarm had come again; and it was not lost on either of the men.

"Your husband, Mme. Legros," said the commissaire, coming brusquely to the point, "he is absent from home. Since how long?"

"Since December, M. le commissaire."

"Where is he?"

"In Belgium."

"Where in Belgium?"

"Monsieur, in Dixmude, as I suppose."

"You suppose? You do not know? You have had no letter from him?"

"No, monsieur."

"That is strange. What took him to Dixmude?"

"Monsieur, he had taken the notion that his family lived perhaps at Dixmude. You know, without doubt, that he had lost his memory. *Eh, bien!* in December, one day, he said to me, 'Suzanne, put a record on the gramophone.' I put on the record of a great *diseuse*, reciting *Le Carillon*, poem of Verhaeren, to music. *C'est un morceau très impressionnant.* At that moment, filled with emotion where the carillons are named turn by turn, my husband cried out: 'Dixmude! there is then a town of Dixmude in Belgium?' 'But certainly,' I replied. He said, 'But that name says something to me! I am convinced, Suzanne, that I have a beloved mother residing in Dixmude. I shall not rest till I have gone to Belgium to make inquiries about this dear mother.' M. le commissaire, he would listen to nothing. He went away, taking with him our small savings, and since that time I have heard nothing from him."

"*Histoire très touchante,*" said the commissaire, drily. "You have my sympathy, madame. But I cannot understand that your husband should be a Belgian. There were no Belgian troops engaged at the third Battle of the Marne."

"Nevertheless, monsieur, his father may have married a Belgian. He may have Belgian relations."

"*C'est vrai.* He left you no address?"

"None, monsieur. He said he would write on his arrival."

"Ah! And he departed how? By the train?"

"Oh, yes, monsieur."

"And you have made no inquiries? From the mayor of Dixmude, for example?"

"Monsieur, you understand that I was sufficiently embarrassed. I did not know where to begin with such an inquiry."

"Nor of us, the police, who exist for that? You did not address yourself to us?"

"M. le commissaire, I did not know—I could not imagine—I told myself every day, 'To-morrow he will write,' and I waited, *et enfin*——"

"*Et enfin*—it did not occur to you to inform yourself. *C'est bien remarquable.* What gave you the idea that your husband was in England?"

"In England, monsieur?"

"In England, madame. You wrote to him under the name of Paul Taylor, did you not? At the town of Valbesch in the county of Laincollone?" The commissaire excelled himself in the rendering of these barbarian place-names. "At Valbesch in Laincollone you address yourself to him in the name of Paul Taylorrr—*voyons, madame, voyons*, and you tell me now that you suppose him to be all the time in Belgium. You will not deny your own handwriting, I suppose? Or the names of your two children? Or the death of the red cow? You do not imagine that you can resurrect the cow?"

"Monsieur——"

"Come, madame. During all these years you have been lying to the police, have you not? You knew very well that your husband was not a Belgian but an Englishman? That his name was actually Paul Taylor? That he had not lost his memory at all? Ah! you think that you can trifle with the police in that way? I assure you, madame, that you will find it a serious matter. You have falsified papers, that is a crime!"

"Monsieur, monsieur——"

"That is your letter?"

"Monsieur, since you have found it, I cannot deny it. But——"

"Good, you admit the letter. Now, what is this about falling into the hands of the military authorities?"

"I do not know, monsieur. My husband—monsieur, I implore you to tell me, where is my husband?"

The commissaire Rozier paused, and glanced at Wimsey, who said:

"Madame, we are greatly afraid that your husband is dead."

"*Ah, mon dieu! je le savais bien.* If he had been alive, he would have written to me."

"If you will help us by telling us the truth about your husband, we may be able to identify him."

The woman stood looking from one to the other. At last she turned to Wimsey.

"You, milord, you are not laying a trap for me? You are sure that my husband is dead?"

"Come, come," said the commissaire, "that makes no difference. You must tell the truth, or it will be the worse for you."

Wimsey took out of the attaché case which he had brought with him the underclothing which had been found upon the corpse.

"Madame," he said, "we do not know whether the man who wore these is your husband, but on my honour, the man who wore these is dead and they were taken from his body."

Suzanne Legros turned the garments over, her work-hardened fingers slowly tracing each patch and darn. Then, as though the sight of them had broken down something in her, she dropped into a chair and laid her head down on the mended vest and burst into loud weeping.

"You recognise the garments?" asked the commissaire presently, in a milder tone.

"Yes, they are his, I mended these garments myself. I understand that he is dead."

"In that case," said Wimsey, "you can do him no harm by speaking."

When Suzanne Legros had recovered herself a little, she made her statement, the commissaire calling in his attendant gendarme to take a shorthand note of it.

"It is true that my husband was not a Frenchman or a Belgian. He was an Englishman. But it is true also that he was wounded in the retreat of 1918. He came to the farm one night. He had lost much blood and was exhausted. Also his nerves were shattered, but it is not true that he had lost his memory. He implored me to help him and hide him, because he did not want to fight any more. I nursed him till he was well and then we arranged what we should say."

"It was shameful, madame, to harbour a deserter."

"I acknowledge it, monsieur, but consider my position. My father was dead, my two brothers killed, and I had no one to help me with the farm. Jean-Marie Picard, that was to have married me, was dead also. There were so few men left in France, and the War had gone on so long. And also, monsieur, I grew to love Jean. And his nerves were greatly deranged. He could not face any more fighting."

"He should have reported to his unit and applied for sick leave," said Wimsey.

"But then," said Suzanne, simply, "they would have sent him back to England and separated us. And besides, the English are very strict. They might have thought him a coward and shot him."

"It appears, at least, that he made you think so," said Monsieur Rozier.

"Yes, monsieur. I thought so and he thought so too. So we arranged that he should pretend to have lost his memory, and since his French accent was not good, we decided to make out that his speech was affected by his injury. And I burnt his uniform and papers in the copper."

"Who invented the story—you or he?"

"He did, monsieur. He was very clever. He thought of everything."

"And the name also?"

"The name also."

"And what was his real name?"

She hesitated. "His papers were burnt, and he never told me anything about himself."

"You do not know his name. Was it then not Taylor?"

"No, monsieur. He adopted that name when he went back to England."

"Ah! and what did he go to England for?"

"Monsieur, we were very poor, and Jean said that he had property in England which could be disposed of for a good sum, if only he could get hold of it without making himself known. For, you see, if he were to reveal himself he would be shot as a deserter."

"But there was a general amnesty for deserters after the War."

"Not in England, monsieur."

"He told you that?" said Wimsey.

"Yes, milord. So it was important that nobody should know him when he went to fetch the property. Also there were difficulties which he did not explain to me, about selling the goods—I do not know what they were—and for that he had to have the help of a friend. So he wrote to this friend and presently he received a reply."

"Have you that letter?"

"No, monsieur. He burnt it without showing it to me. This friend asked him for something—I did not quite understand that, but it was some sort of guarantee, I think. Jean shut himself up in his room for several hours the next day to compose his answer to the letter, but he did not show that to me, either. Then the friend wrote back and said he could help him, but it would not do for Jean's name to appear—neither his own name nor the name of Legros, you understand. So he chose the name of Paul Taylor, and he laughed very much when the idea came to him to call himself so. Then the friend sent him papers made out in the name of Paul Taylor, British subject. I saw those. There was a passport with a photograph; it was not very much like my husband, but he said they would not pay great attention to it. The beard was like his."

"Had your husband a beard when you first knew him?"

"No, he was clean-shaven, like all the English. But of course, he grew his beard when he was ill. It altered him very much, because he had a small chin, and with the beard it looked bigger. Jean took with him no luggage; he said he would buy clothes in England, because then he would again look like an Englishman."

"And you know nothing of the nature of this property in England?"

"Nothing whatever, monsieur."

"Was it land, securities, valuables?"

"I know nothing about it, monsieur. I asked Jean often, but he would never tell me."

"And you expect us to believe that you do not know your husband's real name?"

Again the hesitation. Then: "No, monsieur, I do not know. It is true that I saw it upon his papers, but I burnt those and I do not now remember it. But I think it began with a C, and I should know it if I saw it again."

"Was it Cranton?" asked Wimsey.

"No, I do not think it was that, but I cannot say what it was. As soon as he was able to speak at all, he told me to give him his papers, and I asked him then what his name was, because I could not pronounce it—it was English and difficult—and he said that he would not tell me his name then, but I could call him what I liked. So I called him Jean, which was the name of my *fiancé*, who was killed."

"I see," said Wimsey. He hunted through his pocket-book and laid the official photograph of Cranton before her. "Is that your husband as you first knew him?"

"No, milord. That is not my husband. It is not in the least like him." Her face darkened. "You have deceived me. He is not dead and I have betrayed him."

"He is dead," said Wimsey. "It is this man who is alive."

"And now," said Wimsey, "we are no nearer than before to a solution."

"*Attendez*, milord. She has not yet told all she knows. She does not trust us, and she is concealing the name. Only wait, and we shall find means to make her speak. She still thinks that her husband may be alive. But we shall convince her. We shall have this man traced. It is some months old, the trail, but it will not be too difficult. That he started from here by train to go to Belgium I already know, by my inquiries. When he sailed for England, it was doubtless from Ostend—unless, *voyons*, milord, what resources could this man command?"

"How can I tell? But we believe that this mysterious property had to do with an emerald necklace of many thousands of pounds value."

"*Ah, voilà!* It would be worth while to spend money, then. But this man, you say he is not the man you thought. If that other man was the thief, how does this one come into it?"

"There is the difficulty. But look! There were two men concerned in the theft: one, a London *cambrioleur*, the other, a domestic servant. We do not know which of them had the jewels; it is a long story. But you heard that this Jean Legros wrote to a friend in England, and that friend may have been

Cranton, the burglar. Now Legros cannot have been the servant who stole the jewels in the first place, for that man is dead. But before dying, the thief may have communicated to Legros the secret of where the emeralds are hidden, and also the name of Cranton. Legros then writes to Cranton and proposes a partnership to find the jewels. Cranton does not believe, and asks for proof that Legros really knows something. Legros sends a letter which satisfies Cranton, and Cranton in turn procures the necessary papers for Legros. Then Legros goes to England and meets Cranton. Together they go and discover the jewels. Then Cranton kills his confederate, so as to have all for himself. How is that, monsieur? For Cranton also has disappeared."

"It is very possible, milord. In that case, both the jewels and the murderer are in England—or wherever this Cranton may be. You think, then, that the other dead man, the servant, communicated the hiding-place of the necklace—to whom?"

"Perhaps to some fellow-prisoner who was only in a gaol for a short time."

"And why should he do that?"

"In order that this fellow-prisoner should provide him with a means to escape. And the proof is that the servant did break prison and escape, and afterwards his dead body was found in a pit many miles from the prison."

"Aha! the affair begins to outline itself. And the servant—how did he come to be found dead? Eh?"

"He is supposed to have fallen over the edge of the pit in the dark. But I begin to think that he was killed by Legros."

"Milord, our thoughts chime together. Because, *voyez-vous,* this story of desertion and military authorities will not hold water. There is more than a desertion behind this change of name and this fear of the British police. But if the man was an old gaol-bird, and had committed a murder into the bargain, the thing understands itself. Twice he changes his name, so that he shall not be traced even to France, because he, Legros, under his English name, had enlisted after his release from prison and the record of your Army might reveal him. Only, if he was in the Army, it is strange that he should have found the leisure to plan a prison-breaking for his comrade and commit murder. No, there are still difficulties, but the outline of the plot is clear and will develop itself more clearly still as we proceed. In the meanwhile, I will undertake inquiries here and in Belgium. I think, milord, we must not confine ourselves to the ordinary passenger-routes, or even to the ports. A motor-boat might well make the journey to the coast of Laincollone. Your police, also, will make inquiries on their part. And when we have shown the progress of Legros from the front door of his house to his grave in England, then, I think, Mme. Suzanne will speak a little more. And now, milord, I beg you will honour us by sharing our dinner to-night. My wife is an excellent cook, if you will condescend to a *cuisine bourgeoise* garnished with a tolerable *vin de Bourgogne.* Monsieur Delavigne of the Sûreté informs me that you have the reputation of a *gourmet,* and it is only with a certain diffidence that I make the suggestion, but it would give Mme. Rozier unheard-of delight if you would give her the pleasure of making your acquaintance."

"Monsieur," said Lord Peter, "I am infinitely obliged to you both."

THE SEVENTH PART

Plain Hunting

First, Lucus Mortis; then Terra Tenebrosa; next, Tartarus; after that, Terra Oblivionis; then Herebus; then Barathrum; then Gehenna; and then Stagnum Ignis.

SHERIDAN LEFANU: *Wylder's Hand*

"WELL," SAID SUPERINTENDENT Blundell, "if that's how it is, we've got to find Cranton. But it's a funny thing to me. From what they tell me, I wouldn't have thought Cranton was the man for that sort of job. He's never been suspected of killing anyone, and he never looked to me like a killer. And you know, my lord, that it's very rare for one of them sort of smart burglars to go all off the rails and take to violence. What I mean, it isn't in them as a rule, if you get my meaning. It's true he went for Deacon in the dock but that was more of a scrimmage, as you might say, and I don't think he meant much harm. Supposing as it was the other chap that killed Cranton? He might have changed clothes with him to prevent identification."

"So he might. But what becomes of that old scar on the head? That seems to fit in with the body being this fellow they call Jean Legros. Unless Cranton had a scar too."

"He'd no scar up to last September," said the Superintendent, thoughtfully. "No, I reckon you're right, and that won't work. Some of the measurements seem a bit different, too—though of course, it's not easy to be as accurate as all that when you're comparing a live man with a four-month-old corpse. And there were so many teeth gone and busted from the corpse that we've not got much out of that, either. No, we've got to find Cranton. If he's alive, he's lying uncommon low. Looks as though he'd done something pretty bad—I give you that."

The conversation took place in the churchyard, where Mr. Blundell had been undertaking an exhaustive search for unspecified clues. The Superintendent thoughtfully decapitated a nettle, and resumed:

"Then there's that chap Will Thoday. I can't make him out at all. I'll swear he knows something—but what *can* he know? It's as certain as anything can be that he was sick in bed when it all happened. He sticks to that, and says he knows nothing. What can you do with a man who says he knows nothing? Why, nothing. And as for his wife, *she* couldn't have tied a man up and buried him. She's not a powerful sort of woman by any means. And I've got hold of the children. It went against me to do it, but I did it all the same. And they say their Mother and Dad were both in the house all night. There's one other person might know something, and that's James Thoday. Look here, my lord, here's a queer thing. James Thoday left Fenchurch St. Paul on January 4th, early in the morning, to join his ship. He was seen to go, all right—the station-master saw him. But he never got to Hull that day. I've been on to Lampson & Blake, and they say they had a wire from him to say he couldn't get back in time, but would arrive on the Sunday night—which he did. Had some story of being taken suddenly ill—and they say he looked ill enough when he did arrive. I've told them to get in touch with him as quick as they can."

"Where was the wire sent from?"

"London. From a post-office near Liverpool Street. About the time when the train Jim Thoday took at Dykesey would get up there. Looks as though he'd been taken queer on the way up."

"He might have picked up influenza from his brother."

"So he might. Still, he was fit to sail the next day, and it looks funny, don't you think? He'd have had plenty of time to go up to London and come down here again. He wouldn't come to Dykesey, of course, but he might have come part of the way by train and done the rest by car or motor-bike or what-not."

Wimsey whistled. "You think he was in with Will over the thing. Yes, I see. Will is in a conspiracy with Legros to get the emeralds—is that it? And he gets 'flu and can't do the job himself, so he arranges with Brother Jim to do it for him. Then Jim meets Legros and kills him and buries him and vamooses with the emeralds to Hong Kong. Well, that would explain one thing, and that is, why those infernal stones haven't been put on the European market. He could easily get rid of them over in the East. But look here, Super—how did Will Thoday get into touch with Legros in the first place? It was easy enough when we put it all on Cranton, because he could have got the papers and things made out for Legros by one of his pals in Town. But you can't imagine that Thoday produced forged papers and provided Legros with his passage facilities and all that. How would a fellow like that know how to set about it?"

Mr. Blundell shook his head.

"But there's that two hundred pounds," he said.

"So there is, but that was after Legros had started."

"And when Legros was killed, the money was returned to the bank."

"Was it?"

"Oh, yes. I had a word with Thoday. He made no difficulties. He said he had an idea of purchasing a bit of land and starting to farm again on his own, but that, after his illness, he gave up the idea, thinking that for some time he wouldn't be strong enough. He gave me permission to go over his bank account. It was all in order—no suspicious withdrawals of money up to that £200 on December 31st, and that was paid in again in January, as soon as he was able to get about. And it's true about the land, too. He did think of buying it. All the same, £200 all in one-pound notes——"

The Superintendent broke off, and made a sudden dive behind a tall tombstone. There was a squeak and a scuffle. Mr. Blundell emerged, rather flustered. His large hand held Potty Peake's coat-collar in a firm grip.

"Now, you clear off," said the Superintendent, giving his captive a rough, but not unkindly, shake. "You'll get yourself into trouble, my lad, hanging round the churchyard and listening to private conversations. See?"

"Ar!" said Potty, "you needn't choke a fellow. You needn't choke poor Potty. If you knowed what Potty knows——"

"What do you know?"

Potty's eyes gleamed cunningly.

"I seen him—Number Nine—I seen him a-talking to Will in the church. But the Tailors was too much for him. Him with the rope—he got him, and he'll get you too. Potty knows. Potty ain't lived all these years, in and out of the church, for nothing."

"Who was talking to Will in the Church?"

"Why, him!" Potty jerked his head towards the Thorpe grave. "Him they found over there. The black-bearded man. There's eight in the belfry and one in the grave. That makes nine. You think Potty can't count, but he can. But him as calls the peal—you won't get him, oh, no!"

"See here," said Wimsey, "you're a clever fellow, Potty. When did you see Will Thoday talking to the black-bearded man? See if you can count that far."

Potty Peake grinned at him. "Potty can count all right," he said, with great satisfaction. "Oh, yes." He began an elaborate calculation on his fingers. "Ah! it was a Monday night, that's when it was. There was cold pork and beans for dinner—that's good, cold pork and beans. Ah! Parson he preached about thankfulness. Be thankful for Christmas, he says. There was roast fowl, Christmas Day and boiled pork and greens Sunday and be thankful, that's what Parson says. So Potty slips out at night, for to be thankful again. You got to go to church to be thankful proper, ain't you, sir? And there was the church door standing open. So Potty creeps in, careful-like, see? And there's a light in the vestry. Potty was frightened. There's things hanging in the vestry. Ah! So Potty hides behind ole Batty Thomas, and then Will Thoday comes in, and Potty hears them talking in the vestry. 'Money,' Will says. 'Tis a great wickedness, is money. And then Will Thoday he cries out—he fetches a rope from the chest and—ah! Potty's afraid. He thinks about hanging. Potty don't want to see no one hanged. Potty runs away. He looks in at the vestry window, and there's the black-bearded man a-laying on the floor, and Will a-standing over him with the rope. Ah, dear! oh, dear! Potty don't like ropes. Potty's allus a-dreamin' of ropes. One, two, three, four, five, six, seven, eight—and this one's nine. Potty seen him a-hangin' there. Ooh!"

"I think you was a-dreaming all the time," said the Superintendent. "There's nobody been hanged that I know of."

"I see him a-hanging," persisted Potty. "Terrible it were. But don't you pay no attention. 'Tis only one o' poor Potty's dreams." His face changed. "You lemme go, mister. I gotter feed my pigs."

"Bless my heart," said Superintendent Blundell. "And what do you suppose we're to make of that?"

Wimsey shook his head.

"I think he saw something—or how did he know that the rope was gone from the cope-chest? But as for hanging, no! He's crazed about hanging. Got a hanging complex, or whatever they call it. The man wasn't hanged. Which Monday night do you suppose Potty meant?"

"Can't be January 6th, can it?" said the Superintendent. "The body was buried on the 4th, as far as we can make out. And it can't very well be December 30th, because Legros only got here on January 1st—if that was

Legros you saw. And besides, I can't make out whether he means Sunday or Monday, with his boiled pork."

"I can," said Wimsey. "He had boiled pork and greens on Sunday, and Parson told him to be thankful and so he was. And on Monday, he had the pork cold with beans—probably the tinned variety if I know the modern country-woman—and he felt thankful again. So he went down to the church to be thankful in the proper place. It would be some time in the evening, as there was a light in the vestry."

"That's right. Potty lives with an aunt of his—a decent old soul, but not very sharp. He's always slipping out at night. They're cunning as the devil, these naturals. But which evening was it?"

"The day after Parson had preached on thankfulness," said Wimsey. "Thankfulness for Christmas. That looks like December 30th. Why not? You don't know that Legros didn't get here before January 1st. That's when Cranton got here."

"But I thought we'd washed Cranton out of it," objected Mr. Blundell, "and put Will Thoday in his place."

"Then who was it I met on the road over the bridge?"

"That must have been Legros."

"Well, it may be—though I still think it was Cranton, or his twin-brother. But if I met Legros on January 1st, he can't have been hanged by Will Thoday on December 30th. And in any case, he wasn't hanged. And," said Wimsey, triumphantly, "we still don't know how he did die!"

The Superintendent groaned.

"What I say is, we've got to find Cranton, anyhow. And as for December 30th, how are you going to be sure of that, anyway?"

"I shall ask the Rector which day he preached about thankfulness. Or Mrs. Venables. She's more likely to know."

"And I'd better see Thoday again. Not that I believe a single word Potty says. And how about Jim Thoday? How does he come into it now?"

"I don't know. But one thing I'm sure of, Super. It was no sailor put those knots into Gaude's rope. I'll take my oath on that."

"Oh, well!" said the Superintendent.

Wimsey went back to the house and found the Rector in his study, busily writing out a touch of Treble Bob Major.

"One moment, my dear boy," he said, pushing the tobacco-jar towards his guest, "one moment. I am just pricking this little touch to show Wally Pratt how to do it. He has got himself 'imbrangled' as they call it—fine old English word, that. Now what has the foolish lad done here? The ninth lead should bring Queen's change—let me see, let me see—51732468, 15734286—that's the first thirds and fourths all right—51372468, 15374286—and that's the first fourths and thirds—13547826—ah! here is the trouble! The eighth should be at home. What has happened?—To be sure! What a beetle-headed cuckoo I am! He has forgotten to make the bob. She can't come home till she's called." He ran a red-ink line down the page and started to write figures furiously. "There! 51372468, 15374286—and *now* she comes home like a bird!—13572468. That's better. Now it should come round at the second repeat. I will just check it. Second to fifth, third to second—yes, yes—that brings 15263748, with Tittums at the end of the second course, and repeated once again brings it round. I will just jot down the lead-ends for him to check it by. Second to third, third to fifth, fourth to second, fifth to seventh, sixth to fourth, seventh to eighth, eighth to sixth for the plain lead. Then the bob. Plain, bob, bob, three plain and a bob. I cannot understand why red ink should distribute itself so lavishly over one's person. There! I have a large smear on my cuff! Call her in the middle, in and out and home. Repeat twice. A lovely little touch." He pushed aside several sheets of paper covered with figures, and transferred a quantity of red ink from his fingers to his trouser-legs. "And now, how are you getting along? It there anything I can do to help you?"

"Yes, padre. You can tell me on which Sunday this winter you preached about thankfulness."

"Thankfulness? Well, now, that's rather a favourite subject of mine. Do you know, I find people very much disposed to grumble—I do indeed—and when you come to think of it, they might all be very much worse off. Even the farmers. As I said to them last Harvest Festival—oh! you were asking about my Thankfulness sermon—well, I nearly always preach about it at Harvest Festival. . . . Not so long ago as that? . . . Let me think. My memory is getting very unreliable, I fear . . ." He made a dive for the door. "Agnes, my dear! Agnes! Can you spare us a moment? . . . My wife is sure to remember. . . . My dear, I am so sorry to interrupt you, but can you recollect when I last preached about Thankfulness? I touched on the subject in my Tithe sermon, I remember—would you be thinking of that? Not that we have had any trouble about tithe in this parish. Our farmers are very sensible. A man from St. Peter came to talk to me about it, but I pointed out to him that the 1918 adjustment was made in the farmers' interests and that if they thought they had reason to complain of the 1925 Act, then they should see about getting a fresh adjustment made. But the law, I said, is the law. Oh, on the matter of tithe I assure you I am adamant. Adamant."

"Yes, Theodore," said Mrs. Venables, with rather a wry smile, "but if you didn't so often advance people money to pay the tithe with, they mightn't be as reasonable as they are."

"That's different," said the Rector, hurriedly, "quite different. It's a matter of principle, and any small personal loan has nothing to do with it. Even the best of women don't always grasp the importance of a legal principle, do they, Lord Peter? My sermon dealt with the principle. The text was: 'Render unto Caesar.' Though whether Queen Anne's Bounty is to be regarded as Caesar or as God—and sometimes, I admit, I feel that it is a little unfortunate that the Church should appear to be on Caesar's side, and that dis-establishment and disendowment——"

"A Caesarian operation is indicated, so to speak?" suggested Wimsey.

"A——? Oh, yes! Very good," said the Rector. "My dear, that is very good, don't you think? I must tell the Bishop—no, perhaps not. He is just a leetle bit strait-laced. But it is true—if only one could separate the two things, the temporal and the spiritual—but the question I ask myself is always, the churches themselves—the buildings—our own beautiful church—what would become of it in such a case?"

"My dear," said Mrs. Venables, "Lord Peter was asking about your sermons on Thankfulness. Didn't you preach one on the Sunday after Christmas? About thankfulness for the Christmas message? Surely you remember. The text was taken from the Epistle for the day: 'Thou art no more a servant, but a son.' It was about how happy we ought to be as God's children and about making a habit of saying 'Thank-you Father' for all the pleasant things of life, and being as pleasant-tempered as we should wish our own children to be. I remember it so well, because Jackie and Fred Holliday got quarrelling in church over those prayer-books we gave them and had to be sent out."

"Quite right, my dear. You always remember everything. That was it, Lord Peter. The Sunday after Christmas. It comes back to me very clearly now. Old Mrs. Giddings stopped me in the porch afterwards to complain that there weren't enough plums in her Christmas plum-pudding."

"Mrs. Giddings is an ungrateful old wretch," said his wife.

"Then the next day *was* the 30th December," said Wimsey. "Thanks, Padre, that's very helpful. Do you recollect Will Thoday coming round to see you on the Monday evening, by any chance?"

The Rector looked helplessly at his wife, who replied readily enough:

"Of course he did, Theodore. He came to ask you something about the New Year's peal. Don't you remember saying how queer and ill he looked? Of course, he must have been working up for that attack of 'flu, poor man. He came late—about 9 o'clock—and you said you couldn't understand why he shouldn't have waited till the morning."

"True, true," said the Rector. "Yes, Thoday came round to me on the Monday night. I hope you are not—well! I mustn't ask indiscreet questions, must I?"

"Not when I don't know the answers," said Wimsey, with a smile and a shake of the head. "About Potty Peake, now. Just how potty is he? Can one place any sort of reliance on his account of anything?"

"Well," said Mrs. Venables, "sometimes one can and sometimes one can't. He gets mixed up, you know. He's quite truthful, as far as his understanding goes, but he gets fancies and then tells them as if they were facts. You can't trust anything he says about ropes or hanging—that's his little peculiarity. Otherwise—if it was a question of pigs, for instance, or the church organ—he's quite good and reliable."

"I see," said Wimsey. "Well, he has been talking a good bit about ropes and hanging."

"Then don't believe a word of it," replied Mrs. Venables, robustly. "Dear me! here's that Superintendent coming up the drive. I suppose he wants you."

Wimsey caught Mr. Blundell in the garden and headed him away from the house.

"I've seen Thoday," said the Superintendent. "Of course he denies the whole story. Says Potty was dreaming."

"But how about the rope?"

"There you are! But that Potty was hiding behind the churchyard wall when you and I found the rope in the well, and how much he may have heard, I don't know. Anyway, Thoday denies it, and short of charging him with the murder, I've got to take his word for it. You know these dratted regulations. No bullying of witnesses. That's what they say. And whatever Thoday did or didn't do, he couldn't have buried the body, so where are you? Do you think any jury is going to convict on the word of a village idiot like Potty Peake? No. Our job's clear. We've got to find Cranton."

That afternoon, Lord Peter received a letter.

"DEAR LORD PETER,—I have just thought of something funny you ought to know about, though I don't see how it can have anything to do with the murder. But in detective stories the detective always wants to know about anything funny, so I am sending you the paper. Uncle Edward wouldn't like me writing to you, because he says you encourage me about wanting to be a writer and mixing myself up in police work—he *is* a silly old stick-in-the-mud! So I don't suppose Miss Garstairs—that's our H.M.—would let me send you a letter, but I'm putting this one into one to Penelope Dwight and I do hope she sends it on all right.

"I found the paper lying in the belfry on the Saturday before Easter Day and I meant to show it to Mrs. Venables because it was so funny, but Dad dying made me forget all about it. I thought it must be some rubbish of Potty Peake's, but Jack Godfrey says it isn't Potty's writing, but it's quite mad enough to be him, isn't it? Anyway, I thought you might like to have it. I don't see how Potty could have got hold of that foreign paper, do you?

"I hope you are getting on well with the investigations. Are you still at Fenchurch St. Paul? I am writing a poem about the founding of Tailor Paul. Miss Bowler says it is quite good and I expect they will put it in the School Magazine. That will be one in the eye for Uncle Edward, anyhow. He can't stop me being printed in the School Mag. Please write if you have time and tell me if you find out anything about the paper.

"Yours sincerely,

"HILARY THORPE."

"A colleague, as Sherlock Holmes would say, after my own heart," said Wimsey, as he unfolded the thin enclosure. "Oh, lord! 'I thought to see the fairies in the fields'—a lost work by Sir James Barrie, no doubt! Literary sensation of the year. 'But I saw only the evil elephants with their black backs.' This is neither rhyme nor reason. Hum! there is a certain dismal flavour about it suggestive of Potty, but no reference to hanging, so I conclude that it is not his—he surely couldn't keep King Charles' Head out of it so long. Foreign paper—wait a minute! I seem to know the look of that paper. By God, yes! Susanne Legros' letter! If the paper isn't the dead spit of this, I'm a Dutchman. Let me think. Suppose this was the paper Jean Legros sent to Cranton, or Will Thoday, or whoever it was? Blundell had better have a look at it. Bunter, get the car out. And what do you make of this?"

"Of this, my lord? I should say that it was written by a person of no inconsiderable literary ability, who had studied the works of Sheridan Lefanu and was, if I may be permitted the expression, bats in the belfry, my lord."

"It strikes you that way? It does not look to you like a cipher message, or anything of that kind?"

"It had not occurred to me to regard it in that light, my lord. The style is cramped, certainly, but it is cramped in what I should call a consistent manner, suggestive of—ah!—literary rather than mechanical effort."

"True, Bunter, true. It certainly isn't anything simple and bucolic of the every-third-word type. And it doesn't look as if it was meant to be read with a grid, because, with the possible exception of 'gold', there isn't a single word in it that's significant—or could be significant of anything but moonshine. That bit about the moon is rather good, of its kind. Mannered, but imaginative. 'Frail and faint as a sickle of straw.' Alliteration's artful aid, what? 'So then came minstrels, having gold trumpets, harps and drums. These played very loudly beside me, breaking that spell.' Whoever wrote that had an ear for a cadence. Lefanu, did you say? That's not a bad shot, Bunter. It reminds me a little of that amazing passage in *Wylder's Hand* about Uncle Lorne's dream."

"That was the passage I had in mind, my lord."

"Yes. Well—in that case the victim was due to 'be sent up again, at last, a thousand, a hundred, ten and one, black marble steps, and then it will be the other one's turn'. He *was* sent up again, Bunter, wasn't he?"

"From the grave, my lord? I believe that was so. Like the present unknown individual."

"As you say—very like him. 'Hell gapes, Erebus now lies open,' as our correspondent has it. 'The mouths of Death wait on thy end.' Does he mean anything by that, Bunter?"

"I could not say, my lord."

"The word 'Erebus' occurs in the Lefanu passage too, but there, if I remember rightly, it is spelt with an H. If the man who wrote this got his inspiration there, he knew enough, at any rate, about Erebus to be familiar with both spellings. All very curious, Bunter mine. We'll go along to Leamholt and get the two sheets of paper side by side."

There was a great wind blowing over the fen, and immense white clouds sailing fast in the wide blue dome of sky. As they drew up before the police-station at Leamholt, they met the Superintendent just about to step into his own car.

"Coming to see me, my lord?"

"I was. Were you coming to see me?"

"Yes."

Wimsey laughed.

"Things are moving. What have you got?"

"We've got Cranton."

"No!"

"Yes, my lord. They've run him to earth in a place in London. I heard from them this morning. Seems he's been ill, or something. Anyway, they've found him. I'm going up to interrogate him. Would you like to come?"

"Rather! Shall I run you up there? Save the force a bit of money, you know, on train-fares. And be quicker and more comfortable."

"Thank you very much, my lord."

"Bunter, wire to the Rector that we have gone to Town. Hop in, Super. You will now see how safe and swift modern methods of transport are when there is no speed-limit. Oh, wait a moment. While Bunter is wiring, have a look at this. It reached me this morning."

He handed over Hilary Thorpe's letter and the enclosure.

"Evil elephants?" said Mr. Blundell. "What in the name of goodness is all this about?"

"I don't know. I'm hoping your friend Cranton can tell us."

"But it's potty."

"I don't think Potty could rise to such heights. No, I know what you mean—don't trouble to explain. But the paper, Superintendent, the paper!"

"What about it? Oh, I get you. You think this came from the same place as Suzanne Legros' letter. I shouldn't wonder if you're right. Step in and we'll have a look. By Jove, my lord, and you *are* right. Might have come out of the same packet. Well, I'll be—— Found in the belfry, you say. What do you think it all means, then?"

"I think this is the paper that Legros sent to his friend in England—the 'guarantee' that he composed, shut up in his room for so many hours. And I think it's the clue to where the emeralds were hidden. A cipher, or something of that sort."

"Cipher, eh? It's a queer one, then. Can you read it?"

"No, but I jolly well will. Or find somebody who can. I'm hoping that Cranton will read it for us. I bet he won't, though," added his lordship, thoughtfully. "And even if we do read it, it isn't going to do us much good, I'm afraid."

"Why not?"

"Why, because you can bet your sweet life that the emeralds were taken away by whoever it was killed Legros—whether it was Cranton or Thoday or somebody else we don't know about yet."

"I suppose that's a fact. Anyhow, my lord, if we read the cipher and find the hiding-place, and the stuff's gone, that'll be pretty good proof that we're working along the right lines."

"So it will. But," added Wimsey, as the Superintendent and Bunter piled into the car and were whisked away out of Leamholt at a speed which made the policeman gasp, "if the emeralds are gone, and Cranton says he didn't take them, and we can't prove he did, and we can't find out who Legros really was, or who killed him, why then—where are we?"

"Just where we were before," said Mr. Blundell.

"Yes," said Wimsey. "It's like Looking-Glass Country. Takes all the running we can do to stay in the same place."

The Superintendent glanced about him. Flat as a chess-board, and squared like a chess-board with intersecting dyke and hedge, the fen went flashing past them.

"Very like Looking-Glass Country," he agreed, "same as the picture in the book. But as for staying in the same place—all I can say, it don't look like it, my lord—not where you're concerned."

THE EIGHTH PART

Lord Peter Follows his Course Bell to Lead

> I will again urge on the young conductor the great advantage that it will be to him to write out touches or even whole peals . . . whereby he will gain a great insight into the working of the bells.
>
> TROYTE *On Change-Ringing*

"WELL, OF COURSE," admitted Mr. Cranton, grinning up ruefully from his pillow into Lord Peter's face, "if your lordship recognises me, that's done it. I'll have to come clean, as the sheet said to the patent washer. It's a fact I was in Fenchurch St. Paul on New Year's Day, and a lovely place it is to start a happy New Year in, I don't think. And it's true I failed to report myself as from last September. And if you ask me, I think it's damned slack of you flatties not to have dug me out earlier. What we pay rates and taxes for I don't know."

He stopped and shifted restlessly.

"Don't waste your breath in giving us lip," said Chief Inspector Parker of the C.I.D., kindly enough. "When did you start growing that face-fungus? In September? I thought so. What was the idea? You didn't think it was becoming, did you?"

"I didn't," said Mr. Cranton. "Went to my heart, I may say, to disfigure myself. But I thought, 'They'll never know Nobby Cranton with his handsome features all hidden in black hair.' So I made the sacrifice. It's not so bad now, and I've got used to it, but it looked horrible while it was growing. Made me think of those happy times when I lived on His Majesty's bounty. Ah! and look at my hands. They've never got over it. I ask you, how can a gentleman carry on with his profession after all those years of unrefined manual labour? Taking the bread out of a man's mouth, I call it."

"So you had some game on, which started last September," said Parker, patiently. "What was it, now? Anything to do with the Wilbraham emeralds, eh?"

"Well, to be frank, it was," replied Nobby Cranton. "See here, I'll tell you the truth about that. I didn't mind—I never *have* minded—being put inside for what I did do. But it's offensive to a gentleman's feelings when his word isn't believed. And when I said I never had those emeralds, I meant what I said. I never did have them, and you know it. If I had had them, I wouldn't be living in a hole like this, you can bet your regulation boots. I'd have been living like a gentleman on the fat of the land. Lord!" added Mr. Cranton, "I'd have had 'em cut up and salted away before you could have said 'knife'. Talk about tracing them—you'd never have traced them the way I'd have worked it."

"So you went to Fenchurch St. Paul to try and find them, I suppose?" suggested Wimsey.

"That's right, I did. And why? Because I knew they must be there. That swine—you know who I mean——"

"Deacon?"

"Yes, Deacon." Something that might have been fear and might have been mere anger twisted the sick man's face. "He never left the place. He couldn't have got them away before you pinched him. You watched his correspondence, didn't you? If he'd packed them up and posted them, you'd have known it, eh? No. He had them there—somewhere—I don't know—but he had them. And I meant to get them, see? I meant to get them, and I meant to bring them along and show 'em to you and make you take back what you said about my having had them. Pretty silly, you'd have looked, wouldn't you, when you had to own up that I was right?"

"Indeed?" said Parker. "That was the idea, was it? You were going to find the stuff and bring it along like a good little boy?"

"That's right."

"No idea of making anything out of them, of course?"

"Oh, dear, no," replied Mr. Cranton.

"You didn't come to us in September and suggest that we should help you to find them?"

"Well, I didn't," agreed Mr. Cranton. "I didn't want to be bothered with a lot of clumsy cops. It was my own little game, see? All my own work, as the pavement-artists say."

"Delightful," said Parker. "And what made you think you knew where to look for them?"

"Ah!" said Mr. Cranton, cautiously. "Something Deacon once said gave me an idea. But he was a liar about that, too. I never met such a liar as that fellow was. He was so crooked, you couud have used his spine for a safety-pin. It serves me right for having to do with menials. A mean, sneaking spirit, that's what you find in that sort. No sense of honour at all."

"Very likely," said the Chief Inspector. "Who is Paul Taylor?"

"There you are!" said Mr. Cranton, triumphantly. "Deacon said to me——"

"When?"

"In the—oh, well!—in the dock, if you will excuse my mentioning such a vulgar place. 'Want to know where those shiners are?' he said. 'Ask Paul Taylor or Batty Thomas'—and grinned all over his face. 'Who're they?' said I. 'You'll find 'em in Fenchurch,' he said, grinning still more. 'But you aren't likely to see Fenchurch again in a hurry,' he said. So then I biffed him one—excuse the expression—and the blinking warder interfered."

"Really?" said Parker, incredulously.

"Cross my heart and wish I may die," said Mr. Cranton. "But when I got down to Fenchurch, you see, I found there were no such people—only some rubbish about bells. So I dismissed the matter from my mind."

"And sneaked off on the Saturday night. Why?"

"Well, to be frank with you," replied Mr. Cranton, "there was an individual in that place I didn't like the looks of. I got the idea that my face struck a chord in her mind, in spite of the exterior decorations. So, not wishing for argument—which is always ungentlemanly—I went quietly away."

"And who was the penetrating individual?"

"Why, that woman—Deacon's wife. We had stood shoulder to shoulder, as you might say, under unfortunate circumstances, and I had no wish to renew the acquaintance. I never expected to see *her* in that village, and, candidly, I thought she showed a lack of taste."

"She came back when she married a man named Thoday," said Wimsey.

"Married again, did she?" Cranton's eyes narrowed. "Oh, I see. I didn't know that. Well, I'm damned!"

"Why the surprise?"

"Why?—Oh, well—somebody wasn't too particular, that's all."

"See here," said Parker, "you may as well tell the truth now. Did that woman have anything to do with the theft of the emeralds?"

"How should I know? But to be frank, I don't believe she did. I think she was just a plain fool. Deacon's catspaw. I'm sure the fellow put her on to find out about the stuff, but I don't think she was wise to what she was doing. Honestly, I don't think so, because I can't see that man Deacon giving his game away. But hell! What do I know about it?"

"You don't think she knows where the stuff is?"

Cranton thought for a moment. Then he laughed.

"I'd pretty well take my oath she doesn't."

"Why?"

He hesitated.

"If she knew and was straight, she'd have told the police, wouldn't she? If she knew and was crooked, she'd have told me or my pals. No. You won't get it out of her."

"H'm! You say you think she recognised you?"

"I got a sort of idea that she was beginning to find my face familiar. Mind you, it was only a kind of hunch I got. I might have been wrong. But I anticipated argument, and I have always considered argument ill-bred. So I went away. In the night. I was working for the blacksmith—an excellent fellow, but crude. I didn't want any argument with him, neither. I just went quietly home to think things out, and then I got laid up with rheumatic fever, and it's left my heart dickey, as you see."

"Quite so. How did you get rheumatic fever?"

"Well, wouldn't anybody get rheumatic fever, if he'd fallen into one of those cursed dykes? I never saw such a country, never. Country life never did suit me—particularly in the blasted middle of winter, with a thaw going on. I was damn nearly found dead in a ditch, which is no end for a gentleman."

"You didn't investigate the matter of Batty Thomas and Tailor Paul any further, then?" said Parker, placidly putting aside the eloquence which Mr. Cranton seemed ready to lavish on any side-issue. "I am referring to the bells. You did not, for instance, visit the belfry, to see if the emeralds were hidden up there?"

"No, of course I didn't. Besides," went on Mr. Cranton, much too hastily, "the confounded place was always locked."

"You tried it, then?"

"Well, to be frank, I may just have laid my hand on the door, so to speak."

"You never went up into the bell-chamber?"

"Not me."

"Then how do you account for that?" demanded Parker, suddenly producing the mysterious cipher and thrusting it under the sick man's eyes.

Mr. Cranton turned extremely white.

"That?" he gasped. "That?—I never——" He fought for breath. "My heart—here, give me some of the stuff in that glass——"

"Give it him," said Wimsey, "he's really bad."

Parker gave him the medicine with a grim face. After a time the blue pallor gave place to a healthier colour, and the breathing became more natural.

"That's better," said Cranton. "You startled me. What did you say? That? I never saw that before."

"You're lying," said the Chief Inspector, curtly. "You have seen it. Jean Legros sent it to you, didn't he?"

"Who's he? Never heard of him."

"That's another lie. How much money did you send him to get him to England?"

"I tell you I never heard of him," repeated Cranton, sullenly. "For God's sake, can't you leave me alone? I tell you I'm ill."

He looked ill enough. Parker swore under his breath.

"Look here, Nobby, why not come across with the truth? It'll save us bothering you. I know you're ill. Cough it up and get it over."

"I know nothing about it. I've told you—I went down to Fenchurch and I came away again. I never saw that paper and I never heard of Jean what's-his-name. Does that satisfy you?"

"No, it doesn't."

"Are you charging me with anything?"

Parker hesitated. "Not as yet," he said.

"Then you've got to take my answer," said Mr. Cranton, faintly, but as one who is sure of his position.

"I know that," said Parker, "but, hang it, man! do you *want* to be charged? If you'd rather come down with us to the Yard——"

"What's the idea? What have you got to charge me with? You can try me for stealing those bloody emeralds all over again. I haven't got them. Never seen them——"

"No; but we might charge you with the murder of Jean Legros."

"No—no—no!" cried Cranton. "It's a lie! I never killed him. I never killed anybody. I never——"

"He's fainted," said Wimsey.

"He's dead," said Superintendent Blundell, speaking for the first time.

"I hope to goodness not," said Parker. "No—it's all right, but he looks pretty queer. Better get hold of that girl. Here, Polly!"

A woman came in. She gave one resentful glance at the three men and hurried across to Cranton.

"If you've killed him," she muttered, "it's murder. Coming and threatening one that's as sick as him. You get out, you great bullies. He's done nobody any harm."

"I'll send the doctor along," said Parker. "And I'll be coming to see him again. And when I do come, see that I find him all right. Understand? We shall want him elsewhere, you know, as soon as he's fit to be moved. He hasn't reported himself since last September."

The girl shrugged a disdainful shoulder, and they left her bending over the sick man.

"Well, Superintendent," said Parker. "I'm afraid that's the best we can do for you at the moment. The man's not shamming—he's really ill. But he's holding something out on us. All the same, I don't think it's murder, somehow. That wouldn't be like Cranton. He knew that paper all right."

"Yes," said Wimsey. "Produced quite a reaction, didn't it? He's frightened about something, Charles. What is it?"

"He's frightened about the murder."

"Well," said Blundell, "it looks to me as though he did it. He admits he was there, and that he ran away on the night the body was buried. If he didn't do it, who did? He could have got the key of the crypt from the sexton all right, we know that."

"So he could," said Wimsey, "but he was a stranger to the place. How did he know where the sexton kept his tools? Or where to find the bell-rope? He might have noticed the well, of course, in the day-time, but it's funny that he should have had the whole scheme so pat. And where does Legros come into it? If Deacon told Cranton in the dock where to find the emeralds, where was the sense of bringing Legros to England? He didn't want him. And, if he did for some reason need Legros, and killed him to get the emeralds, where are the emeralds? If he sold them, you ought to have found it out by now. If he's still got them, you'd better have a hunt for them."

"We'll search the house," said Parker, dubiously, "but I don't somehow think he's got them. He wasn't alarmed about the emeralds. It's a puzzle. But we'll turn the place upside-down, and if they're there, we'll get them."

"And if you do," said Blundell, "then you can arrest that chap for the murder. Whoever's got the emeralds did the murder. I'm sure of that."

"Where thy treasure is, there shall thy heart be also," said Wimsey. "The heart of this crime is down at St. Paul. That's my prophecy, Charles. Will you have a bet on it?"

"No, I won't," said the Chief Inspector. "You're right too often, Peter, and I've no money to waste."

Wimsey went back to Fenchurch St. Paul and shut himself up with the cipher. He had untwisted cryptograms before, and he felt certain that this would prove to be a simple one. Whether the inventor was Cranton or Jean Legros or Will Thoday or any other person connected with the affair of the Wilbraham emeralds, he was hardly likely to be an expert in the art of secret writing. Yet the thing had the signs of a cunning hand about it. He had never seen a secret message that looked so innocent. Sherlock Holmes' Little Dancing Men were, by comparison, obviously secretive.

He tried various simple methods, such as taking every second, third or fourth letter, or skipping letters in accordance with a set combination of figures, but without result. He tried assigning a number to each letter and adding the results, word by word and sentence by sentence. This certainly produced enough mathematical problems to satisfy a Senior Wrangler, but none of them seemed to make sense. He took all the bell-inscriptions and added them up also, with and without the dates, but could find nothing significant. He wondered whether the book contained the whole of what was on the bells. Leaving his papers strewn over the table, he went to the Rector to borrow the keys of the belfry. After a slight delay, caused by the keys having been taken downstairs by mistake for the keys of the wine-cellar, he secured them and made his way to the church.

He was still puzzled about the finding of the cryptogram. The keys jingled together in his hand—the two great keys of the west and south doors, all by themselves on a steel chain, and then, in a bunch on a ring together, the keys of the crypt and vestry, the key of the belfry, the key of the ringing-chamber and the key that unlocked the counterpoise of the belfry. How had Cranton known where to find them? He could, of course, have taken them from the sexton's house—if he had known already. But if "Stephen Driver" had been asking questions about the church keys, somebody would have taken notice of it. The sexton had the keys of the west door and of the crypt. Had he the other keys as well? Wimsey suddenly turned back and shot the question through the study window at the Rector, who was struggling with the finances of the Parish Magazine.

Mr. Venables rubbed his forehead.

"No," he said at last. "Gotobed has the west-door key and the key of the crypt, as you say, and he also has the key of the belfry stair and of the ringing-chamber, because he rings the single bell for Early Service and sometimes deputises for Hezekiah when he's ill. And Hezekiah has the keys of the south porch and the belfry stair and the ringing-chamber, too. You see, Hezekiah was sexton before Gotobed, and he likes to keep his privilege of ringing the passing-bell, though he's too old for the other work, and he has the necessary keys. But neither of them has the key to the counterpoise. They don't need it. The only people who have that are Jack Godfrey and myself. I have a complete set of everything, of course, so that if one of the others is lost or mislaid, I can supply it."

"Jack Godfrey—has he the key of the crypt as well?"

"Oh, no—he doesn't need that."

Curiouser and curiouser, thought Wimsey. If the man who left the paper in the bell-chamber was the same man who buried the body, then either he took *all* the Rector's keys, or he had access to *two* sets, and those two sets had to be Jack Godfrey's (for the key of the counterpoise) and Gotobed's (for the key of the crypt). And if the man had been Cranton, then how did he *know*? Of course, the criminal might have brought his own spade (though that added to the complication). If so, he must have had either the Rector's keys or Jack Godfrey's. Wimsey went round to the back and got hold of Emily and Hinkins. They were both quite sure that they had never seen the man who called himself Stephen Driver inside the Rectory gates, much less inside the Rector's study, which was the proper place for the keys when they were in their proper place.

"But they weren't there at all, my lord," said Emily, "because, if you remember, they keys was missing on New Year's night, and it wasn't till near a week after we found them in the vestry—bar the key of the church porch and that was in the lock where Rector left it after choir-practice."

"After choir-practice? On the Saturday?"

"That's right," said Hinkins. "Only, don't you remember, Emily, Rector said it couldn't have been him as left it, because it was gone a-missing, and he didn't have it on Saturday and had to wait for Harry Gotobed?"

"Well, I don't know," said Emily, "but that's where it was. Harry Gotobed said he found it there when he went to ring for Early Service."

More confused than ever, Wimsey trotted back to the study window. Mr. Venables, arrested with a carrying-figure at the tip of his pen, was at first not very clear in his recollection, but said presently that he believed Emily was right.

"I must have left the keys in the vestry the week before," he suggested, "and whoever left the church last after choir-practice must have found the church key and used it—but who that would be, I don't know, unless it was Gotobed. Yes, it would be Gotobed, because he would wait behind to make up the stoves. But it was funny that he should leave the key in the lock. Dear me! You don't think it could have been the murderer, do you?"

"I do, indeed," said Wimsey.

"There now!" exclaimed the Rector. "But if I left the keys in the vestry, how did he get in to find them? He couldn't get in without the church key. Unless he came to choir-practice. Surely, nobody belonging to the choir——"

The Rector looked horribly distressed. Wimsey hastened to comfort him.

"The door would be unlocked during choir-practice. He might have slipped in then."

"Oh, yes—of course! How stupid I am! No doubt that is what occurred. You have relieved my mind very much."

Wimsey had not, however, relieved his own mind. As he resumed his way to the church, he turned the matter over. If the keys had been taken on New Year's Eve, then Cranton had not taken them. Cranton had not arrived till New Year's Day. Will Thoday had come, unnecessarily, to the Rectory on December 30th, and might have taken the keys then, but he had certainly not been in the church on the night of January 4th to restore them. It remained possible that Will Thoday had taken the keys and the mysterious James Thoday had returned them—but in that case, what was Cranton doing in the business? And Wimsey felt sure that Cranton knew something about the paper found in the bell-chamber.

Meditating thus, Wimsey let himself into the church, and, unlocking the door in the tower, made his way up the spiral stair. As he passed through the ringing-chamber, he noticed with a smile that a new board had made its appearance on the wall, announcing that: "On New Year's morning, 19—, a Peal of 15,840 Kent Treble Bob Major was Rung in 9 Hours and 15 Minutes, the Ringers being: Treble, Ezra Wilderspin; 2, Peter D. B. Wimsey; 3, Walter Pratt; 4, Henry Gotobed; 5, Joseph Hinkins; 6, Alfred Donnington; 7, John P. Godfrey; Tenor, Hezekiah Lavender; Theodore Venables, Rector, assisting. Our Mouths shall shew forth Thy Praise." He passed up through the great, bare clock-chamber, released the counter-poise and climbed again till he came out beneath the bells. There he stood for a moment, gazing up into their black mouths while his eyes grew accustomed to the semi-darkness. Presently their hooded silence oppressed him. A vague vertigo seized him. He felt as though they were slowly collapsing together and coming down upon him. Spell-bound, he spoke their names: Gaude, Sabaoth, John, Jericho, Jubilee, Dimity, Batty Thomas and Tailor Paul. A soft and whispering echo seemed to start from the walls and die stealthily among the beams. Suddenly he shouted in a great voice: "Tailor Paul!" and he must somehow have hit upon a harmonic of the scale, for a faint brazen note answered him, remote and menacing, from overhead.

"Come!" said Wimsey, pulling himself together, "this won't do. I'm getting as bad as Potty Peake, coming here and talking to the bells. Let's find the ladder and get to work."

He switched on his torch and turned it on the dim corners of the belfry. It showed him the ladder, and it showed him something else also. In the gloomiest and dustiest corner of the floor, there was a patch that was not so dusty. He stepped eagerly forward, the menace of the bells forgotten. Yes, there was no mistake. A portion of the floor had at some fairly recent time been scrubbed, for the dust which in other places lay centuries thick was here only a thin film.

He knelt to examine it, and new thoughts went swooping and turning through his brain like bats. Why should anybody trouble to swab the floor of a belfry, unless to remove some very sinister stain. He saw Cranton and Legros climbing to the belfry, with the cipher in their hands for guidance. He saw the green glint of the jewels, dragged from their old hiding-place in the light of the lantern. He saw the sudden leap, the brutal blow, and the blood gushing to the floor, the cipher fluttering, unheeded, into a corner. And then the murderer, trembling and glancing over his shoulder, as he snatched the emeralds from dead fingers, took up the body and stumbled panting down the creaking ladders. The sexton's spade from the crypt, the bucket and scrubbing-brush from the vestry, or wherever they were kept, the water from the well——

There he stopped. The well? The well meant the rope, and what had the rope to do with this? Had it been used merely as a convenient means to carry the corpse? But the experts had been so sure that the victim had been bound before he was dead. And besides, there were the blows and the blood. It was all very well making horrible pictures for one's self, but there had been no blow till the man had been dead too long to leave any pool of blood. And if there was no blood, why scrub the floor?

He sat back on his heels and looked up again to the bells. If their tongues could speak, they could tell him what they had seen, but they had neither speech nor language. Disappointed, he again took up the torch and searched further. Then he broke outinto harsh and disgusted laughter. The whole cause of the mystery revealed itself absurdly. An empty quart beer-bottle lay there, rolled into an obscure place behind a quantity of worm-eaten beams that were stacked against the wall. Here was a pretty ending to his dreams! Some unlicensed trespasser on consecrated ground—or possibly some workman legitimately engaged in repairs to the bell-cage—had spilt his beer and had tidily removed the stains, while the bottle, rolling out of sight, had been forgotten. No doubt that was all. Yet a lingering suspicion caused Wimsey to take up the bottle very carefully, by means of a finger inserted into the neck. It was not very dusty. It could not, he thought, have lain there long. It would bear somebody's finger-prints—perhaps.

He examined the rest of the floor very carefully, but could find only a few jumbled footprints in the dust—large, male prints, he thought. They might be Jack Godfrey's or Hezekiah Lavender's, or anybody's. Then he took the ladder and made an exhaustive search of the bells and timbers. He found nothing. No secret mark. No hiding-place for treasure. And nothing whatever suggestive of fairies or elephants, enchanters or Erebus. After several dirty and fatiguing hours, he descended again, carrying the bottle as his sole reward.

Curiously enough, it was the Rector who solved the cipher. He came into the schoolroom that night as the hall-clock struck eleven, thoughtfully bearing a glass of hot toddy in one hand and an old fashioned foot-muff in the other.

"I do hope you are not working yourself to death," he said, apologetically. "I have ventured to bring a little comfort for the inner man. These nights of early summer are so chilly. And my wife thinks you might like to put your feet in this. There is always a draught under the door. Allow me—it is slightly moth-eaten, I fear, but still affords protection. Now, you must not let me disturb you. Dear me! What is that? Are you pricking out a peal? Oh, no—I see they are letters, not figures. My eyesight is not as good as it was. But I am rudely prying into your affairs."

"Not a bit, padre. It does look rather like a peal. It's still this wretched cipher. Finding that the number of letters formed a multiple of eight, I had written it out in eight columns, hoping forlornly that something might come of it. Now you mention it, I suppose one might make a simple sort of cipher out of a set of changes."

"How could you do that?"

"Well, by taking the movements of one bell and writing the letters of your message in the appropriate places and then filling up the places of the other bells with arbitraries. For instance. Take a Plain Course of Grandsire Doubles,* and suppose you want to convey the simple and pious message 'Come and worship'. You would select one bell to carry the significants—let us say, No. 5. Then you would write out the beginning of your plain course, and wherever No. 5 came you would put in one letter of your message. Look."

He rapidly scribbled down the two columns:

* "Doubles" is the name given to a set of changes rung on five bells, the tenor (No. 6) being rung last or "behind" in each change.

```
1 2 3 4 5 6
___________

2 1 3 5 4 6        . . . C . .
2 3 1 4 5 6        . . . . O .
3 2 4 1 5 6        . . . . M .
3 4 2 5 1 6        . . . E . .
4 3 5 2 1 6        . . A . . .
4 5 3 1 2 6        . N . . . .
5 4 1 3 2 6        D . . . . .
5 1 4 2 3 6        W . . . . .
1 5 2 4 3 6        . O . . . .
1 2 5 4 3 6        . . R . . .
2 1 5 4 3 6        . . S . . .
2 5 1 3 4 6        . H . . . .
5 2 3 1 4 6        I . . . . .
5 3 2 4 1 6        P . . . . .
    etc.
```

"Then you could fill up the other places with any sort of nonsense letters—say X L O C M P, J Q I W O N, N A E M M B, T S H E Z P, and so on. Then you would write the whole thing out in one paragraph, dividing it so as to look like words."

"Why?" inquired the Rector.

"Oh, just to make it more difficult. You could write, for example, 'XLOC MPJQI. WON NAE M MBHS! HEZP?' and so on to the end. It wouldn't matter what you did. The man who received the message and had the key would simply divide the letters into six columns again, run his pencil along the course of No. 5, and read the message."

"Dear me!" said Mr. Venables, "so he would! How very ingenious. And I suppose that with a little further ingenuity, the cipher might be made to convey some superficial and misleading information. I see, for instance, that you already have the word WON and the Scotch expression NAE. Could not the idea be extended further, so that the entire passage might appear completely innocuous?"

"Of course it could. It might look like this." Wimsey flicked Jean Legros' communication with his finger.

"Have you——? But pardon me. I am unwarrantably interfering. Still—have you tried this method on the cryptogram?"

"Well, I haven't," admitted Wimsey. "I've only just thought of it. Besides, what would be the good of sending a message like that to Cranton, who probably knows nothing about bell-ringing? And it would take a bell-ringer to write it, and we have no reason to suppose that Jean Legros was a ringer. It is true," he added thoughtfully, "that we have no reason to suppose he was not."

"Well, then," said the Rector. "Why not try? You told me, I think, that this paper was picked up in the belfry. Might not the person to whom it was sent, though not himself a ringer and not knowing how to interpret it, have connected it in his mind with the bells and supposed that the key was to be found in the belfry? No doubt I am very foolish, but it appears to me to be possible."

Wimsey struck his hand on the table.

"Padre, that's an idea! When Cranton came to Fenchurch St. Paul, he asked for Paul Taylor, because Deacon had told him that Tailor Paul or Batty Thomas knew where the emeralds were. Come on! Have at it. We'll ask Tailor Paul ourselves."

He picked up the paper on which he had already written the cryptogram in eight columns.

"We don't know what method the fellow used, or which bell to follow. But we'll take it that the bell is either Batty Thomas or Tailor Paul. If the method is Grandsire Triples, it can't be Tailor Paul, for the Tenor would be rung behind the whole way and we should find the message running down the last column. And it's not like to be Grandsire Major, because you never ring that method here. Let us try Batty Thomas. What does the 7th bell give us? GHILSTETHCWA. That's not very encouraging. For form's sake we'll try the other bells. No. No. No. Could the man possibly have started off with a bob or single?"

"Surely not."

"Well, you never know. He's not pricking a peal, he's only making a cipher and he might do something unusual on purpose."

His pencil traced the letters again.

"No. I can't make anything of it. Wash out Grandsires. And I think we can probably wash out Stedman's, too—that would keep the significants too close together. Try Kent Treble Bob, and we'll take Tailor Paul first, since the Tenor is the usual observation bell for that method. She starts in the 7th place, H. Then 8th place, E. Back to 7th, S; to 6ths, I; to 4ths, T. 'HESIT.' Well, it's pronounceable, at any rate. Dodge up into 6ths place, T again. Down to 5ths, E; to 4ths, T; to 3rds, H. 'HESITTETH.' Hullo, Padre! we've got two words, anyhow. 'He sitteth.' Perhaps 'He' is the necklace. We'll carry on with this."

The Rector, his glasses sliding down his long nose with excitement, pored over the paper as the pencil made its rapid way down the letters.

" 'He sitteth between'—it's part of a verse from Psalm xcix—there, what did I tell you? 'He sitteth between the Cherubims.' Now, what can that mean? Oh, dear! there is some mistake—the next letter should be a B—'be the earth never so unquiet.' "

"Well, it isn't a B; it's another T. There isn't a B anywhere. Wait a moment. THE is coming—no, THEI—no, as you were. It's THE ISLES. I can't help it, Padre. It couldn't come like that by accident. Just a second, and we'll have it all sorted out and then you can say what you like. . . . Oy! what's happened here at the end? Oh, dash it! I was forgetting. This must be the end of the lead. Yes"—he calculated rapidly—"it is, and we've got to make the 3rds and 4ths. There you are. Message complete; and what it means is more than I can tell you."

The Rector polished his glasses and stared.

"It's verses from three psalms," he said. "Most singular. 'He sitteth between

I T H O U G H T	L Y C L O U D B	N Y T E A R S B
T O S E E T H E	U T N O B L I N	E F O R E T H E
F A I R I E S I	D E Y E O F A M	T H I N M O O N
N T H E F I E L	O R T A L W A S	R O S E U P F R
D S B U T I S A	P E R M I T T E	A I L A N D F A
W O N L Y T H E	D T O S P Y T H	I N T A S A S I
E V I L E L E P	E M S O T H E N	C K L E O F S T
H A N T S W I T	C A M E M I N S	R A W N O W T H
H T H E I R B L	T R E L S H A V	O U G H T H E E
A C K B A C K S	I N G G O L D T	N C H A N T E R
W O E H O W T H	R U M P E T S H	G N A S H H I S
A T S I G H T A	A R P S A N D D	T E E T H V A I
W E D M E T H E	R U M S T H E S	N L Y Y E T S H
E L V E S D A N	E P L A Y E D V	A L L H E R E T
C E D A L L A R	E R Y L O U D L	U R N A S T H E
O U N D A N D A	Y B E S I D E M	S P R I N G R E
B O U T W H I L	E B R E A K I N	T U R N S O H W
E I H E A R D V	G T H A T S P E	R E T C H E D M
O I C E S C A L	L L S O T H E D	A N H E L L G A
L I N G C L E A	R E A M V A N I	P E S E R E B U
R L Y H H H O W	S H E D W H E R	S N O W L I E S
I T R I E D T O	E A T I T H A N	O P E N T H E M
S E E T H R O W	K E D H E A V E	O U T H S O F D
O F F T H E U G	N I S H E D M A	E A T H W A I T
		O N T H Y E N D

the cherubims'; that's Ps. xcix. 1. Then 'The isles may be glad thereof'; that's Ps. xcvii. 1. Both those psalms begin alike: 'Dominus regnavit,' 'The Lord is King.' And then we get, 'as the rivers in the south'. That's Ps. cxxvi. 5, 'In convertendo,' 'When the Lord turned the captivity of Sion.' This is a case of *obscurum per obscuriora*——the interpretation is even more perplexing than the cipher."

"Yes," said Wimsey. "Perhaps the figures have something to do with it. We have 99. 1. 97. 1. 126. 5. Are they to be taken as one figure 9919711265? or to be left as they are? or re-divided? The permutations are almost endless. Or perhaps they ought to be added. Or converted into letters on some system we haven't discovered yet. It can't be a simple a=1 substitution. I refuse to believe in a message that runs I I A I G I A B F E. I shall have to wrestle with this quite a lot more. But you have been simply marvellous, Padre. You ought to take to deciphering codes as a profession."

"It was pure accident," said Mr. Venables, simply, "and due entirely to my failing vision. That is a curious thing. It has given me the idea for a sermon about evil being over-ruled for good. But I should never have thought of the possibility that one might make a cipher out of change-ringing. Most ingenious."

"It could have been done still more ingeniously," said Wimsey. "I can think of lots of ways to improve it. Suppose—but I won't waste time with supposing. The point is, what the dickens is one to do with 99. 1. 97. 1. 126. 5.?"

He clutched his head between his hands, and the Rector, after watching him for a few minutes, tiptoed away to bed.

THE NINTH PART

Emily Turns Bunter from Behind

Let the bell that the Treble turns from behind make thirds place, and return behind again.

Rules for Change-Making on Four Bells

"I SHOULD LIKE," panted Emily between her sobs, "to give my week's warning."

"Good gracious, Emily!" cried Mrs. Venables, pausing as she passed through the kitchen with a pail of chicken-feed, "what on earth is the matter with you?"

"I'm sure," said Emily, "I ain't got no fault to find with you and Rector as has always been that kind, but if I'm to be spoken to so by Mr. Bunter, which I'm not his servant and never want to be and ain't no part of my duties, and anyway how was I to know? I'm sure I'd have cut my right hand off rather than disoblige his lordship, but I did ought to have been told and it ain't my fault and so I told Mr. Bunter."

Mrs. Venables turned a little pale. Lord Peter presented no difficulties, but Bunter she found rather alarming. But she was of the bulldog breed, and had been brought up in the knowledge that a servant was a servant, and that to be afraid of a servant (one's own or anybody else's) was the first step to an Avernus of domestic inefficiency. She turned to Bunter, standing white and awful in the background.

"Well now, Bunter," she said, firmly. "What is all this trouble about?"

"I beg your pardon, madam," said Bunter in a stifled manner. "I fear that I forgot myself. But I have been in his lordship's service now for going on fifteen years (counting my service under him in the War), and such a thing has never yet befallen me. In the sudden shock and the bitter mortification of my mind, I spoke with considerable heat. I beg, madam, that you will overlook it. I should have controlled myself better. I assure you that it will not occur again."

Mrs. Venables put down the chicken-pail.

"But what was it all about?"

Emily gulped, and Bunter pointed a tragic finger at a beer-bottle which stood on the kitchen table.

"That bottle, madam, was entrusted to me yesterday by his lordship. I placed it in a cupboard in my bedroom, with the intention of photographing it this morning, before despatching it to Scotland Yard. Yesterday evening, it seems that this young woman entered the room during my absence, investigated the cupboard and removed the bottle. Not content with removing it, she dusted it."

"If you please 'm," said Emily, "how was I to know it was wanted? A nasty, dirty old thing. I was only a-dusting the room, 'm, and I see this old bottle on the cupboard shelf, and I says to myself, 'Look at that dusty old bottle, why, however did that get there? It must have got left accidental.' So I takes it down and when Cook see it she says, 'Why, whatever have you got there, Emily? That'll just do,' she says, 'to put the methylated.' So I gives it a dust——"

"And now the finger-prints have all gone," concluded Bunter in a hollow tone, "and what to say to his lordship I do not know."

"Oh, dear! oh, dear!" said Mrs. Venables, helplessly. Then she seized on the one point of domestic economy which seemed to call for inquiry. "How did you come to leave your dusting so late?"

"If you please 'm, I don't know how it was. I got all behind yesterday, somehow, and I said to myself, 'Better late than never', and I'm sure if I'd only have known——"

She wept loudly, and Bunter was touched.

"I am sorry I expressed myself with so much acerbity," he said, "and I take blame to myself for not removing the key from the cupboard door. But you will understand my feelings, madam, when I think of his lordship innocently waking to a new day, if I may say so, and not knowing of the blow which is in store for him. It goes to my heart, if you will pardon my mentioning the organ in such a connection. There, madam, is his morning tea, only waiting for my hand to put the boiling water to it, and I feel, madam, as though it were the hand of a murderer which no perfumes of Arabia—supposing such to be suitable to my situation—could sweeten. He has rung twice," added Bunter, in desperate tones, "and he will know by the delay that something of a calamitous nature has occurred——"

"Bunter!"

"My lord!" cried Bunter, in a voice like prayer.

"What the devil has happened to my tea? What the——? Oh, I beg your pardon, Mrs. Venables. Excuse my language and my bath-robe, won't you? I didn't know you were here."

"Oh, Lord Peter!" exclaimed Mrs. Venables, "such a dreadful thing's happened. Your man is so terribly upset, and this silly girl—she meant well of course and it's all a mistake—but we've dusted all the finger-prints off your bottle!"

"Wah-ha-ha!" sobbed Emily. "O-oh! Wah-ha-ha! I did it. I dusted it. I didn't know—ho-ho."

"Bunter," said his lordship, "what is the verse about the struck eagle stretched upon the plain, Never through something clouds to soar again? It expresses my feelings exactly. Take up my tea and throw the bottle in the dust-bin. What's done cannot be undone. In any case the finger-prints were probably of no importance. William Morris once wrote a poem called *The Man Who Never Laughed Again.* If the shout of them that triumph, the song of them that feast, should never again be heard upon my lips, you will know why. My friends will probably be devoutly thankful. Let it be a warning to you never to seek for happiness out of a bottle. Emily, if you cry any more, your young man won't know you on Sunday. Don't worry about the bottle, Mrs. Venables—it was a beastly bottle, anyhow, and I always loathed the sight of it. It is a beautiful morning for early rising. Allow me to carry the chicken-pail. I beg you will not give another thought to the bottle, or Emily either. She's a particularly nice girl, isn't she? What is her surname, by the way?"

"Holliday," said Mrs. Venables. "She's a niece of Russell's, the undertaker, you know, and some sort of relation to Mary Thoday, though of course everybody is, in this village, related to somebody or the other, I mean. It comes of being such a small place, though now that they all have motor-bicycles and the 'buses running twice a week it isn't so bad, and there won't be so many unfortunate creatures like Potty Peake. All the Russells are very nice, superior people."

"Just so," said Lord Peter Wimsey. He did a certain amount of thinking as he spooned out mash into the chicken trough.

He spent the early part of the morning in fresh unavailing study of the cryptogram, and as soon as he thought the pubs would be open, went round to the Red Cow for a pint of beer.

"Bitter, my lord?" inquired Mr. Donnington with his hand upon the tap.

Wimsey said No, not to-day. He would have a bottle of Bass for a change.

Mr. Donnington produced the Bass, observing that his lordship would find it in very nice condition.

"Condition is nine-tenths of the bottle," said Wimsey, "and a lot of it depends upon the bottling. Who are your bottlers?"

"Griggs of Walbeach," said Mr. Donnington. "Very sound people they are, too; I've got no complaints to make. Just you try for yourself—though you can tell by the look of it, if you see what I mean. Clear as a bell—though, of course, you have to be able to trust your cellarman. I had a chap once that never could be taught not to pack his Bass 'ead down in the basket, same as if it was stout. Now stout will stand being stood on its 'ead, though it's not a thing I ever would do myself and I don't recommend it, but Bass *must* be stood right ways up and not shook about if you're to do justice to the beer."

"Very true indeed," said Wimsey. "There's certainly nothing wrong with this. Your health. Won't you take something yourself?"

"Thank you, my lord, I don't mind if I do. Here's luck. Now, that," said Mr. Donnington, raising the glass to the light, "is as nice a glass of Bass as you could wish to see."

Wimsey asked whether he did much with quart bottles.

"Quarts?" said Mr. Donnington. "No. Not with quarts, I don't. But I believe Tom Tebbutt down at the Wheatsheaf does a bit. Griggs bottles for him, too."

"Ah!" said Wimsey.

"Yes. There's one or two prefers quarts. Though, mind you, most of the business about here is draught. But there's a farmer here and there as likes the quarts delivered at their homes. Ah! in the old days they all did their own brewing—there's plenty farms now with the big brewing coppers still standing, and there's a few as still cures their own sides of bacon—Mr. Ashton's one on 'em, he won't have nothing new-fangled. But what with these chain stores and their grocery vans, and the girls all wanting to be off to the pictures in their silk stockings and so many things coming in tins, it's not many places where you can see a bit of real home-cured. And look at the price of pig-feed. What I say is, the farmers did ought to have some protection. I was brought up a Free Trader myself, but times has changed. I don't know if you've ever thought of these things, my lord. They may not come your way. Or—there—I'm forgetting. Maybe you sit in the 'Ouse of Lords, now. Harry Gotobed will have it that that's so, but I said as he was mistook—but there! you'll know better than me about that."

Wimsey explained that he was not qualified to sit in the House of Lords. Mr. Donnington observed with pleasure that in that case the sexton owed him half a crown, and while he made a note of the fact on the back of an envelope, Wimsey escaped and made his way to the Wheatsheaf.

Here, by exercising a certain amount of tact, he obtained a list of those households to which Bass was regularly supplied in quarts. Most of the names were those of farmers in outlying places, but as an afterthought, Mrs. Tebbutt mentioned one which made Wimsey prick up his ears.

"Will Thoday, he had a few while Jim was at home—a dozen or so, it might be. He's a nice chap, is Jim Thoday—makes you laugh by the hour telling his tales of foreign parts. He brought back that there parrot for Mary, though as I says to her, that bird ain't no proper example for the children. How it do go on, to be sure. I'm sure, if you'd heard what it said to Rector the other day! I didn't know where to look. But it's my belief, Rector didn't understand half of it. He's a real gentleman, is Mr. Venables, not like old parson. He was a kind man, too, but different from Rector, and they say he used to swear something surprising in a clergyman. But there, poor man! He had a bit of a weakness, as they say. 'Do as I say, don't do as I do'—that's what he used to say in his sermons. Terrible red in the face he were, and died sudden, of a stroke."

Wimsey tried in vain to steer the conversation back to Jim Thoday. Mrs. Tebbutt was fairly launched into reminiscences of Old Rector, and it was half an hour before he was able to make his way out of the Wheatsheaf. Turning back towards the Rectory, he found himself at Will Thoday's gate. Glancing up the path, he saw Mary, engaged in hanging out washing. He suddenly determined on a frontal attack.

"I hope you'll forgive me, Mrs. Thoday," he said, when he had announced himself and been invited to enter, "if I take your mind back to a rather painful episode. I mean to say, bygones are bygones and all that and one hates digging anything up, what? But when it comes to dead bodies in other people's graves and so on, well, sometimes one gets wondering about them and all that sort of thing, don't you know."

"Yes, indeed, my lord. I'm sure if there's anything I can do to help, I will. But as I told Mr. Blundell, I never knew a thing about it, and I can't imagine how it came there. That was the Saturday night he was asking me about, and I'm sure I've thought and thought, but I couldn't call to mind as I'd seen anything."

"Do you remember a man who called himself Stephen Driver?"

"Yes, my lord. Him that was at Ezra Wilderspin's. I remember seeing him once or twice. They said at the inquest that the body might have been him."

"But it wasn't," said Wimsey.

"Wasn't it, my lord?"

"No. Because we've found this chap Driver and he's still alive and kicking. Had you ever seen Driver before he came here?"

"I don't think so, my lord; no, I can't say as I ever did."

"He didn't remind you of anybody?"

"No, my lord."

She appeared to be answering quite frankly, and he could not see any signs of alarm in voice or expression.

"That's odd," said Wimsey, "because he says that he ran away from St. Paul because he thought you had recognised him."

"Did he? Well, that's a strange thing, my lord."

"Did you ever hear him speak?"

"I don't think I ever did, my lord."

"Suppose he hadn't been wearing a beard, now—would he remind you of anybody?"

Mary shook her head. Like most people, she found the effort of imagination beyond her.

"Well, do you recognise this?"

He took out a photograph of Cranton, taken at the time of the Wilbraham emeralds affair.

"That?" Mrs. Thoday turned pale. "Oh, yes, my lord. I remember him. That was Cranton, that took the necklace and was sent to prison same time as —as my first husband, my lord. I expect you know all about that. That's his wicked face. Oh, dear! it's given me quite a turn, seeing that again."

She sat down on a bench and stared at the photograph.

"This isn't—it couldn't be Driver?"

"That's Driver," said Wimsey. "You had no idea of it?"

"That I never had, my lord. If I'd ever had such a thought, I'd have spoken to him, don't you fear! I'd have got out of him where he put those emeralds to. You see, my lord, that was what went so hard against my poor husband, this man saying as my husband had kept the necklace himself. Poor Jeff, there's no doubt he was tempted—all through my fault, my lord, talking so free—and he did take the jewels, I'm sorry to say. But he didn't have them afterwards. It was this Cranton had them all the time. Don't you think it hasn't been a bitter hard cross to me, my lord, all these years, knowing as I was suspected? The jury believed what I said, and so did the judge, but you'll find some as thinks now that I had a hand in it and knew where the necklace was. But I never did, my lord, never. If I'd been able to find it, I'd have crawled to London on my hands and knees to give it back to Mrs. Wilbraham. I know what poor Sir Henry suffered with the loss of it. The police searched our place, and I searched it myself, over and over——"

"Couldn't you take Deacon's word for it?" asked Wimsey, softly.

She hesitated, and her eyes clouded with pain.

"My lord, I did believe him. And yet, all the same—well! it was such a terrible shock to me that he could have done such a thing as rob a lady in the master's house, I didn't know but what he mightn't perhaps have done the other too. I didn't rightly know what to believe, if you understand me, my lord. But *now* I feel quite sure that my husband was telling the truth. He was led away by this wicked Cranton, there's no doubt of that, but that he was deceiving us all, afterwards, I don't believe. Indeed, my lord, I don't think he was—I'm quite sure of it in my own mind."

"And what do you suppose Cranton came down here for?"

"Doesn't that show, my lord, that it was him as hid them after all? He must have got frightened and hid them away in some place that night, before he got away."

"He says himself that Deacon told him in the dock that the emeralds were here, and he was to ask Tailor Paul and Batty Thomas to find them for him."

Mary shook her head. "I don't understand that, my lord. But if my husband had said such a thing to him then, Cranton wouldn't have kept quiet about it. He'd have told the jury, he was that mad with Jeff."

"Would he? I'm not so sure. Suppose Deacon told Cranton where to find the emeralds, don't you think Cranton would have waited in the hope of getting hold of them when he came out of prison? And mightn't he have come down here last January to look for them? And then, thinking you'd spotted him, mightn't he have run away in a fright?"

"Well, my lord, I suppose he might. But then, who would that poor dead man be?"

"The police think he may have been an accomplice of Cranton's, who helped him to find the emeralds and was killed for his pains. Do you know whether Deacon made any friends among the other convicts or the warders at Maidstone?"

"I couldn't say, I'm sure, my lord. He was allowed to write now and again, of course, but naturally he wouldn't tell anybody a thing like that, because his letters would be read."

"Naturally. I wondered whether perhaps you'd had a message from him at some time—through a released prisoner, or anything like that?"

"No, my lord, never."

"Have you ever seen this writing?"

He handed her the cryptogram.

"That writing? Why, of course——"

"Shut up you fool! Shut up you bloody fool! Come on, Joey! Show a leg there!"

"Good Lord!" exclaimed Wimsey, startled. Peering round the door into the inner room, he encountered the bright eye of a grey African parrot fixed knowingly upon him. At sight of a stranger, the bird stopped talking, cocked its head aslant, and began to sidle along its perch.

"Damn your eyes!" said his lordship, pleasantly. "You made me jump."

"Aw!" said the bird, with a long, self-satisfied chuckle.

"Is that the bird your brother-in-law gave you? I've heard about him from Mrs. Tebbutt."

"Yes, my lord, that's him. He's a wonderful talker, but he does swear and that's the truth."

"I've no use for a parrot that doesn't," said Wimsey. "Seems unnatural. Let me see—where were we——? Oh, yes, that bit of writing. You were just saying——"

"I said, of course I'd never seen it before, my lord."

Wimsey could have sworn that she had been going to say just the opposite. She was looking at—no, not at, but through and past him, with the face of someone who sees an incredible catastrophe approaching.

"It's queer-looking stuff, isn't it?" she went on, in a flat voice, "don't seem to mean anything. What made you think I should know anything about the like of that?"

"We had an idea that it might have been written by some man your late husband knew at Maidstone. Did you ever hear of anyone called Jean Legros?"

"No, my lord. That's a French name, isn't it? I've never seen a Frenchman, except a few of those Beljums that came over here in the War."

"And you never knew anyone called Paul Taylor?"

"No, never."

The parrot laughed heartily.

"Shut up, Joey!"

"Shut up, you fool! Joey, Joey, Joey! Scratch a poll, then. Aw!"

"Oh, well," said Wimsey. "I just wondered."

"Where did that come from?"

"What? Oh, this? It was picked up in the church, and we had an idea it might be Cranton's. But he says it isn't, you know."

"In the *church*?"

As though the word were a cue, the parrot picked it up, and began muttering excitedly:

"Must go to church. Must go to church. The bells. Don't tell Mary. Must go to church. Aw! Joey! Joey! Come on, Joey! Must go to church."

Mrs. Thoday stepped hurriedly into the other room and flung a cloth over the cage, while Joey squawked protestingly.

"He goes on like that," she said. "Gets on my nerves. He picked it up the night Will was so bad. They were ringing the peal, and it worried him, like, that he couldn't be there. Will gets that angry with Joey when he starts mocking him. Shut up, now, Joey, do."

Wimsey held out his hand for the cryptogram, which Mary surrendered—reluctantly, he thought, and as though her thoughts were elsewhere.

"Well, I mustn't bother you any more, Mrs. Thoday. I just wanted to clear up that little point about Cranton. I expect you are right after all, and he just came down here to snoop about on his own. Well, you aren't likely to be bothered with him again. He's ill, and in any case, he'll have to go back to prison to work out his time. Forgive my bargin' along and botherin' you about what's best forgotten."

But all the way back to the Rectory, he was haunted by Mary Thoday's eyes and by the hoarse muttering voice of the parrot:

"The bells! the bells! Must go to the church! Don't tell Mary!"

Superintendent Blundell clicked his tongue a good deal over all this.

"It's a pity about the bottle," he said. "Don't suppose it would have told us anything, but you never know. Emily Holliday, eh? Of course, she's a cousin of Mary Thoday's. I'd forgotten that. That woman beats me—Mary, I mean. Damned if I know what to make of her, or her husband either. We're in touch with those people at Hull, and they're arranging to get James Thoday shipped back to England as soon as possible. We told them he might be wanted as a witness. Best way to work it—he can't skip his orders; or, if he does, we'll know there's something wrong and go after him. It's a queer business altogether. As regards that cipher, what do you say to sending it along to the Governor of Maidstone? If this fellow Legros or Taylor or whatever he is was ever in there, they may be able to spot the handwriting."

"So they may," said Wimsey, thoughtfully. "Yes, we'll do that. And I'm hoping we'll hear from M. Rozier again soon. The French haven't any of our inhibitions about dealing with witnesses."

"Lucky them, my lord," replied Mr. Blundell, with fervour.

THE TENTH PART

Lord Peter is Called Wrong

And he set the cherubims within the inner house: and they stretched forth the wings of the cherubims.

I *Kings* vi. 27

And above were costly stones.

I *Kings* vi. 27

"I HOPE," SAID the Rector on the following Sunday morning, "there is nothing wrong with the Thodays. Neither Will nor Mary was at Early Service. I've never known them both miss before, except when he was ill."

"No more they were," said Mrs. Venables. "Perhaps Will has taken a chill again. These winds are very treacherous. Lord Peter, do have another sausage. How are you getting along with your cipher?"

"Don't rub it in, I'm hopelessly stuck."

"I shouldn't worry," said Mr. Venables. "Even if you have to lie still a whole pull now and again, you'll soon find yourself back in the hunt."

"I wouldn't mind that," said Wimsey. "It's lying behind the whole way that gets on my nerves."

"There's always something that lies behind a mystery," said the Rector, mildly enjoying his little witticism. "A solution of some kind."

"What I say is," observed Mrs. Venables darkly, "there are always wheels within wheels."

"And where there's a wheel, there's usually a rope," added his lordship.

"Unhappily," said the Rector, and there was a melancholy pause.

Anxiety about the Thodays was somewhat allayed by their appearance together at Matins, but Wimsey thought he had never seen two people look so ill and unhappy. In wondering about them, he lost all consciousness of what was going on about him, sat down for the Venite, lost the Psalms for the day, embarked on a loud and solitary "For thine is the Kingdom" at the end of the second "Our Father", and only pulled himself together when Mr. Venables came down to preach his sermon. As usual, Mr. Gotobed had failed to sweep the chancel properly, and a hideous crunching of coke proclaimed the Rector's passage to the pulpit. The Invocation was pronounced, and Wimsey sank back with a sigh of relief into the corner of the pew, folded his arms and fixed his gaze firmly on the roof.

"Who hast exalted thine only Son with great triumph into the Heavens. Those words are for the collect for the day. What do they mean to us? What picture do we make of the glory and triumph of Heaven? Last Thursday we prayed that we also might in heart and mind thither ascend and continually dwell, and we hope that after death we shall be admitted—not only in heart and mind but in soul and body—to that blessed state where cherubim and seraphim continually sing their songs of praise. It is a beautiful description that the Bible gives us—the crystal sea and the Lord sitting between the cherubims, and the angels with their harps and crowns of gold, as the old craftsmen imagined them when they built this beautiful roof that we are so proud of—but do we, do you and I really believe——?"

It was hopeless. Wimsey's thoughts were far away again. "He rode upon the cherubim and did fly. He sitteth between the cherubims." He was suddenly reminded of the little architect who had come down to advise about the church roof at Duke's Denver. "You see, your Grace, the rot has got into the timbers; there are holes behind those cherrybims you could put your hand in." *He sitteth between the cherubims.* Why, of course! Fool that he was—climbing up among the bells to look for cherubims when they were here over his head, gazing down at him, their blank golden eyes blind with excess of light. The cherubim? Nave and aisle were thick with cherubim, as autumn leaves in Vallombrosa. Nave and aisle—"the *isles* may be glad thereof"—and then the third text—"as the rivers in the *south*". Between the cherubims in the south aisle—what could be clearer than that? In his excitement he nearly shot out of his seat. It only remained to discover which particular pair of cherubims was concerned, and that ought not to be very difficult. The emeralds themselves would be gone, of course, but if one could find even the empty hiding-place, that would prove that the cryptogram was connected with the necklace and that all the queer tragedy brooding over Fenchurch St. Paul was in some way connected with the emeralds too. Then, if the handwriting of the cryptogram could be traced back to Maidstone Gaol and to Jean Legros, they would know who Legros was, and with luck they could also link him up with Cranton. After that, if Cranton could escape from the murder charge, he would be a lucky man.

Over the Sunday beef and Yorkshire pudding, Wimsey tackled the Rector.

"How long ago was it, sir, that you took away the galleries from the aisles?"

"Let me see," said Mr. Venables, "about ten years ago, I think. Yes, that is right. Ten years. Hideous, cumbersome things they were. They ran right across the aisle windows, obscuring all the upper tracery and blocking the light, and were attached to the arcading. As a matter of fact, what with those horrible great pews, like bathing machines, sprouting up from the floor, and the heavy galleries, you could scarcely see the shafts of the pillars at all."

"Or anything else," said his wife. "I always used to say it was regular blind man's holiday underneath those galleries."

"If you want to see what it was like," added the Rector, "go and look at Upwell Church near Wisbech. You'll find the same sort of gallery in the north aisle there (though ours was larger and uglier), and they have an angel roof, too, though not as fine as ours, because their angels are only attached to the roof itself, instead of being on the hammer-beams. In fact, you can't see the angels in their north aisle at all, unless you climb up into the gallery."

"I suppose there was the usual amount of opposition when you took the galleries down?"

"A certain amount, of course. There are always some people who oppose any change. But it did seem absurd, when the church was far too large for the parish in any case, to have all that unnecessary seating. There was plenty of room for the school-children in the aisle."

"Did anybody sit in the gallery besides the school-children?"

"Oh, yes. The Red House servants and a few of the oldest inhabitants, who had been there from time immemorial. Indeed, we really had to wait for one poor old soul to die before we embarked on the improvements. Poor old Mrs. Wilderspin, Ezra's grandmother. She was ninety-seven and came regularly to Church every Sunday, and it would have broken her heart to have turned her out."

"Which side did the Red House servants sit?"

"At the west end of the south aisle. I never liked that, because one couldn't see what they were doing, and sometimes their behaviour wasn't as reverent as it might have been. I do not think the House of God is a proper place for flirtation, and there was so much nudging and giggling that it really was very unseemly."

"If that woman Gates had done her duty and sat with the servants it would have been all right," said Mrs. Venables, "but she was far too much of a lady. She always has to have her own seat, just inside the south door, for fear she should feel faint and have to go out."

"Mrs. Gates is not a robust woman, my dear."

"Rubbish!" said Mrs. Venables. "She eats too much and gets indigestion, that's all."

"Perhaps you are right, my dear."

"I can't stand the woman," said Mrs. Venables. "The Thorpes ought to sell that place, but apparently they can't under Sir Henry's will. I don't see how it can be kept up, and the money would be more use to Hilary Thorpe than that great tumble-down house. Poor little Hilary! If it hadn't been for that horrible old Wilbraham creature and her necklace—I suppose there's no hope of recovering the necklace, Lord Peter, after all this time?"

"I'm afraid we're a day after the fair. Though I'm pretty sure it was in this parish up to last January."

"In the parish? Where?"

"I think it was in the church," said Wimsey. "That was a very powerful sermon of yours this morning, padre. Very inspiring. It inspired me to guess the riddle of the cryptogram."

"No!" exclaimed the Rector. "How did it do that, I wonder?"

Wimsey explained.

"Good gracious! How very remarkable! We must investigate the place at once."

"Not at once, Theodore."

"Well, no, my dear, I didn't mean to-day. I'm afraid it wouldn't do to take ladders into the church on Sunday. We are still rather touchy here about the Fourth Commandment. Besides, I have the Children's Service this afternoon and three baptisms, and Mrs. Edwards is coming to be churched. But, Lord Peter, how do you suppose the emeralds got up in the roof?"

"Why, I was just thinking about that. Isn't it true that this fellow Deacon was arrested after church on Sunday morning? I expect he got some idea of what was going to happen to him, and concealed his loot somehow during the service."

"Of course, he was sitting up there that morning. Now I understand why you asked so many questions about the gallery. What a sad villain the man must have been! He really did—what is that word they use when one malefactor deceives another?"

"Double-cross?" suggested Wimsey.

"Ah! that is the very expression I was looking for. He did double-cross his accomplice. Poor man! I mean the accomplice. Ten years in prison for a theft of which he never enjoyed the fruits. One cannot help feeling some sympathy for him. But in that case, Lord Peter, who constructed the cryptogram?"

"I think it must have been Deacon, because of the bell-ringing."

"Ah, yes. And then he gave it to this other man, Legros. Why did he do that?"

"Probably as an inducement to Legros to help him to escape from Maidstone."

"And Legros waited all these years before making use of it?"

"Legros obviously had very good reasons for keeping out of England. Eventually he must have passed the cryptogram on to somebody here—Cranton, perhaps. Possibly he couldn't decipher it himself, and in any case he wanted Cranton's help to get back from France."

"I see. Then they found the emeralds and Cranton killed Legros. How sad it makes me to think of all this violence for the sake of a few stones!"

"It makes me still sadder to think of poor Hilary Thorpe and her father," said Mrs. Venables. "You mean to say that while they needed that money so badly, the emeralds were hidden in the church all the time within a few feet of them?"

"I'm afraid so."

"And where are they now? Has this man Cranton got them? Why hasn't somebody found them by now? I can't think what the police are doing."

Sunday seemed an unusually long day. On the Monday morning, a great many things happened at once.

The first thing was the arrival of Superintendent Blundell, in great excitement.

"We've got that letter from Maidstone," he announced, "and whose do you suppose the writing is?"

"I've been thinking it over," said Wimsey. "I think it must have been Deacon's."

"There!" said Mr. Blundell, disappointed. "Well, you're quite right, my lord; it is."

"It must be the original cipher," said Wimsey. "When we found out that it had to do with bell-ringing, I realised that Deacon must be the author. To have two bell-ringing convicts in Maidstone Gaol at once seemed rather too much of a coincidence. And then, when I showed the paper to Mrs. Thoday, I felt sure that she recognised the writing. It might have meant that Legros had written to her, but it was still more likely that she knew it to be her husband's."

"Well, then, how did it come to be written on that foreign paper?"

"Foreign paper is much of a muchness," said Wimsey. "Did Lady Thorpe ever have a foreign maid? Old Lady Thorpe, I mean."

"Sir Charles had a French cook," said the Superintendent.

"At the time of the theft?"

"Yes. She left them when the War broke out, I remember. She wanted to get back to her family, and they scraped her across on one of the last boats."

"Then that's clear enough. Deacon invented his cryptogram before he actually hid the emeralds. He couldn't have taken it into prison with him. He must have handed it to somebody——"

"Mary," said the Superintendent, with a grim smile.

"Perhaps. And she must have sent it to Legros. It's all rather obscure."

"Not so obscure as that, my lord." Mr. Blundell's face grew still grimmer. "I thought it was a bit reckless, if you'll excuse me, showing that paper to Mary Thoday. She's skipped."

"Skipped?"

"First train to town this morning. And Will Thoday with her. A precious pair."

"Good God!"

"You may say so, my lord. Oh, we'll have them, don't you fear. Gone off, that's what they've done, and the emeralds with them."

"I admit," said Wimsey, "I didn't expect that."

"Didn't you?" said Mr. Blundell. "Well, I didn't either, or I'd have kept a sharper eye on them. And by the way, we know now who that Legros fellow was."

"You're a perfect budget of news to-day, Super."

"Ah! well—we've had a letter from your friend M. Rozier. He had that woman's house searched, and what do you think they found? Legros' identification disc—no less. Any more guesses coming, my lord?"

"I might make a guess, but I won't. I'll buy it. What was the name?"

"Name of Arthur Cobbleigh."

"And who's Arthur Cobbleigh when he's at home?"

"You hadn't guessed that, then?"

"No—my guess was quite different. Go on, Super. Spill the beans."

"Well, now. Arthur Cobbleigh—seems he was just a bloke. But can you guess where he came from?"

"I've given up guessing."

"He came from a little place near Dartford—only about half a mile from the wood where Deacon's body was found."

"Oho! now we're coming to it."

"I got on the 'phone straight away as soon as this letter came. Cobbleigh was a chap aged somewhere about twenty-five in 1914. Not a good record. Labourer. Been in trouble once or twice with the police for petty thieving and assault. Joined up in the first year of the War and considered rather a good riddance. Last seen on the last day of his leave in 1918, and that day was just two days after Deacon's escape from prison. Left his home to rejoin his unit.

Never seen again. Last news of him, 'Missing believed killed' in the retreat over the Marne. Officially, that is. Last actual news of him—over there!"

The Superintendent jerked his thumb in the general direction of the churchyard.

Wimsey groaned.

"It makes no sense, Super, it makes no sense! If this man Cobbleigh joins up in the first year of the War, how on earth could he have been elaborately in league with Deacon, who went to Maidstone in 1914? There was no time. Damn it! You don't get a man out of quod in a few spare hours spent on leave. If Cobbleigh had been a warder—if he'd been a fellow-convict—if he'd been anything to do with the prison, I could understand it. Had he a relation in the gaol or anything of that sort? There must have been something more to it than that."

"Must there? Look here, my lord, how's this? I've been working this thing out coming over, and this what I make out of it. Deacon bust away from a working-party, didn't he? He was found still wearing his prison dress, wasn't he? Doesn't that show his escape wasn't planned out elaborately beforehand? They'd have found him fast enough, if he hadn't gone and pitched down that dene-hole, wouldn't they? Now, you listen to this, and see if it don't hold water. I can see it plain as a pike-staff. Here's this Cobbleigh—a hard nut, by all accounts. He's walking through the wood on the way from his mother's cottage, to take the train at Dartford for wherever he might be going to join up with the troops going back to France. Somewhere on that moor he finds a chap lurking about. He collars him, and finds he's pinched the escaped convict that everybody's looking for. The convict says, 'Let me go, and I'll make you a rich man,' see? Cobbleigh's got no objection to that. He says, 'Lead me to it. What is it?' The convict says, 'The Wilbraham emeralds, that's what it is.' Cobbleigh says, 'Coo! tell us some more about that. How'm I to know you ain't kidding me? You tell us where they are and we'll see about it.' Deacon says, 'No fear—catch me telling you, without you helps me first.' Cobbleigh says, 'You can't help yourself,' he says, 'I only got to give you up and then where'll you be?' Deacon says, 'You won't get much out o' that. You stick by me and I'll put hundreds of thousands of pounds in your hands.' They go on talking, and Deacon, like a fool, lets out that he's made a note of the hiding-place and has it on him. 'Oh, have you?' says Cobbleigh, 'then you damn well take that.' And lams him over the head. Then he goes over him and finds the paper, which he's upset to find he can't make head or tail of. Then he has another look at Deacon and sees he's done him in good and proper. 'Oh, hell!' says he, 'that's torn it. I better shove him out of the way and clear off.' So he pops him down the hole and makes tracks for France. How's that, so far?"

"Fine, full-blooded stuff," said Wimsey. "But why should Deacon be carrying a note of the hiding-place about with him? And how did it come to be written on foreign paper?"

"I don't know. Well, say it was like you said before. Say he'd given the paper to his wife. He spills his wife's address, like a fool, and then it all happens the way I said. Cobbleigh goes back to France, deserts, and gets taken care of by Suzanne. He keeps quiet about who he is, because he don't know whether Deacon's body's been found or not and he's afraid of being had up for murder if he goes home. Meanwhile, he's stuck to the paper—no, that's wrong. He writes to Mrs. Deacon and gets the paper out of her."

"Why should she give it up?"

"That's a puzzler. Oh, I know! I've got it this time. He tells her he's got the key to it. That's right. Deacon told him, 'My wife's got the cipher, but she's a babbling fool and I ain't trusted her with the key. I'll give you the key and that'll show you I know what I'm talking about.' Then Cobbleigh kills him, and when he thinks it's safe he writes over to Mary and she sends him the paper."

"The original paper?"

"Why, yes."

"You'd think she'd keep that and send him a copy."

"No. She sends the original, so that he can see it's in Deacon's writing."

"But he wouldn't necessarily know Deacon's writing."

"How's she to know that? Cobbleigh works out the cipher and they help him to get across."

"But we've been into all that and decided the Thodays couldn't do it."

"All right, then. The Thodays bring Cranton into it. Cobbleigh comes over, anyhow, under the name of Paul Taylor, and he comes along to Fenchurch and they get the emeralds. Then Thoday kills him, and *he* takes the emeralds. Meanwhile, along comes Cranton to see what's happening and finds they've been ahead of him. He clears off and the Thodays go about looking innocent till they see we're getting a bit close on their trail. Then *they* clear."

"Who did the killing, then?"

"Any one of them, I should say."

"And who did the burying?"

"Not Will, anyhow."

"And how was it done? And why did they want to tie Cobbleigh up? Why not kill him straight off and with a bang on the head? Why did Thoday take £200 out of the bank and put it back again? When did it all happen? Who was the man Potty Peake saw in the church on the night of the 30th? And, above all, why was the cipher found in the belfry, of all places?"

"I can't answer everything at once, can I? That's the way it was done between 'em, you can take it from me. And now I'm going to have Cranton charged, and get hold of those precious Thodays, and if I don't put my hand on the emeralds among them, I'll eat my hat."

"Oh!" said Wimsey, "that reminds me. Before you came, we were just going to look at the place where Deacon hid those jolly old emeralds. The Rector solved the cipher——"

"Him?"

"He. So, just for fun, and by way of shutting the stable door after the steed was stolen, we're going to climb up aloft and have a hunt among the cherubims. In fact, the Rector is down at the church, champing his bit at this very moment. Shall we go?"

"Sure—though I haven't a lot of time to waste."

"I don't suppose it will take long."

The Rector had procured the sexton's ladder and was already up in the south aisle roof, covering himself with cobwebs as he poked about vaguely among the ancient oak.

"The servants sat just about here," he said, as Wimsey came in with the Superintendent. "But now I come to think of it, we had the painters up here last year, and they ought to have found anything there was to be found."

"Perhaps they did," said Wimsey; and Mr. Blundell uttered a low moan.

"Oh, I hope not. I really think not. They are most honest men." Mr. Venables came down from the ladder. "Perhaps you had better try. I am not clever about these things."

"Beautiful old work this is," said his lordship. "All pegged together. There's a lot of this old rafter work down at Duke's Denver, and when I was a kid I made rather a pretty cache for myself in a corner of the attic. Used to keep tiddly-winks counters in it and pretend it was a pirate's hoard. Only it was a dickens of a job getting them out again. I say! Blundell! do you remember that wire hook you found in the corpse's pocket?"

"Yes, my lord. We never made out what that was for."

"I ought to have known," said Wimsey. "I made a thing very like it for the pirate's hoard." His long fingers were working over the beams, gently pulling at the thick wooden pegs which held them together. "He must have been able to reach it from where he sat. Aha! what did I tell you? This is the one. Wriggle her gently and out she comes. Look!"

He wrenched at one of the pegs, and it came out in his hand. Originally, it had passed right through the beam and must have been over a foot in length, tapering from the size of a penny-piece at one end to something over half-an-inch at the other. But at some time it had been sawn off about three inches from the thick end.

"There you are," said Wimsey. "An old schoolboy cache originally, I expect. Some kid got pushing it from the other end and found it was loose. Probably shoved it clean out. At least, that's what I did, up in the attic. Then he took it home and sawed six inches or so out of the middle of it. Next time he comes to church he brings a short rod with him. He pushes the thin end back again into place with the rod, so that the hole doesn't show from the other side. Then he drops in his marbles or whatever he wanted to hide, and plugs up the big end again with this. And there he is, with a nice little six-inch hidey-hole where nobody would ever dream of looking for it. Or so he thinks. Then—perhaps years afterwards—along comes friend Deacon. He's sitting up here one day, possibly a little bored with the sermon (sorry, padre!). He starts fidgeting with the peg, and out it comes—only three inches of it. Hullo! says he, here's a game! Handy place if you wanted to pop any little thing away in a hurry. Later on, when he does want to pop his little shiners away in a hurry, he thinks of it again. Easy enough. Sits here all quiet and pious, listening to the First Lesson. Puts his hand down at his side, slips out the plug, slides the emeralds out of his pocket, slips them into the hole, pops back the plug. All over before his reverence says 'Here endeth'. Out into the sunshine and slap into the arms of our friend the Super here and his merry men. 'Where are the emeralds?' they say. 'You can search me,' says he. And they do, and they've been searching ever since."

"Amazing!" said the Rector. Mr. Blundell uttered a regrettable expression, remembered his surroundings and coughed loudly.

"So now we see what the hook was for," said Wimsey. "When Legros, or Cobbleigh, whichever you like to call him, came for the loot——"

"Stop a minute," objected the Superintendent. "That cipher didn't mention anything about a hole, did it? It only mentioned cherubims. How did he know he needed a hook to get necklaces out of cherubims?"

"Perhaps he'd had a look at the place first. But of course, we know he did. That must have been what he was doing when Potty Peake saw him and Thoday in the church. He spotted the place then, and came back later. Though why he should have waited five days I couldn't tell you. Possibly something went wrong. Anyway, back he came, armed with his hook, and hitched the necklace out. Then, just as he was coming down the ladder, the accomplice took him from behind, tied him up, and—and then—and then did away with him by some means we can't account for."

The Superintendent scratched his head.

"You'd think he might have waited for a better place to do it in, wouldn't you, my lord? Putting him out here in the church, and all that bother of burying him and what not. Why didn't he go while the going was good, and shove Cobbleigh into the dyke or something on the way home?"

"Heaven knows," said Wimsey. "Anyhow, there's your hiding-place and there's the explanation of your hook." He thrust the end of his fountain pen into the hole. "It's quite deep—no, by Jove, it's not! it's only a shallow hole after all, not much longer than the peg. We can't, surely, have made a mistake. Where's my torch? Dash it! (Sorry, padre). Is that wood? or is it——? Here, Blundell, find me a mallet and a short, stout rod or stick of some kind—not too thick. We'll have this hole clear."

"Run across to the Rectory and ask Hinkins," suggested Mr. Venables, helpfully.

In a few minutes' time, Mr. Blundell returned, panting, with a short iron bar and a heavy wheel-spanner. Wimsey had shifted the ladder and was examining the narrow end of the oaken peg on the east side of the beam. He set one end of the bar firmly against the peg and smote lustily with the spanner. An ecclesiastical bat, startled from its resting place by the jar, swooped out with a shriek, the tapered end of the peg shot smartly through the hole and out at the other side, and something else shot out with it—something that detached itself in falling from its wrapping of brown paper and cascaded in a flash of green and gold to the Rector's feet.

"Bless my heart!" cried Mr. Venables.

"The emeralds!" yelled Mr. Blundell. "The emeralds, by God! And Deacon's fifty pounds with them."

"And we're wrong, Blundell," said Lord Peter. "We've been wrong from start to finish. Nobody found them. Nobody killed anybody for them. Nobody deciphered the cryptogram. We're wrong, wrong, out of the hunt and wrong!"

"But we've got the emeralds," said the Superintendent.

III

A SHORT TOUCH OF STEDMAN'S TRIPLES

(Five Parts)

840

By the Part Ends

5 6 1 2 3 4
3 4 1 5 6 2
6 2 1 3 4 5
4 5 1 6 2 3
2 3 1 4 5 6

Treble the observation.

Call her the last whole turn, out quick, in slow, the second half turn and out slow. Four times repeated.

(TROYTE)

THE FIRST PART

The Quick Work

> The work of each bell is divided in three parts, viz. the quick work, dodging, and slow work.
>
> TROYTE *On Change-Ringing*

LORD PETER WIMSEY passed a restless day and night and was very silent the next day at breakfast.

At the earliest possible moment he got his car and went over to Leamholt.

"Superintendent," he said, "I think I have been the most unmitigated and unconscionable ass that ever brayed in a sleuth-hound's skin. Now, however, I have solved the entire problem, with one trivial exception. Probably you have done so too."

"I'll buy it," said Mr. Blundell. "I'm like you, my lord, I'm doing no more guessing. What's the bit you haven't solved, by the way?"

"Well, the murder," said his lordship, with an embarrassed cough. "I can't quite make out who did that, or how. But that, as I say, is a trifle. I know who the dead man was, why he was tied up, where he died, who sent the cryptogram to whom, why Will Thoday drew £200 out of the bank and put it back again, where the Thodays have gone and why and when they will return, why Jim Thoday missed his train, why Cranton came here, what he did and why he is lying about it and how the beer bottle got into the belfry."

"Anything else?" asked Mr. Blundell.

"Oh, yes. Why Jean Legros was silent about his past, what Arthur Cobbleigh did in the wood at Dartford, what the parrot was talking about and why the Thodays were not at Early Service on Sunday, what Tailor Paul had to do with it and why the face of the corpse was beaten in."

"Excellent," said Mr. Blundell. "Quite a walking library, aren't you, my lord? Couldn't you go just a step further and tell us who we're to put the handcuffs on?"

"I'm sorry. I can't do that. Dash it all, can't I leave one little tit-bit for a friend?"

"Well," said Mr. Blundell, "I don't know that I ought to complain. Let's have the rest of it and perhaps we'll be able to do the last bit on our own."

Lord Peter was silent for a moment.

"Look here, Super," he said at last. "This is going to be a dashed painful sort of story. I think I'd like to test it a bit before I come out with it. Will you do something yourself, first? You've got to do it in any case, but I'd rather not say anything till it is done. After that, I'll say anything you like."

"Well?"

"Will you get hold of a photograph of Arthur Cobbleigh and send it over to France for Suzanne Legros to identify?"

"That's got to be done, naturally. Matter of routine."

"If she identifies it, well and good. But if she's stubborn and refuses, will you give her this note, just as it is, and watch her when she opens it?"

"Well, I don't know about doing that personally, my lord, but I'll see that this Monsieur Rozier does it."

"That will do. And will you also show her the cryptogram?"

"Yes, why not? Anything else?"

"Yes," said Wimsey, more slowly. "The Thodays. I'm a little uncomfortable about the Thodays. You're trailing them, I suppose?"

"What do you think?"

"Exactly. Well, when you've put your hands on them, will you let me know before you do anything drastic? I'd rather like to be there when you question them."

"I've no objection to that, my lord. And this time they'll have to come across with some sort of story, judge's rules or no judge's rules, even if it breaks me."

"You won't have any difficulty about that," said Wimsey. "Provided, that is, you catch them within a fortnight. After that, it will be more difficult."

"Why within a fortnight?"

"Oh, come!" expostulated his lordship. "Isn't it obvious? I show Mrs. Thoday the cipher. On Sunday morning neither she nor her husband attends Holy Communion. On Monday they depart to London by the first train. My dear Watson, it's staring you in the face. The only real danger is——"

"Well?"

"The Archbishop of Canterbury. A haughty prelate, Blundell. An arbitrary prince. But I don't suppose they'll think about him, somehow. I think you may risk him."

"Oh, indeed! And how about Mr. Mussolini and the Emperor of Japan?"

"Negligible. Negligible," replied his lordship, with a wave of the hand. "Likewise the Bishop of Rome. But get on to it, Blundell, get on to it."

"I mean to," said Mr. Blundell, with emphasis. "They'll not get out of the country, that's a certainty."

"So it is, so it is. Of course, they'll be back here by tomorrow fortnight, but that will be too late. How soon do you expect Jim Thoday back? End of the month? Be sure he doesn't give you the slip. I've an idea he may try to."

"You think he's our man?"

"I don't know, I tell you. I don't want him to be. I rather hope it's Cranton."

"Poor old Cranton," said the Superintendent, perversely, "I rather hope it isn't. I don't like to see a perfectly good jewel-thief stepping out of his regular line, so to speak. It's disconcerting, that's what it is. Besides, the man's ill. However, we shall see about that. I'll get on to this Cobbleigh business and settle it."

"Right!" said Wimsey. "And I think, after all, I'll ring up the Archbishop. You never know."

"Dotty!" said Mr. Blundell to himself. "Or pulling my leg. One or the other."

Lord Peter Wimsey communicated with the Archbishop, and appeared to be satisfied with the result. He also wrote to Hilary Thorpe, giving her an account of the finding of the emeralds. "So you see," he said, "your Sherlocking was very successful. How pleased Uncle Edward will be." Hilary's reply informed him that old Mrs. Wilbraham had taken the necklace and restored the money paid in compensation—all without comment or apology. Lord Peter haunted the Rectory like an unhappy ghost. The Superintendent had gone to town in pursuit of the Thodays. On Thursday things began to happen again.

Telegram from Commissaire Rozier to Superintendent Blundell:

Suzanne Legros no knowledge Cobbleigh identifies photograph in sealed envelope as her husband identification supported by mayor here do you desire further action.

Telegram from Superintendent Blundell to Lord Peter Wimsey:

Suzanne Legros rejects Cobbleigh identifies sealed photograph who is it unable to trace Thodays in London.

Telegram from Superintendent Blundell to Commissaire Rozier:

Please return papers immediately detain Legros pending further information.

Telegram from Lord Peter Wimsey to Superintendent Blundell:

Surely you know by this time try all churches registrars.

Telegram from Superintendent Blundell to Lord Peter Wimsey:

Vicar St. Andrews Bloomsbury says asked perform marriage by licence William Thoday Mary Deacon both of that parish was it Deacon.

Telegram from Lord Peter Wimsey to Superintendent Blundell:

Yes of course you juggins charge Cranton at once.

Telegram from Superintendent Blundell to Lord Peter Wimsey:

Agree juggins but why charge Cranton Thodays found and detained for inquiry.

Telegram from Lord Peter Wimsey to Superintendent Blundell:

Charge Cranton first joining you in town.

After dispatching this wire, Lord Peter summoned Bunter to pack up his belongings and asked for a private interview with Mr. Venables, from which both men emerged looking distressed and uneasy.

"So I think I'd better go," said Wimsey. "I rather wish I hadn't come buttin' into this. Some things may be better left alone, don't you think? My sympathies are all in the wrong place and I don't like it. I know all about not doing evil that good may come. It's doin' good that evil may come that is so embarrassin'."

"My dear boy," said the Rector, "it does not do for us to take too much thought for the morrow. It is better to follow the truth and leave the result in the hand of God. He can foresee where we cannot, because He knows all the facts."

"And never has to argue ahead of His data, as Sherlock Holmes would say? Well, padre, I dare say you're right. Probably I'm tryin' to be too clever. That's me every time. I'm sorry to have made so much unpleasantness, anyhow. And I really would rather go away now. I've got that silly modern squeamishness that doesn't like watchin' people suffer. Thanks awfully for everything. Good-bye."

Before leaving Fenchurch St. Paul, he went and stood in the churchyard. The grave of the unknown victim still stood raw and black amid the grass, but the grave of Sir Henry and Lady Thorpe had been roofed in with green turves. Not far away there was an ancient box tomb; Hezekiah Lavender was seated on the slab, carefully cleaning the letters of the inscription. Wimsey went over and shook hands with the old man.

"Makin' old Samuel fine and clean for the summer," said Hezekiah. "Ah! Beaten old Samuel by ten good years, I have. I says to Rector, 'Lay me aside old Samuel,' I says, 'for everybody to see as I beaten him.' An' I got Rector's promise. Ah! so I have. But they don't write no sech beautiful poetry these here times."

He laid a gouty finger on the inscription, which ran:

Here lies the Body of SAMUEL SNELL
That for fifty Years pulled the Tenor Bell.
Through Changes of this Mortal Race
He Laid his Blows and Kept his Place
Till Death that Changes all did Come
To Hunt him down and Call him Home.
His Wheel is broke his Rope is Slackt
His Clapper Mute his Metal Crackt,
Yet when the great Call summons him from Ground
He shall be Raised up Tuneable and Sound.

.MDCXCVIII.
Aged 76 years

"Ringing Tailor Paul seems to be a healthy occupation," said Wimsey. "His servants live to a ripe old age, what?"

"Ah!" said Hezekiah. "So they du, young man, so they du, if so be they're faithful tu 'un an' don't go a-angerin' on 'un. They bells du know well who's a-haulin' of 'un. Wunnerful understandin' they is. They can't abide a wicked man. They lays in wait to overthrow 'un. But old Tailor Paul can't say I ain't done well by her an she allus done well by me. Make righteousness your course bell, my lord, an' keep a-follerin' on her an' she'll see you through your changes till Death calls you to stand. Yew ain't no call to be afeard o' the bells if so be as yew follows righteousness."

"Oh, quite," said Wimsey, a little embarrassed.

He left Hezekiah and went into the church, stepping softly as though he feared to rouse up something from its sleep. Abbot Thomas was quiet in his tomb; the cherubims, open-eyed and open-mouthed, were absorbed in their everlasting contemplation; far over him he felt the patient watchfulness of the bells.

THE SECOND PART

Nobby Goes in Slow and Comes out Quick

It is a frightful plight. Two angels buried him . . . in Vallombrosa by night; I saw it, standing among the lotus and hemlock.

J. SHERIDAN LE FANU: *Wylder's Hand*

MR. CRANTON WAS in an infirmary as the guest of His Majesty the King, and looked better than when they had last seen him. He showed no surprise at being charged with the murder of Geoffrey Deacon, twelve years or so after that gentleman's reputed decease.

"Right!" said Mr. Cranton. "I rather expected you'd get on to it, but I kept on hoping you mightn't. I didn't do it, and I want to make a statement. Do sit down. These quarters aren't what I could wish for a gentleman, but they seem to be the best the Old Country can offer. I'm told they do it much prettier in Sing Sing. England with all thy faults I love thee still. Where do you want me to begin?"

"Begin at the beginning," suggested Wimsey, "go on till you get to the end and then stop. May he have a fag, Charles?"

"Well, my lord and—no," said Mr. Cranton, "I won't say gentlemen. Seems to go against the grain, somehow. Officers, if you like, but not gentlemen. Well, my lord and officers, I don't need to tell you that I'm a deeply injured man. I said I never had those shiners, didn't I? And you see I was right. What you want to know is, how did I first hear that Deacon was still on deck? Well, he wrote me a letter, that's how. Somewhere about last July, that would be. Sent it to the old crib, and it was forwarded on—never you mind who by."

"Gammy Pluck," observed Mr. Parker, distantly.

"I name no names," said Mr. Cranton. "Honour among—gentlemen. I burnt that letter, *being* an honourable gentleman, but it was some story, and I don't know that I can do justice to it. Seems that when Deacon made his get-away, after an unfortunate encounter with a warder, he had to sneak about Kent in a damned uncomfortable sort of way for a day or two. He said the stupidity of the police was almost incredible. Walked right over him twice, he said. One time they trod on him. Said he'd never realised so vividly before why a policeman was called a flattie. Nearly broke his fingers standing on them. Now I," added Mr. Cranton, "have rather small feet. Small and well-shod. You can always tell a gentleman by his feet."

"Go on, Nobby," said Mr. Parker.

"Anyhow, the third night he was out there lying doggo in a wood somewhere, he heard a chap coming along that wasn't a flattie. Rolling drunk, Deacon said he was. So Deacon pops out from behind a tree and pastes the fellow one. He said he didn't mean to do him in, only put him out, but he must have struck a bit harder than what he meant. Mind you, that's only what he said, but Deacon always was a low kind of fellow and he'd laid out one man already and you can't hang a chap twice. Anyway, he found he'd been and gone and done it, and that was that.

"What he wanted, of course, was duds, and when he came to examine the takings, he found he'd bagged a Tommy in uniform with all his kit. Well, that wasn't very surprising, come to think of it. There were a lot of those about in 1918, but it sort of took Deacon aback. Of course, he knew there was a war on—they'd been told all about that—but it hadn't, as you might say, come home to him. This Tommy had some papers and stuff on him and a torch, and from what Deacon could make out, looking into the thing rather hurriedly in a retired spot, he was just coming off his leaf and due to get back to the Front. Well, Deacon thought, any hole's better than Maidstone Gaol, so here goes. So he changes clothes with the Tommy down to his skin, collars his papers and what not, and tips the body down the hole. Deacon was a Kentish man himself, you see, and knew the place. Of course, he didn't know the first thing about soldiering—however, needs must and all that. He thought his best way was to get up to Town and maybe he'd find some old pal up there to look after him. So he tramped off—and eventually he got a lift on a lorry or something to a railway station. He did mention the name, but I've forgotten it. He picked some town he'd never been in—a small place. Anyway, he found a train going to London and he piled into it. That was all right; but somewhere on the way, in got a whole bunch of soldiers, pretty lit-up and cheery, and from the way they talked, Deacon began to find out what he was up against. It came over him, you see, that here he was, all dressed up as a perfectly good Tommy, and not knowing the first thing about the War, or drill or anything, and he knew if he opened his mouth he'd put his foot in it."

"Of course," said Wimsey. "It'd be like dressing up as a Freemason. You couldn't hope to get away with it."

"That's it. Deacon said it was like being among people talking a foreign language. Worse; because Deacon did know a bit about foreign languages. He was an educated sort of bloke. But this Army stuff was beyond him. So all he could do was to pretend to be asleep. He said he just rolled up in his corner and snored, and if anybody spoke to him he swore at them. It worked quite well, he said. There was one very persistent bloke, though, with a bottle of Scotch. He kept on shoving drinks at Deacon and he took a few, and then some more, and by the time he got to London he was pretty genuinely sozzled. You see, he'd had nothing to eat, to speak of, for a coupla days, except some bread he'd managed to scrounge from a cottage."

The policeman who was taking all this down in shorthand scratched stolidly on over the paper. Mr. Cranton took a drink of water and resumed.

"Deacon said he wasn't very clear what happened to him after that. He wanted to get out of the station and go off somewhere, but he found it wasn't so easy. The darkened streets confused him, and the persistent fellow with the bottle of Scotch seemed to have taken a fancy to him. This bloke talked all the time, which was lucky for Deacon. He said he remembered having some more drinks and something about a canteen, and tripping over something and a lot of chaps laughing at him. And after that he must really have fallen asleep. The next thing he knew, he was in a train again, with Tommies all round him, and from what he could make out, they were bound for the Front."

"That's a very remarkable story," said Mr. Parker.

"It's clear enough," said Wimsey. "Some kindly soul must have examined his papers, found he was due back and shoved him on to the nearest transport, bound for Dover, I suppose."

"That's right," said Mr. Cranton. "Caught in the machine, as you might say. Well, all he could do was to lie doggo again. There were plenty of others who seemed to be dog-tired and fairly well canned and he wasn't in any way remarkable. He watched what the others did, and produced his papers at the right time and all that. Fortunately, nobody else seemed to belong to his particular unit. So he got across. Mind you," added Mr. Cranton, "I can't tell you all the details. I wasn't in the War myself, being otherwise engaged. You must fill up the blanks for yourself. He said he was damned seasick on the way over, and after that he slept in a sort of cattle-wagon and finally they bundled him out at last in the dark at some ghastly place or other. After a bit he heard somebody asking if there was anyone belonging to his unit. He knew enough to say 'Yes, sir' and stand forward—and then he found himself foot-slogging over a filthy road full of holes with a small party of men and an officer. God! he said it went on for hours and he thought they must have done about a hundred miles, but I daresay that was an exaggeration. And he said there was a noise like merry hell going on ahead, and the ground began to shake, and he suddenly grasped what he was in for."

"This is an epic," said Wimsey.

"I can't do justice to it," said Mr. Cranton, "because Deacon never knew what he was doing and I don't know enough to make a guess. But I gather he walked straight into a big strafe. Hell let loose, he said, and I shouldn't wonder if he began to think kindly of Maidstone Gaol and even of the condemned cell. Apparently he never got to the trenches, because they were being shelled out of them and he got mixed up in the retreat. He lost his party and something hit him on the head and laid him out. Next thing he knew he was lying in a shell-hole along with somebody who'd been dead some time. I don't know. I couldn't follow it all. But after a bit he crawled out. Everything was quiet and it was coming on dark, so he must have lost a whole day somehow. He'd lost his sense of direction, too, he said. He wandered about, and fell in and out of mud and holes and wire, and in the end he stumbled into a shed where there was some hay and stuff. But he couldn't remember much about that, either, because he'd had a devil of a knock on the head and he was getting feverish. And then a girl found him."

"We know all about that," said the Superintendent.

"Yes, I daresay you do. You seem to know a lot. Well, Deacon was pretty smart about that. He got round the soft side of the girl and they made up a story for him. He said it was fairly easy pretending to have lost his memory. Where the doctor blokes made a mistake was trying to catch him out with bits of Army drill. He'd never done any, so of course he didn't have to pretend not to recognise it. The hardest part was making out that he didn't know any English. They nearly got him on that, once or twice. But he did know French, so he did his best to seem intelligent about that. His French accent was pretty good, but he pretended to have lost his speech, so that any mumbling or stammering might be put down to that, and in the intervals he practised talking to the girl till he was word-perfect. I must say, Deacon had brains."

"We can imagine all that part," said Parker. "Now tell us about the emeralds."

"Oh, yes. The thing that started him on that was getting hold of an old English newspaper which had a mention of the finding of a body in the dene-hole—his own body, as everyone thought. It was a 1918 paper, of course, but he only came across it in 1924—I forget where. It turned up, the way things do. Somebody'd used it to wrap up something sometime, and I think he came across it in an estaminet. He didn't bother about it, because the farm was doing pretty well—he'd married the girl by then, you see—and he was quite happy. But later on, things began to go badly, and it worried him to think about those sparklers all tucked away doing no good to anybody. But he didn't know how to start getting hold of them, and he got a vertical breeze up every time he thought of that dead warder and the chap he'd thrown down the hole. However, in the end, he called to mind yours truly, and figured it out that I'd be out on my own again. So he wrote me a letter. Well, as you know, I wasn't out. I was inside again, owing to a regrettable misunderstanding, so I didn't get the letter for some time, my pals thinking it wasn't quite the sort of thing to send to the place where I was. See? But when I came out again, there was the letter waiting for me."

"I wonder he made *you* his confidant," observed Parker. "There had been —shall we say, ungentlemanly words passed on the subject."

"Ah!" said Mr. Cranton. "There had, and I had something to say about that when I wrote back. But you see, he'd nobody else to go to, had he? When all's said and done, there's nobody like Nobby Cranton to handle a job like that in a refined and competent manner. I give you my word I nearly told him to go and boil himself, but in the end I said, No! let bygones be bygones. So I promised to help the blighter. I told him I could fix him up with money and papers and get him across all right. Only I told him he'd have to give me a bit more dope on the thing first. Otherwise, how was I to know he wouldn't double-cross me again, the dirty skunk?"

"Nothing more likely," said Parker.

"Ah! and he did, too, blast his worm-eaten little soul! I said he'd have to tell me where the stuff was. And would you believe it, the hound wouldn't trust me! Said, if he told me that, I might get in and pinch the bleeding lot before he got there!"

"Incredible!" said Parker. "Of course you wouldn't do such a thing as that."

"Not me," replied Nobby. "What do *you* think?" He winked. "Well, we went on writing backwards and forwards till we reached what they call an impasse. At last he wrote and said he'd send me a what d'you call—a cipher and if I could make out from that where the shiners were, I was welcome. Well, he sent the thing, and I couldn't make head or tail of it, and I told him so. Then he said, All right; if I didn't trust him I could go down to Fenchurch and ask for a tailor called Paul as lived next door to Batty Thomas, and they'd give me the key, but, he says, you'd do better to leave it to me, because I know how to handle them. Well, I didn't know, only I thought to myself if these two chaps come in on it they'll want their share, and they might turn sour on me, and it seemed to me I was safer with Deacon, because he stood to lose more than I did. Call me a mug if you like, but I sent him over the money and some perfectly good papers. Of course, he couldn't come as Deacon and he didn't want to come at Legros, because there might be a spot of trouble over that, and he suggested his papers should be made out as Paul Taylor. I thought it a bit silly myself, but he seemed to think it would be a good joke. Now, of course, I know why. So the papers were made out, with a lovely photograph—a real nice job, that was. Might have been anybody. As a matter of fact, it was a composite. It looked very convincing, and had quite a look of all sorts of people. Oh, yes! and I sent him some clothes to meet him at Ostend, because he said his own things were too Frenchy. He came across on December 29th. I suppose you got on to that?"

"Yes," said Blundell, "we did, but it didn't help us a lot."

"That bit went all right. He sent me a message from Dover. Telephoned from a public call-box—but I'll forgive you for not tracing that. He said he was going straight through and would come along up to London with the stuff next day or the day after, or as soon as he could. Anyway, he would get a message through somehow. I wondered whether I oughtn't to go down to Fenchurch myself—mind you, I never trusted him—but I wasn't altogether keen, in spite of my face-fungus. I'd grown that on spec, you understand. I didn't want you people following me about too much. And besides, I had one or two other irons in the fire. I'm coming clean, you see."

"You'd better," said Parker, ominously.

"I didn't get any message on the 30th, nor yet on the 31st, and I thought I'd been had proper. Only I couldn't see what he had to gain by double-crossing me. He needed me to handle the goods—or so I thought. Only then it struck me he might have picked up some other pal over at Maidstone or abroad."

"In that case, why bring you into it at all?"

"That's what I thought. But I got so windy, I thought I'd better go down to the place and see what was happening. I didn't want to leave a trail, so I went over to Walbeach—never mind how, that's off the point——"

"Probably Sparky Bones or the Fly-Catcher," put in Parker, thoughtfully.

"Ask no questions and you'll hear no lies. My pal decanted me a few miles out and I footslogged it. I made out I was a tramp labourer, looking for work on the New Cut. Thank God, they weren't taking on any hands, so they didn't detain me."

"So we gathered."

"Ah! I suppose you would go nosey-parkering round there. I got a lift part of the way to Fenchurch and walked the rest. Beastly country it is, too, as I said before. I'm not doing my hiking thereabouts, I can tell you."

"That was when we ran across one another, I think," said Wimsey.

"Ah! and if I'd known who I had the pleasure of stopping I'd have walked off home," said Mr. Cranton, handsomely. "But I didn't know, so I trotted along and—but there! I expect you know that part of it."

"You got a job with Ezra Wilderspin and made inquiries for Paul Taylor."

"Yes—and a nice business that was!" exclaimed Nobby with indignation. "Mr. Paul Bleeding Taylor and Mr. Batty Thomas! Bells, if you please! And not a hide nor hair of *my* Paul Taylor to be seen or heard of. I tell you, that made me think a bit. I didn't know if he'd been and gone, or if he'd been pinched on the way, or if he was lurking about round the corner or what. And that chap Wilderspin—he was a good hand at keeping a hardworking man's nose to the grindstone, curse him! 'Driver, come here!' 'Steve, do this!' I didn't have a minute to call my own. All the same, I started to think quite a lot about that cipher. I took the idea that maybe it had to do with those bells. But could I get into the confounded belfry? No, I couldn't. Not openly, I mean. So I made out to do it one night and see if I could make sense of the thing up there. So I made a couple or so of pick-locks, the forge being handy for the job, and on Saturday night I just let myself quietly out of Ezra's back-door.

"Now, look here. What I'm going to tell you is gospel truth. I went down to that church a bit after midnight, and the minute I put my hand on the door, I found it was open. What did I think? Why, I thought Deacon must be in there on the job. Who else was it likely to be, that time of night? I'd been in the place before and made out where the belfry door was, so I went along nice and quiet, and that was open, too. 'That's all right,' I thought. 'Deacon's here, and I'll give him Tailor Paul and Batty Thomas for not keeping me posted.' I got up into a sort of place with ropes in it—damn nasty, I thought they looked. And then there was a ladder and more ropes a-top of that. And then another ladder and a trap-door."

"Was the trap-door open?"

"Yes, and I went up. And I didn't half like it, either. Do you know, when I got up into the next place—Gee! there was a queer feel about it. Not a sound, but like as if there might be people standing round. And dark! It was a pitch-black beast of a night and raining like hell, but I never met anything like the blackness of that place. And I felt as if there was hundreds of eyes watching me. Talk about the heebie-jeebies! Well, there!

"After a bit, with still not a sound, I sort of pulled myself together and put my torch on. Say, have you ever been up in that place? Ever seen those bells? I'm not what you'd call fanciful in a general way, but there was something about the bells that gave me the fantods."

"I know," said Wimsey, "they look as if they were going to come down on you."

"Yes, *you* know," said Nobby, eagerly. "Well, I'd got to where I wanted, but I didn't know where to begin. I didn't know the first thing about bells, or how to get to them or anything. And I couldn't make out what had happened to Deacon. So I looked round on the floor with the torch and—Boo!—there he was!"

"Dead?"

"Dead as a door-nail. Tied up to a big kind of post, and a look on his face—there! I don't want to see a face like that again. Just as though he'd been struck dead and mad all at one go, if you see what I mean."

"I suppose there's no doubt he was dead?"

"Dead?" Mr. Cranton laughed. "I never saw anyone deader."

"Stiff?"

"No, not stiff. But cold, my God! I just touched him. He swung on the ropes and his head had fallen over—well, it looked as if he'd got what was coming to him, anyhow, but worse. Because, to do them justice, they're pretty quick on the drop, but he looked as if it had lasted for a good long time."

"Do you mean the rope was round his neck?" demanded Parker, a little impatiently.

"No. He wasn't hanged. I don't know what killed him. I was just looking to see, when I heard somebody starting to come up the tower. I didn't stop, you bet. There was another ladder, and I legged it up that as high as I could go till I got to a sort of hatch leading out on to the roof, I suppose. I squatted inside that and hoped the other fellow wouldn't take it into his head to come up after me. I wasn't keen on being found up there at all, and the body of my old pal Deacon might want some explaining. Of course, I could have told the truth, and pointed out that the poor bloke was cold before I got there, but me having pick-locks in my pocket rather jiggered up that bit of the alibi. So I sat tight. The chap came up into the place where the body was and started moving round and shuffling about, and once or twice he said 'Oh, God!' in a groaning sort of voice. Then there was a nasty soft sort of thump, and I reckoned he'd got the body down on the floor. Then after a bit I heard him pulling and hauling, and presently his steps went across the floor, very slow and heavy, and a bumping noise, like he was dragging old Deacon after him. I couldn't see him at all from where I was, because from my corner I could only see the ladder and the wall opposite, and he was right away on the other side of the room. After that there was more scuffling, and a sort of bumping and sliding, and I took it he was getting the body down the other ladder. And I didn't envy him the job, neither.

"I waited up there and waited, till I couldn't hear him any more, and then I began to wonder what I should do next. So I tried the door on to the roof. There was a bolt inside, so I undid that and stepped out. It was raining like blazes and pitch-black, but out I crawled and got to the edge of the tower and looked over. How high is that cursed tower? Hundred and thirty feet, eh? Well, it felt like a thousand and thirty. I'm no cat-burglar, nor yet a steeple-jack. I looked down, and I saw a light moving about right away up the other end of the church, miles away beneath me in the graveyard. I tell you I hung on to that blinking parapet with both hands and I got a feeling in my stomach as though me and the tower and everything was crumbling away and going over. I was glad I couldn't see more than I did.

"Well, I thought, you'd better make tracks, Nobby, while the dirty work's going on down there. So I came in again carefully and bolted the door after me and started to come down the ladder. It was awkward going in the dark and after a bit I switched my torch on, and I wished I hadn't. There I was, and those bells just beneath me—and, God! How I hated the look of them. I went all cold and sweaty and the torch slipped out of my hand and went down, and hit one of the bells. I'll never forget the noise it made. It wasn't loud, but kind of terribly sweet and threatening, and it went humming on and on, and a whole lot of other notes seemed to come out of it, high up and clear and close —right in my ears. You'll think I'm loopy, but I tell you that bell was alive. I shut my eyes and hung on to the ladder and wished I'd chosen a different kind of profession—and that'll show you what a state I was in."

"You've got too much imagination, Nobby," said Parker.

"You wait, Charles," said Lord Peter. "You wait till you get stuck on a ladder in a belfry in the dark. Bells are like cats and mirrors—they're always queer, and it doesn't do to think too much about them. Go on, Cranton."

"That's just what I couldn't do," said Nobby, frankly. "Not for a bit. It felt like hours, but I daresay it wasn't more than five minutes. I crawled down at last—in the dark, of course, having lost the torch. I groped round after it and found it, but the bulb had gone, naturally, and I hadn't any matches. So I had to feel for the trap-door, and I was terrified of pitching right down. But I found it at last, and after that it was easier, though I had a nasty time on the spiral staircase. The steps are all worn away, and I slipped about, and the walls were so close I couldn't breathe. My man had left all the doors open, so I knew he'd be coming back, and that didn't cheer me up much, either. When I was out in the church I hared it for all I was worth to the door. I tripped over something on the way, too, that made an awful clatter. Something like a big metal pot."

"The brass ewer at the foot of the font," said Wimsey.

"They didn't ought to keep it there," said Mr. Cranton, indignantly. "And when I got out through the porch, I had to pussyfoot pretty gently over that beastly creaking gravel. In the end I got away and then I ran—golly, how I ran! I hadn't left anything behind at Wilderspin's, bar a shirt they'd lent me and a tooth-brush I'd bought in the village, and I wasn't going back there. I ran and ran like hell, and the rain was something cruel. And it's a hell of a country. Ditches and bridges all over the place. There was a car came past one time, and trying to get out of the light, I missed my footing and rolled down the bank into a ditch full of water. Cold? It was like an ice-bath. I fetched up at last in a barn near a railway station and shivered there till morning, and presently a train came along, so I got on that. I forget the name of the place, but it must have been ten or fifteen miles away from Fenchurch. By the time I got up to London I was in a fever, I can tell you; rheumatic fever, or so they said. And you see what it's done to me. I pretty nearly faded out, and I rather wish I had. I'll never be fit for anything again. But that's the truth and the whole truth, my lord and officers. Except that when I came to look myself over, I couldn't find Deacon's cipher. I thought I'd lost it on the road, but if you picked it up in the belfry, it must have come out of my pocket when I pulled the torch out. I never killed Deacon, but I knew I'd have a job to prove I didn't, and that's why I spun you a different tale the first time you came."

"Well," said Chief Inspector Parker, "let's hope it'll be a lesson to you to keep out of belfries."

"It will," replied Nobby fervently. "Every time I see a church tower now it gives me the jim-jams. I'm done with religion, I am, and if I ever go inside a church-door again, you can take and put me in Broadmoor."

THE THIRD PART

Will Thoday Goes in Quick and Comes out Slow

For while I held my tongue, my bones consumed away through my daily complaining.

Psalm xxxii. 3

WIMSEY THOUGHT HE had never seen such utter despondency on any face as on William Thoday's. It was the face of a man pushed to the last extremity, haggard and grey, and pinched about the nostrils like a dead man's. On Mary's face there was anxiety and distress, but something combative and alert as well. She was still fighting, but Will was obviously beaten.

"Now then, you two," said Superintendent Blundell, "let's hear what you have to say for yourselves."

"We've done nothing we need be ashamed of," said Mary.

"Leave it to me, Mary," said Will. He turned wearily to the Superintendent. "Well," he said, "you've found out about Deacon, I suppose. You know that he done us and ours a wrong that can't be put right. We been trying, Mary and me, to put right as much as we can, but you've stepped in. Reckon we might have known we couldn't keep it quiet, but what else could we do? There's been talk enough about poor Mary down in the village, and we thought the best thing was to slip away, hoping to make an honest woman of her without asking the leaves of all they folk with long tongues as 'ud only be too glad to know something against us. And why shouldn't we? It weren't no fault of ours. What call have you got to stop us?"

"See here, Will," said Mr. Blundell, "it's rough luck on you, and I'm not saying as 'tisn't, but the law's the law. Deacon was a bad lot, as we all know, but the fact remains somebody put him away, and it's our job to find out who did it."

"I ain't got nothing to say about that," said Will Thoday, slowly. "But it's cruel hard if Mary and me——"

"Just a moment," said Wimsey. "I don't think you quite realise the position, Thoday. Mr. Blundell doesn't want to stand in the way of your marriage, but, as he says, somebody did murder Deacon, and the ugly fact remains that you were the man with the best cause to do it. And that means, supposing a charge were laid against you, and brought into court—well, they might want this lady to give evidence."

"And if they did?" said Will.

"Just this," said Wimsey. "The law does not allow a wife to give evidence against her husband." He waited while this sank in. "Have a cigarette, Thoday. Think it out."

"I see," said Thoday, bitterly. "I see. It comes to this—there ain't no end to the wrong that devil done us. He ruined my poor Mary and brought her into the dock once, and he robbed her of her good name and made bastards of our little girls, and now he can come between us again at the altar rails and drive her into the witness-box to put my neck in the rope. If ever a man deserved killing, he's the one, and I hope he's burning in hell for it now."

"Very likely he is," said Wimsey, "but you see the point. If you don't tell us the truth now——"

"I've nothing to tell you but this," broke out Thoday in a kind of desperation. "My wife—and she *is* my wife in God's sight and mine—she never knew nothing about it. Not one word. And she knows nothing now, nothing but the name of the man rotting in that grave. And that's the truth as God sees us."

"Well," said Mr. Blundell, "you'll have to prove that."

"That's not quite true, Blundell," said Wimsey, "but I dare say it could be proved. Mrs. Thoday——"

The woman looked quickly and gratefully at him.

"When did you first realise that your first husband had been alive till the beginning of this year, and that you were, therefore, not legally married to Will Thoday here?"

"Only when you came to see me, my lord, last week."

"When I showed you that piece of writing in Deacon's hand?"

"Yes, my lord."

"But how did that——?" began the Superintendent. Wimsey went on, drowning his voice.

"You realised then that the man buried in Lady Thorpe's grave must be Deacon."

"It came over me, my lord, that that must be the way of it. I seemed to see a lot of things clear that I hadn't understood before."

"Yes. You'd never doubted till that moment that Deacon had died in 1918?"

"Not for a moment, my lord. I'd never have married Will else."

"You have always been a regular communicant?"

"Yes, my lord."

"But last Sunday you stayed away."

"Yes, I did, my lord. I couldn't come there, knowing as me and Will wasn't properly married. It didn't seem right, like."

"Of course not," said Wimsey. "I beg your pardon, Superintendent. I'm afraid I interrupted you," he added, blandly.

"That's all very well," said Mr. Blundell. "You said you didn't recognise that writing when his lordship showed it to you."

"I'm afraid I did. It wasn't true—but I had to make up my mind quick—and I was afraid——"

"I'll bet you were. Afraid of getting Will into trouble, hey? Now, see here, Mary, how did you know that paper wasn't written donkey's years ago? What made you jump so quick to the idea Deacon was the corpse in the Thorpe grave? Just you answer me that, my girl, will you?"

"I don't know," she said faintly. "It came over me all of a sudden."

"Yes, it did," thundered the Superintendent. "And why? Because Will had told you about it already, and you knew the game was up. Because you'd seen that there paper before——"

"No, no!"

"I say, Yes. If you hadn't have known something, you'd have had no cause to deny the writing. You knew *when* it was written—now didn't you?"

"That's a lie!" said Thoday.

"I really don't think you're right about that, Blundell," said Wimsey, mildly, "because, if Mrs. Thoday had known about it all along, why shouldn't she have gone to Church last Sunday morning? I mean, don't you see, if she'd brazened it out all those months, why shouldn't she do it again?"

"Well," retorted the Superintendent, "and how about Will? He's been going to church all right, ain't he? You aren't going to tell me *he* knew nothing about it either."

"Did he, Mrs. Thoday?" inquired Wimsey, gently.

Mary Thoday hesitated.

"I can't tell you about that," she said at last.

"Can't you, by God?" snapped Mr. Blundell. "Well, now, will you tell me——?"

"It's no good, Mary," said Will. "Don't answer him. Don't say nothing. They'll only twist your words round into what you don't mean. We've got nothing to say and if I got to go through it, I got to go through it and that's all about it."

"Not quite," said Wimsey. "Don't you see that if you tell us what you know, and we're satisfied that your wife knows nothing—then there's nothing to prevent your marriage from going through straight away? That's right, isn't it, Super?"

"Can't hold out any inducement, my lord," said the Superintendent, stolidly.

"Of course not, but one can point out an obvious fact. You see," went on Wimsey, "somebody *must* have known something, for your wife to have jumped so quickly to the conclusion that the dead man was Deacon. If she hadn't already been suspicious about you—if *you* were perfectly ignorant and innocent the whole time—then *she* had the guilty knowledge. It would work all right that way, of course. Yes, I see now that it would. If she knew, and told you about it—then *you* would be the one with the sensitive conscience. *You* would have told *her* that you couldn't kneel at the altar with a guilty woman——"

"Stop that!" said Thoday. "You say another word and I'll—— Oh, my God! it wasn't that, my lord. She never knew. I did know. I'll say that much, I won't say no more, only that. As I hope to be saved, she never knew a word about it."

"As you hope to be saved?" said Wimsey. "Well. Well. And you did know, and that's all you've got to tell us?"

"Now, look here," said the Superintendent, "you'll have to go a bit further than that, my lad. When did you know?"

"When the body was found," replied Thoday, "I knew then." He spoke slowly, as though every word were being wrenched out of him. He went on more briskly: "That's when I knew who it was."

"Then why didn't you say so?" demanded Blundell.

"What, and have everybody know me and Mary wasn't married? Likely, ain't it?"

"Ah!" said Wimsey. "But why didn't you get married then?"

Thoday shifted uncomfortably in his chair.

"Well, you see, my lord—I hoped as Mary needn't ever know. It was a bitter hard thing for her, wasn't it? And the children. We couldn't ever put that right, you see. So I made up my mind to say nothing about it and take the sin—if it was a sin—on my shoulders. I didn't want to make no more trouble for her. Can't you understand that? Well, then—when she found it out, through seeing that there paper——" He broke off and started again. "You see, ever since the body was found I've been worried and upset in my mind, like, and I daresay I was a bit queer in my ways and she'd noticed it—when she asked me if the dead man was Deacon after all, why, then I told her as it was, and that's how it all came about."

"And how did you know who the dead man was?"

There was a long silence.

"He was terribly disfigured, you know," went on Wimsey.

"You said you thought he was—that he'd been in prison," stammered Thoday, "and I said to myself——"

"Half a mo'," broke in the Superintendent, "when did you ever hear his lordship say that? It wasn't brought out at the inquest, nor yet at the adjournment, because we were most particularly careful to say nothing about it. Now then!"

"I heard something about it from Rector's Emily," said Thoday, slowly. "She happened to hear something his lordship said to Mr. Bunter."

"Oh, *did* she?" snapped Mr. Blundell. "And how much more did Rector's Emily overhear, I'd like to know. That beer-bottle, now! Who told her to dust the finger-prints off it—come, now!"

"She didn't mean no harm about that," said Will. "It was nothing but girl's curiosity. You know how they are. She came over next day and told Mary all about it. In a rare taking, she was."

"Indeed!" said the Superintendent, unbelievingly. "So *you* say. Never mind. Let's go back to Deacon. You heard that Emily heard something his lordship said to Mr. Bunter about the dead man having been in prison. Was that it? And what did you think of that?"

"I said to myself, it must be Deacon. I said, here's that devil come out of his grave to trouble us again, that's what I said. Mind you, I didn't exactly know, but that's what I said to myself."

"And what did you imagine he had come for?"

"How was I to know? I thought he'd come, that's all."

"You thought he'd come after the emeralds, didn't you?" said the Superintendent.

For the first time a look of genuine surprise and eagerness came into the haunted eyes. "The emeralds? Was *that* what he was after? Do you mean he had them after all? Why, we always thought the other fellow—Cranton—had got them."

"You didn't know that they had been hidden in the church?"

"*In the church?*"

"We found them there on Monday," explained his lordship, placidly, "tucked away in the roof."

"In the roof of the church? Why, then, *that* was what he—— The emeralds found? Thank God for that! They'll not be able to say now as Mary had any hand in it."

"True," said Wimsey. "But you were about to say something else, I rather fancy. 'That was what he——?' What? 'That was what he was after when I found him in the church.' Was that it?"

"No, my lord. I was going to say—— I was just going to say, that was what he did with them." A fresh wave of anger seemed to sweep over him. "The dirty villain! He did double-cross that other fellow after all."

"Yes," agreed his lordship. "I'm afraid there's not much to be said in favour of the late Mr. Deacon. I'm sorry, Mrs. Thoday, but he was really rather an unsatisfactory person. And you're not the only one to suffer. He married another woman over in France, and she's left with three small children too."

"Poor soul!" said Mary.

"The damned scoundrel!" exclaimed Will, "if I'd have known that, I'd——"

"Yes?"

"Never mind," growled the farmer. "How did he come to be in France? How did he——?"

"That's a long story," said Wimsey, "and rather far from the point at issue. Now, let's get your story clear. You heard that the body of a man who might have been a convict had been found in the churchyard, and though the face was quite unrecognisable, you were—shall we say inspired?—to identify him with Geoffrey Deacon, whom you had supposed to have died in 1918. You said nothing about it till your wife, the other day, saw a bit of Deacon's handwriting, which might have been written at any time, and was—shall we again say inspired?—with the same idea. Without waiting for any further verification, you both rushed away to town to get remarried, and that's the only explanation you can give. Is that it?"

"That's all I can say, my lord."

"And a damned thin story too," observed Mr. Blundell, truculently. "Now, get this, Will Thoday. You know where you stand as well as I do. You know you're not bound to answer any questions now unless you like. But there's the inquest on the body; we can have that re-opened, and you can tell your story to the coroner. Or you can be charged with the murder and tell it to a judge and jury. Or you can come clean now. Whichever you like. See?"

"I've nothing more to say, Mr. Blundell."

"I tell thee all, I can no more," observed Wimsey thoughtfully. "That's a pity, because the public prosecutor may get quite a different sort of story fixed in his mind. He may think, for instance, that you knew Deacon was alive because you had met him in the church on the night of December 30th."

He waited to see the effect of this, and resumed:

"There's Potty Peake, you know. I don't suppose he's too potty to give evidence about what he saw and heard that night from behind Abbot Thomas' tomb. The black-bearded man and the voices in the vestry and Will Thoday fetching the rope from the cope-chest. What took you into the church, by the way? You saw a light, perhaps. And went along and found the door open, was that it? And in the vestry, you found a man doing something that looked suspicious. So you challenged him and when he spoke you knew who it was. It was lucky that the fellow didn't shoot you, but probably you took him unawares. Anyway, you threatened to give him up to justice and then he pointed out that that would put your wife and children in an unpleasant position. So you indulged in a little friendly chat—did you speak?—In the end, you compromised. You said you would keep quiet about it and get him out of the country with £200 in pocket, but you hadn't got it at the moment and in the meantime you would put him in a place a safety. Then you fetched a rope and tied him up. I don't know how you kept him quiet while you went to fetch it. Did you give him a straight left to the jaw, or what? . . . You won't help me? . . . Well, never mind. You tied him up and left him in the vestry while you went round to steal Mr. Venables' keys. It's a miracle you found them in the right place, by the way. They seldom are. Then you took him up into the belfry, because the bell-chamber was nice and handy and had several locks to it, and it was easier than escorting him out through the village. After that you brought him some food—perhaps Mrs. Thoday could throw some light on that. Did you miss a quart bottle of beer or so about that time, Mrs. Thoday? Some of those you got in for Jim? By the way, Jim is coming home and we'll have to have a word with him."

Watching Mary's face, the Superintendent saw it contract suddenly with alarm, but she said nothing. Wimsey went on remorselessly.

"The next day you went over to Walbeach to get the money. But you weren't feeling well, and on the way home you broke down completely and couldn't get back to let Deacon out. That was damned awkward for you, wasn't it? You didn't want to confide in your wife. Of course, there was Jim."

Thoday raised his head.

"I'm not saying anything one way or other, my lord, except this. I've never said one word to Jim about Deacon—not one word. Nor he to me. And that's the truth."

"Very well," said Wimsey. "Whatever else happened, in between December 30th and January 4th, somebody killed Deacon. And on the night of the 4th, somebody buried the body. Somebody who knew him and took care to mutilate his face and hands beyond recognition. And what everybody will want to know is, at what moment did Deacon cease to be Deacon and become the body? Because that's rather the point, isn't it? We know that you couldn't very well have buried him yourself, because you were ill, but the killing is a different matter. You see, Thoday, he didn't starve to death. He died with a full tummy. *You* couldn't have fed him after the morning of December 31st. If you didn't kill him then, who took him his rations in the interval? And who, having fed him and killed him, rolled him down the belfry ladder on the night of the 4th, with a witness sitting in the roof of the tower—a witness who had seen him and recognised him? A witness who——"

"Hold on, my lord," said the Superintendent. "The woman's fainted."

THE FOURTH PART

The Slow Work

Who shut up the sea with doors . . . and brake up for it my decreed place?

Job xxxviii. 8, 10

"HE WON'T SAY anything," said Superintendent Blundell.

"I know he won't," said Wimsey. "Have you arrested him?"

"No, my lord, I haven't. I've sent him home and told him to think it over. Of course, we could easily get him on being an accessory after the fact in both cases. I mean, he was shielding a known murderer—that's pretty clear, I fancy; and he's also shielding whoever killed Deacon, if he didn't do it himself. But I'm taking the view that we'll be able to handle him better after we've interrogated James. And we know James will be back in England at the end of the month. His owners have been very sensible. They've given him orders to come home, without saying what he's wanted for. They've arranged for another man to take his place and he's to report himself by the next boat."

"Good! It's a damnable business, the whole thing. If ever a fellow deserved a sticky death, it's this Deacon brute. If the law had found him the law would have hanged him, with loud applause from all citizens. Why should we hang a perfectly decent chap for anticipating the law and doing our dirty work for us?"

"Well, it *is* the law, my lord," replied Mr. Blundell, "and it's not my place to argue about it. In any case, we're going to have a bit of a job to hang Will Thoday, unless it's as an accessory before the fact. Deacon was killed on a full stomach. If Will did away with him on the 30th, or the 31st, why did he go to collect the £200? If Deacon was dead, he wouldn't want it. On the other hand, if Deacon wasn't killed till the 4th, who fed him in the interval? If James killed him, why did he trouble to feed him first? The thing makes no sense."

"Suppose Deacon was being fed by somebody," said Wimsey, "and suppose he said something infuriatin' and the somebody killed him all of a sudden in a frenzy, not meaning to?"

"Yes, but how did he kill him? He wasn't stabbed or shot or clouted over the head."

"Oh, I don't *know*," said Wimsey. "Curse the man! He's a perfect nuisance, dead or alive, and whoever killed him was a public benefactor. I wish I'd killed him myself. Perhaps I did. Perhaps the rector did. Perhaps Hezekiah Lavender did."

"I don't suppose it was any of those," said Mr. Blundell, stolidly. "But it might have been somebody else, of course. There's that Potty, for instance. He's always wandering round the church at night. Only he'd have to get into the bell-chamber, and I don't see how he could. But I'm waiting for James. I've got a hunch that James may have quite a lot to tell us."

"Have you? Oysters have beards, but they don't wag them."

"If it comes to oysters," said the Superintendent, "there's ways and means of opening 'em—*and* you needn't swallow 'em whole, neither. You're not going back to Fenchurch?"

"Not just at present. I don't think there's very much I can do down there for a bit. But my brother Denver and I are going to Walbeach to open the New Cut. I expect we shall see you there."

The only other thing of interest that happened during the next week or so was the sudden death of Mrs. Wilbraham. She died at night and alone—apparently from mere old age—with the emeralds clasped in her hand. She left a will drawn up fifteen years earlier, in which she left the whole of her very considerable estate to her Cousin Henry Thorpe "because he is the only honest man I know". That she should cheerfully have left her only honest relative to suffer the wearing torments of straitened means and anxiety throughout the intervening period seemed to be only what anybody might have expected from her enigmatic and secretive disposition. A codicil, dated on the day after Henry's death, transferred the legacy to Hilary, while a further codicil, executed a few days before her own death, not only directed that the emeralds which had caused all the disturbance should be given to "Lord Peter Wimsey, who seems to be a sensible man and to have acted without interested motives", but also made him Hilary's trustee. Lord Peter made a wry face over this bequest. He offered the necklace to Hilary, but she refused to touch it; it had painful associations for her. It was, indeed, only with difficulty that she was persuaded to accept the Wilbraham estate. She hated the thought of the testatrix; and besides, she had set her heart on earning her own living. "Uncle Edward will be worse than ever," she said. "He will want me to marry some horrible rich man, and if I want to marry a poor one, he'll say he's after the money. And anyway, I don't want to marry anybody."

"Then don't," said Wimsey. "Be a wealthy spinster."

"And get like Aunt Wilbraham? Not me!"

"Of course not. Be a nice wealthy spinster."

"Are there any?"

"Well, there's me. I mean, I'm a nice wealthy bachelor. Fairly nice, anyway. And it's fun to be rich. I find it so. You needn't spend it all on yachts and cocktails, you know. You could build something or endow something or run something or the other. If you don't take it, it will go to some ghastly person—Uncle Edward or somebody—whoever is Mrs. Wilbraham's next-of-kin, and they'd be sure to do something silly with it."

"Uncle Edward would," said Hilary, thoughtfully.

"Well, you've got a few years to think it over," said Wimsey. "When you're of age, you can see about throwing it into the Thames. But what I'm to do with the emeralds I really don't know."

"Beastly things," said Hilary. "They've killed grandfather, and practically killed Dad, and they've killed Deacon and they'll kill somebody else before long. I wouldn't touch them with a barge-pole."

"I'll tell you what. I'll keep them till you're twenty-one, and then we'll form ourselves into a Wilbraham Estate Disposals Committee and do something exciting with the whole lot."

Hilary agreed; but Wimsey felt depressed. So far as he could see, his interference had done no good to anybody and only made extra trouble. It was a thousand pities that the body of Deacon had ever come to light at all. Nobody wanted it.

The New Wash Cut was opened with great rejoicings at the end of the month. The weather was perfect, the Duke of Denver made a speech which was a model of the obvious, and the Regatta was immensely successful. Three people fell into the river, four men and an old woman were had up for being drunk and disorderly, a motor-car became entangled with a tradesman's cart and young Gotobed won First Prize in the Decorated Motor-cycle section of the Sports.

And the River Wale, placidly doing its job in the midst of all the disturbance, set to work to scour its channel to the sea. Wimsey, leaning over the wall at the entry to the Cut, watched the salt water moving upward with the incoming tide, muddied and chafing along its new-made bed. On his left, the crooked channel of the old river lay empty of its waters, a smooth expanse of shining mud.

"Doing all right," said a voice beside him. He turned and found that it was one of the engineers.

"What extra depths have you given her?"

"Only a few feet, but she'll do the rest herself. There's been nothing the matter with this river except the silting of the outfall and the big bend below here. We've shortened her course now by getting on for three miles and driven a channel right out into the Wash beyond the mudbanks. She'll make her own outfall now, if she's left to herself. We're expecting her to grind her channel lower by eight or ten feet—possibly more. It'll make all the difference to the town. It's a scandal, the way the thing's been let go. Why, as it is, the tide scarcely gets up higher than Van Leyden's Sluice. After this, it'll probably run up as far as the Great Leam. The whole secret with these Fen rivers is to bring back all the water you can into its natural course. Where the old Dutchmen went wrong was in dispersing it into canals and letting it lie about all over the place. The smaller the fall of the land, the bigger weight of water you need to keep the outfall scoured. You'd think it was obvious, wouldn't you? But it's taken people hundreds of years to learn it."

"Yes," said Wimsey. "I suppose all this extra water will go up the Thirty-foot?"

"That's right. It's practically a straight run now from the Old Bank Sluice to the New Cut Outfall—thirty-five miles—and this will carry off a lot of the High Level water from Leamholt and Lympsey. At present the Great Leam has to do more work than it should—they've always been afraid to let the Thirty-foot take its fair proportion of the flood-water in winter, because you see, when it got down to this point it would have overflowed the old river-bed and drowned the town. But now the New Cut will carry it clean off, and that will relieve the Great Leam and obviate the floods round Frogglesham, Mere Wash and Lympsey Fen."

"Oh!" said Wimsey. "I suppose the Thirty-foot Dyke will stand the strain?"

"Oh, dear, yes," said the engineer, cheerfully. "It was meant to from the beginning. In fact, at one time, it had to. It's only within the last hundred years that the Wale has got so badly silted up. There's been a good deal of shifting in the Wash—chiefly owing to tidal action, of course, and the Nene Outfall Cut, and that helped to cause the obstruction, don't you see. But the Thirty-foot worked all right in the old days."

"In the Lord Protector's time, I suppose," said Wimsey. "And now you've cleared the Wale Outfall, no doubt the obstruction will go somewhere else."

"Very likely," replied the engineer, with unimpaired cheerfulness. "These mudbanks are always shifting about. But in time I daresay they'll clear the whole thing—unless, of course, they really take it into their heads to drain the Wash and make a job of it."

"Just so," said Wimsey.

"But as far as it goes," continued the engineer, "this looks pretty good. It's to be hoped our dam over there will stand up to the strain. You'd be surprised at the scour you get with these quiet-looking rivers. Anyhow, this embankment is all right—I'll take my oath of that. You watch the tide-mark. We've marked the old low level and the old high level—if you don't see the one lowered and the other raised by three or four feet within the next few months, you can call me—a Dutchman. Excuse me a minute—I just want to see that they're making that dam good over there."

He hurried off to superintend the workmen who were completing the dam across the old course of the river.

"And how about my old sluice-gates?"

"Oh!" said Wimsey, looking round, "it's you, is it?"

"Ah!" The sluice-keeper spat copiously into the rising water. "It's me. That's who it is. Look at all this money they been spending. Thousands. But as for them gates of mine, I reckon I can go and whistle for 'em."

"No answer yet from Geneva?"

"Eh?" said the sluice-keeper. "Oh! Ah! Meaning what I said? Ah! that were a good 'un, weren't it? Why don't they refer it to the League of Nations? Ah! and why don't they? Look at thisher great scour o' water a-comin' up. Where's that a-going to? It's got to go somewhere, ain't it?"

"No doubt," said Wimsey. "I understand it's to go up the Thirty-foot."

"Ah!" said the sluice-keeper. "Always interfering with things, they are."

"They're not interfering with your gates, anyway."

"No, they ain't, and that's just where it is. Once you starts interferin' with things you got to go on. One thing leads to another. Let 'm bide, that's what I say. Don't go digging of 'em up and altering of 'em. Dig up one thing and you got to dig up another."

"At that rate," objected Wimsey, "the Fens would still be all under water."

"Well, in a manner of speaking, so they would," admitted the sluice-keeper.

"That's very true. So they would. But none the more for that, they didn't ought to come a-drowning of us now. It's all right for him to talk about letting the floods out at the Old Bank Sluice. Where's it all a-going to? It comes up, and it's got to go somewhere, and it comes down and it's got to go somewhere, ain't it?"

"At the moment I gather it drowns the Mere Wash and Frogglesham and all those places."

"Well, it's their water, ain't it?" said the sluice-keeper. "They ain't got no call to send it down here."

"Quite," said Wimsey, recognising the spirit that had hampered the Fen drainage for the last few hundred years, "but as you say yourself, it's got to go somewhere."

"It's their water," retorted the man obstinately, "let 'em keep it. It won't do us no good."

"Walbeach seems to want it."

"Ah! them!" The sluice-keeper spat vehemently. "They don't know what they want. They're always awantin' some nonsense or other. And there's always some fool to give it 'em, what's more. All I wants is a new set of gates, but I don't look like getting of 'em. I've asked for 'em time and again. I asked that young feller there. 'Mister,' I says to him, 'how about a new set o' gates for my sluice?' 'That ain't in our contract,' he says. 'No,' I says, 'and drowning half the parish ain't in your contract neither, I suppose.' But he couldn't see it."

"Well, cheer up," said Wimsey. "Have a drink."

He did, however, feel sufficient interest in the matter to speak to the engineer about it when he saw him again.

"Oh, I think it's all right," said the gentleman. "We did, as a matter of fact, recommend that the gates should be repaired and strengthened, but you see, the damned thing's all tied up in some kind of legal bother. The fact is, once you start on a job like this, you never know where it's going to end. It's all piecemeal work. Stop it up in one place and it breaks out in another. But I don't think you need worry about this part of it. What *does* want seeing to is the Old Bank dyke—but that's under a different authority altogether. Still, they've undertaken to make up their embankment and put in some fresh stonework. If they don't, there'll be trouble, but they can't say we haven't warned them."

"Dig up one thing," thought Wimsey, "and you have to dig up another. I wish we'd never dug up Deacon. Once you let the tide in, it's got to go somewhere."

James Thoday, returning to England as instructed by his employers, was informed that the police wanted him as a witness. He was a sturdy man, rather older than William, with bleak blue eyes and a reserved manner. He repeated his original story, without emphasis and without details. He had been taken ill in the train after leaving Fenchurch. He had attributed the trouble to some sort of gastric influenza. When he got to London, he had felt quite unable to proceed, and had telegraphed to that effect. He had spent part of that day huddled over the fire in a public house near Liverpool Street; he thought they might remember him there. They could not give him a bed for the night and, in the evening, feeling a little better, he had gone out and found a room in a back street. He could not recall the address, but it had been a clean, pleasant place. In the morning he found himself fit to continue his journey, though still very weak and tottery. He had, of course, seen English papers mentioning the discovery of the corpse in the churchyard, but knew nothing further about it, except, of course, what he had heard from his brother and sister-in-law, which was very little. He had never had any idea who the dead man was. Would he be surprised to hear that it was Geoffrey Deacon? He would be very much surprised indeed. The news came as a terrible shock to him. That would be a bad job for his people.

Indeed, he looked startled enough. But there had been a tenseness of the muscles about his mouth which persuaded Superintendent Blundell that the shock had been caused, not so much by hearing the dead man's name as by hearing that the police knew it.

Mr. Blundell, aware of the solicitude with which the Law broods over the interests of witnesses, thanked him and proceeded with his inquiries. The public house was found, and substantiated the story of the sick sailor who had sat over the fire all day drinking hot toddies; but the clean and pleasant woman who had let her room to Mr. Thoday was not so easy of identification.

Meanwhile, the slow machinery of the London police revolved and, from many hundreds of reports, ground out the name of a garage proprietor who had hired out a motor-bicycle on the evening of January 4th to a man answering to the description of James Thoday. The bicycle had been returned on the Sunday by a messenger, who had claimed and taken away the deposit, minus the charge for hire and insurance. No, not a district messenger: a youth, who looked like an ordinary out-of-work.

On hearing this, Chief Inspector Parker, who was dealing with the London end of the inquiry, groaned dismally. It was too much to expect this nameless casual to turn up. Ten to one, he had pocketed the surplus deposit and would be particularly unwilling to inform the world of the fact.

Parker was wrong. The man who had hired the bicycle had apparently made the fatal mistake of picking an honest messenger. After prolonged inquiry and advertisement a young Cockney made his appearance at New Scotland Yard. He gave his name as Frank Jenkins, and explained that he had only just seen the advertisement. He had been seeking work in various places, and had drifted back to Town in time to be confronted with the police inquiry on a notice board at the Labour Exchange.

He very well remembered the episode of the motor-bike. It had struck him as funny at the time. He had been hanging round a garridge in Bloomsbury in the early morning of January 5th, hoping to pick up a job, when he see a bloke coming along on this here bike. The bloke was short and stocky, with blue eyes and sounded like he might be the boss of some outfit or other—he spoke sharp and quick, like he might be accustomed to giving orders. Yes, he might have been an officer in the mercantile marine, very likely. Come to think of it, he did look a bit like a sailor. He was dressed in a very wet and dirty motoring coat and wore a cap, pulled down over his face, like. This man had said: "Here, sonny, d'you want a job?" On being told "Yes," he had asked: "Can you ride a motor-bike?" Frank Jenkins had replied, "Lead me to it, guv'nor"; whereupon he had been told to take the machine back to a certain garage, to collect the deposit and to bring it to the stranger outside the Rugby Tavern at the corner of Great James Street and Chapel Street, when he would receive something for his pains. He had done his part of the business, and hadn't took more than an hour, all told (returning by 'bus), but when he arrived at the Rugby Tavern, the stranger was not there, and apparently never had been there. A woman said she had seen him walking away in the direction of Guildford Street. Jenkins had hung about till the middle of the morning, but he had seen no sign of the man in the motor-coat. He had therefore deposited the money with the landlord of the Tavern, with a message to say that he could wait no longer and had kept back half-a-crown—that being the amount he thought fair to award himself for the transaction. The landlord would be able to tell them if the sum had ever been claimed.

The landlord, being interrogated, brought the matter to mind. Nobody answering the description of the stranger had ever called for the money, which, after a little search and delay, was produced intact in a dirty envelope. Enclosed with it was the garage proprietor's receipt, made out in the name of Joseph Smith, at a fictitious address.

The next thing was, obviously, to confront James Thoday with Frank Jenkins. The messenger identified his employer immediately; James Thoday persisted, politely, that there was some mistake. What next, thought Mr. Parker.

He put the question to Lord Peter, who said:

"I think it's time for a spot of dirty work, Charles. Try putting William and James alone in a room with a microphone or whatever you call the beastly gadget. It may not be pretty, but you'll probably find that it works."

In these circumstances, therefore, the brothers met for the first time since James had left William on the morning of January 4th. The scene was a waiting-room at Scotland Yard.

"Well, William," said James.

"Well, James," said William.

There was a silence. Then James said:

"How much do they know?"

"Pretty well everything, by what I can make out."

There was another pause. Then James spoke again in a constrained voice:

"Very well. Then you had better let me take the blame. I'm not married, and there's Mary and the kids to be thought of. But in God's name, man, couldn't you have got rid of the fellow without killing him?"

"That," said William, "is just what I was going to ask *you.*"

"You mean to say, it wasn't you did away with him?"

"Of course not. I'd be a fool to do it. I'd offered the brute two hundred pounds to go back where he came from. If I hadn't a-been ill, I'd a-got him away all right, and that's what I thought you'd a-done. My God! when he come up out o' that grave, like Judgment Day, I wished you'd killed me along of him."

"But I never laid hand on him, Will, till after he was dead. I saw him there, the devil, with that ghastly look on his face, and I never blamed you for what you'd done. I swear I never blamed you, Will—only for being such a fool as to do it. So I broke his ugly face in, so that no one should ever guess who he was. But they've found out, seemingly. It was cursed bad luck, that grave being opened so soon. May be it'd have been better if I'd carried him out and thrown him in the Drain, but it's a long way to go, and I thought we'd be safe enough."

"But, see here, James—if you didn't kill him, who did?"

It was at this point that Superintendent Blundell, Chief Inspector Parker and Lord Peter Wimsey walked in on the pair of them.

THE FIFTH PART

The Dodging

Then whispered they of a violated grave—of a disfigured body.

EDGAR ALLAN POE: *Berenice*

THE ONLY DIFFICULTY was that the two witnesses who had formerly refused to speak could now hardly speak fast enough and spoke both together. Chief Inspector Parker was obliged to call for silence.

"All right," he said. "You've both been suspecting each other and shielding each other. We've grasped that. Now that we've got that clear, let's have the story. William first." He added the usual caution.

"Well, sir," replied William, briskly, "I don't know as I've much to tell you, because his lordship here seems to have worked it all out surprising neat. What my feelings were when he told me just what I did that night I won't say —but what I do want to make as clear as I can is that my poor wife never knew one thing about it, first to last. Why, that was my whole trouble all the time—how to keep it from her.

"I'll begin right at the beginning, with the night of December 30th. I was just coming home, pretty late for me, from seeing to one of the cows that had gone sick up at Sir Henry's place, and as I was passing the church, I thought I saw somebody a-creeping up to the porch and going in. It was a dark night, of course, but if you remember, sir, it had begun to snow, and I could see something moving, like, against the white. So I thinks, that's Potty up to his games again—I better send him off home. So I goes up to the church door, and I sees footmarks going all along the path as far as the porch, and there they seems to stop. So I says, Hallo! and looks round about a bit. That's queer, I says to myself, where's the beggar got to? So I goes round the church, and I sees a light a-moving about and going towards the vestry. Well, I thinks, maybe it's Rector. And then I thinks, well, maybe it ain't. So I comes back to the door, and there's no key in it, like there would be in the ordinary way if

Rector had been inside. So I pushes the door and it opens. And in I goes. And then I hears somebody a-moving about and bumping, like, up in the chancel. I goes along quiet, having rubber boots on, that I was wearing for the fields, and when I gets round behind the chancel screen I sees a light and hears the bloke in the vestry, so in I goes and there's a fellow a-tugging away at the ladder Harry Gotobed uses for seeing to the lamps and that, what's always kept a-lying along the wall. He had his back to me, and on the table I see a kind of a dark lantern and something else as had no right to be there, and that's a revolver. So I catches hold of the revolver and said, loud and sharp, 'What are you doing there?' And he jumped round pretty damn quick and made a dive for the table. 'No, you don't,' I said, 'I've got your gun and I know how to use it. What are you after?' Well, he started some sort of tale about being out of work and tramping about and wanting a place to sleep in, and I said, 'That won't wash. How about this gun? Hands up,' I said, 'let's see what else you've got on you.' So I went through his pockets and brought out what looked to me like a set of pick-locks. 'Well, my lad,' I said, 'that's quite enough for me. You're for it.' And he looked at me, and laughed like hell, and said, 'Think again, Will Thoday.' And I said, 'How do you know my name?' and then I looked again and said, 'My God, it's Jeff Deacon!' And he said, 'Yes; and you're the man that's married my wife.' And he laughed again. And then it come over me just what it all meant."

"How did he know that?" asked Wimsey. "He didn't get it from Cranton."

"That was the other scoundrel? No, he told me he'd meant to come after Mary, but hearing from some fellow at Leamholt that she was married, he'd thought he'd better have a scout round first. I couldn't make out why he'd come back to the place at all, and he wouldn't tell me. I see now, it was the emeralds. He did say something about me keeping quiet and he'd make it worth my while, but I told him I'd have no truck with him. I asked him where he'd been, but he just laughed and said 'Never you mind.' And I asked what he wanted in Fenchurch, and he said he wanted money. So I made out that he'd meant to come blackmailing Mary. Well, that made me see red, and I was in half a mind to give him up to the police and take what was coming to us, but when I thought about Mary and the kids—well, I couldn't face it. I was wrong, of course, but when I remembered all the talk there'd been—well, I wanted to spare her that. He knew just how I stood, the devil, and he stood there grinning at me.

"So in the end, I made a devil's bargain with him. I said I'd hide him and give him money to get out of the country, and then I thought what was I to do with him? I'd got his pick-locks all right, but I didn't trust him none the more for that, and I was afraid to go out of the church with him, where we might run up against somebody. And then I got the idea of putting him up in the bell-chamber. So I told him what I meant to do and he agreed. I thought I could get the keys from Rector all right, so, just for the time being, I pushed him into the cupboard where the surplices hang and locked him in. Then I thought that he might easily break his way out while I was over at the Rectory, so I went down and fetched a rope from the chest and came back and tied him up. You see, I didn't believe that tale of his about sleeping in the vestry.

Robbing the church was what I thought he was after. And besides, if I went away and left him, what was to stop him getting out and hiding somewhere and slugging me over the head when I got back? I'd no key to the church-door, neither, and he might have made off."

"Good thing for you if he had," suggested Mr. Blundell.

"Yes—so long as nobody else caught him. Anyhow, I got the keys. I put up some story to the Rector—it must have been a pretty lame one—the old gentleman was a bit puzzled, I think. He kept on saying how queer I looked, and insisted on getting me a drop of his port. While he was fetching it, I just nipped the keys off the nail by the door. I know what you're going to say—suppose he'd mislaid them as usual? Well, I'd have had to try the same dodge on Jack Godfrey or else change my plans—but there they were and I didn't bother with any ifs. I went back to the church and untied Deacon's legs and made him walk up the belfry stairs in front of me, like taking a pig to market. It wasn't difficult: I had the revolver, you see."

"And you tied him up to a beam in the bell-chamber?"

"Yes, sir, I did. And wouldn't you a-done? Just think of yourself carrying victuals and stuff up one o' they ladders in the dark, with a murderer roaming loose at the top all ready to bash your head in the moment you popped it up above floor-level. I tied him up good and proper, though it was a bit of a job with the rope being so thick. 'Stay you there,' I said, 'and I'll bring you something to eat in the morning and see you out of the country before you're twenty-four hours older.' He cursed like a devil, but I paid no attention to him. It was all I could do to keep my hand offen him, and I'm often minded to think it's a wonder I didn't kill him then and there."

"But had you made any plans for shipping him off?"

"Yes, I had. I'd been over to Walbeach the day before with Jim here, and we'd had a bit of talk with a pal of his—a queer old skipper on a Dutch cargo boat, that was lying there, taking in some sort of freight—I never rightly gathered what it was—but I got the notion the old boy wouldn't find much come amiss to him."

"You're right there, Will," put in Jim, grinning.

"So I found. It wasn't the best plan, maybe, but it was all I could do in the time. I couldn't think very clear, to tell you the truth. I was terrible put about in my mind and my head was buzzing like a thresher. I suppose 'twas the 'flu coming on. I don't know how I got through that evening at home, looking at Mary and the kids and knowing what I knew. Fortunately, she knew I was worried over the cow and put it all down to that—at least, I thought so. I tossed and turned all night, and the only thing to comfort me was the blessed snow coming down and hiding all they footprints we'd left round the church.

"Next morning I was damned ill, but I couldn't stop to think of that. I slipped out well before daybreak, with some bread and cheese and beer in an old tool-bag. Jim heard me and called out to know what was up. So I said I was going over to see the cow—and so I did, only I took the church on the way.

"Deacon was all right, only very bad-tempered and perished wi' cold, so I left him my old coat—not wanting him to be frozen to death. And I tied him up by his elbows and ankles, leaving his hands free, so as he could help himself to his victuals but not untie himself. Then I went on to see to the cow and found her better. After breakfast I got the old car out and ran her over to Walbeach, feeling worse and worse all the time. I found my skipper, just getting ready to sail. I had a word with him, and he agreed to wait till 10 o'clock that night and carry my passenger, no questions asked. Two hundred and fifty pounds was the price he wanted and I agreed to pay it. I got the money and gave him the fifty then and there, promising him the rest when I got Deacon aboard. I got into the car and started back—and you know what happened afterwards."

"That's very clear," said Parker. "I needn't tell you that you were compounding a serious felony by helping a convicted murderer to escape from justice. Speaking as a policeman, I am shocked; speaking as a human being, I have every sympathy for you. Now, you." He turned to Jim. "I imagine your part of it comes in here."

"Yes, sir. Well, as you know, poor Will was brought back in a terrible state and we thought for a day or two he was pretty well gone. He was out of his head and kept on calling out that he must go down to the church, but we put that down to the bell-ringing business. All the time he kept a sort of control over himself and never let out a word about Deacon, but one day, when Mary had gone out of the room, he clutched my hand and said, 'Don't let her know, Jim. Get him away.' 'Get who away?' I said. And he said, 'In the belfry—bitter cold and starving.' And then he sat up in bed and said, quite plain and clear, 'My coat—give me my coat—I must have the keys and the money.' I said, 'All right, Will, I'll see to it'—thinking he was dreaming, and after a bit he seemed to forget about it and go off in a doze. But I thought it was queer, so I had a look in his coat, and there, sure enough, were the Rector's bunch of keys and a whole wad of money.

"Well, I began to think there might be something behind it, so I took the keys, and I thought, before I took them back, I'd just have a look round the church. I went in there——"

"Which day was this?"

"I reckon it was January 2nd. I went up into the belfry—right up to the bell-chamber, and—well! there he was!"

"He must have been pretty fed-up with things by that time."

"Fed up? He was dead and cold."

"Starved to death?"

"Not he. There was a big bit of cheese beside him and near half a loaf of bread and two bottles of beer, one empty and one full. And he hadn't died of cold, neither, as you might expect. I've seen men that had died of exposure, and they died peaceful—curled up like kittens, mostly, as if they'd gone out in their sleep. No. He'd died on his feet, and whatever it was, he'd seen it coming to him. He'd struggled like a tiger against the ropes, working at them till he could get upright, and they had cut through the stuff of his jacket and through his socks. And his face! My God, sir, I've never seen anything like it. His eyes staring open and a look in them as if he'd looked down into hell. It fair shook me.

"I looked him over—and then I saw Will's old coat lying on the floor, thrown off, it might be, in his struggles—and that didn't look like dying of cold, neither. I couldn't tell what to make of it, for I didn't recognise him, you see. I had a look in his breast pocket, and found some papers. There was some made out in the name of Taylor and some in a French name that I've forgotten. I couldn't make head or tail of it. And then I had a look at his hands."

"Ah!" said Wimsey, "now we're coming to it."

"Yes, my lord. You must remember that I knew Deacon. Not very well, but I knew him. And he carried a big scar on one hand, where he'd fallen down one day, carrying a tray with a glass jug on it. I'd seen that scar, and I'd never forget it. When I saw that, my lord, and knew who 'twas—well, there! I hadn't much doubt about what'd happened. Forgive me, Will—I thought you'd done him in, and as God's my witness, I couldn't blame you. Not that I hold with murder, and it came to me then that things could never be the same betwixt you and me—but I didn't blame you. Only I wished it had happened in a fair fight."

"If it had happened, Jim, it would a-been in a fair fight. I might a-killed him, but I wouldn't a-killed him when he was tied up. You might a-known that."

"Well, so I might. But it seemed to me at the time as there was no way out of it. I had to think quick what to do. I found some old boards and beams in a corner, and I stood them up in front of him, so as if anybody came in they might not notice him—not unless they were looking for something—and then I came away and thought hard. I kept the keys. I knew I'd be wanting them, and Rector is so absent-minded, he'd probably think he'd mislaid them.

"I thought all that day—and then I remembered that Lady Thorpe's funeral was fixed for the Saturday. It seemed to me that I might put him in her grave and that he need never be found, barring accidents. I was due to leave on Saturday morning, and I thought I could fix things so as to have an alibi.

"I had a bad moment on Friday. Jack Godfrey told me they were going to ring a muffled peal for Lady Thorpe, and I was all of a shake, thinking he'd see him when he went up to put the leathers on the bells. By a big stroke of luck, he didn't go till after dark, and I suppose he never looked into that dark corner, or he'd have seen the planks had been moved."

"We know what you did on Saturday," said Parker. "You needn't bother with that."

"No, sir. I had an awful ride with that bike. The acetylene lamp worked none too well, and it was raining like the tropics. Still, I got there—much later than I meant, and I went to work. I cut him down——"

"You needn't tell us that, either. There was a witness on the top of the bell-chamber all the time."

"A witness?"

"Yes—and lucky for you, my lad, he was a highly respectable and gentlemanly burglar with the heart of a rabbit and a wholesome fear of bloodshed—otherwise you might be paying blackmail through the nose. But I will say for

Nobby," added Parker reflectively, "that he would consider blackmail beneath him. You got the body down into the churchyard?"

"And glad I was to get it there. Rolling it down the ladders—it gave me the heebie-jeebies. And those bells! I was expecting all the time to hear them speak. I never have liked the sound of bells. There's something—you'd think they were alive, sometimes, and could talk. When I was a boy, I read a story in an old magazine about a bell that called out after a murderer. You'll think I'm soft, talking that way, but it made an impression on me and I can't forget it."

"*The Rosamonde*—I know the story," said Wimsey, gently. "It called, 'Help, Jehan! Help, Jehan!' It gave me the grues, too."

"That's the one, my lord. Anyhow, I got the body down, as I said. I opened the grave and was just going to put him in——"

"You used the sexton's spade, I suppose?"

"Yes, sir. The key of the crypt was on Rector's bunch. As I was saying, I was going to put it in, when I remembered that the grave *might* be opened and the body recognised. So I gave it some good, hard blows with the spade across the face——"

He shuddered.

"That was a bad bit, sir. And the hands. I'd recognised them, and so might other people. I got out my jack-knife, and I—well, there!"

" 'With the big sugar-nippers they nipped off his flippers,' " quoted Wimsey, flippantly.

"Yes, my lord. I made them into a parcel with his papers and slipped it all in my pocket. But I put the ropes and his hat down the old well. Then I filled up the grave and put the wreaths back as tidily as I could, and cleaned the tools. But I can tell you, I didn't care about taking them back into the church. All those gold angels with their eyes open in the darkness—and old Abbot Thomas lying there on his tomb. When my foot crunched on a bit of coke behind the screen, my heart was in my mouth."

"Harry Gotobed really ought to be more careful with the coke," said Wimsey. "It's not for want of telling."

"That damned parcel of stuff was burning my pocket, too. I went up and had a look at the stoves, but they were all stoked up for the night, and the top nowhere near burnt through. I didn't dare put anything in there. Then I had to go up and clean down the belfry. There'd been beer spilt on the floor. Fortunately, Harry Gotobed had left a bucket of water in the coke-house, so I didn't have to draw any from the well, though I've often wondered if he noticed next day that the water was gone. I made everything as clean as I could, and stacked the planks up where I'd found them, and I took away the beer-bottles——"

"Two of them," said Wimsey. "There were three."

"Were there? I couldn't see but the two. I locked up everything tight, and then I wondered what I'd better do with the keys. Finally, I thought I'd best leave them in the vestry, as though Rector had forgotten them—all but the key of the porch, and I left that in the lock. It was the best I could think of."

"And the parcel?"

"Ah! that. I kept the papers and a lot of money that was with them, but the—those other things—I threw into the Thirty-foot, twelve miles off from Fenchurch, and the bottles with them. The papers and notes I burnt when I got back to London. There was a good fire—for a wonder—in the waiting-room at King's Cross and nobody much about. I didn't think anybody would look for them there. I didn't quite know what to do with Will's coat, but in the end I posted it back to him with a note. I just said, 'Many thanks for loan. I've put away what you left in the belfry.' I couldn't be more open you see, for fear Mary might undo the parcel and read the letter."

"I couldn't write much to you, for same reason," said Will. "I thought, you see, you had somehow got Deacon away. It never entered my head that he was dead. And Mary usually reads my letters through before they go, sometimes adding a bit of her own. So I just said: 'Many thanks for all you've done for me'—which might a-been took to refer to you nursing me when I was ill. I see you hadn't took the £200, but I supposed you'd managed some fashion, so I just put that back in the bank where it came from. It was a queer thing to me that your letters had grown so short all of a sudden, but I understand it now."

"I couldn't just feel the same, Will," said Jim. "I didn't blame you, mind—but that rope stuck in my gullet. When did you find out what had happened?"

"Why, when the corpse came up. And—you'll have to forgive *me*, Jim—but, naturally, I fancied you'd done the job yourself, and—why, there! I didn't rightly feel the same, neither. Only I kept on hoping, maybe he'd died natural."

"He didn't do that," said Parker, thoughtfully.

"Then who killed him?" demanded Jim.

"I'm sure you didn't, for one," replied the detective. "If you had, you'd have accepted the suggestion that he died of exposure. And somehow I'm inclined to believe your brother didn't do it either—though you're both accessories after the fact of Deacon's crimes, and you aren't clear of the other thing yet; don't think it. You'd have an awkward time with a prosecuting counsel, both of you. But personally, I'm inclined to believe you both."

"Thank you, sir."

"How about Mrs. Thoday? The truth, mind."

"That's all right, sir. She was uneasy in her mind—I won't say she wasn't, seeing me so queer, especially after the body was found. But it was only when she saw Deacon's handwriting on that paper that the meaning of it all come to her. Then she asked me, and I told her part of the truth. I said I'd found out that the dead man was Deacon and that somebody—not me—must have killed him. And she guessed that Jim was mixed up in it. So I said, maybe, but we must stand together and not make trouble for Jim. And she agreed, only she said we must get married again, because we were living in sin. She's a good woman, and I couldn't reason her out of it, so I gave in about that, and we'd fixed to get it all done quiet-like in London—only you found us out, sir."

"Yes," said Blundell, "you've got to thank his lordship here for that. He seemed to know all about it, and very sorry he was to have to stop you, I must say. Seemed to think whoever put Deacon away ought to get the Wedding March out of Lohengrin and flowers all down the aisle."

"Is there any reason why they shouldn't go on and get married now, Superintendent?"

"I don't know as there is," grunted Mr. Blundell. "Not if these two are telling the truth. Proceedings there may be—you two ain't out of the wood yet, but as to getting married, I don't see no harm in it. We've got their story, and I don't know as poor Mary can add very much to it."

"Thank you very much, sir," said Will again.

"But as to who *did* kill Deacon," went on the Superintendent, "we don't seem very much forrarder. Unless it was Potty or Cranton, after all. I don't know as I ever heard anything queerer than this business. All these three, a-dodging in and out of that old belfry, one up 'tother come on—there's something behind it yet that we don't understand. And you two——" he turned fiercely on the brothers—"you keep your mouths shut about this. It'll have to come out some time, that's a certainty, but if you get talking and obstruct us in our duty of laying hands on the rightful murderer, you're *for* it. Understand?"

He ruminated, sucking his walrus moustache between his large yellow teeth.

"I'd better go down home and grill Potty, I suppose," he muttered, discontentedly. "But if he done it, how did he do it? That's what beats me."

y Seemed to think whoever set Dalton over [illegible] ought to get the [illegible] [illegible] [illegible] how is all over the [illegible]

"Is there any reason why that shouldn't [illegible] [illegible] appointment?"

"I don't know as there is," replied Mr. [illegible]. "Not if these two are doing the math. [illegible] there never [illegible] [illegible] [illegible] [illegible] [illegible] [illegible] [illegible] to know of it. We've got our story [illegible] [illegible] [illegible] and [illegible] [illegible]."

"Thank you very much, Professor Williams."

[illegible] [illegible] the Superintendent. "We don't [illegible] [illegible] [illegible] after all. [illegible] turned [illegible] on the [illegible] [illegible] [illegible] [illegible] [illegible] [illegible] [illegible] [illegible] [illegible] [illegible] [illegible] [illegible] [illegible] [illegible] [illegible] [illegible] [illegible] [illegible] [illegible]"

The [illegible] that [illegible] [illegible]

IV

A FULL PEAL OF KENT TREBLE BOB MAJOR

(Three Parts)

5,376

By the Course Ends

6 5 4 3 2
3 4 5 6 2
2 3 6 4 5
3 5 6 4 2
4 2 3 5 6

8th the Observation.

Call her before, middle with a double, wrong with a double and home; wrong with a double and home with a double; middle with a double, wrong and home with a double; before, middle with a double, wrong and home with a double: before, middle with a double and wrong with a double. Twice repeated.

(J. WILDE)

THE FIRST PART

The Waters are Called Out

> Of clean beasts, and of beasts that are not clean, and of fowls, and of everything that creepeth upon the earth there went in two and two unto Noah into the ark.
>
> *Genesis* vii. 8, 9

THE PUBLIC MEMORY is a short one. The affair of the Corpse in Country Churchyard was succeeded, as the weeks rolled on, by so many Bodies in Blazing Garages, Man-Hunts for Missing Murderers, Tragedies in West-End Flats, Suicide-Pacts in Lonely Woods, Nude Corpses in Caves and Midnight Shots in Fashionable Road-Houses, that nobody gave it another thought, except Superintendent Blundell and the obscure villagers of Fenchurch St. Paul. Even the discovery of the emeralds and the identity of the dead man had been successfully kept out of the papers, and the secret of the Thoday re-marriage lay buried in the discreet breasts of the police, Lord Peter Wimsey and Mr. Venables, none of whom had any inducement to make these matters known.

Potty Peake had been interrogated, but without much success. He was not good at remembering dates, and his conversation, while full of strange hints and prophecies, had a way of escaping from the restraints of logic and playing gruesomely among the dangling bell-ropes. His aunt gave him an alibi, for what her memory and observation were worth, which was not a great deal. Nor did Mr. Blundell feel any great enthusiasm about putting Potty Peake in the dock. It was a hundred to one that he would be pronounced unfit to plead, and the result, in any case, might be to lock him up in an institution. "And you know, old lady," said Mr. Blundell to Mrs. Blundell, "I can't see Potty doing such a thing, poor chap." Mrs. Blundell agreed with him.

As regards the Thodays, the position was highly unsatisfactory. If either were charged separately, there would always be sufficient doubt about the other to secure an acquittal, while, if they were charged together, their joint story might well have the same effect upon the jury that it had already had upon the police. They would be acquitted and left under suspicion in the minds of their neighbours, and that would be unsatisfactory too. Or they might, of course, both be hanged—"and between you and me, sir," said Mr. Blundell to the Chief Constable, "I'd never be easy in my mind if they were." The Chief Constable was uneasy too. "You see, Blundell," he observed, "our difficulty is that we've no real proof of the murder. If you could only be sure what the fellow died of——"

So a period of inaction set in. Jim Thoday returned to his ship; Will Thoday, his marriage ceremory performed, went home and went on with his work. In time the parrot forgot its newly-learnt phrases—only coming out with them at long and infrequent intervals. The Rector carried on with his marrying, churchings and baptisms, and Tailor Paul tolled out a knell or two, or struck her solemn blows as the bells hunted in their courses. And the River Wale, rejoicing in its new opportunity, and swollen by the heavy rains of a wet summer and autumn, ground out its channel inch by inch and foot by foot, nine feet deeper than before, so the water came up brackish at high tide as far as the Great Leam and the Old Bank Sluices were set open to their full extent, draining the Upper Fen.

And it was needed; for in that summer the water lay on the land all through August and September, and the corn sprouted in the stooks, and the sodden ricks took fire and stank horribly, and the Rector of Fenchurch St. Paul, conducting the Harvest Festival, had to modify his favourite sermon upon Thankfulness, for there was scarcely sound wheat enough to lay upon the altar and no great sheaves for the aisle windows or for binding about the stoves, as was customary. Indeed, so late was the harvest and so dank and chill the air, that the stoves were obliged to be lit for the evening service, whereby a giant pumpkin, left incautiously in the direct line of fire, was found to be par-roasted when the time came to send the kindly fruits of the earth to the local hospital.

Wimsey had determined that he would never go back to Fenchurch St. Paul. His memories of it were disquieting, and he felt that there were one or two people in that parish who would be better pleased if they never saw his face again. But when Hilary Thorpe wrote to him and begged him to come and see her during her Christmas holidays, he felt bound to go. His position with regard to her was peculiar. Mr. Edward Thorpe, as Trustee under her father's will and her natural guardian, had rights which no court of law would gainsay; on the other hand Wimsey, as sole trustee to the far greater Wilbraham estate, held a certain advantage. He could, if he chose, make things awkward for Mr. Thorpe. Hilary possessed written evidence of her father's wishes about her education, and Uncle Edward could scarcely now oppose them on the plea of lack of funds. But Wimsey, holding the purse-strings, could refuse to untie them unless those wishes were carried out. If Uncle Edward chose to be obstinate, there was every prospect of a legal dogfight; but Wimsey did not believe that Uncle Edward would be obstinate to that point. It was in Wimsey's power to turn Hilary from an obligation into an asset for Uncle Edward, and it seemed very possible that he would pocket his principles and take the cash. Already he had shown signs of bowing to the rising sun; he had agreed to take Hilary down to spend Christmas at the Red House, instead of with him in London. It was, indeed, not Mr. Thorpe's fault that the Red House was available; he had done his best to let it, but the number of persons desirous of tenanting a large house in ill-repair, situated in a howling desert and encumbered with a dilapidated and heavily mortgaged property, was not very large. Hilary had her way, and Wimsey, while heartily wishing that the whole business could have been settled in London, liked the girl for her determination to stick to the family estate. Here again, Wimsey was a power in the land. He could put the property in order if he liked and pay off the mortgages, and that would no doubt be a satisfaction to Mr. Thorpe, who had no power to sell under the terms of his trust. A final deciding factor was that if Wimsey did not spend Christmas at Fenchurch, he would have no decent excuse for not spending it with his brother's family at Denver, and of all things in the world, a Christmas at Denver was most disagreeable to him.

Accordingly, he looked in at Denver for a day or two, irritated his sister-in-law and her guests as much as, and no more than, usual and thence, on Christmas Eve, made his way across country to Fenchurch St. Paul.

"They seem," said Wimsey, "to keep a special brand of disgusting weather in these parts." He thrust up his hand against the hood of the car, discharging a deluge of water. "Last time it was snowing and now it's pelting cats and dogs. There's a fate in it, Bunter."

"Yes, my lord," said that long-suffering man. He was deeply attached to his master, but sometimes felt his determined dislike of closed cars to be a trifle unreasonable. "A very inclement season, my lord."

"Well, well, we must push on, push on. A merry heart goes all the way. You don't look very merry, Bunter, but then you're one of those sphinx-like people. I've never seen you upset, except about that infernal beer-bottle."

"No, my lord. That hurt my pride very much, if I may say so. A very curious circumstance, that, my lord."

"Pure accident, I think, though it had a suspicious appearance at the time. Whereabouts are we now? Oh, yes, Lympsey, of course; we cross over the Great Leam here by the Old Bank Sluice. We must be just coming to it. Yes, there it is. By Jove! some water coming through here!"

He pulled up the car just beyond the bridge, got out and stood in the downpour staring at the sluice. Its five great gates were open, the iron ratchets on the bridge above drawn up to their full extent. Dark and menacing, the swollen flood-water raced through the sluices, eddying and turning and carrying with them the brown reeds and broken willow-stems and here and there fragments of timber filched from the drowned lands of the Upper Fen. And even while he watched, there came a change. Angry little waves and gurges ruffled the strong flow of the river, with an appearance as of repressed tumult and conflict. A man came out of the gate-house by the bridge and took up his position by the sluice, staring down into the river. Wimsey hailed him.

"Tide coming up?"

"Yes, sir. We has to watch her now if we don't want to get the water all across the causey. But she don't rise very far, not without there's an extraordinary high spring tide. She's just coming up to springs now, so we has to do a bit of manipulation, like." He turned, and began to wind down the sluices.

"You see the idea, Bunter. If they shut this sluice, all the upland water has to go by the Old Leam, which has enough to do as it is. But if they leave it open and the tide's strong enough to carry the flood-water back with it through the sluice, they'll drown all the country above the sluice."

"That's it, sir," said the man with a grin. "And if the flood-water carries the tide back, we might drown *you*. It all depends, you see."

"Then we'll hope you manipulate things in our favour," said Wimsey, cheerfully. The rush of water through the arches was slackening now with the lowering of the sluice-gates, the whirlpools became shallower, and the floating sticks and reeds began to eddy against the piles of the bridge. "Just hold her back for a bit till we get to Fenchurch, there's a good fellow."

"Oh, we'll keep her level, don't you be afraid," said the man, reassuringly. "There ain't nothing wrong wi' *this* here sluice."

He put such marked emphasis on the word "this" that Wimsey looked sharply at him.

"How about Van Leyden's Sluice?"

The man shook his head.

"I dunno, sir, but I did hear as old Joe Massey down there were in a great taking about they old gates of his. There was three gentlemen went down yesterday to look at 'em—from the Conservancy or the Board or something o' that, I reckon. But you can't do nothing much for they gates in flood-time. Mebbe they'll hold, mebbe they won't. It's all according."

"Well, that's jolly," said Wimsey. "Come on, Bunter. Have you made your will? We'd better go while the going's good."

Their way this time lay along the south bank or Fenchurch side of the Thirty-foot. Dyke and drain were everywhere abrim and here and there the water stood in the soaked fields as though they needed but little more to sink back into their ancient desolation of mere and fen. There was little movement on the long, straight road. Here a shabby car met them, splashed with mud and squirting water from every pot-hole; here a slow farm cart plodded ahead with a load of mangel-wurzels, the driver huddled under the rough protection of a sodden sack, and deaf and blind to overtaking traffic; there a solitary labourer, bent with rheumatism, slouched homeward dreaming of fire and beer at the nearest pub. The air was so heavy with water, that not till they had passed Frog's Bridge did they hear the sweet, dull jangle of sound that told them that the ringers were practising their Christmas peal; it drifted through the streaming rain with an aching and intolerable melancholy, like the noise of the bells of a drowned city pulsing up through the overwhelming sea.

They turned the corner beneath the great grey tower and passed by the Rectory wall. As they neared the gate a blast of familiar toots smote upon their ears, and Wimsey slackened speed as the Rector's car came cautiously nosing its way into the road. Mr. Venables recognised the Daimler immediately, and stopped his engine with the Morris half-way across the road. His hand waved cheerfully to them through the side-curtains.

"Here you are! here you are again!" he cried in welcoming accents, as Wimsey got out and came forward to greet him. "How lucky I am to have just caught you. I expect you heard me coming out. I always blow the horn before venturing into the roadway; the entrance is so very abrupt. How are you, my dear fellow, how are you? Just going along to the Red House, I expect. They are eagerly looking forward to your visit. You will come and see us often, I hope, while you're here. My wife and I are dining with you to-night. She will be so pleased to meet you again. I said to her, I wondered if I should meet you on the road. What terrible weather, is it not? I have to hurry off now to baptise a poor little baby at the end of Swamp Drove just the other side of Frog's Bridge. It's not likely to live, they tell me, and the poor mother is desperately ill, too, so I mustn't linger, because I expect I shall have to walk up the Drove with all this mud and it's nearly a mile and I don't walk as fast as I did. Yes, I am quite well, thank you, except for a slight cold. Oh, nothing at all—I got a little damp the other day taking a funeral for poor Watson at St. Stephen—he's laid up with shingles, so painful and distressing, though not dangerous, I'm happy to say. Did you come through St. Ives and Chatteris? Oh, you came direct from Denver. I hope your family are all quite well. I hear they've got the floods out all over the Bedford Level. There'll be skating on Bury Fen if we get any frosts after this—though it doesn't look like it at present, does it? They say a green winter makes a fat churchyard, but I always think the extreme cold is really more trying for the old people. But I really must push on now. I beg your pardon? I didn't catch what you said. The bells are a little loud. That's why I blew my horn so energetically; it is difficult sometimes to hear while the ringing is going on. Yes, we're trying some Stedman's to-night. You don't ring Stedman's, I think. You must come along one day and have a try at them. Most fascinating. Wally Pratt is making great strides. Even Hezekiah says he isn't doing so badly. Will Thoday is ringing to-night. I turned over in my mind what you told me, but I saw no reason for excluding him. He did wrong, of course, but I feel convinced that he committed no *great* sin, and it would arouse so much comment in the village if he left the ringers. Gossip is such a wicked thing, don't you think? Dear me! I am neglecting my duties sadly in the pleasure of seeing you. That poor child! I *must* go. Oh, dear! I hope my engine won't give trouble, it is scarcely warmed up. Oh, please don't trouble. How very good of you. I'm ashamed to trespass on your—ah! she always responds at once to the starting-handle. Well, *au revoir*, *au revoir*! We shall meet this evening."

He chugged off cheerfully, beaming round at them through the discoloured weather curtains and zig-zagging madly across the road in his efforts to drive one way and look another. Wimsey and Bunter went on to the Red House.

THE SECOND PART

The Waters are Called Home

Deep calleth unto deep at the noise of thy waterspouts: all thy waves and thy billows are gone over me.

Psalm xlii. 7

CHRISTMAS WAS OVER. Uncle Edward, sourly and reluctantly, had given way, and Hilary Thorpe's career was decided. Wimsey had exerted himself nobly in other directions. On Christmas Eve, he had gone out with the Rector and the Choir and sung "Good King Wenceslas" in the drenching rain, returning to eat cold roast beef and trifle at the Rectory. He had taken no part in the Stedman's Triples, but had assisted Mrs. Venables to tie wet bunches of holly and ivy to the font, and attended Church twice on Christmas Day, and helped to bring two women and their infants to be churched and christened from a remote and muddy row of cottages two miles beyond the Drain.

On Boxing Day, the rain ceased, and was followed by what the Rector described as "a tempestous wind called Euroclydon". Wimsey, taking advantage of a dry road and a clear sky, ran over to see his friends at Walbeach and stayed the night, hearing great praises of the New Wash Cut and the improvement it had brought to the harbour and the town.

He returned to Fenchurch St. Paul after lunch, skimming merrily along with Euroclydon bowling behind him. Turning across the bridge at Van Leyden's Sluice, he noticed how swift and angry the river ran through the weir, with flood-water and tide-water meeting the wind. Down by the sluice a gang of men were working on a line of barges, which were moored close against the gates and piled high with sandbags. One of the workmen gave a shout as the car passed over the bridge, and another man, seeing him point and gesticulate, came running from the sluice-head across the road, waving his arms. Lord Peter stopped and waited for him to come up. It was Will Thoday.

"My lord!" he cried, "my lord! Thank God you are here! Go and warn them at St. Paul that the sluice gates are going. We've done what we can with sandbags and beams, but we can't do no more and there's a message come down from the old Bank Sluice that the water is over the Great Leam at Lympsey, and they'll have to send it down here or be drowned themselves. She's held this tide, but she'll go the next with this wind and the tide at springs. It'll lay the whole country under water, my lord, and there's no time to lose."

"All right," said Wimsey. "Can I send you more men?"

"A regiment of men couldn't do nothing now, my lord. They old gates is going, and there won't be a foot of dry land in the three Fenchurches six hours from now."

Wimsey glanced at his watch. "I'll tell 'em," he said, and the car leapt forward.

The Rector was in his study when Wimsey burst in upon him with the news.

"Great Heavens!" cried Mr. Venables. "I've been afraid of this. I've warned the drainage authorities over and over again about those gates but they wouldn't listen. But it's no good crying over spilt milk. We must act quickly. If they open the Old Bank Sluice and Van Leyden's Sluice blows up, you see what will happen. All the Upper Water will be turned back up the Wale and drown us ten feet deep or more. My poor parishioners—all those outlying farms and cottages! But we mustn't lose our heads. We have taken our precautions. Two Sundays ago I warned the congregation what might happen and I put a note in the December Parish Magazine. And the Nonconformist minister has cooperated in the most friendly manner with us. Yes, yes. The first thing to do is to ring the alarm. They know what that means, thank God! They learnt it during the War, but He moves in a mysterious way. Ring the bell for Emily, please. The church will be safe, whatever happens, unless we get a rise of over twelve feet, which is hardly likely. Out of the deep, O Lord, out of the deep. Oh, Emily, run and tell Hinkins that Van Leyden's Sluice is giving way. Tell him to fetch one of the other men and ring the alarm on Gaude and Tailor Paul at once. Here are the keys of the church and belfry. Warn your mistress and get all the valuables taken over to the church. Carry them up the tower.

Now keep cool, there's a good girl. I don't think the house will be touched, but one cannot be too careful. Find somebody to help you with this chest—I've secured all the parish registers in it—and see that the church plate is taken up the tower as well. Now, where is my hat? We must get on the telephone to St. Peter and St. Stephen and make sure that they are prepared. And we will see what we can do with the people at the Old Bank Sluice. We haven't a moment to lose. Is your car here?"

They ran the car up to the village, the Rector leaning out perilously and shouting warnings to everyone they met. At the post-office they called up the other Fenchurches and then communicated with the keeper of the Old Bank Sluice. His report was not encouraging.

"Very sorry, sir, but we can't help ourselves. If we don't let the water through there'll be the best part of four miles o' the bank washed away. We've got six gangs a-working on it now, but they can't do a lot with all these thousands o' tons o' water coming down. And there's more to come, so they say."

The Rector made a gesture of despair, and turned to the postmistress.

"You'd best get down to the church, Mrs. West. You know what to do. Documents and valuables in the tower, personal belongings in the nave. Animals in the churchyard. Cats, rabbits and guinea-pigs in *baskets*, *please*—we can't have them running round loose. Ah! There go the alarm bells. Good! I am more alarmed for the remote farms than for the village. Now, Lord Peter, we must go and keep order as best we can at the church."

The village was already a scene of confusion. Furniture was being stacked on handcarts, pigs were being driven down the street, squealing; hens, squawking and terrified, were being huddled into crates. At the door of the schoolhouse Miss Snoot was peering agitatedly out.

"When ought we to go, Mr. Venables?"

"Not yet, not yet—let the people move their heavy things first. I will send you a message when the time comes, and then you will get the children together and march them down in an orderly way. You can rely on me. But keep them cheerful—reassure them and don't on any account let them go home. They are far safer here. Oh, Miss Thorpe! Miss Thorpe! I see you have heard the news."

"Yes, Mr. Venables. Can we do anything?"

"My dear, you are the very person! Could you and Mrs Gates see that the school-children are kept amused and happy, and give them tea later on if necessary? The urns are in the parish-room. Just a moment, I must speak to Mr. Hensman. How are we off for stores, Mr. Hensman?"

"Pretty well stocked, sir," replied the grocer. "We're getting ready to move as you suggested, sir."

"That's fine," said the Rector. "You know where to go. The refreshment room will be in the Lady chapel. Have you the key of the parish-room for the boards and trestles?"

"Yes, sir."

"Good, good. Get a tackle rigged over the church well for your drinking-water, and be sure and remember to boil it first. Or use the Rectory pump, if it is spared to us. Now, Lord Peter, back to the church."

Mrs. Venables had already taken charge in the church. Assisted by Emily and some of the women of the parish, she was busily roping off areas—so many pews for the school-children, so many other pews near the stoves for the sick and aged, the area beneath the tower for furniture, a large placard on the parclose screen REFRESHMENTS. Mr. Gotobed and his son, staggering under buckets of coke, were lighting the stoves. In the churchyard, Jack Godfrey and a couple of other farmers were marking out cattle-pens and erecting shelters among the tombs. Just over the wall which separated the consecrated ground from the bell-field, a squad of volunteer diggers were digging out a handsome set of sanitary trenches.

"Good lord, sir," said Wimsey, impressed, "anybody would think you'd done this all your life."

"I have devoted much prayer and thought to the situation in the last few weeks," said Mr. Venables. "But my wife is the real manager. She has a marvellous head for organisation. Hinkins! right up to the bell-chamber with that plate—it'll be out of the way there. Alf! Alf Donnington! How about that beer?"

"Coming along, sir."

"Splendid—into the Lady chapel, please. You're bringing some of it bottled, I hope. It'll take two days for the casks to settle."

"That's all right, sir. Tabbitt and me are seeing to that."

The Rector nodded, and dodging past some of Mr. Hensman's contingent, who were staggering in with cases of groceries, he went out to the gates, where he encountered P.C. Priest, stolidly directing the traffic.

"We're having all the cars parked along the wall, sir."

"That's right. And we shall want volunteers with cars to run out to outlying places and bring in the women and sick people. Will you see to that?"

"Very good, sir."

"Lord Peter, will you act as our Mercury between here and Van Leyden's Sluice? Keep us posted as to what is happening."

"Right you are," said Wimsey. "I hope, by the way, that Bunter—where is Bunter?"

"Here, my lord. I was about to suggest that I might lend some assistance with the commissariat, if not required elsewhere."

"Do, Bunter, do," said the Rector.

"I understand, my lord, that no immediate trouble is expected at the Rectory, and I was about to suggest that, with the kind help of the butcher, sir, a sufficiency of hot soup might be prepared in the wash-house copper, and brought over in the wheeled watering tub—after the utensil has been adequately scalded, of course. And if there were such a thing as a paraffin-oil stove anywhere——"

"By all means—but be careful with the paraffin. We do not want to escape the water to fall into the fire."

"Certainly not, sir."

"You get paraffin from Wilderspin. Better send some more ringers up to the tower. Let them pull the bells as they like and fire them at intervals. Oh, here are the Chief Constable and Superintendent Blundell—how good of them to come over. We are expecting a little trouble here, Colonel."

"Just so, just so. I see you are handling the situation admirably. I fear a lot of valuable property will be destroyed. Would you like any police sent over?"

"Better patrol the roads between the Fenchurches," suggested Blundell. "St. Peter is greatly alarmed—they're afraid for the bridges. We are arranging a service of ferry-boats. They lie even lower than you do and are, I fear, not so well prepared as you, sir."

"We can offer them shelter here," said the Rector. "The church will hold nearly a thousand at a pinch, but they must bring what food they can. And their bedding, of course. Mrs. Venables is arranging it all. Men's sleeping-quarters on the cantoris side, women and children on the decani side. And we can put the sick and aged people in the Rectory in greater comfort, if all goes well. St. Stephen will be safe enough, I imagine, but if not, we must do our best for them too. And, dear me! We shall rely on you, Superintendent, to send us victuals by boat as soon as it can be arranged. The roads will be clear between Leamholt and the Thirty-foot, and the supplies can be brought from there by water."

"I'll organise a service," said Mr. Blundell.

"If the railway embankment goes, you will have to see to St. Stephen as well. Good-day, Mrs. Giddings, good-day to you! We are having quite an adventure, are we not? So glad to see you here in good time. Well, Mrs. Leach! So here you are! How's baby? Enjoying himself, I expect. You'll find Mrs. Venables in the church. Jack! Jackie Holliday! You must put that kitten in a basket. Run and ask Joe Hinkins to find you one. Ah, Mary! I hear your husband is doing fine work down at the sluice. We must see that he doesn't come to any harm. Yes, my dear, what is it? I am just coming."

For three hours Wimsey worked among the fugitives—fetching and carrying, cheering and exhorting, helping to stall cattle and making himself as useful as he could. At length he remembered his duty as a messenger and extricating his car from the crowd made his way east along the Thirty-foot. It was growing dark, and the road was thronged with carts and cattle, hurrying to the safety of Church Hill. Pigs and cattle impeded his progress.

"The animals went in two by two," sang Wimsey, as he sped through the twilight, "the elephant and the kangaroo. Hurrah!"

Down at the sluice, the situation looked dangerous. Barges had been drawn against both sides of the gates and an attempt had been made to buttress the sluice with beams and sandbags, but the piers were bulging dangerously and as fast as material was lowered into the water, it was swept down by the force of the current. The river was foaming over the top of the weir, and from the east, wind and tide were coming up in violent opposition.

"Can't hold her much longer, now, my lord," gasped a man, plunging up the bank and shaking the water from him like a wet dog. "She's going, God help us!"

The sluice-keeper was wringing his hands.

"I told 'em, I told 'em! What will become on us?"

"How long now?" asked Wimsey.

"An hour, my lord, if that."

"You'd better all get away. Have you cars enough?"

"Yes, my lord, thank you."

Will Thoday came up to him, his face white and working.

"My wife and children—are they safe?"

"Safe as houses, Will. The Rector's doing wonders. You'd better come back with me."

"I'll hang on here till the rest go, my lord, thank you. But tell them to lose no time."

Wimsey turned the car back again. In the short time that he had been away the organisation had almost completed itself. Men, women, children and household goods had been packed into the church. It was nearly seven o'clock and the dusk had fallen. The lamps were lit. Soup and tea were being served in the Lady chapel, babies were crying, the churchyard resounded with the forlorn lowing of cattle and the terrified bleating of sheep. Sides of bacon were being carried in, and thirty wagon-loads of hay and corn were ranged under the church wall. In the only clear space amid the confusion the Rector stood behind the rails of the Sanctuary. And over all, the bells tumbled and wrangled, shouting their alarm across the country. Gaude, Sabaoth, John, Jericho, Jubilee, Dimity, Batty Thomas and Tailor Paul—awake! make haste! save yourselves! The deep waters have gone over us! They call with the noise of the cataracts!

Wimsey made his way up to the altar-rails and gave his message. The Rector nodded. "Get the men away quickly," he said, "tell them they must come at once. Brave lads! I know they hate to give in, but they mustn't sacrifice themselves uselessly. As you go through the village, tell Miss Snoot to bring the school-children down." And as Wimsey turned to go, he called anxiously after him—"and don't let them forget the other two tea-urns!"

The men were already piling into their waiting cars when Lord Peter again arrived at the sluice. The tide was coming up like a race, and in the froth and flurry of water he could see the barges flung like battering rams against the piers. Somebody shouted: "Get out of it, lads, for your lives!" and was answered by a rending crash. The transverse beams that carried the footway over the weir, rocking and swaying upon the bulging piers, cracked and parted. The river poured over in a tumult to meet the battering force of the tide. There was a cry. A dark figure, stepping hurriedly across the reeling barges, plunged and was gone. Another form dived after it, and a rush was made to the bank. Wimsey, flinging off his coat, hurled himself down to the water's edge. Somebody caught and held him.

"No good, my lord, they're gone! My God! did you see that?"

Somebody threw the flare of a headlight across the river. "Caught between the barge and the pier—smashed like egg-shells. Who is it? Johnnie Cross? Who went in after him? Will Thoday? That's bad, and him a married man. Stand back, my lord. We'll have no more lives lost. Save yourselves, lads, you can do them no good. Christ! the sluice gates are going. Drive like hell, men, it's all up!"

Wimsey found himself dragged and hurtled by strong hands to his car. Somebody scrambled in beside him. It was the sluice-keeper, still moaning, "I told 'em, I told 'em!" Another thunderous crash brought down the weir across the Thirty-foot, in a deluge of tossing timbers. Beams and barges were whirled together like straws, and a great spout of water raged over the bank and flung itself across the road. Then the sluice, that held the water back from the Old Wale River, yielded, and the roar of the engines as the cars sped away was lost in the thunder of the meeting and over-riding waters.

The banks of the Thirty-foot held, but the swollen Wale, receiving the full force of the Upper Waters and the spring tide, gave at every point. Before the cars reached St. Paul, the flood was rising and pursuing them. Wimsey's car—the last to start—was submerged to the axles. They fled through the dusk, and behind and on their left, the great silver sheet of water spread and spread.

In the church, the Rector, with the electoral roll-call of the parish in his hand, was numbering his flock. He was robed and stoled, and his anxious old face had taken on a look of great pastoral dignity and serenity.

"Eliza Giddings."

"Here I am, Rector."

"Jack Godfrey and his wife and family."

"All here, sir."

"Henry Gotobed and his family."

"All here, sir."

"Joseph Hinkins . . . Louisa Hitchcock . . . Obadiah Holliday . . . Miss Evelyn Holliday. . . ."

The party from the sluice gathered awkwardly about the door. Wimsey made his way up to where the Rector stood on the chancel steps, and spoke in his ear.

"John Cross and Will Thoday? That is terrible. God rest them, poor, brave fellows. Will you be good enough to tell my wife and ask her to break the sad news to their people? Will went to try and rescue Johnnie? That is just what I should have expected of him. A dear, good fellow in spite of everything."

Wimsey called Mrs. Venables aside. The Rector's voice, shaking a little now, went on with his call:

"Jeremiah Johnson and his family . . . Arthur and Mary Judd . . . Luke Judson . . ."

Then came a long, wailing cry from the back of the church:

"Will! Oh, Will! He didn't want to live! Oh, my poor children—what shall we do?"

Wimsey did not wait to hear any more. He made his way down to the belfry door and climbed the stair to the ringing chamber. The bells were still sounding their frenzied call. He passed the sweating ringers and climbed again—up through the clock-chamber, piled with household goods, and up and on to the bell-chamber itself. As his head rose through the floor, the brazen fury of the bells fell about his ears like the blows from a thousand beating hammers. The whole tower was drenched and drunken with noise. It rocked and reeled with the reeling of the bells, and staggered like a drunken man. Stunned and shaken, Wimsey set his foot on the last ladder.

Half-way up he stopped, clinging desperately with his hands. He was pierced through and buffeted by the clamour. Through the brazen crash and clatter there went one high note, shrill and sustained, that was like a sword in the brain. All the blood of his body seemed to rush to his head, swelling it to bursting-point. He released his hold of the ladder and tried to shut out the uproar with his fingers, but such a sick giddiness overcame him that he swayed, ready to fall. It was not noise—it was brute pain, a grinding, bludgeoning, ran-dan, crazy, intolerable torment. He felt himself screaming, but could not hear his own cry. His ear-drums were cracking; his senses swam away. It was infinitely worse than any roar of heavy artillery. That had beaten and deafened, but this unendurable shrill clangour was a raving madness, an assault of devils. He could move neither forward nor backwards, though his failing wits urged him, "I must get out—I must get out of this." The belfry heaved and wheeled about him as the bells dipped and swung within the reach of an outstretched hand. Mouth up, mouth down, they brawled with their tongues of bronze, and through it all that shrill, high, sweet, relentless note went stabbing and shivering.

He could not go down, for his head dizzied and his stomach retched at the thought of it. With a last, desperate sanity, he clutched at the ladder and forced his tottering limbs upward. Foot by foot, rung by rung, he fought his way to the top. Now the trap-door was close above his head. He raised a leaden hand and thrust the bolt aside. Staggering, feeling as though his bones were turned to water, and with blood running from his nose and ears, he fell, rather than stepped out upon the windy roof. As he flung the door to behind him, the demoniac clamour sank back into the pit, to rise again, transmuted to harmony, through the louvres of the belfry windows.

He lay for some minutes quivering upon the leads, while his senses slowly drifted back to him. At length he wiped the blood from his face, and pulled himself groaningly to his knees, hands fastened upon the fretwork of the parapet. An enormous stillness surrounded him. The moon had risen, and between the battlements the sullen face of the drowned fen showed like a picture in a shifting frame, like the sea seen through the port-hole of a rolling ship, so widely did the tower swing to the relentless battery of the bells.

The whole world was lost now in one vast sheet of water. He hauled himself to his feet and gazed out from horizon to horizon. To the south-west, St. Stephen's tower still brooded over a dark platform of land, like a broken mast upon a sinking ship. Every house in the village was lit up; St. Stephen was riding out the storm. Westward, the thin line of the railway embankment stretched away to Little Dykesey, unvanquished as yet, but perilously besieged. Due south, Fenchurch St. Peter, roofs and spire etched black against the silver, was the centre of a great mere. Close beneath the tower, the village of St. Paul lay abandoned, waiting for its fate. Away to the east, a faint pencilling marked the course of the Potters Lode Bank, and while he watched it, it seemed to waver and vanish beneath the marching tide. The Wale River had sunk from sight in the spreading of the flood, but far beyond it, a dull streak showed where the land billowed up seaward, and thrust the water back upon the Fenchurches. Inward and westward the waters swelled relentlessly from the breach of Van Leyden's Sluice and stood level with the top of the Thirty-foot Bank. Outward and eastward the gold cock on the weather-vane stared and strained, fronting the danger, held to his watch by the relentless pressure of the wind from off the Wash. Somewhere amid that still surge of waters, the broken bodies of Will Thoday and his mate drifted and tumbled with the wreckage of farm and field. The Fen had reclaimed its own.

One after another, the bells jangled into silence. Gaude, Sabaoth, John, Jericho, Jubilee, Dimity and Batty Thomas lowered their shouting mouths and were at peace, and in their sudden stillness, Tailor Paul tolled out the Nine Tailors for two souls passed in the night. The notes of the organ rose solemnly.

Wimsey crept down from the tower. Into the ringing-chamber, where old Hezekiah still stood to his bell, streamed light and sound from the crowded church. The Rector's voice, musical and small, came floating up, past the wings of the floating cherubim:

"Lighten our darkness . . ."

THE THIRD PART

The Bells are Rung Down

The bronze monster had struck him dead.

JULIAN SERMET: *The Rosamonde*

FOR FOURTEEN DAYS and nights the Wale River ran backwards in its bed and the floods stood in the land. They lay all about Fenchurch St. Stephen, a foot above the railway embankment, so that the trains came through snorting and slowly, sending up a wall of water right and left. St. Peter suffered most, its houses being covered to the sills of the upper windows, and its cottages to the eaves. At St. Paul, everything was flooded eight feet deep, except the mound where the church and rectory stood.

The Rector's organisation worked brilliantly. Supplies were ample for three days, after which an improvised service of boats and ferries brought in fresh food regularly from the neighbouring towns. A curious kind of desert-island life was carried on in and about the church, which, in course of time, assumed a rhythm of its own. Each morning was ushered in by a short cheerful flourish of bells, which rang the milkers out to the cowsheds in the graveyard. Hot water for washing was brought in wheeled water-butts from the Rectory copper. Bedding was shaken and rolled under the pews for the day; the tarpaulins dividing the men's side from the women's side of the church were drawn back and a brief service of hymns and prayer was held, to the accompaniment of culinary clinkings and odours from the Lady chapel. Breakfast, prepared under Bunter's directions, was distributed along the pews by members of the Women's Institute, and when this was over, the duties of the day were put in hand. Daily school was carried on in the south aisle; games and drill were organised in the Rectory garden by Lord Peter Wimsey; farmers attended to their cattle; owners of poultry brought the eggs to a communal basket; Mrs. Venables presided over sewing-parties in the Rectory. Two portable wireless sets were available, one in the Rectory, the other in the church; these tirelessly poured out entertainment and instruction, the batteries being kept re-charged by an ingenious device from the engine of Wimsey's Daimler, capably handled by the Wilderspins. Three evenings a week were devoted to concerts and lectures, arranged by Mrs. Venables, Miss Snoot and the combined choirs of St. Stephen and St. Paul, with Miss Hilary Thorpe and Mr. Bunter (comedian) assisting. On Sundays, the routine was varied by an Early Celebration, followed by an undenominational service conducted by the two Church of England priests and the two Nonconformist ministers. A wedding, which happened to fall due in the middle of the fortnight, was made a gala occasion, and a baby, which also happened to fall due, was baptised "Paul" (for the church) "Christopher" (because St. Christopher had to do with rivers and ferries), the Rector strenuously resisting the parents' desire to call it "Van Leyden Flood".

On the fourteenth day, Wimsey, passing early through the churchyard for a morning swim down the village street, noticed that the level of the water had shrunk by an inch, and returned, waving a handful of laurels from somebody's front garden, as the nearest substitute for an olive-branch. That day they rang a merry peal of Kent Treble Bob Major, and across the sundering flood heard the bells of St. Stephen peal merrily back.

"The odour," observed Bunter, gazing out on the twentieth day across the dismal strand of ooze and weed that had once been Fenchurch St. Paul, "is intensely disagreeable, my lord, and I should be inclined to consider it insanitary."

"Nonsense, Bunter," said his master. "At Southend you would call it ozone and pay a pound a sniff for it."

The women of the village looked rueful at the thought of the cleansing and drying that their homes would need, and the men shook their heads over the damage to rick and barn.

The bodies of Will Thoday and John Cross were recovered from the streets of St. Stephen, whither the flood had brought them, and buried beneath the shadow of St. Paul's tower, with all the solemnity of a muffled peal. It was only after they had been laid in the earth that Wimsey opened his mind to the Rector and to Superintendent Blundell.

"Poor Will," he said, "he died finely and his sins died with him. He meant no harm, but I think perhaps he guessed at last how Geoffrey Deacon died and felt himself responsible. But we needn't look for a murderer now."

"What do you mean, my lord?"

"Because," said Wimsey, with a wry smile, "the murderers of Geoffrey Deacon are hanged already, and a good deal higher than Haman."

"Murderers?" asked the Superintendent, quickly. "More than one? Who were they?"

"Gaude, Sabaoth, John, Jericho, Jubilee, Dimity, Batty Thomas and Tailor Paul."

There was an astonished silence. Wimsey added:

"I ought to have guessed. I believe it is at St. Paul's Cathedral that it is said to be death to enter the bell-chamber when a peal is being rung. But I know that if I had stayed ten minutes in the tower that night when they rang the alarm, I should have been dead, too. I don't know exactly what of—stroke, apoplexy, shock—anything you like. The sound of a trumpet laid flat the walls of Jericho and the note of a fiddle will shatter a vessel of glass. I know that no human frame could bear the noise of the bells for more than fifteen minutes—and Deacon was shut up there, roped and tied there, for nine interminable hours between the Old Year and the New."

"My God!" said the Superintendent. "Why then, you were right, my lord, when you said that Rector, or you, or Hezekiah might have murdered him."

"I was right," said Wimsey. "We did." He thought for a moment and spoke again. "The noise must have been worse that night than it was the other day—think how the snow choked the louvres and kept it pent up in the tower. Geoffrey Deacon was a bad man, but when I think of the helpless horror of his lonely and intolerable death-agony——"

The Rector's mild voice came out of the silence.

"There have always," he said, "been legends about Batty Thomas. She has slain two other men in times past, and Hezekiah will tell you that the bells are said to be jealous of the presence of evil. Perhaps God speaks through those mouths of inarticulate metal. He is a righteous judge, strong and patient, and is provoked every day."

"Well," said the Superintendent, striking a note of cheerful commonplace, "seems as if we didn't need to take any more steps in this matter. The man's dead, and the fellow that put him up there is dead too, poor chap, and that's all there is to it. I don't altogether understand about these bells, but I'll take your word for it, my lord. Matter of periods of vibration, I suppose. Yours seems the best solution, and I'll put it up to the Chief Constable. And that's all there is to it."

He rose to his feet.

"I'll wish you good-morning, gentlemen," he said, and went out.

The voice of the bells of Fenchurch St. Paul: Gaude, Gaudy, Domini in laude. Sanctus, sanctus, sanctus Dominus Deus Sabaoth. John Cole made me, John Presbyter paid me, John Evangelist aid me. From Jericho to John a-Groate there is no bell can better my note. Jubilate Deo. Nunc Dimittis, Domine. Abbot Thomas set me here and bad me ring both loud and clear. Paul is my name, honour that same.

Gaude, Sabaoth, John, Jericho, Jubilee, Dimity, Batty Thomas and Tailor Paul.

Nine Tailors Make a Man.